# A Writer's Fantasy

## About This Favorite College Basketball Team & Their Handsome Star Player

By
## TJ Johnson

Copyright © 2009 by TJ Johnson

Library of Congress Control Number:
**2008937333**

ISBN 978-0-9764817-9-9

Published By
Hard Title Publishing


# www.ItsFiction.com

TJ loves college basketball, and the star player of his favorite team is not only exceptionally talented, and a National Player-of-the-Year candidate, he is without argument...handsome! Well, to be honest, he's spectacular! TJ and Shane meet by accident, but the stars must have lined up just for them. They were opposites in talent, height, scoring, rebounding, writing, typing, and designing, but the attraction happen, and fate took an interesting turn.

Though the trend today is for fast romance, quick break-ups, and instant heartache, they were determined to beat the odds for true love, by overcoming their secret relationship in the giant world of ardent fans and mammoth media coverage.

It is a fun story that'll make you laugh, cheer, scream, and applaud as the team seeks the national championship, while the two boys in love seek nothing less than pure joy!

# Books by TJ Johnson

The War Apart - Part I

The War Ahead - Part II

The Will

Stranded

The Raceboys

A Writer's Fantasy
(About His Favorite College Basketball Star)

Coming soon:

Gay Grifters

The Blackfeet Boys

The War Beyond - Part III

Forever Alone...Again

Web Site and Release Information:
**WWW.ItsFiction.com**

# Dedication

There has never been anyone like my favorite college basketball star. If everyone worked as hard, as well, and with such pure determination to be the best at what they do, he'd still be better. Thank you for sharing your heart of a champion with the rest of us. Thank you for making it fun to cheer you on, and applaud your victories great and small.

This story is also dedicated to two longtime friends that made the best sales pitch of their lives by asking the lady of the dreams to marry. Cheers to Gary and Scrappy! (It's about time!)

# INTRODUCTION

The rules of this story are simple and are not open to discussion as this is my fantasy and not yours unless of course you continue to read on, then it might well become yours, too. As the leader of this tale, I have the right to change the facts to suit me. Of course, I immediately changed a few minor but important facts. The writer in the story is now thirty-two years old, has dark brown hair, and though tall at six feet three inches, he weighs just a hundred and ninety-five pounds (just in case my doctor reads this and wonders if I'm sticking to his diet goals and not mine!). From time to time the writer may leap from the story and say something to the reader in clarification as I did in the previous sentence. In my regular stories, I'm not allowed to do such a thing, but for this one story, it might be fun. We'll see.

It would be too obvious if I just told the reader who my favorite team is and the player I so admire, so I've changed the school's name and the player's, as well as the rest of the players, the coaches, and anything else that might give it away, so you could just sit back and enjoy the tale as it is. (Even if you happen to be a Duke fan. If you went to Clemson, perhaps a friend can read the story to you!)

This story was not conceived to hurt anyone's feelings, especially my friends and family members, nor any college for which this story is placed. I hope the player will take my admiration as a sincere compliment, letting him know just how much his fans appreciate all his hard work and dedication. He is by far the exception to the rule when it comes to his skills and talents, as well as his overwhelming class.

# ONE

The two-month vacation trip had been long, hard, adventuresome, and fun, but TJ eventually turned homeward from his marathon journey to the great northwest. After thousands of miles, and for the first time in two months, his compass heading read east. The vacation began in South Dakota in early June after visiting friends in the Midwest. At the start, the Dakotas were indeed beautiful, with the tall grass cascading over the gentle hills of the rolling plains, flowing like a green swelling sea. The journey ended sixty days later in Oregon at the conclusion of a motorcoach convention. The next morning, and still traveling alone except for his dogs, he began six grueling days of cross-country driving before finally crossing the state line into North Carolina. The miles to the white line were like a lighthouse beacon of hope to TJ. He had gone far, crossed through a dozen states, but finally, he and the dogs were in their home state again. He took the exit ramp to the first rest stop to inhale the fine, clean, pine scented air while gazing at the beautiful views of the massive gorge in the heart of the Smokey Mountains. He pulled the motorcoach to a stop near Harmon's Den, applied the parking break, and turned off the engine. As he and the dogs walked across the grass along the edge of the parking lot, he could see Grassy Knob Mountain to his north and High Top Ridge to the south, while overlooking the cold, rambling waters of the French Broad River. As he began his journey home across the west in the later part of a very hot July, he noted the colors of the landscapes were no longer green as they were in early June. Everywhere he looked he saw only shades of mostly medium brown, like the shelves of slacks at a Gap® store in the mall.

On his westward journey, Montana possessed rolling grassy plains in mid June, but now they, too, were dusty in color, and the tall grain lay flat in the summer's triple digit heat wave. Of course, the plains were big, wide, and open, and yes, it did rain every day of his three-day visit to Seattle, but in early July, he discovered snow on the mountains in Glacier National Park. He tried to imagine how impressive and gigantic the peaks must have looked from the worn saddle of an early explorer. However, for all around good weather, he felt better in the middle of good old Western North Carolina. The almost eight thousand mile trip, a mixture of work, education, and vacation, took him to ten state and national parks, plus a dozen Indian reservations and museums. He loved becoming a modern day explorer, visiting places he had never seen before, hiking the trails of our ancestors, circling the excavated pits of a dinosaur, or moving slowly around an enthralling exhibit in a dusty museum.

On this expedition, he saw his first live buffalo herd, and up close as they crossed the highway encircling his parked car, with their new born calves always slightly touching their mother as if timid and shy. He took photos of the big burly beasts from just four feet away while sitting safely beneath his steering wheel. He and the dogs also survived an unexpected encounter with a six-foot long rattlesnake, and lived to tell the tale. At Glacier, he took pictures of a giant moose playing in the cold water of a picturesque lagoon. He recorded his daily observations by typing numerous notes in his laptop journal, while filing away the maps and brochures he collected. He devoured hot, juicy buffalo steaks, and bought bags of tender jerky to munch on. These tidbits of information began the research for future stories, especially his upcoming tales of **The Blackfeet Boys**, and **The War Beyond – Part III**.

In the later part of June, he sat amongst a band of Sioux to watch a reenactment of the Battle of Little Big Horn near Garyowen, Montana. He knew the white man's version of the fight, but thoroughly enjoyed this powerful Indian version, featuring twenty white riders in full authentic cavalry uniforms, including one dressed in buckskins as colorful Custer, and eighty bareback braves wearing loin cloths, hair feathers, and the battle paint of the famous Sioux warriors. The soldiers carried rifles and pistols, while the Indians bravely fought with just their bows and arrows. He found it fascinating, amusing, and inspiring, as if stepping back in time.

In the many towns of North Carolina, some people still wave to a stranger and offer a smile, and willingly offer advice, whether you want it or not. They also never shy away from telling you which ACC College Basketball team they prefer. They'll put a team sticker on the back windshield of every car they own, a championship tag on their vehicle front bumpers, and a university tag frame on the rear. They wear only team colors on game days, receive gifts of team underwear or pajamas for Christmas, and can recite only the alma mater of their school, but may politely hum along weakly to a competitor's poor choice of inferior songs.

All college fans stand on the first note of our country's national anthem, but most will sit when the tune of an opposing team is played, or they may stand, fart, or head for another beer. They cheer their team and jeer everyone else. In my case, next to my own favorite, I will indeed cheer any team that is beating Duke, and will stand up and cheer any time they are beaten, which unfortunately is not often enough, and for that alone, I will reluctantly give them a little credit.

However, their coach looks mean, even when he is saying nice things, and screams at everyone, except of course his lovely daughters. He has an amazing ability to recruit some of the best, but truly ugly basketball players in the country, except for one cute guard on this year's team.

TJ's team, Taylor University is located in the heart of the state, in a town called Lindle, which in 1894 only had fifty residents. A man called Albert Stroupe, a retired professor from Boston, moved south to Lindle, and began what is now called Taylor University, named after its most popular non-athletic alumni member, and a man who donated millions of dollars to the college back when a million bucks did some good. Now the 'town' is a city of about four hundred thousand, and well known around the country, or the world for that matter, for their top-notch university and excellent basketball program, as well as their superb staff, and loyal supporters. This school stands steep in tradition where 'once a fan always a fan' is one of many favorite sayings.

After spending a week in the North Carolina Mountains, TJ felt revived and recovered from the dust of the west and the grime of the highway. Never one to stay too long anywhere, he decided to visit the middle of the state to attend the retirement ceremony for one of his beloved English professors, a woman that knew he was gay even before he did, and encouraged him to write about what he knew, what he felt, and to write it well. TJ always thought two out of three wasn't bad for an above average student chasing after a college professor's lofty goals. Teachers are such demanding people, he thought.

The ceremony was scheduled at three on a Friday afternoon, just before the students returned for their fall term in mid August. It was like the calm before a storm, as the campus was quiet from the blast of dorm stereos, and you could actually hear squirrels chirp and chatter as they scampered from one big oak to the next chasing a brother, friend, or perhaps even a mate if it was mating season. He wondered if squirrels had a calendar carved out inside a tree trunk so they could mate at the right time. After much applause from the group of two hundred invited guests, and twelve boring speeches later, the event concluded with a short but polite speech from his professor. TJ politely shook hands with all, gave his beloved professor a hug, and duty accomplished, he found his car. He toured the campus to refresh old memories of that period in his life when he was not yet paying huge amounts on his college loans, and felt a certain unique freedom to spend cash on beer and pizza, with no worries of interest rates and the dreaded first of the month mortgages.

A few weeks ago, while planning the trip to Lindle, he found a pleasant surprise on the local newspaper's website advertising a huge recreation vehicle and motorhome show at the convention center beginning Saturday morning. He made a call to the show staff to see if overnight parking was available. Of course, they were happy to encourage him to stay in their massive parking lots, so he could attend the show, and perhaps upgrade his RV to a new far more expensive model. He decided to attend, while planning to leave his wallet in the safe.

TJ traveled the country in his motorcoach that served as both his full time home and office. He had a custom cherry wood desk made and installed in the front of the coach so he could comfortably research, write, and edit wherever he happen to be. He traveled with his beloved dogs J-Henry, short and long, and Beeper, just short and fat. J-Henry was tan in color while shading to the orange side of the color chart, but Beeper was mostly dark brown with a lighter contrasting shade of tan under her chin, around her eyes,

3

and the length of her belly. Beeper had four pups and J-Henry was one of them. He looked exactly like his daddy. The lovable dogs never actually grew up, and though they are about ten years old, they preferred to still act and play like a playful puppies.

TJ towed an SUV behind the forty-two motorcoach so he could scout about after hooking up the RV to electrical power, water, and sewer in a nearby resort. The kitchen was fully equipment with Corian® countertops, three-burner gas stove, Speed Cook Microwave oven, and a large two door residential-size refrigerator with ice and water in the door. It was 'home sweet home' to TJ. He bought this coach after selling his last land based home. Now how was somewhere in America, and after ten days anywhere, he was always ready to move on.

TJ parked his RV, as far away from the public parking area as possible so he would be in a safe but quiet area. After putting the slides out, he used the mouse on his desktop computer to tell his Internet satellite dish to scan the skies for a good connection. He then grabbed the dog leashes, hitched the dogs, and took them for a long walk since they had been cooped inside the RV since parking at Taylor University at lunchtime. With their tails wagging feverously, the dogs sniffed and pissed their way along the manicured lawns around the outside edge of the big parking lot. The dogs didn't mean to be so full of piss, but genetics required they mark their way in case a cute dog happen by, and wanted to find them.

Almost an hour later, they completed their journey around the entire facility, and returned to the coach with tongues hanging out. They were ready for a snack and at least a few pints of water. TJ noted the motorized satellite dish locked on to the Internet satellite some 22,500 miles in space, and though he had owned the unit for several years, the technology still amazed him.

He warmed up leftovers from last night's meal, and sat at the table reading the Friday edition of the USA Today® newspaper while listening and watching Brian Williams on NBC's nightly newscast. He read with interest the world and national news, the sports section if they featured something about basketball or NASCAR® racing, and finally the life section for book and movie reviews, and tonight's television lineup.

Later he checked his email and updated his location so that when he wrote friends and family they could easily see where he was located on the North American digital map by clicking a link at the end of his email. He then settled down to work on editing a recent completed story for a new book he had been working on for over a year. He corrected both simple and stupid errors, while adding words of clarification, making a fact easier to understand. Before long, it was time to take the dogs out for a late night pee, and then for TJ to go to bed.

The convention center in Lindle was a huge structure with adjoining multiple buildings allowing the surrounding state RV dealers to place almost all of their units inside the air-conditioned facility. Nearby were similar models in various colors, so if anyone showed interest and wanted their unit to be blue, gold, red, or green, they could whisk the couple away in a nearby golf cart for a tour of their remaining outdoor stock. The markup on a new RV unit was very profitable, but the proceeds from a used one were stupendous. The dealers knew that most folks kept a unit only a few years before trading or giving up the hobby. Either way they would make a large profit on the sales.

TJ entered the first of several big arenas about two hours ago, and immediately visited the new models from what RV folks called SOB units, which meant simply 'Some Other Brand' than the one they were driving. Most RV families are very loyal to their current make and model right up until they upgraded to a different brand. TJ liked saving a visit to his manufacturer last, so he could check out the changes in the Country Coach® line, but nothing more, as he only had about 27,000 miles on his current unit. All new coaches require tweaking, adjusting, education, and training until finally everything works as expected, including extra equipment like the satellite Internet system. He had no interest for moving into a new unit for several years.

After arriving to the large Country Coach® exhibit area, a hostess gave him a new coffee mug as well as an invitation to cocktails later in the day. He didn't like coffee, but thanked her as he placed the cup in his literature bag. TJ always liked to go early to RV shows, while hopefully avoiding the crowds, and the awkward 'you go left and I'll go right' scenario to maneuver down a hall, as more guests came inside the RV units on display. He began evaluating the new models by starting with the cheapest one. He was in the back of a new Intrigue model examining a new bedroom floor plan, when a tall young man about twenty or so years old stepped into the coach and began checking out the front.

It was easy for TJ to feel the vibration of the new visitor as he stepped aboard, but paid the visitor no attention, as he checked out a new wardrobe cabinet. He decided he liked the layout of his current coach better. He especially like his stackable washer and dryer units placed next to the kitchen on the tile floor instead of the bedroom and above the carpeted floor. Surely people occasionally spilled fabric softener on the floor, he wondered, while recalling the time a cabinet above the washer sprung open and a gallon size jug of washing detergent fell out, broke the cap, and the thick liquid began spilling out on the floor while he was driving down the interstate. The dogs said nothing of this catastrophe. It took all the towels in the RV to clean up the mess, and twenty-four loads of washing to get all the soap out of the towels. He thought it gave him the cleanest, sweetest smelling sewer pipes in the world.

As TJ turned to leave the bedroom, the young man in the front began leaving the living room, walking towards the bedroom. They met in the narrow space after the kitchen, and just before the bathroom. It would be like passing a truck in a single lane tunnel.

"Excuse me," said the young man politely, as he backed up so TJ could exit.

"Thank you. This happens all the time at RV shows," replied TJ without looking into the face of the courteous and respected gentleman.

"You're welcome," he replied.

This time the sound of his voice turned on TJ's brain as he recognized his voice. He glanced up and immediately blushed as he smiled at the handsome, but very tall basketball star for his favorite Taylor University team. TJ quickly stuck out his hand while offering it to the talented Shane Bradley. The young man smiled back, and reached out with a hand that looked to TJ like a catcher's mitt. It was so huge, but yet somehow looked warm and soft. TJ cautiously placed his hand in Shane's and shook it firmly, hoping Shane would not accidentally crush it.

Shane arrived at Taylor University as the exception to almost every basketball rule. Sure, he was tall at six feet nine inches, and he weighed in at two hundred fifty pounds, give or take a trip to his favorite restaurant. However, unlike most students, his food choices were all healthy, and about as far removed from the usual college students' love for fast food fare of hamburgers, fry, pizza, ice cream, and beer. He preferred a balanced healthy diet of chicken or sushi, green vegetables, big salads, and low sugar desserts. He did have a love for ice cream, which he enjoyed about once a week.

Shane was also different in his handsome looks and skin texture, and once again, nothing like the pocked faced, crooked nose, bruised and battered warriors common in most college basketball players, especially the Duke dogs. His hair was light brown, with soft thin strands cut short for easy care after a hot workout. His eyebrows were slightly darker and full, and suggested he either plucked or took very good care to brush the short whiskers into place. Though his nose had been bloodied on more than one occasion, especially during a Duke game, his face revealed a straight nose, with soft smooth skin, and just a hint of a summer tan. His arms were long and muscular, as were his legs, and his feet appeared to be at least twice the length of TJ's own pedal pushers.

To see Shane in gym shorts without a shirt revealed his entire body was absent of any sign of baby fat, or adult bulges, but rather displayed an excellent, healthy, strong, and muscular physique that anyone would pay thousands for, if you could shop for it in the mall.

However, Shane's best features were the parts he couldn't really enhance or change, and those were his natural attributes. He displayed a hint of his easygoing soft talking manner in the respectful way he communicated. However, his smile caught TJ's attention first. His beautiful teeth radiated from behind his soft, pink, tender looking lips, that he often parted just slightly when he was pulling someone's leg with a joke, or just being mischievous. His radiant blue eyes were clear and sparkling, alive with excitement, and yet during a game they became extremely focused, in spite of the jeers of thousands of opposing fans and trash talking players. His teammates called him Darth Vader because of his deep unforgiving game-on eyes.

"My name is TJ Johnson, and you're obviously Shane Bradley. I'm a fan, and very happy to meet you in person."

Shane, known as a fierce but fair competitor, would out hustle any of his competitors, out work their attempts to stop him from reaching the goal, and never ever quit on even a busted play. He worked harder, longer, and with greater determination than even his teammates. The opposing team constantly pushed, nudged, poked, elbowed, punched, and knocked him to the floor at least a dozen times more than any other player, and yet he acted as if he felt no pain at all. He always quickly got to his feet, ran the floor on every single possession, and sometimes even beat the shorter and faster guards down the court. His strict diet provided him with maximum muscle strength without resorting to pills or injections. His steely eyes remained focused on winning and nothing else when the whistle blew.

TJ was pleased to discover that Shane was much like a modern day Superman, but today he walked around in his mild mannered, soft toned, Clark Kent mode. He smiled while looking directly into TJ's eyes and replied, "I'm pleased to meet you Mister Johnson."

TJ frowned as if Shane had stuck him with a dagger, "Okay, now you've hurt my feelings. Do I look like I need a cane? You can just call me TJ, unless calling me good looking is too embarrassing for you."

Shane laughed with a striking smile, "I'm sorry, I didn't mean to label you as a senior citizen."

"I know—I just wanted to make you laugh, and I succeeded. You have a great laugh. We don't see it very often during a game, at least not until the horn sounds and you've won."

Shane nodded, "You're probably right. Most fans assume I'm a vicious, tenacious basketball player, but off the court they are surprised that I'm actually human."

"I know what you mean. I get the same response at the laundry when folding my underwear."

"What?" Shane asked and then laughed.

TJ didn't reply, but just kept on talking, "Are you thinking of buying a motorcoach?"

"Not for me. I was thinking that after I turn pro and get a paycheck, I would like to thank my parents for all they have done for me by giving them one. Is this a good one?"

"Well, I'm a motorcoach owner, and I own the brand you're standing in and it is called Country Coach®. I own a different model. May I show you around without a sales pitch?"

7

"That would be great because when a salesman finds out who I am, I swear the price of anything and everything seems to double or even triple."

"I don't want a dime from you. Come on, let's have some fun."

TJ began showing him around the front emphasizing the layout of the television, couch, kitchen, and finally bath and bedroom.

"Come on, I'll show you my model. It's called an Allure."

To this day, TJ wasn't sure why he did the following simple gesture, but out of some reflex, or perhaps a habit from his early days, he did it and Shane did not flinch as TJ took his hand and led him down the hall to the door. He then released his hand as they went down the steps and quickly sidestepped a group of visitors ready to step aboard. It was just TJ's way of taking charge while not allowing or accepting a negative response.

As they approached the Allure model, TJ began opening the bay doors and showing him the huge storage possibilities, the slide out patio television, and the huge battery bays, as well as the utility area. Once inside, Shane liked the forty-two inch LCD high definition television above the driver's head, the sleek design of the driver's compartment, and he quickly noted the marble tiled floors, beautiful window coverings, and the amazingly large residential refrigerator.

"I chose this model primarily because of this refrigerator. On my previous units I couldn't get a pizza box or a watermelon into the refrigerator. This bad boy can handle those favorites with no problem, plus ice and water in the door. I used to have to carry a second freezer unit in a storage bay so I could buy food in bulk from Sam's Club®. Not any more, I have plenty of storage."

He showed Shane the stackable washer dryer machines and the huge shower.

Shane smiled, "I can stand up in that one."

"Yep, and when you get as old as you implied I am, you can sit down on that seat to reach those huge feet of yours."

Shane blushed a little, "You're not going to forgive me for calling you mister, are you?"

TJ quickly answered, "I will, now that you've admitted accidentally implying I was old, but of course, you will have to forgive me for calling your feet huge. They really..." TJ looked down at the basketball star's big feet and continued, "are just, hmm, uh, big feet!"

Shane and TJ laughed as TJ placed his smaller foot next to one of Shane's. He got a slight rush of electricity as their bare legs slightly touched.

"That's the bathroom and this is the first unit for me with the toilet in a separate room than the shower. I like it because if one your friends or family members stink up the toilet, you can just open the vent and close the door until a HAZMAT crew gives you a green light. The bedroom is spacious..." began TJ as Shane suddenly plopped down on the bed. TJ stopped in mid-sentence desperately resisting the urge to jump on top of him.

Shane laughed, "This is a huge bed. What size is it?"

"It's a California King minus an inch or two. Most motorcoaches have custom beds based on design and space. They also come with cheap mattresses. I replaced mine with a custom air unit and it sleeps great," replied TJ.

Shane pushed back until his head reached the top and his feet hung just slightly over the edge.

TJ smiled, "I guess you could sleep diagonally to get your entire frame on there, or do you allow just the top half to sleep."

Shane laughed, "I usually sleep on my side with my knees pulled up slightly to give my back a rest so it is not a problem. Is that another high definition television?"

"Yep, it is a thirty-two inch screen. The speakers are in the ceiling.

Shane and TJ felt the vibration of someone else entering the coach, so Shane leaped off the bed. Shane whispered, "Come on, let's get out of here."

TJ obediently complied by following him as they stepped around the couple in the living room checking out the kitchen, and down the steps to the carpeted convention floor.

TJ said, "Okay that was about the middle of their line, so let's go see a Prevost® coach, and you'll discover the top of the line."

TJ led him across the open area to a coach where the mainframe was made in Montreal, and the coach was converted in Oregon at the Country Coach® factory. The result was a superior ride, with a huge generator, four roof air units, and with first class quality and style all around.

"My gosh! This motorcoach is amazing. It is so opulent."

"Hey, that's a good ten dollar word. It is probably that and more."

"How much is it?"

TJ guessed, "I'd say about one and half million or more. It's what RV folks call the Cadillac® of the industry. This is the kind of unit the big NASCAR® drivers and owners have, as well as movie and music stars."

"It's amazing," Shane said once again as they finished the inside tour, but is it hard to drive?"

TJ replied quickly, "No, but pushing it off to get it started is a bitch. The mother just refuses to roll easy!"

Shane laughed as another couple came aboard. "Time to go," said TJ as he led Shane around the couple checking out the microwave.

A kid recognized Shane and asked for an autograph. Shane smiled and complied. After the kid moved on, Shane said, "I think I have been discovered, and in a few minutes there will be fans coming from all over this building to get an autograph. I need to get out of here now. Can I see your coach?"

TJ was surprised at the request, but managed to say, "Sure, come on. I'll get us out of here."

Together, they walked quickly behind the rows of glistening new motorcoaches and made their way towards an exit on the front of the building, but away from the main entrance to avoid the incoming crowds. Once cleared of the building, they cut through the long rows of the huge parking lot while TJ pointed to his coach way over in the far corner, and away from the traffic flow of the visitors approaching the RV show.

"My goodness your coach was done in a beautiful color. I didn't see shades of blue and gray ones in the show."

"That is just one of the reasons I chose the color, as I like having something a bit different than anyone else, and I already liked the blue of your eyes."

Shane smiled, "Your eyes are blue, too and yes, I like the color of blue—so we have that in common."

"That'll probably be the last of common features because you're tall, good looking, strong, and can play college basketball better than anyone in the country. I'm good at...eating."

Shane laughed at him, "You're tall, too, at least for a non-basketball human."

"Gee, thanks. I was hoping you were going to say I was good looking, too, but I guess one out of four isn't bad."

As they walked closer, Shane asked, "What is that satellite dish on the roof for?"

"That is my Motosat® Internet dish. It sends and receives to the Internet just like your cable or DSL modems at home, but I obtain access from anywhere in North America, as long as I'm not under a huge stand of trees."

"That amazing, what is the dome thing up front?"

"That's probably the most valuable item on the whole coach. That is my in-motion TV satellite system. It allows me to watch or listen to television while traveling down the road, and it gives me high definition and two channels at once. With my DISH® DVR, I can watch two channels at once in split screen mode, record two channels, and watch a recorded show all at the same time. I don't think I could drive all day long, or survive in the coach very long without live high definition television. That's how I watch your games from all over the country. I never miss one. Last season I was traveling in Texas, and it was game time, so I pulled into a big rest area, put out the slides, made lunch, and sat down and watched the game, and then continued on with my trip."

"Wow, that is so cool. Is that a dog in the window?"

"I hope you like dogs. I have two dogs. The brown one in the window is Beeper, and there is a tan one asleep in the passenger seat, and his name is officially Henry Junior, but I call him J-Henry, so they are a team as J-Henry and Beeper. The guests at the RV Resorts just love them."

"I am indeed a dog fan. I had a huge Labrador growing up. He passed away a few years ago."

10

"I'm sorry. Let's head in for a tour. The dogs will smell you up and down, but they won't bite you..." he paused for effect before adding, "unless they're really hungry!"

Shane laughed as TJ opened the door after turning off the alarm and telling the dogs to stay. He stepped quickly up the steps, and told Shane to pull the door to keep the dogs inside.

"They love to escape, and they think it is funny when I'm chasing them around the park. This is Beeper on your right and J-Henry on your left."

Shane laughed as Beeper's tail sped up as Shane petted her head and then woke up J-Henry to give his head a good rub as well. TJ began showing him the front of the coach, explained his custom built business desk with the drop down leaf, desktop mounted computer system and the various printers, as well as the file drawer system he recently put in. All the woodwork throughout the coach is made from beautiful cherry wood.

Shane liked the big Ekornes recliner, the pull out table, the Corian-style counter tops, and opened the big refrigerator to check out a unit with lots of food. He noted the stackable washer and dryer, the big shower, and of course the king size airbed. Shane immediately fell back on TJ's bed to see the difference in the cheap mattress at the show and the custom airbed. He loved it, but the dogs leaped on top of him as they thought he wanted to play, and began giving him kisses and diving all over him.

TJ laughed and said, "I should have warned you that my dogs love attention, and Beeper is a quick kisser!"

Shane began tickling the dogs and they loved it. Somehow, he managed to get out from under them and scramble to his feet.

"Come on," urged TJ. "I'll show you how the Datastorm® satellite system handles my Internet connection."

TJ sat down at his desk and showed him how quickly he could access web pages all over the world.

"That's cool. I assume you can do email?"

"Yeah, I use Outlook® to handle my email accounts. I have eight email addresses."

"Eight? Why so many?"

"I use several for each company, and two for web use only. For example, if I'm just visiting a site that requires an email address, but I don't want any junk mail clogging my in-box, I'll give them one of the web addresses. If I have to register some software, or make an order from a site, then I give them a more secure secondary email address, but not what I consider my permanent ones."

"I should do that because my personal email address soon gets out and suddenly, I get reporters sending requests, as well as fans who want a jersey—like I have boxes of them. "

TJ laughed, "I guess it is tough being a good looking superstar. I never had that problem."

"I appreciate their support, but sometimes it goes a little far. I miss being able to go to the mall, and I have to go movies late at night or odd times, and enter just before the actual movie starts, while heading for the door as soon as it is over. Can I check my email?"

"Sure," replied TJ as he got out of the desk chair. "Do you use a web mail service so you can get it over the Internet?"

"Yeah, I am using Gmail from Google® right now."

Shane sat down and TJ quickly observed how computer efficient he was. He went right on the web, and in a few clicks, he was looking at his email. He began scrolling, reading, and deleting at a frenzy pace. He had at least thirty emails since reading earlier in the day. Shane replied to some messages with super fast keypunching.

"Do you want something to drink? A soda, water, milk, or juice?"

"Water, thanks," replied Shane without missing a beat on skimming through his email.

TJ placed a water bottle near his mouse hand. Shane stopped, twisted the top off, and downed half of it in one gulp. TJ had to smile at him, and his own good fortune in getting a chance to meet Shane, while talking about the motorcoach world. He loved traveling by motorcoach. Everything he needed was right at his fingertips. He often bragged he could vacuum the coach in just six minutes.

Shane finished, spun around and said, "TJ, I'm starving. I had an early weight-training workout, ran about twenty laps around the court, and ate two bowls of cereal on the run, so I could arrive here early. Would you mind if we went to get some lunch and brought it back here to eat? As you probably guessed that would allow me to avoid running into a gang of fans. I've learned to covet my private time alone."

"Sure. My car or yours?"

"Well, I left mine near the convention center. Why don't we hike over and get it, and then I can park it here on the return?"

"I need to pee the dogs, but it will just take a minute," he replied before speaking to the dogs. "Come on boys. Time to pee!"

The dogs quickly ran to the front so he could attach the leash to their collar, and then he opened the door, and they scampered out. "Pee, pee, pee," he commanded.

Shane watched as the dogs obeyed by finding a nearby tree and letting it fly with a dog on each side of the same tree. Once done, TJ praised them and let them back inside. After they were unhitched from the lease, TJ went to the cabinet and gave each dog a small treat.

"Gee nothing for me?" protested Shane.

"Did you pee?"

Shane laughed, "No."

"Then no treat for the hold back boy!" laughed TJ. "Come on, let's go."

They walked across the lot where Shane led them to a brand new Hummer. He hit his beeper to unlock the doors and turn off the alarm, climbed in, and fired up the engine. TJ had just snapped his seatbelt shut when Shane pulled out. He was careful but fast. "How about barbeque? We could do takeout at the Red, White and Blue restaurant."

"That sounds good. You order for me."

Shane smiled as he put on his headset for his cell phone and tapped the button to make a voice call. The restaurant was on his favorite list, so he was soon talking and making the order while we waited at a red light. Twenty minutes later, he pulled through the drive thru and picked up the order, refusing to allow TJ to pay. The lady in the window knew him both as a fan and a regular customer.

After lunch, they took the dogs on a long walk away from the crowds at the convention center with Shane hanging on to Beeper. He loved the walk and the fun the dogs were having as they chased from one scent mark to the other. Beeper soon picked up the scent of a rabbit and began to holler in dog speak, and pulled hard on her leash. Shane had to hang on to keep from losing her. TJ told him a story of how Beeper yanked the leash out of his hand in New Mexico last summer chasing a big old jackrabbit through the cactus fields.

It was about two when they got back to the RV, gave the dogs a bacon treat for a good potty, and lots of water. Shane gave them a good rub and asked TJ a question. "How about going to a movie with me?"

"Sure, what movie? Do I have to be twenty-one to get in?"

Shane laughed, "I think you have that covered. I wanted to go see Rescue Dawn®. It's a true story, and stars one of my favorite actors…"

TJ jumped in, "Christian Bale. Yeah, he is a favorite of mine, too. Did you see him in Batman Begins® last year."

"Yeah, about three times. I love that movie. The movie starts at three thirty, and the theater is about twenty minutes away. I think we could make it."

"Are you going to get swamped with fans?"

"Not if you help me."

"Okay, let's go."

Back in the Hummer they went, as Shane took the back roads to avoid traffic, and arrived at the theater about five minutes from the advertised start of the movie. "Don't worry, we haven't missed any of the movie. I checked the start time, and we have ten more minutes of previews. Here's twenty bucks. Go to the window and buy two tickets, and just as you get to the door I'll be right behind you. We'll dart in and down the hall to the screen, and try to find a seat in the dark."

"Got it, and I'm off."

After getting in through the door to the theater auditorium, Shane felt for TJ's hand, and led him in the darken theater, as the last preview was playing. Using his six foot nine inch viewing height, he spotted two seats in the middle about four rows from the back. He led TJ around the bend and up the stadium steps, and once in view of the crowd he let loose of TJ's hand. The movie started as they sat down. Once their eyes adjusted to the darken theater, they realized there was no one behind them, or on the same row, so Shane was at least safe during the movie.

They made a dash out of the movie right at the end and talked about it as they drove away. They laughed, talked easily, and their day together flew by.

As they waited at a signal light Shane spoke up, "TJ, I hope you're having as much fun as I am. You're a cool guy to get to know."

"Yeah, right, I bet we're heading to a medical supply store to buy me a cane."

Shane laughed, "See, that's what I'm talking about. You always make me laugh. Would it be okay to stop and get some takeout for dinner and go back to your motorcoach? Maybe we could watch a movie or something."

"Sure, but you must have a million things to do besides spending time with me."

"I want to spend time with you, if that is okay." Shane looked over at TJ and smiled earnestly.

"Okay, so what do you want to eat?"

"I was thinking Texas Roadhouse and steaks, potatoes, and salads. Is that good for you?"

"Yeah, I love their steaks. You order but this time I'm paying."

"Okay, but you'll have to go inside for the order, or I'll get mobbed, and we won't get to eat for hours."

"No problem. Let's do it."

The dogs sat patiently on the kitchen floor while the boys ate their meal hoping they would save some steak bites for them. TJ used to give them the t-bone leftovers, but after J-Henry nearly choked on a broken bone, he never gave them a bone again. He did always surprise them with a few morsels of good meat at the end of his meal. He showed Shane how to feed them from his hand, and soon Shane was cutting good meat for them.

After they put away their leftovers, TJ brought Shane a Fat Boy Ice Cream sandwich. Shane almost said no to the dessert, but smiled as he took his first bite. "Hmm...this is good."

"I usually eat just a little small ice cream thing and save this for maybe a good moment during the movie as dessert or something special. I decided you being here was something special enough."

"I have had such a good time. Can I ask you a personal question?"

14

TJ sighed as he guessed the pattern of the upcoming questions. "Sure," he replied.

"How come you aren't married? I am assuming you never were because you don't act like you were married. You picked out all the colors for the coach, and the décor has a male feel to it instead of a female one. I can just imagine how my mom would decorate the coach."

"No, I was never married and don't plan to." TJ finished his last bite, wiped his mouth slowly, and then looked up pensively into Shane's eyes trying to read his line of questions. He had decided years ago, when confronted, to always tell the truth—no matter the consequences. He took a slow breath and said, "Shane, I have admired you for years. You're so talented and so dedicated, and today I've learned you are just the most wonderful, friendly, outgoing, sincere and somehow the smartest person I know."

"What's the punch line? There's a 'but' coming, right?"

TJ smiled, "No, however, I have to be completely honest with my friends, or I'm not really a friend at all. I'm not married because I'm gay. I'm on my second career, so now I travel and write gay fiction novels and sell my books at Amazon.com®, Barnes and Noble®, and my own website ItsFiction.com. I'm not in a relationship, so it is just me and the dogs, and they always love me, as long as I don't run out of food." TJ stopped and waited for Shane to make a fast exit.

Shane finished his last bite and wiped his face on his napkin and smiled, "I thought so. I've been dying to ask you that all day. Let me guess— you thought I would cuss you out, and fly out the door, right?"

"Well, it did cross my mind, but you're too big to fly, but I did keep watching that steak knife next to your plate."

"You're wrong. I think I knew you were gay when we met in that first motorcoach. I think you're a cool, fun loving, happy-go-lucky guy, and I cherish the time we had together today. I'm sorry it was hard for you to tell me, and believe me, I understand how hard."

Shane paused for a moment, and TJ noted the color left Shane's face. "I've never told anyone but my parents what I'm about to tell you, and you must promise me you'll never ever tell anyone, and certainly not the media as they would crucify me." TJ loved the way he added, "Do I have your trust?"

TJ nodded, "Of course you do. I have had a great time today, too. You were so generous to this old fellow."

Shane laughed, "You're far from old." He sighed hard, "TJ, I'm gay, too."

TJ should have said something reflective, calm, comforting, or perhaps supporting, but instead what came out of his mouth was a huge laugh, "Hah, you're teasing me, right? You're pulling my chain, aren't you? This is what the kids call being punk'd, right?"

"No, I'm not. I'm gay. You just wanted me to have to say it twice, didn't you?"

TJ laughed again, "No. I'm in shock. You're so non gay in looks and mannerisms."

"Neither or you—that is something I liked. I like manly men."

TJ grinned, "Oh, that's me all right. I bet I can bench press..." he started looking around the room and finished, "J-Henry! All thirty pounds!"

Shane laughed, "You know what I mean. How long have you known you are gay?"

"Not long enough," replied TJ quickly. "I wish I had known I was gay in college, so I could have dated gays. I dated beautiful young ladies and wasted a ton of money and ego on such pretty girls. I didn't find out I was really gay until years later. I knew I was different, but I just thought it would pass. It was a different time. Now it is cool to come out early. When did you tell your parents?"

"Ninth grade, but I haven't told anyone else. I will one day. My parents were disbelieving at first, but after they told me they loved me anyhow, I expressed more of my feelings, so they knew for sure I was indeed gay, and not just a phase I was going through. However, I have never dated a guy, nor have I been with a guy."

"You mean you haven't had gay sex."

"I fooled around with a guy when I was about twelve at a basketball camp, but that's it."

"Boy, you are a patient soul. You must believe in sex only after marriage."

Shane laughed, "Well, that's a good goal, but I just didn't want to fool around with a stranger. I want to be in love and make love."

"Now you sound like you have been reading my books."

"What does that mean?"

"Well all my books are either action adventure or dramatic stories, but they all are based on the two leading characters being totally in love with the other. None are married because it is mostly illegal in the United States, but they would if they could."

"There, you agree with me. Can I see your books?"

TJ replied, "Sure...just as soon as you start my heart again. It stopped right after you said you were gay." Shane laughed.

TJ stood up to get copies of the books. Shane stood up at the same time. They stood there for an awkward moment until their eyes met. Shane spoke first, "Can I get a hug?"

"Do you need a hug?"

Shane sighed, so TJ added, "I'm just kidding. Come here you big lug."

Shane quickly engulfed TJ in his big arms and pulled him in tight. TJ did his best to hold on as well. They stood there a moment embraced before

16

Shane slowly allowed his hands to wander a little until he had placed them on TJ's butt.

"You have a nice butt," Shane whispered.

"You haven't seen it naked," replied TJ.

Shane stifled a laugh, "But I want to."

TJ allowed his hands to wonder down to Shane's butt. "I have seen this butt on television and web galleries many times. I never thought I could touch your beautiful buns."

"But you haven't seen the bruises underneath the shorts."

TJ grinned, "But I want to."

Shane laughed. Slowly, he pulled his upper chest back from their tight embrace, began looking downward at TJ's hair, smiled sweetly, and placed a kissed on the top of his head.

It was a gentle, tender kiss, but TJ couldn't help himself, "My mom kisses me like that. Could you do something a little sexier? I'm dying here."

Shane laughed again as he brought his hand up, and with the touch of his tender fingers he lifted TJ's chin so he could see into his face. He stared for a long time, as if trying to read TJ's eyes, his sincerity, his heart, or perhaps even to see if there was any love there. Sensing safety, he slowly lowered his lips down and kissed TJ on his cheek, then his nose, and finally to his lips.

The kiss made TJ's penis snap to salute, even before Shane bravely slid his tongue between their teeth and into TJ's warm wet mouth. TJ felt Shane's own erection rise against his upper chest since Shane was much taller. They broke the kiss several times, but returned repeatedly.

It was twenty minutes later before they broke the embrace with TJ suddenly wondering if anyone had seen them, before remembering he had placed the black screens on the windows, so no one could see in during the daytime. He had a curtain for nighttime privacy.

"Show me the books before I mess my pants up," urged Shane.

TJ teased while feigning ecstasy and oblivion, "What books?"

Shane laughed, "Your books, you big dummy."

"I thought you called me smart a few minutes ago."

"That was just to get you to kiss me."

"You big basketball players are all alike. Bounce the ball, and head in for the score."

Shane laughed again. TJ pulled open one of the lateral file cabinets and began retrieving copies of his books. TJ explained the storyline of each one and then said, "Coming soon is **The Raceboys,** and it's about America's top racecar driver who surprisingly falls in love with a new friend. Forced out of the closet, he must endure the anger of the fans and drivers alike to go for another championship. I'll release it this fall, and followed by **Gay Grifters** about a gang of gay thieves in the spring.

Shane looked at the beautiful covers, thumbed through the pages and was shocked to hold gay fiction in his hands, as he had never been brave enough to buy one. "Are these available in Amazon's Kindle® format?"

"Yes, they are."

"Good, because I want to read them all, but I don't think I can take the chance of carrying your beautiful books in my book bag, but I do have a Kindle Reader® and I love it. I have about twenty books on it now and it can hold about ten times that. My unit is password protected so no one can check on what I'm reading. I'll bring it so I can download to it if that's okay?"

"Of course. I hope you enjoy them, but at least by reading them you might understand my wit and humor."

Shane grinned, "I doubt that. Can I have another kiss?"

"Yes, and you never have to ask again your entire life. If you need a kiss, I'm always ready to oblige."

They kissed for several minutes before breaking their embrace. "What time is it?"

TJ looked at his atomic wall clock and replied, "Just after eight o'clock."

"Can I stay here with you tonight?"

TJ almost laughed but kept a straight face, "Yes, you may, and you never have to ask that again either."

Shane did laugh. "I meant sleeping with you."

TJ said quickly, "But I have a nice blow up air mattress we can put right here on the carpet."

Shane frowned, "I meant I want to have sex with you."

"Oh," TJ sighed. "Do you mean all night? I have to get my beauty rest."

Shane laughed hard, "You're in corrigible. Yes, I want to have sex with you all night long."

"Well, if you insist," replied TJ somberly, before busting out laughing and diving into Shane's arms. "But only if you kiss me quick!"

"Yes, sir," he said.

After the kiss TJ added, "You never have to say 'sir' again to me unless we're in a medical supply store shopping for a cane."

Shane laughed. "Should we watch a movie, or…"

"Get naked?" interrupted TJ.

"Yeah," smiled Shane wickedly, "exactly what I was thinking."

"Why of course you were—you're horny. After all, you waited since the ninth grade. Let's pee the dogs and prepare the coach for sleep, and get to it sailor!"

They quickly walked the dogs, and then TJ showed Shane how he locked the door for the evening. Then he pulled a long insulated drape from behind the driver's left side all the way around the front of the coach, following the line of glass and ending at the door. He also pulled down a

18

shade cover on the window next to the passenger. The rest of the window shades he usually left down to prevent sun glare on his computer screen. He longed for the day when he could afford electric shades on all the windows like on the Prevost® motorcoach they saw at the show.

TJ said, "Now no one can see inside." He turned on the light in the back of the coach while turning off the ones in the front. "Come on back to the bedroom. The dogs preceded him and jumped on the bed. "I guess you don't have any clothes or toothbrush, huh?"

"No, I didn't know I was going to fall for a good looking gay man today."

"Good answer," said TJ, "and you win a new, free toothbrush." He reached on to the back of his top shelf of his deep medicine cabinet, and retrieved a brand new brush. "My hygienist always gives me a new one after my cleanings."

"You don't use them?"

TJ smiled, "No, I prefer the rotted look. No, she forgets she sold me a Sonicare® Cordless toothbrush system that uses bristles and sonic sound waves to clean the teeth and gums safely. The only side effect is it makes me get an erection when I use it."

Shane shot back, "By all means, please brush your teeth with that thing."

They both laughed. TJ brushed his teeth and tossed the toothpaste to Shane. After TJ finished, he sat down on the bed, removed his shoes, his polo shirt and hung it up, removed his summer shorts, and pulled off his socks. He then walked back to the toilet to pee.

Shane watched him undress and wasn't ashamed to do so, but it was the first time he watched a man undress without averting his eyes, as he did in the locker room everyday. He followed suit by sitting down and undressing and hanging his shirt in the closet, so it would be wrinkle free in the morning. After TJ flushed, Shane stepped into the toilet room.

"How do I close the door?"

TJ asked, "Are you going to take a dump?"

"No, I just need to pee."

"Well, since in a few seconds I am going to see you naked, don't you think you could pee with me nearby?"

Shane laughed, "Good point. How do you flush?"

"There are two buttons on the left side. The small button is used to put lots of water in the bowl if you're going to take a dump, so it doesn't smell so bad, but if you're just peeing, then once you're done just hit the big button and it'll flush electrically."

Shane peed long and hard, making sure he had every drop out of his bladder, so he wouldn't have to interrupt anything in bed and hit the button. "Cool," he said as the electric toilet disposed of his urine.

He turned around and washed his hands. He then brushed his teeth, and once done, he found TJ sitting on the edge of the bed waiting on him. He came over to him. TJ looked up and smiled, "You're sure you want to sleep with me?"

Shane reached down and took TJ's hands in his, and pulled him to his feet, and kissed him. He broke the kiss and said, "I'm very sure."

They kissed again. Shane broke away and pulled TJ's tee shirt off so TJ did the same to him. After a few kisses, they took turns pulling each other's shorts off, and then fell on the bed scattering the dogs to the far side. With TJ on his back, Shane slid gently over him, putting only part of his weight on him, as he continued kissing him while allowing his right hand to play with TJ's erection.

After a while, TJ pushed Shane onto his back, placed his fingers around Shane's tool, and went down on him. He thought he heard Shane purring, but before long, he heard Shane moaning. He slowed down to keep him from losing his load. TJ spun around so they could perform oral sex at the same time, while carefully stopping just in time.

An hour or so later, TJ reached into the nightstand and removed a new condom and placed it over Shane's huge erection. TJ said, "We're going to have to shop for some super size condom's tomorrow, but this will do for tonight." Shane laughed.

TJ placed a little bit of lubrication in the right place, but soon he was straddling Shane, and gently guiding Shane inside him. TJ watched Shane's eyes, as he waited patiently in anticipation, and grinned when they went wide as he went deep inside. TJ pumped for a while, but stopped from time to time, holding off Shane's climax, and driving the big boy crazy.

About thirty minutes later, he told Shane to swap places. TJ, now lying on his back, showed Shane how to enter him in the same position most heterosexuals used. Once deep inside, the basketball star's primal instinct took over, and he began slowly thrusting while kissing TJ passionately with their tongue's exploring. More than once, TJ had to remind him to hold off until finally Shane felt his body was about to explode, so TJ let the reins out and Shane exploded. Afterwards he collapsed in TJ's arms, but soon began kissing his neck, and explored his ear with his tongue.

Their lovemaking continued most of the night with TJ going in deep, and afterwards, Shane built up steam again and soon he moved once again on top of TJ. By four, they were fast asleep in each other's arms. TJ instantly fell in love while sleeping with his ear pressed to Shane's chest listening to the thump-thump sound of his heart like a new puppy with his mom. It made him feel comfortable, safe, and very much in love.

The next morning TJ's eyes opened before Shane's, and it gave him a moment to reflect over what occurred last night. He knew that Shane, new at gay sex, probably felt both safe and desperate to have male sex for the first time, but now that he had, he felt sure he would want to make a polite exit. He was also relatively sure he would get a few emails from him, and then he would disappear. He wasn't angry at the inevitable conclusion, as the sex had been good for him, too. Shane would not have to worry about him spilling the beans, as he was still a fan of the great basketball player.

Suddenly, Shane's eyes popped open meeting TJ's so he asked, "What time is it?"

TJ smiled and replied, "About eight or so." He slightly hoped Shane might say something sweet or even romantic.

Shane said plainly, with no emotion, "My butt is sore."

TJ smiled again, "So is mine, but after you walk a little and remember how it got sore, you'll learn to like that kind of soreness."

"I already like it. Can we do it again?"

"You did it to me three times last night," replied a protesting TJ, though he was as anxious as Shane was.

Shane added, "Please."

TJ replied, "I hate it when they beg."

Shane laughed. "Put another condom on me."

# TWO

They ate brunch by doing takeout from Bojangles® with TJ eating one bacon, egg, and cheese biscuit, Shane busting his diet by eating two, and the dogs splitting a sausage biscuit, so everyone was full and happy.

After Shane brushed his teeth he surprised TJ by asking, "Do you have to travel today?"

TJ replied honestly, "Well, now that I am making some money from my books, I pretty much do what I want to do, and go where I want to go, whenever I want to. It's a tough job, but somebody has to do it, right? However, no, I don't have to be anywhere for a while. I do have a few book signings coming up, but mostly I'm sending out press releases and such. I am working on a new book, and that takes up most of my time. I do field research like visiting an area where a story takes place, or museums, if it is a period piece, so I can write wherever I am."

"That sounds like a great life. Are you ready for more sex?" Shane asked with a straight face, and then smiled and laughed, "Just kidding, at least for now. Are they going to run you out of the parking lot?"

"No, but I'll need to move to a park soon to fill up with water, dump the tanks, wash clothes, and other chores."

"Is there a resort we can go to that isn't too far away?"

"How about the beach?"

Shane grinned, "That sounds awesome. You can just pick up and go?"

"Absolutely," replied TJ. "I could be underway in about twenty minutes or fifteen if I hurry. Do you want to go to a busy beach or a private one?"

"Private. I want to walk down the beach holding your hand."

TJ smiled, "Daytime or nighttime?"

Shane faked a punch at him, "All the time."

"How about east of Jacksonville, North Carolina?"

Shane wrinkled his nose, "I know there is a Jacksonville in Florida, but you did say North Carolina, right?"

"Yep, it is about as straight east from here as you can get, but on the other side of Raleigh, and not far from Camp Lejeune, where all the good looking young Marine soldiers are."

Shane laughed, "Now you're talking. Is there a good resort there?"

"Pretty good, but with the kids already back in school we might have the place to ourselves before the big Labor Day weekend. Should I call and make reservations?"

"Yes, it sounds great. I can't believe you can just pack up and go. What freedom that must be."

"How many nights can you be gone?"

Shane thought for a second, "I will have to find a place to shoot hoops and work out some, but I don't have class until Wednesday. Can we come back on Tuesday afternoon?"

"Yes we can. Why don't you take the dogs on a quick pee and potty trip while I make the reservations, and then come back here to help me pack up?"

"Okay, but what about my car?"

"When you get back, I'll follow you to your place to drop your car off. Is that okay?"

"Perfect, and thanks. I can grab some clothes, too. Come on J-Henry. Come Beeper." The dogs leaped awake with tails wagging, Shane hitched their leashes, and they went out the door.

TJ managed to catch someone on the third ring at the Atlantic RV Resort and made the reservation. Once done, he brought the GPS map software up on his computer and plotted the course. He knew the town was small where they were going, so he also planned a stop at a huge Super Wal-Mart® to buy groceries. He was printing it out when Shane and the dogs returned.

"Give them a treat. They're in the cabinet above their food bowl."

Shane found the big jar, and gave them both a good rub and a treat. "What are you doing?"

"I plan my trips with CoPilot® software, but this coach has a pitiful Pioneer® GPS system built in. I use CoPilot® to plan and print out the turns and stops, and then program that into the cheesy Pioneer® deck in the dash so we don't get lost. You don't want to make many U-turns in a forty-two foot coach with a SUV in tow. Okay, I'm done. Let's take your Hummer home."

"That sounded like you were stuttering."

"Kiss me quick to cure it."

Shane obliged with a smile and pinched TJ's butt. "I hope you heal up during the trip so we can have lots of sex tonight."

TJ laughed and gently squeezed Shane's bulge, "No problem. I can handle a little dick like this any day."

"Ha! Now that's funny. Let's go."

Two hours later, they finally made it to the other side of Raleigh and away from the big traffic. TJ stopped and put Shane in the driver's seat and showed him how to steer the big coach. Shane was so nervous, but gradually he relaxed, and learned to handle the steering very well. They practiced maneuvering in a big empty rest area parking lot, and then TJ took over when they got down to a two-lane highway leading to the beach.

After they arrived, TJ went to check-in, and then they pulled into the resort. There were about eight hundred sites but only twenty coaches there. They drove through the fancy entrance decorated with lush palm trees and waterfalls, and found their lot not far from the big sand dune that hid the beach.

Shane asked, "Where's the ocean?"

Without hesitation TJ replied, "Damn! Somebody stole it!"

Shane laughed as TJ added, "Hold your horses. You'll see."

TJ smiled as he made a hard turn to the right, then another, and came to their site. He pulled through, while constantly checking his mirrors, until the utility bay was opposite the power pedestal, the water tap, and sewer drains. He stopped the coach, put it in neutral after applying the big yellow knob parking brake, and hit the button for the auto leveling system. "It's over the big dune. There's no ocean view in the park, but the dunes keep the sand and salt from covering the motorcoach. I stayed in a little old place north of Daytona on the beach a few years ago, and my site was right on the beach. Next morning, I couldn't see out the front windows as the salt spray covered the coach. It felt like I was inside a glazed donut trying to see out. I quickly moved, and paid extra to wash my coach. This is best of both worlds. We're close to the beach, so we can walk up and down alongside the water, and this time of the year, we can take the dogs, too. Come on, I'll show you how we set up camp."

With the leveling system fine tuning to a level position, TJ checked to be sure the power breaker was turned off on the utility pedestal, then he undid the little cord door at the rear of the RV, and hit the switch for the cord to roll out. He dragged it to the power box, plugged in, and flipped on the breaker.

"The power will actually kick on inside the coach after a surge and power device checks out the quality of the power from the park's system. It takes about two minutes, and then it pops and we have power. Let's hook up the sewer and water lines."

Opening the utility bay, TJ removed a big plug in the floor, dropped out the black sewage line, and hooked it into the drain in the cement pad. He opened the gray tank valve so the sink, shower, and washing machine water could easily drain. He opened another bay, took out a spare water line, his water softener tank, hooked it up, and turned it on after shutting all the bay doors.

"Okay, before we put out the slides, I always check to make sure we're not going to hit anything now that we're level." He judged the distance to the pedestal to be safe. "We're looking good. Let's go back inside."

He showed Shane the switches for the big slides to go out, he turned off the power generator that had been cooling the coach, and turned off the ignition key to let the diesel start cooling down. They walked to the rear where TJ pushed the buttons for the rear slides to go out. The dogs jumped on the bed. TJ opened the rear cabinet and showed Shane the satellite controller. He hit the search button and Shane heard the dish start up on the roof. The coach was now powered by the pedestal, so the air conditioning units kicked

24

on. They went back up front to pull out the dining table, adjusted the recliner, put up the leaf on the desk, and checked the satellite picture on the front television. In ten minutes, everything was set up and working including the water.

"Time to change clothes and head to the beach. We have exploring to do."

Shane held on to J-Henry's leash as the dog pulled him along the deck ramp leading to the beach. "Boy, he is stronger than he looks."

TJ laughed, "I was thinking the same thing about you!"

"Ha, ha. Can we leave our flip-flops at the end of the deck?"

TJ kicked his off, "Sure. I doubt anyone would steal them, although someone might think your big sandals are surfboards. The beach looks almost deserted. Let's go walking."

They led the two dogs to the water and then turned north as they splashed water, kicked sand, and chatted away. Shane told him about his home and what his friends were like. He talked about high school. He loved his hometown, but he felt trapped there because everyone knew him. They watched him play basketball from as early as the seventh grade. He excelled at the sport early on, and with his teammates, they won the county, state, and regional championships every year. His dad taught him like a coach, but never pushed him like a man trying to live out his own dream.

Shane said he would say things like do you think you can run five miles today, or do you think the few players that will make it to college ball would run six.

TJ smiled, and asked, "How far did you run?"

Shane grinned, "Seven miles."

TJ laughed, "I doubt I could walk that far. I guess running for me is like taking the car and 'running' to Wal-Mart®. I guess your dad was pretty smart as most kids would rebel from being told what to do, but allowing you to make the decision was good training for then and now. Nowadays, kids can't learn how to make a good decision, if they aren't allowed to make lots of decisions…with guidance of course."

Shane replied, "My folks and I are very close, but I am especially close to my dad. We are fortunate because he worked so hard in his early years, that he had the time and money to never miss one of my games. He flies in to most of my home games, and any other games within a few hundred miles of home."

"Was it hard telling them you are gay?"

"I know it is for many kids, but I really feel like my folks are some of my best friends. We all cried after I told them—not so much for what I told them…" he paused remembering "but after they quickly replied by telling me how much they still loved me. Everywhere we go girls yell out how much they love me, and I smile and say thank you, but none of them really know me. In a way, because of my folks, I didn't seek out a girl that would easily have sex with me, but rather I sought love.

"I discovered I was gay just as I was about to start high school, so I couldn't find love without exposing myself to constant homophobic abuse. My town isn't a huge town like Lindle, Charlotte, or Raleigh where you can almost hide due to the numbers. Our population was about twenty thousand, and though I didn't know all their names—they knew mine. You should see the scrapbooks my mom has put together. There was one book just for junior high and the occasional sports page clipping. In high school, there were so many news stories she had to do a book a year, and she doing the same for my college years.

"How'd you find out you were gay? Did you hit your head and it popped out? Did you accidentally buy a tie that actually goes with your suit? Did you learn how to cook a pound cake? Did you start shopping for coordinating colors of paint for your room?"

Shane was laughing. "I have never met anyone like you. You find humor in everything, and I mean everything. No, I just began noticing certain good looking guys on various teams."

"What about the locker rooms?"

"No, it wasn't on my mine because I was afraid I might get an erection if I saw someone cute. I showered, dressed and got out of there as fast I could. During my junior high years, I was at a basketball camp in a neighboring state. It was a camp known to attract various college coaches and recruiters. I became friends with this guy from Florida. He was a guard with awesome legs."

"Ah, a legs man. Me, too, but I like them long and naked."

Shane blushed and added, "Me, too." He picked up a stick and flung it out into the crashing waves. "He just kept staring at me. I smiled back. He winked at me. I winked back. I had to go home the next day, but the night before, he and I went for a walk, stepped off the trail, and kissed and felt each other. It was the most natural thing in the world to me. I knew it was guys for me from then on.

"High school basketball players are often treated like gods, and the girls are trying to score on you while you're trying to score some points for your team. I had to fake a relationship with a good friend. She may have had thoughts we would get married, but I never tried to have sex with her. I believe she thought I was just well mannered, maybe chivalrous. I don't know.

"My dad and I always watched all the Taylor University games on television, and it was really the only place I wanted to go to college. I'm thankful it was far away from home so I could back off a little from the relationship pressure. I have a lot of friends who are girls, wonderful girls, but I was only drawn to guys."

TJ said, "I came out pretty late about six years after college. I missed out on dating during college when I still had my natural good looks." TJ pretended to pose like a GQ model. They both laughed.

Shane smiled, "I think you're still very good looking."

TJ spoke to the dogs, "You hear that. Write that down. This boy is smart—smart enough to brag on the chef that is doing the cooking tonight." They laughed again while the dogs pricked up their ears trying their best to figure out what TJ was talking about. "Let's turn around. We're grilling steaks tonight and you're going to help."

"No problem. I'm a good steak turner."

"Salad and baked potatoes okay?"

"Perfect. I don't usually eat too much red meat, but every now and then, a good steak is fine. As I get closer to team practice starting, I begin sticking to a very rigid but a great diet designed for hard work. I became great friends with the team dietician and together, we created a lean and mean menu system, and I stick to it no matter how tempted I am to fall back on old habits. I believe it gives me a twenty percent advantage over my competition. I can run up and down the floor all night long without getting tired, while still jumping and fighting for every rebound and loose ball. I love the fight to win. I love to score. I love to out hustle the competition. I love the game."

TJ grinned at him, "Yeah, like I said, you and I have a lot in common, because I love watching you do all that, and I especially like it when you're on top of me. If you keep making me having sex eight times a night, I'm going to have to make an appointment with your diet guru!" Shane laughed so TJ added, "Or a proctologist!"

Shane laughed harder, slipped his hand into TJ's and squeezed it. The beach was almost deserted and near twilight. They walked holding hands until someone approached. They were both happy, and silly. They laughed, poked fun at each other, and yes, they were getting hungry and horny.

Each day at the beach they went exploring, driving to see the local attractions and landmarks, and taking daily walks on the beach. Every morning they went to a local park so Shane could shoot for a while. TJ was smart enough not to play against Shane one-on-one, but rather kept feeding him the balls as they swished through the net about ninety-eight percent of the time. TJ counted a hundred foul line shots, a hundred shots from fifteen feet away from the goal, and he finished almost two hundred shots within six feet. He also ran and jogged his way all around the park with the dogs chasing him for a while, but soon they would tire, so TJ would snatch up their leashes and lead them back to the SUV and their water bowl.

TJ and Shane took a swim in the ocean before moving to the pool where most of the time they found themselves alone. Late one night, they went skinny-dipping and made out in the Jacuzzi. In just a few days, they had become closer than some couples dating a month or more. They began finishing each other's sentences, and thinking alike. In privacy, they touched each other tenderly on the arm, shoulder, hand, or a thigh. They kissed often, sometimes deeply and other times gently, by planting a butterfly kiss to the other's eyelids, cheeks, forehead, ears, neck, and lips.

They never tired of their lovemaking, sleeping side by side by cuddling close, and taking long naps with the dogs on the other side of the bed. They also napped in the shade of the palm trees, watched movies, held hands, and teased and laughed all day long.

TJ explained the plots of various gay movies, and one by one, they watched and discussed them. They started with TJ's all-time favorite "Torch Song Trilogy" and Shane loved Harvey Fierstein's wonderful, hilarious and touching story. After enjoying "Long Time Companion" Shane asked many questions about AIDS, as well as the success rate for gay couples to stay together.

TJ explained some gay couples are just like heterosexuals using the speed dating practices of the younger generation where couples fell in and out of love about as fast as they changed the songs on their digital music players. He estimated about thirty percent of the straight world stayed together an entire lifetime, but it was a higher percentage in the gay world after they made it through the first five years. He told him he wanted to be in a relationship like his parents. They were already on their way to their sixtieth wedding anniversary.

Shane asked why TJ failed to fall in love before. TJ sighed and rolled his eyes. "I thought I was in a love a time or two, but in most cases I loved them more than they loved me."

Shane smiled, "Their lost. My gain. I win again."

TJ deadpanned, "What makes you think I love you?"

Shane slide his hand in TJ's pants and wrapped his fingers around his penis, "Because if you don't I'm going to give this little wiener a big old yank!"

TJ laughed, "Okay, you win. I love you."

Shane relaxed his grip but kept his hand in place, "I love you, too. Now get your clothes off."

TJ laughed as they both rapidly stripped for the second time that day. The dogs trotted off the bed to the living room as they already seen enough naked human butts to last them a while.

Monday night before they fell asleep, Shane pulled TJ tighter into his arms, kissed him lightly, pulled away and said, "I have something to say."

TJ didn't catch the serious tone of Shane's voice, assuming there was something funny he was about to say, or he had to fart and replied, "You're not pregnant are you?"

Shane smiled, "No, but you should be. Hush up and listen to me because I'm dreading going back to school tomorrow."

"Why? You love Taylor University and soon it will be basketball season—your favorite time of the year."

Shane sighed, "I repeat politely—shut up."

"Yes, dear," replied TJ sweetly.

"I dread going back because I don't want you to go away."

TJ's expression changed, "I see."

"Is there an RV resort near campus? Can you stay longer? I don't want to lose you."

TJ smiled, "You can't lose me—I'm too big." Shane didn't laugh. TJ winked at him, "To be honest I have been thinking the same thing all day as well, but since you're the younger one and the superstar, I felt I should hold back on my thoughts."

"That's stupid. We're partners. I'm just taller..." he paused before adding, "and better looking, but don't ever do that again. We should never lie to each other, and we should always say exactly what we're thinking."

"When did you get so smart?"

"I want us to be one of those rare couples that stay together for a lifetime. That's why I've been worried all day. I know you have to travel for book signings and research, but could you stay longer. I feel like we're just getting started on a wonderful relationship. Tell me you can stay."

TJ replied, "You're sure?"

"Very sure." Shane kissed him.

TJ replied, "Okay, let me up."

"Where you going?"

"I'm going to the computer to see if there is an RV park near your school. I'll be right back."

Shane laughed as TJ walked naked down the hall. He called after him, "The leather is going to be cold."

TJ flipped a light on, and moved to his chair to sit down, "Ow! That's cold."

"I told you," laughed Shane from the bedroom.

Soon TJ returned to the bed. "There were two parks, but after reading the reviews, I think we're better off putting the coach in Twin Lakes. It has longer sites for big rigs, less trees for better satellite reception, and it is about seven miles from your school."

"That's great. Did they have a vacancy?"

"Too late to call, so I sent them an email requesting a reservation. How long do you want me to stay?"

Shane went pensive for a long second before smiling just slightly and replying, "Forever."

# THREE

TJ was thankful the inner city older RV resort was nicer than he thought it might be. They remodeled it a few years ago putting in a row of eighty foot cement pads with new fifty amp power pedestals while clearing out some ugly old trees in the process. The boys were also pleased to have a corner lot providing a little more privacy.

Their neighbors, Bob and Sue, were from South Dakota as residents, and originally from the far southwest, but spent part of each year traveling. They had a relative going through surgery and recovery at Duke Medical Center and volunteered to travel south to help look after him. They traveled with cats, but loved TJ's dogs, and together, the four of them made friends quickly.

On the weekend, Bob grilled chicken breasts on their grill, and TJ made his mother's famous recipe for mustard potato salad. Sue made corn on the cob in their microwave while slow cooking green beans on the stove. Shane made a fresh bowl of salad, and a platter of various raw vegetables to nibble own while waiting for the chicken to cook. He even brought out several bottles of salad dressing—all fat free.

As the sun began to set, Sue turned on their patio lantern lights with their globes of rainbow colors. The foursome laughed and talked throughout dinner, and though they were from different generations, they bonded quickly. They had the fun of traveling and living aboard an RV in common. Bob showed them many tricks for maintenance on the outside of the motorcoach while Sue helped with organization inside, and quick meal tips.

They were almost done with the meal when Sue, displaying a bit of her wonderful wit, simply asked how long the boys had been dating. Shane nearly choked on the ear of corn he was working on, but TJ, with a bit more experience on receiving such questions replied they had only been together about eight days. Bob and Sue smiled as Sue offered that she and Bob suspected they were gay on day one. When Shane asked how, she said they just had the look of someone in love, and since there were no girls around, she assumed they were in love with each other. She noted the silent smiles they gave each other, and the look of their enduring eyes. Bob said she missed nothing, but he said even an old fart like him would have bet they were a couple. He said now that their secret was out, they should know that both Bob and Sue were not homophobic, but rather the opposite, and completely supportive. He told them if there was anything they could do to help, they would. Shane sighed heavily as the number of people on the planet that knew he was gay had just grown from four to six: his parents, the player at camp, TJ, and now Bob and Sue.

Shane, like the rest of the team, had taken a full load of summer classes to make his winter season easier. Though required to live in the athlete's dorm, he spent all of his spare time with TJ. Shane rose early each morning taking both an eight o'clock and nine-thirty classes. He was in the weight room by eleven, and after lunch he spent about two hours shooting before joining various pick up games with the rest of his team. After his games, he would begin his running workout by doing various sprints, ending with a long run for stamina, and finishing with a cool down walk followed by lots of stretching. He also followed a routine of stretching before beginning any workout. He religiously took special care of his body, determined to prevent any possible muscle, ligament, tendon, cartilage, or joint damage. No one on the team came close to his workout regime, his strict diet system, his inner drive, his purposeful discipline, and his heart and love for the game.

During the summer sessions, former Taylor players often returned to the campus for a few days to take on the younger players, many of whom were NBA starters, which gave the Taylor University players excellent, challenging, and demanding workouts. They also picked up tips and tricks, as well as new trash talk as the older players enjoyed razing the new younger ones, but it was a mutual admiration society. The young players dreamed of making it to the NBA and making all that money, while the pros with all that money wished they could play one more year of college basketball.

If he felt he needed work on a particular shot during these outside pickup games, he would return to the gym after supper, and spend hours shooting that shot, or perfecting a move repeatedly. Team managers took turns helping him by tossing him another ball, while retrieving the last shot. Two hours of working out with Shane left the student manager exhausted and drenched with sweat. With Shane's lean body mass, and extraordinary muscle tone, he rarely showed signs of sweat, even during an intense up and down the court ballgame. After a quick shower, he returned to the athlete's cafeteria for a snack of fruits and raw vegetables.

Shane followed the daily workout schedule seven days a week including holidays. During the season, if the team received a rare day off from practice, Shane could be found on the wood floor practicing his shots. Not a single team manager ever said no when Shane asked if they would workout with him. They instinctively knew that one day they would be able to tell their kids they helped develop one of the NBA's major stars.

Shane also possessed impeccable manners, unique for today's college kids, and was generous with his time when meeting someone new. He occasionally yelled on the basketball court, but mostly remained soft spoken, polite, and almost tender in his responses to the sportswriters' questions. His gentleness was just part of a long list of admirable qualities his coach loved. Shane, he once said, was a coach's dream by buying into the coach's strict system with more than a hundred percent effort. The coach just wished he could put some of Shane's heart in his other players.

With his starlike persona, something he never asked for, he remained completely loyal to his fellow players, and did all he could to help when asked, while never presuming he knew more, or better than they were. He knew he could not carry success on his shoulders alone, but rather he hoped he would at least be the first to pick success up, and wait for his team to join him on the path to the top as well. He believed his coach's adage that the player's name on the back of a jersey was not nearly as important the team's name on the front.

When TJ heard that, he looked at the tag in the back of Shane's tee shirt and said, "Hey, this misspelled your name. Instead of Shane, it says Hanes. They need to move that "S" to the front of the word!"

The first weekend after school started, they remained in town so Shane could get a jump-start on the pile of homework his professors put on at the beginning of a semester, and so TJ could catch up on days of no writing during their early getting acquainted days. TJ still couldn't believe the chance meeting with Shane, but falling in love with him was just something he would never have bet on. Everyday, he woke up and glanced to his right to see if this adventure might be a dream, and if Shane remained asleep at his side. Seeing Shane's soft, smooth face early in the morning, with his short hair askew, always made TJ smile with a great sense of relief. It wasn't a dream, a fictitious aberration, a delusional hallucination, or even a mirage. In TJ's opinion, Shane, the most beautiful, wonderful, exciting college basketball player in the country, did indeed sleep with one of his long muscular arms wrapped around TJ's chest.

This weekend, however, TJ packed up and waited for Shane to finish his workouts at the gym. Shane arrived at the RV park to find TJ's car hitched up and ready for towing, as well as the power, water and sewer lines disconnected and put away, the satellite internet dish stowed, the curtains tied back, and the windows screens removed. He spotted TJ finishing a long walk with the dogs.

Shane parked in the rear of their site to hold it, and together, they gave Bob and Sue a hug goodbye. They were going to Wilmington for the weekend to enjoy another of North Carolina's spectacular beautiful beaches. TJ told Shane as they pulled off the on ramp for I-40 that North Carolina was one of those special states possessing three amazing terrains within the state borders. To the east were broad beautiful beaches producing glowing sunrises and stupendous sunsets, while the west produces some of most serene mountain views in the country, with lush green trees and plants, and hundreds of waterfalls, pristine creeks and streams, and amazing rock structures. The middle section of North Carolina was a bit of both with easy going rolling hills that were once under the ocean floor, and the occasional big hill, a mere little cousin to the big mountains of the west, but still green and pretty even in the September sun.

Shane began driving after they passed Raleigh, while TJ studied the route on his laptop, memorizing the key turns, and hoping they would be ahead of the beach traffic. With the football season already underway, most of the beach crowd diminished to about twenty percent of normal load, and perfect for TJ and Shane.

TJ left the crock-pot sitting in the one of the dual sinks and plugged in so it could continue to cook while they rolled down the highway thanks to either the power inverter or generator. The smell of Swiss steak nearly drove the boys and dogs crazy. Beeper stopped at the sink and barked, as if to say she should be allowed to taste the food her nostrils inhaled.

Several hours later, they found the RV resort and checked in. TJ's research and conversation with the manager paid off, and they were rewarded with a beautiful long pull thru lot off to the side, and away from the guests that would wander up and down the long aisles of recreational vehicles. Starving, they quickly set up camp as TJ called it, and began working on dinner. TJ made a large batch of mashed potatoes, with Shane heating up a green bean casserole TJ prepared the night before, while cooking more corn on the cob in the microwave, and together they sat down to eat. The dogs sat in the aisle as if blocking the boys' way from the table to the kitchen, and hoping and praying for some bites of the sweet smelling steak.

Shane ate several bites of everything before commenting. "Oh my, this is really good. You're quite the cook."

TJ smiled, "Thanks, but I'm limited as to what I can cook for friends. By myself, I do many one-pot meals, combining vegetables and such to make it fast and easy. I still consider you company, and I am afraid that if my cooking happens to poison you, the university would tar and feather me."

"I doubt that."

TJ added, "Well, to be selfish and honest at the same time, if I did accidentally poison you, I sort of doubted you would want to have sex with me tonight."

Without a moment of hesitation Shane replied dryly between bites of foods, "I doubt that, too."

TJ laughed, as Shane smiled with a mouthful of the potatoes. "This is really good. We make a good team in the kitchen. Did I tell you I love you today."

TJ frowned, "Only twelve times. I feel so neglected."

Shane laughed loudly almost choking on his food, but quickly added, "I love you. I love you and I love you. Now can I go back to chewing?"

"Yes, that'll do—for now."

After dinner, they took the dogs to the beach a half hour before sunset and enjoyed another long walk exploring, occasionally holding hands in secret, while laughing and talking together. This was there favorite time of the day at the beach, as they took in the view, and laughed as the dogs sniffed everything from seaweed to crabs.

Later, TJ surprised Shane with a bowl of banana pudding he made earlier in the day and placed on the bottom shelf of refrigerator, deliberately hiding the dish with other groceries.

Shane ate a spoonful that produced a bright gleam to his eyes and huge grin to his face. "This isn't on my diet—except for the bananas."

"It's got milk in it, too," protested TJ.

"I know, but it also has sugar and fat stuff."

TJ frowned, "Who doesn't like sugar?" He leaned over and kissed Shane quickly.

"I certainly like that kind of sugar, but I just saying that refined sugars aren't good for the human body."

TJ sighed, and replied as he yanked Shane's bowl of banana pudding from his hand, "Well, if that is the case, I'll feed yours to the dogs."

Shane's hand leaped liked he was going for a steal in a tie game with Duke and snatched the bowl back, "That's okay. I'll make an exception for your cooking because, hmm, because, hmm, because…"

TJ interrupted him, "You've already said 'because' three times. Good grief let me help you. You'll make an exception because you LOVE my cooking. Is that right, or do you plan to sleep alone tonight?"

Shane laughed, but wisely answered, "I love your cooking, I love this banana pudding, and I love you. Now can I eat?"

"Yes, you may, but I get to be the top first tonight."

"That's a deal. I need someone to stretch out my lower back."

"I'll do that and more," laughed TJ.

At the end of a few weeks, TJ wondered if he should get back on the road, but Shane urged him to check into a monthly rate, as Sue told him they could stay cheaper at the park if they paid by the month. Later that night, they talked about how things were going.

Shane was rubbing TJ's back, something no one in his dating life had ever done for more than sixty seconds, and yet TJ was an excellent masseuse, and everyone loved what he could do to their sore backs, so it finally felt great to be on the receiving end. He taught Shane how to put his thumbs in deep at the bottom of the spine between his buns, and push upward, slowly following the spine to the neck. Shane purred every time TJ did it to him, but now it was TJ's turn to purr, and boy did he like it. He also liked the way Shane put his big hands to use on TJ's shoulders.

"So are you going to start renting by the month?"

TJ teased him, "Aren't you tired of me yet?"

Shane replied instantly, "No, I'll never tire of you. I love you, you big knucklehead."

"Gee, you're good with romantic talk, aren't you? I know you do, and I love you, too, but I'm older than you, and perhaps, you would like to date someone your age."

"Is that what you want to do? You want to date someone your age?"

TJ grinned, "No, all the guys my age are losing their hair and gaining a spare tire in their midsection. I like dating guys your age, especially those with big hands that don't mind rubbing my back."

Shane gave TJ's naked butt a playful swipe. "You're incorrigible. I'm trying to tell you I love you, that I want you stay forever, and I want to be with you as often as I can. I don't want you to go away. What do you want to do? Do you really love me?"

TJ turned over so he could look into Shane's eyes and smiled. "Yes, I really love you. I just want to be fair to you. I missed my chance to date guys in college by coming out late, and I don't think it is smart to just fall head over heels with the first gay guy you meet."

"You're my second. The first was cuter," Shane deadpanned.

"Oh, I forgot," replied TJ.

"TJ, I'm smarter than you look."

"What?"

"I meant smarter than I look, but now that I said it, I like smarter than you look. If there is one thing I do well in this world, it is make decisions. I am slow and methodical about making the important decisions in my life. For example, everyone thinks I'll turn pro at the end of this season, but I think there's more to learn from our coach, and more growing to do as a young man safe in the college world. I'm not ready emotionally to handle the stress and pressure of the NBA, but I'm ready for a real relationship with the man I love most on the entire planet. I don't have a clue how to work things out because I know you love to travel and so do I...at least by your motorcoach. I've never been a fan of flying in airplanes. If God meant for us to fly..."

TJ injected, "he'd a put a turbine engine up our butt!"

Shane laughed, "So help me figure out our future together, and please start by renting by the month. That'll give us time to come up with plan B. As a matter of fact, practice starts soon followed by the season, and I think I could concentrate more on my game if I knew I didn't have to worry about you leaving."

TJ felt he gave Shane plenty of excuses to dump him and now felt confident that wasn't going to happen. "Okay, I'll stay. I love you very much as I have never loved anyone else, but if you ever stop loving me please tell me straight up. I don't want you to hold back your game, your studies, or your career."

Shane replied, "I don't think I'll ever stop loving you. I don't want to stop loving you. Now can we make love?"

"Boy, I give you my heart and that is still not enough. You insist on having my body, too."

"Such as it is," grinned Shane. "Come give me a big kiss."

They decided to celebrate their decision by leaving early on Friday and heading west to Lake Toxaway, a beautiful area just west of Brevard and Rosman in the Blue Ridge Mountains of western North Carolina. They left after Shane's last class, as the Friday afternoon traffic on I-40 could be exhausting. They drove west to Asheville, and then southwest on highway 191. Shane drove some of the interstate route, but as they approached Asheville, TJ took over so Shane could look at the mountain views.

The last few miles of the journey on highway 64 west were loaded with tight mountain turns, and some amazing hairpins turns. They were fun in a car, but in a big RV, it required a lot of work on TJ's part. He constantly checked for oncoming traffic, while doing his best to hug the center lane. He watched the rear tires of the motorcoach to make sure they were staying on the pavement. He was worried about his SUV in tow, but there was little he could do, as he knew it would just follow wherever he steered the coach. He did glance at the rearview television monitor to check on the car from time to time.

As they went over the spillway Shane grinned, "Wow, what a view. What a river!"

TJ laughed, "That's actually the spillway for Lake Toxaway."

"Where's the lake?"

TJ pointed over Shane's head on the right side. "Way up there above your head."

"Oh my gosh. If the dam broke right now, we would be dead, huh?"

"Well, let's just say I hope you know how to swim. Hang on, more turns."

"Oh my!" exclaimed Shane, as he held tight to the armrests and watched the views out the window.

About ten turns later, TJ made a sharp left and turned down a hill that to Shane felt like they had just topped the hill of a big rollercoaster at an amusement park. TJ slowed down, eased down the hill, and pulled to a stop at the office for the beautiful Outdoor Resorts at Lake Toxaway. This was one of the most beautiful RV spots that TJ liked to visit, and he wanted to share it with Shane.

After TJ checked in, he pulled the coach off to the side of the road, and together, they unhitched the SUV. Shane drove the car and followed TJ to their site where he helped TJ back into their site on the top of a small mountain. Shane walked around to the front of the coach after hooking up the power, water, and sewer lines while TJ leveled the coach, ran out the slides, shut down the engine, and started up the DirecWay® Internet satellite dish. He came out of the coach with the dogs on their leashes so they could find a nearby bush to pee on.

TJ asked Shane, "So what do you think?"

Shane turned in a slow circle. This is one of the most beautiful places I have ever been to. The surrounding mountains are just magnificent."

"We timed it perfectly, missing all the traffic in Lindle, and through Greensboro, Winston-Salem, and even Asheville. The coach handled all the mountain turns with ease although my arms are tired. Are you ready for a hike around the resort?"

"Sure. Let's go."

TJ locked the car and the coach. Shane put a hat on with his sunglasses, hoping to avoid discovery, but the resort wasn't busy this time of year, as summer was over and too soon for the leaves to start changing. TJ wisely led them up the hill of their street that was the highest point of the park, affording another spectacular view of the valleys and gorges of the mountains to the south. The dogs appeared oblivious to the views as they had hundreds of new places to sniff and mark, and soon poop on. Shane did the pick up duty with their blue recycle bags on a roll on their leash holder, and he soon found a dumpster to put them in. TJ was pleased how quickly Shane fell in love with his dogs as well. He played with them, rubbed their ears and their bellies, gave them treats, and cuddled up and took naps with them. TJ sometimes remarked that Shane kissed the dogs more than he kissed him to which Shane shot back that the dogs were cuter.

They grilled some chicken breasts on the furnished deck grill and ate rice pilaf, fresh corn, and green beans, and began it all with a salad Shane made. They were sitting at the outside table as the sun began to set behind a mountain to the west. The hues of orange color were postcard perfect. After dark, they moved inside the coach and closed the front curtain so they could kiss whenever they wanted to, and settled down to watch another gay movie called "Trick." It starred Christian Campbell, one of TJ's favorite actors, and was the story of a down on his luck songwriter who meets the perfect guy, but has nowhere to go as the boy lived with his mom, and Christian's roommate is straight with a friend already there for the evening. Everywhere they tried to shack up is booked. It is a fun, but sometimes a sad story, that gave Shane another view of the gay world.

After it was over Shane said, "Boy, I'm sure glad we have a bed to go to."

"Me, too. Are you ready for sex?"

"No," Shane said with a straight face, "I'm tired. I think my hormones are kicking in."

TJ busted out laughing. "Yeah, right. Let's go pee the dogs and turn off the lights. You're not fooling me. I'm still top tonight!"

They left the motorcoach early the next morning with the dogs in the backseat, a water bowl and a small backpack with doggie treats and water bottles, and a second backpack for the boys for their snacks and water, and camera. TJ turned west out of the resort, taking them through another section of hairpin turns that were easier to handle in the SUV and continued on to the town of Franklin. There they turned north to head to Moonville State Park. TJ hiked the park when he was in college and knew it well. The park possessed numerous waterfalls, as well as beautiful views, and TJ planned to show Shane all of them.

They unloaded in the parking lot, let the dogs pee, and gave them some water. They picked up their small backpacks, while Shane pulled his hat down low as usual, and wore his dark sunglasses to help hide his identity, and out the door they went. TJ knew there would be people there, but they hoped they were early enough to miss a large group. They counted only four cars in the parking lot, so they were confident they would be alone most of the time.

TJ decided to hike to two of biggest falls in a counter clockwise route starting with Rainbow Falls. They walked the bridge right over the top of the falls, where the water ran from smooth to whitewater in less than a second, and began the hundred and twenty-five foot fall to the pool below, while bouncing numerous times on the rocks as it descended. TJ took several pictures with Shane and the dogs, with the waterfall in the background. They returned to the near side, and took the new path to picnic area on the far side so they could look straight across the pool at the bottom and the river bed, and up towards the waterfall. It was a great sight.

After a while, they followed the tight trail along the stream as it worked its way through the mountainous hillside and around to the top of Quad Falls. Shane was aghast at the huge waterfall that fell to a second waterfall, and on to a third waterfall, and then a final fourth one. They kept to the trail for safety sake until they were across from second falls. TJ led them down a steep set of steps, and out onto some huge rocks where they could look back and see the first and second falls, and they were overlooking the water traveling quickly to the last of the falls. The dogs wanted to run, but TJ warned Shane to keep a tight lease as the algae and moss made the rocks slippery. TJ took a bunch of pictures before they went back up the steps, and hiked around to another picnic shelter allowing them to sit down, eat a snack, and take in all four falls.

The dogs ate their treats and drank lots of water, but when the boys were ready to hike, the dogs began wagging their tails rapidly as they were still ready for action. They made it back to the car, drove out of the front of the park, and began making left turns until they were on the backside of the park, reentered the park, unloaded the dogs, and hiked through the woods to Cascade falls. Unlike the cliff-like waterfalls they had seen earlier, this was a long huge massive waterfall that if it wasn't so dangerous, a visitor might think you could slide down it. Of course, beside the jagged rocks you would encounter on the way down, there wasn't a beautiful pool to land in. At the bottom were giant chunks of granite that had been ice wedged away from the top of the falls perhaps centuries ago. The dogs barked at the falls as they carefully made their way around the side, and climbed up about halfway so they could see the spread of water as it cascaded down the falls.

A Writer's Fantasy

After they returned to the car, they turned south on US 76 and crossed the state line into South Carolina, and worked their way to Nickel Ridge. This park featured no waterfalls, but they make the short walk to viewing area. Once Shane and the dogs made it to the outer edge, he realized they were on the top of a big mountain. The viewing area was out a ways from the peak of the mountain providing an amazing view of the Piedmont area of the upper art of South Carolina.

Their last stop before lunch sent them back to the north. TJ carefully slowed down so that he wouldn't miss the off-road parking area. TJ, Shane, and the dogs scampered across the highway and began the mile long hike to the waterfall. They could hear the roar before they could see it. It wasn't a huge amount of water like all the other falls, but it was a very tall one, about two hundred feet or more, and it cascaded much like the falls you might see in Hawaii. The falls were beautiful with the bright white, air-mixed water in front of the dark, wet wall of rocks, and framed by beautiful lush green vegetation of the mountain trees, laurel, and almost subtropical plants. They sat on a picnic table to take in the view and rest a bit. The dogs drank more water before they began the hike back to the car.

After lunch and a brief nap on a blanket in the shade of a tree, they set out again using a map TJ printed for a shortcut up the through a gorge in the mountains and onto the Blue Ridge Parkway. They turned left on highway 281 towards Balsam Grove and onto highway 215 continuing their northward direction. There were lots of turns and beautiful green mountain farms, and traffic was very low allowing the journey to feel like a big adventure. When they reached the ridge, they turned right on the Blue Ridge Parkway turning north, and drove just a mile to the big parking lot for Devil's Courthouse.

They gazed upward at the top of the small mountain sitting on top of a huge mountain and realized the view there would indeed be scenic.

"How far to the top?" asked Shane as he helped water the dogs.

"Only a mile, but it is upward all the way. I'll be puffing by the time we get to the top, but I have to remind myself that many senior citizens make the same hike every day, and if they can do it—I can do it."

Shane laughed, "Let's go. This looks like fun."

The paved path was easy at first as the trail meandered along the edge of the highway before entering a cavern-like canopy of beautiful trees and mountain laurel, but immediately the trail turned steep as they climbed upward on the steps. TJ grinned as the dogs used their four-paw power gear to make it easy for them, but in a few minutes, their tongues seem to grow longer as they panted to cool themselves. TJ stopped a few times to slow his heart rate, and hide his embarrassing heavy breathing while Shane had yet to break a sweat.

"Are you alright? You're not going to have a heart attack or something, or you?" Shane was grinning at TJ, but a little worried.

"Don't you ever tire of having sex? We're on the trail for Pete's sake," replied TJ.

Confused, Shane asked, "What?"

"You're hoping I have a heart attack so you can feel up my chest and give me mouth to mouth, weren't you."

Shane laughed, "You're crazy. Absolutely crazy."

TJ panned up and down the trail, and finding no one replied, "Crazy for you." He leaned into Shane and gave him a kiss. TJ announced, "Okay, now that I have some sugar I'm ready. Let's go."

Shane rounded the last of the trail, stepped out on the rocks and suddenly, he left the confining canopy and found himself in the midst of a circle of rocks providing him a full three hundred and sixty degree view of the mountains in a place where he could see both the Blue Ridge and Pisgah Mountains.

Shane exclaimed, "Oh my gosh! This is spectacular. What a view!"

"I thought you might like it, replied TJ, relieved to find they were alone with no other visitors at the top. He handed Shane Beeper's dog leash, and pulled out his camera from the backpack. Shane posed at various spots on the compass. They sat down and rested a while. They enjoyed the freedom of holding hands together. Shane put his arm around TJ, and planted a big French kiss on his lips. About twenty minutes later, two women stepped out the forest and on the rocks for their view. TJ immediately picked up they were lesbians he had seen at a support group for gay people when he lived in Hendersonville. They recognized him, and said hello.

TJ introduced Shane, "Janet and Susie, this is my boyfriend Shane."

Shane blushed at the surprised introduction, "Hi," he managed.

The girls replied hello as well. Janet asked, "Shall I take your picture for you?"

TJ answered, "Yes, that would be great. He showed her where to push the button on his camera as he handed it to her."

She took the first picture, but Susie frowned, "You guys look like bored Republicans. You're gay. You're in love. Action."

They all laughed and Shane finally realized they were gay, too. He turned to TJ, and planted a kiss to his lips. TJ moved around in front of Shane, and then sitting down he leaned back into him as Shane's long arms enveloped his body. Shane leaned down and put his head alongside TJ's for yet another picture. All together, they took a dozen shots before TJ began taking pictures for the girls with their camera.

Back on the parkway and heading north, they went through several tunnels before turning south towards Cullowhee, and driving straight through Cullowhee National Forest. After a few miles, they turned into the parking lot for Slippery Rock. As they got out of the car, TJ turned to Shane and told him to get in the backseat of the car where the windows were heavily tinted and more room, and told him to change into his bathing suit.

40

Shane returned in a few minutes and asked, "Aren't you going to change?"

"Naw, I want to stay dry so I can take some good pictures. I'll also handle the dogs. Grab that beach towel. You're going to need it."

"Is this safe? I don't want to break my leg."

TJ laughed, "Your legs and arms will be fine, but I'm not sure about your butt!"

They crossed the parking lot, stepped around the changing rooms, and immediately caught sight of Slippery Rock. It was about seventy feet long, with a gentle angle, and the folks already sliding were landing in a big pool. They all crashed into the water and came up screaming. Shane assumed they were just elated at the fun of the ride.

TJ pointed to the line at the top where Shane should go, while he took the dogs and followed the path to the bottom to prepare for the pictures. Shane had left his hat and sunglasses on, and hoped no one would recognize him, and he was right, at least for a while, as no one expected the candidate for National Player of the Year Award to be sliding next to them.

The line kept moving and near the end of it Shane stepped into the stream feeding the waterslide and instantly realized the water was a cool fifty seven degrees even in early fall. He watched the kids ahead of him as they carefully sat down on the slide and pushed off. TJ snapped a picture of him waiting for his turn at the top.

Shane sat down and the rush of water instantly surrounded his lower body, turning his entire body into a sea of giant goose bumps. He pushed off and laughed heartily as he rode the rock and the water down the slide. TJ kept snapping pictures as the dogs barked at Shane, wishing they could get in the water, too.

Finally, Shane reached the bottom and made a huge splash into the water, as he held on to his hat with one hand, and his glasses with the other. He came up screaming as his entire body was immersed into the very cold pool of water. TJ laughed, but kept clicking the button for his digital camera.

Shane made his way out of the water and around the platform where TJ had his towel wrapped around his neck. Shane quickly retrieved it, and began attempting to dry his body off.

"How was the ride?"

Shane laughed, "You didn't tell me how cold it was. It is freezing, but yes, it was fun."

"Do you want to do it again?" TJ tempted his male ego by adding, "Is it too cold for your skinny little ass? Are you a wimp?"

Shane laughed, "You're baiting me, aren't you? I'll go one more time, and that's it." He gave TJ the towel, and began making his way to the top.

This time he was shivering while waiting his turn, but gleefully sat down in the cold water, and rode the rock with all the speed possible before crashing once again into the pool. Shane leaped up and quickly made his way out of the water and ran to TJ for the towel. As he dried off, the dogs began licking the water from his legs.

TJ was laughing as they made their way back to the car. Shane changed clothes and came out of the car still cold. TJ led him to a bench at the edge of the parking lot where they could sit in the sun so Shane could warm up.

"Every visitor has done the same thing you did for more than a hundred years."

Shane replied, "Is it always this cold?"

"Yes, even in July. The water comes out of the ground not too far upstream, so it is crystal clear, but a cold fifty-seven degrees."

TJ noted a kid of about fourteen standing not far away with his parents and a younger sister. They were pointing at them and talking. At first, TJ thought they might have assumed they were gay, but when Shane saw them, he proclaimed the right assumption.

"I've been spotted. They know I play basketball."

The family began walking over to him. The boy was red headed with bright blue eyes, and a face filled with tiny freckles. His sister possessed similar features with a beautiful smile. The boy asked, "Are you Shane Bradley?"

"Yes, I am."

"We saw you go down Slippery Rock. I never thought I would meet you here."

"My friend here talked me into trying it—he just failed to mention how cold it is?"

"May I have your autography?"

"Sure," replied Shane as he retrieved a short Sharpie pen from his pocket. TJ had never noticed the pen before. "Do you want me to sign your Taylor University hat?"

"Yes, please." The boy handed Shane his hat.

"What is your name?"

"Larry."

Shane began writing as he spoke politely to the rest of the family. "Are you guys going down the slide, too?"

The little girl replied, "No, only an idiot would go this time of year. It's too cold."

The parents blushed as Shane handed the signed cap back to the boy. "What is your name?"

"I'm Kathy."

Shane smiled as he shook her hand, "Well, Kathy, you're looking at one big idiot, as I did the slide twice and lived to tell the tale, and you're right—it is very cold, and I don't recommend it unless you're very brave."

They all laughed as Shane and TJ stood, and began making their way to the car. "I'm pleased to have a chance to meet you, and I hope you have a great day," added Shane.

They waved goodbye as they drove out of the lot. "Where to?" asked Shane.

"Butt Buster Falls," replied TJ stoically.

"What? You're kidding—another sliding rock?"

"Yes, but I doubt you're brave enough to slide this one."

"Is the water freezing there as well?"

TJ smiled, but didn't answer, as he turned right to go through the sleepy college town of Millersville, and back towards Lake Toxaway. Carefully, he watched the highway signs and made a left and before long, they were parked along the side of the road with a dozen other cars. The dogs anxiously leaped out of the car, and TJ led them down a path until they were standing near a clearing. They could hear the rush of the giant waterfall. It was about eighty feet wide and more than a hundred feet tall. It was pitched at a much sharper angle than Sliding Rock, and Shane noted there were several teenagers indeed sliding down the rock.

"Do you see that lift of water about twenty feet before you crash into the pool of water? That is a little fin of rock, and if you don't ride it correctly your butt will get quite a smack—hence the name Butt Buster Falls. You lift your butt by pressing down and back with your trailing hands to avoid the smack. It is one of the most exhilarating things I have ever done. While working at camp, we would bring busloads of kids over for the ride, but we put climbing ropes down the side of the rock to make it easier to climb up for another ride, and kept a lifeguard at the bottom with a buoy and rope. No one was ever hurt from our group, but there have been tourists that have been killed here. Usually alcohol was involved, and they did everything wrong by going off the usual path, didn't lift, or somehow got turned over on their side or tummy, and smacked the rock with their head. We'll just watch this one because I love your pretty head just the way it is."

Shane gulped, "I'm glad. That looks pretty scary."

TJ grinned slyly, "You mean you rather play against Duke for the title that go down this waterfall?"

"Hell yes," laughed Shane.

After dinner, they took the dogs on a doggie walk around the RV resort and politely waved at other guests. TJ was sure they noted how tall Shane was, but they may not have caught on that he was the number one college basketball player in the country. They enjoyed the beautiful landscaped sites, and numerous upscale motorcoaches.

"There's a Prevost®," stated Shane.

"Yes, a new one. It appears packed up so most likely they own the lot it is parked on, and leave it here from time to time to fly back for family visits or business, and let 's hope not for an illness or death in the family."

"Why do people buy a lot? Don't they want to travel all the time?"

TJ smiled, "Everybody has different goals. Some love the travel and I'm in that group, but others travel for a year or two, and then settle down in two spots."

"Why two spots?"

TJ smiled, "In the winter they go south to Florida, Texas, or Arizona to avoid the cold winters of the north, but by April, they all head north to the escape the heat of the south. Some folks live in a big Prevost® motorcoach, and five years later, they only have six thousand miles on it. They just don't travel around and see the country. I'm the opposite of that. I love the road. I love to see new things, and stay in new places. Until I met you, and fell in love, and I did mention I loved you, didn't I? Well, anyhow if I was scheduled to stay somewhere for two weeks, by the tenth day, I had an itch for the road. If I was supposed to stay five days, I was ready to go by the third day. I just love it."

Shane thought for a minute before speaking, "So maybe we can make a big trip after basketball season, or better yet, after the end of the spring semester. Can we make a plan to go somewhere for fun?"

TJ laughed, "Now you're talking. Yes, we'll make a big plan to hit the open road and have some fun. I think we need to work on merging the data for both of our calendars. I have a great deal of work to do on the final editing of **The Raceboys** my newest book, and get it to press as it releases the Tuesday after Thanksgiving for folks to buy for Christmas gifts. I'm also editing **Gay Grifters**, my next book, so I can ship it to my editor who will work on it, and get the manuscript back to me for my final edit before printing. I like to write the press releases and promo materials myself so I have that to do, too."

"When does it release?"

"It is scheduled for a spring release of April fifteen or so."

"I've read your first two books, and I'm working on the third one. They are just like you, funny, sad, and page turners."

"I am currently writing **The Blackfeet Boys,** but some tall cute guy has slowed me down a little. Now that you're in school, I'll have my days free to write. I hate to admit this, but since I'm not traveling, I have more time to do research for the story. I also began working on a storyline about a guy that falls in love, but suddenly they breakup months later. This happens to the poor man over and over again. It is very funny, but filled with sad heart wrenching moments as well. It is called **Forever Alone, Again**."

"How do you come up with the stories?"

TJ grinned, "The first draft is what I call the fun part. I often write a chapter in my head while driving, and later when parked, I punch it out on the computer keyboard. I have never experienced what some call writer's block. If I am not sure of where to go in the story, I take the dogs for a walk, or just take a nap, and before long, I'm writing again. Normally, I see the entire story like a video of a movie in my head; so typing almost slows me down, as the story rolls out of my head rapidly. It is fun, and perhaps even good therapy for me. I can't do all the things my characters get to do, but when I write, it is like I'm experiencing it myself."

"I doubt I could write a book," stated Shane.

"Well, I doubt I could run up and down the court with the Taylor team for more than sixty seconds, and I know I couldn't pull up and shoot a fifteen foot jumper, or stop a seven foot giant from scoring like you do."

"Yeah, I doubt you could do that, too. I guess we're built different."

"But our differences is what makes our relationship fun. If we were just alike, we'd be bored to death."

Shane knew he was sore from the hiking to the waterfalls, and a little sore from the sex they had last night, but he was up early stretching and feeling his muscles before heading out for a run around the resort. By the time he returned, TJ had finished his shower, walked the dogs, and started on breakfast. Shane came up behind him at the sink and squeezed TJ's butt.

"I see you're hungry," teased TJ.

"Do you mean for food or sex?"

TJ turned around so Shane could kiss him. Shane slipped his right hand into TJ's underwear and began playing with TJ's penis. After they broke away from the deep kiss, TJ said, "I see you're still horny, but boy do you need a shower! Did you have a good run?"

"Yes, but the hills were tough, but a great challenge. I loved the views. It was good for me. I'm heading to the shower."

TJ protested, "But you already got me hard!"

Shane dropped to a knee, yanked TJ's shorts down, and began oral sex on him. TJ began running his fingers through Shane's short hair. He loved him so much. It didn't take long for TJ to come.

Shane stood up, "Okay, I'm in the shower. What are you cooking for breakfast?"

TJ laughed, "Why? You just ate."

"That was an appetizer. I'm starved." He began stripping out of his clothes allowing TJ to watch.

"Did I tell you how sexy you are?"

"Thanks," replied Shane, as he pretended to play with his penis. "What's for breakfast?"

"Omelets, ham and cheese, grits, and fresh fruit."

"Excellent. I'll be out of the shower in a minute."

Shane heard the trumpet signaling the beginning of the CBS Sunday Morning Show that was a favorite of TJ's, but now a favorite of Shane's, too.

He came to the table wearing only his boxer shorts, gave TJ a fresh kiss, and sat down to eat. TJ sat the orange juice and milk containers on the edge of the table knowing Shane would refill his glass more than once.

The boys had talked about saying a blessing at their meals early on, as both came from families that did pray at the table, and the team prayed as well when they were traveling and eating together. Shane said the blessing, and they dove into the food. The dogs sat obediently nearby in case Shane left some food for them.

They started on their journey home right after breakfast to avoid as much traffic as possible. It had been a great getaway weekend for them, and perhaps, the last time until after the long winter basketball season. Though their relationship was still new, they were learning to cherish their quiet time together.

Bob and Sue came out of their motorcoach to meet them as they pulled into their lot after Shane moved his Hummer out of the way. He and Bob began hooking up the utilities while Sue came aboard to collect the dogs to let them pee, and TJ set up the inside by moving the slides out, the satellite up, and placing the furniture in the usual spots. In just a few minutes, they were all set up. TJ came out of the coach to say hi.

"Did you have a good weekend?" asked Sue.

Shane spoke up quickly, "It was the best. Have you been there? It is so beautiful. I've lost count as to how many waterfalls we saw, but my friend tricked me into going down Slippery Rock in Cullowhee National Forest. It was the coldest water I have ever experienced in my life. Just talking about it gives me goose bumps, but it was also fun. That area of North Carolina is just so beautiful."

Bob spoke up, "How did the coach do on all those hairpin turns?"

TJ grinned, "Like a Cadillac®. I kept watching my line and staying just as close to the centerline as I could. I never saw a rear tire come off the pavement but it sure came close. It was a lot of fun and the resort is as beautiful as ever."

Shane added, "That was probably our last weekend to bolt for freedom until after the NCAA tournament. I'll miss it, but I also look forward to our next journey. We're going to take a big trip when we do head out in the spring."

Sue asked, "Where you going?"

TJ spoke up, "I think we'll go down to Key West, but we'll have to wait and see how much time we have."

Sue grinned, "Are you boys hungry? I have a pot roast in the Crockpot, and it's ready. I also made a green been casserole."

Shane rolled his tongue across his lips, "Hmm, that sounds wonderful, and you know I'm always hungry. What do you think?"

46

TJ smiled back, "We have plenty of stuff to make a salad, and we'll make a plate of fresh fruit. We could cook some ears of corn we bought, too. Can you give us twenty minutes?"

"Sure, just come on over when you're ready."

The boys loved their impromptu dinners with Bob and Sue. They were well experienced, always knew something about somewhere in the country, and TJ loved picking Sue's head about her photography and her Mac® computer. They all liked each other's company, and the boys were excited to share another meal with them.

# FOUR

Shane was looking forward to beginning of their practice agenda, as he had for every day since the abrupt end of last season at the Elite Eight Tournament. The sudden unexpected loss, left him and his fellow players feeling completely lost, empty, void of completion, and for the seniors soon to graduate, an opportunity lost forever. Shane promised everyone this year's Taylor team would make it all the way. It was a bold boast, as so much could happen, but he liked putting himself on the line, and then fighting to make his predictions come true. It challenged him to try just a little harder on every possession, touch of the ball, dribble, leap, rebound, and shot. He would win. They would win, and a lost like last time would not happen.

However, the night before the first practice was something Shane dreaded more than a flu shot, and almost as much as a ride on an airplane during bad weather. They called it 'Take Back' as in it was time to start taking back the title. It became the official kickoff of the new basketball season. The fans filled the basketball arena full of enthusiasm, energy, and excitement for the upcoming season. However, the performances tonight were not highlighting Shane's tremendous basketball talent, but rather his not so good dancing feet, his pathetic acting skills, and his total lost for comedic timing. Every team member prayed no one would ask Shane to sing as well! TJ knew he could sing, but in front of huge crowds, Shane suddenly became tone deaf. It embarrassed him immensely.

Members of the public relations staff, along with the cheerleaders, and few other souls, wrote and directed the evening that ended by introducing the coaches along with this year's team. They performed various skits, and finally a little light scrimmage with lots of huge dunks. Nevertheless, someone had to imitate and impersonate the coach, and the staff begged Shane to do it, but he absolutely refused. He actually threatened to transfer to another school, but he was joking. TJ agreed with his decision. So did the team. They got a poor freshman to do it.

The media arrived in full force to cover the event with ESPN® doing a live video uplink, as well as an interview with Shane and Dick Vitale. Dick, an over the top wonderful broadcaster, genuinely love great players and their families. He predicted big things for Shane back when he was in high school, and with Shane on the roster, he picked Taylor University to win the NCAA championship next spring.

Shane brought TJ in through a back door to the complex, and led him into the arena so he could get a seat before the doors opened. This gave TJ a chance to watch Shane's interviews with the media before tonight's event began. TJ thought Shane did well, but looked uncomfortable. He thought he might try to help Shane as he had done radio, television, and live concerts in his 'other' life as he called it. He also taught and directed a sales team for many years, but now enjoyed selling his novels. He also loved the freedom of traveling the highways of America to see beyond the next crest of the hill, over the mountain, around the lake, or along the shoreline.

Once "Take Back" began, TJ laughed at the silly skits, but he loved watching Shane blush repeatedly as he said his memorized lines with little dramatic effect. He and TJ had gone over them many times the night before. He hoped Shane would somehow get through it.

Later, when the lights dimmed, the cheerleaders moved towards the tunnel entrance to take their positions forming two lines, the band blew the spit out of their water valves, and lifted their instruments to their mouths as they prepared to play the school's fight song. The announcer introduced the assistant coaches, and followed with a big introduction for head coach, Ryan Timmons.

A few years ago, TJ followed the hiring of the coach with great interest. He is a veteran coach with a remarkable winning record, with knowledge of Taylor University, as he played here decades ago. His coaching career began by sitting on the far end of the bench as a manager, but a year later, he moved to the other end of the bench as an assistant coach. He left the university he loved after two years, so he could continue learning by becoming a head coach. Now he was home again, and the Taylor team was winning. He and his staff worked long hours, traveled for days, ate cold dinners, and sat on uncomfortable couches on the recruiting trail, but they were successful. Shane was one of their first recruiting accomplishments, a player that was both an outstanding student in class, as well as a student of the game. His attitude, his excellent manners, and his heart impressed all the coaches, as well as the players when he came to visit Taylor University. Shane was impressed, too. First with Coach Timmons, the school, but also his players and staff, but after visiting other schools, in his eyes, none measured up to the high bar Taylor University possessed.

Coach Ryan Timmons walked out of the tunnel to thunderous applause and a standing ovation by all. TJ noted in person he was six feet tall, but on television, he looked far shorter standing next to the giant players he recruited. The shortest freshman was at least four inches taller. He had gray hair, sparkling blue eyes, gold rim glasses, and appeared to be in excellent physical shape. He had a reputation of being tough, tenacious, charming, and hard working. He displayed excellent people skills, and a leader on the court, behind the desk, in the locker room, and in his own home. He was proud to be a family man with a great love for the young men who played and worked for him. Many of his players described him as a father figure, someone they admired and trusted. Timmons often said he really cared how they succeeded in life more than in basketball, but oh did he love to win.

Coach Timmons smiled and after taking a bow, he mouthed 'thank you' to his fans as he made his way to his customary seat at the head of basketball's bench row. Soon they began introducing the new freshmen, followed by each class. Though Shane was twenty-one by a few months, having started school a year behind some of his friends, he was at that awkward stage where he was half boy and man. He had the charm and good looks to beat out most of the boys in his class, but the discipline of a man far older. No one hustled on every play, pushup, or lap as he did. This desire is not teachable, as the coach often said of his star player, because either you're born with it, or develop it at a very early age. He compared Shane to the story about Rudy that wanted to play a Notre Dame, so he played on the practice squad that prepared the first team for their games by running against them all week along.

Later than night, Shane came by the motorcoach because he was still wound up with excitement. After telling some of the behind the scenes stories, he announced he was going to bed because he had to be up at six for their real first practice, and it would be a tough one. He ate a snack of fresh fruit that TJ learned to keep handy along with chopped fresh vegetables. They moved to the bedroom where Shane was anxious to make-out and after twenty minutes, they were pulling off their clothes and moving on to sex. About midnight, Shane left for his dorm and ready for bed.

TJ managed to catch up on his writing and editing over the next few weeks as Shane went to class in the mornings, then weights, lunch, spent two hours working on certain shots with his favorite team manager, and then full practice with the team in the afternoon. Afterwards, he ate dinner in the athlete's cafeteria adhering to his strict diet plans. Once completed, he went to his room and began his homework. He was asleep by ten on most nights after completing his to-do list for the next day. He always wrote down what he planned to work on with his manager friend before practice. This year he was developing his outside shot because he knew his opponents would double and triple team him in the lane or the paint as he called it, so for him to score, he would have to make the defense come farther out or away from the goal to block his shot. He explained to TJ the more shots he could count on for success, the better threat he was as a scorer.

Practice ended with lots of running, hitting the floor and sliding, going for loose balls, and Shane loved every minute of it. He wasn't afraid to get his big old frame on the wood to scrub out the ball from a little old guard as he called them. While some players during the first week may have gotten sick from so much running, Shane thrived on it. He was in superb shape from head to toe including his brain and attitude. He could never get enough of working hard for success.

Three weeks later, they won their first pre-season game on their home court, and Shane was as hyped up and excited about playing this game as a game during tournament season. Working with the front office, Shane pulled some strings until he had a seat for TJ right across the court from the home team bench. Usually seats for players were behind the team, but Shane

50

experienced that for two seasons already with his parents sitting behind him. He wanted TJ in front, so when sitting he could glance up and see him without someone catching on. He thought if he had to keep turning around to see him, someone would clue in. He also knew that if it was just a time-out, he could see TJ when they broke the huddle and went back out on the court.

Shane played well in the game, but the other team was good. The Taylor team made many mistakes, none of which made Coach Timmons very happy. The team knew his stern evaluation from his speech in the meeting before the next practice, and the prepared video clips of the game displaying their mistakes, that the tough, no nonsense coach was not about to let them get away with lousy play. The practice was tough, but Shane flourished.

They had another game Friday, followed by a Saturday practice, and Sunday off. Shane arrived right after the practice. They grilled out on the patio, as the afternoon was still warm though it was early November. Bob and Sue joined them as they ate barbequed chicken, potato salad, corn, and a huge salad. TJ made a batch of banana pudding, and they all devoured it.

Sensing the boys needed to be alone; Bob and Sue were smart to say an early good night. TJ and Shane took the dogs on their long walk of the day. They returned and put on a movie to watch, but thirty minutes later, they decided to head for the bedroom. They made up for almost a week of no sex, and then lay side-by-side, cooling down in each other's arms, cuddling and talking. Shane was concerned that TJ would get bored being by himself, while Shane went to school and practice, but TJ replied he had lived by himself all of his adult life, and to rest assured he would be fine. TJ told him about all the work he accomplished that week, and felt like by this time next week, he would be back on schedule.

He said he also took time to work on his new story, which was always his favorite part of the writing job. He said Bob and Sue helped him as he washed the motorcoach, and then did the chrome and tires until everything shined. They were going to do Bob and Sue's motorcoach next week. Therefore, he looked Shane right in the eyes, kissed his nose gently, and told him not to worry that he would be fine. He told him to concentrate on making this season the best in his life because if he didn't, every Taylor fan in the world would hate him and maybe use tar and feathers to express their dissatisfaction. He had to do well this year. He had to be better than last year. He had to win.

Shane got so excited listening to TJ talk like he felt on the inside, but he felt grateful that he could work as hard as he wanted to without worrying about TJ. He kissed TJ deeply, passionately, and then they went for round two, as if making up for lots of missed opportunities.

Their first game was tomorrow night, so the coach ordered a shorter and lighter practice, although he felt the team still had more conditioning work to accomplish. He wanted to keep working on his long-range plans while also making sure they didn't lose any games due to practice exhaustion—a dilemma he fought every season.

Shane came over so they could eat takeout together from their favorite Italian restaurant. He arrived just thirty minutes before dark so they decided to hold their dinner in the microwave while they took the dogs on their long walk. Shane enjoyed hanging on to Beeper as her tail wagged as she picked up the scents of every dog having passed the same way in the past month. Shane thought Beeper was grinning as she went from spot to spot until she couldn't let out another pee drop.

During dinner they talked about the upcoming game, and Shane gave TJ the inside scoop on what he thought would happen, and the players he would be responsible for guarding, and how he thought their team would do.

The next night, TJ found his usual seat a little early so he could watch the team warm-up. Shane winked at him but went right back to his serious face as he methodically and carefully began his stretch routine, one in which he slowly moved every single muscle in his body as carefully as a surgeon working on brain surgery. TJ was impressed with the strict professional attention Shane gave himself. When he finally picked up a basketball, he began shooting from just a few feet out, with another player or a manager feeding him one ball after another, as he worked his way around the front of the goal area in a semi-circle while still moving a step back at a time. Everyone paid attention when he started hitting one eighteen-foot jumper after another, missing only two out of twenty-five. TJ knew Shane would not be happy he missed any, and would shoot five hundred of the same shots over the next few days to improve it. He completed his warm-up with twenty-five foul shots, a little team workout, and then he jogged back to the locker room.

Shane told TJ the only thing he didn't like about game day was the waiting. He could handle the work of running up and down the court on every possession, but to sit still in their nice locker room, or a not so nice visitor locker room on the road, was always boring. The only thing more boring was the waiting in a hotel room before they traveled to the arena. He watched the clock and took a final pee, the team said a prayer, the coach made a short speech including his goals for the game, and soon they were in the tunnel waiting for introductions.

Shane missed a foul shot in the first half but made six others. He would talk about the missed shot after the game for a long while. The team did very well against a team not in the top twenty, and though the players understood they would face many teams far tougher than they would face their opponent, they enjoyed the game and the win anyhow. They were happy in the locker room afterwards, but not jubilant like they were after making the Sweet 16 in the spring.

They had the next day off so Shane came home after the game and arrived not long after TJ. Shane had eaten dinner at the cafeteria, but ate a fruit dessert with TJ before sitting down to watch a movie and unwind from the week. On Sunday morning, after their favorite big Sunday breakfast, they read the newspaper before Shane went to work on a term paper he had to write for one of his classes, and TJ did some writing he had been working on.

After lunch, they loaded up the dogs, went to a favorite large park about thirty minutes away, and began hiking all over the grounds while laughing at the dogs searching everywhere for scent marks, and trying to leave a new scent of their own.

It was a good day for Shane, as there was nothing like being out in nature to settle him down, to walk and laugh with the dogs, and to hold TJ's hand when they felt they were alone. In the car, he often put one of his big hands on TJ's thighs to show his affection for him, especially when a kiss might be inappropriate. Their love grew though they were as busy as a married couple working hard on their careers might be. They began finishing their partner's sentences by filling in words not yet thought of and verbalized. They also helped where needed and without asking, held hands when possible, and gently leaned into the other to share a laugh. They slept soundly in the others embrace. They felt and cherished their love. A love that made the couple feel stronger, more vibrant and alive, but they were also happier at little things, delirious with big things, and so very confident and contented.

Their first away game had been more on Shane's mind than TJ's even though he had the schedule right there on his computer screen. He just assumed Shane would be away for a few days, and he was thinking about getting the carpet steam cleaned. He placed a yellow sticky note on his desk to call the carpet service. On the weekend before, Shane said he had talked to his parents and told them of his falling in love with a crazy man, as he teasingly put it to TJ, but that he was so happy, he wanted them to know. They asked all about TJ, and Shane gleefully began bragging about all of TJ's work, his cooking, his dogs, his motorcoach, and more. He then told his dad he wanted to find a way for TJ to be at every away game because he was the rock that kept Shane glued to his goal, but he didn't know how to manage it. His dad wanted to help his son, so he said he would call him back in a day or two with a plan, and for him not to worry about it. He hinted they might be able to use TJ's talents with the research on Shane's future NBA career.

Shane's family was well off financially, but he never acted like it. His parents trained him to do his chores, carry his dishes to the kitchen, and help out where he could. His dad didn't have any money as a boy, but after he completed four years in the Air Force, he came home, married his sweetheart, and built his first hardware store. Ten years later, he opened his twenty-fifth store, and managed to find time to help his eight-year-old son shoot hoops. Today, Al owned over two hundred and fifty stores, and his now twenty-one-year-old son could shoot amazing hoops against America's best collegiate athletes.

All his life Shane and his dad talked about basketball business and his future. They knew that in two more years, the NBA would offer Shane a big contract. This would include a big signing bonus, and a six-year contract worth about a hundred and twenty-five million or more. Al knew this would set his son up for life.

The next day Al called Shane with his plan, and that night Shane came to the motorcoach to ask a favor of TJ by explaining their plan.

Shane began, "Honey, did I tell you how good looking you are today?"

TJ's eyebrows went up while a sly grin began opening across his mouth, "What are you up to? I ain't falling for that line."

Shane laughed, "Well, you are handsome and you're right, I am up to something."

"Well, spill the beans. Tell me what you're thinking."

"Let's eat some ice cream, and sit at the table and talk." Shane grabbed the ice cream from the refrigerator, and fixed two bowls topped with fresh strawberries. He brought them to the table.

"Ah, so you really are trying to butter me up. What did you do—hit the motorcoach with the Hummer?"

"No, of course not—I'm an excellent driver, and I know you'd kill me if I accidentally did that. I talked with my dad yesterday about something important. They know all about you, and they are very excited I have a boyfriend, and someone that really loves me. I told dad you already sacrificed a lot for me by staying here, changing your schedule along with your work and travel habits, and I know you did it because you love me, and I appreciate it. I have also come to depend on you both on and off the court. To look up and see your reassuring eyes gives me just the boost I need, and I selfishly want you at every game.

TJ interrupted, "But that would mean…"

"Hold on. Please hear me out. Dad thinks there is a way to accomplish this and some other goals at the same time. He knows you're a writer, and of course, he is doing all he can to start the publicity machine for when I get ready to go to the NBA and prepare for the draft.

"We think it would be cool if you wrote a book that was almost like a journal of this entire basketball season starting with last summer's practice right up and through the NCAA tournament. It would be like a behind the scenes book that every player, coach, and broadcaster will want to read. I will tell you the facts as I see them, and then you put them in the book. There have been a few books like this in the past few years, but none by an All-American and potential National Player of the Year." Shane blushed, "That would be me, of course.

"So if you agree to write the book, then we have to figure out how to get you to all the games. They fly me on the team plane, but we don't think they would allow a writer onboard. Commercial flights would take too much of your time because you'd have to leave so early, and get back so late, that we'd have even less time together than we do now. Especially since half our games are on the weekends.

"I'm not allowed to talk to a sports agent yet, and can't do so until after I declare early for the draft, or after the last game of my last year, or senior year. Dad went to lunch with several agents to get a feel of where they think I'll stack up in the draft, and what kind of money we should expect. The money is very high.

"Based on his research, Dad secured a million dollar loan in his name that I'll pay back after I get the sign in bonus, which could be five million or more. He'll pay the monthly payments on the loan so I don't have to worry about it. He has several business partners and together, they share a lease for Learjet. The partners split the cost and each man pays an hourly rate. Dad has made us one of their partners. Therefore, we now have a private jet at our disposal.

"If you agree to the book, and attend every game, I'll talk to the Public Relations Director, and if you want, he can set up interviews with the players and coaches. However, I'm buying a ticket for you at every away game across the court from my team bench, just as we have set up for home games.

Shane set the spoon down and gave TJ his most earnest look he could muster up, "So please, tell me you'll write the book, and take advantage of the jet, and be at all my games. Will you?"

TJ was shocked and sat there in astonished surprise, not even eating the rest of his ice cream. He finally spoke, "Are you sure this is what you want?"

"Absolutely, it was my idea, but I needed dad to help me figure out a way."

"And the book—you want to open yourself up to how you are feeling as the season progresses, and reveal that behind the scenes look?"

"I can trust you with what I say, because you won't let me look stupid. I think it will be good for the sport. The book should release right after March Madness when the hype for college basketball reaches a huge peak. The book will push my name out front with the NBA folks, their scouts, and even the agents. If we win the championship this year, it might be in my best interest to leave college, and put my name in the draft. It'll be hard to ignore me when this book is in every bookstore in the country."

"What are you hoping for?"

"I'm hoping to win the championship, but I would also like to finish my senior year and graduate, but I have to weigh the risk of getting hurt during my senior year, and blowing my career and a lot of money—about a hundred and twenty-five million or more."

"Oh my, and your dad can really afford to rent a Learjet for us?"

"Yep, he already has it in the works so you can do the first game this weekend. All you have to do is say yes."

"I haven't written a biography or a non-fiction sports book before."

"Yeah, we know, but we think with your background in fiction you'll be able to take boring facts about practice and game strategy, and make it interesting so everyone will want to read the book."

Tom sat silent and still for a long minute before breaking a smile and saying, "Okay. I'll do it."

Shane laughed, "Yeah! That's what I wanted to hear."

"Are you going to call your dad, and tell him I said yes?"

Shane grinned slyly, "I already told him you would say yes. Of course, I didn't tell him if you said no, I wouldn't have sex with you for a week."

"You couldn't hold out that long," teased TJ.

"You're right and speaking of which, come on. I'm sex deprived. Let's go to the bedroom and get those clothes off!"

# FIVE

TJ drove to the private airport in Lindle after lunch with a bit of trepidation and uneasiness about flying on the Learjet alone. He had flown on every commercial airliner in the world except the Concorde, including several water planes in the Caribbean that nearly jarred his teeth loose. He didn't feel like a big wig, as he called it, a business executive, or even a rich man, but Shane told him he would be fine, and he would love it. TJ smirked, and said the only love he was sure of was his love for Shane.

Coach Ryan maintained discipline even when the team was not on the court by insisting they all wear suits and ties when traveling, so they could look and act professional at all times. TJ followed his guidelines and wore a nice lightweight suit, and carried a garment bag with pockets for his small stuff, since he would only be spending one night in the hotel. He already owned an excellent laptop-briefcase because before he went full time with his motorcoach, he flew on vacation to the islands southeast of Florida, the islands in the Pacific, or the fun cities of New York and Las Vegas. He carried an extended battery in the case, as well as lots of cords and adapters so he could watch movies while traveling or connectors for the hotel television. He also carried a good lightweight showerhead and a small pair of Robo-Grip® pliers, because he hated the new water-saver showerheads that barely rinsed the soap out of your hair. He liked hot water and plenty of it in the mornings. The security detail at the airport always had a field day with his laptop and bag when he went through the x-ray machines.

He arrived early after finding the private parking area for executives, and walked into a plush waiting area that was clean, and sported a nice bar and restaurant at one end. The lady at the counter checked his identification, made a quick phone call, and then smiled and said, "Mr. Johnson, your flight crew are ready for you at gate one." She pointed behind him as he thanked her, and then walked across the carpet to find a stewardess waiting for him.

She led him directly to the plane without having to go through any security whatsoever. On the tarmac he saw a beautiful white sleek Learjet with the steps extended and waiting for him. She helped him stow his luggage, and the pilot came out of his cabin to welcome TJ aboard. The captain stowed the ladder with the press of a button, pulled in the door, and sealed it until a light came on indicating it was tight and locked.

Steve, the pilot, said, "Sir, we'll take off in about three minutes if that is okay with you."

TJ smiled and replied, "Thank you. That is perfect."

The captain left to prepare for takeoff while the stewardess brought TJ a soft drink after he turned down all forms of alcohol including beer and wine. His seat was large, plush, and most comfortable, and Susie, the pretty stewardess, showed him how to recline the fancy electric seat should he want to sleep. She also showed him where he could plug in his laptop should he have work to do.

He buckled his seatbelt and she took her seat across from the galley as the jet began moving out to the runway where it paused only briefly before receiving clearance for takeoff. TJ grinned as the last time he had taken off from Charlotte his commercial airliner had to wait in a line of twenty planes for takeoff. They flew rapidly down the runway, but surprisingly, inside it was amazingly smooth, as if riding in an expensive car, and it seem to just float off the runway like a big bird taking flight. The pilot quickly climbed to his assigned altitude, giving TJ a wonderful view of Lindle, but only for a minute or so, as they were racing through the sky to his destination in Connecticut.

About fifteen minutes into the flight, Susie brought him a lunch tray with freshly made club sandwiches quarter cut, mustard potato salad, and a fruit bowl. She also brought him a USA Today® newspaper and refilled his Diet Pepsi® glass before disappearing to the galley. She waited about fifteen minutes and reappeared with a fresh slice of apple pie with vanilla ice cream on top. TJ soon realized he could probably gain weight from the many flights he would have to take to keep up with Shane and the team playing on the road.

The Learjet leasing company always reserved a car service standing by for his arrival at the Connecticut airport, and not more than twenty minutes after landing he was standing in the lobby of the hotel for the team. After a recent home game, Shane introduced him to the Taylor University Athletic Public Relations Director's secretary who gave TJ a list of their hotels for their away games, while tournament hotels would be determined at a later time.

Shane, more experienced at staying in the hotel with the team, suggested TJ make a reservation two floors above the team, so if Shane could sneak away, and he was sure he could, there was far less chance of anyone seeing him enter TJ's room.

TJ checked into the hotel using the new MasterCard® Shane's dad sent him by a courier service, urging him to use it for all his expenses. His room was on the fourth floor and in the back of the hotel, chosen again by Shane. He hoped they could avoid a chance meeting of the athletic staff by using the back elevator.

He unpacked his clothes and hung them in the closet, made a bathroom stop, and left the room in search of a nearby store. He saw some of the team in the lobby, but walked a few blocks south to find a small grocery store. He bought a two liter bottle of Diet Mountain Dew®, some packs of crackers, a few apples, the local newspaper, and a pack of Bit O'Honey®, one of his favorite chew candies. As he walked back to the hotel, he noted a few restaurants across the street, and one of those ice cream stores called a creamery. Once in his room, he fired up his computer, grabbed the ice bucket, and left to find the ice machine. He returned as his computer completed downloading his email. He stripped out of his clothes, put on a pair of lightweight warm-ups and a long sleeve Taylor University t-shirt, and settled down to read his email.

He was surprised to find an email from Shane checking to make sure that all went well with his flight. TJ immediately wrote back everything was perfect, and thanked him yet again. He had done the same several times on the phone as they worked out the details. He also received edited versions of several press release materials by the media staff to provide him facts and details for the new book, but knowing he had the afternoon to himself, as the game wasn't until tomorrow afternoon, he began writing a chapter for his new story. He was enjoying the adventure of discovering how the story would unfold as it fell out of this brain and onto the keyboard. He had been thinking about this chapter off and on over the past few days so it felt good to finally punch it out on the keyboard.

Hours later, he jumped when his cell phone rang. He glanced at the caller ID and smiled, "Hey, how are you?"

Shane grinned from the lobby where he walked away from the team rooms. "We just got back from practice in their arena."

"How did it go?"

"It's a big building, but the coach always reminds us the floor length is the same as back home, and so is the rim height. All of us have seen the movie **Hoosiers** a dozen times where the team arrives for a championship game, and the coach has them measure the goals to assure the players it may be a bigger place, but the game is the same. We worked out a little harder than we usually do before a game, but I think that is because Coach still is trying to whip us into shape."

"You're way beyond in shape," smiled TJ. "You're fitter and stronger than anyone on the team."

"Yeah, but I can get better, and I must help my teammates get better, too. How was the Learjet?"

"It was awesome. I think it was brand new. Susie, the stewardess, spoiled me. I ate a nice sandwich for lunch, and afterwards pie and ice cream. I was also able to use my laptop flying and finished some editing that I needed to do. I'm working on the new story now."

"What room are you in?"

"467. Why?"

TJ heard a knock at the door. He laughed while still talking on the phone and walking towards the door. "Is that you or that good looking room service waiter I saw when I checked in." TJ opened the door.

"It's me!" Shane laughed as he quickly stepped in before seeing anyone in the hallway. He closed the door as they both hung up their phones. TJ started to speak, but Shane planted a deep wet kiss to his lips while slowly picking TJ up and walking him to the bed where they both fell back on the mattress. Shane began undressing TJ while TJ tried to get Shane's shirt off. It took longer to get naked, but they just didn't want to stop kissing.

TJ did manage to get his hand on the condoms in his pocket so Shane could enter him, and together, they made love for a long hour before Shane had to leave for the team dinner.

TJ watched Shane dress. "I didn't think we'd get to do this on the road."

"It depends on the situation, but sometimes we get a break after study hall or practice, so that's why I wanted you to stay in the same hotel, and up a few floors from the team."

"Ah," replied TJ, "so you were planning to rape me."

Shane laughed and kissed him again, "I was planning on making love to the man I love most on the entire planet."

"And who would that be? I'll whip the bastard's butt. Where is he?"

Shane laughed as TJ pretended to be jealous. "I love you, but I have to go. I'll call you later. I'm so glad you're here."

"Me, too. I love you."

With the game at two on live television, the team pre-game meal was at nine, and it was sort of a brunch with breakfast fare mixed in with lunch. Shane ate steak and eggs, a bowl of fruit, and plenty of milk and orange juice. Afterwards, he kept bottles of water handy and took sips often. He finished working on his homework to help make the time past quicker. About eleven, he packed up his school bag, his luggage, and set it at the door. His roommate did the same, and together, they left the room and made their way to the lobby, where their personal stuff was loaded on the team bus. A manager checked their names off his list and soon they were off to the arena.

TJ ate breakfast in his room, and went back to writing on his story. When it came time to leave, he arranged for the desk clerk to keep his things in their storeroom, checked out of the hotel, and left the lobby catching a cab to the arena.

The building was vast, but TJ managed to find his way to his seat, so he watched Shane begin his long warm-up, stretching his muscles until he was confident they would perform well for him. TJ didn't bother to count the endless practice shots Shane made, but he loved how graceful and confident he was. TJ made some mental notes about Shane's routine, and thought he might write about it on the way home for the book.

He and Shane began talking about practice for a few minutes every day, and Shane told him what to watch for in their play against Connecticut. He also told him who he was defending and why, as well as what he thought his opponents strengths and weaknesses were. TJ completed two chapters of the new basketball story: one on the summer workouts and pre-season practices, and another on preparing for this game. He hoped to catch up from the summer workouts to current practices soon.

60

Shane helped download the team's huge media guide to TJ's laptop. At five hundred plus pages, it contained everything about the team's history, the records, and all about each player, coach, and manager. TJ read it quickly, but stored it on his laptop for future research. It was then he wished he had his laptop at the arena.

The team was doing some pre-game drills while TJ sat alone in his seat directly across from the team and three rows up. He hadn't noticed the tall man coming down the steps from behind him until he stopped and spoke to him. "Excuse me, sir. Are you Mr. Johnson?"

TJ looked up to see Walter Mills, Director of Public Relations for the athletic department, and a former star player himself a few decades ago. He was still tall, with a few more golf freckles on his face, and thinning red hair on his head, possessed a warm smile, and his gold rim glasses almost masked his green eyes. He stuck out his hand as TJ stood up.

"Yes, I'm TJ Johnson." TJ recognized the face as someone he had seen at the home games, but didn't know his name.

"I'm Walter Mills, head of the Public Relations for the Athletic Department, and I have been hearing quite a lot about you from Shane. He said you had an idea for a book. I'm very pleased to meet you."

TJ blushed a little, "Yes, Shane is confident the team is going to the final four, and perhaps win the championship, if they can all stay healthy, so we felt that this might be a great year for a book."

"He said you had a different take on the book."

TJ wasn't sure what he meant but took a guess, "Well, I do intend to write about all the games, but we thought we might call the book," he paused as if thinking hard, which he was, "A backstage pass to an NCAA championship with Shane Bradley. Or in other words, we want to allow the reader to get a feel of what happens in the days before the games and afterwards as seen through Shane's eyes."

"I see. That's very interesting. So he'll report to you after games and practices as to what he is thinking and how he observed different events."

"Yes, but we hope to keep it from becoming boring by putting in some of the team and coaches comments and quips along the way. Shane says they all have quite a sense of humor."

"Yes, they do. I am very pleased to hear of this project, and I am here to help you any way I can. What can I do to be of assistance?"

TJ thought for a second, "Well, I won't pretend to be a student of the game, and I don't want to slow Shane down from his studies, but after I write about a game, would you mind if I emailed it to you for your perusal? I want to be sure I have the facts right as well as the feel for the game."

"I would be most happy to do so. Most of the time, I don't know what is in a story until I see it in the paper. I would enjoy reading your take on this season. Do you write on pads or a laptop?"

"Well, I'll have to take notes at the game, but I write on my laptop?"

"Well, I think we need to make some changes to make that possible. Do you have a moment? I have an idea, and I want to show you something and explain."

"Sure," replied TJ as he followed him up the steps and into the big hallway that went all the way around the arena. He pushed through a door into a room with a sign taped to the door that said Pressroom. Inside TJ saw rows of workstations with various reporters typing and working on their stories. Across the way he saw a food buffet, and on another wall was a large LCD television screen displaying the basketball court.

"This is where the press is before a game, at half time and afterwards. Every arena has a similar setup. Most of the writers file their stories from here as the room has an excellent Wi-Fi signal for the Internet. There are lockers on the wall here so they lock up their laptops during the game, if they wish, though some of them set up down near the court and write as the game is being played. The only folks allowed in here are reporters with press credentials, and that is where my idea comes into play.

"I'm sorry we didn't arrange this service for this game, but if you'll come by my office on Monday afternoon, I'll provide you press credentials for the rest of the season. We'll take your picture for your identification badge, and we'll put your name on the press list representing the university so you'll be expected everywhere we go. Will this be of help to you?"

"Oh yes," replied TJ, feeling quite astonished with his generosity, "this will be most helpful."

"If you'll bring your email address, I'll put you on our press mailing list so you'll get notices of press conferences and other team news throughout the season. I shall look forward to seeing on Monday."

"Thank you very much," replied TJ as he shook Walter's hand firmly, and met his eyes with his own and smiled. TJ returned to his seat in time to see the team return from the locker room, and noted the arena was now almost full. He had never thought of himself as a reporter, but the press pass would give him access to far more information and detail, making the book accurate and exciting to read. He realized the job he was doing was not going to be easy, but he was looking forward to the challenge.

TJ could tell Shane was pumped up for this game. He was excited and fidgeting on the sideline before the start of team introductions. He looked up at TJ and smiled at him. TJ wished he could do something to make Shane relax, but all he could do was wink and smile.

Taylor got the tip in their backcourt to Jerry Karnes, known around basketball circles as the fastest guard in the country with deep shooting ability and an amazing assist numbers. He was also fingered as a bit of a rascal, full of mischief, and always pulling small pranks and telling jokes, and watched cartoons to chill out.

As the very split second Shane's eye focused on the tip going to Jerry, he broke for the basket at a full run, and just as he looked back he saw the ball coming rapidly over his shoulder. He snatched it as his feet left the floor, and he flung in a powerful two handed dunk that silenced the home team fans, but brought the thousand or so Taylor fans to their feet. Shane hustled down the floor, and setup their defense before the other team managed to bring the ball in.

Shane picked up his man and was all over the guy, forcing their guards to risk taking a wild shot since they could not move the ball into their big man. Shane snatched the rebound and flipped the ball to Jerry who brought the ball down the court in less than three seconds, made a big cut between two tall men, and rolled in a layup before their enormous center made it to the paint. Shane grinned as he came back down the court.

They double-teamed Shane the moment the ball was flung to him. He tried to shake loose before spotting Larry McKenzie open in the corner. Larry caught the pass and leaped upward from behind the three-point line. Larry had a soft touch with his jump shot that broadcasters described as smooth as silk. The ball arched perfectly just like the coaches drew on the chalkboard, and hit nothing but net, as the Taylor fans said 'swish' in unison. Larry, hailing from Binghamton New York, seemed shy until you got to know him, remained the third fastest man on the team, could dribble between two men, change direction in the blink of an eye, and just when it appeared he was going to charge the lane, in a flash, he would pull up and shoot another swish. He was also deeply in love to a pretty girl by the name of Janet. Shane thought they were perfect together. He liked the team policy of rotating roommates, but he and Larry always had a good time when they got together.

The Taylor team put in fourteen points before Connecticut finally scored a basket. Their coach called a timeout to try and slow down the powerful momentum Shane's team exhibited on the court. The opposition began the defensive tactic of applying a full court press, and to their credit on the first possession, they caught Jerry off guard. He pushed hard up the sideline, but ran into one of their forwards blocking his path, and as he tried to stop, he stepped out of bounds creating their first turnover. Jerry quickly signaled his team to shift to full court offense.

Shane rushed back down the court as the referee blew his whistle and handed the ball to their player to throw it in. They brought the ball in quickly, but the Taylor defense dug in their heels, stayed hard on their assigned players, and with the thirty-second clock winding down, Connecticut took a long three-point attempt that bounced high off the rim. Their tallest man was four inches taller than Shane, but Shane was not to be out hustled. Shane leaped hard and snatched the ball twelve inches above the rim, and as he twisted his body away from their big guy to prevent a steal or jump ball, he caught sight of Larry on the run. He quickly flung the ball like a quarterback, and all the fans stood as the ball sailed over everyone's head and into the hands of Larry who took one step, leaped into the air, and slammed the dunk so hard the goal actually shook and vibrated like a cartoon.

It was only two points, but the play-by-play broadcaster noted he could see the wind dissipate from Connecticut's sails. They looked defeated with only five minutes off the clock in the first half. They began to foul Shane every time he got the ball. Normally this was a big mistake, as he was the second best foul shooter on the team, and in top the three in the ACC last year. This was quite unusual for a big man, but it was a shot he started working on when he was just eight years old.

However, when the two shot foul was awarded he went to the line, and TJ noted that he was still very excited and pumped up. Though it appeared to the fans that he performed the shot as he had done all last season with great success, Shane knew instantly the shot was just slightly off, and it embarrassed him. He tried to settle his jitters down a notch. Jerry leaned in and smiled at him and said, "Come on you sissy, put the ball in the hoop. It's a simple game even a ten-year-old understands!"

Shane laughed and smiled. He sighed hard, focused, and made the second shot, but didn't gloat or even act like he had done something special. He rushed to the sideline where the other team would bring the ball in, and began waving his arms to block a long throw to the backcourt. He had been studying the big guy as he brought the ball in, and noted he threw across the court about eighty-five percent of the time. He watched him carefully and although the player faked throwing it in with quick pumps of his arm, when he was ready to throw he would lean forward. As he did, this time Shane leaped to his right and got a hand on the ball, knocking it to the floor. He quickly scooped it up and before anyone could stop him, he dunked it viciously. The Taylor fans were on their feet again. The half ended with Taylor at twenty-one points ahead of Connecticut.

The second half was worst for the opposing team. During halftime, Shane assessed his first half performance and was not all happy with his play. He chastised himself and decided he would do far better. Coach Timmons wasn't happy with his team's execution, and didn't mind telling them. He had the ability to rant and rave a little, while still explaining they were better than the skills they displayed in the first half. He also began telling each man exactly what he would do in the next twenty minutes of play to improve.

The opposing team began the second half with a quickness to their step and scored the first basket, but Taylor went on a run and scored the next ten after a huge block on their best shooter by Larry. The end-of-the-bench squad checked in the game for the final minutes, and though the Connecticut players scored a few points in the final minutes with the younger squad, Taylor ended the game with a thirty-point lead.

TJ took a cab back to the hotel to pick up his luggage and laptop, and made his way to the executive airport. The team showered and changed, ate a quick meal in the locker room, and boarded the bus to the airport for their chartered flight home. TJ followed Captain Steve's instructions by calling him so he could get the jet ready and warm for his arrival. TJ made the call on the way to the hotel to pick up his luggage, but still felt amazed he could simply walk from the cab, through the small terminal and over to the Learjet. Susie greeted him with her usual smile, and stowed his luggage while Steve asked if there were any flight deviations, and TJ replied no, as he buckled his seatbelt, sat back, and relaxed as the jet took off a few minutes later.

Once in the air, TJ pulled out his laptop and began writing his thoughts about the game. He didn't try to put the facts in finished paragraphs, but instead, he just wanted to get his memories stored on the hard drive. After he finished the rough draft, Susie brought him his dinner. As he ate the rib eye steak, baked potato, and fresh salad, TJ realized he had not eaten anything since breakfast. After completing the last bite, he pulled the laptop to him, read his notes, and made minor corrections. Afterwards, he began writing about Shane's thoughts before the game, his preparation for the game, the practice in the arena, and game day jitters. He explained Shane's focus prior to the game, the mistakes in the first half, and their amazing play in the second half.

He heard Steve on the intercom say they would be landing in ten minutes so he completed his last paragraph, and stowed his computer as Susie put away his drink glass. Five minutes later, he was on the ground and on his way home. It had been an amazing first journey.

Shane came home to the motorcoach about an hour later, excited for the win, down on his play, but so thrilled TJ was able to join him there. TJ related the conversation he had with Walter, and it shocked Shane they were going to give TJ a press pass, making TJ's accessibility to the team much easier. They were still taking about it as they moved to the bedroom and began undressing. After sex, they cuddled up into their favorite spooning position, the dogs returned to their side of the bed, and all slept well.

# SIX

Shane ate breakfast with TJ on Sunday morning and enjoyed a long walk with the dogs on a cool fall morning. He then drove to the gym, and though they the team had the day off, he managed to catch Brandon, one of the team managers on his cell phone, and talked him into meeting him there. For the next three hours, he worked on every shot he missed, shooting it over and over again with Brandon rapidly bouncing the next ball to him. He stopped for a water break from time to time, but he kept practicing until he could make each of the shots perfectly and repeatedly.

Shane picked up takeout from his favorite barbeque place on the way home. TJ cooked several ears of fresh corn in the microwave, made a salad, cut some fresh fruit, and took the dogs out for a pee just as Shane drove up. Seeing the takeout bags, the dogs peed quickly and headed for the door with their tails wagging.

After a nap, Shane went to work on more homework while TJ first paid the bills, then began editing a dozen pages on the gay fiction book soon to be going to his editor, and finally spent two hours writing on the new basketball book after talking with Shane about the trip and the game.

The practice on Monday had been very hard, with high energy, a new level of expectations, but Shane expected the workout, as it was still early in the season. He knew the team needed more strength and endurance training. The coach removed the rims from the goals so they worked hard on defense for most of the workout. He knew they would do the same the next day before preparing for the upcoming game. He never resented extra work, as he remained steadfast to accept any challenge presenting him as a player and athlete.

Shane called home after eating dinner and explained to TJ how the practices were going before talking about his schoolwork and his day. Shane was always very careful to also ask about TJ's day. He ended with how much he missed him. They had a home game on Wednesday night, and he told him he would see him there.

The next day, TJ spent all morning writing and editing, by using the information he picked up from his first visit on Monday to Walter Mills in the public relations office. He now had a printed media book, folders on all the team's travel plans, including times and flights, as well as hotels and reservations phone numbers. TJ created a spreadsheet on his computer to keep up with everything with columns for the game location, date and time leaving, for return date and time confirmed, hotel name, reservation number, and confirmed. He did not want to either embarrass himself, or Shane by missing a game. He couldn't imagine writing a detailed book on the season if he failed to be witness a single second. He always used spreadsheets as a way of freeing his mind of detail and clutter, so he could go back to concentrating on his writing.

For many years he used a database contact manager to keep up with all of his contacts, so he created a new contact file for Taylor University Basketball, inputting everyone's name, telephone number, and email address he came across while covering Shane's games. He created a methodical, systematic, and orderly report for all the flights required for the season, and emailed the details to his new contact at the Learjet leasing company. In a few hours, he received confirmation for all his flights.

In the meantime, he patiently called every hotel on the away game list, and lined up his reservations, making sure the room retained was two floors above the team and near the back of the building. He also learned the executive airports provided their passengers with a car service to the hotel in all the cities he was flying to, so no rental cars were required, and he was set to go.

He walked the dogs early, loaded his laptop in the car, and drove to the campus two hours before game time. He placed the lanyard holding his new press-pass over his head, and the press-parking-card Walter's secretary prepared for him inside the front windshield. He made his way into the arena via a door marked press entry, walked up to the lady at the counter showing her his new press-pass.

"Ah, Mister Johnson, we're so glad you're here. It is going to be a great game tonight. My notes tell me you're new, so I've arranged a tour of the building for you. It'll help you find your way around. Is that okay?"

"Excellent," he replied, "thank you."

"Very good," she said to TJ, and then into her walkie-talkie, "Mark? I have Mister Johnson ready for you. Are you on the way back?"

Mark, a work-study student from Lakeland Florida replied, "I'll be right there."

TJ sat on a sofa behind the counter and in a few minutes a good looking Mark arrived in a hurry. He was average height, bright blue eyes, short red hair with just a flip up in the front like a big Labrador had licked the upper part of his face, two pierced rings in his left ear, and he came up quickly, stuck out his hand, and smiled, "I'm sorry it took me so long. Are you ready to go?"

TJ stood and shook his hand, "I was fine, and yes, I'm ready to go, but I didn't know I needed to pee to start the tour."

Mark laughed, "I guess I should have been more specific. Please walk this way." Mark turned and let TJ through a door and into the hall.

They walked up a flight of stairs and down the hall where Mark pointed out the coach's office, as well as offices for all his assistants and team support members down the hall from where TJ visited Walter on Monday. He visited the basketball museum before they walked out into the arena. Mark showed him the layout of the floor, pointed to the tunnel the Taylor team came through, and then up to the pressroom.

They returned to the hallway and went down several flights of stairs to the main floor, and moved around the building to the far side. As he continued the tour, he pointed out the opposing team's locker room, and the locker room for Taylor. He was told he could go in the locker room after the game to interview the players, but never before or at halftime.

After returning to the main floor, they made their way to the back of the arena and through a door marked pressroom. Inside, Mark showed him to a locker explaining it was much like a bus locker where the key comes out when locked but not when open. He pointed to the location of the bathrooms, over to the desk area, gave him his password for an Internet connection, and together they went over to the food area.

"Well, this ends the tour. You can see the video live feed of the basketball court overhead as the clock counts down to tipoff time so you don't miss it." Mark handed his business card to him, "If you need anything, just call me on my cell number. I'm here to help in any way."

"Thank you, Mark. Excellent tour," said TJ as he shook his hand and watched him leave.

He sat down at an empty workstation and unloaded his laptop. He tested his new password and sure enough, he was online. He looked up at the clock, and it was sixty-five minutes until game time. On the desk was a press release for the game where he discovered one of Shane's teammates would not play tonight due to a stomach virus. He hoped Shane and the rest of the team didn't catch it.

Realizing he was hungry, he walked over to the buffet line, picked up a plate, and loaded his plate with prime rib, mashed potatoes, cream corn, and green beans. He added a spoonful of a chicken and rice casserole, picked up a glass of sweet ice tea, and went over to a table to sit down and watch the television monitors while he ate. By the time he finished there was a line at the buffet and almost all of the workstations were taken. He realized how well the press covered the Taylor basketball teams, and feeling like a novice in this room full of veteran reporters, he hoped they didn't ask him too many questions.

After seeing the team take the floor to warm-up on the big television screen, TJ locked his laptop in a locker, made his way to the arena, and walked down the aisle to his seat to watch. Shane spotted him and smiled. TJ replied with a wink as he sat down. Shane finished his stretching and began shooting close in as usual before working his way to almost the three-point line. After a few drills, the team left the floor as the fans began filling up the seats.

TJ went back to the pressroom and decided to eat dessert. He found a delicious piece of pecan pie, added a scoop of ice cream, and sat down to eat. He watched the press members as they told stories to each other and laughed.

There were a few reporters typing on their laptops, but mostly they were enjoying the calm before the game. He put his empty plate down, chose a water bottle from a barrel of ice, and returned to his seat in the arena.

Taylor was playing Davidson, a school just a few hours away and not in the ACC league, but each time they played Taylor as if each player would win a new car if they won. They were feisty, scrappy, determined, pushy, and many times successful, though they had never made it to the final four.

Shane thought the tipoff ball was coming to him when suddenly one of Davidson's senior players leaped in front of him stealing the ball. The move pissed Shane off, but he picked up his man as the Taylor team set up their man-to-man defense. One of their guards posted up in the corner and hit a beautiful swish shot putting their team on the scoreboard first. Shane brought the ball into Jerry, who quickly moved the ball up the court, but as he crossed between their guards, he lost control of the ball. A Davidson player snatched the ball and made a quick run and layup, and now Taylor was down five points.

Most coaches would have called timeout to settle their team down, but coach Timmons liked for his players to work out their problems on the court. It was also a silent sign he displayed to his players that he wasn't worried, and they shouldn't be worried, because he knew they would find a way to overcome their poor start.

Jerry snapped the ball over to Larry, but the Wildcats immediately covered him, and he couldn't get a shot off. The ball went back to Jerry and over to the far court and then back again. Shane broke free near the foul line, and Jerry bounced the ball to him. Shane snatched it up and turned while spinning, leaped upward, and fired a shot he had done a hundred times in practice. It hit the backboard and fell away without even touching the rim.

The crowd anticipated their first score and signed heavily. The miss embarrassed Shane, and though he knew he should have shaken the failure off, he couldn't. TJ noted Shane's face remained red as he went down the court. The ball was tossed to the player he was defending, he tried too hard to steal it, and fouled him as the player went up to shoot. This made Shane even angrier as he walked to the line to wait for his opponent to shoot. To rub salt in the wound, Davidson made both shots, and it was now seven to nothing—so much for Taylor's home team advantage. Journalists around the country listed Taylor in the number one slot for their first ranking of the year, and the Wildcats were absolutely nowhere on the list, and yet they were beating Taylor.

Shane fought hard trying to shake his defensive player. When he finally got the ball, he drove hard to the basket—some would say too hard, because he loss control, accidentally knocked down a Davidson player, and called for a charging foul. Two fouls on their star player in less than a minute. Coach Timmons sent a substitute to take Shane's place. Reluctantly, Shane made his way to the bench and sat sound full of anger.

TJ wished players were allowed to carry a cell phone, as he never wanted to talk to Shane so bad as now. A few plays later, Taylor began to score, but by halftime, Davidson led by six points. The long sit on the bench did wonders for Shane. The coach hooked his elbow before he went into the locker room. He waited for the rest of the team to go on by. Shane assumed he was about to get a well-deserved ass kicking, but wisely, the coach leaned into him and whispered. "What did you learn out there?"

The question and the lack of angry tone surprised him. He thought for a second while searching his coach's eyes for the correct answer. Then it dawned on him, and he replied, "That any idiot can lose his temper and lose a game."

The coach smiled, "Well put. What else?"

Shane began searching his coach's eyes once more. He sighed and replied, "That trying to win the game in the first two minutes is impossible as there are forty minutes of playing time."

Coach Ryan replied, "And one more time, what did you forget?"

Shane brow wrinkled, his brain was racing, and his heart pumping, but the coach never backed off. Shane said, "That no one can win a basketball game by themselves. After all, who would bring the ball in?" All of Shane's replies were direct quotes from sayings the coach taught them in practice. Lessons Shane had learned well, and in the span of a few minutes forgot them all. He would not neglect them again.

The coach smiled, "I could not have said that better. Now get in there and prepare for a better second half. We're down six, and you have two fouls and zero points. Can you do better?"

"Yes sir I can."

"Good. I'll look forward to watching."

Coach Timmons met with his assistant coaches while Shane took a piss, and then he sat down on the bench in the corner to think. Shane spoke to no one, but returned to the group when the coach came in to speak to them. He was hard on them as a group, and then carefully selected players to speak to. By the time he finished, Taylor University was ready to start this evening over.

TJ had gone to the pressroom where a female student gave him a press release with the first half statistics. He read it after getting a bowl of yogurt ice cream, and sitting down at his desk. After his laptop came to life from hibernation mode, he began writing the facts of the first half as he recalled them, and below that, he began writing the story behind the facts, explaining what had happen to Shane and to the team. By the time he finished, he looked up to see the countdown clock to the second half at two minutes. He saved his work, packed up his laptop, and placed it in the locker. He made it down to his seat as Taylor broke their sideline huddle. Shane turned around and immediately spotted TJ.

70

TJ had been thinking of something he could say that would help, or something that would bring comfort, but in the moment, he smiled as big as he could, winked at him, and then taking both hands he stuck them out and a little downward, and raised and lowered them just slightly, while mouthing the word 'chill'. Shane understood and smiled back as he nodded approvingly.

Twenty seconds later, Shane caught the tip, flung the ball to Larry, who through it back to Jerry, as Shane set up a screen. Jerry ran his man into Shane, and flung the ball in a fast bounce pass to Larry in the corner, who went up and hit a beautiful three point swish. The crowd cheered, and Shane rushed to cover the man bringing the ball in, as they had planned a full court press on the first possession. Shane jumped and waved his hands, making his six foot nine inch body the size of a small billboard. Frantically, the Davidson player attempted to find someone to throw it to, knowing the referee was counting to five seconds.

Shane's intensity increased. Desperate to get the ball in, the player made a mistake by bringing the ball way back with his right hand to throw way down the court. Shane timed it perfectly, leaped as high as he could, and caught the ball one handed. As he came down, he spun around counter clockwise, dribbled the ball twice as he made his way towards the basket, leaped high into the air, flung the ball through the goal, and hung on to the rim to keep from falling on his back.

The home team crowd leaped to their feet and cheered. The players and coaches quickly leaped to their feet and cheered. Shane ran to the corner to prepare to press the inbound player once more, and coach Timmons smiled, because he knew his star player was now focused, and ready to play ball.

Shane stole the ball three times in the second half, completed sixteen points from the field, and put in another ten points from the foul line. Larry hit twenty-two points, and Jerry ended with sixteen points, fourteen assists, and even six rebounds for the shortest guy on the court. The rest of the team contributed to the victory as well. The final score resulted in Taylor winning by sixteen points.

Shane shook hands with each of Davidson players, and then looked up to the stands to see a smiling TJ beaming proudly. Shane shook his fist in the air and smiled back before turning towards the locker room.

TJ went up to the pressroom and found the media reporters rapidly typing away at their laptops, trying to say in words a description of the amazing Taylor play in the second half. They ran out of adjectives to describe Shane's performance, but it didn't stop them from typing.

He passed behind two of several photographers as they flipped digitally through one game photo after another on their Mac Book® laptop using Adobe's Lightroom® software to sort through hundreds of shots until they found the ones they wanted. Quickly they enhanced, cropped, and completed the photos with such ease and artistic talent that TJ just stood there and watched, mesmerized with their skills.

Once done, they used Stuffit® to compress the photos before uploading the bundle to their boss at the Associated Press® in Charlotte. Thirty minutes later, the photos would arrive at every newspaper and affiliated magazine office in the country.

TJ hesitated, but when one of the photographers left, he asked the remaining one if he could speak to him.

"My name is TJ Johnson. I'm writing a book about the Taylor team this season, and I was wondering how I go about getting permission to use some of your pictures? You and your partners' camera skills are amazing. The photos are works of art."

The photographer smiled, "I'm glad you liked them. Shooting the Taylor team is one of our favorite projects. We use top quality digital cameras with large zoom lens, so it appears as if we are standing on the court when they shoot a thirty-foot jumper. It is a lot of fun, and everyone seems to like our work. We're Associated Press® photographers, so our shots belong to them, but usually a courtesy is extended to book writers, as long as our photos are properly credited." He stopped talking, fished into his pocket, and came up with a business card. He wrote a name on the back and a phone number. He handed the card to TJ.

"This is the phone number for my boss. Call and tell him you met me here, what your publication plans are, and I'm sure he'll approve you, and if so, he'll give you a password to our photography website where you can scan all our photos, and download the ones you are interested in. Our software makes a list of your downloads, and they'll check with you from time to time for status of your work."

"The book is like a backstage pass to a championship season through the eyes of Shane Bradley. Every day he and I talk about his individual workouts, his personal progress, and team practice. We also talk about what he was thinking during the game, and how he assessed the opposition, and specifically the players he was defending and attacking."

The photographer smiled, "Okay, you got me. I'm hooked. Where do I order the book?"

TJ laughed, "Well, first we have to win a championship, or we don't have a book."

"You mean you are writing on the book all a season, and if they lose, you end up with nothing?"

TJ grinned, "Well, Shane doesn't plan on losing to anyone this season. He says he and his team will indeed win the championship."

"That's a big boast, but if anyone can make it happen—it is Shane. He is incredible and a photographers dream. He gives us the best shots, and the fact that he is also good looking makes our pictures even better. Okay, my email and contact information is on my card, so please keep me posted on the progress. I'll look forward to reading the book after the championship game next spring. It was great to meet you."

72

Shane arrived at the motorcoach about ten-thirty. He was tired, not from running, but from the anxiety he created in the first half, and the enthusiasm he exploded with in the second half. He looked at TJ as if ashamed of his first half performance. TJ was outside letting the dogs pee when Shane drove up.

TJ smiled and gave him a half hug as he held on to the dogs. "Well that was an interesting game. I learned so much tonight."

Shane grinned, "So did I, but I learned it the hard way."

TJ pulled the dogs as they made their way to the door. "Come on in, and tell me about it. I know what I saw, but what did you see."

"I have never been so stupid in my life," began Shane, but TJ interrupted.

"I doubt that."

"You doubt I was stupid."

TJ laughed, "I doubt that tonight's event was less stupid than some other brain fart moment you experienced!"

Shane looked stunned at the comment, felt a bit angry at first, and then smiled, "You are wise, my friend, and you are right. It was bad tonight, but I have done worst."

"More importantly, you proved in the second half you can learn from your mistakes, and you can excel from having done so. I would say the lessons you learned were almost as important as the win—but we love the win, don't we."

Shane hugged and kissed him. "Yes—we do love to win, and we love to make love to tall skinny guys…"

TJ interrupted between a break in the kiss, "with great dogs?"

Shane laughed, "Yes, they are great dogs, but their owner has a great ass."

"Now be careful. You'll make me get an erection."

"I plan for you to do more than that. Let's go to bed."

"Hang on, I have to give the dogs a treat before I give you one!"

# SEVEN

The coach scheduled a practice the next day, and it was another hard one. They began in the meeting room looking at selected clips of their performance with Davidson, the reading of their stats, and a list of what they planned to accomplish in today's practice. They always received the list in writing so they would know that what they were doing had nothing to do with the coach becoming angry at their performance, but rather an assignment of a task that must be completed, and completed well, so the team as a whole could improve. Shane told TJ that the plan put everyone on the same page, and thus, the same goal. He did the same thing for his shooting practice, writing down what he planned to do before he arrived at the gym. Sometimes, he gave the list to the manager feeding the balls to him. Other times, he folded the list up, and placed it in the top of his socks.

Near the end of practice the coach told them to stop, take a knee, and then he said good teams often lose in the championship tournament because they don't learn to play through difficulty. He smiled and continued, "Everyone in the stands last night, and everyone watching on television wanted me to call a timeout when things began so badly for us. Hell, he added, my assistant coaches wanted me to call a timeout, but I resisted the temptation because this was the first opportunity I have had so far this year to teach you to work through your difficulty. While you were just a little behind at the half, it was actually a big comeback from your rough start, and you did it without Shane's help, as he was sitting on his ass on the bench.

"Now if we graph our performance from tipoff to the end of the game, it would go from the bottom to the top, and that is exactly what I wanted you to do—find a way to move the ball and start getting some points. I wasn't happy with your play in the first half," he paused to be sure he had their attention, "and neither were you. You knew you could do better, but I can't always make you do better—you have to want to do better.

"And one last thing. If you make mistakes and get yourself in a hole, I expect the team to find a solution. Not a single player, but the team. A championship can sometimes appear to be lost by a single player's mistake, but I guarantee no one player as ever won a championship by himself. Not a single time. We must pull together when a player is down.

"Now granted, Shane didn't give us much time to help him in that first half, but from now on, I want you to be on guard when a player's timing is off, when he makes a stupid mistake, and when his usual finesse is forgotten. You must recognize your fellow player's fall, quickly get around him, and let him know he has your confidence. Encourage him to settle down, chill out, and be cool, as they said in my playing days, and to let the game come to them—especially in the first few minutes of the first half with so much game to be played. After practice, I want each of you to create a list of at list three things you could say to a player that is in trouble, helping get back in the right frame of mind. We'll go over them in the team meeting.

"If you will continue to maintain the attitude that we all have a lot to learn, then we'll all continue to grow together, and we will be successful." He paused for a full two minutes allowing them to think about what he had just taught, and then he grinned, "Okay, toe the line."

The team rushed to the court line to begin their end of practice running drills, and they did so with great enthusiasm. Shane beat the guards down the line, and vocally yelled at the team to run. He beat them again and the coaches loved it. Everyone began yelling, and running harder and harder. Sweat soaked their practice shirts, but they kept pushing. When the coach finally said for them to cool down and stretch, they knew they had just moved their knowledge, skill, and team spirit one step farther up the ladder towards success.

Shane left the gym for the dining hall feeling far better about his performance than he had all year. He could not wait to play the next game.

The night before they were both scheduled to fly to Rochelle, New York for the Iona game, TJ and Shane agreed on a few secret signals for future games. If TJ held up five fingers it meant for Shane to chill, relax, and the game will come to you, while three fingers meant go, go, go! One finger meant TJ loved him. Two fingers was designed to make Shane laugh, and it could mean two things at once, hence the choice of number two: it could either mean Shane's pants were down at his ankles and his ass was showing, or TJ was going to be the top tonight! Every time they practiced it, Shane laughed. TJ later created a third option of imagining everyone on the court naked; just to make Shane relax with a bit of humor.

If Shane saw any of the signals, he was to respond by pulling his ear, and a wink if he agreed, and a shake of the head left and right indicating no he didn't agree.

On Friday, Shane left after his second class about ten-thirty, while TJ flew out at noon. The team immediately noted the difference in temperature as they left Lindle at a balmy fifty-nine degrees, but they landed in Rochelle at twenty-eight degrees, and found themselves in a cold wet wind. They dropped their bags in their room, returned to a rented conference room for lunch, and followed by a team meeting where they saw highlights of several scout films for the Iona team. Their opponents were quick on the inside with two big men ready to take on Shane. The coach followed the film by giving each man his defensive assignment. He also diagramed a refresher on a few plays they already used this season, but would specifically use in tomorrow's game, plus two inbound plays when the ball is under their own goal. He also reminded everyone of the team's strategy should they go into overtime. This is something he did before every game because no one could predict when a tied ballgame might occur.

They loaded the team's chartered bus at two and went to the arena to practice on the court. They did a one hour shoot and run practice so they could get the feel of the floor and the dynamics of the shot. Although the distance from a shot to the rim and from the floor beneath the rim were the same as home, how large of a building and how far to the ceiling above, seemed to play into their depth of field, so they practiced many long shots until satisfied they were ready.

They returned about four for study time for two hours followed by dinner, and then free time.

TJ was glad to see that Steve was back as his pilot, but Janet was now the stewardess as Susie enjoyed some time off. He found her charming as well. She came from Alabama, and while she possessed and displayed a thick accent, her smile and blue eyes appeared to be electrically charged. True to her state, she served him fried chicken with rice and gravy, green beans, and cream corn, as well as a salad, and brought him banana pudding for dessert. He loved the meal, and the quiet time to write and study. He left the big media book at home on purpose, as it was just too heavy for travel, but the Acrobat PDF® version remained loaded on his laptop. He studied and reread the notes on Iona, as well as the press releases he received from Walter's staff. He even studied the floor plan of the gym, so he knew how to find the team's locker room, where the Taylor team would appear before taking the floor, and finally how to find the pressroom.

He landed safely, said goodbye to Steve and Janet, and then the car service took him to his hotel. He warmed up his laptop and loaded his GPS software called TravRoute®. He typed in the address of hotel, did a search of the surrounding streets, found a grocery store one block north, and for future reference, he spotted a creamery in case he had a craving for ice cream. He thought the weather too cold for ice cream, as he chilled from the plane to the car, but he might change his mind later.

After he left the hotel, he walked quickly because he had not brought an overcoat, and made it to the store in three minutes. He shopped quickly, obtaining a two liter bottle of Diet Mountain Dew®, a bottle of water, a few snacks, and a local newspaper. He returned to his room, filled the ice bucket, and changed clothes after turning the heat up in the room. He began reading the newspaper while his computer downloaded his email.

When his cell phone rang, he nearly fell off chair he had been typing from. He picked it up and looked at the caller ID.

"Hello?" he asked, and though he knew whose phone was calling, he still played it safe in case someone else was using Shane's phone.

"Me, of course," replied Shane.

"What does 'me' look like?"

Shane smiled, "Me looks good."

TJ said, "Me thinks me lies."

Shane laughed. "What are you doing?"

"I'm writing the new book. I had a good flight, and you?"

"Yes, I did, too."

"It is cold as hell up here. Are there polar bears about?"

Shane grinned, "No. I think it is too cold for them."

"I went to the store for supplies and nearly froze to death. How did practice go."

"Very well. I have been doing homework the rest of the afternoon, but we're fixing to eat dinner, and then we'll get some free time. I called to see what room you're in."

"423. What time do think you can come? I need to eat some supper."

"I'm sorry we can't eat together. Probably about seven."

"Okay, enjoy your dinner, and I'll see you later tonight. I love you."

"I love you, too. Bye."

TJ smiled as he hung up the phone, checked his watch, and went over to the dresser to see what restaurants were in the hotel. He didn't see anything that excited him, and he didn't want to go back out in the cold, so he picked up the room service menu, ordered stir fry chicken with vegetables, fried rice, a salad, and a diet Pepsi® to drink.

He had been working on this past week's practice, the drills, the attitude of the players, and the lessons learned from Shane's perspective. He then described Rochelle, New York, and the weather. He read his work and saved it.

He then opened the new book he had been working on, and began writing a new chapter until he heard the knock on the door. He checked the peephole to be sure, and opened the door for the room service man. He was short, probably a high school kid working on the weekend, dark haired, and fairly nice looking, thought TJ as the young man pushed the cart into the room.

"Is it always this cold up here?"

The waiter smiled, "It's only November. It'll be very cold by January. This is balmy to us."

"Yeah, right. Are you a Taylor University basketball fan?"

"Yes, except when they are playing Iona. I have to pull for the local team."

"That'll hurt your tip," teased TJ. "I'm here for the big game tomorrow. Are you going?"

"I wish. I have to work."

"I understand. Just roll the tray over here so I can see the television while eating." TJ signed the bill and gave him a good tip. "Thank you very much. Go Taylor."

The boy smiled as he left the room.

TJ had just finished brushing his teeth when there was another knock at the door. He rolled the food cart to the door and opened it.

"Oh, jeez, it's only you. I thought it was the cute waiter again."

Shane laughed, "You are so funny." Shane pulled the cart into the hall, stepped in, picked up TJ, and hauled him to the bed, where together, they fell down and started making out.

An hour later, clothes in a piles on both sides of the bed, naked bodies sweating on the sheets, they cradled each other as if they hadn't seen each other in a year instead of just the other day. Shane playfully bit one of TJ's nipples, so TJ leaned over and bit just a piece of Shane's ear.

"Okay, okay," said Shane quickly. "You win."

TJ laughed because in a basketball game Shane could be beaten over and over again, knocked hard to the floor, pushed into the bleachers, and stepped on. He might be punched, by accident of course, and perhaps poked in the eye, making an eye contact fly to the floor. He never once complained about pain, but a little pinch or nibble by TJ, and he began his mister please don't hurt me plea mode. He was also ticklish, though none of his teammates knew it, and TJ put a finger into his armpit.

Shane rolled off, grabbed TJ's leg, and pulled him to him. They kissed again before Shane broke it off and said, "One more time."

TJ sighed, "You really have some juice left?"

"Yeah, it's been thirty minutes."

"Okay, okay, face up or down?"

"Down this time. I want to see if it feels different."

"I'll squeeze my legs if you don't squish me into the mattress."

They moved back to the center of the bed and before long Shane was pumping hard before finally groaning loudly as he came. Afterwards, he carried TJ to the shower so they could enjoy the hot water, and so he could gently wash his boyfriend.

Shane spent five minutes blow-drying his short hair, so his roommate couldn't tell he had taken a shower out of their room. It was almost ten and time for him to go. They kissed several more times, then again at the door, and he was off.

TJ locked the door, brushed his teeth, and made his way to the bed. He was sore from their love making, but happier than he could remember. He fell asleep thinking only of Shane.

The gym was on campus in an old building, and TJ didn't think it very warm for the team to be running up and down on the court, but the staff was nice and led him to the pressroom. It wasn't as pleasant as the one at the Taylor Dome, but it was warm, the food looked good, and he had an Internet connection in seconds. He read the press releases, made a few notes, and typed them as well as his thoughts on the campus and the building into his laptop.

He looked up at the clock and decided he had time to eat lunch before the team worked out. He chose a grilled cheese sandwich, a hot bowl of vegetable beef soup, a salad, and a slice of lemon meringue pie for dessert. He decided to choose Diet Pepsi® to drink, as they didn't serve sweet ice tea this far north.

After his meal, he locked his laptop in a locker and made his way down to watch the team warm-up. Finishing his stretch routine, Shane sat on the floor looking up the aisle where TJ descended. As their eyes met, they both smiled. TJ took a single finger and pretended to rub his nose with it. Shane winked at him as TJ sat down to watch.

Forty minutes later, the game started with the Taylor team scoring the first goal with a pretty three-pointer from the corner by Larry. Jerry tossed the ball inside to Shane, but Iona double-teamed him, and it was too early for him to fight his way to the goal, so he flicked it out to Larry who caught it and shot.

That was the last of the easy shots as Iona proved to be very scrappy, hustling hard on defense, and staying close on offense by hitting some beautiful three-point shots. Shane tried to do too much too fast and missed a three-foot shot, a hook shot, and somehow missed a dunk. The coach was livid, and took him Shane out for a little rest, and to give him time to calm down and think.

Brandon handed a cup of Gator-Aid® over his shoulder and a towel. Shane took a long drink of it, and as he held the cup, he caught site of TJ sitting on the other side of the court. He pulled the cup down, wiped the sweat from his face with the towel, and saw TJ signaling with the numbers. He pulled his earlobe acknowledging he needed to chill. Coach Timmons was not pleased with their defense, so during a television timeout he explained exactly what he expected of the team in the first half. They came out of their sideline huddle ready to play ball. TJ first gave him five fingers. Shane nodded approvingly like a pitcher accepting the catcher's choice for a fastball, and tugged at his earlobe to let TJ know he saw it.

TJ grinned, gave him two fingers, and laughed. Shane's face wrinkled in a puzzled look before he remember the meaning of the two, and now the three choices: either's Shane's pants were down and his ass was showing, the players on the court were naked, or TJ was going to be the top tonight. Shane laughed hard, and tugged at his ear. He leaned over towards the coach and said, "I'm sorry, Coach. I was trying to win the game…"

The coach interrupted him, "In the first five minutes?"

Shane blushed a little and nodded, "Yes sir. I'm ready."

The coach looked at him to be sure Shane understood. "Let the game come to you and it will. Now get in there."

Shane ran to the scoring table, dropped to a knee, and waited for the first break in the play. As he waited, he looked back at TJ who was signaling with one finger then five, then again one and then five—I love you and chill. Shane tugged his earlobe and winked at him.

The buzzer blew and in he went. He set up a screen and Jerry downed a beautiful three. He snagged a rebound and flung it out to Larry for a layup. He got another rebound and flung it out to Jerry, sprinted down the court, and Jerry gave him a hard bounce down the lane. Shane snagged it like a shortstop, turned, and dunked it. The three hundred Taylor fans present stood and cheered.

He was fouled two plays later, kept his cool, and hit both shots with nothing but net. He was back to his old self, and he was having fun. He actually smiled as he came down the court.

Taylor led by six at the half. Coach Timmons had plenty to teach the team during the break, and the team returned to the floor and won the game by twenty-six points. Shane had twenty-eight points, and Larry had twenty-four. Shane also had twelve rebounds, and hit sixteen foul shots without a single miss.

Shane waved at TJ as he left the court. TJ hustled to the pressroom, and picked up the last press release with the game's statistics. He snagged a water bottle and left the gym for the street. He caught a cab and made his way back to the hotel, picked up his luggage, and rode to the airport.

Later that night, after they were in bed in the motorcoach and making out, Shane stopped and told him TJ's signaling calmed him perfectly, and he thanked him.

TJ laughed, "I liked the last signals the best. I love you and I'm the top! So turn on your back, dude!"

Shane and TJ laughed as he rolled over, and spread his legs as TJ dove on top, and began kissing him before their lovemaking began.

# EIGHT

The last of the autumn leaves covered the ground, and two to three days a week, the morning temperatures dropped below freezing. Though basketball filled most of their daily activities, they knew Thanksgiving was coming. They both came from families that enjoyed big holiday dinners and spending time together. Every other year the team would travel to Hawaii or Alaska for a tournament, but not this year. Shane and TJ discussed the holiday, and came up with what they thought was a workable plan for both families and the boys. They called their families to explain, and they graciously agreed with their timetable. Afterwards, TJ made the flight arrangements, and emailed their parents their arrival and departure times, so there would be no misunderstanding as to when they had to leave.

They were scheduled to fly to Las Vegas for a tournament the weekend before Thanksgiving with the final game set for Tuesday night. Shane flew out at noon after the players had a chance to attend morning classes, and TJ flew out early that morning to avoid the weekend flight traffic. They checked the forecast the night before with Shane studying the radar maps, as he hated to fly in bad weather. He gave Friday a thumb up for flying.

TJ learned to look ahead at his flight schedule, and then checked out the local gay bookstores in the cities they were traveling. He would call them on the phone and arrange a book promotion and signing if they were interested. The gay bookstore in Las Vegas had been very interested, but so was the large Barnes and Noble® store. He shipped in extra books to both stores as well as posters advertising the signing. He arrived at ten thirty Las Vegas time, checked in, and arrived at the Barnes and Noble® by three and signed books for an hour. He caught a cab to the gay bookstore, laughed with the manager and staff for a while, and began signing books about four-thirty. He was back at the hotel at six, while hoping the stores would begin to promote his books a bit more.

TJ kept a detailed contact record in his computer for everyone he met in the book business. He made sure he had the store managers contact information and their email addresses for promos of upcoming books. He also sent thank you notes for their assistance in promoting his books. Just as he finished, his phone rang. He looked at the caller ID and smiled.

"Well, hello. How was your flight?"

Shane grinned, "Excellent and the views today were awesome. Sometimes I don't look at the ground, but I enjoyed seeing the mountains and desert valleys. I'm sure yours was fine, too."

"Yeah, my flight crew today was Steve and Susie, and I enjoyed prime rib and stewed potatoes for lunch. It is a tough job, but somebody has to do it."

"We had mystery meat so I ate the salad and vegetables. Practice was good and the arena is huge. I hope they sell a lot of tickets."

"I wouldn't be surprised because the hotels have put together ticket packages for the tournament, gambling, shows, and hotel stay. Are you free for dinner?"

Shane deadpanned, "No, I'm expensive." TJ laughed. Shane continued, "I thought we were going to have a team meal, etc., but since the first game isn't until Sunday afternoon, he gave us tonight off. He knew many of the players haven't been to Las Vegas. Have you been before?"

"Yeah, a couple of times. I love the shows—especially the magic shows. I got to see Siegfried and Roy before the tiger tasted Roy and spit him out!"

"Funny. I have been once. What can we do for dinner?"

TJ thought for a second, "I think we should go to another hotel, take in a nice dinner but not the typical buffets to avoid the autograph seekers, and if you want, I can try to get tickets to something."

"Do it, I'm on the way up. What room?"

"2332."

"Good grief, they have over a two thousand rooms. My lord they're raking in the dough. See you soon. Bye."

"Bye. I love you, and I know you can't say it—so I said it for both of us. Wear a sports coat."

TJ let Shane in having just got up from his laptop. I made a few calls and the magic shows were sold out tonight, but I got lucky at one. It's at the Bellagio®, where the outdoor dancing fountains are, and we're eating at a nice Japanese steakhouse for dinner, and I got two tickets from a scalper service for the eight o'clock show for Elton John. You interested?"

"Elton John! Hell yes. That's great. Kiss me quick!"

Shane and TJ embraced, TJ quickly changed clothes, and they were out the door. A limo picked them up at the side entrance, and whisked them to the Bellagio® celebrity entrance. They told the driver when the show was supposed to be over, but he gave them a card with his number on it to call him. TJ tipped him nicely.

Earlier, TJ used Shane's name to arrange the dinner reservations so there was a pretty hotel hostess waiting for them. She shook their hands and began giving them a brief tour of the hotel while making her way to their restaurant. Inside, she bypassed the line waiting at the maître d' station, and led them to a beautiful table near the back providing privacy. TJ tipped her as well.

A waiter arrived in full Japanese costume, took their drink orders which was diet drinks, and gave them a few minutes to check out the menu. They ordered the fireworks meal that included cooking the meal on the hot table before them with all the flair. The waiter disappeared and soon a private chef arrived with a platter of shrimp, chicken, raw vegetables, and more, and began cooking. He threw things in his hat with his knives, chopped vegetables rapidly, and Shane thought dangerously, but they began eating everything he threw on their plates and loved it all. TJ tipped him very well, too.

They walked to a creamery for dessert where they both chose ice cream sundaes with Shane sticking with strawberries and bananas, and TJ going for butter pecan and bananas. It was a lot of ice cream, but it was very good.

Near the end of their sundaes, TJ dialed the hostess cell number she gave him. In a few minutes, she arrived and let them down a hallway and into the concert hall for tonight's show. She took them directly to their seats through a side entrance, so they never had to wait in line to get in. This helped Shane stay incognito for a while longer. She told them to meet her at the same entrance door she brought them in after the show.

A waiter appeared with a thick program book for each of them and a flute of champagne. He then took free drink orders, but they stayed with their diet drinks, as Shane wasn't allowed to drink on the road while representing the team. The crowd began filing in, and soon the auditorium was packed and the Red Piano show began. Elton went from one hit to the next without stopping for forty-five minutes, and somehow changed costumes while singing behind a bamboo blind. Shane and TJ loved it.

He then did a few numbers from an upcoming album, and finished with another non-stop menagerie of his amazing songs. The boys stood with the rest of the audience, giving him many ovations until finally the lights went up. A few fans recognized Shane and asked for autographs, so he politely signed as they made their way to their awaiting hostess.

She asked if they enjoyed the show and of course, they said yes.

She smiled, "Would you like to meet him?"

Shane replied, "Yes, of course, but isn't that impossible?"

She laughed, "Not in Las Vegas. Anything is possible, but to be fair, Elton recognized you from the stage, and his associate sent me a note to bring you backstage."

Shane's face went white, "You're kidding. He recognized me? Of course, we'd love to meet him."

She led them backstage where about a dozen other folks were standing outside his door. Quickly, an aide took the guests into his dressing room, where they talked to Elton briefly, obtained his autograph, and were led back outside. It took about ten minutes, but soon the line was finished. The aide brought Shane and TJ in, and at first Elton thought it was just another hotel courtesy guest, but as he looked up, and up some more, he smiled as he saw Shane's face at the top of his six feet nine inch frame.

Elton stood up and came over to Shane, "My lord, you're so tall and good looking." He nodded to his aide. "Shut the door, honey. These boys are the last ones." He turned back to Shane. "I have seen you play on television many times because I'm a Taylor fan—unless you're playing Georgia Tech. I live in Atlanta when I'm not here or in London, and I love college basketball.

You are the man when it comes to playing basketball. Are you going to win the championship this year?"

Shane laughed, "Well, I hope so. This is my junior year and the team is coming along just fine."

Elton noticed TJ standing back a step to Shane's side. At first he thought, he was a manager or an assistant, but then he smiled, "And who is this handsome young man."

Shane grinned sheepishly as he looked to see if anyone else was in the room, "Elton, this is TJ—my partner."

Elton did a double take kind of a look, "Partner as in business partner, or partner as in…"

Shane couldn't help himself, "Partner as in boyfriend."

Elton slowly sat down in his seat. "Well, you're the first this month to surprise me, but what a pleasant surprise. TJ, come shake my hand. I want to meet the lucky fellow, and I do mean lucky."

TJ did as requested. "Shane and I are such big fans of your songs. He doesn't like rock music, prefers songs he can either sing to like yours, or some smooth jazz when he is relaxing before a game."

Elton laughed, "You should sing 'Rocketman' before a game because that is who you are flying up and down that court. In addition, I just love it when you get a chance to do a huge dunk! Come here boys, and sit down with me. I have a second show in a while, but this is a treat. How long have you been together?"

Shane answered, "Since August. We met by chance or by…"

Elton jumped in, "Fate. Love is a funny thing. I have been unlucky many times, but I wasn't a very good catch back in my drug binge days, but now I am clean and sober, and have a great husband. I wish he were here. He is a fan, too. I'm so happy for you. I assume you are still in the closet."

"Yes, I'm afraid so. I doubt Taylor is ready for a gay basketball player."

"Times are changing, slowly, but they are," added Elton. "TJ, what do you do?"

"I write gay fiction, at least normally, but this season I'm writing a book about Shane that is sort of a backstage pass to a championship season. It'll be out in April."

"Oh, that sounds great. Put me down for a copy. Gay fiction? Wait a minute, I know you. You wrote the **The War Apart** series. I just loved that. Since I'm English, I just didn't know much about the Civil War in America, and never thought about the poor gay boys who had to fight and die. How interesting, and now the lovers are in Colorado. Is there a third book coming, pardon the pun?"

TJ smiled, "Yes, it is called **The War Beyond** and should be out in another year."

Shane jumped in, "He's releasing **The Raceboys** next month. It's about America's first young gay racecar driver, and it is a fun read."

"Ah, there's a promoter in the family. I like that. I assume you're playing in the tournament."

"Yes, our first game is tomorrow afternoon."

"Okay, you came to see me, so I'll come to see you play tomorrow."

Shane beamed, "That would be fantastic."

Elton got a card from his desk, "Now this is my private card with my contact information. I wish we could do lunch or something, but I assume you have to eat well before the game so we'll try that next time. TJ, you call me if you're going to be here, or in Atlanta sometime, and we'll get together at my house so you can meet my boyfriend. It was so great to meet you."

"And we loved your show," added TJ.

"Thank you," said Elton. "Now come give me a group hug."

They hustled back to the hotel, but after kissing goodnight, Shane rushed out the door and down two floors to his room to keep from being late. He never missed a curfew, and didn't want to raise suspicions by missing one now.

The following day they had an early practice while TJ remained in the room working hard on updating Shane's story, along with editing his own book. He worked on the press releases until he felt they were ready, and would go out Thanksgiving weekend. The book would come out the first Tuesday in December, and he hoped sales would go well. Both Amazon® and Barnes and Noble® already had a supply of the books, and the book cover was on their website and taking advance orders. TJ uploaded the new book on his website, and actually started processing orders both for the electronic version and for books. He also put a package together for multi-book orders for Christmas gifts, and a designed a way to autograph his books if requested.

Recently, he created a bookmark advertising his books and website, and gave them away everywhere he went, and added the item to his mailing list program. Every book purchased online received a bookmark as well.

Friday night's game was against Oregon State, and they had two big men who were ready to do battle with Shane. While their guards were good, they were not as good as Jerry and Mike. Mike grew up in New Hampshire, and though he was not as fast as Jerry, he was a great assist man, and offered a beautiful jump shot. He was six feet four inches, a hundred and ninety pounds, blond hair and blue eyes, and although he appeared quiet and shy, he had tremendous wit. He usually found something funny to say at any occasion.

Beginning with this first game with Oregon, TJ changed his pre-game habits. He still went to the pressroom before the teams warmed up and stretched, but now ate his lunch or dinner prior to the game at the press buffet, read the press releases, and wrote details for the book. He would walk down and watch the pre-game warm-up, and head back up to the pressroom during the break. Just before game time, he would return to the arena and walk over to the tunnel where the Taylor team would often be waiting to return to the court.

Using his press identification badge, he would step just a little into the tunnel until his eyes met Shane's. TJ was aware that Shane could do little to acknowledge him, but TJ would scratch his nose or the edge of his face while using five fingers for him to chill, and followed by one finger indicating he loved him. Shane would respond with a tug of his earlobe and sometimes he would smile and wink.

Before team introductions, TJ hastened to his seat and prepared to watch the game.

Taylor didn't have a man that could out jump Oregon's tallest man at seven feet one inch, but as the ball tipped towards one of their forwards, Shane leaped inside and stole the ball. The moment Jerry saw Shane's quick move, he took off running towards their goal. Shane flung the ball down the court allowing Jerry to catch it on the run and dunk it. He gave Shane a high five with open palms as Shane went to block the man bringing the ball in, and Jerry waited on his guard to make his way down to receive the ball. The two Taylor players made it tough on the throw in by Shane waving his arms and Jerry closely guarding his man.

Afraid of another steal, the player on the sidelines threw the ball too hard and too far to the right, and away from Shane, and his guard could not hustle to it fast enough as the ball bounced out of bounds. It was now Taylor's ball. Shane threw it in quickly. Jerry flipped it to Mike, who faked a drive to the basket, and kicked it out to Larry in the corner, who hit a beautiful three-point shot. Swish!

Taylor got an eight-point lead before Oregon settled down and started playing ball. From time to time, they would get close to tying the score, but then Taylor would go on another run and score sixteen points before Oregon scored a single basket. At the half, Taylor was up by eighteen points.

Shane had ten points, two from fouls shots, and six rebounds so he was off to a good start. The coach was pleased with most of their effort, but this was early in the season, and he was determined to keep teaching. Sometimes during the play of the game, he would turn his back to the court and speak to the players on the bench, instructing them in something he had seen and wanted them to see, learn, and remember.

They returned to the court with great enthusiasm. TJ signaled again to chill, but added the three-finger signal which meant go, go, go! Shane laughed, and he took his game up a notch and scored twelve points in four minutes, blocked two shots, and made two steals. The final score had Taylor winning by forty points, and everybody on the bench got to play but the coaches.

Shane felt great about his game, and as soon as they had eaten the after game meal, they were awarded with free time, so Shane rushed to TJ's room. TJ quickly asked him several questions about the game that he added to his notes, but once he was done, they began stripping out of their clothes to celebrate in their own private way.

The second game in the series was Sunday afternoon, and they were playing Brigham Young, the team from the Mormon college. It was the first time Shane played an all white team since moving into college ball, but those players were scrappy, tough, agile, in excellent shape, and they would steal the ball from you in the flash of an eye. Unfortunately, they didn't have big inside men, and all the Taylor team had to do was feed Shane the ball at every opportunity, and he either pulled up and shot a short jumper or dunked it. They led by ten at the half, and won by twenty-four points.

Shane had been shaking hands with all the opposing players for years, but this time every single player said "God Bless You" instead of the usual "good game" most players offered. It touched him to see their sincerity. Like many religions around the world, Shane and TJ knew the Mormons did not like homosexuals. It bothered Shane that people were so nice, warm, and friendly on the court, but if they knew about him, they could hate him for being gay. TJ reminded him that all religions treat homosexuals pretty much the same.

They had Monday off because none of the television networks wanted to go up against Monday night football. The entire team had tickets to see a Cirque de Soleil® performance at Treasure Island. TJ had a ticket as well, but sat by himself. Afterwards, he and TJ had a car service lined up, and they went to the Stratosphere Hotel to eat a late dinner in the roof restaurant that gradually turned while they ate. They also had a rollercoaster on top of the restaurant, but neither boy wanted to try it. They returned to their hotel for a little quiet time until Shane's curfew.

Tuesday was a long day for the team as they had an easy morning practice, some study time, and then waited for the night game. They were playing Colorado State for the tournament championship, and the game was at six o'clock local time, or eight o'clock Eastern Time for prime time television.

TJ enjoyed the pressroom in Las Vegas as they set up awesome buffets, and their excellent technical facilities made an easy connection to the Internet. He wore his team press badge as well as a tournament press badge because security was high as Las Vegas was well prepared to protect visiting athletes.

Colorado proved tenacious, and Shane suddenly lost his temper when one of their men just kept hanging on to him, and the referees didn't call a single foul in Shane's favor the entire first half.

After the coach took him out of the game for a few minutes of rest, Shane glanced up, and TJ gave him the five fingers chill sign followed by two fingers. Shane's face portrayed a puzzled look, as TJ had not given him this signal in a while. TJ was smiling when he did so, and when Shane suddenly remembered, he started laughing, and his anger fell away. He wasn't sure if TJ meant his pants were around his ankle, or about sex, but later that night he found out that TJ meant the later—meaning that TJ would be the top, and they laughed about it as they made love to celebrate the victory. The team won by fifteen points and had a trophy to ship home.

Shane told the team manager his flight wasn't leaving until midnight, while the rest of the team was making various flights to their hometowns right after the game. They wished him well. He took a cab back to the hotel and made his way to TJ's room with his luggage.

After kissing for a while, they went downstairs and ate at one of the casino buffets as Shane was starving. TJ had eaten well in the pressroom so he ate some fruit and together, they had dessert.

Keeping his hat and sunglasses on, they managed to tour the casino and shops for a while before heading to bed about midnight where they began an hour of lovemaking, set the alarm for six, and instantly fell asleep in their usual spooning position.

They checked out by seven, and the car service took them to the executive airport. Their bags were quickly stowed as Steve warmed up the engines. Janet greeted them at the door, stowed their carry-on luggage, and made suggestions for breakfast. She brought them large glasses of freshly squeezed orange juice right after Steve took off, and settled into their high altitude slot, along with fresh blue berry muffins that were about the size of softballs. They were hot and delicious. Soon she brought the boys ham and cheese omelets, crisp bacon, whole-wheat toast, and a tray of fresh fruit, and large glasses of milk.

Afterwards, TJ pulled out his laptop and interviewed Shane about the behind the scenes stuff for the championship victory last night over Colorado State. Fifteen minutes later, TJ went to work assembling the notes he took from the game, along with Shane's inside knowledge and tidbits, and began weaving them into what he called the Las Vegas games. Shane hit the button to lower his seat to a reclining position, and Janet brought him a warm blanket and a few pillows. She laughed when she saw that the blanket only covered part of his large frame, so she brought a second one for his lower half.

The plan for Thanksgiving was simple on paper, but the weather could be a big factor, but so far, there was no snow in the forecast. If they had tried to do this on a commercial airliner with first class tickets, they would still be sitting on the runway waiting to takeoff, as the day before Thanksgiving was considered America's business flying day of the year. Thankfully, they were riding in the private Learjet, and they were the only passengers aboard.

Together, they would fly from Las Vegas to Shane's home in the Midwest where they would stay Wednesday and celebrate a Thanksgiving dinner that night. The next morning they would fly to South Carolina arriving in time for Thanksgiving lunch with TJ's folks. They would stay the night and fly back to Lindle the next morning. There was a practice scheduled for five followed by a Thanksgiving meal in the dining hall for the team, managers, and coaches.

About half past eleven, they landed in Almont, Missouri where they were met by Shane's parents in the family SUV. Shane began by introducing his father, Al Bradley, who stood about TJ's height that made TJ wonder where Shane got his super height. He also appeared to be in good shape, same hair color, and eyes as Shane, and smiled a lot. Barbara Bradley was in her late forties, same blue eyes, dark hair, short at five feet seven inches, and a warm radiant smile that she displayed as she refused to shake TJ's hand, preferring to give him a big hug. TJ felt at ease with both parents immediately. They quickly climbed in the warm car, and Al gave TJ a short tour of Almont. Shane teased them as he mentioned the population was only about twenty thousand. TJ saw it as a beautiful, but typical 'Leave It To Beaver' kind of small town, where probably everyone knew each other by face and maybe name, too.

They ate lunch at the country club overlooking the snow-covered golf course. Al and Shane told stories about each other's worst days on the golf course. TJ and Barbara laughed as the father and son teased each other, and it was easy for TJ to surmise Shane obtained his wit and basketball experience from his dad, but his smile and glowing eyes from his mom. However, she also played high school basketball and a star player as well in her day.

They drove to their house, and the boys carried their bags to Shane's old room. Thankfully, he had been sleeping on a king-size bed since the ninth grade, and Al and Barbara had no reservations about TJ sleeping with their son in the room. She put fresh linens on the bed, towels in the bathroom, and urged them to settle in, and then come down for something warm to drink.

They walked into the den, but soon TJ moved to the kitchen table as Barbara gleefully pulled out early scrapbooks and pictures of Shane as a baby and on through high school. Meanwhile, Al and Shane talked about Shane's game, his practices, how he liked this year's team, what he was hearing about NBA showing interest, and so on.

TJ Johnson

TJ returned to the den and sat by Shane as they talked about going to the pro teams after Shane's rein at Taylor. TJ quickly learned that everyone in this family said exactly what they were thinking at anytime.

Shane replied to his dad, "The newspapers, magazines, and television journalists are all predicting I will leave Taylor at the end of my junior year and enter the NBA draft, but I don't think so."

His mom jumped in quickly, "I think it would be smart to graduate as I doubt you'll ever have time to do so once your turn pro. Their seasons start in late summer or so, and if you make the playoffs, the final games are early June. That is a long season. I would love to see my son graduate."

Al smiled as he had heard what she said many times before, "I agree, and hopefully he can graduate, but just for discussion, and maybe plan B, let's talk about what-ifs. For example, let's say Shane has an excellent year, wins many awards, and his team makes the final four in March. In addition, if he is really lucky, they win the championship. Now he is a hot commodity, all the pro teams will want him, and they'll pay big bucks for him."

Barbara scoffed, "I don't like talking about our son as a commodity. He's our flesh and blood, although cuter than his dad," she teased, "and again, graduation is important."

Shane jumped in while TJ eagerly listened, "I agree with both of you, I want to graduate, and if I left after we won the championship, I would attend summer school each year until I graduate. I would only have about six courses to complete, so it wouldn't take very long to finish. I might finish some over the Internet as the university is expanding the at-home-anywhere curriculum."

Al spoke up again, "If Shane plays his senior year, and God forbid he gets hurt, the value of his selection could go way down, or they might pass on him forever. That is a huge risk."

Shane replied, "Dad, I have never been hurt playing basketball since the sixth grade, and that's when I started my strict stretching exercises, hard weight room work, strenuous running, and methodical cool down periods. I also changed my diet in the eight grade, and my body fat is nil, my strength is through the roof, and the team managers and strength coaches agree, I'm as fit as possible."

"Yeah," jumped in his mom, "but you took quite a hit in the nose in that Duke game last year."

Shane laughed, "Yeah, I know. I don't think he meant to. I am hit in the face all the time because as the arms go up and we all clash together, eventually an elbow to the face happens unintentionally. It just made me mad that I was bleeding. It didn't really hurt me. It certainly didn't hurt my game."

"A broken arm or leg would. Or a pulled tendon, strained knee, or hurt back," replied Al. "I'm just saying, we must make a careful decision for your future. Of course, I'm assuming you still way to play in the NBA. Has those goals changed since you met TJ?"

90

A Writer's Fantasy

Shane couldn't help but frown. TJ winked at him as he sat across from Shane on the sofa with Barbara. Shane smiled slightly, "TJ and I have talked about it some, but he is just like you guys. He wants what is best for me, and only wants me to do what I want to do. I told him I think by the end of my senior year, I will have accomplished all my goals in college ball. I will then be ready to take on my next challenge, which is playing well in the NBA. I don't want to just make the team—I want to start. I know there are a lot bigger guys than me, very talented guys, but I see that as a positive challenge, and it will happen when I no longer have to go to class and write papers. I will be able to concentrate on my strength and my play, and become a better ball player than I am right now. TJ is behind me one hundred percent."

Al smiled, "I knew that, but forgive an old man for just wanting to hear it."

Shane smiled back, "I don't doubt you in the least. We love each other, and thankfully, his career is more flexible than mine, and he has been willing to make huge sacrifices for me."

"Not that huge," interjected TJ. "I can write anywhere I can sit and have a little power for my laptop. I am as excited as anyone at watching your son play, and I was a huge Taylor University fan before he came there, and I certainly don't want him to leave earlier than he wants to because the team, the university, and the fans will miss him so much. I plan to stay out of the decision to stay or go, because I suspect I'm a bit stingy as a fan, and hope he'll stay, but as someone that absolutely loves your son, I just want him to be happy and successful."

Barbara grinned, "Here, here! Well said, TJ. So we're all in agreement at wanting what is best, and hopefully it'll work out where he can play his senior year and graduate, and then go make those huge piles of money!"

They all laughed. She added, "Let's talk about something else."

TJ said, "I have some questions. I want to write about Shane's home and his hometown, and of course, about his wonderful family. Could I interview each of you separately for about a half hour?"

"Sure," replied Al. "Honey, why don't you go first as your memory is better than mine."

"Okay. TJ, let's go to the kitchen and get some cinnamon tea."

Al and Shane talked more about basketball, but stayed away from the turning pro subject for now.

TJ sat at the kitchen table asking about incidents in Shane's childhood, any signs of his athlete ability, when did he grow tall, and tales of early years. He wrote quickly in his laptop while she talked, enjoying every morsel of her memories of her beautiful son.

Al took her place about forty-five minutes later while she went to the stove to check on her Thanksgiving dinner. TJ learned Al began tossing

91

basketballs to Shane when he was about five, and by eight years old, he was swishing shots from nine feet back. At eleven, he started growing faster than his pants could keep up with him. His parents had to buy Shane new pants about every sixty days during his sixth grade year.

In the seventh grade, he began playing on a school team and excelled immediately, because he had a good coach that showed him how to improve his game. He began working out before practice and running more after practice, and as he got stronger, his game became better.

He joined the high school team in the ninth grade as a starter at six feet five inches tall. He still holds the school points record as a freshman. He broke that mark every succeeding year until he graduated. All four records have never been broken, and Al didn't think they ever would be. TJ smiled at how proud Al was of his son.

TJ enjoyed the banter at dinner, as well as Shane and Al teasing each other and their mother about almost everything, and together, they laughed and smiled at each other. The food was delicious, so TJ and Shane couldn't help but eat well, as a mother's cooking was not something they had a chance to enjoy very often.

Al set up a movie projector after dinner and soon they were all laughing at Shane's play from an early age. During the entire evening, TJ learned so much about Shane. He now felt as if he had known Shane all his life. They stayed up late while laughing, talking, and enjoying a bowl of late night ice cream. Altogether, Shane had broken almost all of his nutrition guidelines in the last twenty-four hours, but TJ knew that Shane could account for every calorie over his normal intake, and in short order he would work it off, but not tomorrow.

Thursday morning came all too soon, and Barbara shed a few tears on the way to the airport, but Al kept reminding her they would see one of Shane's games in two weeks, but she was still his mother, and it was hard to say goodbye. She held on tight to Shane as she hugged him goodbye, and did the same for TJ. Both boys waved as Steve pulled the stairwell in and closed the door to the Learjet. Soon they were in the air and on their way to Greenville.

They had no memory of the flight as they both fell asleep as soon as they were in the air. Susie woke them as they approached the Greenville-Spartanburg airport. A few minutes later, they were on the ground. As Steve opened the door and lowered the steps, TJ looked out to see his parents, his sister, and her son. He smiled and waved as they came walking up to the jet as the engines died down. TJ received hugs from his mom, sister, and nephew while his dad gave him a friendly handshake. TJ shook his hand and then hugged him anyhow. He then made the introductions, "Shane, this is my parents Bill and Alma, and I let you guess which is which." They all laughed, "And then this is my favorite sister Debbie."

She piped in, "I'm your only sister!"

"And this is my favorite nephew, huh, what is his name?" They all laughed again. "This is the infamous Greg."

Shane asked with a grin, "How do you put up with him?"

TJ grinned slyly, ignoring Shane and said, "And everyone, this is the Shane Bradley." Consider the introductions complete."

Shane shook hands and as polite as ever he said how happy he was to meet everyone. They brought two cars to get everyone to the house so they loaded up their overnight bags, and piled into the cars to head to the house. Once they arrived, Shane's nose immediately picked up the scent of a turkey cooking. They placed their stuff in the hall and returned to the living room so they could sit down and talk before dinner.

TJ felt just a bit slighted as all the talk was about Shane, as they already knew about him, but he enjoyed laughing and talking with his family as well. They watched him play on television ever since TJ had written he had fallen in love with Shane. The parents had a hard time with the love part, but they were happy TJ finally had someone to enjoy life with as they put it. When TJ came out to his parents and announced he was gay, he did it in the form of a letter, as he was too afraid they would disown him, even though he was a grown adult.

His parents told their minister about it, and he told them as long as TJ didn't do any gay things like having sex, and then he could still go to heaven. TJ's dad mentioned it to him and TJ sighed heavily, and replied, "So the church wants me to live totally alone, never have anyone love me, never feel the comfort of having the person I love most sleeping in my arms at night, and never enjoy the gifts God gave us?" Dad sighed, and never brought it up again.

Early on, in his gay dating, he thought perhaps his parents prayed he would not find someone and experience sex, and if so, TJ thought, perhaps their prayers had indeed been answered. He would say, "I found people to have sex with, but finding someone that will love you as much as you love them—now that is the hard part." He had never been able to do so until Shane came into his life. They felt that after an hour of talking to Shane and watching him look at their son with loving eyes, they knew TJ and Shane were perfect for each other. They would now pray that perhaps God would make an exception, and allow them into heaven anyhow.

His nephew, Greg, was enamored with Shane and his success. He knew nothing of basketball stars after attending college in Manhattan at a top-of-the-line university specializing in the performing arts. His friends were dancers, singers, actors, writers, musicians, set builders, and graphic arts designers. He loved the theater and everything to do with it, and using his student card, he was able to obtain great seats to all the best Broadway shows.

He graduated from school just last year and now worked for a wonderful doctor, who adored him, and her clients were mostly the rich and famous, so he had other benefits from time to time like opportunities to go backstage and meet the cast.

TJ visited him about once a year or so as he, too, loved to visit New York City and see the shows as well as the museums. Last visit Greg took him to the Bronx Zoo. TJ was shocked at how big and wonderful it was in the heart of city, but as much as TJ loved visiting, he could not imagine living in New York. He always felt successful if he could visit the bit city and get out alive.

Dinner was ready and the boys worked their way through a big buffet filled with food. They chose sliced butterball turkey, rice, cornbread dressing, and gravy. They added green beans, sweet potato soufflé with melted marshmallows and roasted pecans on top, and cranberry sauce. On a second plate, they chose a three-bean salad, tossed salad; a peach congealed salad made with Jell-O, fruit, and whipped cream. They managed to snatch a few buttermilk biscuits, and sweet ice tea, plus a bowl of ambrosia made with fruit, coconut, and lots of other wholesome stuff. Their dessert choices were coconut cake, German chocolate cake, red velvet cake, and a few leftover slices of pecan pie. Shane picked up a piece of coconut cake as his first choice.

TJ laughed as Shane filled two plates and made his way to the dining room to find a seat. He had to come back with a saucer to load up on biscuits that he soon filled with butter, and waited patiently for everyone to finish working their way through the line. He blushed when they teased him about his three plates of food, but after a moving blessing by TJ's father, Shane went to work, chewing carefully as he always did, but nonetheless, the food began disappearing one big bite at a time.

By the time, everyone began their dessert, Shane excused himself and went back for a piece of the pecan pie. Mom got up to help him by putting his slice in the microwave to heat it, and then adding a scoop of vanilla ice cream to the top before handing it back to him. Shane returned to the table grinning, and soon he was eating delicious bites of the pie as well. She refilled his tea glass at least three times, as she loved to see folks eat her wonderful food. Cooking and sharing was Alma's way of showing how much she loved and cared about someone. Of course, dad had to shop and buy the groceries so he did his part as well.

Everyone helped clear the table and put the food away, but soon TJ snagged Shane away as well as Greg, and borrowing his sister's car he began showing TJ around Greenville. They drove by his old high school, and he explained there was a time when their only two white high schools and one black one. The two white schools maintained a huge fierce rivalry that gradually fell away in the early seventies when the county finally built more high schools.

94

He drove through his boyhood neighborhood, and crossed a new road through what used to be a forest and swamp where TJ hiked and played as a young boy.

He drove by the YMCA where he grew up and worked during high school, and then went by a small but favorite restaurant's of TJ's even though closed for Thanksgiving Day. Known as Tanner's Orange®, they made a real fruit punch drink from freshly squeezed oranges, and featured roasted peanuts, and the best sandwiches in town. TJ used to buy gallons of the punch, take them back to college, and sell for a huge profit.

When they returned home, they sat in the living room and began telling everyone where they had been. Mom disappeared and soon returned with large glasses of crushed ice filled with Tanner's Orange® punch for TJ and Shane. As they tasted the fresh juice she bought the day before, they waited for Shane's evaluation.

Shane stopped drinking long enough to exclaim, "Oh my, that is awesome!" They all laughed.

They filled the afternoon with stories of TJ's childhood, and this time it was TJ that blushed as he kept telling Shane not to believe a word they were saying, but of course, he did and laughed along with everyone.

By late afternoon, Shane needed a stretch, so Greg borrowed a basketball from a neighbor, and crossed a block to a local playground with a basketball goal with a rusted chain net. Shane felt the ball and almost instantly knew it was at least a half pound down in air but it would do. Greg stood under the goal and fed Shane the ball as he began shooting close to the goal as he did during warm-ups before a game. Gradually, he began moving back a step or two at a time. The rest of the family walked over, sat on the hill, and watched as Shane hit twenty-three straight shots from eighteen feet, before moving back another three feet and starting over. He hit seventeen out of twenty from that distance. He finished by doing several awesome dunks just to make Greg laugh. The family audience clapped and cheered, as did some of the neighborhood boys who watched the big player in awe.

By seven o'clock, they lined up to work their way through the food line again, but TJ and Shane used only a half of one plate, as they remained stuffed from lunch. They did, however, enjoy one more piece of the coconut cake. The talk around the table was fun and boisterous, and Shane enjoyed all the teasing that bounced from one member to the next and found himself in the middle of it most of the time.

TJ called the week before and told his parents he made a reservation at the nearby Sheraton® so he and TJ could sleep there because there wasn't room for his sister and nephew, his parents, and them, and besides Shane needed to sleep in a big king size bed, he added. He wisely left out that Shane would want to ravish their son's body all night long. They left for the hotel about eleven, promising to be back for breakfast at nine before heading to the airport.

Borrowing Debbie's car once more, they began their drive to the hotel.

TJ jokingly asked, "Are you hungry? Do you want to stop for a burger?"

"You've got to be kidding," replied Shane. "I shouldn't have to eat for a week. I must run after we get home tomorrow."

"Thank you for coming," said TJ. "I really enjoyed showing you off."

"It was fun. Your family is hilarious. I can see where you get your wit and humor. I don't see how your dad stands it."

"He laughs, but every now and then he'll toss in a gem."

They checked in, found their room, locked the door, and got naked fast. After a period of making out, they slowly shifted into their lovemaking roles, as Shane wanted to be the top first.

They returned to Lindle near eleven the following morning and made their way to the motorcoach. Bob and Sue had taken care of their dogs, by feeding and walking them as needed. As soon as they drove up, Beeper jumped on the dash and started barking rapidly at them with great excitement. J-Henry didn't like to get on the dash, but missing the boys, he made an exception; so together, they barked and wagged their tails as fast as they could.

TJ and Shane dropped their bags at the door, ran up the steps, and began hugging and kissing their dogs. They rubbed them quickly, and then the dogs would switch positions so they could get love from both boys. They leashed the dogs, and came outside as Bob and Sue came over to greet them.

"Thank you so much for taking of the dogs for us," said TJ.

Sue said, "It was our pleasure. They're such good dogs. Did you have good time?"

"Yes, a wonderful time. Bob, the car is open. You'll find a bag of goodies for you in the back seat. My mom baked everything in the bag. I guarantee you'll gain a pound or two."

# NINE

The next several practices were physically some of the hardest to survive, according to Shane, but also mentally, as the coaches added a few more plays, and began working on final thirty seconds game drills. When they began making consistent progress against the second team, they began working on overtime drills.

In two of the practices, the coach decided they were not concentrating hard enough on defense so he once again removed the goals, forcing the young minds to focus entirely on defense. TJ felt surprise and admiration, as Shane described all the hard work he did in practice, and then added that he loved every minute of it. In just a few months with Shane, TJ learned more about college basketball than in his entire life.

Shane explained that at first, many new players didn't buy into the coach's methods, and his superior experience and game intelligence, but Shane did. He said it happened for him when the coach came to see his parents at his house. He didn't talk down to anyone, but spent a lot of time bragging on the hard work that my parents did raising their wonderful well-mannered son. The coach surprised him by spending the first fifteen minutes talking with his parents about every day things, and never once mentioned basketball. He told TJ the coach spoke highly of my manners, my schoolwork, the recommendations of my teachers, my exam scores, and then talked about my personal discipline, my drive, and my determination to excel. Next, he talked about the high academic standards of Taylor University, promising all his players received the very best college education, stating profoundly that Shane would graduate. He didn't get around to talking about playing basketball until after my mom refilled his coffee cup.

After the short Thanksgiving break, the team flew out after practice on Tuesday, so they would have two full days of classes before hitting the road. TJ left about noon on the Learjet for Columbus, Ohio, and easily discovered he liked flying on the private jet with no other guests onboard. He fired up laptop before they left the ground and wrote another chapter in the new book before landing.

They approached the runway as the rain fell, but Steve put the plane down smooth and safe, and cautiously coasted up to the gate. Susie found a large umbrella and stepped out of the plane first, waiting for TJ to join her. Together, they practically hugged their way to the terminal. TJ thanked her several times before heading out to the waiting car like a movie star. Ten minutes later, he checked into a huge Marriot close to the Ohio State arena.

The elevator took him to the seventh floor. After setting his bag and computer briefcase on the sofa, he undressed, and fell on the bed and immediately began working on a serious nap. Unfortunately, he dreamed the rainstorm turned to ice, affecting the team's flight to Ohio. He knew Shane would not be pleased with a precarious flight in the rain. Suddenly, a bolt of

TJ Johnson

lightning hit the starboard engine setting it on fire. The plane began to rapidly descend. He could see Shane screaming, but he couldn't hear him.

TJ suddenly woke with a start and with sweat drops on his forehead. He rolled out of bed, went to the bathroom, and washed his face. He decided he had enough of naps, booted his laptop, and searched the area with his GPS software until he found a grocery to visit. He looked out the window, discovering the rain stopped, the sky became brighter, and the clouds were breaking up and letting a little blue sky through.

He put on the warm coat he remembered to bring, and made his way to the street. He had two blocks to walk, but the wind died down so he enjoyed the walk. He bought a couple of apples, some grapes, four bananas, a local newspaper, and one of his favorite newspapers a USA Today®. He spotted a Mexican restaurant down a side street and thought he might try it for dinner.

He stopped at the front desk and asked the clerk about the restaurant, and the ladies behind the counter gave the restaurant a good grade so he made his way to the room.

Shane checked into his room after the team ate dinner and told his roommate he was going for a walk to stretch his legs after the flight. They had about forty-five minutes until study hall. He walked to the back of hotel and found an elevator. He dialed TJ on his cell phone and obtained the room number.

Shane knocked on the room door a few minutes later. TJ opened the door and said abruptly, "Forget sex—I have a headache."

Shane grinned as he calmly came in the room, shut the door, and kissed him, "We're not married…yet! You can't get a headache if we're not married."

TJ laughed, "I am so glad you're here. I had a bad dream during my nap. I thought the storm would play havoc with your flight. How was it?"

Shane replied, "Great actually. I slept the whole way." TJ sighed greatly.

They moved to the bed and sat down, talked a little more before they kissed a few times, and then began pulling clothes off, playing with each other, achieving erections, and then Shane spotted the clock by the bed.

"Oh my gosh! I only have fourteen minutes until study hall. This is like an overtime drill. Spread your legs!"

TJ laughed as he grabbed a condom and barely got it on Shane's dick before TJ fell back and Shane slid forward. TJ moaned, Shane groaned, and soon the loose headboard began bumping the wall. Six minutes later, Shane exploded, TJ laughed, they kissed deeply, and then reluctantly, Shane rolled off, cleaned himself up, dressed, came back and kissed TJ again, and headed for the door grinning like a sly fox.

TJ ate dinner with Shane's parents who had flown in for the game. They had a grand time talking about TJ and Shane's adventures, but his dad asked how Shane was handling the pressure with such great expectations for the team. Almost everyday, Al read in a newspaper, magazine, or online about the predications for this year's squad. Dick Vitale of ESPN® picked Taylor University to win it all: the season championship, the league tourney, the regional tournament, and the final four championships.

TJ smiled, "Well, you know your son better than I, but from my point of view he acts like there's nothing more important going on in his life than getting his homework done. Sometimes I get hyperactive before a game, and then I look at him, and discover he is the epitome of calmness, appearing tranquil, quiet, and smooth. I don't know how he does it. However, just as soon as the referee blows his whistle and tosses the ball up starting the game, a switch is thrown somewhere deep inside Shane, and magically and mesmerizingly, he becomes this giant basketball machine. It is amazing to watch, talk and write about, and although I have yet to earn the right, I am so proud of him."

Al and Barbara laughed. She spoke first, "You should put that in your book. It sums him up beautifully."

Al added, "We know exactly what you're talking about. I guess we're asking you to let us know if you see something different from his current emotional state. We hope and pray he never changes, but the media exposure, fan support, and high expectations have to break his shell at some point."

"To continue the metaphor," began TJ with a sly grin, "the shell you're talking about is not an eggshell, but rather tough and hard—more like a giant tortoise shell. He's like a reversible winter jacket; one minute he is hard on the outside and soft on the inside, and minutes later, he is soft on outside, and tough on the inside. He is amazing." TJ smiled and added, "I know I'm not telling you anything you don't already know, so I will also tell you he is the product of two great parents both nature and nurture. He possesses impeccable manners, and a great jump shot. He is a ball of fire and gentle tenderness."

The parents beamed. Barbara sighed heavily, "After seeing the two of you together at Thanksgiving, and seeing the interaction between you, I began noting the unspoken words of communication that transfers between you. I also saw the slight hint of smiles that happen as your eyes meet. This makes me feel so wonderful to know my son is in love with you, and you, in turn, are very much in love with him."

TJ blushed and deadpanned, "Is it that obvious?" They all laughed.

Al asked a favor, "Please, TJ, just let us know if the pressure gets too much for him, and tell us what we can do to help."

"I promise if you'll promise not to ever change how you feel about him right now, no matter how famous he becomes, and that you'll continue to pray for his safety both on the court, and in the planes, buses, limousines, and cars he travels in. You might also pray he survives my limited cooking skills, but maybe you should pray I don't get food poisoning either as he is learning to cook, too. He loves stir-frying anything."

They all laughed again, finished their dinner, and walked to the Schottenstein Center for the Ohio State game. They parted company upon arrival so TJ could head to the pressroom with his laptop and prepare for the game. TJ arrived in the room and immediately greeted warmly by a pretty college coed handing out the game notes, and a last minute press release. He found an open seat, set up his laptop, glanced up at the television monitors displaying both the court behind him, and a count down clock to game time. He highlighted quotes and facts he liked as he read the four-page document. He began typing those facts into his computer. He kept a journal of facts for each game in case he needed to refer back as he completed the book. He went to work adding the feel and timbre of the center and campus atmosphere for the game. He finished after noting the Taylor team arriving for their warm-up period. He locked his laptop in the locker, grabbed a Diet Coke® from a barrel of ice, and walked down the steps leading to the court, stopping about four rows from the floor, so he could see over the heads of the players in the foreground. Shane immediately smiled at him. TJ returned the smile and a single finger on his nose for I love you. He wished he could tell Shane about the dinner and conversations with his folks, but that would have to wait until later.

The team was flying out immediately after the game so the boys could attend class early the next morning. TJ checked out of his room earlier, leaving his bags in storage near the front entrance. Shane stretched for twenty minutes, and then began shooting and actually missed his first three shots. Jerry walked over to him and with clown-like, exaggerated hand motions; he pretended he was wiping clean Shane's glasses, though he wore contacts. They both laughed. Shane scratched his head, moved in closer to the goal, and stared at the rim as if it was crooked, smiled, backed up a few steps, and began swishing shots, as he gradually worked his way in a semi-circle around the floor in front of the goal. He moved back another step or two, and continued working on his shots. For the next twenty minutes, he only missed four shots out of hundred. This restored his confidence, so his smile morphed into his game face. TJ called his somber look, his mug shot face.

After the team left the court, TJ walked around the edge of the sparkling wood floor, and up the aisle to sit alongside Al and Barbara for a little while. They chatted until time for the team to return for the game. TJ wished them a safe trip home, walked down to the corner, spotted Shane, gave him the chill sign as well as the sign for his love, Shane pulled his earlobe in acknowledgement, smiled, and winked at him. TJ just made it off the floor on the way to his seat as the team rushed onto the court.

Ohio State had the same starting lineups as last year and plenty of experience. They won the tipoff and scored with a beautiful three from way outside the three-point line. Shane brought the ball in by giving it a hard throw to Jerry who caught it and sped up court at his usual lighting speed. Shane rushed up the court behind him, and just in time to provide a big boy screen, catching the Ohio player guarding Jerry unaware. He crashed into Shane as if he had run into a wall. A referee almost called a charging foul on a defensive player, but caught himself as Jerry took advantage of the screen, quickly squared up, and leaped upward while firing off his jump shot. Shane, barely feeling the thump of their falling guard, rushed down the lane for a possible rebound, but Jerry's shot was on target and swished through the net tying the game. Shane rushed to cover the inbound throw of the ball, as the rest of the Taylor squad began a full court press.

The Ohio State inbound player had trouble bringing the ball in with Shane's frantic waving of his arms and occasional legs as he jumped up and down. Ohio finally made a bad toss that Jerry scooped up. Shane rushed towards the goal, and Jerry instantly threw a hard bounce pass to him. Shane caught it on the fly, leaped, and performed a violent and vicious dunk. The five hundred Taylor fans in the midst of the vastly filled sea of thousands of Ohio State fans leaped to their feet, as did the Taylor bench, and the coaches, because they knew that Jerry and Shane just lit the fire the team needed to win.

The halftime score displayed a ten-point lead by Taylor, and continued to grow during the second half. The end of game came with a long swish by Larry, putting the score at the hundred and eight for Taylor and seventy-five by the beaten Ohio State team.

TJ waved at the Bradley family as he made his way to the pressroom. He picked up the final game statistics, grabbed his laptop, and made his way down the steps to the court. The Ohio fans quickly left, leaving the court empty except for the press talking to some of the Taylor fans. Shane saw TJ and spoke to him about game stuff, but the eyes and the smiles portrayed deeper feelings that no one noticed. Shane went over to see his parents while TJ made his way to the exit.

TJ found a cab, picked up his luggage, and was in the air forty minutes after the end of the game. Susie prepared a prime rib dinner for him, plus bacon and cheddar mashed potatoes, a beautiful salad, and French bread. He ate well while reading the game data. Susie cleared the table as he finished, so he could set up his laptop and type in the statistics, and then began finishing the first of this week's chapter, describing the emotion of the game, especially the turning point on their second possession and the huge dunk.

The Taylor team ate sub sandwiches in the locker room while changing and packing. They hauled their gear out to the waiting bus, and sixty minutes after the end of the game, they were in the air. After landing, Shane picked up a snack before leaving the athlete's dining hall, and made his way to his room. He quickly typed an email to TJ checking to see if he arrived safely. At home, TJ continued working on his writings after walking the dogs when he heard the chime for his email. He responded immediately. Shane bade him goodnight, set his alarm clock for his early class, and fell asleep in seconds. It had been a good trip, a great win, and another one with TJ's smiling face just across the court providing comfort, solace, and the encouragement, inspiration, and motivation he trusted.

The next few days were a blur for Shane as he attended classes and hard practices with the team flying to Lexington, Kentucky at noon on Friday for Saturday's game. TJ flew out about the same time, checked into the Hyatt Regency on West High Street, and very close to the famous Rupp Center, the off-campus home for the famous Kentucky Wildcats. Tomorrow's two o'clock game would pack the huge arena to the gills with twenty-three thousand fans. The Kentucky fans were planning a bigger facility for the year 2018, as basketball was king in this part of the country. They named it for their famous coach, Adolph Rupp, a year before he died in 1976. Rupp won many games, far more than most, but perhaps more famous for coaching the losing team against the first all black team to win the NCAA championship in the midst of our country's racial conversion.

The team landed, boarded their bus, and went straight to the center for practice. Shane visited the colossal center two years ago as a freshman and it made a huge impact upon him. In his opinion it was not one of his best games, although he scored eighteen points, snatched eight rebounds, and shot eight of his points from the foul shot line, but he knew could have done better. Taylor nearly lost, but a last minute shot by Larry from the corner, put them over the top and a victory. Kentucky remembered that lost a year later when they played on Taylor's home court and lost again by two points. Seething with anger and frustration, the Wildcat fans expected their team to give Taylor a solid thrashing in tomorrow's afternoon televised game.

TJ walked to the center, and took in the museum displays in the foyer, while waiting for the team to take to the court for practice. Using his press pass, he spotted Walter Mills as he arrived, and received his approval for TJ to sit in the stands to watch the team practice. Technically, this was a closed practice so there were only forty people in the vast arena, and most of those were Taylor University personnel. He saw the ESPN® crew sitting in the center of the arena about twenty rows up so they could talk without disturbing the coach. TJ saw Mike Patrick, their play-by-play announcer, sitting amongst several staff members making notes for his call of the game. To his left sat Walter Mills with a big notebook, flipping back and forth, as he sought the answers to their questions. To his right was Walter's counterpart for the Wildcats.

TJ noted broadcaster Dick Vitale sitting with a smaller group of network researchers and writers away from the larger group. What caught

TJ's attention was not the normally never lost for words Dickie V style, but rather a calm man, studying intensely the Taylor team on the floor. He possessed a photographic memory, and it was as if he was downloading each player's photo and bio as an associate read him the info on each player as he requested it. Dick loved college basketball. Many critics panned and abused him all the time, but not a word from their hot tongues ever discouraged him. He had a great job, great family, and he truly didn't mind putting his emotions on his sleeve. He had thousands of fans that came up and gave him hugs, and before game time, sometimes students would lift his body and pass him over their heads through the bleachers, while being careful to avoid dropping their hero.

He talked to players about their jump shot or defense, as well as their family and their high school teams. He recalled these gems of information at crucial points in the game when the player he discussed was facing great adversity or excelling with amazing skill. He never criticized or denounced a player's talent or skill, but while saying what the player should have done, he followed it with a great story about the player's heart, and his love for the game. He told them about the support of their parents, and how confident he was the player would indeed grow, develop, and succeed in future games.

At the end of practice, Dick walked down to the court to talk to a few of the players and Shane in particular. TJ stood off to the side so he could hear both sides of the conversation, while looking for a few quotes he could add in the book. Shane could see TJ in his peripheral vision, but he gave Dick his complete attention. As they finished, Shane told him he wanted to introduce a friend of his to him.

"Mr. Vitale. This is my friend TJ Johnson. He's writing a behind the scenes book about our road to the championship."

Dick turned and immediately shook TJ's hand and smiled at him, "Well, it appears you have the same vibes I do about the Taylor squad. A book for this year's team is most appropriate. I hope I can provide a few quotes for your tale of their adventures. I am so pleased to meet a friend of Shane's."

TJ grinned, "The pleasure is mine, and yes, some of your comments will indeed be in the story. Thank you for being so kind to the Taylor team and Shane in particular."

"I must say I'm envious, TJ, because you're getting the in depth and comprehensive back story a commentator like me would kill for."

"Would you like to peruse a chapter from time to time? I could email them to you. We would love to add a Dick Vitale quote about the team and Shane in particular."

Dick smiled as he fished a private business card out of his pocket. "Down at the bottom is my private email address as well as my home and cell number. If there is anything I can do to assist with the book, or help the both of you, please give me a call."

TJ Johnson

He turned back to Shane, "So you're feeling good about winning tomorrow?"

Shane grinned, "Of course, we came here to win."

Dick smiled, "But tomorrow there will be twenty-three thousand plus fans yelling for the Wildcats, and they're mad as hell at your Taylor squad after losing the last two games."

"But that just makes us more determined than ever to stop their fan momentum. You'll see. We're going to win."

Dick laughed as he shook their hands. "Okay, I believe you. Are your folks coming tomorrow?"

"Yes, they are. They were in Ohio as well so this has been a big week of travel for them, but they are not that far from home."

"Good, I'll look forward to seeing them. Good luck tomorrow. It is going to be a fun game. It was nice to meet you TJ. Good luck on the book as well. I am sure it will be great."

"Same here. Thank you."

The team ate a great dinner, attended a team meeting on assignments, plays to use, working through scouting reports, and film clips to watch, and followed by a mandatory ninety-minute study hall. After dinner in his room, TJ read his email, including checking the sales of his new book that had begun earlier in the week. He turned down a few book signing opportunities that he could have made using the Learjet to fly in and out, but he couldn't justify the expense in his mind, even though he wasn't paying for it. A few weeks ago, he mailed out press releases and stories for the periodicals that might carry information about the new book, and followed it up with info kits for some of the major gay bookstores. Amazon®, and Barnes and Noble® displayed the new book online, and TJ checked their info about the book to be sure it was correct.

He then went to his book website that he maintained and found about twenty-five orders. He would ship those books out when he got back home tomorrow. Those customers ordering directly from him received an autographed copy, and custom bookmark featuring a gloss book cover shot, and details on one side, and information about his other books on the back, along with the release date of his next story.

About nine-thirty, he heard a knock at the door and smiled. He checked the peephole and laughed. Shane anticipated he would check the viewing glass, so he opened his mouth wide covering the view. TJ was literally looking down his throat.

TJ opened the door, "Yeah, it's big enough." He reached and grabbed Shane arms and pulled him into the room, closed the door, and kissed him.

Shane broke the embrace and asked, "Big enough for what?"

104

TJ smiled slyly, "Big enough for my dick. Now get busy. I'm horny."

Shane laughed, picked TJ up, and hauled him to the bed where he stripped him, and then TJ returned the favor. They fell on the bed and their lovemaking began.

The team meal seemed way early at nine o'clock, but Shane was used to it, as weekend games were often in early or mid afternoon. This game was at two o'clock. TJ checked out of his room and stored his stuff at the front desk as usual. He arrived at the pressroom ninety minutes before game time. He got a good seat, read the pre-game press releases, typed the facts into this laptop, and made his way to the buffet line. He dined on fried chicken, mustard potato salad, green beans, cream corn, and fresh salad. He would save dessert for after warm-ups.

Feeling full, he went for a walk around the big arena while stopping to read notes under the pictures and displays for the history of Wildcat basketball. He then walked into the stands and sat in his game seat. Shane was stretching with his back to him, but soon turned around and smiled. TJ winked at him.

"How's your boy?"

TJ turned to his left, and in the aisle was Dick Vitale. TJ grinned." He's fine and ready to win."

"May I sit down?"

TJ politely stood up as Shane watched them, "Of course, please."

Dick shook his hand before sitting down, "I just had lunch with Sean May. He has a game here later tonight so we talked Taylor basketball, and he could not stop bragging about Shane. You might want to get a quote from him. He's a big fan."

"Thank you, and I will. I hope you had a good lunch."

Dick feigned being stuffed, "I did, and I hope I digest some of it before game time. I told him about your book. I was talking to my wife last night, and I told her as well. She's a big Taylor fan, too. I told her how polite you and Shane are. I'm impressed. I think the book will be big. Do you want to put my picture on the cover?"

TJ didn't know what to say. Dick jumped back in, "It's a joke. You're going to put Shane's picture on the cover, as he is a way better looking than I am. Which company is publishing for you?"

"I don't have a publisher yet. We're only telling a few friends we're doing the book as we want the team to concentrate on the championship, and I want fair assessments and comments, and not contrived views in hopes of getting in the book."

"That's smart, but I have an idea for you when it comes time to get hard work published. Do you have an agent?"

TJ sheepishly replied, "No, not yet."

"Do you have a pen and something to write on?"

TJ took out his reporter pad that he brought to all the games for notes during the game. He flipped it open and clicked the button on his pen.

"Very good, now let me think a second. Ah yes, I suggest you call Jake Tidwell. He is one of the top sport agents in the country when it comes to publishing. He is sharp, brutal in negotiations, and you'll like him. Call him, and say Dick Vitale said for you to do so. Tell him I think an auction would work for your book."

TJ asked, "An auction? How does that work?"

"You write the book, and when you're about three weeks from finishing it, which I assume is the championship, you let Jake contact all the key publishers offering a chance to bid on your book with a seven day deadline. This creates a chaotic buzz about your book, and drives the price up. Yeah—it'll work. You'll see."

TJ saw the Bradley family taking their seats across the court. He smiled at them. Dick noted it. "You recognized the Bradley family. Do you know them?"

"Yes indeed. They are wonderful supporters for Shane. They are so proud and happy."

"Would you mind introducing me?"

TJ grinned, "Of course. Shall we walk over?"

"Yes, that would be great."

TJ and Dick made their way around the court as Dick called the names of various Taylor players as they were warming up. He called to Shane and said, "Shane I know you're trying your best, but you're going to have to give up, as there is no way you're ever going to be better looking than me!"

The Taylor team laughed, as did Shane. Dick shook his hand, laughed with him, and said softly, "You see, a laugh makes it far easier for a great player to relax, so whenever you're tense, just think of this face…" he point to his cheek, "and laugh, and you'll be great that day."

"Thanks, Mister Vitale."

"You can call me Dick."

Shane replied as politely as ever, "Right, Mister Vitale."

Dick shook his head. "Go ahead and shoot a few threes to make the Wildcats nervous. Come on TJ. Let's go see this boy's family."

As they approached, TJ made the introductions. Dick spoke up quickly, "You have raised one of the finest examples of what college basketball is all about when it comes to his athleticism, but when it comes to being a gentleman, you have really outdone yourselves. I give my sincere and hearty congratulations."

They beamed with pride as Dick continued, "Al, when did he start shooting?"

"About eight I think. He could swish it from ten feet out by then."

"My goodness," replied Dick, "and Barbara what did you feed him to make him grow so tall and strong?"

She laughed and replied, "Anything he wanted. We could not keep food in the cupboards. He ate and worked, and ate and worked. Now he has a nutritionist to make sure he eats properly, so he'll continue his strength training, but for me, I was just trying to fill him up."

"Well, the both of you did an excellent job. Thank you for allowing me to visit a few moments. Good luck in today's game. I think he is going to win."

Al beamed, "Yes, we hope so, too. It was a pleasure to meet you."

Dick shook their hands and then TJ's, "Well, sport, I have to get to work. I enjoyed our chat. I will see you at the next opportunity and call me if I can be of help."

"Thank you, especially for Jake's name."

"My pleasure, but if you're not happy with him, let me know and I will find another agent."

Dick left and TJ sat down with the Bradleys, as Shane and the team ran through several drills. TJ spoke up first, "Dick has a great idea on publishing the book. He suggested the name of a top publishing agent in New York, and told me to encourage him to auction the book about three weeks before the championship game when all eyes are on the tournament play."

"Auction?"

"Yeah, he said it would drive the price way up."

"Boy, we just keep learning in this business don't we? Are you going to call him?"

"Yes, first thing Monday morning. A lead from Dick Vitale is not something to be ignored."

The game began with Jerry catching the tip and flinging a bullet pass down the court to Shane on the run. He caught it over his shoulder, took one quick step, and into the air for a dunk. Dick went wild with excitement, and began talking about Shane once again in his commentary before Mike Patrick took over once more.

The Wildcat fans began standing and yelling for their team. They scored a pretty three-shot off the right corner over Larry. The coach gave Larry a holler as they went down the court. Jerry brought the ball down the court, and as he flew by his man, he did a head fake to the left, and suddenly saw an opening down the lane, and drove down it at lightening speed for an easy layout.

The crowd sighed heavily as Taylor began their full court press. Shane knew he had little chance of a steal, but he kept up the strong defensive position. The player he was guarding was a senior and a good one. However, Jerry and Larry made it difficult for him to get the ball in the near court, and at four seconds, he gave it a big heave to mid-court. Their big center caught it. Taylor quickly fell back into their man-to-man defense.

The Wildcats kept the game close, but with three minutes to play in the half, Taylor went on a tear, racking up twelve points in five possessions, put three fouls on their center, and two fouls on Shane's man. Taylor led by fourteen points at the half and the entire Rupp Arena was fuming.

TJ could feel the tension in the pressroom, as most of the press was from the local media. TJ kept to himself and just listened. He got a bowl of hot peach cobbler topped with vanilla ice cream. He let it begin to melt as he typed out his synopsis of the first half. He finished, closed and locked his laptop, gobbled down the delicious dessert, snatched up a water bottle, and made his way to his seat, as Shane and the team broke their huddle to begin the second half.

TJ gave him three fingers for go, go, go signal for the second half play! Shane grinned and pulled his earlobe acknowledging and agreeing. For the next fourteen minutes, however, the Wildcats clawed their way back, and with four minutes to go, and during television time-out, they were sniffing for blood. Vitale was having a field day with the tight exciting game, while TJ was working on an ulcer. Shane came out of the huddle and this time TJ give him two signals: the first was to chill and Shane knew it was the right strategy. There was plenty of time to play and win. The second was the rare two fingers on the nose, and Shane laughed as he took it to mean the entire Wildcat team was standing naked on the floor.

Shane spoke to his teammates as they crossed the court to bring the ball in. "We're going to win this one. Are you with me?" The team yelled back affirmatively, though they were barely able to hear their fellow players over the screaming twenty-three thousand fans.

Shane flung the ball into Jerry who broke their full court press, veered around Shane's screen at the half court, and threw it hard to Larry in the corner. Larry's man covered him quickly. Shane broke from the top of the key down the right side of the lane with Jerry on his tail. The defense quickly double-teamed Shane leaving Jerry open. Larry flung the ball over his head into Jerry's hands, and the shortest man on the team dunked it. Shane caught him as he came down.

Jerry laughed, "Thanks for caboose ride. It was fun. Come on let's get these guys. Taylor was up by four.

They continued tough defense but with two minutes left, the game remained tied, Taylor's shooting went cold, while missing their last three shots. Everyone thought the coach would call a timeout, but it was still early in the season, and he still wanted to teach his team a lesson, though risking a lost. Shane threw the ball into Jerry and sprinted down court. He began working left and right of the lane, and each time he had a chance to get the ball, the Wildcats double-teamed him.

Finally, he was open and to his surprise, the Kentucky boys quickly triple-teamed him, and then Shane made a mistake and tried to go up with the ball with all three around him. There was no doubt they fouled him, but the referees didn't blow the whistle. He missed the shot, and the Wildcats got the rebound.

The coach was screaming at the nearest referee about not calling a foul, but he knew they were in trouble. Still, he refused to call a timeout. "Get tough. We need a stop!"

Jerry relayed the call, but it wasn't required, as the Taylor team knew they had to stop the Wildcats from scoring. Shane was all over his man, but being careful not to foul. With two seconds remaining on the thirty-second clock, the Kentucky team attempted a three-point shot from the outside corner. Shane quickly pushed his way back from the goal to protect it for a rebound, and to prevent an easy toss up from beneath the goal. Larry had done the same on the other side. The ball bounced high off the rim, and as it started to fall, five mixed team members went into the air, but it was Shane who had leaped higher than anyone else, and just barely got his fingers on the ball. He rolled it down his hands, and pulled it tight to his chest to prevent a steal.

His feet hit the floor, and he spun to avoid anyone grasping it, and flung it out to Jerry who was grinning. They stopped the mighty Wildcats with twenty-nine seconds to play, the score tied, and Taylor with the ball. Now the coach called a timeout.

They were expecting him to chew on them, create a trick play, but he said, "Are you boys having fun yet?" He paused and continued as he grinned, "This is why you work in the heat of the summer. This is why you train hard in the weight room. This is why we sweat the workouts in practice. This is why we push, study, and motivate. This is the kind of moment every kid with a basketball goal dreams about in his backyard. The score is tied, and my favorite team has the ball. So what do we do?"

Shane spoke up first. "We fake it to me going down the lane. They will jump all over me, and somebody else better score while I'm getting beat up!"

The coach and the team laughed, but coach Timmons knew they just learned another lesson. "Two options: Jerry set up Shane down the lane and either kick it out to Larry for three, but I'd rather have a sure thing, so if you get free would you mind laying that thing in the basket so we can go home with a win?"

The team grinned as they broke the huddle, and that grin unnerved the Wildcat team, as they were afraid to lose for the third time in a row. Dick noticed the confidence as the director hustled a shot on the television monitor of Shane with that grin on his face. Shane winked at TJ. Shane brought the ball into Jerry. The defense was tough, but Jerry weaved back and forth, eating up as much of the clock as possible. At the ten seconds mark, he moved to the top of the circle, and put up five fingers, that at this point of the game meant nothing. In preparing for the game, the Kentucky boys read a report that the Taylor team used a play that would get the ball to Shane, and assumed the signal was the play. Shane came around under the goal, spun around up to the foul line, and started down the lane.

Jerry looked out to Larry, but his man was smart and stayed with him. Jerry's man suddenly broke away, trying to cover Shane from the side. Jerry crossed dribble and left the floor just a yard into the paint. He used the goal as part of his defense and went to the left side for an easy layup. By the time his feet touched the wood floor, the buzzer sounded, and Taylor won by two.

Shane gave Jerry a hug, "You owe me for two train tickets!"

Jerry laughed, "Boy, that was so much fun. The coach is right. This is a fun game!"

TJ picked up his laptop and came down to the floor of the arena. The disappointed Wildcat fans fled the building like a plaque. He crossed the court and said goodbye to Al and Barbara. He turned around and ran into Dick.

"How'd you like the game?"

TJ replied, "I nearly wet my pants, but it was fun."

Dick laughed, "That's the kind of game we live for. Both teams fought hard, but my prediction was right. Shane was on his game tonight with twenty-eight points, twelve rebounds, and twelve straight foul shots. Oh my, what a guy! Have a safe flight."

TJ wished him the same as they shook hands. TJ turned, and Shane winked at him and ran to the locker room. TJ used his press pass to go out the back of the arena, caught a cab to the hotel, picked up his gear, and headed to the executive airport for the flight home.

With Sunday off, Shane arrived at the motorcoach about seven o'clock. He told TJ about the team's plan for the final score in the Kentucky game. He recalled what the coach said in the huddle about basketball and the fun of a tight scoring game. After TJ made his notes, they went to bed early. Shane had many sore spots from the banging in the paint under the goal, so TJ gave him a sexy massage followed by great sex together. It was good week, two great games, two more wins, and their love continued to grow.

110

# TEN

They were home for just a one and half days before flying out again Monday afternoon after practice. They were in route to Philadelphia to play the University of Pennsylvania at the old but famous Palestra basketball center. The building played host to more NCAA tournament games than any other arena in the country. It possessed a large barracks feel to it with exposed quarter moon shaped beams crossing high overhead.

The game was Tuesday night so the coach scheduled an afternoon practice before an early dinner, and the team flew out at six. TJ arrived that afternoon and settled into the Sheraton hotel, found some groceries, and went to work writing on his book. Shane called right after they landed to obtain TJ's room number. After they settled in their room, the players received ninety minutes of free time to unwind from the hectic day, and their practice. They had to be in their room by eleven o'clock curfew.

Shane knocked on the door and waited for TJ to answer. Once the door was opened, Shane bear hugged him, closed the door with a foot, and together, they made their way to the bed where they fell down laughing. They talked about the day, went over details for the schedule tomorrow, and watched some television before making out. Shane wanted to sleep with TJ badly, but settled for a massage and sex. He kissed TJ goodnight about fifteen minutes before curfew to make sure he got to his room in time.

TJ ate breakfast in his room, worked hard on editing his new book **Gay Grifters** to be released May 1st. They moved the date around so the new release date would be after the championship and before the end of exams. TJ considered going on the road to promote his book while Shane prepared for exams, but not yet committed to doing a tour. He needed to get the book to his editor some time in January, but TJ was busy rewriting his second draft, embellishing details, and expanding character attributes. TJ tended to write new stories extremely fast so the first draft often portrayed very little of the character's physical description, although TJ could see the character's face in his head. Eventually he had to slow down and make it easy for the reader to envision the same thing.

He had been working all morning when Shane called on his way back from lunch.

"How are you?"

TJ replied, "Fine. I've been so busy working on **Gay Grifters** that I forgot to order lunch. I'll do that shortly. How did the shoot around go?"

"This is an amazing place. I love the architecture of this old building, but it messes with your shooting aim until you get used to it. The coach has been there many times, and he knew about the depth of perception problem, so he had us shoot far more shots that we usually do for a pre-game practice. I felt I was pretty good at the top of the circle, but spent a lot of time at the foul

111

line, and my regular shots before backing up to the three-point line. I doubt I shoot any that far tonight, but you never know. Let's hope the game isn't close, so they don't need a last minute shot from me. Boy, I need a back rub."

"I'm available, but are you?"

"I wish, but I have study hall shortly, then we eat the team meal, followed by a required nap for ninety minutes so we'll be rested. I hope to get some free time before we check out and head to the arena. What time are you checking out?"

"I managed to get a late check out of five o'clock since they weren't busy. I was prepared to pay for a second night even though I am flying back after the game just as you are, but they were nice. They probably experience this every week for college games. Your dad called this morning. He said to tell you hi."

"How is he doing and what is he up to?"

TJ smiled, "He and your mom are doing fine and wished they could be here, but that is a long flight, and he has a conference to attend tomorrow. They are going to miss the next several games, but will join us in Lindle for our first home game in a while. They can't wait to see the motorcoach. We'll have to clean up."

"It's always clean. You're a great housekeeper, and a better lover."

"Now don't you go talking sexy to me on the phone and getting me horny when you're not around to do anything with."

They both laughed. Shane said, "Well, I'd better go. It always makes me sad when I can't see you, but I'll come as soon as I can."

TJ answered quickly, "I prefer that you not come too fast, as I like delaying climax and ejaculation when possible!"

Shane laughed as he hung up.

Shane didn't usually sleep well before a game, but feeling comfortable with TJ nearby, he actually slept hard during his nap, and didn't wake up until time for them to leave. He quickly packed his stuff while sending a text message to TJ apologizing for missing him and promising to make it up to him.

TJ, though disappointed, smiled. He knew their schedules would constantly conflict during the season, so he didn't let something like this get him down. He knew that Shane fell asleep because his body needed to rest. However, it threw off his rhythm during the first few minutes of the game, and he felt embarrassed after missing three close shots and two foul shots. Everyone on the bench could not believe it. The coach took him out and let him think about his game for a little while.

Aggravated at his poor performance, it was whole minute before Shane looked up at TJ who was signaling with five fingers to chill out. He then sent the one finger for love, and the two single for the naked players.

A Writer's Fantasy

Shane smiled, pulled his earlobe, took a sip of his Gator Aid®, wiped the sweat from his face, and nodded at the coach.

"Are you ready to play?"

Shane smiled at the coach, "Yes, sir. I'm sorry. I'm not sure what happen."

The coach grinned, "I think you were in a different zip code. Are you ready to win?"

"Yes sir. No problem."

"Get in there."

Shane hustled to the scoring table and waited for a break in the action. After the next buzzer, he took to the floor and began moving up and down the court with ease, but the team fell behind Penn by six points. His first opportunity to score came a minute later as he caught an offensive rebound six feet from the basket. He faked going up to try to throw off the defense and then leaped hard. He carried three Penn players on his shoulders, but he hit the shot as the referee blew the whistle for a foul. He hit the foul shot making it a three-point opportunity.

Two possessions later, he pulled up about twelve feet from the goal, and dropped a pretty swish shot for two more points. The Taylor team suddenly went into a full court press with Shane on the inbound player. He had been studying him in the film they watched yesterday, and today in the game. Five out of six times he threw it across the court with a bounce pass. Shane waited patiently, and then suddenly leaped as the boy drew his arm back just a little farther. Before the planned bounce pass hit the floor Shane got a hand on it and scooped it up, but it fell from his hand, and bounced off the floor as he began moving. In a flash, he snatched it up and dunked it hard.

Seemingly, all by himself, he just scored the last seven points for his team, and Taylor was now up by one, but Shane later told them he would not have scored any without the help of his teammates. This began a sixteen-point run that frustrated the Penn players and their fans. They began to push harder on Shane, beating, and banging his shoulders, back, arms, but not a single foul called by referees. Finally, the coach had enough of the abuse, called a timeout, and spent almost the entire break giving one of the referees an earful of his displeasure in their performance.

The referees responded to his complaint by doing the opposite and calling more fouls on Taylor than on Penn, some of which were not fouls at all. The coach actually laughed at one ridiculous call. The ESPN® broadcasters noted the problem as they, too, mentioned the lack of fouls called from the beating Shane took, and then acknowledged the retaliation the referees seemed to be making.

Just before the end of the half, one of the Penn boys caught Shane hard in the jaw as Shane was going up for a dunk. It knocked him off the court and sent him tumbling into the stands. He cut his arm on a chair and came back on the court bleeding. The referee signaled for time, but once again no foul. Coach Ryan became very upset as was TJ, but TJ knew he should be patient, even though Shane may be bleeding a little. A few weeks ago, Shane told him about a similar game in which the referees never called a foul, but he laughed because in the end, Taylor won by forty points. A little blood for that victory was a small price to pay, he thought. The coach screamed at the referee who immediately called a technical foul. This made the coach extremely angry, but he settled down and signaled for another referee to come talk to him.

Meanwhile, the trainer and the doctor took Shane to the locker room. The cut took four stitches, but Shane wanted to return to the game. The doctor held him back, as there was only thirty seconds until half, and he felt Shane might need to build up his fluids. As the team came into the locker room, they all wanted to see his cut, but the doctor already put a bandage on the cut, and taped his arm so that it would not come off in the second half. The players told him about the technical, and they all grinned.

By the time the coach came to talk to him, he had already calmed down. The coach asked, "Shane can you play?"

"Yes sir," he replied quickly.

"Can you play well?"

"Well enough to beat these bums."

The team and the coach laughed. "Well boys, I really don't have a lot to add to that comment. Are your ready to win?"

"Yes sir!" they screamed.

Shane hit eighteen points in the second half for a total of thirty points. He snatched twelve rebounds and four steals, and hit fourteen straight foul shots without a single miss.

TJ grabbed the final stat sheet, and made his way out of the frustrated pressroom, as Taylor just whipped the homeboys by twenty-six points. He caught a cab as usual, and was in the air in thirty minutes. He wrote his summation of the game during the flight, while eating an ice cream desert Susie made. She definitely found his weakness for ice cream.

After landing he received an email press release from Taylor University Athletic Department Director. He announced he filed a formal complaint against the officiating in the Penn game with NCAA. He demanded they be reprimanded for their poor performance and allowing a player to get hurt. TJ grinned. He didn't expect anything to happen, but it would look good in the newspapers.

It was a school night so Shane didn't come over to TJ's after he landed. He picked up a snack and went right to bed so he could get up to study the next morning. The next day began their exam break, and his first test was Friday. He got up at the usual class time and began studying. By noon, he was in the gym doing his weight workout, then three hundred shots before a short team shooting practice. He worked hard in the two hour abbreviated practice, and then ran for thirty minutes, showered, ate dinner, and he was in his room studying once again for the rest of the evening. He sent TJ several emails and a final text message to say goodnight.

The weekend between exam weeks might be the last weekend they had off for a long time, depending of course, on how far the Taylor team went in the championship games in March. TJ caught up on his bills, paperwork, and somehow found the energy to work on his taxes even though he had a few weeks left in the tax year. He assumed he would have no time in January to get his numbers together for his accountant, so now was as good a time as any.

With Bob's direction and help, he also decided it was time to do a little cleaning and waxing on the exterior of the coach, as the weekend promised to be one of the their last warm weather days for a long while, too. Bob operated the hose like a retired fireman with a death grip, as if TJ would take it away from him. TJ, as usual, hauled the mop bucket around the coach, and used his long extension pole and a ladder to scrub the top of the coach. Wisely, he retreated out of the way while Bob went up the ladder to spray the soap bubbles and dirt off. After he finished, Bob went around the coach spraying the dirty water from the roof off the sides while TJ began cleaning the sides of the coach all the way around.

Sue came out of her coach with refreshments, and gave them a freshly made brownie and a bottle of water. Bob maintained a sour look on his face, as if she was interfering with progress until he tasted the brownie, and then he politely said, "Yum-Yum, honey bun, these are great!" She and TJ laughed at him, but not too loudly, as he still had the grip on the water hose.

Sue picked up the leashes for the dogs and took them on a long walk, so the water noise wouldn't frighten them. TJ thought that Sue was very clever, because she also avoided helping to wipe down the coach after the last rinse.

TJ used a pole squeegee to get most of the water off the coach, while Bob began using another pole with a towel over the mop end to dry away the water spots. It took them thirty minutes to dry all the windows, sides, and chrome. They tackled the wheels and tires next after comparing notes. TJ put a wax substance on the chrome wheels, and Bob sprayed it off. After they went all the way around TJ used a tire dressing spray to make the tires black and protect them from the sun. Bob watched.

TJ then used several rags to buff the chrome wheels to a bright finish and sprayed a clear sealant protector on to help keep the dirt from sticking.

Sue returned with the dogs and pronounced the coach beautiful. TJ and Bob ended up washing his car and Bob's car before they put the hose and buckets away. TJ thanked Bob and Sue, and went inside to start cleaning windows, dusting, vacuuming, scrubbing counters, microwave, stove top, sinks, bathroom and the shower before deciding that was enough for the day.

Shane went through an unusual Saturday afternoon practice since a few players had exams that morning. He came over to the motorcoach afterwards for dinner, and hit the books to study for a while at the table. TJ quietly pecked away at on an outline for a new story. He titled the future novel "**The Blackfeet Boys**" but felt the storyline required more work. Quiet digital satellite music played on the stereo from his favorite smooth jazz station, the dogs were asleep, and TJ nearly was, as he preferred to work with some background noise like the History channel. However, he admired Shane's tenacious discipline on the court and off, as he remained oblivious to anything and everything around him as he went back and forth through his exam notes. When he forgot something, he wrote it down on paper as if writing it permanently in his brain.

Shane only had one more exam on Tuesday, but he felt determined to earn an A in the class. He kept class notes in a spiral book, research notes in his laptop, and flash cards for things he must memorize. Three hours later, he closed everything up and said he was done for tonight.

He fixed himself something to drink and said, "Let's take the dogs for a walk. My brain is exhausted."

"It's dark, but I guess we can stay on the road under the lights. I'll get my coat and a flashlight. He thought the weather had been a nice today, but tonight, it was already in the low forties with clear skies and slight breeze."

Shane put on his coat, a hat, and began hitching up the dogs. TJ took a pee he had been holding for a long while, because he didn't want to disturb Shane's concentration on his studies. Shane took the dogs outside as TJ came down the hall, locked the door, and Shane handed Beeper's leash to TJ as they began their walk.

TJ bravely asked, "How's the exam studying coming?"

Shane smiled, "I must apologize. I knew I wouldn't be much fun while I study. I want to make an A in this class, but this one is a tough one, and so I must concentrate very hard. But then again, I probably do the same on all my studies. My roommates call me a nerd. I'm sorry."

"You were fine. I managed to do some storyline writing, but my work is not as hard as yours. I'm writing fiction and make it up as I go along. You have to remember what people did in history many years ago. I am just so glad to have you here, so I can sneak a peek at your gorgeous face every now and then."

Shane laughed, "Yeah, I bet. I must act like an old fart."

"Not to me. Just a few more days, and you'll be free of studies until mid January."

"You're right about that, but as soon as exams are over, then the coaches will act like it is the beginning of the season again. We'll work out twice a day, since we don't have homework, and we'll catch up on things we have yet to master. I promise you by January and league play, we'll be ten times better than we are now."

"Do you dread the heavy workout?"

"Hell no, although all players whine about it. It is actually when I'm really at peace, practicing and playing as hard as I can, and hopefully improving. It'll be fun. We need to talk about Christmas."

TJ smiled as he had thought about the upcoming holiday, but didn't bring it up, as he felt Shane had enough on his mine. Since going off to college, TJ was always caught between enjoying Christmas with his family and friends, and dreading the holiday, and all the questions from relatives as to when he planned to find the right girl, marry, and settle down.

There was a lot to like about Christmas, he thought. Great fellowship, good food, sharing presents, and laughter, and a lot to hate like not being able to discuss gay issues at the table, and trying to buy presents for everyone, without a clue for what to buy. Some of his relatives were just too lazy to make a list. He also knew he would gain ten pounds from all the good, home cooked food.

Deep down, he felt envious that most of his adult family and friends had someone they loved with them, and he didn't. He wasn't sure if he had a partner would they be welcome to attend the family gatherings, but he would bring them anyhow, and to hell with what they thought. Every family holiday beginning with Thanksgiving, Christmas, Valentines, and ending with Easter, left him feeling sort of left out. He had no one to blame but himself, as he could have found someone, even if they weren't perfect, or close to perfect, he thought. Maybe if I look through the wrong end of a pair of binoculars, every available man would look picture perfect! He laughed at his weird thoughts.

TJ could handle living alone, as long as during the holidays he was actually alone. However, oddly, in the company of both friends and family, he often fell silent, and just listened to the others talk about all the fun things they were doing. He wished he could get his dogs to talk, so they could talk about all the fun things they did with TJ, but they had yet to master that trick.

Finally fed up, and annoyed with the lack of wish lists, in the last few years, TJ began skipping the secular part of Christmas, and celebrating only the religious part of the holiday, that should have been the most important part, but he received no sympathy for his decision. His loved ones and co-workers called him a scrooge. He told them he just got tired of trying to shop for everyone, and listening to all the Christmas gossip. It just wasn't fun anymore. He took the money he used to spend on presents, and gave it to charities, but he never told anyone. He let them call him all the names they wanted. At least he was somewhat happier and besides, he no longer had to fight the traffic to the mall, or return another pile of ugly sweaters or loud argyle socks.

He prepared for Shane's anticipated need for spending time alone with his family, but he hoped perhaps Shane would return for New Year's

TJ Johnson

Eve. Soon it dawned on him that Shane would be back for sure because he already booked all the hotels for the away games, and had practically memorized the schedule, and there was a game on December 27$^{th}$ this year, so Shane would be back early. He could handle that, he thought. He waited for Shane to continue.

"Well, we can do whatever you like, but I'll tell you what I was thinking. Mom and Dad are flying down here for the Sunday game on the 16$^{th}$. Our next two games are also at home on the 19$^{th}$ and 22$^{nd}$. The later game time is one o'clock. That means we could fly out about five to start our holidays. I thought perhaps we could do the reverse of our Thanksgiving schedule, if it works out okay for your family. We could spend the night of the 22$^{nd}$ and 23$^{rd}$ with your folks and fly out Christmas Eve morning to my house to spend the 24$^{th}$ and 25$^{th}$ with them. We could then fly out the morning of the 26$^{th}$ for home, as I have practice that afternoon at three sharp. We have a game on 27$^{th}$ but it is here in Lindle. I don't know how we got such a run on home games during the holidays, but it sure made holiday scheduling a whole lot easier. So what did you have in mine?" Shane looked into TJ's face and realized his eyes had watered, and it looked like he was about to cry. Shane became worried. Rapidly he said, "Oh my gosh, did I screw this up? We can change the schedule. I'll do whatever you want. I'm sorry."

TJ smiled, "I not sad at all. These are tears of joy, and I know it is hard to tell the difference, but I'll give you a hint. If I frown and cry, then I'm sad, but do you see this smile? It means I am very, very happy and I love you so much. I like the schedule, and I'm excited about it."

"If you're happy, why the tears?"

"I have never spent Christmas with the person I love most in the world, but this year, thanks to you, I will."

Shane didn't care if the paparazzi were ready with flash cameras and videos. He went to TJ in the middle of the darken road, kissed him on the lips, and held it for the longest time.

He finally broke the embrace and said softly, "I don't want to go anywhere, or celebrate a single holiday or family gathering, without you by my side. Remember that, and I hope you feel the same way."

TJ smiled and kissed him again, "I do feel the same way. I love you."

Shane waited for his grades to post on the computer, and he knew he had five minutes to go, but he acted like an expectant father. Finally, he called TJ with the news. "I got an A in both classes. Can you believe it?"

TJ laughed as he could hear the excitement in Shane's voice. "I'm so happy and proud of you. You worked so hard. You earned it."

"Yep. I had to call you but I'm on the way to the gym. I'll see you later tonight. I love you."

"Way to go. I'll see you then. I love you, too."

118

Practice was hard, as Shane predicated, as no one had any homework to do. They ran, worked on drills, and ran some more. The coach scheduled two practices a day for the rest of the week, and a Saturday morning practice before their flight to New Jersey at noon.

TJ flew up that morning, and read all about the Rutgers team in the digital media guide on his laptop, while eating a grilled chicken salad with a plate of fresh cut fruit. Susie spoiled him with a piece of hot pecan pie and ice cream on top.

The team stayed at the Long Haven Hotel on Broad Street with a nice view of the town. The newspaper said Taylor would wipe them all over the court, but Shane knew better, as everyone played their best when they went up against the tradition of Taylor. Many times the coach suggested they avoid reading the newspaper and magazine articles about predictions and performance. He said the stories would depress them, and might even make them angry.

The hotel room was furnished beautifully including a thick, white bathrobe hanging on the wall in the bathroom. TJ made his run for some snacks and drinks, bought the local newspaper, and began making notes in the computer for the next chapter in the book. He included his thoughts on how exams stressed out the players, and quoted Shane as saying he was looking forward to two-a-day practices to get them in shape for the bigger games coming up.

The team arrived at three due to a delay at the airport, but thankfully, the weather was good but very cold. Coach Timmons took the team directly to the arena so they could do about an hour shoot around. The game was at two the next day, so he didn't want his players practicing the morning of the game.

They ate the team dinner at six, watched some scouting video tapes on Rutgers, went over assignments, and to everyone's surprise, the rest of the evening to themselves. Shane went straight to TJ's room.

After he knocked on the door, TJ appeared wearing the white robe. "How much time do we have?"

"Three hours!"

TJ flung the robe off and Shane discovered he was naked.

Shane laughed, "Well let's get started! I'm as horny as hell!"

The Rutgers game started in a fury with Shane diving for a loose ball, crashing into the coaches sitting on the bench, and tumbling everyone over backwards. He came up scratched but unhurt, and took a lot of ribbing after knocking over the coach, and messing up his always perfect hair. Shane had been a little nervous before the game, but the accidental incident made him laugh, and when Shane laughs, he's relaxed.

Two plays later, he unloaded a huge dunk over Rutgers' big guy, followed with a steal in the far court that he tossed out to Jerry, who sped down the sideline. As Shane headed for the goal, Jerry threw a hard bounce pass right into his hands, and he laid it up as well. Fouled on the play, Shane tossed in the extra point as well.

Larry hit four beautiful three-point shots in the first half, and the Taylor team led forty-six to thirty eight at the buzzer. While the first half may have been fun for the players, the coach wasn't happy with their defensive effort, and felt they gave up almost twenty easy points. He promised long runs in tomorrows practice if improvement didn't occur in the second half.

Shane and the boys went to work, putting pressure on the ball at all times, always running the full court press, and adding traps at odd times to catch a single player in a tight court. To accomplish this, on secret signal from the coach, Shane would race away from guarding his man to the corner near the scoring table. Along with the man assigned to the Rutger player, Shane would sneak up on his blind side so that when he turned, he had nothing but a six foot nine inch wall to run into. As the Taylor boys frantically waved their hands, the unsuspecting player was indeed caught in a trap, and either he gave up the ball, called a timeout, or was caught by the five-second rule. The later happened, and Shane went out of bounds to bring the ball in for his team, as the coach shouted enthusiastically while applauding his team's effort.

The second half ended up being a romp with the Taylor team scoring a game total of a hundred and four points, and held Rutgers to just fourteen second half points for a total of fifty-two points. It was a great second half defensive effort.

The team flew back immediately after the game with dual practices planned again for Monday, but they had the night off.

Shane picked up takeout on the way to the motorcoach. TJ arrived home almost two hours earlier, walked the dogs before dark, chatted a while with Bob and Sue, and answered a few emails. He had completed his work on the game on the plane so he spent the rest of the time editing **Gay Grifters**. He heard Shane drive up so he marked his spot, saved the file, and greeted Shane as he came in the door with the bags of food.

He gave TJ a kiss, handed him the food, and knelt down and played with dogs, as they rapidly swished their tails back and forth like windshield wipers in their excitement to see Shane.

It was barbeque night, something Shane rarely ate on the road, as they usually ate what he called safe digestive foods, and certainly nothing that could create gas like pinto beans. They talked about the game, how much fun it was, and TJ noted the three Band-Aids® Shane wore on his arm from his tumble over the Taylor bench in the first half. They both had a good laugh about it. Shane picked up the remote and changed the channel to ESPN's SportsCenter® to see if it made the highlights.

TJ had gone through the mail, and there he found a Netflix® copy of **Charlie Wilson's War** with TJ Hanks and Julie Roberts. They decided they would watch it after dinner. Shane felt greatly relieved he didn't have any homework to worry with, and it would be almost a month before he would have to pick up the books again. He hardly knew what to do with his free time, but the coach did, by scheduling so many dual daily practices.

They loved the movie and made their way to bed just before eleven o'clock. Shane told the other players he was 'staying with a friend' during the holidays, so they were together every night and they loved it. They especially loved that practice wasn't until nine thirty in the mornings.

The game was at seven. Shane ate the game meal at two that afternoon, and enjoyed a fruit snack about ninety minutes before game time. He watched the scouting report film six times, and studied intensively each of the three possible players he would be required to guard defensively. He was anxious to play, and though he tried not to, he glanced at the wall clock once again.

Nicholls State hailed from Thibodaux, Louisiana. They were a great middle ranked college team with one amazing player. His name was Adonis Gray, and he was on target to score over twelve hundred points in this his final season as a senior. He was also going to pull down over four hundred rebounds. However, both of their centers were sophomores, and Shane noted both good and bad habits with these two boys. Shane's big concern was Ryan Bathie from Australia. He was a six-feet six-inch forward, with a thick accent that managed to run his mouth during most of his games, but he was deadly as the leading scorer with a determination to break four hundred points this season.

Shane watched the tape one final time and looked up at the clock, and it was now down to sixty minutes to go. He was ready to hit the gym and stretch, because he would be in a routine he had done over and over again since high school. It began with long careful stretches by himself, and then additional work with the help of a manager. After twenty minutes, he would begin shooting easy shots near the goal, and working farther back as the clock to game time ticked away. Near the end of the pre-game rituals, he and the rest of the team would go through several well-practiced drills before heading to the locker room for a final trip to the bathroom, closing comments by the head coach, and then into tunnel to wait for team introductions.

TJ felt spoiled to have so many games at home, allowing him to wait until ninety minutes before game time to drive over to the university's arena. He used the car pass to park in the rear lot, made his way into the building using his press pass, and climbed the steps up to the pressroom. He learned not to eat at home, as the food at the buffet was always good. Tonight he ate fried chicken, rice and gravy, green beans, sweet potato casserole, and macaroni and cheese. In Lindle you don't have to worry about asking if the ice tea was sweeten, as they were in the heart of the south, and sweet tea was practically a law.

121

He ate well, but decided to hold off tackling dessert until halftime. He set up his laptop, read Walter Mill's pre-game statistics and facts about the matchup, and began writing about the upcoming game. He glanced up from time to time, while checking the clock counting down until game time. Shane would be coming out of the dressing room soon.

He locked away his laptop and began walking to the door, when behind him, he heard the unmistakable voice of Dick Vitale, who was in town to provide color commentary. TJ turned to see him just as Dick walked right up to TJ.

"I thought that was you. How are you?" Dick stuck out a hand bigger than TJ's, engulfing his, while shaking it vigorously with a big huge smile on his face.

TJ smiled and replied, "I'm great and you?"

"Don't I look great?" He always made jokes about himself and added, "I have to like this face…it's the only one God had left. Tell me about your boy. How's he doing?"

"Better than ever. He made A's on his exams and classes, and he amazes me in the fact that he actually enjoyed the two-a-day practices since exams were over. He even likes the hard running they've done, and he shoots for two hours before practice, and takes a long jog afterwards. He is as fit as anyone I know. I wish I was."

"I know what you mean. I am winded climbing the steps in these arenas, but I am doing the treadmill every morning at home, and exercising in the hotel room as well. So what does he think about the matchup tonight?"

TJ smiled, "Well, I can't speak for him as I'm not tall enough." Dick laughed as TJ continued, "But from what I have been reading, and what he has been explaining to me, Nicholls State is good defensively, and he has a good match up with their big Aussie forward. I think we'll win on our home court, but you never take any game for granted."

Dick smiled, "Spoken like a politician. How's the book coming?"

"I'm ready to send you the first few chapters, if that is okay with you."

"Of course it is. I'll look forward to seeing your insight into the Taylor team through Shane's eyes." He laughed at himself, "Hey, look at that alliteration. I'm good."

TJ laughed, "Yes you are, and your fans love you. Dick, please don't ever change. Your support of college basketball, and your verbal description of the players and their families is priceless."

"Thank you. Let's go watch old Shane warm-up. I bet that's where you were heading. Am I right?"

"Yes, you are. I was watching the countdown clock on the monitors while typing up my notes leading up to the game."

As they made their way down the steps Dick asked, "Do you have house here in Lindle, or do you have to fly in like I do?"

122

They sat down on the same row that TJ had a ticket for. "No, I live full time in a motorcoach, and I've parked it in a RV Resort not far from here, so home games are easy. I just have to fly to the away games."

"Now that must be nice. I'd like to see it some time. How long is it?"

"It's forty-two feet and it's a Country Coach® Allure 470, and I'd be happy to show it to you."

"You know John Madden, the football color guy for a lot of the major NFL broadcasts, travels only in a big Prevost® unit as he will not fly. He has it equipped with multi television monitors so he can watch game films while in route. On game night, he walks from his coach right into the stadium for the game. He's asleep within an hour after the game ends. I have to look into that. I'm getting tired of flying, and I miss my honey. My wife and I have been married forty years, but she rarely flies to a game with me unless it is an all weekend event in the same town so she can shop. Boy, I lose a lot of cash when she does that," he teased.

"The next time you're coming to town just call me, and I'll pick you up and show you my setup. My cabinets are made from cherry wood so I had a cabinetmaker create a desk I designed. It has a drop down leaf for travel, but when parked, it creates a u-shape work area for me. I write everything on a computer using an Apple iMac® desktop computer on the RV, and Mac Book® laptop when I'm not at home. I gave up on IBM® compatibles and Microsoft® operating systems. A Mac® is more reliable."

"I'll look forward to seeing your coach, desk and you. So is Shane matching up with Ryan Bathie tonight?"

"Yep, at least most of the time. He's a big boy and their leading scorer, but the team has to watch out for Adonis Gray. He's the senior and a big leader for them."

"You're right about that. He has a sweet shot. I bet he hits sixteen or eighteen points tonight."

The Taylor team came out of the locker room wearing their warm-up suits. Shane caught sight of TJ and Dick sitting in the stands. He walked over to shake their hands like he was just seeing TJ for the first time in a while, which was really only an hour ago.

"Hey, champ," began Dick, "I looking for a great game tonight. How are you feeling? Those exams didn't wear that brain of yours out did it."

Shane knew he was teasing, "I'm great, and my little old brain is ready to go, too. I think it will be a good one."

"Got a score prediction?"

Shane grinned, "I know better than that. Whatever I said could jinx us. I'd better go stretch. It was great to see you. It's nice knowing you're doing commentating tonight. I always DVR our game when you're on, but never Billy Packer's broadcast. He just makes all of us mad."

Dick laughed, "Hey, he makes me look good!"

They all laughed. Shane trotted over to a favorite spot on the floor to begin his routine.

Dick said to TJ, "I've watched him do that workout before. He is unhurried, careful, and methodical. He really takes care of his body. I've seen good players go down with a cramp, a pulled muscle, or limp from a bad step, but never Shane. He is like a machine. You turn the key on and he just gets the job done, and nothing fazes him. I bet he gets knocked down more than all the other players combined."

"You're right about that. Did you see him take out the bench on Sunday? He has taken a lot of ribbing for knocking the coach over and messing up his hair."

"I bet he did," laughed Dick. "I guess I don't have to worry about my hair if he runs over me. I just hope he doesn't mess up this pretty mug!"

TJ and Dick both laughed.

About forty-five minutes later, TJ sat in the midst of thousands of Taylor University fans. He had just returned from the edge of the court where he spotted Shane waiting in the wings to come onto the court. TJ signaled a five for him to chill, and the usual one finger for love by scratching his nose. Shane pulled his earlobe and smiled for a second before returning to his stoic game face.

The tip-off might have been an indicator of how tough the game was going to be. Shane caught the ball, but as he came down from his leap into the air, Ryan Bathie yanked the ball from Shane's hand and sprinted to his goal. The Taylor team had already started running towards their goal after seeing Shane grab the ball in the air, leaving the Nicholls goal unprotected. He scored the first two points of the game. Shane wasn't happy at the steal, but after he threw the ball in to Jerry, Ryan picked Shane up at half court for defense and began running his mouth at Shane.

"I guess you're not as good as people like to think. You muscles look weak compared to mine. I'm going to run over you all night long."

Shane knew it was just trash talk, but it pissed him off anyhow. The team worked the ball left and right before tossing it into the paint to Shane. Nicholls immediately swamped him by double-teaming him, leaving Larry open in the corner. Shane should have tossed it out to him, but instead he pushed upwards through the State boys hoping to score and get the first foul on Bathie.

Shane missed the shot, was obviously fouled, but the referees didn't call anything, so the score remain zero to two. The coach said something to Shane as he went up court, but TJ couldn't make it out. Two plays later, they finally scored. As the ball came down the court, Shane attempted a steal, leaving the lane wide open. When he missed the opportunity, the ball was tossed to Ryan for an easy dunk. The score was now two to eight.

124

On the next possession, Shane was again double-teamed when he got the ball, but this time he did toss it out to Larry who dropped a three with a swish. Immediately, the Taylor team went to a full court press. Shane was guarding Bathie as he attempted to throw the ball in. He came close to a steal by just tipping the ball. The Colonels made the next points with a nice three-point shot of their own. Ryan, who made it look like he was tripped, bumped Shane hard and again no foul was called, even though Shane was knocked to the floor.

TJ knew Shane was getting mad and was relieved when the first television timeout came. The coach talked to his team about settling down, moving the ball quickly on offense, and running them hard. He warned Shane that State has hopes of him fouling out, and that he should be aggressive, but under control.

When Shane came out of the huddle, TJ was holding five fingers up trying to encourage him to just relax. Shane smiled slightly. Jerry brought the ball down court after calling a play. Shane moved to the top of the key to provide a big body screen for Jerry. This put Jerry open for a half second and that was all the time he needed for a beautiful three-point jump shot.

On the other end of the court, State's guard shot the ball. Shane prepared to jump up for the rebound, but Ryan stepped on his foot just as Shane started up. It threw Shane off his balance, and he fell into another State player, and called for a foul. Shane protested, but the referee wouldn't talk with him.

On the next possession, Shane went down low until the ball had been passed back and forth looking for an opening. At the ten-second mark, he suddenly left Ryan under the goal, sprinted to the top of the circle. Jerry flung him the ball. Shane leaped, spun, and dropped a beautiful two-point shot. TJ grinned.

Back and forth, the lead changed hands but at the half, Shane had twelve hard fought points, six rebounds, and one foul. Ryan had fourteen points, five rebounds, and two fouls. The coach thought Ryan had committed at least six more uncalled fouls, and he wasn't happy about it.

TJ ate his planned dessert at the half, but he was worried about the game. Ryan had become increasingly aggressive both physically and verbally in the first half. He wrote his notes in the laptop, spoke to the photographer friend he had met on a previous game, and came back to his seat as Shane was warming up.

TJ smiled at him, gave him the two finger sign, and Shane nodded and smiled. Shane had a plan for the second half, and he was ready to go to work on Ryan.

Shane threw the ball in to Jerry, who immediately threw it to Larry in the corner, who dropped a quick three-point swish shot. Taylor took the lead. Shane was all over Ryan as he tried to bring the ball in. The rest of the Taylor team swarmed like bees around their man, preventing a safe throw of the ball to them. As time was running out, Ryan reared back and gave the ball a hard throw to the backcourt.

Larry's man was running to catch the ball, but Larry timed it perfectly, and intercepted the pass. Shane swung around switching from his defensive role to an offensive one, and broke on a run to the basket. Larry spotted him, and threw the ball hard down the court to him.

Humiliated at the interception of his pass, Ryan ran hard to stop Shane, but he was a half step late. As Shane went up, Ryan hit him with his body, caught his left shoulder with his elbow, the whistle blew, and somehow Shane managed to put the ball in the goal and score.

Shane dropped the foul shot into the net cleanly. A seething Ryan, who now had three fouls, picked up the ball. Again, the full court press was on, but as time almost ran out, State's coach called a timeout. The Taylor team applauded their efforts as did the fans, and on television Dick Vitale was explaining the spirit he could see in the Taylor team's attitude.

The game returned to a slugfest for the next twelve minutes and Taylor was up by four. Shane had two fouls, but Ryan had three, and had to be careful with just over three minutes to play. Shane took advantage of that. He told Jerry to throw him the ball in the paint. Jerry assumed Shane would kick it back out, but instead he turned, and leaped high into the air, but slightly inward to Ryan causing a collision.

The whistle blew once more. Ryan expected the foul to be called on Shane, but the referee was on the other side of the play, and he called the foul against Ryan giving him four fouls. Then the player from Australia made a big mistake, and began arguing with the referee, who was polite at the first, but before his Nicholls teammates could pull him away, Ryan cussed the referee, and immediately drew a technical foul.

His coach was furious at the call to start with, but came unglued and yelled at Ryan to get his butt to the bench. Frustrated, Ryan stomped his way across the court, Ryan had four fouls, and there were two minutes on the clock. Jerry made the technical foul shot, followed by Shane making his foul shot, and Taylor had the ball. Ryan stayed on the bench thirty seconds before the coach put him back in, because they were down twelve points.

Shane said nothing to Ryan, but continued to play good solid defense, and hit two jumpers near the foul line that Ryan didn't come out to block. The game ended with Taylor winning by fourteen points. Shane looked up at TJ as the buzzer sounded and smiled. TJ smiled back in return, while scratching his nose with a single finger indicating love. Shane pulled his earlobe, shook the hands of the Nicholls State team, and made his way to the locker room.

The next morning, TJ emailed the entire book through last night's game to both Walter Mills in the Public Relations Office for the Athletic Department, and to Dick Vitale. He asked them to peruse and write any comments, suggestions, and arguments they could, but to please give him an honest opinion.

TJ enjoyed designing his book covers, and for weeks he worked on a several designs for the basketball book before finally deciding on his favorite. He prepared an Acrobat® PDF file with the cover and the partial book. He then sent a copy to Jacob Tidwell, the book-publishing agent that Dick Vitale recommended. He prepared a plan for the book, information about his writings, and he was honest by saying most of his previous work had been gay fiction. He also gave Jacob the website address for his other books, and asked if he would be interested in representing him for Shane's book.

He then grabbed the dog leashes, hitched J-Henry and Beeper, and took them for a walk to stretch his legs, as he had been writing all morning. Shane arrived after finishing his morning practice. TJ came in with the dogs that made a dash for the water bowl. TJ and Shane began putting lunch together. TJ had been cooking a homemade beef, tomato, and vegetable soup that smelled wonderful when they opened the door to the coach. Shane made a big salad, while TJ prepared a tray of fruit, and then dipped out bowls of the hot soup, followed by a saucer of hot cornbread that his mother taught him to make.

They both broke the cornbread into small pieces and added it to their soup to thicken it, and ate their salads while the soup cooled. Shane ended up eating two bowls of soup, and most of the fruit, as the double practices were burning up lots of calories. TJ gave him a natural fruit Popsicle® for dessert. The dogs enjoyed licking the soup bowls.

Shane went to the computer to check his email and called to TJ. "You've got mail!" he said as if imitating the AOL® voice on the commercials. TJ came over to see, and there was an email back from Jacob already.

"Go ahead and open it. Read it to me," urged TJ as he sat down in the recliner, and began preparing for bad news.

Shane began reading aloud, "TJ, this Jacob and please call me Jake. Only my mom calls me Jacob. If my dad calls me Jacob that means I usually did something wrong, but at least nowadays I can out run him. I was anxious to hear from you as Dick Vitale called a few weeks back and told me about your project. I stopped everything I was doing and read it straight through. I'm a speed-reader so I read it for content and a feel for the story. Later today, I'll go through it again and mark my suggestions, although I doubt there will be many as you write very well. The premise intrigues me, and Dick was correct in assuming I would be interested. I think this book could be huge, and needs to be released as soon after the championship game as possible. However, we're getting ahead of ourselves, as we first have to find a publisher.

"I also agree that an auction would be a smart move, but it is too early to attempt it. I think you should prepare the book for press as you go.

Get the editing done every week, so that as you finish the book, and Taylor wins the title, then the book can be ready for press quickly. I think we should do bids about the last week of the season. If Taylor wins the league title, and the ACC tournament, we'll score a gold mine.

"I would like to meet you in person at your earliest convenience in my office in New York City. I'll draw up a standard contract and email it to you so you can have your attorney look it over. Just email me back, and I'll take care of the rest.

"I'm looking forward to working on this project with you. Best wishes to Shane, yourself and the Taylor team!"

"Wow," added Shane. "The book is a go."

"Yes," grinned TJ, "although I had my doubts, I knew the subject would have strong appeal. I guess everyone has heard of old Shane."

Shane came to the recliner and kissed TJ, "What do you mean old?"

"As in famous," teased TJ.

"Yeah, right. Let's go take a nap mister author. I'm feeling old after this morning's practice. Will you massage my back and legs?"

"Yes, dear," laughed TJ. "Anything else need massaging?"

TJ had done most of the local Christmas shopping while Shane did the Internet online orders, but by Thursday, they had all the shopping done for both families. Sue came over and helped them with the wrapping, including wrapping her own present. TJ had told a fib that the dinner for two at a famous Greek Restaurant in town was for his aunt when it was really for Bob and Sue.

They organized the boxes according to the family they were heading to, and then set about packing their clothes on Friday. The UC Santa Barbara game was set for Saturday at one o'clock, and thankfully still at home. Shane ate the team meal at nine, and now paced the locker room while waiting for stretch time. TJ ate a late lunch in the pressroom after taking the dogs for a long walk. This time they were taking the dogs with them for Christmas as Bob and Sue had relatives coming in to stay with them, and they all were going to Charlotte for Christmas.

TJ read the press release, and just as he was finishing, Walter Mills walked up and sat down. After shaking hands Walter said, "I must admit, I didn't get to sit down and read your chapters until last night. It has been a hectic week, but all the players are booked and ready to fly out after the game for the holidays and back again afterwards. The book is exciting, insightful, and though I know you're not known as a sportswriter, I think it makes your look into our sports world more creative, and perhaps easier for a novice to understand. I noted a few facts that weren't wrong, but need a little clarification, and sent it back to you just a little while ago. If we can just win the National Title, this book will be a huge seller."

"Thank you for help. I'll look forward to seeing your suggestions."

"What happens if we don't win?"

TJ smiled, "Believe me, Shane and I have talked about that, but a behind the scenes pass means you see victories and losses from an inside view. I don't know how it would sell, but the story remains the same. It would allow us to explain why we think we lost, but let's don't get ahead of ourselves. Shane says we're going to win. I'm betting nine months of work on it."

"You're right. They are going to win."

"Dick Vitale is reading the same chapters, and is going to do a quote for the cover and press releases. He is a big fan of Shane."

Walter smiled, "Excellent."

"Walter, I may need a favor."

"Sure, what can I do?"

"I think the book would start off on the right foot if coach Timmons were willing to write the introduction. Do you think you could ask him for us?"

"Sure. May I show him what I read?"

"Absolutely. I realize if he writes it now, it may need editing later on, but at least we'll know he is onboard with it."

"I will talk to him at the first opportunity." Walter stood up and shook hands again. "I hope you have a great Christmas, and I'll look forward to the next installment."

"Same to you, and thanks again."


The first half had been sloppy, and the coach was not happy about it. Jerry attempted a behind the back pass he had done a thousand times, but lost control of the ball, and it fell out of bounds. Larry pulled up for a jumper while standing on the out of bounds line. Shane went up for a dunk, but was too far under the rim and fell back out of bounds. The entire team appeared to have one foot already in the plane for the ride home to Christmas with their families. They were winning by ten points, but to hear the coach in the locker room at the half, you would have thought they were losing by a hundred.

TJ ate dessert at the half, and returned to his seat as the team came out to warm-up. Shane looked up at TJ expecting to see the five fingers for chill, as that was exactly what he needed to do. However, TJ had two fingers up and pointing at the other team indicating he should imagine the other team naked on the court. Shane laughed, and in the moment he did so, he began to chill out.

Shane and the team went on a tear from the moment they brought the ball in. For the next ten minutes, Taylor controlled the ballgame completely. They held UC Santa Barbara to zero points while they scored eighteen points. By the end of the game, they won hundred and eight points to forty-seven. It was an embarrassing lost for the visitors, but a sign of how strong the Taylor team really was.

TJ hustled to the motorcoach while calling Steve on the phone. Steve had been watching the game in the pilot's lounge so he was ready to go as soon as they arrived. TJ went over and gave Bob and Sue a big hug, gave them their gift, and Sue laughed when she saw it, opened it up, and smiled at the deception.

TJ then walked the dogs, loaded the car, and about the time he finished, Shane drove up. He ran over to give Bob and Sue holiday wishes, and hugs as well. With the dogs aboard, they drove to the executive airport, and loaded their stuff onboard. Shane walked the dogs once again while TJ parked the car.

Once onboard, Steve and Janet greeted their new four legged guests, and stowed everything away. Shane and TJ presented them with gifts, and soon they were ready for the short flight to Greenville. The dogs did great in flight, but soon fell fast asleep, as did Shane. It had been a stressful game, but though displeased with his first half performance, he was glad they played at such a high quality the second half.

They landed less than an hour later, and TJ's family helped them load their stuff in the car. Because Steve had two more flights to fly, they had to take all their stuff for Shane's family, too. Everyone teased them by saying they needed a sleigh to carry everything.

TJ's mother had dinner ready when they got to her house, and Shane ate a double helping of everything. Even food he wasn't too fond of he ate because she was such a wonderful cook. Shane had never eaten a German chocolate cake, but he ate two slices of the gooey, messy, but wonderful dessert.

After they cleared the table, the whole family sat around, laughing, and chatting about what happen in the family since Thanksgiving. Of course, now they all watched Shane play on television, and tried to spot TJ in the stands. TJ's nephew played with the dogs after the pups help clean up the kitchen by chewing on the minor morsels left on the plates. Beeper practically climbed inside the dishwasher.

By ten, TJ, Shane, and the dogs made their way to the hotel, took the dogs on a long walk, and settled in for a much-needed cozy sleep. The next day was a frenzy of activity, as TJ's mom and sister hustled about with last minute shopping, and the boys helped with some chores. Later, Shane watched a basketball game while TJ worked on his parents' computer. He always kept their computer running up to date, as they loved receiving email from family and friends, and did research on the web for things they wanted, or treatments various doctors suggested.

TJ and Shane braved the traffic as they went to Tanner's to bring home lunch for everyone, and gallons of the orange drink they all loved. He bought an extra gallon to take to his parents. The dogs rarely had time for a nap, as there was always someone ready to play with them. They returned to the hotel about two and took a big nap. Afterwards, Shane dressed and went for a jog, while TJ and the dogs watched as they did their long doggie walk of the day.

Shane returned to get a shower so he would smell better during dinner. Together, they arrived back at his folks house for round two, and this time, it was an early version of her Christmas dinner including a big ham, meatloaf, mashed potatoes, green bean casserole, corn on the cob, strawberry congealed salad, and big buttermilk biscuits, plus more of the chocolate cake along with a pecan pie. Shane and TJ ate well as did the dogs.

Afterwards, they shared gifts so everybody began opening packages. J-Henry and Beeper ran from box to box smelling the packages looking for doggie treats, and they weren't disappointed as not one, but four boxes were just for them. TJ's sister bought lighted, tiny reindeer doggie headbands, but the dogs weren't very excited about that gift. They preferred the new pile of doggie rawhide chews.

By ten, they gave everyone hugs, and Debbie and her son said they would pick them up at seven for their flight the next morning.

After getting ready for bed, Shane and TJ began making out, and before long making love. They slept soundly until the alarm rang at six.

Their flight to Missouri had been a good one, with bright blue skies, but very cold temperatures. Steve expertly put the plane down on the runway, though recently cleared of snow. His parents met their flight, and once again they loaded the up the car. This time Susie handled the hostess duties so they gave her a Christmas gift, and wished Steve and Susie a safe holiday as watched them takeoff.

Their Christmas Eve dinner was barbeque, a family custom, and TJ could see that the love of barbeque ran through Shane's genes as well. His parents adored the dogs, and TJ and Shane got pictures of them playing in the snow.

They watched a ballgame until about ten when the boys and the dogs headed to Shane's room for sleep. They made out for a while, cuddled in tight while feeling warm and cozy, and slept soundly until about eight the next morning. Shane lifted his nose and smelled sausage on the stove. Together, they got up, showered, dressed, and came down in time for Barbara to bring the first stack of pecan pancakes to the table along with a platter of sausages. The boys ate, the dogs nibbled, and the family enjoyed a good time together.

Later in the day, TJ talked to Al about Jake and the need to go to New York. Al agreed and told TJ to make the arrangements when he could.

Friends and other family members came over for a big nighttime Christmas dinner. They all ate too much of the wonderful food and found themselves sleepy.

Steve landed the jet on time and their received gifts were loaded for the trip home. TJ and Shane gave Al and Barbara big hugs and thanked for a great time. They were home by noon.

# ELEVEN

Shane took a nap, and left for the gym at two. Practice wasn't until four, but by then, Shane hit eighty of his hundred practice shots. Their next game was tomorrow night at seven, so the practice was designed to get the team back in the rhythm of playing and working together as a team now that the holidays were over. They did fast break drills, full court press offensive and defensive drills, overtime plays, and thirty seconds end of the game maneuvers.

After ninety minutes, the practice was over, but they moved to the meeting room to take a first look at scouting tapes, and player assignments. An hour later, the coach began an earnest talk about the fact that the holidays were done, and it was just one last week before the ACC league season would begin.

Shane arrived home about six and ready for supper. He called TJ on the way to his car to see if he wanted to do takeout, but TJ said no he had a cooked a pot roast in the Crockpot, with stewed potatoes, carrots, green beans, and Shane laughed and told him he would be there in ten minutes.

They devoured their salad, ate a good solid meal, and TJ surprised Shane with a slices of fruit with orange sherbet on top, and they both enjoyed it all. The dogs licked the juice from the plates, the boys settled in to watch a movie, and they were in bed by ten. After being on the road with their families, they were enjoying being home and some serious lengthy lovemaking. They both would walk with a hint of soreness in the morning.

After breakfast, Shane told TJ his thoughts about the after Christmas practice, and how he matched up for tonight's game. Shane then began watching ESPN's SportsCenter® while TJ did some writing on the book, and preparing for tonight's game.

About eleven, they decided to watch a movie together, nibbling a little on snacks, but not too much as Shane had a team meal scheduled for two. After the movie, they bundled up as it only about thirty-six degrees with some wind, walked the dogs all the way around the park, and returned to the RV. Shane changed clothes, and drove to the dining hall to eat the team meal. TJ fixed some of the leftovers from last night's meal for his own enjoyment.

Shane returned just before three and found TJ asleep on the bed. He quietly pulled off his shoes, nice slacks, and sweater, and crawled up beside him, pulled a light Polartec® blanket over them, cuddled in closely and promptly fell asleep.

They awoke about two hours later after hearing Beeper barking in the front window. TJ got up, looked out, and saw a big Great Dane on a leash with a small lady making the rounds of the park. She apparently just arrived.

TJ laughed, "Shane, come see the horse in our front yard."

"A horse?" Shane yawned and stretched as he got up, and walked to the front of the coach. He looked out the window and laughed. Where's the saddle? My gosh, I would hate picking up a turd after that thing."

"I could have slept until game time."

Shane grinned, "Me, too. Will you give me a massage?"

"Yes, I will. Go get naked."

Shane took off running to the bedroom with the dogs chasing him. He retrieved an older sheet they kept handy for massage treatments, and flung it over the bedspread. TJ stripped down as well, rubbed the lotion in his palms until it was warm, and began working on Shane's massive muscled legs by pushing, squeezing, and rubbing his thumbs deep into his big leg muscles until all felt smooth again.

He worked his way up to his buttocks and rubbed them hard, and then worked on his spine to the base of his neck and back again. Shane cooed as TJ did it better and sexier than any of the trainers in the locker room. Shane left at five for the game feeling loose and ready to play.

TJ showered as he worked up a sweat massaging Shane. He dressed, took the dogs to pee, and drove to the arena. They decorated the pressroom in holiday stuff, and his dinner could not have been better with turkey and dressing, rice and gravy, vegetables, and salad. He would once again have to wait until halftime for dessert.

They were playing Nevada and it was on ESPN2® at seven o'clock. TJ said hi to Walter, and several other press members who he knew by face, but not as friends. Dick was still on holiday so Lane Soward was doing the color commentating work.

TJ went down to his seat to watch the warm-ups. Shane was already there shooting foul shots. He didn't quit until he hit twenty-five in a row. He then went to work on other shots, turn and shoot jumpers, front jumpers, his hook shot, and then the team came out to stretch. He went to his usual spot on the floor, looked in TJ's direction, and smiled. He loved having him there, and thankful his seat had been secured at all the home games, and pretty close to the same seat in the away games. He would have to work on the tournament games.

Nevada's team had flown in yesterday afternoon from wherever their players' homes were to save time. The team manager met all their flights until everyone was safe in their hotel. They practiced last night in the arena, rested, and had just come out for their pregame drills.

Ten minutes into the game, Jerry was charging down for a layout, and made the shot, but as he came down, he stepped on a player's foot causing his ankle to give. Jerry managed to walk off the court on his own, but the coach sent him to the locker room with the doctor.

Billy had been the backup point guard for three years. He had tremendous wit, the ability to lead, but he was not as fast as Jerry, but improved tremendously from last year. After coming in to play, he threw an amazing lightning bounce pass to Shane on the next play for an easy layup. The fans cheered and the coach sighed heavily.

By halftime, Taylor was leading by twenty points, so they decided not to put Jerry back in the game so his ankle would have more time to heal.

The second half started with a surprising turn of events as Nevada score fifteen points to Taylor's two cutting severely into their lead. There wasn't a lot of shoving and fighting going on under the goals, but with six minutes to play, and Taylor eight points ahead, a Nevada player went up to block Shane's shot, and accidentally caught him with an elbow to the nose. It bled instantly.

TJ, like most fans was mad, but Shane experienced this many times in his career, and he knew the player didn't mean to do it. The Nevada boy helped Shane to his feet while apologizing. Shane immediately went to the locker room, leaving two essential and seemingly indispensable Taylor players out of the game, and six minutes of playing time left. The coach made the substitution, but TJ could see worry lines on his face from across the court.

The Nevada team took advantage and cut the lead to just two points with ninety seconds to go. Shane came out of the locker room and walked over to the coach. He said, "Hey, coach, do you have a spot on this team for me?"

The coach said later he could have kissed him, as seeing him ready to play with blood on his shirt brightened his spirit immediately. He put him right in after laughing and patting him on the back. Shane scored three times in ninety seconds putting the team up by seven, and the team got tough on defense and held Nevada to zero points. The game was won, but the cost had been heavy as Jerry was going to be out for a while.

Later that night TJ put a frozen bag of mixed vegetables inside a dishtowel and gently placed it against Shane's nose as he lay on the couch watching SportsCenter®. TJ sat at the computer updating his notes from the game, adding many of Shane's comments about the incident, and the more serious problem of losing Jerry for a while.

They were enjoying living like a real couple going to sleep and waking up together, though the days of such pleasure would soon end when classes started again.

The coach was still pushing the team's endurance and fitness to the max with quick fast-paced drills and plays, while running, jumping, and working them harder than ever on their defense. At some point in the scrimmage, he would call for a stop that meant no matter what the offense attempted to do collectively, the defense would not allow them to score, no matter what.

The coaches knew the entire squad was improving, but Jerry, his star point guard, sat in a chair on the sidelines with his ankle propped up. He was doing therapy every day on his ankle, but unfortunately, it was going to take time.

Their last game was on Thursday night, and tomorrow's game on Sunday afternoon felt like it was just too soon after the injuries of the last contest, but Shane woke up ready to play, feeling stronger, and more confident with Billy filling in for Jerry.

The team meal was at nine, followed by another viewing of the scouting report of the Valparaiso team. Shane memorized the traits and habits of the three men he could end up guarding, and he had their routine seared into his brain. He returned home to help the time past a little faster. They took the dogs for a good walk, but as Shane left for the game, it began to rain. Though the students were still home for holidays, the tickets were sold out, so he hoped the arena filled up.

TJ arrived about an hour before game time, ate lunch in the pressroom, and made his way down to watch Shane workout. The team seemed quiet, and TJ suspected they were genuinely tired both mentally and physically, as the mid-winter workouts had been hard to make them tough enough to get through the last half of the season. But Shane also thought they were far better prepared for this season than last year's team, and he expected them to go all the way to the finals and maybe even win.

TJ returned to the pressroom, and began reading through the media guide about Valparaiso, which he wrongly thought the university was on the west coast. The small school with just over four thousand students, with a strong Lutheran heritage, was built in Valparaiso Indiana near the shores of Lake Michigan. The school possessed a proud history dating back to 1859 while maintained an amazing student success rate.

TJ wondered how such a small school produced a fine, stoic basketball program with eight-conference tournament championships, and ten season titles. They were known as fierce fighters on the court, and like David in the Bible, they were always willing to go against the Goliath-like schools like Taylor. Coach Homer Drew, one of the winningest in the college game, was in the midst of his thirty-first season. He wasn't about to let the team embarrass their school in their play in Lindle.

Shane knew they had a big seven-foot one-inch giant from New Zealand on their team. Calum MacLeod struggled early in his career, but came on strong last year, and he could be a big threat inside, especially when pulling down rebounds. Shane would have to help box him out of the lane on defense.

Shawn Huff was Shane's most likely match up. He was a great scorer, who liked to block shots, and didn't mind hustling for a steal or rebound. Guard Jake Diebler would also have to be contained by Billy, and everyone on the Taylor team knew that Billy was an excellent defender.

The holidays were almost over with New Years Eve just a day away, but the Taylor fans were already cheering and screaming for their team to score. For all of ten minutes the Taylor first team looked like they were running on a quart low, an expression TJ had used for years, but aptly applied. The coach screamed, clapped, balled his fists up, and yelled repeatedly at the team, but nothing seem to get their attention.

Finally, Coach Timmons had seen enough. He took out the entire first team, all five of the starters, and sat them on the bench. He put in the next five that generally ran against the first team in every practice. They were indeed like a second team, knowing where each player was going to run, when they were ready to shoot, and cohesively ran a very tight effective defense.

The second team slowed down the Valpo team, and scored eight points, while the coach was facing his first team on the bench, ranting and raving about their poor performance. Meanwhile, the second team was showing up the performance of the elite first team. Shane felt embarrassed, as were his teammates, and that was exactly what the coach intended. When he had made his point, and a very long four minutes later, he put the first team back in with the score Taylor thirty-eight, and Valparaiso thirty-five.

Shane's team hit the court with a fire in their belly. They ran hard, played tenacious defense, scored on almost every possession, and picked up the tempo of the game by three fold. This was not good for the Valpo boys. At half, the score was fifty-two to forty.

After a strawberry sundae made with frozen yogurt, TJ returned to his seat to watch a wild and wonderful second half. Shane held Shawn Huff to just four points and three rebounds. Big guy Calum MacLeod did get four rebounds, but not a single point. They had shut down their seven-foot center.

Shane got fourteen rebounds, eleven points from foul shots, hitting a hundred percent of his shots, and scored twelve from the field, including a non-scripted three-point shot from two feet behind the line that lifted the team off the bench into a standing rousing ovation. The fan were also treated to a three hundred and sixty degree dunk that Shane made as easy an Olympic ice skater going for the gold. It made the SportsCenter® highlight reel, and played over and over for the next twelve hours.

Shane arrived home about ninety minutes after the end of the game, and told TJ his thoughts about their poor start and amazing recovery. If they had lost, Shane would have been upset for quite a while, but the turn around performance of his team lifted his spirits.

He was still fired up when they went to bed, where sex was fun for both for over an hour. They would both be a little sore in the morning.

# TWELVE

The fifth home game in a row was set for Wednesday night, and Taylor's last non-conference game before pre-league-seasonal play. The early season games helped tune up the team before the games really began to count. They knew their total season record would always show in the sports pages and polls, and perhaps even taken into account by the NCAA tournament selection committee for seeding. However, on Sunday, the ACC league play would begin with a tough tenacious opponent when the Taylor team arrived in Clemson. Their last non-conference game of the season would be after the Clemson game, and against UNC at Asheville, a sister university in the state system. This pairing would be what the staff called a goodwill game, promoting basketball at the smaller school, and increasing their bank account for team sports at the same time.

Their immediate next match-up was against Kent State. Their team arrived in Lindle the Tuesday afternoon before the game, and practiced later that night in the arena to get the feel of the floor. Any team visiting the famous Taylor Arena did the same thing, as there was a mystique about playing at this field house, as there was for the likes of Duke, Maryland, Indiana, and many others. The fact that the Taylor team maintained an eighty-four percent winning record at home in this arena, put a lot of fear in the visiting teams.

The Golden Flames were part of a large campus of thirty-three thousand students, and nearing their centennial mark as a university in 2010. They were not a large team, but made up for it in their drive and determination under the tutelage and instruction of coach Jim Christian. TJ wrote that the Taylor team knew better than to take this non-conference game lightly. The coach chose this opponent specifically as the last opportunity to toughen up his squad, deepen their drive, while filling their hearts and minds with fervor to win by excelling, determination, and practiced skill, and push for teamwork far above what others hoped to achieve.

Shane, placed opposite Kent State's Mike Scott, knew the top scorer was also a senior with lots of experience. As teenagers, Shane and Mike played on opposite teams at a sports camp, and looked forward to the duel in the Taylor Arena.

TJ arrived in time for dinner as usual in the pressroom. Walter Mills, the teams marketing director came over to eat with him.

"TJ, may I join you?"

"Why of course. I welcome the company. I usually eat alone amongst such senior newspaper and television sportswriters. I doubt they know my name, and probably think I'm a grad student working on a thesis."

Walter smiled as he set down, and opened his utensils in the cloth napkin, "That will all change come spring when your book is released. Look around and note their faces, as each one of them will read every single page if they have any common sense at all. I finished the most recent installment and emailed it back this very afternoon, and I loved it. I hope you don't mind, but I have sent the coach all that you have written to date. He, too, was thrilled for the opportunity and will write the requested introduction."

TJ smiled, "That is excellent news, as to the coach helping us, and thank you for inspiring a writer who faces the blank pages on the screen alone, day after day. I am truly trying to write as Shane sees it, and at the same time give the fans that backstage promise into Taylor basketball. If they're like most fans, they can't get enough tidbits and morsels of news when it comes to this team."

Walter laughed, "Especially of Shane. We are averaging over four thousand autograph picture requests a week for him. Of course, the university's autograph policy saves him from having to sit down and sign them like a NBA pro player or a NASCAR® driver."

"How does the policy work? He hasn't mentioned it."

"The problem started a few decades ago, but with the advent of eBay® we had to come up with a rule. You see, the players are happy to sign an autograph for individual fans, but sly salesman were getting the boys to sign multiple copies of their photographs, and putting them on eBay® and selling them for hundreds of dollars. It wasn't fair to the players to sign so many out of courtesy, only to be robbed by these guys. The rule states they can only sign at official events, and the autograph has to be made out to the person standing before them and asking for it. As in to Bobby, to Jimmy, to Mary, and so forth."

"I see. I suppose Shane's autograph must go for a pretty good price on eBay®. Is that right?"

"Yes, he signed a basketball at a mall one day that ended up on eBay® for over a thousand dollars. Shane didn't receive a penny of that money, and by NCAA rules, he shouldn't have, but it still wasn't fair." Changing the subject after another bite of prime rib, he continued, "TJ, have you given any thought to the cover picture, or perhaps a section of pictures on the inside."

TJ laughed, "Well, I told Shane his head was too big to put on the cover, and that we'd have to use a zoomed out shot. I think we envision the team, an insert picture of Shane, and the championship trophy, and I have talked with a few of the photographers that cover the games, but no decisions have been made. I have a card for their boss, but I haven't contacted them."

"Well, if they give you any trouble about licensing fees, just give me a call. As a matter of fact, I will send you a letter this week authorizing you to use any game shots. I was thinking perhaps a few pages in the center of the book displaying highlights of the year might add to value of the book."

"What about some behind the scenes shots, as well such as watching game film, a team meeting, getting on the bus or plane, eating on the road, an inside the plane shot, and of course we'll need game shots as well."

A Writer's Fantasy

"Now that is something that hasn't been done. I think I should assign one of our photographers to keep this in mind as they travel with the team. I'll set up a few shots and email them to you. You'll have many game shots to sort out, but we can help you with it if you like. The next day after a game, and after we have put out all the game stories, stats, and information about the next game, we spend a lot of time going through the game shots, looking for those we'll use for our media guides, publicity for the athletic department, recruiting, and our support clubs."

"That would be great, and thank you for the help," replied TJ. "So give me the inside feel for tonight's game with Kent State."

Walter lost the smile just a little, "Between you and me, it is going to be a tough one, especially if the Taylor boys start out sluggish like the last game."

TJ laughed, "That will not happen. Shane said they learned their lesson and learned it well. He said they got too pumped up for the game, and by the time the whistle blew, their adrenalin sagged, and he said it felt like the blood had thickened in his veins. Of course, the coach fired them up again, and the results were amazing."

"I hope you're right. Well, I have to run. I enjoyed our chat. Again, if there's anything I can do to help, please let me know."

"The pleasure was mine, and thank you. I'll see you later."

The game began with Taylor on a run. Shane scored eight points in the first three minutes, but then Mike Scott got tougher on defense, and hot on offense hitting six points of his own. Back and forth the lead changed hands, and though Taylor was up by two points with just twenty seconds before the half, Scott hit a long three-point shot just as the buzzer blew, giving the Kent team the lead by one.

The coach wasn't upset with their play, but he also knew Taylor could play better. He made some key adjustments, called several plays, and though the second half remained a close game for a while, as the minutes ticked by, the score began to widen. Two minutes to go, Shane topped twenty-six points with a twelve-foot jumper and a foul shot.

Mike Scott collected eighteen points as Kent's leading scorer, but his team basically ran out of gas. The Taylor boys were taking advantage of their extensive running and working in practice, and they cruised to a sixteen-point victory over the Ohio squad.

Shane later told TJ the key to the game was their hard earned endurance, and Billy's command as the point guard, as Jerry remained on the sick list. Billy only scored nine points, but he had sixteen assists, two rebounds, and not once did he throw the ball away. The coach mentioned his play in the locker room, and the team applauded him. It was the kind of a moment coaches and players live for.

TJ Johnson

The Sunday night game at Clemson was not one that Shane was looking forward to, except for his determination to whip them on their home court. The big Taylor team had been beaten before, while assuming they were going to just walk into Littlejohn Coliseum and tame the Tigers, and yes, they were beaten badly. For some reason, they just had trouble being as ferocious as the Clemson boys. The coach was not about to let that happen this time, and he warned them during their practice time after the Kent game.

They arrived the day before their Sunday night televised game. TJ had done the same, checking into his hotel on Lake Hartwell, and enjoying the view, though the wind off the water was cold. TJ knew the area well, water-skied on the lake as a teenager, and his brother went to Clemson. He hated Clemson and almost said a prayer for victory, but prayed for all the players' safety instead.

The Taylor team experienced a good practice in the late afternoon in the coliseum before having dinner together, and then went through the scouting report and footage. Shane would have James Mays to guard in the forward position. He was their second leading scorer, following behind K.C. Rivers. He might also take on Karolis Petrukonis, a six-feet eleven-inch tough player. He was a sophomore but learning fast, and he didn't mind pushing his weight around. The coach told Shane when James Mays needed a breather, Tiger Coach Oliver Purnell would probably send Karolis in to beat and bang with him. He was told to hold his ground, but watch his fouls.

Shane got an hour of free time to make his way up to TJ's room and spend some time relaxing. TJ massaged Shane's back, they made-out a while, and Shane went back to his room early.

The team meal was at two, and the wait time seemed to dribble along slowly like a slow leaking faucet. Shane watched some other games, and as usual, he got very excited at some of them. He questioned calls, and took pleasure in telling the referee off, though so far, the poor referee had not been able to hear him through the television.

They arrived at the coliseum about two and half hours before game time, and already there were Tiger fans there to boo them. By the time, they were ready for warm-ups were about eight hundred Taylor fans in the coliseum, but the rest of the seats were filled with thousands of orange clad, diehard Tiger fans, and they were very vocal.

TJ felt outnumbered in the pressroom before the game, but soon saw a few friendly faces. TJ never wore team colors, creating an appearance of neutrality, which of course was completely false.

The Tigers got off to a roaring start, scoring the first eight points before Taylor finally put some points on the board with a beautiful three-point shot by Larry from deep in the corner. The following opportunity, Shane took Mays with him to the rim. Shane scored, Mays obtained his first foul, and Shane also scored his first foul shot.

Taylor went on a run fourteen minutes into the game and went up ten points, but coach Purnell called a timeout, chastised his team, built up their spirits, and they respond with an eight point run of their own. The halftime score put Taylor in the lead by three, though not much comfort to anyone.

Clemson was no longer an agriculture school, and now offered a long list of majors in business, technology, arts, science and more. However, they were still known to produce the best ice cream in the state from their student run diaries. TJ enjoyed fresh butter-pecan ice cream at the half, but said almost nothing to anyone. He updated his notes, grabbed a water bottle, and went back to his seat for the later half of the battle.

Shane picked up a foul in the first half, and now his second at the beginning of the second half on an unintended foul after tripping on his way to the basket. The charging foul pissed him off, as he didn't think it was his fault, but after asking the referee about it, he dropped it and went to work on their full court press.

James May is not a player that makes many mistakes, but all players do at some point in the game. With eight minutes to play, the score often tied, he threw the ball in one too many times to the right of Shane's outstretched hand. This time Shane anticipated, gambled, and won by getting just his fingertips on the ball, letting it bounce down to the floor as he took two quick steps, picked up the ball, and beat James to the basket for a nasty dunk. May, angry at his mistake, fouled Shane unnecessarily. He now had three fouls, and Coach Purnell was not happy with his team's play. He called time.

Coach Timmons told the Taylor team to settle down and have fun. He urged the team to chill out, and let the game come to them, at least that's how he started, but before they returned to the court, he told them they could beat those guys, if they wanted it more than the Tigers did. That pissed them off.

Shane looked up at TJ who was giving him the go, go, go signal. Both teams received similar pep talks, but as the game wound down, the score remained close, and at the end of the game, the Tigers missed a shot that would have won the game for him, but the buzzer sounded with the score tied. The Taylor teamed sighed greatly, while realizing they now had a second chance, or five extra minutes to beat the Tigers on their home court.

TJ saw Shane in the huddle and realized he was trying to fire up his team. He came out of the cluster and scored the first basket. They pushed hard on defense, too hard, and Larry fouled May with just two seconds left on the possession clock, and way outside the three-point line. It was an unnecessary foul, and Larry knew he had made a huge mistake. While May missed the long shot, he was awarded three chances to get three points from standing still on the foul line. Thankfully, he only got two of three, but it put Clemson up by two.

Back and forth, they hustled and if Taylor got two, Clemson got three, then Taylor got three, and Clemson got two. Shane dropped a foul shot, and that tied the game with fifty seconds to go.

The Tigers came down the court with the ball, and Coach Purnell called a timeout, set a play before they returned to the court, and though Taylor defended hard, the Clemson team made the shot, earning a two-point lead. Shane looked up at the clock and realized they had only twenty-four seconds to tie or win the game.

He called to his teammates, as Billy brought the ball down. They knew the play and the options. With ten seconds to go, the ball was thrown back to Billy at the top of the key. Shane drifted out wide, but suddenly broke on a run to the center, and turned to start down the lane. Two Clemson players swarmed him to prevent him from getting the ball, and perhaps an easy shot. This left Larry open as he had just run from one corner under the goal and out to the other side. The play was simple, and Tim stepped back from the man guarding him, and momentarily blocked Larry's man from catching up with him. Billy flung the ball to the corner before Larry got there. He caught the ball on the run with two seconds to go, turned, jumped, and fired off a beautiful shot.

Suddenly, all the noise in the coliseum stopped as if time stood still, or you're watching a movie, and the sound suddenly went off. Slowly, the ball arched and started down. Larry felt good about the shot, but his heart nearly stopped anyhow. The team on the bench stood in anticipation. The Clemson squad prayed it would miss. Shane flung himself around as if there would be a rebound, but the buzzer sounded just a half second before the ball fell through the net with a soft swish.

The rule is simple. A ball in the air and on the way to the goal is still a score. If the buzzer sounds, the goal counts, and both teams know the rules. The fans know the rule, but it didn't change the disappointment in their faces, as it was a three-point play putting the Taylor team ahead by one. They won the difficult, hard fought game in overtime.

The eight hundred Taylor fans stood and cheered, while the shocked Clemson fans turned and left. TJ stood there completely amazed, and yes, overjoyed. In sixty seconds, there wasn't a single orange fan left in the building. He laughed when Shane looked up at him, as the players shook the hands of the defeated Tiger team. He complimented James May and his play, and then made his way to the locker room. It had been a big win, and the team and the coaches celebrated in the locker room.

TJ was waiting on Shane when he got back to the motorcoach later that night after their flights home. TJ had already walked the dogs, so Shane gave them a good rub. He told TJ some of the stories in the locker room, things that happened in the game that TJ might have missed, and then they went to bed while winding down from a hard battle in Clemson, and the first win of their quest to win the league title.

# THIRTEEN

TJ made the flight arrangement for ten, but still had trouble believing that in the morning he was flying to New York City for his first visit with Jake Tidwell, the publishing agent interested in representing him for their basketball book. Last Friday, TJ met with athletic department's attorney who made an appointment in New York City for an author attorney with vast experience in the publishing contracts and royalties, especially in the world of sports. To TJ's surprise, and something he and Shane had never thought about, he also arranged for a visit with a top sports accountant. TJ was most grateful for Walter's continual help and advice with their project.

After the meeting with the team's attorney, TJ explained all that transpired to Shane and together, they decided to call Al Bradley to seek his advice. On a conference call, they explained the purpose of the trip to New York City, the meeting with Jake, and the meetings with an attorney and accountant.

Al said he had been reading and researching all he could about sports agents and NBA contract, procedures, and policies, and he said it was a nightmare to try to figure out. He thought all he heard from TJ was a good idea, and quite frankly a great relief, as began to feel like this stuff was way over his head.

Shane asked how they pay for it all since Shane will have no money until he signs an NBA contract a least a six or eighteen months away, depending on whether they win a championship this year, and after he decides on returning for his senior year.

Al said he anticipated the situation, and working with his accountant, he secured a credit line loan for Shane for up to five million dollars. He said the loan was in Al's name to make sure they carefully followed NCAA regulations, preventing him and Taylor University from receiving any penalties. Al stopped and asked Shane one more time, did he want to play pro basketball in the NBA. Shane didn't hesitate saying yes he did, and that he was looking forward to the challenge, but he wanted to finish his college career first. This pleased Al and his mother, as they always dreamed he would become a college graduate. His success at basketball went way beyond their hopes and dreams.

Al encouraged TJ to explain to the attorney about the credit line he arranged, and if he approves, then explain it to the accountant, and see what his thoughts were. "Give me the times of your meetings, and I'll make sure I'm in my office and ready for a conference call if you need me. Shane, I suggest you do the same, but remember we can only sign in TJ's name, and nothing in Shane's name. If they need me to sign something, I'd be more than happy to do so. They can fax or overnight a package to me."

144

After they hung up with Al, Shane and TJ felt much better, but this would be an exciting adventure for all, while TJ felt both the stress and excitement of actually going there and attending the meetings.

TJ got up at four as Shane groaned at the early hour, but after TJ finished his shower, Shane sat up and watched him dress. TJ skipped breakfast knowing Susie would have something for him on the plane. He played with the dogs, kissed Shane goodbye several times, and picked up his laptop briefcase and made it out the door. As he cranked the car, he wished Shane was going with him, but he knew that if a photographer snapped a picture of him going in and out of the appointments, the implications could be a mess for all, so he backed out of the drive, and made his way to the airport.

Steve landed at five o'clock, refueled, and waited for TJ's arrival. He waved as he saw him park in the executive parking lot. TJ locked the car and made the cold walk to the waiting jet.

"Good morning. Are you ready for the trip to the big apple?"

TJ smiled, "How can you be so cheerful at this hour? What time did you have to fly out?"

"We left about four thirty. Susie and I will have to get some sleep while you're in your meetings. The airport in New York has a nice lounge, so we'll check in, get some rest, and be ready for the return flight this afternoon."

"Thank you for your patience and diligence. How's the weather for the flight?"

"Clear skies, but cold. It'll be thirty-five degrees when we land."

"Brrr, that is cold." TJ stepped aboard as Susie greeted him.

"Good morning. How are you?"

"I'm fine, but my goodness it is early."

Steve pulled the door close, keeping the heat in the plane, and went forward to prepare for takeoff. Susie asked TJ, "Do you want breakfast now so you can a nap or the reverse?"

"I guess now, so maybe I can go back to sleep. How about some hot tea to drink afterwards? I still prefer juice and milk for the meal. What's on the menu?"

"How about a ham and cheese omelet?"

"Excellent."

"Okay, you know the drill, so fasten that seatbelt, and we'll be in the air in just a few minutes, and I'll bring your breakfast shortly thereafter."

TJ settled in after securing his laptop in the floor by his seat, as he felt Steve push the throttle forward, and in seconds, they were in the air and climbing rapidly looking for smooth air.

After leveling out, Susie brought his drinks, followed by breakfast. TJ ate well, drank some of the hot tea, and settled back to snooze. He always had trouble falling asleep on commercial flights, but not on the Learjet. It was quiet, the seats were overstuffed, real leather, and very comfortable, and he loved the way they reclined.

Ninety minutes later, Susie woke him with another cup of hot tea, and then whisked the remains away just before they landed.

Steve opened the door while Susie handed TJ a twelve-ounce bottle of Diet Mountain Dew®, his favorite way to obtain caffeine. He thanked them both for their service and encouraged them to get some sleep.

He walked through the large terminal and saw a nice looking guy holding a sign with his name on it. It was the chauffeur for the car service he arranged. He introduced himself and was led to the car. He knew the itinerary by heart, but not the addresses. He gave the driver the printed itinerary and addresses, with the attorney's office his first stop, and settled back to enjoy the view of New York City on the cold morning. He bravely left his long coat in the car as the limo was warm and cozy, and he assumed the offices would be as well.

TJ had been to New York several times, while attending the Broadway shows he loved and admired, but also to see his nephew in college there, and later his graduation. He loved to visit New York, but there was no way he could ever live there. It was home for too many people for him, but the list of fun things to do was long. Years ago, he began visiting some of the classic museums to add to his list of tourist sites. Sadly, his last visit to the World Trade Center had been in late June before the September 11th disaster. He still could not believe the towers and all those people were gone.

His first meeting was at nine and he arrived at Livingstone, Smith, and Wadsworth on time. The receptionist led him down a long hallway with beautiful offices on the left and right. He was introduced to Maggie Callaway, Jerome Wadsworth's secretary. He sat briefly while Jerome finished a call, and then was led into his massive office with beautiful oak walls, luxury carpet, and a view out the back of the office of the New York skyline.

Jerome was about fifty or so, shorter than TJ at five feet eight inches, a bit chubby, and hair only on the sides of his head. He had a warm smile, large hands, and he quickly came around his desk and reached out to TJ. They shook hands as Jerome led him over to a sitting area. TJ sat on the couch, Jerome took a leather chair opposite him, and Maggie sat in the other chair with her steno pad and pen ready.

"TJ, it is a pleasure to meet you. Walter spoke highly of your book as well as yourself, and your friend Shane. He is one heck of a ball player. I understand, of course, that officially, we are talking only about engaging my firm for the purpose of 'your' book, but when the opportunity arrives, I hope we can help Shane as well.

"Just a brief history, I graduated from the University of Chicago a few decades ago, graduated from Harvard Law, and the firm that hired me stuck me with real estate contracts. I was bored out of my mind. One day, a client arrived wanting help on a sports contract. No one in the firm wanted to mess with it, so they gave it to me. The guy's name was Joe Norman. He was fresh from college, entering the draft for the NFL, and was selected in the top

A Writer's Fantasy

ten. That account turned out to be huge, requiring immense research. I loved it. It was exciting and it came with benefits, as I got tickets for all of his home games.

"I left the firm and formed my own law firm specializes in sport related work that developed into some entertainment clients as well. Now we're sixteen lawyers and staff of associates of forty.

"I talked with Walter at length about your situation. Shane can't receive any funds from the book, so everything is in your name and rightly so, as you're the one doing the work and the writing. What can I do to help?"

TJ smiled as he opened his legal pad to glance at his prepared notes, "Dick Vitale has lined up an appointment this afternoon with Jake Tidwell, a book publishing agent who also specializes in sports publications as well as other books. Dick also suggested I talk with him about representation, and perhaps considering an auction for the book."

Jerome smiled, "I can certainly help you with negotiations with Jake, I know him, and his contract. He is standard on his fees and paperwork, so legally he'll be easy to work with. He is also very, very good, so he is an excellent choice for you. I'm pleased that he is interested as he is always busy. Tell me about the book."

TJ gave him a quick synopsis of the behind the scenes stories with insight from Shane, and his comments about practice, training, strategy, scouting, out of season work, locker room insights, and as much unknown information as possible. "Coach Timmons has given his approval and he will write the introduction, and Dick Vitale will make a comment as well. Dick has been most helpful, as well as Walter Mills. I met with the Taylor athletic attorney who suggested you, as well as a sports accountant by the name of Sam Minton. I have a meeting with him later this morning." TJ noted that Maggie wrote everything he said down.

"I know him as well, and he is also very good. Therefore, you'll have a good team, and you'll need all of us for the book deal, and making sure you're paid, but also when the time comes for Shane to put his name in the draft, then we'll all have to be on our game.

"Here's what I suggest: from now on, please do not sign any contracts without giving me the opportunity to peruse the documents for you. That includes book agents, accountants, banks, real estate, and even cars. Let's make sure we don't trip up on a technicality in a long boring contract. That's my job to protect you. What questions do you have?"

"Well, you answered the big ones already as we have no legal experience for a book deal. Shane's father has set up a credit line for me to draw off that is in his name. We have used it sparingly so far, as I attend all the games at home and away. Normally, I travel writing my own books, which brings me to a question for you. My other work is gay fiction. Do you have any trouble representing a gay person?"

Jerome laughed. "No, I don't. This is New York City, and there are gay people everywhere. My brother is gay. I have a nephew that is gay. I think I have an uncle that is gay, and still in the closet at sixty years old. Maggie, how many gay people work for us?"

She smiled, "Six that I know of, and two more that are suspect."

Jerome grinned, "Maggie, please make sure those suspects are made to feel that it is okay if they decide to come out of the closet at work." He turned back to TJ, "Does that answer your question?"

TJ smiled, "Yes, it does. So what happens next?"

"Are you ready to sign the agreement for our services?"

"Yes, would you explain your fees?"

Jerome reached for a file folder on the coffee table in front of him. "We ask for a retainer of five thousand to start, and a thousand a month. This means you get the entire staff you see on this floor at your disposal. If you have a problem, a question, or even a what-if thought, you call us. Maggie will give you a list of our contact information and several of my business cards. You'll note my home and cell number are on the cards, as I represent you twenty-four hours a day. How does this sound?"

"It's exactly what the attorney at school told me to expect, and so there were no surprises. Where do I sign and who do I make the check out to?" Al had opened a bank account for TJ, and ordered checks a few weeks before, but this was the first time TJ actually used one.

Jerome turned the file around and began pointing at the pages for TJ to sign and once complete, he said, "Very good and welcome aboard. We're so glad to have you with us. The check is made out to Livingstone, Smith, and Wadsworth. We'll bill you monthly. Please fill out your address information at the bottom as well as all your contact information. Of course, the bills will go to your new accountant."

TJ began signing while adding, "I'll put Al Bradley's information down as well. He and Barbara are wonderful, supportive parents, and have helped me so much." TJ was been careful not say 'we' at any point in the conversation, and Jerome was smart enough not to ask if Shane was gay as well, or if they were partners.

After more handshakes, TJ followed Maggie to her desk where she presented a folder to him of all their contact information, and handed a business card for his wallet, and other cards for his associates and meetings later in the day. "Just tell them to fax over the contracts, I'll prepare them for Jerome, and we'll make corrections and fax them right back. Once the paperwork is completed, we'll overnight copies to you. Now, if you'll give me a minute, I want to make copies of the signature pages for you." She already made copies of their standard agreement for him.

She returned a few minutes later with the completed copies and gave it to him. She also gave him some of her business cards with her email address and phone numbers. "TJ, please feel free to email any question to me twenty-four seven or call me. Email has become the modern way for instant communication. Jerome and I carry Blackberry® units so we can email on the run. You're paying us to work for you so use us. It was a pleasure to meet you and we'll look forward to seeing you next time in town."

"The pleasure was mine."

TJ checked his watch on the way down in the elevator, and smiled when he realized he was on schedule. The limo began taking him across town. TJ called Al and related the details of his first meeting. Al was reassuring to TJ about the money, and told him not to worry, as he had it all covered and wished him good luck with the accountant.

TJ arrived at Sam Minton's office just before his eleven o'clock appointment. He smiled as he took the elevator, and walked across the lobby to a very nice office. He sat for just a few minutes before meeting Sally Rush, Sam's secretary, and was ushered into his office. The layout was similar with a beautiful clean office, and a great view of New York City. Sam was taller than TJ, and played college basketball in college. He was six feet five inches, but TJ had grown used to living and working with giant basketball players. Sam had gray hair, wore wire rim gold glasses, and had his jacket off, looking like a guy that wasn't afraid to work. He came around the desk to meet TJ.

"How are you and welcome to New York City? Did you have a good flight?"

"Yes, thank you, and it is a pleasure to meet you. Thank you for seeing me."

They moved over to a seating area where Sally sat in adjacent chair with a steno pad ready to go. TJ felt like he was back in Jerome's office, but immediately comfortable. Sam said, "I just a call from Jerome a few minutes ago letting me know that you're one of his boys. He's good and you'll like him. He protect you," he paused, "and so will I."

"Excellent. I have a meeting after lunch with a book-publishing agent. His name is Jake Tidwell. Do you know him?"

"Yes, of course, and he is very good, too. Dick Vitale and your team at Taylor University made excellent recommendations for you. Do you have any questions, or shall I explain how we work for you?"

TJ had a list of questions in his pad, but he smiled and said, "I made a list of questions, but I surmise you're about to answer them for me."

Sam smiled, "I hope so, but if you have any questions, just stop me and I'll explain. Most of my clients are sports related via players, coaches, reporters, media personalities, and such, and I love working for them. While the basics are the same, such as handling their finances, bills, contracts, payments and royalties, and of course taxes, the element of sports keeps it exciting for me, and far more than just handling numbers. We'll handle everything for you involving money, from credit cards to investments. Our goal is to save you money, prevent tax problems, and help your money grow."

TJ said, "You come highly recommended so I am most grateful to meet you. Shane's dad has set up a line of credit for me, so I can write the book while being extremely careful to avoid having Shane financially involved in anyway. W must protect his NCAA status. Once he joins the draft for the NBA, sometime in the future, then we'll need far more help. I have a Learjet available as part of a lease with Al Bradley's company, so I attend all the away games as well. He gave me a credit card for the bills, but mostly, I now have the time to work on the book, while trying not to worry about the bills."

"Excellent choice of words because you should never have to worry about legal with Jerome, Jake with publishing, and old Sam here for accounting. Here's how it works: I know you have some of this set up already, but we'll take over, and it'll be easier for me to handle things with a bank right here in New York and rates and fees we approve of.

"I charge two thousand to set everything up, and we'll bill you five hundred a month. When Shane joins us, I'm presuming of course, I'll charge him a one time fee of twenty-five hundred to set up an LLC corporation to protect him or both of you.

"I know you have the credit card from Al and the checks, but just put those in a safe for now. I've already arranged a line of credit for you at our bank, so we'll pay the bills for you, etc. When Jake gives you a contract, fax it to me so I can check the numbers, although Jake does only first-rate business, and I assume you'll fax it over to Jerome as well. This will make sure we don't have any problems down the road." He sighed, "What questions did I miss?"

"Just one. Do you have any problem with a gay client?"

Sam grinned, "TJ, I'll be honest with you. I knew you were gay before you arrived. I check out my potential clients thoroughly. I have your credit information, social security info, and by this afternoon, I'll have a copy of your last three tax returns. My researcher discovered your website, your books at Amazon®, and Barnes and Noble®, and I've read the synopsis of your stories, and I have no problem whatsoever representing you. I have a family member that is gay, two of our associates are gay, and so we're fine."

"That's it. Where do I sign?"

Sam smiled, "That was easy."

TJ grinned, "With the recommendations I received for you, it was an easy decision. I'm also relieved, as worrying about the bills, making the payments, figuring out taxes, and all that stuff is a headache for me."

Sam flipped a folder around, TJ signed on several pages, and checked a sheet of contact information Sam's team already filled out for him."

"Are you going to keep using the mailing service in Florida?"

150

"That's a good question. I normally travel by motorcoach all year, and so I needed the mailing service. The project with Shane has forced me to park the coach in a nice RV resort, and I will be there until spring or longer. I would have the bills comes here."

"Very well, I do the address transfers for you. I spoke with Walter Mills. He assures me the book will do well, and it will experience phenomenal sales if Taylor University wins the National Championship. You'll rake in millions. You might consider looking for land to build on near the university, and setting up a home / office for tax and convenience considerations. If the first book does well, you'll be there another year writing the sequel."

"The sequel?"

Sam laughed. "TJ, if the first book sells millions, your publishers are going to want you to write a sequel, especially if Shane stays for his senior year. Can you just imagine if Taylor won the title back to back? Oh my, you'll make a ton of cash, and his value to the NBA will be astounding. He'll easily be the first round draft pick."

TJ mouth dropped, as he never thought about a sequel.

Sam continued, "Okay, here's the drill, Sally is going to lead you to her office, and she has prepared a folder of all my contact information. You'll have access to me any time you have a question. Please remember, don't sign anything financial without telling me or asking me a question. She is going to give you new credit cards for both Master Card® and Visa® through our bank, new business and personal checks, and she'll take your picture so we can add picture identification to your credit cards and your new bank cards. We'll over-night those cards tomorrow. "

"Whom do I make the check out to?"

Sam stood and smiled, "Sally will help you with that. Thank you so much for coming, and I am excited to have you with our firm for now, and we hope to have Shane join us down the road after he wins a couple of championships. Welcome aboard."

They shook hands and then TJ followed Sally to her desk. She added her information to the folder, gave TJ a handful of business cards, took him to a wall and snapped his picture, and prepared copies of their service contract, and told him to call if he had any questions, or gets lost in New York City, and please email her anytime.

TJ smiled as he got on the elevator and started down. He was on schedule, and felt they were safe with Sam. It was lunchtime when he got back to the limo, and his last appointment of the day was at two with Jake. He got in the back of the limo, and pressed the button to slide down the privacy glass and called out to the driver. We have an hour before my next appointment and I'm hungry. Where should we go?"

"Sit down or fast food?"

"Well, I'd love to get a couple of good calzones. Is there somewhere we can eat in or out easily?"

"No problem. I know just where to go. I'll have you there in ten minutes."

TJ laughed as he called Al and brought him up to date on the appointment with Sam. He told Al that Sam was going to call him after lunch to explain to him how the line of credit will work with his bank, and what he needs. He then called Shane and brought him up to date as well. He sure missed Shane, and couldn't wait to get back home that night.

The driver pulled up to the curb in front of a small Italian place. Customers were going in and out rapidly with bags of food, as it was indeed lunchtime in the city. The driver leaned back and said, "Sir, the food here is awesome. I eat here at least twice a week. Just go in, tell them what you want, and you'll have it in seconds. You can sit at a counter on the opposite wall, or come back here and eat in the car."

"I think I'll eat in the car. What do you want?"

"Sir?"

"I'm not going to eat in front of you without offering you some food. I'm from the south. My mom would whack me if I didn't feed you. So what do you want?"

The driver laughed and ordered a hot Italian sub, and a large Pepsi. TJ made his way into the restaurant. Four minutes later, he came out with two bags of food, and a tray carrying the drinks. He climbed in and asked the driver, "How far to Central Park?"

"Just five minutes."

"Is there somewhere we can park without getting a ticket?"

"Of course, no problem. Hold on."

TJ set the food down, and put both hands on the drinks. The driver made a series of turns, and minutes later he drifted into the park. Immediately, TJ began enjoying the view, and even though the weather was cold outside, they were nice and warm inside.

After the driver parked the car, TJ handed him his drink, and his bag with the sub. TJ flipped down a tray, set his food on it, spread out napkins to protect his clothes, and began eating the first of his hot calzones. He got pepperoni and cheese in the first one, and ham and cheese in the second. The food was excellent and he ate every bite of it.

He arrived at Jake's office just a few minutes before his appointment. He rode the elevator to the floor, but once he stepped out, he began looking for a bathroom for a much-needed pee. He cleaned up, washed his hands, checked his teeth to be sure he found no morsels of food left there, inspected his hair, and made his way down the hall.

The receptionist once again led him down a second hall, and into a small waiting area where he was introduced to Alice Sherwood. She told him she had been Jake's secretary for fifteen years, and she was here to help TJ in any way possible. She picked up a pile of folders and led him into Jake's office.

TJ smiled as once again Jake had a beautiful chrome office, with bright blue carpet, and a wide view of New York City. Jake was a former quarterback at Auburn University about twenty years ago, but only played two years in the NFL when he decided to retire early, and start his agency after spending a few years working for another book publishing agent. He learned a lot, but knew he could do it better.

Jake was also tall at six-feet five-inches, blond hair, just hit forty-two, had a golf tan, and broke into a huge smile as TJ followed Alice into his office. "TJ, we're so glad you're here, and we're ready to go to work for you.

"Thank you for seeing me. Dick Vitale sure speaks highly of you, and so did my attorney, Jerome Wadsworth and my accountant, Sam Minton."

"Ah, you've been busy. Very good, and they're all the best at what they do. We'll work well with them and have many times before. My job is to represent you when it comes to publishing, and find a company willing to give us the most bangs for the buck. For example, we want them to publish the book, but we also have to be concerned about their plans for publicizing the book, their marketing and promotion schemes, bookstore tours, cover designs, book settings, galley proofs, and keeping up with all of it. We'll also take charge when it is time for the sequel. I think Dick's idea of an auction is a good one, but I think we need to wait a while longer to see how Taylor does this year. The more games they win, and the better Shane plays, the more power we'll have asking for more money. I always treat every book deal as the only opportunity we have for income, so we go to bat and swing hard for the most money."

"How do this all transpire?"

"Dick said he saw a few earlier chapters and was impressed. I'd like for you to send me your work as you continue writing so that I have time to formulate a plan, and start creating buzz. Near the time of releasing the auction idea, I will leak that a book is in the works. After that, my phone will ring from various folks as they ask questions, and start trying to guess what our plans are. Is that okay with you?"

"Sure, I'm open to suggestions. Walter Mills, the athletic marketing director, gets a copy so he can correct any mistakes when quoting scores, statistics, and records. I also send it to Dick as his knowledge of college basketball is huge, and I'll be happy to put you on the email list. It will be in Acrobat PDF® format if that is okay with you?"

"That's perfect. I work on a commission, or a percentage of the deal. You probably wrote checks to my associates Sam and Jerome, but not here. Based on my research, I am confident I'll recoup my investment in a few months. If Taylor wins, the sequel will be even bigger, and we'll make more. That is how it works. Any questions?"

"I assume in the end, the deal with the publisher is mine to approve."

"Absolutely, and I'll explain everything to you. We fight for everything we can get our authors, as that is how I get paid."

"Very good. No, I'm excited! Shane has a lot of work to do for his team to win the championship. I'm lucky to be along for the ride."

"And you have a lot to do to, getting it down, and finding something no one else has written about. It has to be fresh, different, and exciting to read. You'll have just as many women reading this book as well. Women are big sports fans."

TJ laughed, "Okay, let's do it."

Jake flipped around the folder that Alice handed him. The contracts were all prepared. "Whoops, I almost forgot, I'm suppose to send this to Sam and Jerome before signing."

Jake laughed, "I know. Alice took care of both of them during lunch after receiving phone calls from them. You'll see here where they have both made minor corrections, initialed, and hand wrote a note to you."

"My goodness. That's great. I was embarrassed to ask."

"Don't ever be embarrassed to ask me anything. I'm here to work for you, so you just ask away."

"I do have one last question, do you have any problem working with a gay client?"

"I'm sorry, I should have brought that up. After you mentioned you write gay fiction, I went to your website. I suspect you're not moving many books on your own. Is that right?"

"Yeah, that's right. I do some signings but most are sold online. I sell more from my website than the bookstores."

Jake smiled, "You did a great job designing your covers, writing your promo materials, and I bet you designed your website, but from now on we're going to help you sell a lot more books. You'll note in the paperwork, I have agreed to work on your gay fiction as well. I have some contacts for this genre as well, and I think we may be able to republish them with a gay publisher that has the skills to get those books promoted correctly."

TJ smiled, "Very good." He confidently signed the paperwork, and then received the usual folder with all the contact information. They shook hands and twenty minutes later, he in was in the limo and on the way to the airport. He first called Steve so he could get the jet ready, and then called Al once more to bring him up to date. He checked his watch and knew he couldn't call Shane, as he would be in the middle of practice. He tipped his driver well, walked through the terminal and on to the tarmac for the flight home.

He ate roasted chicken, mashed potatoes, green beans, a salad, and strawberry shortcake on the flight home. He spent time on his laptop writing down all the details taken during his meeting in New York City. By the time he landed, he was ready to go home.

Shane was in the motorcoach after just finishing walking the dogs. TJ waved at Bob and Sue as he walked to the coach. He went inside and immediately hugged and kissed Shane, missing him so much throughout the day. Shane ate in the athlete's dining hall after practice, so they sat down while TJ continued telling him about each of the meetings. J-Henry jumped in TJ's lap first, anxious for some attention, and TJ provided kisses, hugs, and backrubs for him. Then he leaped out of his lap, and Beeper took his place for the same procedures.

Shane called his dad for a conference call on the day's events and together, they all felt good about the plans. Al said he talked to Sam and everything was set with the bank. He was relieved Sam would be taking care of the financial decisions and preparing his son's and TJ's future. They were all satisfied with the trip, and their new team in New York that TJ lined up. TJ sent emails to Walter and the team's attorney, thanking them for their assistance, and the same note to Dick Vitale.

The next morning, TJ began handling requests from Jake on details of each of the books he published under **Hard Title Publishing®** and the stories in varies stages of completion. Preparing this information took TJ two days, as he wanted it to be perfect. He knew Jake would be using this information to go after a publisher for his gay fiction. However, once completed, he emailed the report to New York, and then went right back to work on the basketball book.

Now that the regular league season was underway, the new couple had little time together. Shane stayed in the athletes' dorm Monday through Thursday night, and if in town, Shane stayed with TJ on the weekends. However, the schedule seemed to have them in town one weekend and out of town the next, but not necessarily. The only true statement was Taylor played two basketball games a week for all of January, February and most of March, and during ACC tournament time, they would play three straight games with no days off if they kept winning.

They talked several times a day, and sent a few text messages, but they longed to just hold each other. They missed being together, and talking and laughing. Sometimes TJ would write a long email telling Shane just how much fun he was having since meeting him, while trying to describe how much he loved him.

When Shane did make it to the motorcoach, or up to TJ's hotel room, their lovemaking was very passionate, lengthy, fun, and they enjoyed it immensely. When sexually excited, Shane could be both tender and aggressive, and TJ would laugh at how caveman he could be at times. They held nothing back in their frank discussions about religion, sex, and politics.

It was easy to see they were in love, so in public, they rarely stood close to the other, gesturing with their eyes, or a nod of their head. It was difficult, but interesting, TJ would say. Shane would simply say the time apart was frustrating. He wanted to live with TJ full time, but he knew a request to move out of the special dorm would send up a huge red flag.

In the next two weeks, they beat NC State, UNC Asheville, and a difficult game at Georgia Tech. They came home to play Maryland, and they didn't play with their usual drive and determination. They slipped up, fell behind, failed to recover, and suffered a loss on their home court. Shane felt so humiliated at the way they played.

Shane remained depressed after he arrived home that night, skipped the sex, and went straight to bed. He simply wanted to embrace TJ. TJ felt a warm tear on his chest as he stroke Shane's soft hair. To most, he was a giant, a fierce competitor, and a warrior, and these descriptions are usually true, but he was also tender, kind, gentle, and loving. He cared more than most about a win and especially a lost. Another day passed until his personality returned to normal.

TJ wisely said little during the process, but remained ready to listen at a moment's notice. In the end, he made excuses for Shane to doggie sit, take them for a walk, or together, they took the dogs to a park or a field. The outdoors and his gentle nature towards the dogs brought him back from his temporary depression.

The next two weeks were almost a blur for both. They traveled to Coral Cables to take on Miami and it was a tough battle, but Taylor came away with the win. A few days later at home they took on Boston College and whipped the tar out of them, and Shane said he felt like the team turned a corner on their confidence level.

Four days later, they returned to Florida playing Florida State. They experienced trouble with the Seminoles in the past but not this year. Taylor was doing well, and the coach gained confidence in his team, but stayed on their backs nonetheless.

Taylor's most tenacious rival remained Duke University, and for many reasons. They had been playing each other for decades—almost a century. Rumors developed the two competing coaches did not get alone, but it was the nature of their fierce competition between the teams that made a real friendship between coaches impossible. Many of Shane's teammates played in summer leagues with Duke players, but he rarely did. He would see them from time to time at his favorite sushi bar, but that was about it.

Taylor won more overall contests, but in the past two decades the point scores were closer, the battles intense, and the wounds bloody, because pride counted on every possession. The first meeting for the two basketball giants for this season was on Taylor's home court, and theoretically, they had the advantage, but many times an advantage meant nothing in such combative competitive wars.

TJ arrived early because he knew every seat would be taken in the pressroom. He ate dinner quickly, went to work on the last minute media notes, and then put his laptop in the desk locker and went down to his seat to watch Shane work out. He wanted to see if Shane was relaxed and confident, or a bundle of nerves like TJ was.

Shane saw him walking down the steps, dropped his game face for just a moment, and smiled. TJ scratched his nose with one finger letting Shane know he loved him even though it wasn't necessary. Shane knew TJ loved him if they won or loss, if Shane scored a lot or none at all, or even if he fouled out or got the most rebounds. He took great confidence the love would always be there.

TJ spotted Al and Barbara as they walked down to their seats a few rows up and behind the team. TJ walked down and around the floor, close to Shane so he could wink at him, and up to Shane's parents. He gave Barbara a big hug, and Al a big handshake. He sat down with them, and they began to talk about the week, and the forthcoming battle with Duke.

They turned to watch the Blue Devils team enter the arena to begin their workouts and rituals in preparation for the game.

Barbara asked, "I think this is going to be a close one. Taylor won both games last year, so the Duke team will be out for revenge."

Al concurred, "I agree, but we have the home court advantage, and the team has played great since the lost to Maryland."

TJ grinned, "Shane says it will be close, but there is no way they are going to lose. They want three victories against Duke in a row, and they want it bad. He said the coach told them if they could beat Duke, they could beat anybody in the country. I think we'll win, but I may lose a few fingernails in the process, as it is going to be a nail biting contest."

Barbara asked him about his trip to New York and how things were going since his return. He explained the trip, his impressions, and said he was thrilled at how fast and efficient all three teams were. Jake had indeed been busy with gay publishing companies, and TJ had a phone interview the following day with one of them. He also said Sam, the accountant, had everything squared away, so all the bills now went to him to confirm and pay. TJ said his new bank and debit cards were working just fine.

The arena staff began letting the fans into the arena, so TJ knew that soon every one of the twenty thousand seats would have a body in it. Across the court, he saw his friends Gary and Chris with their girlfriends coming down the steps on his side of the court. He bade goodbye to the Bradleys and made his way back across the court. Just as he went under the goal, Shane made a layup as part of a team drill, and took the ball and lightly tapped TJ's back with it.

TJ turned, smiled, and quickly said to him. "I'm pulling for Taylor. If you want to hit somebody in the back, go down to the other end of the court and pick on someone your size!"

Shane laughed and ran back to his place in line. It was a good laugh, a calming laugh, and he needed it to help him chill out for this big game.

Gary and TJ had been friends for a dozen years or so, and Chris has been Gary's friend for even longer. Together, they had enjoyed the lake, helped TJ with chores, and from time to time traveled to the beach together. They even attended a couple of Taylor games last year. Shane somehow managed to get four tickets for the Duke game after meeting them on a previous weekend when they came down for a home game in December. He liked TJ's friends very much. All six of them had the best time cutting up and laughing over dinner.

TJ came up to his seat and gave Tammy and Meagan hugs, and then hugged Gary and Chris as well. There was manly love between them, they all knew he was gay, and they were still getting over finding out that Shane was gay, after TJ had sworn them all to secrecy under penalty of death.

They chatted away until almost game time when TJ excused himself, ran to the pressroom bathroom for a much needed pee, snagged a cold water bottle from an ice barrel, and came down the steps as the teams were being introduced.

Shane glanced up from the bench huddle right before the start of the game and saw TJ holdup five fingers in his hair for Shane to chill. Shane pulled his earlobe to acknowledge, but his face remained in what TJ told his friends was his game face.

Duke captured the ball first and went right down the court with Jon Scheyer hitting a beautiful three-point shot. Billy came down the court for Taylor, threw the ball hard to Larry in the corner and he shot a three. The score was tied and remained so until the last two minutes of the half when McFadden got his third foul, and Coach K of the Duke team took him out. Shane and Billy went on a run. Shane stole the ball tapping it to Billy for a quick layup. Shane got a rebound, tossed it out to Billy. He fought the Duke guard off him and managed to shake free. Meanwhile Shane ran the full length of the court, no one picked him up, Billy fired it to him, and Shane went up hard for a huge dunk, and by the buzzer Taylor was up ten points over Duke. Coach K was still arguing with the referees for the lack of fouls called as they left the court.

Shane would later say that having that big of a lead at half made it very tough on the Taylor squad in the second half. He knew Duke would return fired up and ready for revenge. Coach K blistered his boys in the locker room, and they returned ready for war, and went on a sixteen point to zero run over Taylor and now led by six points.

Shane tried too hard on his on own in the lane and got caught on a charging foul. Jerry set on the bench wishing he could get in there as he knew he could beat the Duke player guarding Billy. The Duke guard successfully frustrated Billy. He threw away the ball twice, lost his dribble on a drive, and had the ball stolen for him. Temporarily, the coach took him out of the game to calm him down, and Larry brought the ball down with Shane's help. Shane brought it in, set a screen for Larry, ran to half court, and if Larry was in trouble he would fling the ball to Shane. Together, they got the ball in their court to set up their offense.

Duke usually double-teamed Shane, if he got the ball within ten feet of the goal, making it difficult for him to score, but he still had ten points from the field and eight foul shot points. Billy came back into the game and began to play with more confidence. Four minutes later, they tied the game again.

Back and forth, the lead changed, the fans were going crazy, and at the four-minute mark, the play stopped for a television timeout with Taylor up by two. Once back on the court, the tide changed. Shane missed a short shot, which was very uncharacteristic for him, and it miffed him. Larry missed a pair of three-point shots and before anyone knew what happen, Taylor had gone cold, and didn't score a single point for the next three minutes, while Duke took the lead and now led by ten.

It was too much to overcome, though Taylor did their best to catch up, but they lost to the Duke Blue Devils on their home court. It was hard for the entire squad and fans to stomach. Slowly and somberly, they filed out of the building. TJ gave each of his friends one last hug, waved across court at the Al and Barbara, and made his way to the pressroom. He picked up the notes from the game, and left for the parking lot and his ride home.

The coach gave Shane and the team the next day off because he knew they were completely emotionally spent. Shane arrived home later that night, his spirit broken, and together, they just lay in the bed until they both finally fell asleep.

# FOURTEEN

Clemson planned to come to Lindle for revenge, but suffered the unfortunate scheduling nightmare of having to play Taylor University four days after their lost to Duke. The fired up Taylor squad played like they were in the NBA. Shane scored thirty points, and Larry twenty-eight in their thirty-point victory over the Tigers.

Next they flew to Charlottesville, VA to play Virginia University and though a tough fought game for thirty-four minutes, Taylor went on a run and score sixteen points before the end of the game and won by twenty-two. Shane later said the games were played with odd taste of revenge in their mouths after heartbreaking lost to Duke. Their foes paid for Taylor's lost with their own defeat.

The next day Shane went with TJ to take the dogs to the vet for their annual shots, toe nails trimmed, and a physical, or as TJ called it a 'go-over' as the vet went over their whole body.

The vet's assistant took the dogs back to trim the nails while they waited for their doctor appointment. TJ warned Shane that J-Henry would do just fine, rarely making a noise, but when they cut Beeper's nails, she would scream and whine like they were gutting her with a dull knife. Shane didn't believe him.

About five minutes later, Beeper rattled the entire veterinarian office with wails and squeals until all her toes were trimmed. The lady returned Beeper with her hair askew and looking a bit flabbergasted. Once Shane saw that Beeper was okay, he started laughing and couldn't stop.

When they took the dogs into the examining room, Shane set Beeper on the table. All was fine as the doctor looked at her teeth, her ears, and felt for growths. TJ told him Beeper had one anal gland left and asked him to check it. Shane about passed out when the doctor put on a rubber glove, placed lubricant on his forefinger, and stuck his finger in Beeper's butt. TJ held the poor dog still. Beeper looked up at Shane with a sad look as if to say she was not a gay dog, and the man should get his finger out of her butt. Beeper whimpered, but she always felt better once the squeezed gland gave up the stinky stuff. Shane held his nose at the awful odor the gland produced.

TJ lifted J-Henry onto the table, asked the doctor about his cysts, but the dog said they were all fine until he got to one on his rear hindquarters. "TJ, this one might be cancer. I think we should remove it and send it to the lab. Is that all right with you?"

TJ thought for a second, "Will you have to knock him out?"

"No, will give him a Novocain shot, and then remove it. Will you hold him?"

"Sure." The doctor prepared the shot. TJ looked up at Shane and realized he was about to cry. "Don't worry. Old J-Henry will be fine. We've

160

done this before on him and me," grinned TJ. "Although, mine was doesn't by our veterinarian." The doctor and TJ laughed. "It won't hurt."

Five minutes later, Shane set J-Henry down carefully on the floor, they shook hands with the vet, paid the bill, and off they went to McDonalds®.

"Why are we going here?"

"I always take the dogs to McDonalds® after the vet for being good. I get them a cheese burger and split it."

As they waited their turn through the drive-thru, TJ told him how J-Henry once jumped across his lap when he went to pay the girl in the window, and he suddenly leaped towards the window into McDonalds kitchen. TJ caught him by the hind legs. He said he could not imagine how much havoc J-Henry would have caused running around trying to get burgers and fries back there.

Two days later, the lab tests were negative on the cancer. Shane drove back to McDonalds® and bought the dogs another cheeseburger to celebrate.

Next up was Virginia Tech on Taylor's home court. Everyone in the Taylor University team still felt so bad for the Virginia Tech family after the awful shooting the previous spring that left so many fellow students dead. They placed a patch on their uniform to show the visiting team their university was still in the hearts and prayers of the Taylor squad.

However, when the whistle blew, Taylor went to work. After the lost to Maryland and later to Duke, the team knew they could not afford to lose another game if they hoped to win the season conference title. Jerry was still on the bench, though beginning to work out some in practice, but mostly just shooting. During the rest of the practice, he rode a stationary bike to build up his stamina, as well as listening and learning from the coaches.

Billy had the best game of his career. He hit eighteen points from the field, six more at the foul line, twelve assists, and not once did he have an error. The team again cheered him, as the coach gave him high praise in their twenty-eight-point victory.

The campus was covered in snow, and most companies and schools closed for the day. No one was going anywhere, which is precisely why TJ announced they were going to see the new Bourne movie starring Matt Damon. They went in Shane's Hummer, allowing the use of his four-wheel drive feature, and arrived at the theater just a few minutes before show time. To their delight, there were only six cars in the parking lot.

They sat down in the empty auditorium, held hands, and loved the movie. It was the first real date they enjoyed since meeting way back near the end of summer in August.

The lovemaking that night was long and special, but the next day, it was back to war as they traveled over to Raleigh for the second meeting of NC State at their home court in the giant Raleigh RBC Arena. Their fans filled the place, while hoping to take a bite of Taylor, and indeed the first half went back and forth, as the Wolf Pack came for blood.

However, Shane and his teammates had other plans. With four minutes left in the half, he yelled at his teammates to put this team away, and they went on a run scoring twelve points to zero and now led by sixteen.

The second half was even worst for NC State, as Shane kept scoring about every other possession, and ended up with thirty points, including three big dunks, and three steals. It was a great game for everyone but the NC State Wolf Pack.

They were down to the last two weeks of the regular schedule with Wake Forest coming to Lindle for the next game. Dick Vitale flew in a day early to scout out the teams, and to visit TJ and see his motorcoach. He loved it, the office setup, and the dogs.

He also sat down and critiqued the latest chapters of the book, and like his comments on television, he said the truth followed by how much he enjoyed the narrative, and what a great book it would be. TJ grinned at Dick's expert, carefully delivered advice, and felt thankful to count Dick as his friend.

Arranged by Walter, TJ and Dick ate in the athletes' dining hall with Shane. Dick asked him questions about his early life, playing high school ball, his family, and his friends, but the interview was more like a good old dinner conversation with friends, and TJ remained impressed how easy Dick made his job appear.

Dick insisted they go to one of his favorite ice cream creameries nearby for dessert. It was twenty-eight degrees outside, but inside the store with no other customers, they were warm, cozy, and laughing at Dick's stories. They enjoyed having the place to themselves as they laughed and talked about their lives together so far.

The next day, the Taylor squad once again put a special patch on their uniform to memorialize long time coach and friend of Coach Timmons, Skip Prosser, who died suddenly in late summer. The Wake Forest team lacked the fire normally seen by this year's squad, and Taylor defeated them. It was an emotional victory for coach Timmons. Shane recognized his coach's despair, and so the big guy put his arm around his coach as they left the floor for the locker room.

Two days later, they were on a plane to Chestnut Hills, Massachusetts to play Boston College in the Conte Forum. It was cold and snowing when they landed, and Shane was not at all comfortable on the flight after watching them de-ice the plane before takeoff. They worked out that very afternoon after braving the cold to get there.

Boston College had a great guard in Tyrese Rice, and Dick Vitale warned Shane in the dinner meeting that if Tyrese got hot, to look out. Unfortunately, Dick's prophecy came true. In the first half, the Taylor defense just could not stop him, and he scored forty points in twenty minutes of play. The team walked around the locker room completely shell-shocked. Coach Timmons decided to play Jerry a bit in the second half.

The coach ranted and raved in the locker room, and they started the second half with Jerry on the court for the first time since his injury. He did not have his usual speed, but his perception of the game was as strong as ever. He made a few mistakes, but somehow he got his team fired up, and they went on two long runs leaving Boston scoreless, and won the game by fifteen points. Jerry and Billy took turns guarding Tyrese and together, they held him to just a few points in the second half. It was an amazing comeback, but due to the snowy weather, the Taylor boys were glad to be heading home to Lindle.

After the cold trip to the north, they wished they were playing Florida State back in sunny Florida, but it was their last home game of the season, and time to pay tribute to the seniors, all three of them. Billy got the most applause after doing an excellent job filling in for Jerry. For the next two games, Billy stayed in about half the time to help Jerry build up his stamina.

Florida State arrived with eagerness and ready to whip Taylor on their home court. Of course, the Taylor boys were not about to let that happen, as they were in a tie for first place with Duke for the league championship.

Shane became flustered on a foul he didn't think he made, went down the court and tried too hard to steal the ball, and got caught for a second foul, all in the course of the first six minutes of the game. The coach sat him down.

The Seminoles took this as a sign, stepped up both their offense and defense, and just about caught the Taylor team at the half.

Shane evaluated his play at the half and was not all happy. He decided to make several key adjustments after talking to his coach and some of his friends on the bench. Midway through the second half, he already led all scorers at twenty-two points, and Taylor was up twelve. They continued to push the ball, and gained a commanding lead of twenty-four points with two minutes to play. The coach called a timeout, put Billy and the two seniors who rarely got to play on the court, along with a few other boys on the bench, and they went to work racking up six more points before the buzzer. The starting five gave the team on the floor several standing ovations, lots of applause, and some laughing as well.

TJ Johnson

Billy spoke to the crowd afterwards with tears in his eyes, while his team and fans cheered him and the other seniors for all their hard work as players for Taylor University.

The final game of the season was another big one by playing Duke at on their home court at Cameron Indoor Stadium that was really an overgrown field house. It was always packed to the gills with the rowdy but clever Blue Devil fans, and after losing to them a month ago, the Taylor squad arrived with stoic game faces on the all the players, coaches, and even the managers.

Shane had trouble sleeping the night before, even after a long massage, longer sex, both playing top and bottom roles, and curling up in their favorite spooning sleeping position. He was just too pumped for the event.

Walter did TJ a favor and got him a seat on the team bus to make it easier for him to get into the game. The pressroom was packed, but he managed to eat some dinner with Dick Vitale and Walter.

Shane looked good in warm-up and came out of the locker room ready to play. This was his second trip to Cameron, and the last time he got his nose bloodied. He was not about to let that happen again.

Shane caught the tip, flung it to Jerry, and ran hard down the lane. Jerry flipped a behind the back pass to him, and Shane dunked it. The exciting precision play was meant to be a statement and it was. Shane guarded his man on the inbound pass and nearly stole it. Taylor pressed hard and sure enough, the Duke player made a bad pass that his coach caught on the sidelines. Coach K yelled obscenities. The battle had begun.

Taylor was up by six at the first four-minute mark for a television timeout. TJ had begun measuring play in four-minute intervals, as Taylor was always on television, and had grown used to the timing. Coach Timmons rarely called early timeouts, preferring to keep his team running up and down the court, and wearing out the competition. Taylor kept at least eight men in rotation and sometimes ten. Duke ran six. Coach Timmons knew that somewhere in the game, Duke was going to run out of gas.

He yelled at his team to keep up the speed, and to hustle hard on defense. Just before half, a frustrated Duke player fouled Shane hard after missing his shot the previous possession. Shane fell into the throng of Duke Students behind the goal. Everyone got out of his way. He missed the shot he had been attempting, and the students yelled and screamed as he shot the two fouls shots. Shane dished their jeers by making both shots. Taylor led by six points and in a Taylor-Duke game that was huge.

TJ barely made his way through the tightly packed crowd to the press room, finally took his chance to pee after standing in line, grabbed two water bottles and made his way back to his seat for the second half.

The coaches successfully fired up their teams in the locker room and for ten minutes, they traded shots back and forth, but just before the second television timeout, Shane was knocked down hard after completing one of his hook shots successfully. Coach Timmons called for an intentional foul, or two shots for a rough foul, but the referee gave him the usual one shot after making a completed goal.

TJ had flinched when Shane hit the floor hard on his side and skidded out of bounds into the feet of his fellow players as they sat on the bench. He got up a little slower than usual, and walked gingerly back to the foul line. He took his time, bounced the ball a time or two, and put the shot in the net.

There were eight minutes to play. During a timeout, Shane drank several gulps from his Gator-Aid® cup. He looked up to TJ as they came out on the floor. TJ gave him first the three sign for go, go, go, and followed by a two sign that made Shane grin.

Duke was bringing the ball in, and Shane was guarding the inbound pass. He had been watching his man carefully all night. He saw that he was still breathing hard although they just had a timeout. He gambled and dove hard to his right as the man through the ball in. Shane got just a finger on the ball, tapped it once to deflect and slow it down, then got a hand on it, and took off on a run. He dribbled just two times, leaped, and dunked it hard. It was a huge, emotional point.

TJ felt like he could see the backs of the Duke players' slump. The game continued to go back and forth, but Taylor began to spread their lead.

Jerry received the inbound pass with thirty-two seconds to go. Carefully, he weaved back and forth, passing the ball and then receiving it again, as they wasted the time clock. Finally, he took the last successful shot of the game with a beautiful three-point swish, announcing to all that he was back and ready to play. Duke attempted a follow-up shot that bounced short off the rim and fell out. The buzzer blew, and the disappointed Duke fans began to file out like they had just attended a funeral.

Shane jumped into the air, pumping his fist high over his head, leaping and smiling like he'd just a million bucks. He was so overwhelmed at beating Duke on their home court after losing to them four weeks prior. In the locker room, the entire team including the coaches did a silly jump drill they often did after a big game.

TJ rode with the team back on the bus, and he was thrilled to see the players so jubilant and excited. Once home, he wrote a long chapter on the victory and waited for Shane. They talked about the game, laughed, and were still excited at midnight. Shane struggled out of bed the next morning from the nerve wrecking game, his body bruised, his limbs sore, but it had been fun and they were victorious, and that made it worth the price he paid.

# FIFTEEN

They were no more games until their first game Friday night in the ACC tournament weekend. They were the top seed after beating Duke and winning the season title. They endured very hard practices on Monday, Tuesday, and Wednesday leaving little time to celebrate the victory over Duke.

On Sunday before tournament week, TJ surprised Shane with a dinner at Shane's favorite steakhouse. TJ met with the manager and arranged a dinner for two in the private area. On Sunday night, the room would be empty. He wouldn't answer any of Shane's probing inquisitive questions, but forced him to clean up and get in the car.

He parked at the side of the restaurant, and walked in through a side door, using a key loaned to him by the manager.

Shane laughed, "You stole the key?"

TJ grinned, "No, my friend loaned it to me so I could bring Mister Superstar in through a private door. Come on before someone spots us."

Once inside, Ron glanced over from the counter where he was preparing some drinks, picked up two menus, and introduced himself. "Hello TJ and Shane. I am so glad you came to join us for dinner tonight. No one knows you are here. Let me lead you to the table."

TJ gave Ron the key to the door and thanked him again for his help. They sat down, ordered ice tea, and began studying the menu. Shane said, "This may be the first time we have sat down in a restaurant to eat by ourselves in I don't know how long. This is fun."

TJ smiled, "You see it is possible to go out. You just have to do a little advanced planning. I'm starved. I hope you're hungry."

"I could probably eat anything as I know the coach is going to run the extra weight off in tomorrow's practice, but I will still eat healthy. I am thinking of having a T-bone steak, baked potato, mixed vegetables, salad, and some fruit. What are you ordering?"

"I'd like to have Shane on a stick," teased TJ, "but I doubt they serve that here. I'm going to have a rib-eye steak, creamy potatoes, green bean casserole, and salad."

"Hmm, that sounds good, too. I may have to eat off your plate as well! I'm so glad you thought of this. What a week we had beating Duke on their home court after such a close game. We really shut them down at the end. That was so much fun."

"How do you think you'll fair in the tournament?"

Ron came back for their orders after setting their drinks down. Once he was gone to the kitchen they continued with Shane saying, "I know better than to be confident, as many a good team has lost in the first game. The ACC teams are always at their best for the tournament. I think we will win the first and second round and play for the championship."

"How about the competition? Will you play Duke, Maryland, Clemson or Boston College?"

"Any of those could make it. I would hate to play Duke so soon after beating them, but it would solve the 'who's better' question by the winner achieving the best of the three games. Clemson is getting better every week, so I predict we'll end up playing them, as long as we don't get the big head and mess up."

"Jake called on Friday after you left for practice. I haven't had a chance to talk with you about it. We had a conference call last week with a potential publisher, he sent them copies of my gay books, and with his help and professional promotion, they are going to sign me to a five-year agreement, take over the current books with new releases and covers, and they want me to write and deliver two new books a year. They will heavily promote the gay fiction in all the gay publications, plus key websites, and send out press releases to all the gay periodicals. They want to do a promotional tie-in with the re-release of **Raceboys,** and they will be releasing **Gay Grifters** the first week of May. They want me to go on a tour of about ten major cities doing several books signing each day.

"Jake thinks we'll get a publisher for our basketball book that will release it the following week after the tournament winner, and they want me to on tour for that one as well. As a matter of fact, they want you to attend all the books signing you can, but they know you'll be pushing for exams."

"This is great news. I'm so happy about your books going mainstream. I could use the Learjet and catch up with you on the road. If I work ahead, I could leave after classes on Thursday. We'll see. Man, I'm so proud of you."

"I didn't do anything. I already wrote the books they are going to publish, but none of this would happen without the story about your backstage view of Taylor University Basketball. Of course, Dick Vitale and Walter Mills have been a big help, too. Jake is really delivering on his promises."

"I'll say. When you get the tour schedule worked out, send it to me so I can start trying to work it into my schedule. This will be a big change for us. All winter you have been following me around, and in the spring, I'll end up following your cute tail around. I guess that is fair."

"Two more things I have to tell you. Jake has sent **The War Apart - Part I** to three key directors he has worked with in the past on movie projects. He thinks that book will make a very good movie. At the least, it could end up on HBO, Showtime, or even the LOGO gay channel."

"Now that would be cool. I wonder who they will get to play Josh and Zeke?"

"I can't imagine. Of course, when I write, I often see my stories as movies in my head, and so it would be weird to see them as actual movies after I wrote the book."

"This is amazing news. What was the other thing?"

TJ waited while Ron placed their salads on the table along with a basket of hot yeast rolls, and platter of honey butter. TJ teased Shane by suddenly snatching the basket. "You shouldn't eat these, as they are not on your nutritious diet."

Shane grabbed the basket back, "I have you to know I need some carbohydrates, too. Pass the honey butter," he added with a grin.

TJ laughed at him and then began, "Well, we're going to be very busy right through to your exams. I know you will also have a busy time in the pickup games all summer. I was wondering what you thought about making a trip with me in the motorcoach right after your last exam. We could make a journey down the coast of Florida, spend some time in Key West, Miami, and Fort Lauderdale, then up the west coast to Naples, Pensacola, and maybe over to New Orleans. Would you like to?"

Shane grinned and said loudly, "Yes I would! That would be great."

"Wonderful. When is your last exam, and when do you have to be back for summer workouts?"

Shane thought for a second, "Well, believe it or not, just a few days after the end of the tournament we start playing our pickup games. It slows down some during exams, and then most folks disappear for a while to go home and spend time with their families. I think we could be gone three weeks in May, and return the first of June for summer league play, plus I'm taking four classes this summer to keep my senior year load down to a minimum."

"If you'll get me the dates, I'll plan our itinerary, and send it to you for you to agree on or make suggestions, etc. Nothing will be written in stone, so if you'd rather skip a town or visit one I didn't put on the list, that's easy to do. Alternatively, we can stay as long as we like anywhere. It will be fun to just get away. Would you like to go to a gay resort?"

"They have those?"

TJ waited while Ron removed their empty salad bowls, and set hot plates of their food before them. "Hmm, this smells so good. Yes, they do. There are several gay RV resorts around the country, although some of them are really just primitive campgrounds, and my motorcoach can't get in and out of them safely. I have been to one north of Johnson City and it was okay. I went to one in Georgia, just of north I-85 and it was much bigger. They have a very tight entrance that makes it tough on my coach, but plenty of open land once you're inside. They make a joke about the 'tight entrance' being a gay campground. They have a nice pool, cookouts, live shows, and it was fun, but I have to warn you that eighty percent of the crowd are the kind of gays that like leather and such, although they don't wear any at the park. It is also a clothes optional park, so you will see people walking everywhere in the nude. Once you get used to it, you almost forget about it. I wore shorts, but I did sunbathe and swim in the nude. It was fun. I met some nice guys, but no one I ever called.

168

"There are also several gay bed and breakfast places in Key West and Fort Lauderdale. I once stayed in a gay hotel in Miami and that was wild. There were men doing the nasty in the elevator. They had three dance bars, so the nighttime fun ends at dawn."

"I would probably be recognized," replied Shane between bites of the wonderful food.

"Perhaps, but I'm fine with you deciding to do something or not. It will be totally up to you. However, I think you could put a big sunhat on, dark glasses, and you might be okay. We'll see."

"Ok, but tell me about the trip plan. What ideas and destinations do you have?"

TJ finished another bite, sat back to sip on his ice tea, and replied, "I thought we would drive from here to Hilton Head and stay a day or two and hang out with my sister. My nephew might want to fly in to join us. On the island she has a longtime gay couple as best friends that would be very discrete should you want to have a quiet meal at their house, but we can swim, go to the beach, and go deep-sea fishing, although I'm not very good at it. The last time I went I caught a small stingray, and I couldn't get it off my hook. I also caught an old tire. Everybody laughed at my fishing abilities. Then we could go on down to Jacksonville and visit some longtime friends of mine that will just love meeting you. They are a very funny straight couple that has many gay friends. I was in their wedding when I was just seventeen so we have been friends a long time.

"Next up would be Daytona to visit my longtime best friend Rick and his partner Paul. They have a beautiful home just off the beach. Rick has helped me so many times through the years. You'll like them. Then we're on our own. We could cut over to Orlando and do a couple of fun things if you want to."

"Like what. I've been to Disney World®. I don't fit in the rides anymore."

TJ laughed, "I hadn't thought of that. What I was thinking of is they have an early morning Segway® tour before Disney opens. They go in groups of about twenty. Are you familiar with Segway®?"

"No, what's that?"

"It's those two wheel modern things you stand on and it drives you around based on which way you lean. Lean forward it goes forward. I have always wanted to try it while zooming around Disney World®."

"That sounds cool. What else?"

"Have you been to Sea World®?"

"No, we didn't have time when I was a kid to stop there."

"It is wonderful. So many amazing animal shows and exhibits to see. I could use your fame and maybe get you in the water with Shamu the killer whale."

Shane laughed, "Don't go doing me any favors."

TJ grinned. "After that I would head south to Fort Lauderdale. There is a gay RV resort there I have always wanted to stay in, but then we could just hang in the gay district. It is huge. They even have a gay shopping mall. There are thousands of gay people who live there. Next would be Key West. We'd stay in Bluewater Key, a very exclusive motorcoach only RV resort, and go in and out of Key West as much as we want. There is plenty to do in Key West. We could rent scooters to scout about the town, and take you on a resort scuba dive where you don't have to be certified while diving with a safely instructor."

"Are you certified?"

TJ smiled, "Yes, I'm certifiably crazy and in love with you."

Ron arrived with a huge bowl of ice cream. TJ said, "I took the liberty of ordering their giant banana split ice cream bonanza. We each get a spoon, so dig in."

Shane tasted his side of the big dish, "Yummy. This is so good."

TJ continued, "Yeah, I'm a certified diver. If you like the resort dives, we could arrange for you to be certified. It's not hard and you're good with math and learning stuff. I just hope they have fins in your size. Next would be Naples. It is on the Gulf Coast, and it is a beautiful and very rich area. We could do some shopping and eat very well there.

"In Pensacola, I was thinking of taking you to the Air Museum and the home of the Navy's Blue Angels. They have an IMAX® theater that is also cool, and the airplane museum is huge. We could gamble in Biloxi Mississippi at the casinos, or make it on over New Orleans. There are lots gay activities there if you're up to it.

"On the way home we could stop in the mountains, spend a few days, and just enjoy ourselves No timetables, no boarding passes, no security tags, and no deadlines to meet. How does that sound?"

"I can't wait to go. Thank you for the evening. The food, the conversation, the dessert, and your smiling wonderful face are all great."

TJ grinned wickedly, "You can thank me when we get home because I'm going to be the top first!"

TJ knew the tension inside Shane was growing as each day of pre-tournament practice became more intense. Shane agreed with some of the coaches that winning the season title should be the highest goal, as it far harder to win league games against your opponents than to win three games in a row at the end of a long season. However, they knew that once the first tip-off occurred on Thursday night between perhaps two teams with the worst records in the league, the competition began growing like a snowball rolling down a big hill.

For many college athletes, playing for three or four days in a row, against the best teams in arguably the toughest league in the country, is very difficult, tough on their bodies, and ending just four days before some of the

170

winners will play their first game in the NCAA's end of the year three weekend road to the championship.

Coach Timmons wanted to win every game, but he would not sacrifice the health of a player in the ACC Tournament, because winning the NCAA tournament was far more important. As he has said many times, and relayed by Shane to TJ, a game is still a game and we still want to win, so we'll play to win, and hope we are lucky enough to take the trophy home.

Taylor's first game was at noon on Friday and everybody in sports writing questioned how the number one seed ended up in one of the worst television spots in the tournament. Most of the Taylor fans and even those that hate them, would still be at work trying to sneak a peek at the game. Shane feared no one would be in the arena, as he often felt like the team fed off the energy of the their fans. However, he knew that even if no one were there, Taylor would win because they had the bigger heart, the larger drive, and the supreme goal of winning the national title.

After supper, Shane came over to the RV. He had just finished the last of their hard practices before tomorrow's trip to the tournament city. He hugged TJ as if he was either exhausted physically or mentally, so he held on to TJ longer than usual, kissed him longer, and then hugged him some more.

TJ smiled as Shane sat down in the recliner with a seemingly thud. TJ smiled and said, "I take it practice today was as hard as those on Monday and Tuesday?"

"Yeah it was, and yet it was the best practice ever. The team is fired up, and I don't mean just the starting five, but the squad we go against all season is pumped up as well. The beating and banging, the running and defending, the flow, the run, the fast break, and the full court press—all were elevated to a much higher level. We all knew it was good for us, but that's like saying if you run ten miles instead of five it will be better for you, but it is twice the distance."

"So you are saying the Taylor team is more than ready to play and win?"

Shane smiled, "Yes, we will win, because the tournament will be easier than going through those three days of practice. No one in the league will push as hard as our coaches and practice squad were."

"What time are you leaving in the morning?"

"We leave at nine, practice at eleven in the arena, and at two at a local gym. What time are you going?"

"I'm going to leave about the same time because rush hour will be awful both here and in Charlotte. I'm actually looking forward to driving, as I'll get a chance to see the countryside. I'm not looking forward to the traffic near the hotel so I'll get in there before lunch and hopefully the traffic will be down."

Shane stood, "If I beg, would you massage me?"

TJ laughed, "The price is far higher. You'll have to make love to me when I get done."

"I think I can do that," replied Shane slyly. "Come on, let's give it a try."

The team's bus got there faster than TJ, as they had a police escort and drove about eighty miles an hour on the interstate, and waited for no signal lights when they hit the local streets. Shane was surprised that so many Taylor fans were waiting for their arrival at the hotel, and cheered for them as they made their way to their rooms.

Thirty minutes later, the fans were still there cheering when they boarded the bus for the arena. This was the second time this season the Taylor team was scheduled to play a game in the big building that was home to the NBA's Bobcats. It was a massive place, but once on the court, Shane felt at home. This was a public practice, the kind the coach hated the most, but it was supposed to be good for the fans and thus good for the game. They did a long shoot around, and the last fifteen minutes of the scheduled hour, they ran some drills, and then made their exit to the bus.

They would eat lunch, rest an hour, attend a team meeting for going over scouting reports for their first opponent, receive their player assignments, and then board the bus once more for a trip to a local high school gym for a private practice. The team managers, the athletic department leaders, and their hired security team arrived an hour earlier to secure the building.

No one was allowed in the gym including the school principal. Local police took care of the parking lot, and patrolled the building. Taylor's people guarded every door. This assured the coaches they could talk as freely as they did in their home gym.

This practice was not as hard as those earlier in the week, but they were important. Plays were run until perfection was achieved. Defense strategies were put into practice and achieved. The later half of the practice was dedicated to the unknowns: tied games, overtime drills, key players fouled out, injuries, and inbound ball players both offensively and defensively. The coach expected the team to be confronted with at least one overtime game, as the competition in the ACC had never been higher. He also knew that Murphy's Law would happen in all three games when a solid experienced player would make a dumb mistake. He'd shoot when there was plenty of time on the clock, step out of bounds when the score was tied, he'd miss foul shots when he was the best shooter on the team, or he'd let his man disappear for a dunk. It happened all the time, but the pain of these mental breakdowns remained with him for most of the off-season.

TJ stopped at a grocery store a few miles from his hotel to stock enough groceries to get him through four days in Charlotte. He also knew Shane would have many opportunities to camp out in the room with him, so

172

he bought more food than usual, including fresh fruit and vegetables. In the last few blocks of his long drive, he noted the nearby restaurants and spotted an ice cream creamery just a block away. He was looking forward to making a sweet stop one night before or after a game.

He was also looking forward to some meals with Shane's folks, as well as TJ's friends from Asheville. He talked to Gary on the way down, and the longtime Taylor fan was already pumped up about the upcoming game on Friday. All four managed to get off of work and would arrive early so they wouldn't miss a single moment of the game.

He checked in, set up his laptop, and took a moment to test his high-speed connection, as some hotels advertised Wi-Fi, but had poor signal quality. He recently began calling and quizzing the hotels carefully about their Internet service after a bad experience in Boston. After that experience, he began carrying an air card as a backup. After unpacking his clothes to avoid some wrinkles, he grabbed his jacket, made his way down the elevator, out of the beautiful hotel with the vast lobby the size of a football field, and walked to a Mexican restaurant he noted on his way in. He stopped and bought a pile of newspapers from a local vender including the Charlotte Observer, the USA Today, and the Atlanta Constitution.

He read the first paper while waiting for his lunch order of his favorite chimichanga with beans and rice. The coverage for the ACC tournament was amazingly huge, especially when compared to the other similar league contests taking place around the country. An entire special section had been created in the newspapers, and TJ read every article about the Taylor team, Shane in particular, the ACC teams, and the other college teams receiving coverage.

If he read a particular point or view he liked, he marked it with his pen. Upon returning to his room, he would put the comments into his laptop for review, as the march to the title continued. Shane teased him about his new yellow highlighter that was shaped just like a regular pen, telling TJ he looked like a geek with two pens in his pocket. It wasn't long of course, until Shane was using the same pen on his homework. TJ grinned as he bought a whole a dozen of the markers.

The meal was good and cheap for downtown tournament prices and he tipped the waiter generously. He buttoned up his coat as the wind was blowing as it should in March, stacked up his newspapers, and made his way back to the hotel.

He changed to comfortable clothes, poured a glass of caffeine free Diet Pepsi®, and sat down at the computer to write in what he learned from the newspapers. Once completed, he began going online reading the national reporters and sportscasters. He started with his friend Dick Vitale's article on the ESPN® site, followed by Fox Sports®, and on to Sports Illustrated®.

He then read the volume of information the Taylor athletic office put together on the history of Taylor in past tournaments, and the latest releases for tomorrow's starting game. He finished by thumbing through the media tournament book produced by the league's office. Walter left a copy for him at the front desk.

By six, he was exhausted with information overload. He stood up and walked to the window to check out the sun setting over the mountains to the west when the phone rang. He flipped open his cell phone and smiled as he saw the caller ID.

"Hey, how are you? I missed you."

Shane replied, "I missed you, too. What room are you in?"

TJ toyed with him, "I'm on the seventh floor. Just knock on doors until you find me."

Shane laughed, "I could do that, or I could tell you that I'm very horny."

TJ grinned, "In that case I'm in seven twenty-two. I will hold the door for you."

Shane busted out laughing, "I'll be there in a minute."

"Hurry," replied TJ as he hung up and walked to the door.

Friday morning came too soon for the team after a hard week of practice and eating a team meal at eight in the morning was always weird according to Shane. He dined on steak and eggs, grits, whole-wheat toast, and his favorite strawberry jam, and finished with a plate of fruit.

There was a brief team meeting afterwards, followed by a mandatory study hall with the teachers working with them, as it was a school day. The coaches felt studying might be the only way to try and take the game off their minds, as the long wait until game time would be tough. He also didn't want them to go back to a deep sleep, but he would allow a good thirty-minute nap. They boarded the bus at ten and feeling a bit odd to prepare so early for a tournament game. They had done things like this when they were on the west coast or even Alaska or Hawaii, but in their own time zone, it just felt weird to them. They were all yawning as the left the bus for the locker room.

TJ took a cab to the arena, and came in through the back using both his team authorized press pass and more importantly to the ACC guys, his official ACC press pass presented to him by Walter in person. In recent years, security at the tournaments had become a top priority. They knew that one day, a diehard fan might step over the line and injure an upcoming opponent's star player. Taylor officials took this seriously as well and were always on guard for their team's security. Walter brought along four state highway patrolmen for additional protection for players and coaches. During the tournament, he would double that guardianship.

TJ made his way to the basketball court, walked around it, and up to the pressroom floor. The room was larger than any he had seen during the season. He felt it was size of a Walgreens pharmacy. He was given a press kit as he entered the room, found a desk, put his laptop in the cabinet, and went to the buffet line before it became a sea of hungry newsmen. The food was spectacular with lots of variety, and he chose roast beef, mashed potatoes with a little gravy, cream corn, green beans, and apple pie for dessert.

He had almost finished when a big guy walked up behind him placing his hands on his shoulders. "How's my favorite writer doing?"

TJ turned to see the smiling, friendly face of Dick Vitale, "I'm great. How are you?"

Dick sat down beside him, "I'm nervous. Before a game, I feel like a player, and I pace back and forth while mentally psyched to play. I can't wait for game time to come, although this is an unnatural hour to be playing. Taylor is the top team in the country and they put them at noon. What were they thinking?"

TJ laughed, "I know. Shane managed to sleep, but let's hope he's awake when the whistle blows."

"I doubt we have to worry about that. He could score in his sleep. He's a champion and the champions always soar. He'll do great. It's me I'm worried about. I hope I don't yawn when the camera is on me."

"I think you'll do fine."

"Listen, I'm glad I caught you. The last chapter on the Duke game was fantastic. You gave the reader a great feel for what it is like in the Duke hot box. I must lose twenty pounds of water during that game. I have watched it twice already. Our coverage was good, but your writing made the game come alive. You're good. Did you get my comment for your book jacket sleeve?"

"Yes, and it was perfect. I assume after they win you'll want to up date it."

"Yes, of course. How's the food? I'm starved."

TJ smiled, "The roast beef was great and the apple pie melts in your mouth."

"Okay, I'll try that, but don't tell my wife about the pie. She's coming to the game by the way. She is doing some shopping in Charlotte while she is here. I bet she spends an easy thousand dollars. Well, I'd better go eat. Go Taylor, and I'll see you later."

"Thank you. Good luck on the broadcast."

Florida State had been beaten twice already by Taylor this year, and they were not happy about it. They came to the arena ready for revenge. The Taylor team would have trouble shaking off the fact they had beaten Florida State already, and may not have taken seriously their determination to whip them in the first round of the tournament.

Florida won the tip with a huge leap by their center, knocking the ball to their point guard, who flung the ball to a sprinting forward, who promptly dunked the ball over Shane. This did not sit well with him. He took the ball out and threw it to Jerry, who was almost back to his normal speed, and he needed it, as Florida applied a full court press.

Shane wisely moved to half court and waited for a screen for Jerry or a toss to him if Jerry became cornered. Jerry breezed by him at full speed and so close that the man guarding him ran smack into Shane who was at least six inches taller. It knocked him to the floor, leaving Shane smiling as he sprinted down the court. For a few seconds, Taylor had Florida five to four on the floor. Their big guy picked up Shane. Jerry threw the ball hard to Larry, but as Shane broke down the line, Larry tossed it to him. Shane sensed a double team on him and tossed it right back to Larry who immediately fired off a three-point shot.

For the next twelve minutes, the game went back and forth until Taylor pulled to a ten-point lead. Florida called a timeout hoping to stem the flow of the game. They changed to a zone defense, but this made it a little easier for Shane to shake free, and in the closing minutes of the first half, he put in six points including two foul shots. Taylor led by eight at the half.

The coach knew they were not playing up to speed at this early hour, but they showed signs of normalcy near the end of the half so he let it go. He did point out their mistakes, made some changes to their strategy, and sent them back to win the game.

Shane went dry for four minutes on offense, but his defense had been outstanding. He stole the ball twice in the second half, pulled down seven rebounds, three assists, four straight foul shots, and led all scorers at twenty-eight points. Taylor won eighty-two to seventy.

Shane and two other players were selected for the after game press conference. If there was anything Shane hated in the game of basketball, it was press conferences. He barely tolerated interviews, but at least those were one to one, and he enjoyed the conversation style interviews. He'd grown accustom to microphones stuck in his face after a game, but sitting in a room filled with a hundred media folks firing off questions was a bit unsettling, but he did the best he could. He wouldn't know until he saw the replays that he never once smiled during his time on the camera.

TJ attended the press conference as a spectator with no intention of asking any questions, but anxious to hear how Shane responded, as well as to the longer responses from his coach. Afterwards, he returned to the pressroom to retrieve his laptop, stopped at the dessert table, and received a tall cone of frozen strawberry yogurt. He began licking and walking, and finished it by the time he made it out of the big building and onto the street. He tossed the remains in the trash, caught a cab, and made his way to hotel.

TJ had been writing for over an hour about the game when Shane appeared at his door. They had known he would have dinnertime free, so TJ changed clothes after a barrage of kisses from his favorite top scorer—both on and off the court. They went down the back stairs, caught a cab, and made their way to Vince's Italian Restaurant.

As they got out of the cab, Shane immediately spotted his mother and walked over to give her a hug. TJ caught up after paying for the cab, and hugged her as well just as Al walked up from parking their rental car. Together, they went inside and found Gary and his gang in the far corner at a table set for eight. TJ and Shane gave Gary, Chris, Tammy, and Scrappy big hugs, introduced them to Shane's parents, and they all sat down to study the menus and talk about the game.

TJ ordered chicken Francesca pasta with salad. Shane went for chicken Parmesan and when the salads arrived, they all dug in. Shane ate all of his salad and half of TJ's. His mother laughed at his voracious appetite, but she had seen him eat like this all his life, and knew he would burn it off about as fast as he chewed. Surprisingly, he declined dessert, as he and TJ had a plan for afterwards.

Gary asked many questions about the game, as well as the match up with Virginia Tech tomorrow. Shane answered politely, but quickly asked how things were going in Asheville, and wondered if the leaves were returning to the trees with spring fast approaching. He longed to return to the mountains once more, and maybe even go down the waterslide and land in the cold pool.

TJ talked with Al and Barbara about the basketball book, and the response he was getting from the pre-book readers. They were as excited as he was. TJ said he would them a copy by email this weekend. They agreed to meet TJ for lunch the following day, but Shane would be waiting for practice to start.

Shane and TJ asked the cab driver to let them out about a block from the hotel. They rushed inside the creamery TJ spotted on arrival, went in, and immediately made their order. Shane got a banana split with extra strawberries, TJ settle in for an order of pistachio ice cream with bananas, nuts and a dash of whipped cream. They walked to the back entrance of the hotel eating their delicious dessert.

TJ made his way to the bathroom, so Shane set up his laptop for him. He planned to go online to check his email, but on a lark decided he would read TJ's pages on the game, something he had done many times, so he clicked on documents to find it. He always had trouble with the sensitive mouse pad on TJ's laptop and scrolled too far down. When the list stopped, he noted a folder marked "RV Port Home." He had never heard this phrase and clicked on the file out of curiosity.

Inside the folder, he found several files labeled: floor plan one, floor plan two, building view, home view, outside view, and so forth. He double-clicked the first one and a drawing software package opened the file. On the screen, he saw a large top view of a building TJ had drawn. He clicked on a button marked three-sixty view, and instantly the angle dropped to the ground and began rotating around the building. Shane quickly realized the front of the building had a long porch leading to the front door, it moved counter-clockwise where he could see a double car garage and next to it was a large garage door. He realized this taller door was for the motorcoach. The view continued around the back where he could see utilities drawn in, and on to the far side where he saw a second garage door. He zoomed out noting a long slow curve driveway to enter the building from one side and exit the other.

Shane clicked on the next file, which was a vertical view looking down into the structure as if the roof had been removed. He could see the motorcoach parked in the rear of the building, two cars in the garage, and inside he noted the kitchen, office, bedrooms, great room, wet area for Jacuzzi, sauna, and such, and storage in the back of the building.

TJ came up behind him, put his hands on his big shoulders, and leaned over. "Ah, you found my drawings."

"This is amazing. I didn't know you were working on this. It is beautiful."

"I started it about two years ago. I guess I missed having a home building for maintenance of the coach, as well as updating. I had to teach myself this simpler CAD program, but slowly I'm getting better at it. "Watch this. This is a virtual view of the house."

TJ clicked on a button and the screen became like a camera taking Shane through the front door, into the various rooms, and eventually through the kitchen into the car garage and into the RV garage.

"This is so cool. I love the house. We should build it."

"I don't think I can afford to build a house. Maybe after the book is released, and if we get lucky with sales."

Shane's face lit up, he turned and kissed TJ, and led him to the couch where they made out for a while. Finally, he was ready to talk, "I guess I've been so busy getting through the basketball season, and trying hard to improve my play, that I didn't stop and think about you and me after the season. I know you have two book tours while I get ready for my exams, then we have a three-week vacation planned, but what are you going to do during summer league play?"

TJ replied quickly, "I thought I'd fly to Africa and chase some elephants around. Why? What did you have in mind?"

Shane laughed and playfully squeezed his knee. "You're weird. I don't want you to go far without me. I'd be going to class in the mornings, workouts, and playing some hot games in the afternoon, but my evenings and weekends would be free. I will be able to sleep with you every night. I think we should build this house."

"I don't even know what it would cost. I was going to do most of the work myself, but you only have one more year here, and then you'll be gone to some big city that has a pro team."

178

"Wrong! We'll be going somewhere to play pro ball. I am not going without you."

TJ smiled, "Are you sure? You've only known me about eight months."

"Eight wonderful months, and besides I know you intimately, or should I say inside and out."

TJ laughed, "Don't go getting me horny again."

"TJ, I love you with all my heart. I think having a home will make it easier for us next year. We could keep the home when I go pro, or sell it and make a profit."

"Where would we get the money?"

"Well, I'll run it by my dad, but I think we should call Sam Minton, and let him figure out how we can do it. If we had a construction crew build it, take a guess at how much it would cost."

"Half million maybe seven hundred thousand. We'd know more after an architect worked on it?"

"Your plans look ready to go, why do we need an architect?"

"Because I'm not licensed, and we have to obtain building permits and there are codes for electrical, plumbing, and so forth that I don't have the knowledge for. He'll take my drawings, figure out any mistakes I made, bring it up to code, and then he can give us a cost analysis."

"Well, why don't you get started on that when we get home? I'm going to call dad to see what he thinks."

Shane made the call while TJ went to his laptop to check on his email, and make some notes in the computer. Shane talked to his dad for about a half hour before saying goodbye.

"Well, dad agrees with me. He thinks there would be a tax advantage for me to own a home when we sign with the NBA. He said we should call Sam, too. Here, use my phone. Call him."

TJ laughed, "It's ten o'clock. I will email him and see if he wants to talk about it, or I'll call him tomorrow."

"Okay, but you'll do it, right? We'll have to find some land when we get back. I hope we can stay close to Taylor to make it easy for me to go back and forth. I want to spend as many nights with you as possible. I am beginning to hate living in the dorm." He stopped and looked at his watch. "I've got to go."

TJ stood and Shane bear hugged him, they kissed long and deep, and said goodnight.

TJ returned to his laptop and typed out a paragraph to Sam asking his thoughts about building a house with the motorcoach facility, an office, and could he arrange a loan?"

He sent the email, undressed, and went to the bathroom. Just as he was finishing, his cell phone rang.

"Hello?"

"TJ, this is Sam. How are you?"

"I'm great."

"That was a fantastic game. Are we winning tomorrow, too?"

"Shane says yes, though Virginia Tech will be a tough one."

"I received your note on the house. What kind of money do you need?"

TJ swallowed hard, "I'm going to get my plans to an architect to bring it up to code, and give me a cost analysis, but I'm guessing five to seven hundred thousand plus the land cost."

"Okay, so let's say a million. I don't think that would be a problem. I'll get the loan set up so they're no payments until we see how much the book brings in, or we wait until Shane gets his signing bonus. So this is not a problem, go for it. Keep me posted and I'll be watching tomorrow."

"Thanks Sam. I appreciate it. I'll be in touch."

TJ hung up in shellshock from just receiving approval to build the RV home he had been dreaming about for years. It would be tough going to sleep, as his head spun with all kinds of ideas floating around for tweaking construction of his dream house.

Shane was allowed to sleep in and ate the team meal at ten with the game time set for two o'clock. TJ tried to sleep in but dreams of the house kept running through his head. He ordered room service breakfast, and snatched up the newspaper under his door. He read all the articles on the game, and put the notes in the computer.

After breakfast, he began searching for land for sale near the university. He knew that it wouldn't be easy, as the school was constantly expanding, and there were huge housing developments under construction to handle the growth. Two hours later, he listed several sites he wanted to view. He called the realtors listing the land, and had them email him the plats and any pictures they had. He really hit it off with the last realtor, so he explained what he was planning to build, and asked for a suggestion for an architect that would use his drawings. She gave him her top choice.

He began searching the web for this guy's work. He found a website for him and began scrolling through picture after picture of his designs. TJ didn't see a single home for less than million and immediately became worried. On a lark, he dialed the number listed.

He almost hung up after third ring when a man answered, "This Bobby Jenkins. May I help you?"

TJ grinned, as he had the man he wanted on the phone. He told the guy he had been referred by the realtor. He described the RV port home to him, his floor plan, and asked if he would be interested in taking a look and perhaps drawing the final plans for the house. To his surprise, the man said yes. He had seen a few port homes in Florida and wondered why they hadn't caught on in North Carolina with so many folks moving here. TJ made an appointment for Monday afternoon. He already had several appointments to go look at the land he found. He felt it was going to be an exciting day.

Shane called about ten-thirty, and just before time to head to the arena. TJ related all he found starting with Sam's approval, the realtors, and finally the architect. Shane was as excited as he was, but he also had a game to think about. They discussed how he felt, was the team ready, and soon had to say goodbye.

TJ had some time left, so he worked on the plans a bit more, and called the front to see if they could print them out for him. They gave him a password to their business center in-house website. He sent the files to the printer, and then walked downstairs to pick them up. He ran into Al and Barbara who had arrived for their lunch date in the hotel restaurant.

They ordered their lunch, and Al began asking about the house. TJ made room on the table and began showing the plans to them. They had never heard of a RV port home. TJ explained what Sam said, Al and Barbara had apparently talked about it, too and they agreed the house would be good for their son and TJ. After the meal, they took the elevator up to TJ's room where he demonstrated the virtual view of the home on the laptop. He also showed pictures of the land he found. He thought for a second and asked them, "This house was drawn when it is was only me moving in. What does Shane need in a house to be happy and enjoy it as much as I would? I already figured I would redraw the office and make it big enough for both of us, as well as the walk-in closet, as he has lots of stuff."

Barbara replied immediately, "He'll need a lot of shoe and hat storage, and his clothes are long so the closet bars need to be up high."

TJ grinned, "There you go. I hadn't thought of that. Thanks."

Al spoke up, "I've built a few metal buildings in my time, and it seems to me if you add to the length of it you could expand the wet area for exercise machines, weights, and perhaps build a basketball half court."

TJ's face lit up. "Oh my gosh! Yes, then he could practice at home on his shooting skills. Way to go, Al. I'll start redrawing later tonight. I'd better put in an extra car garage, too. Whew, this is exciting!"

Together, they took a cab to the arena, but separated as they dropped TJ off at the rear, while Al and Barbara drove around to the front with the rest of the ticket holders. TJ made his was to the pressroom, picked up his media notes for the game, locked his laptop in the locker, and looked up at the video display to see Shane making his way onto the court. TJ walked down the steps to watch him warm up.

Shane smiled at him as he began stretching, but he had his game face on, expecting a hard battle from the Virginia Tech team.

After warm-up, TJ secured a water bottle from pressroom and made his way down the steps to the floor, walked around to the entrance to the tunnel, and caught sight of Shane. He gave him a five-finger sign for Shane to chill, and then the one sign for love. Shane pulled his ear acknowledging the signal and winked at him. TJ went back to his seat as they took the floor.

The game began with a big mess for Shane. The ball was tipped towards him. He just put his hands on it and ready for a fast break for a score, but slipped on the ACC decal in the center court, and fell flat on his face losing the ball to a Tech player. It was so sudden, he didn't prepare to slide as they practiced, and receive an elbow and knee burn, as well as lots of embarrassment. He jumped to his feet and began his defense of their goal by picking up and guarding his man.

Shane kept his cool, but Tech scored a two-point shot from the top of the key. Shane bought the ball in quickly to Jerry who sprinted up the floor. Shane rushed up behind him and just as Jerry tossed it to Larry, Shane continued his run down the lane. Larry tossed him the ball and Shane went up to shoot, and was blocked hard by their big man and a foul was called as hands scraped Shane's face. Shane was pissed at the block. However, he settled down and made both foul shots tying the game.

Back and forth, the lead changed hands. Shane stayed on his man hard, but didn't foul him. Their big man had two fouls in first fourteen minutes of the game, and his coach took him out. Shane saw this as a break, and told the starters in a huddle he thought he could get open. The ball was thrown back and forth, and then in to Shane. He shot a short jumper and made it. Two plays later, he was farther out at fourteen feet and made it. The next time he got the ball, he drove hard and dunked it. Taylor led at the half by four.

The tech boys returned for the second half fired up, and after several mistakes, the Virginia boys took the lead by six. After the second television timeout, Taylor re-fired their play, and did a ten-point run that put them up by four. Nevertheless, they couldn't relax as Tech soon tied it up.

At four minutes to go, Shane was called for a foul, and their big guy put both shots in. They were up by two. The coach used the television timeout to settle his team down. He told them they would win, and they should just chill out and play their game, but at the end of the speech, he asked them for a stop. He did not want Tech to score for the next three minutes.

Shane looked up to TJ who signaled a three for go, go, go and Shane was ready to do just that. Taylor had the ball so Shane brought it in. He tossed it to Jerry who made his way into his home court. The ball went back and forth and with the clock ticking down, Jerry flung it to Shane at the top of the key. Shane turned, jumped, shot, and sunk a two-point shot tying the game.

Taylor went into their full court press with their talent knob turned way up. Shane had been watching his man carefully bring the ball in throughout the game. Shane had yet to take advantage of a little hint of a throw he picked up. Now was the time. As the guy prepared to toss it to the mid court, Shane jumped, got a hand on the ball, and dropped it beside him.

He picked it up, dribbled once, and sailed through the air. Their big man tried to block it, but caught Shane hard on the shoulder knocking him to the ground. The ball fell through the net. He got up quickly and walked to the foul line with a grin. He sank the extra shot and now they were up by three.

Tech brought the ball in again, but they could not make the play, and shot wildly before the shot clock buzzed, and Shane pulled down the rebound. Jerry set up a play call the green monster. They tossed the ball in to Shane in the paint, and he was immediately double-teamed. Larry's man had been a part of that. Larry quickly ran to the corner and Shane flung the ball to him. Larry caught it, jumped, shot and it was a swish. They were now up six.

Taylor was still holding Tech to zero points, but at the one-minute mark, Larry fell while guarding his man, and the Tech player hit a three, dropping the score to Taylor up by just three.

Down the court, they went with Jerry trying to use up as much time as possible. He shot as the last few seconds ticked off the shot clock, and it hit the rim and fell out. Shane was boxed out, and Tech had the ball with twenty-eight seconds to play. If they hit a three, they could tie the game. If they shot a three and Taylor fouled the shooter, they could shoot a foul shot to win.

The coach called for a stop. Shane was all over his man, but being careful not to foul. Larry had his man contained until he was caught in a screen. In an effort to catch his man, he ran too fast, and bumped him before he could prepare to shoot. The whistle blew for a foul. The coached sighed heavily as the infamous Murphy's Law error had just happened to his team.

Tech's player was very nervous but because of the Taylor's team fouls; he had a one and one situation. If he hit the first shot, he would get a second one. Swish! He hit the first and Taylor now only led by two. He fired his second shot. Rim! The ball bounced off. Shane had the rebound but came down in a pile of Tech boys who ripped the ball from his hands with ten seconds to go.

They tossed the ball out to their guard who shot for a three. Rim! Shane went up for the rebound, but Tech got it again. They tossed it back out with four seconds to go. Rim! They missed a final time. Shane jumped hard and came down with the ball as the buzzer blew. Taylor had won by two in a very hard fought game.

# SIXTEEN

The game was at one o'clock, so the team meal was at nine. Shane ate carefully, trying not to chew too quickly, and avoiding any digestive problems. Afterwards, he came up to TJ's room. They talked over the plans TJ made to see the land and architect. Shane looked at the pictures of the houses Bobby Jenkins designed, and felt confident the man could do the job if they could afford him. TJ showed Shane some changes he made to the house including a bigger car garage, office and master walk-in closet, but finally the wet area as he called it with the workout stuff, and the half court for basketball practice. He asked Shane how tall the ceiling had to be. TJ made a note while Shane grinned as he went back over the plans. He was already looking forward to living there with TJ.

They talked about the game while TJ made some notes until TJ's breakfast arrived via room service. Somehow, Shane was still hungry and ate some of TJ's fresh fruit. Together, they read the articles about the game in the newspaper, and TJ once again made notes as to what Shane thought about the articles.

Shane laughed at a quote. TJ asked what was so funny.

Shane replied, "The reporter asked if I thought Clemson was as good as last year. I said they were better than last year, and the year before since this is the third year I've played against the Tigers. The newspaper says I said Clemson is far better than last year."

TJ grinned, "I guess the writer went to Clemson, or the editor needed to shorten the sentence."

"But it is a quote," protested Shane. "It should be exactly as I said it."

"Yeah, I know. I guess times are changing and everything is printed in short sentences and sound bites. I guess this is a good reason to be careful about your responses to media questions. Don't feel you have to answer quickly, pause and maybe repeat the question to give you more time to think. For example, do you think Clemson is better than last year, you would reply, you're asking if I think Clemson is better than last year, and while repeating the question, your brain is thinking about a good answer."

Shane asked, "What would have been your response?"

"Clemson sucks!"

The short sharp reply bowled Shane over with laugher. "Now that is what I should have said!" They both laughed hard.

TJ added slyly, "However, Clemson does make good ice cream." Shane laughed again. The comic relief helped him greatly with his pre-game tension.

Shane left at ten-thirty to return to his room, pack, and head down the elevator to the team bus. TJ hauled his stuff to his car, then returned to the front desk to check out, and made his way to the arena. It was almost two hours before game time, and fans were already arriving, but he managed to get a good parking spot in a nearby parking garage.

The pressroom was a buzz when he arrived there so he ate lunch, and then sat down at his laptop to read and make notes on the pregame press release. This game attracted at lot of press, particularly from South Carolina and parts of George where thousands of fans supported Clemson. Walter came by for a chat as did Dick, but they all seemed as nervous as he was. This was the last game before the NCAA tournament committee made their final choices, and hopefully, they would pick Taylor as the number one seed, and put them in the bracket that was closer to home for the first four games.

Later, TJ walked down to watch Shane warm-up the court, and around the court to sit with Shane's parents after they arrived for the game. They talked about next week's travel plans, assuming Taylor ended up the number one seed. They would be flying in each of the next three tournament weekends, as long as Taylor kept winning.

TJ waved at Dick Vitale as he came around the court. He politely came up the aisle and shook hands with Shane's parents, and had many good things to say about their son's performance, drive, and discipline. He then added, "TJ's writings about your son's thoughts behind the scenes has been wonderful. I can't wait for the finished edition. Well, time for me to get to work. I think Taylor is going to pull off another victory, but who knows in the ACC. It was nice to see you again."

Al and Barbara were pleased to see Dick, while enjoying his comments about their son and TJ. TJ replied that Dick only knows one way to act, so he is the same on and off the air.

TJ winked at Shane as he made his way around the court, while returning to the pressroom. He nervously decided to eat dessert and chose a slice of pecan pie with ice cream. He devoured it, grabbed a water bottle, and walked down to his seat.

He watched the time clock before finally making his way to the tunnel where he found Shane in the back of a long line of Taylor players waiting on introductions of the team. TJ gave him a five and one sign. Shane could only wink in a reply. He was excited and wanted to keep his mind focused on his game.

The Taylor team already beat Clemson twice this year by two-points at their home field, and a last minute shot, and in overtime by ten-points on Taylor's home court. However, ACC Tournament history showed that all bets were off when it came to championship play. The sportswriters picked Taylor to win, but only by two points. They described the game as a battlefield. Clemson had no intention of losing three in a row to Taylor, and Taylor needed a win, assuring their number one seed in the NCAA tournament.

Shane was introduced with great applause from the Taylor fans and TJ cheered as loudly as he could. It helped release some of the stress swirling inside him.

Shane came out of the team huddle with a forbearing face displaying no emotion, a face that almost scared his Clemson counterpoint as Shane looked as if he had gone psycho, and was about to commit murder. Clemson caught the tip and scored the first basket. Taylor countered with a basket. Back and forth, the game progressed and Taylor led at the half by four. Shane had one foul but Clemson's forward had two. Jerry had been on fire scoring ten points, eight assists, and no turnovers. Larry put in eight, and Shane had ten with four fouls shots.

The coach had been a bit harsh at some obvious mental mistakes by his team in the first half, but he also criticized their lack of drive and effort. He told them if they didn't improve in those areas quickly, they would not go far in the NCAA tournament. However, he followed those comments with many positive ones. He finished by telling them he knew they could win if they became tougher on defense, and worked the ball for the great shots on offense. The team returned to the floor with substantial determination to play better and win.

The next eight minutes Taylor was flawless, pushing the lead up to eight points, but Clemson fought back. Shane picked up two fouls, but the Taylor defense did a miraculous job of holding back Clemson's good shooters, often preventing their team from getting more than one attempt per possession.

With four minutes to play, Shane was fouled going up for a layout, and to everyone's surprise Shane made the shot with not one, but three Clemson players hanging on to his shoulders for the ride. Unfortunately, he came down hard on the floor knocking the breath out of him. Shane knew he was okay, but until he got some wind in his lungs, he remained still. The loud boisterous fans filling the arena fell silent, including the fans of Clemson. Taylor's biggest star remained motionless on the court.

Suddenly Shane stirred, gasped hard, took a few quick breaths, and rolled on to his knees and stood up. He face was pale, but with more breaths, his color returned. The referee asked if he was okay, and Shane replied with a bit of wit, "Where'd that freight train come from?"

The referee grinned and said he was shooting one shot. The audience sighed. Shane's teammates huddled around him, called for a full court press after the shot, and Shane reassured his teammates they were going to win the game. They smiled and asked if enjoyed his nap. Shane laughed, the referee threw him the ball, and he made the shot.

The battle was far from over, as Clemson continued to score well, but Taylor kept making their defense as aggressive as ever. Finally, Shane managed a steal, and tossed the ball to a running Larry for an easy layout. A minute later, the game was over, with Taylor winning by only five points. It had been a great game, and Clemson had nothing to hang their heads for. They had fought very well, but Taylor was just too strong.

Most tournament winners are ecstatic over a tournament victory, but Taylor remained subdued by only cutting down one net. Winning had been their desire, but their goal for the year was to win the NCAA title, so the tournament was just a stepping stone on their way to success for the year.

Shane slept over Sunday night after returning home from the excitement and commotion after the NCAA tournament committee announced the Taylor team as the number seed in the nation. Walter and his staff immediately went to work following through with their plans for hotels, restaurants, practice gyms and security staff. TJ drove home safely, and forced himself to write the end of the tournament chapter in the book. Together, they enjoyed a long massage and sex session before falling asleep. Shane was up at seven and made his way to class. TJ took care of confirming his hotel for the week, as they would be playing the following weekend in Raleigh. The NCAA had a block of hotel rooms reserved, but Walter forwarded the information to TJ, while relaying he placed a reservation in TJ's name. TJ was most grateful for Walter's help, because the hotel was sold out. However, TJ stayed on the phone for twenty minutes, while the reservation clerk moved him to a different floor, and to the rear of the building, with floor with no teams staying on it.

By nine, he left the RV with a folder in hand of the printouts of the land he was going to look at it. He called the realtor of the first lot and together, they drove to a lot that was about the right size, but it was too steep for his motorcoach plans. He thanked her and moved on to the next one.

A male realtor met him for this one, but the road there was very curvy and in bad shape with many potholes. The property was a virtual forest requiring a lot of work. TJ declined, thanked the realtor, and moved on.

This pattern of rejection continued all morning, until he met Jennifer at noon. The road in was in good shape. The location was just a few miles from their current location, but only a mile from the interstate, making access for the motorcoach a breeze. TJ knew it would also make runs to the airport easier. He brought it up on the GPS software on his laptop, and it measured just over nine miles from Shane's dorm, making it a doable drive for the basketball star.

He stood on the road in front of the property with the plat of the lot in his hands. It was five acres and for the most part the property was level, with just a slight decline to the rear of the property. TJ began to envision his RV port home on the property. He turned his head left and right, imagining the entrance and exit of the motorcoach. He turned around to see the view they would see out the breakfast room windows. It was of a small forest of beautiful trees.

Wisely, Jennifer said, "The lot on this side of the road is pretty, but not capable of building on, as it has an underground spring. It will always be a forest, and you won't have to buy it to keep it that way."

He smiled as he turned around to look at the five acres again. "Let's walk to the back of the lot. I want to see where the water is going to drain when the rains come."

Jennifer anticipated this and slipped from her heels to her hiking boots. TJ arrived with his boots on. Together, they walked down the right side of the property. Every fifty feet or so, TJ would turn and look back towards the road checking the roll of the land. He noted the soil seemed hard and absent of muck, with no standing water or mud holes. He liked what he saw so far. They continued walking until they found the back of the property and a small creek with high banks.

"Nature has carved a nice barrier for hard rains. I don't see any bent grass," began Jennifer, "which means rainwater has not exceeded the banks."

They walked along the creek to the far left corner, and TJ once again looked up the property line to the street. He was beginning to feel good about this lot. It was also the last one on his list. He walked up the line to about where the port home would be built, and then strayed to the center searching the ground for any problems.

He turned to Jennifer and said, "How much?" TJ knew the listing price.

"A hundred and twenty-five thousand. It has approval for a septic tank, and electrical, telephone, cable, water, and gas lines are buried along the road. It is a good safe area with easy access to the interstate. There are twenty restaurants within four miles of this location, plus four grocery stores, banks, etc. An elementary school is six miles away. Two churches within ten miles, and I think you could get it for less."

"Do I make an offer?" TJ had bought and sold rental properties a few years ago, and developed lots at a lake. He knew the drill.

"Precisely."

"I'll offer ninety thousand with immediate closing and no loan approval. I will pay cash."

Jennifer smiled, "Let's walk to my car and do the paperwork. I don't know if they'll accept it, but cash always gets everyone's attention. I'll need a deposit."

TJ produced a check from his pocket that he brought along just in case he found the right spot. He wrote the check for five thousand, handed it to Jennifer, and signed the papers. She said she would call the buyers and call him back as soon as they decided. She asked for forty-eight hours. TJ told her to tell them he was going to spend the afternoon looking at other lots. She winked at him, knowing he was bluffing.

TJ made his way back to the RV and walked the dogs. He ate a sandwich, answered Shane's call, and left for his appointment with Bobby Jenkins. He arrived fifteen minutes later. The architect's office was beautifully designed with lots of natural rock and exposed beams. TJ loved the wooden floors.

Bobby won numerous awards for his designs. He was sixty-three years old, displayed a soft, down home kind of look to his demeanor, and could have easily played a look-a-like for Andy Griffith. He warmly shook TJ's hand as they met in the lobby surrounded countless pictures of his work. They went into his office and after formalities; TJ explained the building he and his friend wanted to construct. He began showing him his designs, as well as his virtual tour on his laptop.

After some discussion, Bobby suddenly asked, "How long have you guys been a couple?"

TJ's face flushed, so Bobby continued. "My partner and I have been together for over thirty years. His name is James. My staff knows I'm gay, but the public doesn't. The way you designed the house indicates you have only males in mind, and the guest room, though nice, was not created for a roommate. Am I right?" Bobby knew he was.

"Yes you are," confessed TJ. "I am relieved that I can be open about it with you."

"You have nothing to fear. Does your guy have a name?"

TJ thought for a second, "Yes, but he is, huh, a public figure that must remain the closet."

Bobby sighed, "That's too bad, but I know how he feels. I only know one other gay architect, but I suspect more, but as more gay college kids graduate, will soon have an out of the closet bunch of designers, and that'll take some pressure off of me."

"You must keep his name in the strictest confidence. Do I have your word?"

"Yes, you do. I prefer to work closely with both of my clients so this will help him join us in our meetings."

TJ smiled, "His name is Shane and he's the most wonderful guy in the world."

Bobby sat back, "You don't mean THE Shane?" Bobby was a huge fan of Taylor basketball and had season tickets. Currently, he only knew one Shane, and it was Taylor's star player.

TJ nodded his head affirmatively.

"Well, I'll be. I am shocked actually. What is he like?"

"I'll try to bring him next time, but his schedule is very tight with the title on the line. He'll look forward to meeting you, but he is counting on me to handle construction, as he is way too busy trying to win the title."

"And we're going to win it. Okay, let's get to work. I have a few suggestions and options for you."

They began to discuss TJ's drawings. Bobby used a large pad and made rapid sketches, corrections, changes, and in a few hours, the design ideas were hashed out. TJ apologized and told him this was a rush job, as they wanted to move in by June first. He then asked Bobby for a construction company he could count on for discretion, performance, and speed. He was given two names.

Shane stayed at school after a hard practice and a big meal, and began getting his homework done. They talked on the phone for a while with TJ bringing Shane up to speed on the property.

The following morning, TJ got a call from Jennifer. The seller accepted his office. He asked her to fax or email the contract to both his accountant and lawyer in New York City. She was impressed and promised to do so in a few minutes. He called Sam and Jerome explaining the details of his purchase. He also told Sam about Bobby's fee for the drawing. Sam said he would overnight a check to Bobby's address. Jerome would prepare the closing on the land. They would sign the papers on Wednesday. Jerome had a contact in Lindle to secure the research on the land title, and would hand deliver all the required paperwork to the courthouse. All the paperwork would be in TJ's name only, securing Shane's privacy.

Shane's workouts were hard, but he felt great about the practices. The team's progress was going very well, and he knew he was in the best shape of his life no matter how hard the coaches pushed him.

Later that day, TJ got a call from Jake Tidwell, his book-publishing agent. He took a minute to bring TJ up to date on the republishing of his gay books, and the plans for the **Gay Grifters** release on May first. TJ thought the publisher's choice of his new titles to promote first was a good one. Then Jake sighed and said he was ready to start the auction of his basketball book.

TJ asked, "You think the timing is right?"

"Yes, after Taylor won the season title, and the ACC tournament, and I believe they will easily make it to the Sweet Sixteen after this weekend's game in Raleigh. Hype for Shane has never been higher. He is nominated for almost every basketball award except team manager and coach of the year. It's time."

"How does this work?"

Jake replied, "I have prepared packages including ten chapters from your book. My in-house editors have poured over the book and made a few minor corrections. We have done a cover mockup to give them an on the shelf visual. We have bios of you and Shane, as well as the history of the team. I'll send those overnight to only the top ten publishers. Bids will end a week from Friday. Are you ready?"

"Yes, I guess so. I would like a copy of the corrections you made."

"No problem, I'll email a Acrobat PDF® file for you, and we've highlighted the changes in yellow to make it easy for you to find them. No content was changed. I'll keep you posted on the response. I'm also sending you a link for several publishing websites because this is going to be topic one for about ten days. Congratulations. Step one is about to being."

TJ thanked him and hung up. He sat down in the recliner to absorb all that was happening. He had bought the land of his dreams to build the RV port home he had spent so much time on. He had secured a top architect to finish the final plans, and he was about to be the subject of the publishing world as the media jumped on the auction.

After a few moment of reflection, he went back to his desk and made the calls to the construction companies Bobby gave him. He made afternoon appointments, packed up his stuff, ate some lunch, walked the dogs, and set off on his journey.

Each meeting took over an hour. He promised to have final plans soon, told them Bobby Jenkins was working on the designs, and the owners of the companies were immediately impressed. TJ relayed he would seek bids from only two companies and time was critical. He would be paying cash for the construction so he wanted a good company that could do a great job, and be ready to break ground in a week.

They were all shocked at the requested speed, but they could work it out. The housing market had slowed over the past year, and they were having a difficult time keeping their crews busy. The winner of the bid would see TJ's project as a lifesaver. He shook hands firmly with each man assuring him his project was sincere, and he suggested they confirm the details, both with Jennifer and Bobby as well as his accountant and lawyer in New York. They were once again impressed.

Shane and the team took a bus to Raleigh after a morning practice in their home gym. They would attend a shoot around in the RBC arena that afternoon before the night games. The team arrived at their hotel amongst a crowd of fans, the team's cheerleaders and mascot, and the pep band.

TJ drove over that morning and parked in the hotel's parking garage. He picked up an assortment of newspapers and groceries as usual. He would be there through Sunday's game, assuming Taylor University kept winning. Their first game would be against Mount Saint Mary's University.

TJ ate lunch in the room and began reading his emails. He read several from Jake with links to various articles in the press. The first was a front-page story for Publishers Weekly, and an interior page in the New York Times. The later links were online stories for publishing, especially in the sports related fields. Both stories said the author was unavailable for comment. TJ smiled, and was a bit thankful he wasn't. Jake advised him to stay low until the auction completed, adding to the suspense of the bidding.

Though the school and the arena were only an hour away, the team elected to stay in town to get the feel for tournament hype and atmosphere. They did not want to play just like another away game. They wanted to be away from everyone so they could concentrate on their mission.

TJ received a call from Bobby on Thursday afternoon telling him the plans were ready. TJ decided he would drive back to Lindle Friday morning to meet with Bobby. TJ asked him to prepare three sets of the drawings for the two construction companies to prepare their bids, and for him to show Shane and begin making notes. He also asked for digital copies of the plans so he could send key pages to the wire installers for all their special electronic features. TJ had been through this process before in the design and construction of his long time home in Hendersonville, but this project was going to be a big one, and he was very excited.

Shane returned to his room about five and called his parents to confirm dinner at six. He then called TJ to do the same and get his room number. When Shane arrived, TJ explained all the latest news on the house as well as the book. He asked about the team and learned Jerry had taken a hard fall to the floor, but his ankle appeared to be fine, to the relief of all.

They took a cab to a restaurant outside the loop around Raleigh, and hopefully away from the large crowd of fans near the arena. They had a table in the back, and praying for privacy. Shane hugged his parents and they in turn hugged TJ. They had begun acting like a family of four, and TJ liked the feeling of acceptance they gave him. They were thrilled at the latest news on the book and the house, and couldn't wait to see the plans from the architect.

Shane chose a steakhouse for dinner and ate most of his rib eye, but ate all of his salad and potato. He skipped dessert and together, they sat there talking about their plans for after the season ended. TJ explained the tour for two books, Shane flying in for the weekends, Shane preparing for exams, and their three-week vacation. They targeted the move-in for June first or as soon as possible.

After their return to the hotel, TJ and Shane went up the back elevator to TJ's room. They talked basketball briefly, the book, the house, the land, and their future for about an hour before Shane began unbuttoning TJ's clothes. He called it tournament fever, but TJ called him just horny as usual. Their lovemaking was both fun and passionate. Shane wished he could have stayed all night, but he had a curfew, and reluctantly struggled from their bed to dress. They kissed goodbye several times.

Early the next morning TJ drove back to Lindle to meet with Bobby. They met in a conference room set up for presentations. They went through the plans page by page, and TJ liked what he saw.

Bobby then sat him down and dimmed the lights. "I thought you might like to see your plans come alive with more detail." He clicked a remote control device for his laptop that sent the image to his high definition projector hanging from the ceiling. The picture projected an image eighty inches diagonal on the wall.

192

The presentation started from the front of the property taking in both driveways. It then zoomed to an overhead so everyone could see the driveways leading to the building and its placement on the property. Bobby had driven to the lot earlier and took pictures to use for his designs and presentation. He recalled TJ's description of keeping a gradual drive with a just a slight hint of a slop to allow water to drain off the pavement.

Bobby clicked the next sequence and they went through the entry door to the RV building, and once inside, they did a vertical circle to see all the walls before exiting. TJ explained the importance of accurate measurements for drains and power to the coach, as well as the rectangle lighting, framing the coach to make it easy to clean and maintain. Bobby then went in through the front door of the house and zoomed in for each room. TJ was thrilled with his work.

With the lights back up, Bobby handed him a computer disk of the presentation for him to study, plus three large rolls and digital disc of the plans. He also received an invoice for his services. TJ asked him to fax the invoice to his accountant, and told him they would overnight a check to him. TJ shook his hand warmly, and thanked him several times.

Bobby walked him to the door, "I hope you like the plans, but we can change and fix anything you want. I'll see you at the game tonight."

"Great. I'll look forward to celebrating another win. Thank you for the excellent job and quick service. I'll be in touch soon."

TJ drove to both construction companies and dropped off copies of the plans. He had called earlier to let them know he would be doing so. They had their staffs standing by, and went to work immediately doing a cost analysis. He would meet with them again on Tuesday for their bids. TJ drove by to check on the dogs. Bob and Sue were walking them around the park. He stopped and received many doggie kisses. He spread his copy of the house plans on the hood of car so Bob and Sue could see them. He thanked them for taking care of the dogs, and then drove back to Raleigh.

TJ ate an early dinner with Gary and his friends from Asheville. Somehow they all piled in a cab afterwards for the ride to the arena. TJ excused himself and made his way to the pressroom to pickup any last minute media notes, and to stow his laptop for the game. He picked up a water bottle and went down to watch Shane warm-up. Gary and his gang had already taken their seats, as had most of the Taylor fans.

Later, he made his usual pre-game trip to the tunnel, signaled to Shane with a smile, and got out of the way before they ran out to the court. Shane caught the tip, flung the ball hard down court to Jerry, who tossed it to his right to Larry, who tossed it across the paint to Shane who went high and dunked it. The fans went wild with excitement, and the Taylor team kept on rolling. They made huge defensive stops, fast scoring runs, and won the game a hundred thirteen to seventy-four. It was a signal they were sending to all their opponents that Taylor came to win and win big.

TJ made a stop at the creamery and bought two large ice sundaes, and then made his way to the hotel with the desserts in a bag. Shane made it up to his room shortly thereafter. He was as excited as he had ever been. He grabbed TJ and swung him around the room, and then kissed him deeply. He was so happy with his performance in tonight's game, and especially the efforts of his team. It was a thrilling start.

TJ opened the bag to surprise him with the dessert. Shane smiled a giddy smile like a two-year-old on Christmas morning. They sat on the couch and watched ESPN's SportsCenter® as they reviewed outstanding plays including many dunks by Shane. However, he was more proud of his outside shooting, hitting twelve points from the field, fifteen foul shots, and eight points from close in. It had been a great game, but he knew the next game would be tougher.

At ten minutes to eleven, Shane kissed TJ goodnight and made his way to his room to sleep. TJ went to his laptop and wrote down his impressions as Shane relayed his thoughts about the game, his enthusiasm, and his pride. Shane and TJ slept well, but sadly two floors apart.

Saturday was a slower day for the team with an afternoon practice at a local gym. Arkansas had a great season and made it into the tournament, and came ready to play.

That night Gary and his crowd met Al and Barbara, along with TJ and Shane, for dinner at a seafood restaurant. Shane grinned when he realized they offered sushi, but not TJ. He still called the raw food fresh bait. The gang laughed about the previous game, and they told stories about each other. Shane delighted in hearing Gary talk about some dumb things he and TJ had done. His favorite was about Christmas trees and the tale was in two parts.

TJ used to like going into the high country, cutting his own Christmas tree from land owned by a friend of his. Each year the chosen tree height became a little taller, and they were now shopping for a fourteen-foot tree. Gary and his brother Greg lived with TJ from time to time, and always helped with the tree. They were being silly when they finally found this year's tree. TJ got on the ground with his rough blade saw, and began sawing away at the tree. After it fell, he started back up the hill, slipped on a fallen branch, and fell awkwardly into the grove of trees, knocking his hat off. In seconds, he was buried in the limbs, and almost out of sight except his feet. Gary and Greg laughed so hard they had to sit down, remaining completely helpless and giddy as to getting TJ out of this predicament.

The next day Greg spent the greater part of an afternoon taking delicate care to decorate the tree perfectly. He was so proud of it he took pictures. Later after he went to work, TJ and Gary were watching an action movie, and noticed there was no bass sound coming from the subwoofer that was hidden in the corner behind the Christmas tree.

Gary moved the packages out of the way, and on his back, he crawled under the tree, and found the problem and plugged the subwoofer power cord into the wall. TJ turned to walk over to the stereo to turn up the volume to test it when Gary suddenly screamed.

TJ quickly turned around and immediately the falling Christmas tree hit him in the face. Gary tried to hang on to the tree from beneath, but couldn't stop it. The lighted star on the top hit the ceiling fan, throwing parts all over the room. Hundreds of blinking lights and piles of green electrical wires fell on TJ like green slime, and glass balls hit the floor popping and breaking everywhere. The dogs scattered into the kitchen.

TJ caught the tree and with Gary's help, they struggled to get it back up, but now all the decorations were in a heap on the carpet. It took a while for them to stop laughing, but they knew Greg would be home soon. Quickly, they went to work and redecorated the tree as best they could after making a urgent trip to Kmart® to replace the broken pieces.

When Greg came home, he plopped down on the couch, and started talking about how beautiful the tree was. He never noticed that there was a new star on top, or that some of the glass balls were now different colors. They didn't tell him about the falling tree until after Christmas. Shane laughed hard as TJ blushed a bit, but it was a good relaxing time by all. Al and Barbara thought TJ had the best friends, adding more to their confidence in Shane's choice for a partner.

TJ and Shane had an hour after they returned to the hotel, and they made love passionately. Shane felt for the rest of his team who probably didn't get as much sex as he did. He loved it all.

They ate the team meal at one, as the game was scheduled for approximately five based on the games ahead of them. TJ made his way to the arena about three o'clock anticipating a traffic jam. He ate an early dinner, read and typed away on his notes, chatted with Walter about the game and the book, and laughed with Dick Vitale about some of Shane's dunks in the previous game.

The game started uneventful. Shane again caught the tip, flung it to Jerry, who cut hard around his man with a behind the back dribble, and laid it up left handed for their first two points. The Taylor defense was again tenacious; holding Arkansas to just thirty points in the first half. Shane and his group scored fifty-four points.

During the second half, the Taylor team was even stronger, as they ran the Arkansas boys up and down the court, and soon Shane noted the man assigned to guard him was often just at half court by the time Shane was under his goal. Jerry began throwing the ball to him for short shots, layups, and dunks. At the four-minute mark, the coach took the starters out, and played the rest of the team, as they rarely got on the court in a tournament game. They won a hundred and eight to seventy-seven.

It had been an impressive weekend, and they had already won two of the six games required to become National Championship, and the next games would be much tougher, but for now, they were deliriously happy. They knew that every game they won led to a far more difficult game. They would have three days to prepare for the next weekend, but for tonight, they would celebrate and enjoy the victories.

The next morning the newspaper announced Shane was one of five candidates for the Player-of-the-Year award. Shane, as well as all his family and friends were excited and happy for his nomination, and hoped he would win the award.


On Tuesday morning, Jake called TJ and told him he handled numerous calls and questions about the auction from the book publishers, but no bids yet. He said they would mostly come in on the last day, and that he wasn't worried. TJ was. What if no one wanted to publish the book? He wondered how embarrassing would that might be.

He left at nine and drove to his least favorite construction company for their bid. He had judged and rated the companies after speaking to some of their clients and studying their project pictures. He knew either one came highly recommended, and would do a great job for them, but his first choice offered some great suggestions. He had also noted two gay folks working for them in the office.

The first quote came in at eight hundred thousand dollars. TJ thought that price was very high, but was polite and thanked them for their efforts. He said he would meet with his accountant and attorney, and call back tomorrow. He drove hastily to the second one.

The second company prepared a quick presentation with charts and slides, and several staffers took part. TJ was impressed with their organization skills. Their bid game in at six hundred ninety-five thousand, and TJ was relieved, but he didn't show it. He began asking more detailed questions included materials, insulation R-values, time frame, land grading, and especially the drain slope of the RV floor and car garages to a center drain. He had built several garages in his lifetime, and not one sloped as designed. As much as he washed the motorcoach, he wanted the water to slide down to the drain rapidly so the floor would dry fast.

They answered all his questions quickly and with great confidence. He asked to see their contract, and quickly read the entire six-page document with attached pages of the floor plans. He noted approximate completion date of ninety days. He asked if they received a quick okay on the contract, could they move in June first. The answer was yes.

He noted the money was a third down, a third at dry in, and balance after completion. TJ asked them to include a water test on the cement floors

196

for drainage to the center before the second payment. They agreed. He warned them politely, if it failed to drain, it would have to be dug up and done over. They gulped, but agreed. He asked them to put all his requests in a modified agreement.

He read the requested and revised amendment, asked them to sign it, and handed them a card to fax it to his attorney and accountant. Someone fetched him a cold water bottle while they waited. Each party was nervous. Eight long minutes later Sam called. TJ spoke to him. Sam gave it his blessings, and told him he could handle the money once Jerome approved.

Just as he hung up the phone, Jerome called. He liked the agreement, made a few changes to the water test, and final approval before payment, and faxed the changes to the company. A secretary brought it to TJ while he was still on the phone. TJ read them, but had no questions. He thanked Jerome for his quick response.

He handed the changes to the boss. He read them and smiled. He signed the new last page, inserted it into the agreement, and TJ signed it. He asked him to have his secretary fax the signed agreement to Sam and Jerome, and prepare a copy for him to take with him.

TJ explained that Sam would deliver the deposit on their desk by courier in the morning. They decided to follow TJ out to the property to get an idea of where he wanted the building on the land. He stopped in front of what he called gate one, and then moved down to the future gate two location, and parked his car. Gate two would become the main entrance for cars and guests, while gate one would be just for the motorcoach entry. After arrival, they began walking the property. He wanted the house set back at least a hundred and fifty feet from the street for privacy. There would be a fence around the entire property, electric gates with remote controls, and a dog pen area with gates indicated on his plans.

They walked the area for the building, noted the nearest electrical power box on the road and wrote down the identity number. They placed flags for the location he chose for the building. They all shook hands and left. TJ sighed as he drove away. It was the biggest transaction he had ever handled, even bigger than the deal for his motorcoach. He felt like his twenty-four hour deodorant had long ago failed him.

On Wednesday, Shane came by late in the morning after class and rode with TJ to the property. To their delight, a grading crew was already working on the building site, the two driveways had been carved in the soil, multi loads of gravel had been put down, and a plumbing team had arrived and was working on the plumbing that would be roughed in before the slab. The plans also called for the plumber to handle the underground wiring conduits as well other networking and phone conduits, and a yard sprinkler system. A truck from the power company installed a temporary pole and ran a power line from the transformer box to the pole.

TJ and Shane left the site impressed with how quick the construction team went to work. TJ confirmed the arrival of the check that morning, as well as called the other company, and politely told them he appreciated their bid, but he chose another company.

After their visit to the site, TJ and Shane picked up takeout and went back to the coach to eat. Shane took a nap and then left for practice. The team would leave later that afternoon for Charlotte, and the site of the second round of NCAA tournament play, or what was known around the country as the Sweet Sixteen.

TJ and Shane met with the Al and Barbara for dinner Thursday night. Shane didn't want to talk basketball as his nerves were already growing as the game approached. He had twenty-four more hours to worry about it so they talked about the house and the plans. Barbara suggested they hire an interior designer to help plan, and order furniture for the house as well as picking colors for wall paint.

Shane acted offended and then laughed, as he didn't have a clue how to pick out colors. Barbara reminded both of them that Shane needed a long bed to accommodate his height. Shane had been tempted to tell her they didn't need a tall bed, as they actually only used about four by six feet as they slept spooning every night, but decided not to say anything. TJ agreed he could use a designer's help with the furnishings.

Barbara liked the high ceilings the plans called for, since her son was tall. Al thought they might want a big television in the great room to watch the games. TJ explained he planned to use a high definition projector, and told him the picture would be at least a hundred and twenty inches diagonally. He thought that was fantastic.

The game was at seven and CBS had the broadcasting rights, but in the pressroom, ESPN's Dick Vitale walked up to TJ who was already sitting at a table eating dinner.

"Hey, TJ. May I join you?"

"Of course, please do, and how are you?"

"I'm great. It feels good to be here as a fan, and I have a column to write, so just a little bit of work involved. Are you ready for the big game?"

"Yes. The team has worked hard, but Shane is nervous. He thinks they will do well, but they are all afraid last weekend's big wins might have given the team the big head and made them a bit lazy."

"I hope not. I doubt it. Coach Timmons isn't about to let that happen. Let me guess. He practiced and ran them hard for three days. Is that right?"

"Yep, Shane wasn't complaining, but boy was he tired."

"What's new with you?"

TJ set his fork down and smiled, "Let's see, hmm, I bought five acres of land, signed a contract to build an RV Port home and move in by June first, and ..." he looked at his watch, "The auction for the book ends in about fifteen minutes. I hope Jake can reach me here."

"Oh my! You had a busy week for sure. What's an RV port home?"

You build a normal home with a big double garage for cars, and one long and taller garage for the motorcoach to pull in. Once the doors are closed, people could drive by and not even know the coach is there. The large garage makes it easier to maintain and load the motorcoach."

"Hey, I've got to see that. Put me on the tour list when it is done."

"Of course, we would love to have you come see us. We're building a large office in the house so I can write, and keep up with Shane. If the book does well, there could be a sequel."

Dick thought for a second, "Shane is going to live with you isn't he?"

TJ looked around and noted they were alone, "Well, part of the time. He has to stay in the dorm during the season, except for weekends and days off, and some holidays."

Dick paused for a second as he looked left and right, making sure they were out of earshot of anyone before speaking. "Did I ever tell you about my favorite nephew. He is about your age now. He is gay. He has a partner of twelve years. They are perfect together, just like my wife and me. I love both of them. They are so smart, so happy, and I certainly wish all married couples were as much in love and blissful as they are.

"In my business, all the old farts like me are probably straight, but a large part of the technicians behind the scenes are gay. I love 'em. They do such a great job for me.

"I hope I'm not about to offend you and if so, we'll drop it, and I'll never bring it up again. You are gay, aren't you?"

TJ put down his fork, and nodded at him. "Yes, I was born that way."

"Of course you were. I never bought in to the idea that people choose to be gay. They only choose whether to keep it a secret or not. I've seen the way you and Shane look at each other. Magic happens, and that is hard to hide. He's gay, too?"

"I would have preferred he answer that question, but Dick, you have been such a good friend to us that I would not want to lie to you. Do you promise to keep this off the record from everyone?"

Dick smiled, "I can promise except for one person...my wife. She knows everything and says nothing. Secondly, I promise it is off the record, but if he decides to come out, I'd appreciate the opportunity to break the story. I think I could help."

"Okay, that's a deal. Yes, he is and yes, we are a couple. It happened by accident. I met him at a motorcoach show. He was about to be swamped by fans, so I showed him my coach. We hit it off immediately. We love each other very much."

"Excellent. It is so important to have someone in this world that loves you."

"Yes, but it is hard as a gay person to find someone that loves you as much as you love them. Shane does that for me. We have so much fun together. There is so much support there."

"I can tell. Okay, it is my secret. Are you going to tell Shane I know?"

"Yes, of course. We keep no secrets."

"That's why I have to tell my wife. So, you're going to build an office. If Taylor wins the championship, and your book sales explode like I predict, and Shane decides to come back for a senior year, he is going to be in hot demand for interviews. Wait a minute, do you know if he is coming back?"

TJ laughed, "Boy, you just can't lay that reporter curiosity down can you?"

Dick grinned, "Nope, but I often try to."

"I don't know. Shane doesn't know. He won't discuss it until after the tournament."

"Good answer. Stick to it if anyone asks and they will. What I was getting at is that you could put in a big phone line, I think they call it a T something…"

TJ jumped in, "A T1?"

"Yeah, that's it. Anyhow, that would give you several phones and fax lines and a superior Internet connection. I have this at home. Then you could put in a very small studio for Shane to do on-air interviews right from your home. This would make him accessible for publicity sake, and keep him from having to go out of his way to meet reporters face to face. Interested?"

"Yes, of course. I had been debating on going online via cable or satellite. I have worked with T1 lines in my earlier career. That is an excellent suggestion."

Dick took out one of his business cards and turned it over, and wrote a name and telephone number on the back and handed it to TJ. "Call Brian Kenny at this number. He is a longtime friend and technical guru for ESPN®. Tell him I said for you to call. Explain that as his uncle you're handling Shane's media requests, and that Dick said for him to put a studio hookup in your new house. He'll know what to do, and will make a few requests and suggestions for you. He'll fly in and hook it all up when the house is done."

"Thanks, that is a great idea," replied TJ pocketing the card. "Are you ready for the game?"

"Yep. I'd better run. I have some ESPN® folks waiting on me. Enjoyed dinner with you, and I'll see you soon."

"Same here, and thanks."

200

# SEVENTEEN

Their third game of the tournament started off with Shane attempting to chase down a runaway ball and crashing in and over the scoring table. The referees immediately blew a whistle, as he had accidentally knocked over several time and scoring officials. Shane came up unhurt, apologized as he checked on the people he knocked over, but as he came back to the court, his team stood and applauded. The rest of the fans joined in, and that's when Shane finally blushed.

The coach feared he might have hurt himself, but he drilled into his players to go after the ball and that every possession counted. The other team retained possession, but when their guard went to throw it to the man Shane was guarding, Shane quickly cut the pass off, stole it, and made a dash down the court. With his long legs and big feet, it only took about six giant steps, a couple of dribbles, and boom he dunked it. The fans went wild, as they applauded and cheered him.

Taylor jumped out to a ten-point to nothing lead, but soon their opponent settled down. At the half, Taylor only led by two. The coach was on the players about their defense, shot selection, teamwork, and most importantly, their drive to win. He told them he thought the other team wanted to win more. The later comment charged up the team. Coach Timmons smiled.

Shane had sat silently at his locker after changing into dry socks and laced his shoes. He personally evaluated his play in the first half and decided he could do much better. This ability to critique and make corrections to his play, without direction from anyone, was part of the reason Shane was so good.

The second half started with Taylor on a roll, running up the lead to twelve. Shane stole the ball again in the second half, the defense held strong, and they won by six. It wasn't pretty, said the coach, but it was a win.

At the half, TJ had looked at his phone several times, as he hadn't heard from Jake. He finally noted he had no phone signal. After the game, he walked to the windows in the hallway, and immediately his voice mail flashed. The message was from Jake.

"Hey, TJ. I guess you're in the arena. Please call me. The auction is over. I have great news."

TJ instantly hit the button to dial Jake and waited. "Hello?"

"Jake, this is TJ. Can you hear me?"

"Yes I can. Taylor did great. Shane hit twenty-six points. Excellent win. Only three more wins to go. Well, the auction turned into a frenzy of rapid activity this afternoon, and the final bid was two and half million dollars. You get one million up front if Taylor wins the championship, and a half million if they don't."

"That's great news. They are going to win."

"Yes, they are. I've emailed the contract to Jerome and you for perusal, and over to Sam as well. Please try to get it back to me on Monday. I'll have a check over to Sam on Tuesday. Congratulations."

"Thank you," replied TJ, though shocked from the news. "Goodbye."

Later that night, Shane received some free time, and went up to see TJ. After a round of kisses, TJ told him about the book news. They were so excited that they immediately called Al and Barbara, and related the news as well. TJ held back on the split deal for the down payment, and told them he got a half million up front, trying to avoid putting any more pressure on Shane. It would be the first time he had done so, but he hoped Shane would forgive him, and he would come clean promptly after the tournament.

The weekend became a blur with so much for TJ to think about and for Shane to do. Taylor won the second game and left Charlotte for home having won four of the six required games to win it all. They would have just one more weekend of basketball for this season. That alone brought some sadness to Shane, as he really enjoyed working out, practicing, shooting, and sweating. He loved the competition, but he also loved winning. He was looking forward to the championship in San Antonio.

TJ signed the approved book contract on Monday. Jake had forgotten to tell him about the sequel so they discussed it before TJ signed. If book one went well, then TJ would receive three million, with half upfront for the sequel. This huge amount of cash shocked TJ, bringing tears to his eyes.

After he emailed the final copy to Jake his phone rang. It was Henry at the construction site. He told TJ they were pouring the cement in the morning for the slab, and wondered if he could come over to be sure everything was in the proper place. TJ agreed, so he walked the dogs, grabbed his copy of the plans, and his notes for measurements for the RV parking, and then drove over.

Together, TJ and Henry looked at every drain and pipe in the slab, and then Henry explained how the red wire stakes were used to make sure the floor slanted correctly in the RV building and the triple garage. It took ninety minutes for them to cover the entire slab of the hundred by hundred twenty-foot building. They went over the ditch from the road to the house for the utilities, the drain field for the septic, the conduit to the gates, the field lights, and the slope for the dog area. Two crews from a fence company were already working on putting the entire five acres inside a fence, plus two gates at the driveways, a fence splitting off the front property from the back with gates, and they had already put the posts in the for the dog area. The posts were one foot inside of the frame in slab area so the dogs could not dig under the fence.

TJ was thrilled at the progress and signed off on the pre-slab inspection. The county building inspector had already done the same, so unless it rained hard, the cement trucks would start arriving at eight in the morning.

TJ returned to the motorcoach, walked the dogs, chatted with Sue for a while, as Bob had gone to change the oil in their car, and then went in to get his email and work a while. He got a message from Jake requesting TJ send everything he had written on the basketball book to an editor at the publishing company. He also asked to be sent a copy as well. TJ had just received the last chapter from Walter and Dick, so he made corrections, added some new thoughts, and sent it along as requested.

About twenty minute later, he received a call from Janet Wilson from Over-The-Fence Publishing, a subsidiary of Double Tree. She was TJ's project manager and would handle all correspondence on the production of his book. She said two editors were already pouring through the book, and would email corrections or suggested changes to him tomorrow.

She asked if he had any ideas for the cover and were there to be any inside pictures.

"Well, I thought the cover should reflect the championship win with the trophy, team and coaches. An insert of Shane's picture should also be on the cover as it his insight that give us the behind the scenes story. The back cover should also be a picture of a massive Shane dunk, a picture of the coach and so on. Actually, we'd better prepare two covers, one if they win, and a different version if they failed to win the national championship."

"We anticipated doing the two covers. The coach is doing the introduction right?"

"Yes, he has already written it so I included it, but he has the right to change it depending on the outcome of the next two games. There is also a comment paragraph from Dick Vitale for the jacket flap."

"Wow," she said, "nothing like knowing a few key sports celebrities. I'll send them a form to sign off on so we can use their words in our publicity campaign. Please send along their contact information. What about the inside of the back jacket? Do you want to put your bio there? Do you have a picture?"

"Ugh, I knew this would come up. Reluctantly, I can send you a picture. I would put it on the inside back page and very small. Can I be honest with you?"

"Sure."

TJ swallowed hard and said, "I also write gay fiction, so I think it is best that we keep my picture hidden on the inside. My name should also be small, as the book is about Taylor University and Shane, and not me."

"Well, you're being humble. I'll see what we can do. On the inside front cover flap, we might put an excerpt from the book, or quotes for sports personalities like Dick Vitale, etc. I understand you'll continue to write as these final games are played. We're going to send you some things to look at and approve, and will be standing by for the last few chapters.

"I'll also be coordinating with our promotion department on your tour. I'll send you an email itinerary as soon as I can. I understand they are almost done, but as Taylor and Shane continue winning, more stores are signing up for the tour."

TJ replied, "Thank you. I welcome any and all advice on the book. I want it to be as perfect as possible."

"My boss has arranged for a top sports photographer to cover these last two games, hoping for the perfect shots for the cover and maybe the inside. We'll own the pictures so that'll avoid delays in copyright approval. I saw your notes and contact information for Walter Mills at Taylor University and the Associated Press. We like the pictures you have selected for the picture section in the middle of the book. I will be in touch with these organizations as well." She hung up after promising to stay in touch with him, and wished him good luck on the tournament.

TJ and Shane talked after he had completed his homework and before going to bed in the dorm. They missed each other. TJ tried to keep his news to a minimum, feeling Shane had enough to worry and get excited about, but Shane said he would meet him at the site after lunch while he digested, and before his shooting practice and team workout. He said the media was everywhere trying to obtain interviews, stories, and photos. He was trying his best to avoid the onslaught of the media, but some interviews were required. Thankfully, Walter's office handled the requests, the selections, and the schedule.

TJ woke up early on Tuesday and went over his reservations for this weekend. He received an email schedule from Janet for the book tour. She also sent him a Word® document of his book with comments from the editors in the margin. He spent a few hours working on their suggestions and making the corrections. As hard as he tried proofing his own work, he missed some simple errors. This always irritated him, feeling he should do better. Walter and Dick missed them, too, but of course, they were mostly reading for content. He was ever so grateful to have a team of editors helping him, and hopefully they prevented him from looking stupid.

He walked the dogs early, ate a quick lunch, and waited for Shane's call. He had just sat down in the recliner when Shane called saying he was leaving now for the property.

Fifteen minutes later, they both parked behind each other along the side of their property. Their land looked like a war zone with at least twenty men working on the slab by hand and with a machine spinning flat blades to tighten the cement while removing air bubbles. More men were completing the second of the two long driveways that went from an eighteen-foot wide at the entrance where it fanned out to the street, and another wide fan out as they approached the building. They also were creating a huge parking area. They had finished two parking pads for motorcoach guests, and another twenty-foot by twenty-foot slab for an exterior shed for TJ's truck, tractor, and accessories for the moving, tilling and such.

TJ and Shane carefully stepped around the stonemasons working on the two pillars that would hide the housing for the electric gates on each side of the driveway entrances. The fencing crew completed the entire property, but they would be back in a few days to install the gates.

Shane could not believe how big the slab was without a building on it, but as they walked up, Henry spotted them and waved them over. He shook hands with TJ and Shane, and told them all had gone well with the pouring. TJ asked about the slant for water drainage, and Henry once again indicated all precautions had been made, and they could test it in the morning.

TJ trusted Henry but was still apprehensive. He knelt down at the corner of the car garages to see the angle for himself. Visually he could see the slight slant, but a test he would make for sure. He did the same for the RV floor. He liked the long center drain. He explained to Shane the importance of keeping the coach washed and maintained, and how easy it was for the floor to dry if it drained by gravity to the center. This would keep wet footprints and paw prints out of the motorcoach and off the carpet. They also poured a slight down slope cement slab for the new dog pen. TJ designed it so the rainwater from the metal building would cascade off the roof and onto the cement to wash away the dog debris.

TJ hated cutting grass because after a few years of living in a home he had bought that had over an acre of grass on very good soil. It had to be cut weekly, or it would be too deep the following week. He told his friends that on his next house he was going to asphalt all the way around the house, and paint it green and put out plastic plants, so he wouldn't have to cut anything, nor would he have to water as well.

They soon retreated out of everyone's way, feeling completely confident in Henry's team and their skills. TJ headed home and Shane drove to the gym. He had just two more home practices for the season, and felt sad that the games would soon be over. He loved everything about being on a team, working and sweating together, outrunning and outhustling his teammates, and often felt very lucky to be playing for coach Timmons and the Taylor team. He knew in just a year his college years would be over for life.

He changed clothes, did his physical work, and then found his favorite team manager. Together, they went to the practice gym to shoot alone. Over and over, he shot from every possible position and various feet away from the goal, while gaining confidence with each swish.

Practice began with a team meeting. They were shown scouting reports and edited videos of the first team they would play this coming weekend. It would be Kansas, a very tough opponent, and coach Timmons reminded his players they should not be taken lightly. He told them it would be three times harder to win than last weekend, and seven times harder as compared to their first weekend of the tournament when they scored over a hundred points in both games. He said this game would be tough in every facet of the game, from offense to defense, and would require maximum effort from every person on the team, whether they were in the game or not.

He got them fired up, excited, and told them to go the gym. Coach Timmons was a methodical man. He and his coaches had met for hours on the schedule for today's practice. Everything during the practice was segmented, goals defined, tactics approved, and allotted time carefully scheduled. They left nothing to chance or whim. Shave loved this type of regimen. He thrived on goals and the determination to accomplish them. He exhorted, encouraged, and entreated his teammates to try harder, push farther, and strive for excellence. Off the court, he continued his highly disciplined motivation by eating correctly to strengthen his body from within, as well as working hard with a strength coach to make his muscles as strong as possible.

TJ went back to the new home site the next morning for the water test. Only he and Henry were there, as the crews had been told to stay off the concrete for three days. Henry set up a long water hose, and waved at TJ as he parked on the street. The top layer of the concrete was hard and resilient to the water spray as he shot streams of water from all sides and corners of the big multi-car garage. He then shut the water off and together they watched the water slide to the drains correctly. There was not a standing puddle anywhere. TJ was thrilled.

They moved to the big garage and began a test down the short exit side. Henry sprayed a lot of water and then waited once again while the water moved to the drain. He went down a long side, the entrance side, and finally the other side and each case the water moved to the center drain. The drain around the Jacuzzi area also drained correctly so that any splashing or dripping water from exiting would slide to the drain as well. TJ had never seen this done successfully on any of his past projects. He was overjoyed and very impressed with Henry. He felt if Henry paid this much attention to concrete, he would certainly do the same for the house. He shook Henry's hand repeatedly, and signed off on the paperwork.

TJ returned home, made a few calls, including one to Sam as to the status of the construction, walked the dogs, spoke with Bob and Sue, and then drove to the airport. Steve and Susie flew him to San Antonio. She fed him a great lunch, and though he had some in-flight writing planned, exhausted from the stress of all he was involved in, he promptly fell asleep.

The car service brought him to the Hyatt Regency Hotel in ten minutes. He checked in, fired up the laptop, and sent Shane a note, though looking at his watch he knew he was in the middle of their last team practice in the home gym. He put his things away, checked his email, brought up the GPS software, and realized he was close to a grocery store a block behind the hotel. He made his usual trip, picking up local newspapers, fruits, drinks, and snacks, watched for restaurants, and enjoyed the spring weather on his way back to his room.

He sat down and made some phone calls, answered all his email, and began reading and researching the newspapers and Internet for all the stories, angles, and comments on the games. About five, he received a reply email from Shane that he was heading back to the gym from his dorm room to fly to Texas.

TJ wrote numerous notes into his research file on the computer, wrote down his impressions, and began writing new pages leading up to the first of two possible games.

The team's flight arrived about nine o'clock local time, and promptly took the bus to the hotel. They had a shoot around in the arena scheduled for in the morning with the public watching. They would do this for about an hour, go through a press conference with the largest press corps of the year, and then take the bus to an arranged private practice in a college gym.

TJ ate dinner in the room, set aside his work on the basketball book, and began working on the final edition of **Gay Grifters**. He made all the changes his editor friend marked in the manuscript, but was reading through every single page looking for anything that might stand out as incorrect, or spot a typo. He hated the later most of all, believing that with two editors and his personal work of going through the manuscript at least five times, plus all the rewrites, he should have caught and fixed everything. This was the first book the gay publishing team would also edit, so he sought the additional goal of making a good first impression.

Shane came up to the room about ten and though they only had an hour before his curfew, they wasted no time getting naked. After their lovemaking, they held each other and talked about the day, the new house, new book, and how things were going. They didn't talk about the upcoming game.

There had been a lot press and fan coverage, and though the team arrived a few days early, they were determined to stay focused on their mission. They practiced Thursday and Friday with shoot-around time in the arena, as well as private, far more serious practices in a local college gym. The team meetings were longer and checklists were used. The lengthy scouting report covered every detail of their opponent. They watched many video clips from various games with emphasis on all their starters and substitutes. The coach devised several new plays, and they practiced each many times.

The coaches were also studying videos and making charts as to what percentage of the time the opposing coach made a certain call. They wanted to know what he was going to do in response to any situation. Most of this research concerned the last two minutes of a close game, and overtime calls.

Near the end of practice, they did several running drills, and surprisingly the coach called for a two minutes end-of-game scrimmage. He followed that with more running and over time drills, and thirty-second drills. He wanted the team to perform well though close to exhaustion. He smiled as they did all he asked very well. He challenged and complimented the team, often in the same sentence. At this moment, he thought, they were the best they have been all year.

TJ spent his days working hard on the book. He had begun going back through the entire basketball book, editing chapters before signing off on them by noon on Friday. The publishing team prepared the completed chapters for press, and by five the galley proofs returned. Now he was looking at electronic galleys, so he studied each page for layout perfection, header, and footer placement, and page numbering, especially for odd and even spots. He also made sure bold and italic words printed correctly. He liked the font they chose as it made the writing look clean and easy to read.

He also received cover number one and two inside and out. He liked everything but his picture. He felt tempted to buy a picture frame from Kmart®, scan a headshot of the model inside the frame, and replace it with his own mug. The front cover pictures were primarily for placement purpose, as the publisher's photographer would be shooting high quality pictures at both of the final games, assuming Taylor won the first one.

He began going through the middle of the book collage of pictures of Shane, the coaches, and the team pictures as well as many action shots that Walter's staff picked out. The end of the book supplement displayed the result stats for the year and included space for the final games update. It also had a team roster. He sent this middle section to Walter to make sure the pictures titles were labeled correctly. Walter and his staff already spent hours preparing the statistic pages for the book, so he sent the galley proofs for his perusal as well.

TJ finished the book with a personal note thanking Shane, the team, the coaches, Walter Mills, and Dick Vitale as well as his new team of Jake, Jerome, and Sam. He added a personal thank you to Al and Barbara, Bob and Sue, and his family.

After finishing last minute notes, he emailed it all to Janet Wilson who would be standing by all weekend with the editors as they planned to go to press on Tuesday after the championship game the night before. TJ looked at the clock and realized the time for dinner with Shane and his folks had crept up on him. He hurried to change clothes, and just finished fixing his hair when there was a loud knock at the door. He knew from the tone and temper of the knock his boyfriend had arrived.

They hugged after closing the door and kissed passionately. "How was practice?"

Shane smiled, "It was very hard, but a good one. The team has done well, and the immense preparation by the coaches gives you a great perspective of the team we're about to play. I think it will be a tough battle, as Kansas is a great team, but I believe we are more determined to win than they are."

"Let's go. I'm starved."

As they walked to the back elevator TJ brought Shane up to date on the book's progress. Shane couldn't wait to see the final product. TJ told him he would show him the cover layout when they returned, but reminded him all the cover shots will come from his final two games. Shane laughed and said he had better brush his teeth and brush his eyebrows so he would look good.

Shane wanted to eat Italian tonight so Al booked a reservation way across town, and hopefully away from as many fans as possible. The cab let them out at a side door so Shane and TJ could slip into a private dining room undetected. His parents were waiting for them.

After hugs and kisses, they sat down to study the menu, and talk about all that was happening. Shane talked about the practices for about fifteen minutes and then asked the group to change the subject. He had done this before, and they responded quickly by asking TJ about the book and the house.

Not wanting to brag, he gave a brief synopsis on the progress of the book, and delighted greatly in explaining the progress of the house. He received an update email from Henry stating the big steal beams and fabrication arrived on Thursday. A crane would arrive early Friday morning so the crews would start installing the posts and beams shortly thereafter. They would also work throughout the weekend.

TJ and Shane both ate Fettuccini Alfredo with grilled chicken, large salads, and hot garlic rolls. After the table was cleared, they continued talking like a family, with TJ being careful to ask how things were going back home in Missouri.

On the way back to the hotel, TJ and Shane asked the cab driver to stop at an ice cream creamery where they selected banana splits, and returned to TJ's room to eat and spend some quiet time together. Shane loved the cover of the book and the inside pictures, but all too soon, it was time for him to return to his room to sleep, leaving TJ alone again.

# EIGHTEEN

Game day arrived quickly, but the day itself moved along at a snail's pace. The team did a shoot around at one, and ate their game meal at three. They had two team meetings and some study hall time to help with their homework and assist the day along. They watched television in their rooms, doing their best to relax. However, with the pressure of the game, they were not allowed to even visit with family members for dinner. They feared a player catching a cold, eating bad food, or overeating good food. Every morsel they ate endured testing by the team's doctor and their dietician.

TJ worked at a frenzy pace making final changes to the chapter leading up to the game, and by mid afternoon, he sent it on to Walter and Dick, begging for a quick reply, and finally sent it on to Janet in New York.

He spent the rest of the day working on the basketball book tour. Shane had decided he wanted to join TJ on the weekends of the tour. This absolutely thrilled the publishing company. They modified press releases for the weekend appearances. They would fly a Learjet down to pick him up after Friday morning classes, and fly him to the next stop on the tour so he could catch up with TJ.

TJ studied the itinerary, the hotels list, the airports, and finally the stores for the signings. He tried to find any mistakes in the tour, but Janet's team did an excellent job. He verified Wi-Fi service at every hotel. He suggested they use his flying service and they did. He sent the schedule to the Learjet leasing office two weeks ago, but once again reconfirmed all the stops and details, and the hotel reservations for the flight crew. TJ grinned when he gave the air travel company the billing address for the publishing company, as they would be paying for all his expenses. This was a first for his short writing career.

Once satisfied all was set, he smiled as he looked at the itinerary for the first tour covering eighteen days and approximately seven thousand miles. They lined up numerous radio, television, and newspaper interviews to do alone the way, at least two or more signing per day, and three or four on the weekends. He began to think the tour might be harder than writing the book. Shane used his Kindle® EBook reader to read the most recent chapters of the basketball book. He read the entire book over the past two weeks, and gave TJ high reviews for his descriptions and narrative of the things that happen off the court. He also read **Gay Grifters,** while waiting endlessly in the hotels during the tournaments.

Jake sent the travel schedule for his second tour promoting his new gay fiction novel. This would be a two-week tour and TJ would have to do this one alone, as Shane needed to continue to stay in the closet. There would be no radio and television interviews on the road, but he would do a few interviews for gay periodicals, and one television interview for Logo Channel.

Over the past few weeks he had already done several phone interviews for both tours, so they could print in advance of his arrival.

He checked for conformations at each of the hotels. Both tours would begin in New York City on a Monday, with the first one starting just seven days after the championship game. The high-speed printing presses would begin running Tuesday night, after the Monday night championship game. The entire book would be ready for press and just waiting on the outcome of the games, and TJ's final installment. By Friday of the same week, every bookstore in the country would have a supply of basketball books, posters for their windows, and cardboard displays with Shane's picture on it. They made cutouts that were Shane's actual size to attract attention and let kids pose for a picture with Shane. The tour stops would receive larger book shipments. The first tour included special press releases to the sports directors of all the television stations. TJ would spend two days in New York working with Janet's team practicing interviews for all mediums. TJ found himself excited and a bit nervous for all the work he would have to do.

He ate an early dinner with Al, Barbara, and Gary's friends, who arrived that day for the tournament. They all talked about the game for a while before shifting to news on the house and the upcoming tours.

TJ returned to the hotel to dress for the game. Shane called on his cell so they were able to talk for a little while. Afterwards, he took an after dinner nap and wished he had the dogs with him, as they all liked taking naps together.

He arrived at the arena by cab about seven o'clock for the eight o'clock game. The arena was already eighty percent filled. He made his way to the pressroom, found an available desk and locker. He read the press releases, made his notes, and typed them in the computer.

He watched the monitors and left the room for the arena by walking down to his seat to watch Shane warm up. Shane winked at him, but otherwise kept his game face on. He looked serious, almost grave, TJ thought, as if he had just received bad news about a family member. This made TJ nervous, but he knew Shane had far more experience at preparing for big games than he did.

After the warm-ups, the team returned to the locker room and TJ to the pressroom. He had about thirty minutes to kill so he visited the dessert section of the big buffet, and made himself a bowl of fresh strawberries and bananas, and topped it with frozen vanilla yogurt. He watched the game clock countdown that had begun at the end of the first game. If they beat Kansas, they would play Memphis who won the first game. Both teams were big and powerful, and though Taylor received favorable odds, there were no safe bets.

A few minutes before player introductions, TJ walked down to the tunnel using his press pass, spotted Shane and gave him the chill sign, and the

TJ Johnson

single finger on the nose for love, smiled and returned to his seat. Shane responded with a wink.

TJ sat down in his seat with his friends from Asheville. He waved across the court to Al and Barbara just before the lights went down and the teams were announced.

Beginning with the tipoff, Kansas began to show Taylor they came to win by scoring two quick three-point shots, and a pair of inside shots. They were leading Taylor ten to zero. The Taylor fans appeared shocked. Everyone thought coach Timmons should call a timeout, and find out what is going on with his team, but he didn't. He called a play, a full court press, and finally for a defensive trap.

The team met at the foul line after Shane received a foul, after he scored his team's first basket from a rebound put back in. Two of the Kansas players rode his back up trying to block while fouling him. He told his teammates it was time to flip the switch. Time to score, time to hold, and time to win, he said. Shane made the foul shot putting the score at ten to three.

Shane got a steal on the inbound, tossed it to Jerry, who drove hard on his man and flipped it back to Shane for a dunk. Taylor put the full court press on Kansas, and their guard accidentally stepped out of bounds. Jerry brought the ball down the court quickly. He threw it to Shane, who was immediately double teamed, so he tossed it to Larry, who put a beautiful three-point shot in from the corner.

On the next possession, Taylor sprung their trap with Shane coming way out on a run, so he and Jerry could corner the Kansas player with the ball near the scoring table. When the Kansas player desperately tried to pass, Jerry stole the ball and made a quick run for a layup and tying the score. Kansas immediately called a timeout.

Shane and his teammates were now fired up and came out of the huddle ready to hustle and score. Back and forth, the score continued to climb. At the half, Taylor had Kansas by six.

TJ spoke to Dick in the pressroom. "How'd you like that first half?"

Dick replied, "I don't know about you, but I'm as nervous as a cat. I love great ballgames, close scores, but with all you have riding on this game, I find myself nervous for you. The book will soar up the charts if Taylor wins, but I have no idea how it will do if they lose."

TJ smiled, "They'll win—I hope!"

"Me, too. Is the book ready?"

"Yes, we've done all we can do except write about these last two games. The publisher has a top photographer getting the game shots to help with the final design of the cover. I leave next week for New York to start the tour."

"Well, I know it will be fine but again, I'm nervous. I'll see you later. I have to get something to eat. I'm starved."

212

TJ said goodbye as he found his workstation, opened his laptop, and wrote his impressions of the first half. He finished as the team returned for the second half play. He quickly made his way to his seat. Shane spotted him as they broke their huddle. TJ smiled, gave him the two-finger signal to make him laugh, and the three-finger signal for go, go, go. Shane tugged his ear in response.

Kansas did a good job of planning ways to break Taylor's full court press, and how to handle the trap, so coach Timmons pulled back from these defensive efforts and let the game run the course. He encouraged Jerry to move the ball as fast as possible. He wanted to wear down their opponent, as he knew his team was superior in strength and stamina.

The game stayed close for twelve minutes of the second half. After a television time out with just over seven minutes to play, coach Timmons told them it was time to step up the run on offense, and time to double up their defensive efforts. The full court press and the trap option were put back in to play.

Two plays later, Shane got another steal, and ran the full court in eight steps and leaped for a dunk. It was at turning point in the game. Dick would later write he could see the Kansas player's breathing hard after that amazing dunk. He thought they looked winded. TJ was not as confident, as Kansas got a bit of a second wind, and almost tied the ball game with sixty seconds to play, but Larry leaped hard into the air, and got just the slightest touch of a finger to deflect a three-point shot from their opponents best shooter.

Shane pulled down the rebound with fifty seconds to play. Jerry brought the ball up quickly. Taylor had three-point lead. Coach Timmons wanted to call a timeout, but seeing a sag in the Kansas top players' steps as they came down the court, he knew Taylor had finally worn them out. He called a play from the sidelines.

Jerry knew they should use as many seconds as possible before shooting, while trying to keep the ball out of the hands of the determined, but exhausted Kansas players. Their energy spent, they were playing on heart alone. Back and forth, the ball went from one side court to the other. At six seconds in their allotted possession, Jerry tapped his head, indicating time for the play to run.

Shane broke to the top of the key and Jerry tossed him the ball. Two Kansas players rushed to double team him. If they failed to do so, Shane would turn and shoot, but as they came up the court, he saw Larry's man fall back to prevent a lane drive. Shane flung the ball hard to Larry who caught it and went up instantly for a shot before his man could return to guard him.

Shane moved to prepare for a rebound, but none was needed as the ball swished the net. Shane set up to guard the inbound play, but with a six-point lead, it became their game to lose. They applied their usual full court press to force Kansas to use up a lot of clock. They made it across the half court line with twenty seconds to play.

They were forced to make a quick three-point shot. Amazingly, it went in, even though Jerry had been all over his man, but desperately trying not to foul him. With eight seconds left, and Taylor winning by just three, Kansas called a timeout.

Coach Timmons reminded them to keep cool heads, as Kansas would have to foul someone and to not take it personally, as it was just a defensive play. He instructed the team to keep the ball in Larry's hands if possible, as he was their best shooter, followed by Shane's soft touch hands.

Shane brought the ball in to Jerry who kept it only two seconds before flinging it to Larry as Kansas rushed to foul him. He kept it only a second before throwing it to Shane as he rushed up the court. In the rush to foul Jerry and Larry, Kansas lost sight of Shane. He caught the ball on the run, and quickly dribbled down the court eating up precious seconds. As Kansas rushed to foul him, he leaped in the air and shot a short six-foot jumper with a swish as the buzzer sounded. Taylor won by five. They actually fouled him, but the referees didn't call it, as it wouldn't change the outcome.

TJ, Gary, and their friends leaped into the air. Across the court Barbara and Al were cheering as while. Shane looked quickly to see his parents and smiled, and then turned and found TJ. The team quickly formed a line and shook hands with the Kansas team and staff. Shane then ran across the court and into the stands where he gave TJ and his guests hugs. He was very excited Taylor would now be playing in the championship game against Memphis on Monday night.

TJ said goodbye to Gary and their friends, and returned to the pressroom where Dick Vitale bear hugged him while laughing. "Whew, that was close, but what a game. I loved it, and you can quote me on that."

TJ waited for the game stats before heading out of the arena and back to the hotel. It was late, but he turned the television to the ESPN's SportsCenter® and began typing away at the chapter on the game.

Shane devoured the after game celebratory meal, ate a dessert of bananas and strawberries, and then excused himself as he made his way up the back elevator to TJ's room.

Shane entered the room by bear hugging TJ and kissing him over and over again. They celebrated for several minutes before Shane fixed himself a soft drink and plopped down on the couch to watch the replays of the game highlights. He told TJ about the final team meetings earlier that day, their discussions in the locker room before the game and at the half, and how it felt to make the last shot, sealing the victory.

TJ typed away the quotes, but delayed adding them to this chapter for tomorrow when he would be fresh. He shut down his laptop and smiled wickedly at Shane. Shane looked around him watching a dunk he had made earlier in the game. TJ began pulling his shirt off, then his pants, and finally his underwear before finally Shane laughed, turned off the television, and rapidly stripped out of his clothes.

Their lovemaking lasted a long time, as TJ gave Shane a deep and wonderful massage to help sooth his muscles. They took turns pleasing each other, delighting in the soft moans, and watching their lover's toes flinch as they came. They ended the night by taking a shower together, creating lots of lather, as they took turns washing each other.

It had been a long boring day for Shane, a busy day for TJ, but an exciting night for the couple, and a wonderful celebration after an amazing victory. Back in his room, Shane fell asleep with the memory of the coach drawing a large numerical one on the chalk board in the locker indicating there was only one game left to a championship.

Sunday began late for both boys as they slept in. TJ arose and ate breakfast about ten, read the newspaper accounts of the game, downloaded other stories from the national press, and snatched quotes from time to time. He fixed a large glass of Diet Mountain Dew® and began to write his final thoughts on the semi-final victory.

It was about one o'clock when he emailed the chapter to Walter and Dick, after calling both to see if they would have a minute to check it for him. They immediately read it through, made a few comments, and TJ made some corrections before sending it on to Janet and her team. He ate lunch in his room, took a much needed nap, and by four, the chapter had been returned with a few more corrections. He pondered each carefully before making his re-writes, and sending it back.

Shane began his day with a very late breakfast and a team meeting. They returned to the scene of the most recent victory with another press filled shooting practice. The coach and several players did a reluctant but required press conference. The team boarded the bus and returned to the college gym for a private practice to prepare for the championship game with Memphis.

They returned to the hotel for a late lunch and scouting reports. Shane was free by three, but exhausted and took a long two-hour nap. He was also free for dinner and made his way to TJ's room just after five.

They talked over the day's events and Shane sat down with TJ's laptop to read the new chapter. TJ then showed him a slide show of about two hundred game photographs shot by the publisher's photographer. They were all high quality shots and captured the action extremely well. Janet and her team were pouring over the shots as well, trying to find the right ones for the cover, but knowing a second batch would come from the final game. It took them two hours to narrow the shots down to three they could use.

TJ and Shane met his parents and Gary's gang at steakhouse for dinner. They chose top quality thick steaks since they were in the heart of Texas, then made a trip to a huge salad and fruit bar, and devoured pecan pie for dessert. They laughed and talked about basketball for a half hour before moving on to the book and the construction of the house. The meal lasted two hours, but they laughed and enjoyed each other's company and support, and the time just flew by. Shane relaxed, smiled, and laughed, but in twenty-four hours, he would be going to war with a strong Memphis team for the title.

TJ and Shane made out in TJ's room until the end of Shane's curfew. Tomorrow would be a long day of waiting and worrying.

TJ tried to sleep in the following morning, but unable to do so. He reluctantly got up, ordered breakfast via room service, and began answering his emails. It was noon by the time he completed all, and began working on the final chapter of the book beginning with Shane's thoughts on the upcoming game with Memphis.

Meanwhile, the Taylor team spent ninety minutes shooting in the arena, and then moved to the college gym for a run through on their defensive assignments, thirty-second drills, and finally, their overtime plays.

They returned to the hotel for their team meal at five. The rest of the day, the anxious but nervous players were forced to lie around and sleep.

TJ had done all he could on the basketball book and put it aside. He also finished the last check of the galley proof for **Gay Grifters** and uploaded his approval to his new gay publishers. He had now written and published several gay books since publishing **The War Apart – Part I**. He spent most of last summer researching part three for this series, visiting a dozen northwestern Indian museums, as well as numerous towns and trails in northern Colorado, Wyoming, Montana, Idaho, and east into the Dakotas. He spent time going to see the buffalo in the South Dakota State Park just south of Rapid City, and saw big herds of buffalo in Yellowstone. He especially loved the new memorial museum for Chief Crazy Horse, and the Kevin Costner Museum about the buffalo and the amazing bronze sculptors on the museum's grounds. His rough draft of **The Blackfeet Boys** also contained much of his research.

He had been writing a story in his head when he had time, and now reached his favorite part of creating a new story with the writing of the first draft. He typed fast, and though he corrected some errors, generally, he just pushed to get the story in digital format. Later he would begin the editing and polishing of the story.

He did the mechanics to get ready by creating a new folder for current projects, and transferred all his research materials to that folder. He created a second folder for pictures and transferred all the photos he took of Indian crafts, bows, arrows, and smoke pipes. He opened Word® and began creating several simple documents that he would use as he worked through the creation process and later during editing.

He started a new story journal that he would update with each day's writing, noting the page numbers of new chapters, and ended each day with the page he stopped on. He then created a character page by transferring key characters from the previous books so it would be easy to refresh his memory as to their description and age. He started a new storyline document and began quickly writing short sentences describing the events he had been working on his head. Finally, he opened a new master story document and set up the formatting, as he tended to enjoy writing in a book format, so he could see what the story looked like as he wrote, and he liked the tighter margins to visually edit within the margins. He created the header and footer. He called the book **The War Beyond – Part III**.

Now he stared at the blank page for almost a minute before describing the opening sequence that would begin the story. He forced himself to write about the main characters, as if this was the first book and not the third in case someone read this book first, or perhaps a reader forgot what the characters looked like.

It was six by the time he stopped for the day. Caught up in the story, he couldn't stop writing. Over the past few months, he had grown tired of editing, and reveled in the joy of freely writing fiction. He changed clothes, gathered up his laptop, his press pass, and identification cards, and made his way out of the hotel. He caught a cab and arrived before the fans swarmed the place. Tonight, there would be just one game at eight o'clock central time. He made his way to the pressroom, found a desk, stowed his laptop, and placed the final press releases on the desk to be read shortly.

He made his way to the buffet line and snatched up a plate and silverware. He made a healthy salad and took it to a nearby table, and returned to fix a plate of food. He decided to eat southwestern barbecue chicken, potato salad, coleslaw, cream corn, and green beans. He got a big glass of sweet tea, sat down, and glanced up at the television monitors displaying pre-games sports shows.

He finished eating, went to the bathroom to wash up, and made his way into the arena to watch the Taylor team warm-up. As he came down the steps, Shane came out of the tunnel and waved at him. Slowly and methodically, he began his long stretching routine with the help of a trainer. TJ knew he would soon begin his close shooting practice followed by foul shots, and farther away jump shots. Other team members began joining him, as did the Memphis team on the far end.

TJ saw Al and Barbara enter on the other side of the court, so TJ made his way down the steps and around the court. Shane came close enough to smile at him, but said nothing. TJ went up and gave Al and Barbara a hug, and sat down to chat while they watched the boy they all loved warm-up. TJ told them about the final work he had done on the book, but said nothing about his gay books. They knew he wrote gay fiction, but he wasn't sure they would be interested.

The stands began to fill up as the teams retreated to the locker room. TJ said his goodbyes, and made his way back around the court and up to the pressroom. He went back to the buffet, got a bowl of strawberries, and put ice cream on top. He feverously devoured it. Some people can't eat when nervous, but in his family, nervousness was just another reason to eat. He snatched a bottle of water from a barrel of ice, and made his way to his seat, where he found Gary and his friends. He chatted briefly. They were all excited about the game.

TJ glanced at his watch and made his way to the tunnel entrance. It was just a minute before the team made their way to the court, but TJ could see Shane. He gave him the chill sign and the two sign to imagine the refs are naked. Shane smiled and knew TJ was trying to tell him to calm down and let the game come to him.

TJ got out of the way as the lights went down. The team was introduced and ran out of the tunnel. They used spotlights to introduce the players for the starting lineups, followed by coaches and the rest of the players. After a long television break, the team broke their huddle and made their way to center court. Shane looked one more time at TJ who gave him the one finger symbol for love. Shane pulled his earlobe to acknowledge, but kept his game face on. He would be guarding a man three inches taller than he, but Shane had more experience and scored more points this season, but it would still be a tough battle.

Shane caught the tip, flipped the ball to Jerry, who moved it quickly down the court with Shane tracing him. Jerry was so fast that he blew by his man and laid it up. Taylor University was first on the board. Taylor went immediately into a full court press. Shane had studied the film on his man over and over, and now he finally stood in front of him like a moving semi truck blocking his vision of the floor with his body and windmill waving arms.

They achieved getting the ball in, but Jerry managed a steal from his man as Shane began sprinting down the court. He quickly changed direction, as Jerry worked to shake off the man he had stolen the ball from. Jerry quickly flung a long bounce pass that came up and into Shane's hands. He caught it, took one step, and left the floor and slammed down a hard thunderous dunk. They now led four to nothing. This brought the Taylor exuberant fans to their feet.

They brought the ball in and quickly moved it up court. Shane stayed with his man the whole way, preventing him from getting the ball, and blocking him out of the paint as much as possible. Their high-speed guard made a run for the basket. Shane quickly stepped over and planted both feet, blocking his path. The boy had run so hard that he couldn't stop and ran right into Shane. The whistle blew and the Memphis guard received a charging foul, and Shane took the ball out of bounds. He tossed it into Jerry while their guard was still arguing with the referee. They came down the court and set up with Shane setting two screens until Larry was finally opened. He dropped a three-point shot making it seven to nothing.

The Memphis coach was pissed and called a timeout. Coach Timmons told the Taylor boys to keep it up. He wanted to see many defensive stops in tonight's game and urged them to keep up the pressure.

This time, however, Memphis got the ball down the court and set up their offense. They moved the ball expertly left and right and set up a beautiful three-point shot. They decided to begin their full court press. Shane took the ball out, quickly got the ball to Jerry. He moved half way up the court, stopping to create a screen for Jerry if he needed it, or to catch a quick pass and go if Jerry got himself in a pickle.

This time Jerry breezed to him with rapid dribbles, and his man bumped Shane, allowing Jerry to run free into the Taylor court. Two of their players came to the top of the lane to stop him. Jerry saw this but plowed ahead. Larry broke down the sideline and Jerry bounced the ball to him. Larry went under the goal and threw it back up over his head for a nice layup.

Memphis hit a pretty three from way back of three-point line, and the announcer for CBS Sports® said he shot it from another area code. Near the end of the half, with Taylor up by four, Shane went for a quick layup, expecting to get fouled, but two Memphis players had gone up so hard, they hit Shane, knocking him into the stands. He bumped his elbow on a metal chair and it hurt. He caught his breath, retrieved his body from the folks he had fallen on, and walked slowly to the foul line.

He rubbed his left elbow several times as it continued to sting. He bounced the ball and missed the first shot. This pissed him off, but he stayed in control and made the next one. Memphis brought the ball down quickly, ran a play, and put a two-point shot in just in front of Shane. After he brought the ball in, the cameras and the fans watched Jerry received Shane's throw, but few were watching Shane as he began sprinting down the court. The man guarding him was being outrun, and feared Shane would sprint for a pass and a layup. He bumped Shane twice to slow him down without a foul called, and finally tripped him.

This sent Shane sprawling to the floor right in front of his bench. Coach Timmons had seen the foul, but not a single referee saw it, or if they did, they didn't call it. Shane had bit his lip in the fall, and came up quickly with blood dripping down his chin. Jerry shot a pretty three-point shot, but as it went through the net, the referee called time, and told Shane to get help to stop the bleeding.

He went to the trainer as the coach put in a substitute. Shane was not happy at being tripped, but he kept calm, and let the trainer put some stinging stuff on the wound to stop the bleeding. It was inside his lip. He then rolled some gauze and told Shane to put it between his teeth and gum.

The coach started to put him back in, but Memphis tied up the game, and with just thirty seconds to go in the first half, he decided to give Shane a rest. Jerry attempted a last minute shot that went in the rim and rolled out. The scored remained tied.

The doctor looked at Shane's lip in the locker room, but said it didn't need a stitch. He put a new gauze pad in, and told him to try to keep his lip still for a while. Shane went to the bathroom and washed the blood off his face and hands. He then sat in front of his locker and evaluated his performance in the first half. He made a mental list of the things he thought he could improve.

The coaches met while the players talked and then finally, Coach Timmons faced them for the last time this season. The players fell silent before he spoke, "Boys, this is one exciting game. This is what I live for. Excitement, major competition, hard play, beautiful shots, and the only thing better—is winning the darn thing. Okay, we're going to change out a few assignments, and we're going to apply even more pressure to them. They say they like to run, but I saw them panting hard near the end of the half. They can't keep up with us all night. You're in better shape. You're tougher and more disciplined. We're going to run their legs off.

"Jerry, every possession is a fast break. I want the team to hustle down the court at lighting speed. Shane, we're going to assume they are going to keep two-timing you when you get the ball. When this happens, I need my forwards to get to the corners and get ready to shoot. Two men on Shane means one of our boys is open, and without a man guarding him. Get it to that man.

"If we do this enough, they'll stop the double-team, and that'll allow us to get the ball into Shane and score. I think this game is going to go to the wire. Expect a thirty-second play at the end. Expect overtime. Above all, expect to win. Are you ready?"

The team yelled yes in unison.

TJ had been so nervous that he picked at a bowl of ice cream and slowly ate it. He went to the bathroom to pee, and returned to the arena with a fresh bottle of water. Gary and Scrappy were so excited they rarely sat down.

The teams kicked off the second half at a frantic pace. Up and down the court they went. Both teams were shooting well from way out, but Taylor began working the ball to Shane, but as coach predicted, the Memphis double-team appeared. Shane worked his way left and right to force them to guard him tightly, and then he jumped and flung it out to the open man. Larry dropped in another beautiful three-point swish. He had already hit three in the second half from the corner. Taylor had a six-point lead with three minutes to play.

On a fast break, Shane broke for the basket on a full run, but again fouled hard by Memphis trying to prevent him from scoring. He came down on a player's shoulder with his face, knocking a contact out. Shane immediately spotted it on the floor, picked it up, ran to the bench for some water, rinsed it, and put it back in. He then walked to the foul line, and to the marvel of all, he put both shots in. The announcers could not believe how calm he was after being fouled so harshly, plus the disadvantage of having to put a contact in with millions of fans and viewers watching.

At sixty seconds to go, Taylor went up by three, but their guard got loose on a screen, and hit a long three tying the game.

Coach Timmons called time, but carefully watched the other team as they left the floor. They bent over in their huddle and he knew they were tired. "Keep up the running. They are spent. They have nothing left. Okay, run the blue plate special after using at lot of the clock, stay tight on defense, don't foul, but don't let them have a good shot either. If we play smart, we're going to win. Are you ready to win?"

The team yelled yes in unison and took the floor. Shane looked up at TJ and winked. TJ gave him three fingers for go as hard as he can. Shane brought the ball in. He knew they had to score, and they had to get a defensive stop afterwards. Jerry worked the ball up the court safely. Shane stopped at the top of the circle to set up a screen, and then moved down the right line. His man was all over him trying hard to prevent him from getting into a scoring position. Shane moved under the goal, and then backed up and across the other side. He looked up at the possession clock. Twelve seconds to go. He rushed to the top of the circle again to set up a screen. Jerry came from the far left and ran pass Shane at a blazing speed losing his man by a step as he made his way around Shane.

Shane broke to the left and got his hands up and ready to catch a quick pass from Jerry, but Jerry went in for the layup. The ball went off the glass, rolled around the rim twice before flopping out. Shane went up hard, snatched the ball, and with his soft touch put it in the center of net. Taylor was up by two with thirty seconds left.

Memphis called time to plan how they were going to use up the clock, and take the last shot to tie the game once again. They were also thinking the last shot might be a three for a win, but coach Timmons knew better. A three-point shot was too big a risk. They would want to move the ball in close for a better shot at tying the game. Therefore, he warned his boys to be careful not to foul the shooter, or they would give them a chance to win by one at the foul line.

They broke the huddle and set up their full court press, forcing Memphis to use up some of the clock, so they had less time to set up their offense. The man-to-man pressure kept up all the way down the court. Shane kept his man from getting the ball. Every Taylor hand was up and they were pushing as hard as they could, but at five seconds to go, their guard made a fake drive to the lane hoping Taylor would converge on him, and he could toss the ball to one of their big men for a layup, short shot, or a solid dunk. However, they didn't fall for it. Two seconds to go. He quickly came up and shot, but Jerry accidentally bumped him just slightly. The ball swished tying the game. One second on the clock, and Memphis shooting one.

Jerry felt awful. He just couldn't stop his momentum when the boy pulled up to shoot. The championship was on the line. With one second to go, Taylor would have no chance to get the ball in and shoot. Shane felt sick. The team huddled and reminded each other not to foul, but to not let the team get a rebound tip in.

The Memphis team was excited. They knew they had a chance at winning. This was a shot their guard made eighty percent of the time. They were smiling. TJ looked down at the Taylor bench and already they were assuming they might just lose this thing by one-point.

The referee stepped into the lane and reminded the players it was just one shot. Just as he about to pass the ball to the shooter, coach Timmons yelled for a timeout. The team hustled to the sidelines. His intention was to rattle the shooter, and remind his team to block out and no fouls. They returned to the court. The fans behind the goal stood to make as much upsetting noise as possible. Every person in the arena stood.

Once again the referee reminded the players this was just one shot. He tossed the ball to the Memphis player. The player sighed hard, harder than he had done all night, and Shane knew it. He bounced the ball four times, but earlier he had only bounced it twice. Shane knew that as well. His felt the boy's nerves were getting to him.

The boy brought the ball up with the championship on the line, brought the ball back and shot. It hit the front of the rim and could have gone forward into the net or backwards off the rim. Shane was in the air the moment it left the boy's fingers. The ball fell back towards him and he snatched it, and started down but a Memphis player hit him in the air while trying to get the ball. The referee's whistle blew just a half second before the buzzer sounded.

Pandemonium swept across the court and into the stands. The replay team in the video truck outside the arena rapidly turned their knobs rewinding the tape. The producer asked for video and they rolled the first feed. In the distance, you could see the possession clock counting down, but that clock was no longer important. In the lower right corner was the game clock. The clock began to run when the ball touched the rim. It fell back and Shane grabbed it, and then he received a shot to the back of the head from the elbow of the Memphis center. They froze the frame at the moment of impact. They could see Shane's hand roll forward from the blow. The clock showed one and half seconds. The officials watched it on the overhead monitors as over and over from various angles the replay continued. All three officials went to the scoring table and carefully watched a replay monitor there. Then they discussed it, and declared the foul on Memphis. They put one second on the clock.

The teams slowly walked to the other end of the court. Just a second ago, Memphis shot for the championship and failed, and now Taylor possessed one last chance at the championship. Shane waited calmly at the foul line. Shane had shot eighty-three percent all year. If anyone on the team could stay cool in this situation, it was Shane. Probably no one else in the arena or at home on television was as calm as Shane was. He practiced similar possible outcomes in his backyard as a boy. He won two high school championships by shooting the final shot. He just sighed and waited.

The announcers talked about how Shane had just one shot to win the game. The arena announcers did the same. The coach talked about the one shot. The teams lined up as Shane walked to the foul line and waited for the referee to pass him the ball.

The referee with the ball stepped under the rim and said, "Okay, gentlemen, don't leave the line too soon, and remember he is shooting one."

Everyone lined up, arms up, and knees bent. Every person in the stands stood to watch. The tension on the sidelines was at an all time high. The announcers finally ran out of anything to say.

Just as the referee pulled his arms back to throw Shane the ball, Shane suddenly said, "Sir, I'm sorry. You're mistaken."

The referee had to quickly hold onto the ball. "What do you mean I'm mistaken?"

"You said one shot. I have two shots."

The referee replied, "You weren't in the act of shooting. It is a one shot foul."

"I know that, but that was there tenth foul. It is one and one."

The referee's face turned pale. He held the ball and walked through the lane and back to the scoring table. They discussed it and Shane was right. It was one and one." He returned to the waiting teams.

He grinned, "You're right. It is one and one, but if you make the first one there is no need for the second one."

Wisely Shane corrected the referee to give himself another thirty seconds to relax. Shane took the toss. His routine for foul shooting for almost a decade was always two bounces, set and shoot. It was something he did about five hundred times a week. Very few big men could shoot fouls shots as well as he could.

He bounced the ball once, twice, flexed and brought the ball back and shot. The ball arched beautifully. It was a textbook shot. The crowd fell silent. Coach Timmons was sure his heart had stopped.

Swish!

For a half second no one in the arena reacted. Shane sighed and smiled. The fans suddenly cheered. The Taylor coaches and players at the bench leaped into the air. The referee held the ball, and then as promised, he tossed it one last time to Shane. With one second on the clock, he had no choice but to give Shane that second shot. Shane bounced it twice, flexed, and shot. Swish! Taylor now led by two.

Memphis went out of bounds and spread their players across the court. Their only strategy was to catch the ball, turn, and shoot hoping Taylor fouled them.

The referee tossed the player the ball. The Memphis player faked left and right, but Shane was right with him swinging his arms wildly, trying to prevent a clear shot. Finally, the player threw the ball to half court. Their guard caught the ball on his way up. He twisted in the air as the buzzer sounded, and shot the ball.

Shane held his breath. There was no chance of a foul, as Jerry had backed away from the player's body, but leaped up in hopes of getting a finger on the ball.

The ball sailed down the court in a good arc, but fell one foot short of a swish shot. Taylor won by two. They were the new National Champions.

Shane leaped into the air. The players on the court rushed to him and they bear hugged each other. The bench spilled and the rest of the team joined them.

TJ smiled as his friends gave him hugs. The fans cheered. It had been one heck of a game and an amazing finish.

Taylor quickly lined up for the customary handshaking, but once completed Shane made a dash to give his parents a hug, and then darted across court and gave TJ, Gary, and his gang a hug as well. He even hugged a few fans on the way back to the court.

TJ sat down. His energy spent. Ladders were brought out and the team began cutting the nets, one player and one string at a time, and then the coach. A stage was assembled and soon the trophy was given to the team. They presented Shane with the Most Valuable Player award. Then they announced he also won Player of the Year Award, and presented that trophy as well. It was an hour before they made it to the locker room for a team celebration, and then the coach, Shane, Jerry and Larry made it to the press conference room to answer the media's questions. This lasted another hour.

TJ bade goodbye to his friends and climbed the stairs to the pressroom that was a buzz of activity as reporters were filing their stories. Some had just rushed in from the press conference. TJ was handed the final stats for the game, and walked to his desk. Exhausted, he walked over to the buffet and secured a fudge brownie, and added a scoop of ice cream to the top. He grabbed a Diet Pepsi®, and sat down to eat it slowly.

Once done, he unlocked his laptop, placed it and the press release in his briefcase, and made his way out of an arena for the last time this season. He took a cab to the hotel, made his way to the room, and heard the team arrive as the fans cheered in the lobby.

He set up his laptop and began getting out of clothes. He fixed himself another Diet Pepsi®, and sat down to write the end of the book.

Shane and the team had their final road meal together as they continued to celebrate their championship. There were speeches by coaches and players. Shane was grinning from ear to ear the entire time.

Ninety minutes after setting up his laptop TJ was done. He called Walter on his cell to see if the coach wanted to change his introduction. Walter had remembered to ask and said no, the coach would let it stand.

Just as he hung up, there was a knock at the door. Wearing only tee shirt and boxers, TJ went to the door. Shane entered and shut the door and bear hugged him. He almost started crying he was so happy. He began planting kisses on TJ's face, while a hand slipped into TJ's shorts.

After their celebration continued, TJ begged him to sit down on the couch and tell him about it. TJ made quick notes and added them to his final chapter. Once satisfied, he told Shane to get naked.

TJ attached the chapter to an email for Walter. He called him again and asked him to read it as soon as he could. Walter was in his room and had his laptop ready. He read it, made one change, and sent it back. TJ made the correction, and sent it to Janet.

He watched the email leave his machine with the attachment, and turned to see a tall naked man with a silly smile on his face lying on his bed. TJ pulled off his shirt, dropped his shorts, and flung himself on to the bed, bounced once and landed on top of Shane.

Their sexual celebration lasted quite a while, and they both would be sore the following day, but it was a once in a life time achievement, and with no curfew, they slept soundly in each other's arms.

Shane had

# NINETEEN

TJ's flight arrived just minutes before noon after a late start from San Antonio. He drove to the house and called Shane on his cell phone. Shane had crawled out of bed first as the team planned an early flight. He missed his classes, but went online and obtained his homework assignments, plus he watched an online video of the class presentation. He took notes as if he had been sitting there. Once completed, he filled out a form to obtain credit for 'attending' class. He then took a nap, as he was still exhausted from the game, the victory, and the celebration. His telephone rang.

"Hello?"

"You sound asleep. I call back when you're asleep," teased TJ.

"No, no," yawned Shane, "Don't go doing me any favors. I'm awake. Are you home?"

"Yes, safe and sound. I just walked the dogs and was going to head over to the construction site to see how they are coming. Would you like to meet me there?"

"Yes, of course. I forgot about it. I slept all the way home, did a class, and went to sleep. I'll be there in fifteen minutes. Bye."

"I love you. Bye." TJ knew that if Shane didn't say whom he was talking to, or say goodbye, by saying something about love, that there was someone else in the room. In this case, it was most likely his roommate. It didn't bother him at all. He preferred to keep Shane safe, and he knew Shane loved him. He met gay couples that felt unloved if their partner didn't say they loved them about twenty times a day. TJ thought once a day was enough and any more than that was icing on the cake.

He gave the dogs a treat and went next door to thank Bob and Sue for watching J-Henry and Beeper. They chatted for a while and then he drove over to the construction zone.

As he came around the last slow curve, the construction came into view. He slowed down and his jaw dropped. He looked into the rearview mirror and Shane was right behind him. Slowly, they drove in the entrance through the newly completed gates that were open for the construction crews. They drove to the building and instead of finding a few pieces of steel erected, they found the entire house and coach building constructed and it had the metal skin on it. They were working on the soffit on the left side. Another group was installing the outside heat and air units for the west end of the building. The same units were already completed on the east side. They walked into the twenty-foot wide motorcoach entrance. Eight men were working on completing the insulation of the interior of the building. Six more men were installing the lighting fixtures after the installation of the insulation, and were installing outlets and switches all the way around the building.

A plumbing crew was hooking up the waterspouts, laundry sinks, and bathroom fixtures. They had already installed two tank-less hot water systems, providing energy efficient, instant on demand, unlimited hot water for the residence and RV garage. They also installed the piping for the big air compressor with air hose wheels on each side of the coach and the tow vehicle. Next to that were water hose wheels hooked to a restaurant-style, big sink water valve, so they could adjust the hot water to warm for washing. TJ knew that sometimes very hot water was excellent for getting grease off the coach, and warm water did wonders for washing away the bugs.

They walked through the building while turning in slow circles and feeling amazed at the progress since they left for San Antonio. On the right side, the framing crew completed a floor to the ceiling interior wall and insulated it. Inside the wall and all the way around the inside of the RV garage, brick masons installed cement blocks to a height of four feet. They used spray guns to coat the block with a thick waterproofing product that made the rough block smooth and watertight. TJ failed to do this on his previous building, which meant that the water spray hit the wooden walls causing mildew. He explained to Shane the concrete walls would allow them to wash away spiders and bugs, as well as dirt and dust down the floor drains.

TJ and Bobby Jenkins designed the lighting with particular concern to providing bright light all the way around the parking zone of the coach and tow vehicle for washing and especially detailing. Henry placed over a dozen canvas tarps over the new cement to keep it clean during construction. After construction, the paint crews would paint the floor with two coats of gray epoxy. He set up temporary wood blocks as marks for where the coach should park. Off to the left on the floor was a recessed floor drain for connecting the sewer hose, but capped with a spring-loaded hard plastic lid that pulled up. A foot away was a second recessed six-inch square compartment, housing a water spigot for the RV quick disconnect water hose for filling the onboard freshwater tank. A third recessed watertight compartment housed an Ethernet connection for Internet access, telephone port for their phone system, and coax for satellite television. TJ explained this would allow them to see and do all the things they could do in the open sky while inside the garage, plus have the ability for a wired telephone and Internet access.

Henry spotted TJ and Shane and came over to shake their hands, "Welcome to your new RV garage."

"I can't believe how fast you have put this up. It is amazing."

Henry smiled, "Well, once a metal building is engineered, it is all computerized manufacturing after that. The steel went up in two days and I had plenty of men on hand to get it dried in. Once that was done, most of the work is on the inside. I figured we would finish the RV garage first and use it for a staging area for the home construction your new home. Your home section will take longer to build, as we have to finish framing it out, do the electrical and specialty wiring, plumbing, heated floor, and all the bells and whistles. Then sheet rock and wooden walls are finished, flooring, cabinetry, bath and kitchen stuff, well, there will be a lot to do, and it has to look and feel perfect. Would you like a tour of the house?"

"Sure."

Henry walked led them towards the exit of the RV garage on the east side and pointed out, "That is where the utility stuff come in underground. There will be air units outside and an automatic start generator. We will step through this door into the car garage. It'll handle three vehicles. We'll be putting lots of cabinetry in here to store the things there's no room for the in the house. As they came through the second door frame he showed them the laundry on the right, pantry on the left, then the large kitchen on the right, and dining area on the left, and a window frame to see out the front of the house across the covered long porch. The rooms were only framed in with metal studs, but the floor plan TJ had drawn became a reality to him. He could envision even the furniture in its intended place.

They saw the great room on the right and the long office on the left. Through the office, they found the foyer leading to the porch and main entrance to the left. On the right was the hallway with a hall closet, guest room on the left, hall bath, and then into the master bedroom. They saw the large walk-in closet, huge bathroom, and to the left and out the far side of the house a doorway led to a wet area for Jacuzzi, sauna, weights, treadmill, and half court for basketball practice.

Henry delighted in showing it to them. "I think you should come back now and then to check on our work. If you want to change something, now is the time."

TJ grinned, "Don't worry. It looks perfect to me, almost like I drew it, but better."

Henry said, "The outside areas are almost done. The gates are working, and I close them at the end of the day. The yard is totally fenced in, as is the half fence going from side to side and touch the rear corners of the building, and the fenced in dog pen. There is underground lighting along the two entrances, and intercom to the gate pedestals. We also put in the utility pedestals for the two RV parking spots, and wiring to the shed. The big garage doors will arrive on Thursday and we'll get them up right away so we can start locking things up. Do you have any questions?"

Shane spoke up, "Are we still on schedule?"

Henry grinned, "I don't get to say this very often, but I'd say we're ahead of schedule. Have you got your furniture ordered?"

TJ blushed, "No, I haven't even started on it. We had too much basketball to worry about. But I'll get it done before I leave for New York on Sunday."

"Very good. I'll see you next time. Congratulations on the national title!" The boys shook his hand, thanking him repeatedly for an outstanding job.

Henry took off to go meet with the plumber. Shane and TJ wandered through the house once more before heading home. Their new home was going to be spectacular, and they couldn't wait to see it finished. TJ planned to come almost every night to take pictures of the wiring and plumbing in the walls, in case they experienced problems later on.

Shane returned to school to get busy on his homework and would work out afterwards. He had just finished winning a national championship on Monday, but couldn't wait to work out, as he made a list of things he wanted to work on that he couldn't during the season. He also wanted to maintain the physical shape he was in, and increase his strength, speed, and endurance throughout the off-season.

TJ returned home and pulled out the contacts he had been given for furniture for athletes—especially tall ones like his boyfriend. He quickly opened a blank spreadsheet, and opened the plans for the house. He modified the office to suit two people, but he decided to work room by room. After selling his previous house, he sold most of his stuff when he went full-time on the road, rather than pay large storage fees. In each room, he added to the spreadsheet the items he thought they needed.

Once he completed the list, he made a call to the lady who sold him the land. He asked for references for an interior decorator that could make the house look great but not too feminine. She laughed and said Leslie would be perfect. He thanked her five times, hung up, and dialed Leslie.

"Hello?"

"Leslie, my name is TJ Johnson, and I building an unusual RV Port Home in Lindle. It is under construction with move in day scheduled on or before June first. My partner is very tall at six feet nine inches. We don't want the house to be too feminine, but not completely a man's place either with beer signs flashing everywhere."

She laughed, "I think I can handle that. How soon can I see your plans?"

"I'm free this afternoon."

She laughed again, "That sounds like a man. Anxious to get me checked off their list."

This time TJ laughed. "Well, yeah, and I have to fly to New York on Sunday, and will be gone three weeks, home for a few days, and gone two more weeks, so yes I do have a long list to accomplish as quickly as I can."

"Where are you?"

He gave her the name of the RV Resort and she knew it. "I'm just five minutes from there right now. Should I come ahead?"

"By all means—I'm in lot 89 on the back row. It's a blue and gray motorcoach with a big satellite dish on top. I'll see you soon."

TJ quickly walked the dogs so they could pee, and she drove up as they were walking back to the RV. He introduced the dogs to her. She knelt down and petted them. In TJ's mind, she just passed her first test—a dog friendly person.

He showed her the plans on paper, and then the virtual tour the architect produced for him. She had never seen anything like his designs, but loved the concept. She went over the height restrictions and then he asked, "Leslie, I must be up front with you on an important point, "My partner and I are gay. Is that a problem for you?"

She laughed, "Of course not. My brother is gay and I hate anti-gay people. I'm fine with that."

TJ smiled, "One last thing, my partner is not out of the closet and is a bit of a celebrity. We must keep his name a secret. Will you do that for us?"

Her face expressed a puzzled look as who that might be, but answered honestly, "Of course I will. That will not be a problem."

"Very good. TJ showed her the printout of the furniture he thought they needed, but she quickly pointed out he didn't have anything down for windows like blinds, drapes, sheers, and no end tables, or even a coffee table. He did have all the office furniture down. She made several quick suggestions and asked, "How far along is the construction?"

"It just about framed in. Would you like to see it?"

"Yes, I would. It would help me get a feel for the house."

She followed TJ to the house in her car, brought along a camera and notepad, and began snapping pictures as they went from room to room, measuring for furniture, and asking about cabinetry. After the walk through, they went back and sat in TJ's car. He gave her a slip of paper with the name of the big and tall furniture galleries.

"I hope these help when it comes to a bed. We'll order a custom air flex mattress once you give us the measurements."

"What's that?"

"Well, that's not the right name, I think it is called Sleep Bear®, but anyhow I'll look it up for you. You're familiar with Sleep Number® Beds I'm sure. Well, this is a simpler system, with an easier fill and deflate air system. I have owned two Sleep Number® beds, and I like this air system better. Each side has a manual control and the firmness or softness changes in seconds. It uses a vacuum cleaner motor. It's cool. I'll email you the spec sheet on it."

"When is our completion date?"

"Well, the big work is ahead of schedule, but there is a lot of finishing on the inside, especially the house. I'd like the furniture here no later than the third week of May. We'll be out of town and are due back by June 1st. I hope you can move everything in, and have it working and in place before we get home. I'll put you in touch with the project director. His name is Henry and he is excellent." TJ pointed at Henry through the windshield, "That's him in the Taylor University ball cap."

She left with promises to get back to him by email with her suggestions next week. TJ explained the tour, but said he would receive email several times a day. He gave her all his contact information. He also gave her the info for his accountant for the bills. They shook hands and Leslie left to get busy. She was excited to take on this unique project, while TJ couldn't resist walking through the house one more time.

Since Monday night following the championship game, TJ and Shane slept together every single night. Shane all but moved out of the dorm, leaving only some clothes for workouts or going to the dining hall. They enjoyed the six nights together so much, and couldn't wait for the tours to be done and exams, so they could leave on their extended vacation.

They said their goodbyes in the motorcoach with lots of kisses. Shane and Sue would be taking care of the dogs, but TJ kissed the dogs goodbye like they were his own children. He drove to the airport feeling sad at leaving the ones he loved most behind, but excited to begin his first professional book tour.

It was an early flight so Susie prepared breakfast for him once Steve leveled out the Learjet. He would be using two flight crews for the three-week journey, but was thankful to start out the journey with his old friends. A car service carried him to his hotel where he checked in, dropped his bags, and then the driver took him to the publisher's office. All his previous visits to the big apple included battles for finding a cab, having the right change, and money for a tip. Like his previous trip to meet his new publishing team, he would enjoy the pleasure of a chauffeur.

TJ thought it felt weird to be arriving in New York City on a Sunday morning, as traffic was only about ten percent of normal, many folks were either in church or just waking up, but as they cut through Central park he could see lots of families walking and enjoying the spring day. He was thankful he would not need an overcoat on this tour.

He met Janet Wilson in the lobby of Over-the-Top Publishing. He found her to be about five feet six inches tall, dark hair, and dark eyes with a good tan. With a father as her dentist, she also possessed bright white teeth and smiled at him all the time. After introductions, she took him on the company tour, but there wasn't that much to show off as the printing division was actually in New Jersey. This office prepared the books for printing and sent the files digitally to the printer. They maintained a full graphics department that on Sunday looked like a long row of dark monitors.

He noted they had a large marketing department and that impressed him because publicizing the book was always the hardest part. The last stop on the tour was in a room that looked like a library, but was rows and rows of copies of the books they published. There were far too many for TJ to count but he would guess in the thousands. This impressed him.

She then took him to a conference room where he met several of the key people working on his project. The first thing they did was hand him a copy of his new book. TJ was thrilled with the front and back cover. Winning the championship certainly helped, as there was a big picture of the team holding the trophy on the front, with an insert picture of Shane slamming a dunk down. The rear featured another team picture, a picture of coach Timmons, and headshot of Shane. The inside front contain a list of quotes they obtained for the book with Dick Vitale's comment at the top, and the rear inside featured TJ's picture at the top, a brief bio, and a paragraph from the book.

TJ flipped through the opening pages and finally through the book. He looked and smiled as the group silently waited for his decision, "This is perfect. Way to go. I can't imagine how you printed it in six days, but it is terrific. I'm am very pleased with everyone's hard work."

The group collectively sighed. Janet spoke up first, "We're thrilled that you like it, and you may think the hardest part of the job is over, but it is really only the beginning. For all of us to make a living at writing and publishing, we have to sell books. That is what this tour is all about. We have prepared short instructional periods, with practice time on each segment. We'll do the same tomorrow. The tour officially kicks off Tuesday morning with a segment on the Today show."

TJ whispered, "The Today Show? Holy cow."

"Just this morning a producer called me, and they have Shane set up with a remote camera from the campus, so you'll be on the air with Shane and the coach. It should be fun. Are you ready to get started?"

"I'll do anything you say. I'm ready to learn."

"Great," she replied. "Tim is going to train you for interviews. Tim, this is TJ Johnson, and he is all yours. Call me when you need me?"

TJ took his coat off and sat down as Tim began telling him about the key elements of an interview. He explained the differences between a news print interview and live medium like television or radio. His group prepared numerous practice interviews, and they setup a camera, lights, and monitor for his rehearsals. They attached a microphone to his shirt, and placed an earpiece into his ear, so he could receive instructions from the television director or producer, and the bright lights. TJ didn't tell them he had done stints at both radio and television stations in his early employment career.

He smiled as they introduced him and asked the first question. TJ listened well and replied smoothly. Tim loved it. He asked TJ to think of a longer answer and they recorded it, and then a shorter answer. He was pleased that TJ could think on the fly. TJ thought Tim should be happy TJ could think at all.

Since the live medium is where an author might screw up the most profoundly by inserting his foot in his mouth, Tim spent three hours on interviewing. This was followed by a late lunch, and TJ was then introduced to Sarah for print medium training. She gave him two pages of a short synopsis they wrote for his book. He read it and smiled. He liked most of it, but already prepared a series of quotes from his book on his laptop that he had been working with that he liked better. He blended their work with his. Over and over, they practiced for the next two hours.

After some refreshments, he went to the other end of the conference room where they set up a simulated signing table. They told him to imagine sitting in a big bookstore like Barnes and Noble®, a long line before him all wanting his autograph, and what he must do to keep them happy and moving along, so everyone obtains what they had stood in line for.

Janet told him to imagine that each person waiting was like a nonpaid marketing person. If they obtained his autograph, they would tell dozens of people they see every day, including relatives and friends, and email friends around the globes, bragging about meeting the author.

TJ got the message and he knew the key points. Smile, look them in the eye, and pay attention to their name. He placed a pad on the table to write unusual names allowing a chance for correcting the spelling before writing their name in a book. He sat down behind a stack of his book with single blank sheets inserted in the front for practicing autographs. He asked about writing a phrase and immediately Janet answered, "If the line is short, write a good phrase so the line backs up a little. This will encourage others to take note. If the line is long, please write dear Sally and your name, and move on by saying thank you."

TJ smiled, "I've got it. Shall we practice?"

This final session of the day took two hours. Janet studied each paper he signed, and watched as his signature and his writing improved.

Satisfied with his progress, she announced, "That's it. I'll see everyone right back here at eight o'clock tomorrow." The employees began filing out of the room after shaking TJ's hand. She turned to TJ, "Well, I must say I'm impressed, and we're ahead of schedule. We'll do more of the same tomorrow, but not as long. We'll have several key people here from our company to meet you, and tomorrow at four you'll do your first interview with a reporter from the New York Times®."

"Oh, my. Starting at the top, are we?"

"Yes, he'll be writing a story about you that will come out Tuesday morning, so we'll be blitzing for both mediums from the get-go. We'll go over the schedule tomorrow. Tuesday you have the Today Show®, a noon local show on a superstation, and an interview at ESPN® with Dick Vitale and Shane again on a remote. We have four bookstores to do in New York. Afterwards you'll fly to Philadelphia for the next stop on the tour. Get plenty of rest and I'll see you tomorrow. You did great and thank you for your patience with us."

"It was my pleasure and thank you."

TJ left the building with the adrenalin still pumping through his veins, but by the time he settled into the backseat of the limo, he realized just how tired he was. He made it to his room, ordered room service for dinner, and called Shane.

Shane was anxious to tell him about the two interviews he would be doing with TJ, and together they laughed and talked about TJ's training, as well as Shane's schoolwork. They both missed the other very much, but reluctantly hung up so Shane and TJ could study and prepare for the next day.

The next morning TJ was there a few minutes early impressing Janet once more. Many a time her authors began to act like divas showing up very late with everybody on her team waiting to go. They practiced the television interviews first, stopped for meeting with the big wigs in the company, and back to work on newsprint, and signings. After lunch, he met with the royalty department where a nice lady, who acted like an accountant in a doctor's office, spoke very softly to him as she explained the reports he would receive monthly on the sales of his books. TJ expected this and immediately produced his accountant's business card and asked her to send everything to him. She smiled, knowing this was a common request. She asked if he would like an Acrobat PDF® file of his reports emailed to him, and he said he would.

The first interview with New York Times® went well, and he was hoping the reporter would make him look good.

By the end of the day, he was exhausted, but prepared for the tour and especially for his big day tomorrow.

He told Shane all about the day on the phone and wished he were there with him. TJ also wished Shane was in the bed with him, as he was nervous about tomorrow and all the work he had to do. He didn't sleep well in the bed alone.

The limo picked him up at six and took him to Rockefeller Center with the sun creeping between the giant skyscrapers. Even at this early hour, traffic had already picked up. Janet met him at the underground entrance along with an assistant NBC® producer, and led him into the green room where he would wait until they were ready for makeup. He sipped some hot tea, and ate a croissant and fresh fruit, while the producer prepared TJ for the interview by asking questions one of the show's hosts might ask. He performed well, making Janet feel both relieved and pleased. Once rehearsal was completed, he begged for a Diet Mountain Dew® to get some cold caffeine in his veins. Several bottles appeared shortly thereafter.

He watched the first of the show in the green room, and then off he went to makeup, and back to the green room. At eight-forty, they whisked him to the set where he met Meredith, one of the co-hosts, as his microphone and earpiece were attached, and he sat down across from her. They made minor lighting changes to adjust for his height, he tested his sound level during a commercial, and soon Meredith was given a cue. She began introducing his book and finally she talked about him.

"Welcome, TJ, we're delighted to have you with us."

"Thank you. It's great to be in New York."

She smiled, "My family members are huge college basketball fans. I know several of the guys on our crew have been reading your book all morning. I cheated as I got an advance copy and had to hide from my husband. You give us an interesting look behind the curtain of college basketball. How did you come up with the idea?"

"I became friends with Shane Bradley last summer, and when he found out I like to write, he jokingly said I should do a book about Taylor University winning the National Championship."

She interjected, "He predicted they would win last summer?"

"Yes, and he never doubted it. Each week he would tell me how workouts were going, the pickup games with the NBA players last summer, and once the season started, he told me about practices, locker room talks, strategies, and then after a game he gave his perspective from a player on the floor."

"Well, speaking of Shane we have him on remote from Lindle, North Carolina. Shane, welcome to the Today Show®."

TJ could see a monitor just over Meredith's head as they did a split screen with her and Shane. TJ smiled as Shane spoke, "Thank you. I wish I could be there, but I have classes to attend."

Meredith asked, "Did you reveal any team secrets to TJ for this book?"

"No, the staff and coach cleared the book from the beginning. My thought was to make the book much like a behind-the-scenes feature on a movie DVD, giving the fans an interesting way of learning what the players do to prepare for a game and a championship."

"I read that when you have a night game, except for some shooting practice, you mostly lay around the hotel room all day bored to death. Is that right?"

Shane grinned, "Well, we do go to classes and study halls for our assignments, but yeah, we bring along DVD's to watch and iPods filled with our favorite music to listen to. I usually read about twenty books during the season while waiting for a game."

Meredith turned back to TJ, "What surprised you most about working with Shane on the book?"

"I have been a big Taylor basketball fan for most of my life. It is a North Carolina tradition to support one of the college teams in the state. I knew they probably worked hard, ran some laps, and did some pushups, but I never imagined how hard Shane and the team worked in the off-season. He attends his classes, does his weight room workouts, strength workouts, then he shoots thousands of practice shots with a manager tossing the balls to him, and sometimes does over five hundred shots in two hours. He has been known to shoot thirty-five free throws without a miss. After all that, he goes through practice with the rest of the team. Sometimes, he even practices his shot after a long hard team practice. Several times this year when the coach gave the team a day off, you could still find Shane in the gym shooting. He eats very healthy, stretches his muscles carefully before practice, and takes excellent care of his body. He is tenacious on the court as well as off the court when it comes to basketball."

"TJ, thank you for telling us about your book." She spoke to Shane, "Shane, and thank you for joining us. It is a great book. Now you get to class," she teased.

As only Shane could say with sincerity, "Yes ma'am!"

Once the producer announced clear, Meredith shook TJ's hand and wished him well. They whisked TJ to makeup to get the stuff off, and then Janet took him out the door and into the limo to head to the ESPN® studios.

Essentially the same things happened: green room, makeup, pre-interview with a producer, on to the set, live interview with Shane and Dick Vitale. It went great. Obviously, TJ felt very relaxed working with his old friend Dick.

Janet took him back to the limo where they ate a box lunch in the back seat in route to her office, and followed by a press conference in the lobby of the publishing company with all their staff on hand. There were many photographs, an unveiling of a Shane size cutout to display the books. Hundreds of pictures were taken, and all the questions were pretty close to his training.

TJ went back into the limo, drove to a huge Barnes and Noble® store, and was quickly ushered in through a back door. There he met the management that led him to a table set up with stacks of books and two helpers. A minute later a red rope was removed, and the line of seventy-five people began filing pass him. He signed quickly, smiled, and chatted with everyone, and the line continued to grow. Janet was counting heads and filling out forms for their marketing department, and checking her watch every five minutes.

Ninety minutes later, he was in the limo drinking more Diet Mountain Dew® while making their way across town for the next store. By eight o'clock, he had been to four stores and signed three thousand books. Janet dropped him off at the hotel. TJ made his way to the room, ordered room service dinner, and called Shane.

They talked until his dinner arrived, mostly about TJ's day, but also about Shane's classes, homework, and the dogs. TJ fell asleep by ten, but was up at six for the ride to the airport. The flight to Philadelphia was short. TJ did a local morning television show, and checked into his hotel, but was soon off to his first signing at noon, another at three, and the last at six. He ate when he could.

Each day he was in a new city doing basically the same thing. On Friday morning, Janet had a USA Today® newspaper waiting for him in the limo. She showed him a full-page full color ad promoting the book. He couldn't stop laughing when he saw that. He called Shane and told him to go buy the paper—several he said for family members.

As soon as the jet landed in Baltimore and TJ stepped off, Steve and Susie took off again heading to Lindle. Shane finished his second class, and drove his Hummer to the airport. He watched the jet land, boarded with his weekend luggage, and they took off again.

TJ did the television show and was resting in his hotel. He got a text message from Shane as he was taking off. The limo picked TJ up and took him to another Barnes and Noble®, and then sped away to the airport. TJ was about halfway through the noon signing session when Shane entered the bookstore and sat down beside him. Pandemonium resulted and Janet was glad she insisted on extra guards. TJ and Shane signed a thousand books before heading out the back door. They did two more signings that day before retiring to the hotel.

They ate dinner in the room, stripped naked and made love. They set a clock for the next day, and slept well in each other's arms.

Saturday and Sunday were done with early flights, three or four signing, and late dinners. Unfortunately, Shane flew home Sunday night to attend classes Monday morning, and TJ hated to see him go. He missed him immediately.

The next five days, TJ bounced across the nation performing very well at all the stops, and Janet and her boss were very pleased. Jake flew out and met him spending a day with him talking some business, but most of all checking to see how he was holding up.

Shane arrived Friday about noon in Cincinnati, and they spent the weekend at signings, television shows, and flying. When they could, they made love with great passion.

The next week was the same routine followed by Shane on the weekend. TJ again hated to see Shane fly home on Sunday night, but he knew he would be home Wednesday after flying in from the west coast ending the tour. Their reunion was a joyous one.

TJ slept the rest of Wednesday, all night, and late the next morning. He finally woke up in time to walk the dogs before lunch, chat with Bob and Sue, eat brunch, and met Shane at the new house to see how things were going.

The framing crew finished two weeks ago, the big panels of sheetrock were installed, and the crews were doing cornering and finish work in preparation for painting in the bedroom areas. The bathroom tubs and showers were installed. In the huge wet area of the house, the men were installing the final long sections of sheetrock, while other teams were doing the mudding and smoothing out the seams, corners, screw dimples, and making it all look like one perfect piece. Two coats of paint had already been applied to the kitchen, laundry, pantry, office, and bathrooms a few days earlier. A cabinet installation crew began installing the kitchen and office cabinetry, and TJ noted the big garage doors were installed in the RV building as well as for the car garages. All the outside doors for the entire structure were installed. TJ walked through the building with Henry and Shane, feeling euphoric at the progress. Henry told him that Leslie, their interior decorator, had been by earlier. The boys marveled at the amazing work and shook Henry's hand vigorously while thanking him.

On Friday, TJ flew out for the gay tour. There was no training for this one, but he applied what he had learned before and went right to work. He had fourteen cities to stop at, but unfortunately, Shane would not be along on the weekends. This distressed him, but he was excited about finally promoting his new gay book, as well as the re-release of his others. In the gay bookstores, his company sent larger posters to help with the promotion, and TJ was pleased with the lines at each signing opportunity. He gave data cards to every bookstore manager so he could add their store to his gay database for future promotions. He also gave away bookmarks promoting future books and his website.

Shane made it a personal goal to earn top grades in all his classes and finish with excellent grades on his exams. With TJ out of town, he studied for long hours, and performed as he hoped. He called TJ with the news of his grades. TJ was so proud of him and always thrilled to hear from him. They talked about the upcoming vacation, the house construction, and how they missed each other.

Shane told Bob and Sue that he was going to surprise TJ by washing and waxing the coach so they would be ready for their vacation trip. Bob told him he would help, so the next morning, they emptied the black and gray tanks, sprayed them out, and filled the freshwater tank to the brim. They pulled a ladder out and sprayed off the top of the coach, and then began washing the walls of the coach all the way around just as TJ and Bob did last winter.

Sue decided to help and went inside and cleaned the kitchen, the bathrooms, and began dusting all the way around the coach. She finished by vacuuming the entire motorcoach using the built-in vacuum system. She liked how easy it was to use.

They used water from the filtered salt tank to rinse the RV, eliminating many spots. Shane and Bob finished the sides, and using the squeegee, they pulled the water off the coach to avoid water spots. They used quite a few towels to get it shiny and clean. Then they set out to make the rims and tires look good. Shane scrubbed all the dirt and mud away, and then Bob hooked up a small leaf blower to blow away the water. They put a tire dressing on the tires to make them shiny and black, while also helping to avoid UV damage. The rims were treated with a cleaner, then a buffing agent, and rinsed. Finally, they sprayed on a clear lacquer type sealant that would make it easier to wash the dirt off for about four months. They finished by cleaning all the glass and mirrors with a new product Bob found that made the glass crystal-clear. They did the inside glass as well, but Beeper had already messed it up with her nose trying to get their attention.

Satisfied all was clean inside and out, Shane took them to dinner to celebrate. While Shane and TJ were gone on their upcoming vacation journey, Bob and Sue were going to head to Washington to spend a few weeks sightseeing. Sue especially wanted to spend more time in the Smithsonian Museum, and Bob wanted to see the World War II memorial. Weeks ago, TJ talked them into visiting the new Air & Space Museum to the west of the city outside the loop. He knew they would enjoy the beautiful gigantic facility.

# TWENTY

For the second time in the past few weeks, TJ flew across the country, meeting thousands of nice gay readers, and learning what they liked about each book. It made him feel absolutely great that he could write gay fiction and people actually enjoyed reading his books. Many times buyers stood around after the signing just talk to him. He learned quickly to ask about their lives, and if they were in love, as he thought listening to their stories was more fun than repeating tales of his adventures. The days of the tour flew as he racked up thousands of miles, but today, the second tour ended in Atlanta with three signings. He flew home and landed in Lindle at eight o'clock. He drove straight home from the airport, anxious to see Shane, the dogs, as well as Bob and Sue. They were ready to see him, too.

Shane came running out of the coach and bear hugged TJ and swung him around, but refrained from kissing him in public. Sue gave TJ a big hug, too. They talked for a while, and then TJ went inside and knelt down and let the dogs welcome him home.

Beeper would run up and kiss him, and then take off down the hall in a full run, and return quickly to kiss him again. Meanwhile J-Henry would come up and give him a small kiss, but stick around for some quality rubbing, before more kisses. TJ and the dogs played for twenty minutes while Shane heated up the takeout he brought home from the barbeque restaurant he loved.

They sat down, ate, and talked about what was going on in their lives as if they had been apart for a year. After they cleared the table, Shane sprung his surprise by telling TJ that he, Bob and Sue had cleaned the coach inside and out, and this afternoon he bought groceries so the coach was ready to leave tomorrow morning on their vacation.

TJ laughed and gave him a hug for all his hard work. Although he had done a ton of travel by plane over the past five weeks, he was ready to get behind the wheel, and get on the road with an easier schedule. TJ undressed for bed feeling exhausted, but Shane was rested and took over. He gave TJ a very loving, deep massage, and then they made love, and fell asleep cuddled together. For the first time in five weeks, TJ did not set an alarm clock.

They didn't stir until ten o'clock. TJ took a lot hot shower while Shane made breakfast. After breakfast, Shane took his shower, and they began stowing the final stuff away and bringing in the slides. Out of habit, TJ checked the levels on the tanks, feeling thrilled and spoiled that Shane and Bob emptied the gray and black tanks, and filled the freshwater tank for him. He stowed the office stuff, moved chairs, and pushed in the dining table until it locked. They went outside and met Bob and Sue, and talked for a while. They disconnected everything but the power cord as the air-conditioning continued cooling RV.

A Writer's Fantasy

TJ invited Bob and Sue to go with them to see the progress on the house. Shane drove, while TJ used his phone to see if Henry was around. He said he would meet them there.

As they pulled in the gate, it appeared the outside of the house was finished. The gates and fencing completed, the outdoor lighting, remote gate, and intercom control units were in, and so were the security cameras. They noted the cameras at the gates, and on the corners of the building. There were at least seven trucks backed up to the house, and they could hear the sound of saws and drills working.

TJ took Bob and Sue through the RV building first, after pointing out the guest RV parking areas, and Shane told them they were welcome to stay any time they wanted. They couldn't believe how big the building was, and all the features installed from a washing machine, dryer, instant hot water units for RV and house, air compressor lines on both sides of the coach, as well as hot and cold water, floor drains, lighting and more. This time the RV garage bathroom was finished, as were the storage cabinets, tool bench, and high storage near the rear of the building.

They walked to the back so they could see the doggie pen and the back of the property. They returned to the car garage and found it painted and all the cabinetry installed. They came into the house through the garage entry door and looked into the laundry. The plumbing was finished, the painting done, and cabinetry installed. Across the hall, the pantry and all the shelves painted and the electrical done for the freezer that would be in the back of the pantry.

Sue marveled at the kitchen. The walls were painted, the cabinets hung, but the countertop was not yet installed. They realized the flooring was not complete either, as an orange waffling mesh covered all the floor area in the house. Henry came out of the office to welcome them.

After introductions for Bob and Sue, he told them they were working on the heated floor. He insisted the entire system be put down and tested before the tile floor began, as he wanted no errors that would require pulling the tile back up again. He said all the countertops were due in next week. He walked with them from room to room and almost all of it was complete. There were a few more lights and ceiling fans to hang, but it was working and beautiful.

TJ and Shane loved the office. Except for the countertops, they could see the layout and they were very excited with the design and space. Shane asked about the wires hanging from the ceiling on his side of the room.

TJ replied, "Dick Vitale suggested we put in a remote studio system that will allow you to do television interviews from right here to save you from wasting time heading to a local television station. Brian Kenny from the ESPN® technical crew will be here in two weeks to install it."

Henry broke in, "Actually, he was in town last week and came by just to see how things were going. The telephone company finished and tested

241

the wiring for the T1, and your other technical stuff including the security company. Brian will be back as mentioned.

"Leslie has been by several times, measuring, taking pictures. Next week, most of your furniture is arriving and we're going to store it in the RV garage until the flooring and countertops are completed. The appliances are in town and waiting for me to call and give the clearance to bring them in after the flooring is cured. She said to tell you everything is on schedule and have a great vacation."

TJ grinned, "Thank you. Let's see the rest of the house."

They walked down the hall, into the guest room, hall bath, and on to the master bedroom with the large walk-in closet, and huge bathroom. They went out the far door to the wet area. Shane grinned as he saw their Jacuzzi, sauna room, steam room, weight room, treadmill, and four men were working on a new wood floor for the basketball half court and goal for him to practice on. Of course, Shane felt this area was the most important part of the house.

They thanked Henry for all his hard work and drove back to the RV Resort. TJ and Shane gave Sue a big hug and Bob a big handshake. Shane hitched up the dogs so they could pee. TJ fired up the engine, letting it warm up, while filling the air tanks for the air ride and the brakes. He then went outside to unhook the power line. Shane and Bob had already hooked up TJ's SUV, and Bob had the keys to Shane's car so he could park it next to their car for now, but to be moved to the new house closer to move in day.

TJ blew the horn and waved at their friends as they pulled out of the RV resort for the first time since basketball season started early last fall. They made their turns before reaching the freeway.

TJ was driving, while Shane fired up the laptop in the front passenger seat. TJ asked, "Where to?"

"I already plugged in your itinerary plans. We're just going to Hilton Head today, and I called your sister. We're having dinner with her. That puts us at three hundred twenty miles and not a bad trip for the first day. We'll be in Daytona tomorrow night. Is that okay with you?"

"Yes, did you make a reservation for Hilton Head Motorcoach Resort?"

"Yes, I did. I'll go ahead and confirm for Daytona. We're staying at International RV Resort, right?"

"That's right. You will make a great co-pilot. Do you want to drive some today?"

"Yeah, I need to get better at it. I hope I can eventually relax and drive."

"You'll do fine."

A few hours later, they crossed the state line. Once in South Carolina they pulled into the Welcome Center, walked the dogs, and Shane sat down behind the wheel. TJ tried to remain quiet while Shane went through his checklist, adjusted his seat, checked his mirrors, and turned on his turn signal blinker. He looked behind into the rear camera monitor, as well as left and right in the big truck mirrors, and pulled out of their parking spot and moved onto the highway. Shane was clinching the steering wheel like it might get away from him, so TJ reminded him to relax and just keep checking his lanes for alignment, but too look farther down the road to keep a straight line.

Fifty miles later, Shane began to relax and his driving became smoother. They stopped for lunch in another rest area near mile marker forty-seven, and then TJ drove the final leg into Hilton Head, as the park was a little tight for their entry. After they registered, TJ put on his headset with microphone phone, while Shane snatched up a walkie-talkie from the cabinet over the dash. They quickly tested their ability to talk to each other. They unhitched the car, and Shane followed TJ to their spot. He parked down a few spots, and then walked down to guide TJ into the tight spot. This was a beautiful ownership park, and they did not want their guests trampling their grass with his big truck tires. TJ could listen to Shane, as well as see him. He expertly backed into their spot, and adjusted their depth so they would have room for their car up front. Not long after they set up the RV and walked the dogs, TJ's sister Elagene drove up.

Shane became a big fan of her amazing energy level. They laughed and cut up, played with the dogs, and then drove off in her Lexus® for dinner. They ate seafood followed by a walk around the famous harbor. By the time they made it back to the coach and walked the dogs, they quickly settled down to sleep.

The drive the next day included a fuel stop, and then on to Daytona. They set up the RV, downloaded their email, walked the dogs, and then Rick and Paul showed up. Rick was TJ's best friend for over twenty-five years. They sat around the RV and talked for a while. TJ showed some of the pictures of the new house, and they promised to come up for a visit this summer. They talked during dinner and even longer in the coach afterwards, as they had a lot to catch up on.

The next morning they were back on the road heading south and making their way to Fort Lauderdale area for another overnight stay in a nice resort. They walked the dogs, unhitched the car, and TJ took Shane on a tour of the gay beach area of Fort Lauderdale. Shane pulled his hat on tight while wearing a big pair of sunglasses. He could not believe how many gay people were out of the closet and having fun in the beach area. They saw gay bars, hundreds of gay friendly restaurants with the familiar rainbow in the windows, and even a shopping mall primarily for gay people. They ate dinner at a wonderful Italian restaurant, and then went back to the coach to go over their travel plans.

Shane made reservations at Bluewater Key Motorcoach Resort at mile marker fifteen on south US 1, but there wasn't an interstate to travel on after Homestead for their journey, plus they had a few key turns to worry about in route. They also planned an early morning fuel stop, so they wouldn't have to worry about finding diesel in the keys. TJ had made this trip several times for mid-winter vacations, but he always felt better after studying the required exits and turns.

They left early the next morning and immediately felt thankful the south Florida morning rush hour was heading towards and not with them. They headed west until they picked up Interstate Ninety-Five, where they turned south. The last time they drove on a two-lane road was in the early fall on their route to Lake Toxaway in the mountains. As they began to reach the long bridges, Shane was blown away at the incredible view of the tropical blue water and white sand around the motorcoach, but he kept worrying about the guardrails and oncoming traffic. Island by island they leaped from one bridge to the next until they reached their destination just fifteen miles north of the end of US 1 in the heart of Key West, Florida.

The resort staff led them into their spectacular spot, surrounded by lush tropical palms with a commanding view of the ocean just twenty feet in front of the motorcoach. They set up camp including the awnings as they were going to spend most of the week here. They walked the dogs, met some of the other guests, and cooled off in the resort's swimming pool. After grilling steaks, they drove into Key West. TJ quickly took him to the boardwalk and dock area where everyone gathers to watch the sun go down. A dozen street performers, telling corny jokes to attraction attention before dazzling the crowd with stunts, tricks, entertained the huge crowds and even a tight rope walking or juggling fire sticks. Tips were earned and expected.

They bought frozen daiquiris and enjoyed the various groups of performers until the sun went down. Afterwards, they began walking Key West's main street called Duval Street, and found a creamery where they both purchased fruit sundaes and ate while walking. They enjoyed seeing the people from all over the world, and Shane was amazed that all the stores were gay friendly. He spotted gay people everywhere. They went about ten blocks before crossing over and starting back.

It was their first evening in downtown Key West and they experienced a great time. Shane had never been to a city where being gay was actually cool and comfortable. It didn't mean he could be out of the closet, at least not yet, but he discovered there were places they could go and be free to be who they really were. They drove back to the coach with only minimal plans for tomorrow. TJ told Shane they were going to rent motor scooters to make it easy to get around downtown, but they were also going to do a scuba dive in the late morning.

They drove into Key West early the next morning with their swimsuits and towels in the back seat, plus TJ's scuba gear. They found the new location for Point South Dive Shop and went into the shop. Shane began looking at the diving gear while TJ talked to the manager about their reservations for diving.

"I see by our records you are certified diver but your partner is not," began the manager with the great tan and blue eyes.

TJ smiled, "I signed Shane up for the resort dive training at nine and our ocean dives at eleven."

"Yes, you're quite right. We'd better get him ready. Are you paying by credit card?"

TJ presented his card for the swipe, he signed the printout, and then Shane came over and signed a dive waiver. Together, they went into a changing room to get ready. The manager took Shane to their rental equipment room, found a mask that fit his head, huge fins for his big feet, and together they walked out to the pool in the back. He was introduced to Mark Elmore his diving instructor. Mark was about five feet eight inches, great tan, dark curly hair, big smile, and apparently lifted weights, as he was cut with beautiful muscles. TJ felt a tinge of jealousy, but not enough to doubt the love he and Shane shared.

Mark began teaching Shane the mechanics of diving, safety tips, rules, and how to handle his equipment, and within the hour, Shane was underwater and swimming around the pool and having a great time.

As they came out of the pool Mark, told TJ that Shane was a natural and he would do well. They put his gear on board the boat at the dock, along with TJ's, cast off the lines, and they began leaving the harbor for the open ocean. TJ and Shane were enjoying the scenic view of Key West when Mark brought them plastic cups of an orange punch they served on all their dives. He told them they would have a snack after their first dive.

Shane's first dive would be to a depth of forty-five feet with Mark swimming next to him the entire time so he could monitor Shane's equipment and movement. TJ would also be nearby as Shane's official dive buddy. They planned a diving excursion at the underwater national park where the tropical warm water coral was known to be beautiful.

After they reached their destination they tied off the boat to a permanent anchor buoy, so they could avoid damaging the coral by dragging an anchor. Shane and TJ put their gear on, and checked each other's buckles—all under the watchful and attentive eye of Mark. Once ready, they made their way to the edge of the boat. Mark stepped off first, followed by Shane, and then TJ. All three gave the captain of the boat an 'okay' sign with their thumb touching their index finger, and then they began their gentle descent down the anchor line. Shane cleared his ears as instructed and TJ grinned when he saw Shane's eyes, as he stared at the thousands of tropical fish swimming around him. Once they reached their bottom target depth, Mark pointed the direction he wanted them to swim. It took Shane a few tries, but soon he mastered neutral buoyancy, so he wouldn't rise or sink, and he began to follow TJ.

It wasn't long until TJ noted a lobster swimming in a crevice and showed it Shane. Next up was a small octopus Mark found. The big coral sponges amazed Shane, as well as the large brain coral. It was just so fascinating to the number one basketball player in the country and the recent winner of the National Championship. TJ knew the joy of a first ocean dive, the freedom to float freely along the coral beds, watching carefully for sea creatures, and mesmerized to be swimming amongst the beautiful colorful fish.

Near the end of the dive, they suddenly spotted something large ahead and to the right a bit. Mark signaled for the boys to hold still as the creature became larger, and soon they realized it was a huge manatee. It was the first time for both boys to see such a beautiful animal in the open water. Later, they saw a big sea turtle and pretended to chase it for a few yards.

Back in the boat, Mark gave them a big thumb up for Shane's first dive. The captain moved the boat to their next dive spot while they began resting. Mark brought out a Tupperware container of fresh cut pineapple and oranges, along with some croissants, and the boys devoured them. He explained that breathing the tank air always makes you thirsty, and kicking and pulling makes you hungry.

The second dive began as easy as the first, and Shane couldn't help but get excited. The shallow dive placed the boys at a depth of just twenty-five feet. Suddenly, Mark grabbed Shane's arm to halt him and waved at TJ. He pointed off to his right and downward where they saw a huge Moray Eel feeding on a fish the animal just snatched. They swam on after watching the eel for a minute.

A big grouper came by to investigate and later a silver barracuda. Shane was just fascinated with everything he saw, and TJ realized he should have rented an underwater camera. As they made their turn to head back, Mark suddenly tapped Shane again. As Shane looked right, he sighed heavily creating a huge stream of bubbles. TJ looked over his back to where Mark pointed. Out of the deeper water was a sand shark. He was about six feet long, but to Shane he was still a shark. He turned to be sure TJ was looking and smiling as best he could with the regulator stuck in his mouth. TJ nodded approvingly.

They laughed all the way back to the dock with Shane telling tales of the shark that almost ate him, and each time he told the story the shark became another foot longer.

TJ tipped the captain and Mark for their patience and expertise. It was a good first dive for his boyfriend.

They drove back to the motorcoach to walk the dogs, as well as shower and change. After lunch, they took a nap, took the dogs for a quick pee, and then drove back to Key West in the late afternoon. They parked the car at a motor scooter rental place and rented two bright yellow motor scooters. They practiced in the parking lot before heading out. Shane was sure

246

he had never done anything as dangerous. Carefully, he followed TJ as they drove towards the beach while weaving in and out of traffic. They went away from the crowds and drove to the absolute end of US Highway One. They asked a tourist to take a picture of the couple with their camera. Shane was wearing a big hat and sunglasses, so no one would recognize him, but everyone noted the tall, good-looking, athletic man on the scooter. Gay men were waving at him at almost every block they passed.

TJ led the way as they rode to the AIDS memorial near the entrance to the pier. They parked their scooters and began reading the memorial plaques. It made them feel sad that so many died before the medical doctors began to understand the disease. TJ could still recall a Christian evangelists calling AIDS a gay disease, and a punishment for their perverted ways.

They rode leisurely down the wide sidewalk, but stopped every now and then to look across the beautiful beach at the blue water surrounding Key West. Shane could not get used to seeing so many gay people. They were working in every field from a doctor to a policeman, shipping clerks and servers, and as well as tourists.

They safely returned the scooters before dark, and made their way on foot to the Crabby Dicks restaurant. It was up a flight of stairs and they were ushered to a table overlooking Duval Street. Shane and TJ pointed out various good-looking men walking up and down the street Shane saw couples holding hands, kissing, and nobody said anything, or least not a local. There were times when they would see someone scoff at a gay couple, but the boys immediately knew they were tourists and not accustomed to the openly gay friendly society surrounding Key West.

After dinner, they did a bit of shopping and then drove back to the motorcoach. They decided to change clothes, and head to the Jacuzzi. The mostly older crowd in the resort settled in early leaving the pool to themselves. They enjoying lounging and working on their tans, however, after their skin became hot, they dove in the pool, swam some laps, and splashed each other. The pool wasn't very long so it only took Shane about five strokes to reach the other side. They returned to the hot water and soaked awhile before heading to the motorcoach. Now that the sun was way down in the horizon, and finally cooler, they took the dogs on a long walk. After dinner, they showered to get the chlorine off their skin, and went to bed so they could make love and fall asleep.

They loved cooking on the grill while looking at the beautiful blue water in front of their coach. The seagulls rode the ocean wind currents above the water, and every now and then, they would see a dolphin crest the water surface. It had been a long time since Shane felt this relaxed, comfortable, mellow, and calm, and he loved it. He had yet to check his computer calendar to see his to do list. He always cherished the time he and TJ had together, while dreading the moments they had to part. To be together twenty-fours a day became like a treasure of time to Shane. He felt so blessed to simply have seconds, minutes, and hours to hold hands, lean against TJ, take a nap with his boyfriend, walk side by side, kiss for the fun of it, touching foreheads together, and especially liked not having to say hello or goodbye to TJ as one of them left town.

After a few days, he began jogging in the mornings. He started by running laps around the resort, but it wasn't that big so he talked TJ into joining him. It had been a long time since TJ had done any running. He was pretty sure it was in the eighth grade. His idea of running involved a list, a car, and heading to a grocery store, Sam's Club®, Home Depot®, or Wal-Mart®. Shane made him stretch for a while, and then they slowly began jogging out to the sidewalk along the highway US1 leading to downtown. The sea breeze blew across their sweating bodies and surprisingly, TJ did better than he thought he would, but Shane wisely stopped from time to time to keep TJ from becoming winded.

After thirty minutes, they began walking for another half hour before picking up the pace again. By the time they returned to the motorcoach, TJ's legs were spent and Shane was grinning. From then on, TJ joined Shane's on his light runs, though sometimes Shane would tell him he was going on a long run for endurance, so TJ would walk the dogs or write another chapter on his new story.

The next day they did their second scuba dive trip, and experienced as much fun as the first. That night they decided to eat on Duval Street again. Afterwards, they walked through the Wyland Museum® and decided to purchase a large picture for their new house. TJ shipped the painting home, but with instructions to hold shipping for another week. He would later email Leslie so she could figure out where to put it. The manager emailed TJ an Acrobat PDF® file of the picture so he could send it to her.

Shane had gone out to the street, while TJ took care of the paperwork for purchasing and shipping. TJ joined him on the street.

"Let's go get some ice cream," urged TJ.

"Naw, let's go home," replied Shane with a surprising cold tone to his voice.

TJ noted a change in Shane's tone and a quiet demeanor. "Okay, but what's wrong?"

Shane waited until they turned up a side street in search of their parked car. "Did you see that older couple in the museum. They kept staring at us. I thought they had made me, but when I had my back to them, I heard the man say that we were another fucking gay couple. He told her this town was full of faggots."

TJ caught on, "And how did it make you feel?"

"Angry. I wanted to punch his lights out."

TJ grinned, "I could see the headline after that. Sports Star Beats Old Fart For Calling Him A Faggot!"

Shane smiled slightly, "But they didn't even know us. Why did they talk about us like we were crap? Our love matters just as much as theirs."

"I don't think they can make love as much as we do, so probably that's what made them irritable." He tried to make Shane laugh, but it didn't work. "I know you're not used to it, and maybe I shouldn't get used to it, but a long time ago I just learned to ignore bigotry. There's not much we can do about it, but slowly, we should try to keep educating the world."

"That'll take too long."

"Not if every gay person tried to change the hearts and mind of their family, friends, and co-workers. If they do that, then like dominoes, as time goes by, the world will have changed without anyone really knowing it."

"You're full of it," said Shane. "I think I would rather bash some heads."

TJ laughed, "Yeah, you're probably right, but the world is changing. You'll see. One day we will be able to marry."

Shane laughed as he got in the car, "Now you're talking. I love you with all my heart, and I would not be afraid to marry you. If we do that, do we get to have sex all night to celebrate?"

"We can do that now."

Shane looked pensive and puzzled, "Oh," he sighed while musing, and then quickly added. "Well, hurry and get me home. I am horny as I can be."

TJ gave him a mock salute, "Yes, sir. Right away, sir."

They laughed as made their way through the island traffic, and drove the fifteen miles to the motorcoach as safely as they could, and still in a hurry.

The next morning they left their island paradise ready to explore the mainland, while enjoying the spectacular morning scenery as the crossed the many bridges heading north on US Highway One. They pulled into a beautiful huge luxury motorcoach facility in Naples just after two. They took the dogs on a long walk around the gorgeous park and grinned at the numerous huge beautiful motorcoaches. Shane pointed at the Prevost® units as well as the cars like Hummers, Porsche, Jaguars, and even a Bentley.

Shane said, "You know this time next year we can buy one of those Prevost® motorcoaches—especially after the NBA draft. If I have a great year and get the number one pick, the contract could be for big figures."

TJ laughed, "How would that work? You'll be flying all over the country with the team. You'll play several nights in a row. There won't be time for a motorcoach ride."

"You make that sound bad," replied Shane.

"I'm sorry. I just meant that you hardly had any free time this season, and probably even less in the NBA. They play more games and for a longer season."

"Yeah, but we'll have plenty of time together because I won't have to study, and we'll have at least five months off a year. We can go anywhere we want to either by motorcoach or by jet. You'll see. It'll be fun."

"I know. Come on, let's go cook dinner. I'm starving."

"I thought we'd go for a jog," teased Shane.

"In the morning when it is cooler. I'd die of a heat stroke if we went now."

"Okay, what's for dinner?"

"I thought we'd grill some chicken."

"Good, I'll make the salads and slice up a bunch of fruit. That cantaloupe we bought is awesome. It is so sweet and melts in your mouth."

TJ grinned slyly, "You're trying to get me horny again, aren't you!"

The next morning they did their morning jog, ate breakfast, took their showers, and then TJ wanted to drive to the Apple® store in Naples. They used the GPS software and found it in a huge new outdoor mall that was more like a new city. Shane immediately saw an iMac® like TJ's but TJ drifted over to the laptops. Shane followed him as TJ began looking at a MacBook Pro® with a large screen, fast dual processors, plenty of RAM and a big hard drive. Shane on the other hand discovered the new MacBook Air® that weighed only three pounds.

The clerk began showing the boys the features of both computers and hooked Shane right away. He couldn't believe how much lighter it was than his old PC laptop, and he had been on TJ's iMac® enough to know that it was a superior computer. He began asking what software came with it, all of which was cool, but not what he was used to. He used Microsoft's Office® products to do his schoolwork. TJ told him that he used the new Office version on his iMac® and Shane grinned, well, that is what I want on this one. Shane grinned mischievously and said, "Sir, how much is this MacBook Air® with Office installed?"

The clerk used an iPhone® to quickly add up the order plus tax and told Shane it would be twenty-seven hundred dollars or eighty-two dollars a month. Shane didn't hesitate, "I'll take it." He turned to TJ, "Which one do you want?"

TJ laughed, "You're kidding."

"No, I'm not. We deserve it. We just had a very hard winter, you just worked your tail off doing five weeks on the road, we're making good money, and we deserve it."

"You're hilarious. Are you sure?"

"As sure as I love you." Shane suddenly blushed knowing the clerk heard him, "Well, I do, so which one do you want? I would think you need something more robust than the model I chose, as you have to handle graphics, drawing, and word processing. You practically wore out your current laptop."

250

TJ smiled and winked at him, "I think the MacBook Pro® with the seventeen inch screen so I can leave open a research window while I'm writing in a word processing window. It should also have Office loaded, as well as VMware Fusion® so I can run my Windows programs like our GPS and financial software. Add Fusion to Shane's order, too, and AppleCare® to both."

The clerk tapped away and soon had a total. "We can have this ready in about an hour. Perhaps you would like to shop a while or have some lunch."

Shane handed the clerk his credit card, "We'll do just that." He checked the time on his watch. "We'll see you in an hour."

Shane pocked the receipt and led TJ out of the store. Once outside they laughed heartily at their big decision to order new MacBook® laptops. They found a Mexican restaurant and ordered lunch. Afterwards, they stopped in Barnes and Noble® just to see if their books were on display. It was easy to find the section for Shane, as it was right up front with his big cardboard life-size display. They both giggled and Shane was thankful he had his hat and sunglasses on. TJ took his picture standing next to it. They made their way to the gay fiction area and found a poster on the end of a row featuring TJ's new book **Gay Grifters**. It made TJ's day to see it along with a row of all his books on display.

After they picked up their new laptops, they drove around Naples to see the sights, and then made their way to see the Gulf of Mexico. Eventually, they made their way back to the motorcoach after picking up some groceries. They both went to work playing with their new computers, loading additional software, and making everything work. They felt like kids on Christmas morning.

The next morning, they drove to Orlando, staying at a resort away from the traffic on Interstate I-4, and on the west side of Disney World®. They set up the coach, walked the dogs, and drove to Sea World®. Shane had never been to the giant water and animal park. They wore out the map with the show schedules, hustling from one to the next. Shane loved Shamu, the killer whale show, and also all the smaller otter and sea lion shows. He also enjoyed the water ski show. They did the whole park in three hours and left.

They grilled chicken breasts outside when they got back to the motorcoach resort, ate a nice dinner, and then took the dogs on long hike all the way around the RV resort. The dogs were sufficiently worn out and slept well.

TJ set an alarm for the first time on their vacation. They were up at six and arrived at a back gate at Disney World® by seven thirty. They were given special passes, picked up in a fancy golf cart, and taken to a training facility. They watched a video along with the other eighteen guests on the special tour about safety on a Segway®. Their guides appeared and told them about a few key rules. Afterwards, they went outside to pick up their Segway® units. TJ and Shane quickly got the hang of the units, as they were encouraged to practice for a few minutes. They were soon following each other like on a snow slalom course, weaving and grinning the whole time.

Soon they lined up and began following their tour guide on their behind the scenes tour via the Segway® two-wheel motorized personal transport vehicles. They had seen postmen use them, and even a few cops, but this was the first time they actually rode one and took the special Disney® tour. They had a blast chasing each other and breezing in and out of the tour route.

After the tour, they quickly made a run to Space Mountain to ride the rollercoaster before the crowds got there. Afterwards, they boarded a tram and went to Epcot and did the full tour, and finished with MGM stunt show. They got back to the motorcoach and rescued the dogs that were ready to pee.

They managed to take in a few summer movies at several of the local twenty screen giant movie theaters by entering early in the day or late at night. They spent a few days in Orlando, and had a great time, but soon they were loaded up and heading west to Pensacola. They stayed in Perdido Beach for several days because they loved walking on the sand that looked and felt like they were walking on sugar. The dogs loved the beach early in the morning and near sundown so that it wouldn't be hot on their paws. They spent a half day at the Naval Air Museum, and watched two IMAX® shows.

The following week they arrived in Biloxi and stayed a few days in a beautiful new motorcoach resort, and found time to visit one of the many casinos in the area. They watched the big buck tables, but played it safe by spending nickels and quarters on the slot machines. They were having so much fun on their vacation that they often had to ask the other what day it was.

TJ did check his email and the reports coming in from Janet on the basketball book sales absolutely amazed and amused him. Yesterday, they hit the second million sales mark and still climbing up the bestseller list. The report on his new gay fiction books of course produced far less numbers, but a respectable hundred and twenty-five thousand and growing. He tinged with excitement after learning readers were buying many of his earlier books as well, especially the series starting with **The War Ahead – Part I**. This made him anxious to work harder on part three **The War Beyond**. He was thinking he might subtitle it as **Mountain Posse,** but he had other things to write first.

They did enjoy many quiet times together, too. Shane read two books on his electronic reader, and TJ did some writing. He called it therapy and after the basketball season, the two books tours, and the fun and adventure of building the house, well, it all just mentally strained his brain. Writing tended to relax him, especially his gray matter.

He got a note from Jake congratulating him on his success and wondered what his plans were for next year. TJ wrote back that he and Shane agreed to do a sequel to the basketball book called **Twice Is Nice**. He wrote he hoped to finish his next gay fiction book by Labor Day for a Christmas release, and freeing him to start work on the second basketball book. All this was good news to Jake. He knew the bid for the second book was going to be big, forcing the current publisher to offer far more to prevent an auction, thanks to a clause Jake and Jerome worked out before TJ signed his publishing agreement for the basketball book. The clause was simple, if the book sold more than a million copies, then the publisher could increase their second offer to four million and half up front. On the other hand, the publisher could decide to pass, and if so, the book would go to auction. Jacob told TJ there was no way the company would allow that to happen. They had until September first to make the decision and deposit the two million in TJ's bank account.

Shane and TJ moved on to New Orleans staying in an exclusive a new motorcoach resort in the downtown district. They walked Bourbon Street, enjoying all the food and jazz. They were surprised to find how open and gay friendly the city was. Shane thought that maybe one day he could visit a gay dance club and have some fun, but first he had another championship to win.

In their final week, they reluctantly turned northeast by working their way back to the Carolinas with a stop in Birmingham, Atlanta, Greenville, but two days later, they would arrive at their new home on May thirty-first at noon. Thankfully, Henry and Leslie agreed to meet them. Brian Kenny was flying down the next day for the final testing of the new television gear, and train TJ how to engineer it.

# TWENTY-ONE

Shane called Henry on his cell phone, as they took the final exit leading to their new house. Henry, waiting at the house, hit the button in the office to open the entry gate as he saw them approaching on the bank of monitors on the ceiling above TJ's desk. The gate and intercom buttons were blinking on the multiline digital phone. He walked through the house and into the RV garage, hitting the buttons to open the big garage doors. He strolled out the entry door to wave them in.

TJ carefully maneuvered through their new driveway gates while he and Shane took in the view of the beautiful property. There were no trucks or workers anywhere, only Henry and Leslie's cars. Henry gave them a final wave, and then jogged down to the other end of the RV garage to guide TJ in like an airport runway worker parking a big jet. There were markings and lane lines on the floor and rubber tire stops to make it easy for TJ to stop at the right point. Henry turned on all the lights so the place would be bright and beautiful.

TJ easily pulled in, centered the coach between the white lines, and pulled to a stop with Henry's help, with his tires just barely touching the bumps. As instructed by TJ's phone call, Henry went over and hit the garage doors to let them come down. TJ hit the level button but with the flat floor it didn't take but a second. Shane put the slides out and TJ shut down the engine. Together, they went out the door, checked to see if the big doors were down, and let the dogs out.

"Henry, how are you?"

Henry took Shane's big hand in his and replied, "I've very excited and have excellent news. The entire house is done. We'll do the papers later this week, but the job is finished as far I can tell."

TJ came down the steps and shook his hand as well. "Henry, we're so glad to see you."

"I'm glad to see you as well. Here, these remotes are for your coach, and your cars." He handed them a plastic bag filled with remote control devices for all the garage doors in the RV and car garages and the gate controllers. TJ put the one for the coach inside and shut the door.

"Thank you. Let's hook up the coach to keep it cool and we'll take the house tour." Shane quickly led the dogs to the door leading to the new doggy pen. Gleefully, they ran into the new pen and began marking territory. Shane returned to help TJ hook up the coach.

They walked around to the street side of the coach. TJ opened the utility bay while noting the floor plates aligned underneath. In just a few seconds, he hooked up the sewer line as well as the freshwater line. TJ noted the cap marked with an E for electrical. Inside he found the connections for satellite television, telephone, and Ethernet. He hooked short cables to each. At the rear of the coach but towards the outside wall, Shane found a big black wire at an angle attached to a hook on the wall. It was the master fifty-amp power cord. He unhooked it and walked to the small rear door noting the new cord was a perfect measurement. He easily hooked the power cord to it. In just a few minutes, all the utilities were hooked up and operational.

"Now that was cool. Everything lined up perfectly. Way to go Henry." TJ walked to the wall, and hit the big door opener buttons, allowing the air to flow through the RV building, blowing away the fumes and allowing the engine and generator to cool.

"I hope you'll wash this coach soon, so we can see all that water rush down the drains. Are you ready for the house tour?"

"Yes, sir. Lead the way."

As they came into the house they found Leslie in the kitchen. TJ spoke up first, "Leslie, how are you? I can't wait to see what you've done."

"Hello, and welcome to your new home. You must be Shane, as I already know Henry. Welcome to your home, too. It is nice to meet you."

"It's nice to meet you as well. Let's do the tour. I'm so excited."

Henry showed them the laundry with the big washer and dryers sitting on their pedestals, the laundry sink with the long drain shelf with a small rail overhead, the shelving, and the permanent ironing board and steamer.

Shane asked, "What's the rail for?"

TJ grinned, "That's so you can wash the dogs. You hook a short leash to their collar and the rail, and they will stand right there why you wash them."

Shane grinned as he turned around and looked into the pantry. It was big, beautiful, and bare. Shane said, "I guess we need to go grocery shopping. I like the freezer in the back. We're can buy lots of big quantity stuff."

Next door to the pantry was the dining area. They called it a breakfast room because it wasn't a formal dining room. They had a long table, and chairs that Leslie selected after sending pictures of several choices to the boys on the road. Along the sides were two levels of cabinetry stacked with dishes and other kitchen things. At the right entry was a chef's desk for planning meals and paying bills.

Behind them was the kitchen, featuring a huge forty-nine cubic foot refrigerator, ice machine, lots of cabinets, big gas stove with eight burners and a grilling station, dishwasher, trash compactor, large sinks and dual microwaves and ovens. They were prepared to do some serious cooking.

Leslie showed the things she had in the drawers including rows of silverware and utensils. Shane opened the refrigerator and found a single can of Diet Coke®. "We definitely have to go to the store or we'll starve."

They all laughed as he shut the door. Next up was the great room. Leslie showed off all the furniture she and TJ picked, including he-man recliners, couches, tables and chairs. TJ quickly looked at the shelving and cabinetry Henry installed and noted the high definition projector. Hidden cabling ran to the audio/video cabinet across the room. TJ picked up a remote and hit a few buttons, and soon they saw bold a high definition picture take up most of the wall on the far side of the room. It was an hundred and forty inch picture. He hit another button to dim the lights, and a final button to turn on the Bose® surround sound system. The room came alive with a bright screen and beautiful sound. Shane just stood there shaking his head in disbelief.

"I can't wait to see a ball game on that system."

They laughed as they walked around the corner to the hall and back to the office. The left interior wall was a long row of high and low cabinets with a beautiful countertop. The back wall had a long power strip, as well as plug-ins for phone or Internet. The office equipment included a big digital printer, copier, scanner, and fax machine at one end. TJ's desk area was on the right. It was a big U-shape area with lots of cabinetry and new iMAC® at his main desk area. Between his area and Shane's on the wall was a thirty-two inch LCD High Definition television screen. Shane's desk was smaller as he had less to do there—mostly homework, and another iMac® computer. Between the entry to the kitchen and Shane's desk was a stool, with several backdrops rolled like a window shade in frame attached to the wall. On the ceiling were three lights like stage lights but smaller. Between them hung a small television monitor, and on the shelf next to the stool, Shane found a small audio amplifier, lapel microphones, and two headset-hearing pieces. Shane had worn similar ones before doing interviews. TJ explained this was his new mini-studio for remote broadcasts.

They went down the hall and saw the charming guest bedroom, and the hall bath, all of which Leslie had done a beautiful job decorating. The hall veered left leading to the recreation room, but they went right into the master bedroom suite. She placed a big bed in the center against the west wall with a dresser on each side, along with sitting chairs, and a fifty-two inch LCD High Definition television on the opposite wall so they could see the TV while in bed. Under the television was a door leading into a huge walk-in closet. The lights came on automatically as they entered. The room was divided in half with Shane's on the right with tall rails for clothes, lots of shoe racks, and shelves for shirts and sweaters, plus room for his huge ball cap collection. Between them was a huge set of dresser drawers for various smaller items, including shorts, socks, tee shirts, and underwear. In the middle were chairs and benches like a shoe store, cool track lighting, and stereo speakers.

The master bath was next with double sinks, urinal, toilet, cabinetry and both a walk-in dual person shower with multiple directional showerheads, and a one person Jacuzzi tub for soaking. On the back wall was another television and speakers mounted high in the corners. The boys were seriously impressed with the master suite.

They went back into the hallway and made a right towards the wet area. Henry showed off the big Jacuzzi, sauna, steam room, weight room, and outside the door were treadmills, stationary bikes, and other machines. In the center of the room, facing the middle of the building, Shane noted a beautiful special made wooden basketball half-court. The goal was mounted on the high point wall leading to the RV garage. There was a rolling rack full of basketballs, just like at the university.

Shane grinned, "Well, we know for whom this court was built. I'll get to practice more than ever."

Henry turned and pointed back at the door they led to the house and the doggie door just to the right of it. He then pointed to another one to the left of the court at the rear of the building. They went out the people door to the right of it. He showed them a clear circular device much like a slinky, but bigger and enveloped in clear plastic with lots of holes for air. He pulled the one near him across the floor to the center. He went to the far side and picked up a second and walked it to where he had left the first one. Carefully he pulled them together. They were magnetic and snapped in place.

"Here's how this works, and I assume you can train the dogs to do this, but they come through the house, through the wet area, through this tunnel, and out the back to their own doggie pen. Come I'll show you."

They went out a people door through the back of the building and were now standing in the dog pen. The cement leaned slightly downward. Henry showed them how the rainwater would wash the poop away. There was also a farm spigot and hose wheel in case nature needed a little help.

Shane laughed and asked, "Why are they marking in a brand new dog pen?"

TJ grinned, "I asked Henry to bring his dogs over and get them to mark up the pen. I knew our dogs would smell their scent and get busy making marks of their own, but it'll take some work to teach them how to use the tunnel."

They left the dogs in the pen while they went to the exit of the RV garage and cut back through the car garage. Henry opened the doors. "You have room for three cars and a golf cart. Out here, there are two parking spots for RV guests complete with water, electrical, network, satellite television, phone, and sewer. The garage is for your yard tractor and other stuff."

He turned back to the new home, "The building has been sealed with the best insulation available. It will easily heat and cool. He walked over to a fenced in area with many bushes around it. Inside they found several working air conditioning units, and the generator. "This is a twenty kilowatt generator with auto start. It won't run everything in the building, but all the essential stuff. Tomorrow, there is an electronic expert coming by to train you on the operation of the battery bank installed in the corner of RV garage on the other side of the wall here, as well as all the security, telephone, intercom, Ethernet, and other systems. The guy is crazy to talk to, wears weird clothes, but he is a technical genius. Just call him Buddy.

"Well, I'll get out of your way and let you get settled. I'll stop in tomorrow to see how you're doing. If you find anything that needs adjusting, just make a list and I'll get it fixed for you. Welcome to your new home."

"Henry, thank you so much. It is spectacular," said TJ as he shook his hand.

Shane shook hands as well, "I've got to admit I couldn't quite imagine a metal building home, but you've made TJ's dream a beautiful reality."

"Thank you. I hope you enjoy it, and I hope you win a second championship next year, too."

Leslie told TJ and Shane about some of things she bought for them. She, too, said she would head home, but would return tomorrow to see if she could help them find stuff. They thanked her as well, and soon they were alone.

Shane jogged to the dog pen door and let the dogs into the RV garage. They began unloading some of their personal stuff they needed in the house, and then began discovering new things in the house. They would leave most of their stuff on the coach, so that it was always ready to go. TJ went to train the dogs on the new doggie doors using a handful of their favorite beef treats while Shane made a called to Bob and Sue, and asked them to bring his car over, and come take a tour of the house. They were delighted to do so.

Shane laughed as TJ stuck his head through the first doggie door, and called the dogs, stuck his hand through the rubber flap offering a tiny treat, and soon he had them going out. He would then come in and call them again. Once inside, they obtained another treat. Over and over, he did it until they were comfortable with going in and out of the door. He told Shane to go in the RV building and push the tubes apart and up to the wall to make the dog tunnel short. He went into the RV building, and climbed in the last three feet of compressed tube, and stuck his hand through the doggie door and called them. He had treats in this hand. They were cautious, but soon pushed into the garage and into TJ's face. He backed out and went inside.

He reached through the door and called them and they came in through the tube. He did this six times, before having Shane stretch the tube a foot. Over and over, they went until they would come through the entire tube without hesitation. Finally, they put the tubes together and TJ went outside into the pen, and stuck his hand through and called them. They were already in the tube when they heard him, and sprinted through the clear plastic tube.

"Here they come," said Shane as he followed them, while laughing.

Shane laughed when he saw them go through the last door and into the pen. TJ gave them a good treat and repeated the drill over and over.

258

"Now they will do it on their own. Come on, we need to make a grocery and supply list."

They had just started on the list when Bob and Sue arrived at the gate. They heard them on the intercom. TJ walked over to the phone and hit the button marked 'gate one' and together, they watched on the monitor as the two cars pulled in the main entrance. They went through the kitchen, leaving the dogs behind, and hit a button for a garage door.

"Hey," called Sue as she stepped out of her car. Bob was right behind her in Shane's Hummer.

"How are you?" TJ went over and gave her a big hug. Shane did the same.

"Thank you for bringing my car over," said Shane to Bob as he shook his hand. TJ did the same.

"My goodness, this is quite a place," said Sue.

"We offering free tours today," grinned TJ, "but first I have to show you something. Walk this way." They walked over towards the garage where Bob and Sue assumed they were going to look at the back of the property. They noted the garage, but TJ stopped near the end of the asphalt. "We built two RV parking spots including utility pedestals for our favorite guests. I know you guys are soon leaving to go to your South Dakota home, but I hope you'll come back this fall and if so, you can stay here for free."

Sue laughed, "You're kidding. My goodness, what a beautiful spot."

Shane added, "Well, it just wouldn't be the same if we didn't have Bob and Sue next door."

TJ grinned slyly, "We may also will need some help from time to time checking up on the dogs. They have a new dog pen, and several doggie doors, but still, this is a big place, and I think having you guys come and go will discourage uninvited folks. You'd be doing us a big favor, so we reserved the spot for you, and I hope you'll take us up on it. Of course, you could still make this a jumping off spot to travel to Florida or north. How was the Washington trip by the way?"

They started walking through the car garage to see the house. Sue said, "It was fun, and I learned a lot, but that town has way too many cars for me."

"Did you ride the metro from Cherry Hill like I showed you?"

"Yes, and you were right. In most cases, we either went underground or by bus to get to everything, but even getting groceries we met a lot of traffic. We left at five in the morning to try and beat the traffic around the outer loop to head back south."

Bob added, "It was nice to see where all our tax dollars have been going. I did enjoy seeing the war memorials, and the Indian museum."

Sue chimed in, "And the Smithsonian was even better than the last time I did it. We also liked the new Air and Space Museum. You were right, it is huge."

Shane pulled his car into the garage. The tour continued with the laundry, pantry, kitchen, and on into the great room, office, and all the way to the wet area. When they stepped into the RV garage Bob and Sue's mouths dropped open. They were seeing every RVer's dream—an enclosed building with a slanted floor, great lighting, and all the stuff to make it easy to wash and maintain. Bob thought the rolling ladder was really cool, too.

After they had made a full circle of the new house, TJ said, "We need food and supplies, and we're starving. Would you guys go with us to shop, and we'll pick up some takeout for dinner?"

"Sure," replied Sue.

"Let's go in two groups, "Shane you take Bob and you guys take on Sam's Club®. I have a list for you. Do you have your membership card?" TJ gave him the spreadsheet printout he had been working on during their trip.

Shane replied, "Yep, and I'll put it on Mister Plastic."

Sue laughed, "Now that's funny. Where are we going?"

TJ said, "We have to pick up a lot of groceries as the house has nothing in the way of food. The guys are picking up some office supplies on the list, but I need to get a few more things at Office Depot® and maybe Best Buy® first, plus stuff for the dogs. Are you ready?"

They gave the dogs a hug, made sure they had water and Shane brought some dog food from the motorcoach for them. TJ made a note to buy dog food. TJ gave Shane the remote unit for the gates and garage for his car. He and Sue went into the RV garage and unhitched the car, and backed out of the building, hitting buttons to close the doors and open the gate.

Shane and Bob loaded his Hummer down with two cases of copier paper, twenty A to Z file dividers, a dozen boxes of file folders, boxes of pens, pencils, tape, paper clips, staplers, and various other office stuff, plus tons of paper towels, toilet tissue, cleaning supplies, and finally bags of frozen chicken, and fresh vegetables, fruit, and meat. The back of the Hummer was full.

TJ and Sue made a run to the office store and came out with bags of stuff, a second stop to Best Buy for electronic supplies, and finally to a big Super Wal-Mart®. Thankfully, Leslie had taken care of towels, linens, and bath mats and such, plus towels for the kitchen. They took two carts and loaded up on dog food and chewies, and then took on the grocery section.

Bob and Shane unloaded the Hummer with their loads, and then drove over to the storage unit where TJ moved his personal things last winter from Hendersonville and found the boxes TJ wanted. It included his Caphalon pots and pans and the overhead rack, his small appliances, and more stuff as he called it.

They all arrived home, backed into the garage and shut the door so the dogs could walk back and forth with them. The food and house supplies stuff came in first with TJ telling folks where to put it. Soon it was all stored in the cabinets, drawers, refrigerator, freezer or pantry. The office stuff went on the counter in the office to sort out later.

Bob and Shane got the stepladder from the RV and began putting up the pot rack in the kitchen. TJ began a second list for things he thought of as they were working. He added a small stepladder for kitchen, and a bigger stepladder for house projects, and another one to work on the RV, especially for cleaning the windshield and mirrors.

Sue and TJ put the bathroom stuff away including the guest bath, and then came back to the office to begin putting away all the new supplies. Sue said, "I have never seen so many empty file cabinets."

"I'll begin filling them next week. We have a lot of files we can now take off the coach, and I have two tall file cabinets in storage. We also needed room to store books for sale, and I'm looking forward to unpacking my reading book collection, my CD music collection, and especially my DVD collection. I have over a thousand movies on disc."

"I bet you put them in alphabetical order, don't you?" Sue grinned.

"Of course, how else would you find the one you want?" They both laughed. "I guess it is a gay gene thing. I can't wait for you to see our High Definition system. It is really cool."

TJ came in the kitchen as Shane announced they were finished with installing the rack. TJ looked at their work and smiled as he gave the project a big thumb up. "Why don't you guys go get some dinner and we'll put the pots and pans on the rack?"

Shane replied, "What should we get? Let's eat Italian tonight"

Bob and Sue concurred so Bob and Shane left to get dinner. TJ began washing the pots in one of the big sinks. Sue stretched out some towels on the counter for them to drip on, but also took another big towel and began toweling each one dry. TJ showed her one of the wide drawers to put the lids in, and once he completed the washing, he began hooking the pots on the rack.

Dinner arrived about the time they finished and cleaned up their mess. Soon they were sitting at their new table enjoying the hot food and the conversation with their friends. Bob and Sue announced they were leaving for the Dakotas tomorrow, after admitting they planned to leave last week, but wanted to wait until the boys returned.

After dinner, they said their goodbyes, promised to stay in touch, and the boys reminded them of their free parking offer for next winter. They were sad to wave goodbye as Bob and Sue drove down their drive and would miss them, but hoped they would have a safe trip to the north.

TJ practiced the dogs a few more times on getting through the dog tunnel. Shane put some music on the new Bose® system and went around the house hitting buttons so the music would play in all the rooms. They decided it was time to enjoy the wet area. Shane turned on the sauna and the steam room. It would take about thirty minutes to get the temperature up. He checked the Jacuzzi to make sure it was warm as well.

TJ returned from playing with the dogs and found Shane shooting hoops. He wasn't surprised to see him back at work on the sport he loved most. "How's the new floor?"

"It is absolutely great, and with a unique sound when I dribble. I love it," added Shane.

TJ took the dogs to the pantry and gave them a bacon treat. He return to the gym to try out the treadmill, but tired quickly after long journey home, the spent adrenaline rush of seeing their home completed, and moving in.

Shane suggested they try the sauna first. They went to their room, stripped naked in the new walk-in closet and put their dirty clothes in a rolling hamper. They turned on the big television screen in the wet area to watch ESPN's SportsCenter® and stepped into the hot sauna. TJ added some vanilla scented water to the hot rocks, and the boys moved to the highest level. In twenty minutes, they were drenched in sweat from head to toe. They kissed several times before moving to the steam room. Again, they were sweating profusely, but now their skin felt moist from the hot steam.

TJ and Shane breathed in slowly letting the steam go deep into their nasal passages and into their lungs. After twenty minutes, they rinsed in the glass thick block enclosed shower, and walked over to the Jacuzzi. Together, they flipped the big lid over and off to a shelf rack Henry had made for them, and slipped into the bubbling water. They each found a recliner section to enjoy the water jets pulsating into their backs high and low, as streams of water and bubbles began cascading around their legs and arms. They enjoyed the Jacuzzi for thirty minutes, before climbing out and replacing the cover.

Shane said, "I think we need a refrigerator right there." He pointed near the door. "It'll be easy to service at that spot, plus it will remind everyone to grab a water bottle when they enter, because you can lose water weight in these areas fast. Come on, let's go get some water."

They dried off, stopped in the bedroom and put on some clean shorts, shirts, and socks and then Shane went to the kitchen. TJ went to the office and fired up the new iMac® computer on his desk. He had been in communication with the network guy who had set up their home network in a secure way, but he already had the links and passwords installed on the RV iMac®. Shane brought him a water bottle, removed their laptops from the cases, and set them up on the counter on each side of their desks. Shane turned his iMac® on as well.

TJ did a check and soon he could see the files on the RV computer system, as well as the laptops, and Shane's iMac®. He could also see the new digital printer. He told Shane to send something to the printer from his desk unit and then his laptop. TJ did the same and grinned when it all worked perfectly. Shane made his laptop since with his new workstation, grinning at the huge size and colors of the new screen. Shane saw a couple of remote controls to the right of his desk, glanced over at the same ones on TJ's desk, and hit the button for the HD LCD television mounted between their desk about five off the floor on the wall. Instantly, the screen came to life with HBO playing.

TJ said, "Use the white remote and turn on the Bose® system."

Shane picked up the remote, hit on, and after two seconds, the sound of the movie flooded the room. "Wow, the sound is amazing."

TJ grinned, "Up air in all four corners of the room are the small white speakers and base woofer is under the counter between our desk, near the middle of the room. There is a center speaker mounted under the television. Change the channel to an action movie and listen."

Shane played with the system for a while before ending up on ESPN's SportsCenter®. He began retrieving office supplies to set up his desk and drawers, while together, they began downloading their email to their iMac® workstations. TJ moved his writings, planning files, house notes, and banking files to the home network. In a high cabinet to the right of his desk was the network short equipment rack. In there, he saw the twenty-four station network switch, a patch panel for all the network connections in the house and garage, plus the wireless router and access points that led to sub units throughout the house and the RV garage. He also saw the equipment controlling the T1 high communications phone line, handling their phones and fax communications, as well as sixteen channels that handled their super high-speed Internet service. Finally, he noted a RAID backup system for their computer data. He was impressed to see it all working with their tiny LED lights blinking green.

He opened a spreadsheet for supplies and needs, checked off the things they already secured, added the refrigerator for the gym, and cases of water bottles. They both answered their emails. TJ stopped to read out the latest reports on their book sales and grinning as the sales numbers continued to climb.

He answered a confirmation email for Buddy and Brian for visiting in the morning. The boys were tiring so they left the office for the great room. Shane fixed some bowls of bananas and strawberries, and a few scoops of ice cream, while TJ selected the movie **Dances With Wolves** for it scenic beauty and awesome soundtrack, dimmed the lights, and had it cued up when Shane joined him. They sat in matching supersize recliners. Shane looked perfect in his, while TJ looked small in his big chair, but it was very comfortable. The dogs knelt down in front of them hoping to get a lick of the ice cream. TJ hit the button and the movie started.

"Oh my!" exclaimed Shane. "That picture is incredible. I love the sound, too. Now this is living well."

"Yes, it is and so is the ice cream, and the good looking boy to my right is nice, too."

Shane grinned, "You meant very good looking boy, didn't you?"

TJ added, "My mistake. The lights are indeed dim, so to be completely honest, the boy on the right is very good looking."

"Your turn tonight."

"How so?" asked TJ?

Shane grinned, "Because I was the bottom last night. Now it is your turn tonight."

"Now you're getting me hot and my ice cream will melt."

They both laughed, but after they finished their dessert, they turned everything off, and headed to bed, feeling too tired and too horny, but very happy to be home.

# TWENTY-TW0

Not long after a breakfast of cereal and fresh fruit, the intercom chime sounded. TJ walked to the office where he could see a car. He hit the reply button, "Yes, may I help you?"

"My name is Buddy Bell from Super Cool Electronics."

"Yes, I'll hit the gate for you." TJ hit the button and watched the gate open. He walked through the kitchen and into the garage where he went out the exterior door to meet Buddy's car.

Buddy was getting out of the car. He had a short ponytail banded with green rubber bands, wore long well worn cargo shorts, a tee shirt from a rock band tour, and was short at five-feet eight-inches, and very thin at maybe a hundred and thirty pounds, fair skin, and a big smile.

"My name is TJ." He stuck out his hand to shake.

Buddy took his hand, "I'm of course, Buddy. I really love your new home. It is an amazing design and layout. Let's go to work. Let's start at the beginning." He carried a well-worn laptop case and a second small parts satchel with his tools. He turned to face the street. "All your utilities come in from the left corner of the driveway and underground in a twelve inch pipe that goes under the pavement, and comes up in the utility area. That was Henry's suggestion to prevent someone from planting a tree and digging up the pipe. I doubt anything will harm the wiring under the cement." They walked down the drive to the fence gate controls hidden behind the bushes. The weather boxes prevent moisture from getting to the circuit boards, and he had the boxes locked to prevent vandals and thieves from tampering. They returned to the building and Buddy showed him the utility area including the generator, and the various boxes on the exterior wall of the building for electrical and telephone, as well as the gate and intercom, and the security monitors.

He walked over to the generator, and turned a handle and opened a side door exposing the engine. This system will crank itself once a week at noon to keep everything lubricated and ready to go. It calls for the oil and filter to be changed once a year. I put it on a maintenance list for you, or you can sign up for our maintenance program, and we'll do it for you." He pushed a button to start the big motor. It instantly sprang to life. He spoke louder, "It runs clean off of natural gas so if you lose power it'll fire up, and you'll be able to have electricity for the essential stuff." He turned it off and closed the generator door.

They left the outside and went inside the RV building. TJ turned on the lights. To their immediate left was a small cement block room with a steel door. The exterior walls were treated with white waterproofing paint to prevent any wash water from soaking through. Inside Buddy turned on another light. "This is where the electrical and electronic stuff is controlled. You have four breaker boxes on the wall. The two on the left are the ones that the generator will keep working in event of a power failure. The two on the right do not have backup power. They are not essential services like Jacuzzi, steam room, etc."

He opened a big steel cabinet. TJ saw row after row of the big maintenance free gel batteries like the ones on the motorcoach. Buddy began pointing while talking. "Now you can see a power line coming into the left side that feeds several five thousand watt inverters. They charge all these rows of twelve-volt batteries. The power comes out of the batteries, and into a second set of inverters. Now the power is converted back to normal, but it is a very clean, reliable hundred twenty-volt AC. The clean line goes out the right side and into the last breaker box that feeds every electronic thing in the house. In theory, you should never have a voltage spike, brownout, or surge get through your batteries and on to your electronic equipment. This means your computer and phone network stays up at all times, as does your alarm, surveillance, stereo, telephone, Internet, and video equipment. I also put whole house surge protection on the main breaker boxes. That last big box is full of bypass switches, so when the times comes to replace batteries we'll be able to use the bypass to keep you running while servicing."

Buddy continued, "Because all your electronics are running off batteries, if you lost power from the street transformer, your equipment will never know it as they will be running off the batteries, and they can do so for days. Of course, the generator will kick on and start charging so they should never go down. This gives you the cleanest power possible even in thunder and ice storms." Buddy pointed at an electronic Ethernet network switch with an Ethernet wire coming out of it. There were numerous wires to all the sensors on all the inverters, chargers, and voltage regulators. "That wire feeds the network, and there is software on the network monitoring everything in here, and it provides warnings and reports, and in our maintenance program it sends me notices as well."

He closed the cabinet, and opened the next one on the wall, but it was much smaller. "This houses all the connections for the telephones, intercom, security cameras, electric gates, alarm system, and fire and smoke detectors. All the wirings comes here to this patch panel in case we need to change or add something, or run some tests in the case of a bad wire. I did the wiring and personally tested every wire. I also ran numerous extra wires, especially to the office, and great room as you'll probably make changes or additions as new electronic toys come out."

They walked over to the coach, "Now that is a beautiful coach. Did you hook up when you arrived?"

"Yes, of course. I have tested the computer network and could access my RV system from the office successfully."

Buddy grinned, "Excellent. Let's check out the phone system."

They went onboard after TJ turned on some lights. Buddy laughed, "Wow, I'd love to wire one of these up."

266

"It uses digital wiring for all the lights and stuff to cut down on the miles of wire in the coach. Here's the phone."

Buddy looked at the phone and smiled, "We need to swap out this analog phone for a digital one like in the house. That way you can access everything from here just like in the house. By the way there are a few of these phones on the walls around the RV building in case you get a call or a visitor at the gate while out here working." He took a phone out of his satchel, and quickly swapped it out and tested it. "It is working fine. Can you turn on the television for me?"

TJ picked up the remote and turned it on, and handed Buddy the remote. "You probably watch satellite the most followed by DVD, is that right?"

"Yep."

"Well, if you're watching the satellite, just punch in channel 001." He hit the buttons as he spoke and instantly, they were now looking at all the security cameras at the same time in twelve small squares. "This allows viewing of the entire property from any television in the house. You can hit the right button and each box will go to full screen and each rotate as you select, and finally back to all of them."

"Wow, that's a nice feature. So if we hear a noise in the night…"

"You can search the property without getting out of bed. You can also see an alarm status report, and hit a panic button to reach your security company or the police."

"Amazing."

"Come on, let's go inside the house."

As they came out of the coach, Buddy pointed to two cameras covering the inside of the RV building as well as sensors for smoke and fire, as well as door and motion sensors. He knelt and petted the dogs as they entered the house, but he had missed Shane, who had left early that morning for his first summer school classes, then workouts, and pickup games.

Buddy pointed out heat sensors in the laundry and kitchen before they made their way into the great room. TJ had some questions for him concerning the equipment. Buddy showed him to bring up a display screen through the projected picture that showed him the operation of all the audio and video equipment in the house. He also explained the multi-remote unit that controlled everything in the great room. With the push of one button, the lights would dim, the projector would come on, and the Bose® surround sound system would turn on. He answered all of TJ's questions, leaving him amazed at what they could do with all the electronic gear.

They moved to the office where Buddy went over the devices in the network cabinet. "You probably noted there are no UPS or uninterrupted power supply units for anything in the house like you have been using. There is no need for them because of the big battery system you have. He showed him how to add additional computers to the network, password protection, and the DRS spam and anti-virus device.

"The T1 comes into the utility cabinet, goes through a surge device, and comes up here. It first goes through the DRS so that all spam and virus stuff is stopped cold, right before it gets to any computer or digital device in the house." Buddy pulled a manual notebook from a slot on the right side of the smoked glass cabinet. "This book has all your passwords, setups, and how-to notes for all the systems—just in case I get hit by a big truck."

"Please don't let that happen. Look both ways before crossing the street."

Buddy grinned, "No problem, but our company has other guys that can help in case I'm on vacation or a seminar." He checked out both of their computers, printers, scanners, and security cameras via the large LCD television on the wall. "I had a bad camera switch on entrance gate one, but I tracked it down and got a new one flown in yesterday. Everything is under a one-year warranty and we have extended warranty service in our maintenance plan. Do you have any questions?"

"Not yet. You have done an excellent job."

"Okay, well here is my business card, and the maintenance program is explained in this folder, and if you think of something let me know. If you decided you want to sign up for our program, you can do it online. I can fix a lot of things remotely, and you can call my boss with questions about the maintenance contract. Good luck and I hope you enjoy your new home."

TJ walked him out and noted the gate would open automatically by ground sensors for anyone leaving. It also closed itself after the vehicle crossed over a second ground sensor near the road. He went back inside, grabbed a water bottle and waited for Brian Kenny to arrive. Just for the fun of it, he clicked on the security icon, then chose gate, then logs, and instantly saw a print out of all the times each gate opened and closed. Using the software, he created a few additional gates codes for friends and workers, read up on a code he could give temporary workers that last just for the day.

TJ heard the gate chime as he returned from a trip to the bathroom and saw Brian at the gate. He buzzed him in and walked out to meet him. Brian was in a rental car and had flown in to see him on the way back from a remote ESPN® had done in Charlotte for their NASCAR® race coverage. TJ greeted him with a handshake. He had spoken to Brian several times on the phone and through many emails as they planned the office setup prior to and during the house construction.

"I'm so pleased to meet you," said TJ.

"And I. You have such an amazing place. Most folks would think a plumbing contractor stored supplies in your building and not your house. It is beautiful. Is you motorcoach here?"

"Yes, would you like to see it?"

"Of course."

"We just got in yesterday and went right to work moving in, so we haven't had a chance to wash off the bugs, but come on we'll go in through the garage door."

They stepped inside and as they stepped into the RV building, TJ hit the light switch, and suddenly, the coach appeared. Brian grinned. "Now that is a beautiful coach."

They walked all the way around and Brian noted the phone and Ethernet connections, as well as the satellite connection. "Now that is nice."

TJ took him inside and he was amazed. After they came back to the front he said, "You know I could do the same thing I'm doing in your office in this coach so you could have network access from anywhere using your Datastorm® unit."

"Now that sounds like a good idea, but one step at a time. Let's get the office working first."

In the office, Brian set his stuff on the counter. He had already been through the house a few days before. Brian said, "I brought a new audio/video controller for your desk corner. It goes over here."

If someone entered their office from the kitchen the desk area was to front of the house or the left, and it was like an odd shape W with Shane's side first with a tight U loop, and then TJ's side with a wider U, as he had far more equipment and cabinetry than Shane wanted or needed. Just as you stepped in the office on the wall to the left was the studio set up area with stools and back drops, and it faced the center of the room with the lights and monitor on the ceiling as well as the camera facing Shane's stool. Just beneath the ceiling mounted equipment was the beginning of TJ's section, where Brian mounted the controls for the lights, camera remote controller, and the audio-headset controls. He also had another phone there, and Brian told him Buddy had wired a button on that phone that killed the ringer in that part of the house, and killed the audio from Bose® sound system. TJ was impressed.

Brian hooked up the new controller, tested everything, and then said to TJ, "Okay, this is how this works. First you flip on the lights with this switch, the camera on switch is next so it can warm up, and this switch turns the audio and headset system on. Shane has a controller next to his stool. He can place the microphone under his shirt or clipped to it, and stick the headset piece in his ear, and let the cord fall behind his back and out of sight. You can turn that controller on and off from here.

He handed TJ a headset with a boom microphone on one side, "This headset will let you hear Shane in the right ear, and the director or producer in the left. The microphone is normally off, so if you need to say something you push and hold the green button to talk.

"Now we need something to practice with." Brian walked over to the backdrops that were like a series of window blinds or slide screens, and he pulled down the first one. TJ laughed as realized it was a huge poster of Shane. "Nice subject."

Brian grinned, "He works cheap and holds very still." He came around and sat beside TJ at the controller. Now using the joystick we can zoom in and out by going forward and back, and by using this joystick we can pan left and right, or up and down, and we can do all that at the same time. Once you have a good headshot of Shane, then you ready to adjust his microphone level. Make sure your headset is on your head and over your ears, so that you're not hearing him live, but only through your headset. What you hear is probably what they are getting in control in New York. I'll put on his microphone and do a test for audio and his hearing. You can control both with these two slide switches."

TJ put the headset on. Brian did a test by saying one, two, and three, and then said some fake copy. "Be sure you watch the meter as it should be bouncing in the high green side but not staying in the red. It can bounce a little in the red, but if it stayed there it would be heavily distorted.

Brian came back around to TJ and said, "Okay, all the gear is ready, our model is ready, so now it time to connect to ESPN® control to set up the interview. This starts from your computer. Buddy has it set up so that you're using eight of the twenty-four T1 channels for telephone and fax service. You have four voice lines, and some security and control lines. The rest are for Internet. This gives us several channels for audio and High Definition video feed, as well as communications.

"I put the software on your iMac® as well as Shane's as a backup. I put some notes on your desk for procedures and connections in case something crashes, but otherwise you just double click the link for ESPN® Network, and the software will open and test out the connections for camera, audio, and communications. That's why you turn on the lights, camera, and audio first. You'll get a green light once that is done. If you're wondering, the camera and audio circuits, along with communication, are digitized and sent down an Ethernet wire to the switch and comes into your computer where it is processed and sent to New York at blazing speeds.

"However, you control who can connect to your remote studio. Obviously, you will probably connect to ESPN® most of the time, but you'll have requests from other networks, and sports reporters at television stations when Taylor is playing their local team. Once you have their director on the phone, you'll give him a password and a link the software will generate for you. The password is good for one connection only so we don't have to worry about someone connecting at odd times. This is an extremely secured network.

"Are you ready to give it a try?" TJ nodded yes and hit the button to generate the password and link. Brian said, "I put ESPN® control on your phone for you, so just hit the memory button twice and spell ESPN® on the keyboard and it will connect. This number is also on your notes. Put it on speakerphone so we can both hear.

"Hello, this is Fred Archer in ESPN® control, may I help you?"

"Fred, this is Brian Kenny. I'm in Lindle, North Carolina at the new home for Shane Bradley's uncle. His name is TJ Johnson, and we have just finished setting up a new remote studio."

Fred replied, "Hello TJ, and welcome aboard our remote network. I assume you guys are ready to test, so if you'll give me the link and the password, we'll get the test started."

TJ gave him the information and hit a button for his software to go in receive mode. In seconds, it showed that ESPN® was connected. Brian walked over to the control station and put the headset on. "Can you hear me on the communication channel?"

"Roger, loud and clear. Can you hear me?"

"Yes, we're good. TJ hang up the phone and come put the headset on. I'll go put on Shane's microphone and headset for the test."

TJ rolled his desk chair over to the control station and put the headset on. Fred said, "TJ, can you hear me okay?"

"Yes, sir, loud and clear."

Brian hooked himself up and added, "Okay, fellows, I'm on Shane's setup. I can hear Fred in New York. Can you hear me?"

Fred replied, "Yes, but I need a little more level. TJ, can you bring up the volume just a little while Brian talks to us?" Brian began speaking and TJ gently brought the level up."

"Okay that is good. Okay, let's run a video test. Everybody ready?"

Brian said, "TJ hit the audio mute switch on the phone."

Fred immediately said. "A mute switch. What is that for?"

Brian grinned, "Fred, you want believe this house. It has Bose® audio speakers systems in every room and a digital phone system running off this T1. The mute switch kills the phone from ringing in this part of the house, and the audio so there are no surprises during taping."

TJ said as he looked at the flashing red light on the phone, "Audio secured. I'm ready."

"We're rolling," began Fred, "and we're on in five, four, three, two…"

Brian began speaking as if he was a reporter, and rattled on for a full minute before Fred cut in, "Okay, guys, let's roll that back and take a look." He paused for a few seconds and they said, "The signal is beautiful though you might want to calibrate the camera again. Red was a little hot. Here we go."

Brian quickly turned on the LCD High Definition television on the wall between their workstations, and hit an auxiliary input button that he showed TJ, and said. "You can have the video on during recording, but you must mute the sound to avoid feedback. Mute my microphone and pull the headset off and let's watch and listen."

TJ thought the signal and audio were great, but the experts had some tweaking to do. Brian took over TJ's headset and listening to Fred, they made some adjustments to the camera until the signal and clarity were at a hundred percent. He gave the headset back to TJ, as they made two more tests, and pronounced it good to go. Brian said goodbye to Fred.

"That's all there is to it. Once you're offline with the network, you should kill the audio and video on your control unit. Take the mute off your phone. Kill the lights and camera, and you can close the software on your iMac®. I have left several of my business cards for you in case you have a question or a problem. I'm always ready to help you.

"I've got to catch a flight to New York. One last thing, Dick Vitale said for you to call him when we had your new studio up and running. He is coming to town and wants to interview Shane if that is possible. Just give him a call. Thank you and I'll be watching for your interviews."

TJ walked him out and thanked him several times for the free equipment and setup. After the gate closed, TJ decided he wanted to walk the property to be sure the fence was good, and the construction stuff cleaned up. He went back in the house, but left the garage door open and called the dogs. They came running and followed him over to the shed so he could check out the building, the lights, and power, and then he checked out the RV pedestals, and finally he opened a big gate to the backyard and the dogs scampered through. He shut the gate behind him and together, he and the dogs began walking down the far right fence line to the rear of the property. Grass had been seeded weeks ago and was growing nicely. He knew they would have to start cutting it before long.

They made it to the corner, and he was thankful that all depressions had been wired with fence to keep the dogs in, and strangers out. He also saw drain pipes that would take all the rainwater off the house and the cement, and send it down the pipe to the creek. Henry turned the pipe so that it almost paralleled the creek and brought in a truck of riprap, and placed the rocks on both banks of the creek and the bottom, preventing the pipe water from eroding the soil. They made their way all the way across the back of the lot and began moving up the far corner. The dogs were darting left and right and smelling for scents on their new property. Up the slight hill they came to the mid fence. TJ could see the dog pen and noted the slight grade to make the water run away from the house. There was a six-foot slab of cement all the way around the house for the same reason. TJ didn't want any gutters to clean, so the rain bounced off the cement, and then soaked into a French drain that ran to the big pipe that took the water to the creek.

He opened the gate and called the dogs. Their tongues were getting longer from their hot run in the June sun, but they hustled through the gate. He walked down the entrance drive and inspected the electric gate mechanism, noting the wide pit and the round three-inch solid steel pipes that covered it just like the ones used at horse and cattle farms. He knew the dogs would never go near the gate or try to get under it, nor would they dart across if it suddenly opened. There was a small side fence to prevent any attempted jumps from the side.

He walked along the front of the property noting the ground lights and the cameras, and checked the main gate as well. Finally, he came up the drive to the house, but used the porch leading to the front door. Leslie placed rocking chairs, a swing, and small tables out for guests to enjoy.

He came in the front door with the dogs behind him. They quickly darted in the house, and made a run to the kitchen for their auto-fill water jug. He gave the dogs a treat, and then fixed himself something to drink. He changed clothes to shorts and socks, as he wasn't expecting any more company. He picked up the pamphlet for programming his workstation phone, and put Dick's number in the system, saved it, and put on his new Bluetooth® earpiece. He hit line one, and the speed dial button for Dick, and listened as it dialed Dick's cell phone.

"Hello? Dick here."

"Hey Dick. This is TJ Johnson. How are you?" TJ smiled at the sound of Dick's voice.

"I'm great, Buddy, how are you?"

"We're good. We just got back from vacation and moved in the new house. Brian just left after training me on the new remote studio. He said you have the same setup in your house."

"Yes, and I use it all the time instead of flying to New York, or begging the local station for some satellite time. I'm on the golf course, but the reason I told Brian to have you call me is that I'm flying up tomorrow to interview the coach about next season, and to find out about his recruits. I thought I would swing by and see your new house, and if it is okay with Shane, I'd like to do an interview with him, a few promos, and a tag for the show I'm doing on this year's recruiting in the ACC. Is that okay with you?"

"Absolutely. What time?"

"I'm doing the coach thing at ten and could probably be at your place by noon."

"That's good, as Shane gets out of class at eleven thirty and can easily be here in time. I'll email directions for you."

"Perfect. I'll see you tomorrow."

"Great, and thanks for the help on the remote studio."

"My pleasure. See you soon. Bye."

"Bye."

TJ hung up and put Shane's cell number in the new phone system, and then dialed him. "Hey. Are you out of class?"

"Yep, just finished. How'd it go this morning?"

"It was awesome. I can't wait to show you what I learned. Are you on the way to lunch?"

"Yeah, I thought I would eat a small meal, then do my physical workout, weights, and some running, and then shoot a while. I'll be home about three, as I'm not doing a pick up game today."

"Dick Vitale is coming to town in the morning to interview the coach and wants to do an interview with you in our new remote studio about noon. Is that okay with you?"

"Sure, that'll be fine. I'll come home after class, do the interview, and eat lunch before heading back to my gym."

"Perfect. I miss you. I had gotten use to seeing you all day long."

"I miss you, too. I'll see you soon. I love you. Bye."

TJ knew Shane was alone for him to say he loved him. "I love you, too."

TJ spent the afternoon moving boxes of files from the RV he needed in the office, plus some of the book supplies he carried on the road. It had taken an hour just to catch up on all the emails that had come in now that he was no longer on vacation. Sales for all the books were still climbing, and Jake was almost as excited as TJ was.

He organized the files and supplies, and then took the car and drove to the storage unit where he loaded the rest of his office stuff and boxes of books until he had no more room in the back of his SUV. He backed into the garage, closed the door and began moving books to the storage cabinets in the garage, while taking the office stuff inside.

He had just carried the last box in when the phone rang. He flopped down in the desk chair to rest a bit and answered the phone. "Hello?"

"TJ, this is Barbara. How are you?"

TJ easily recognized Mrs. Bradley's voice. "I'm great. We had such a good time. Shane is rested, and on day one he is back in the gym working after attending class this morning."

"I'm so glad you had a good time. Thank you for teaching us how to follow you on the Internet with the GPS software. That was cool."

"You're welcome. How is Al?"

"He's doing great. Tell me about the house."

TJ grinned and teased her, "No, I can't tell you about the house. You have to come see us. I will say it is all that we hoped it would be and more. We have the guest room made up and waiting for you."

"Well, if you're sure you don't mind, we were thinking of flying down this weekend."

"That would be great. Just email me your flight schedule, and I'll pick you up. Dress casual as it is summertime here and about eighty degrees."

"Are you sure this is okay?"

"It is fine. I'll tell Shane when he gets home. He is going to love giving you the tour."

"Okay, we'll I'll see you soon. I love you."

"I love you too. Fly safe."

TJ grinned at how easy it was to say he loved the Bradleys because they had welcomed him so effortlessly into their family. He was looking forward to seeing them, as he last saw them the night after the championship game.

The short rest period helped a little, so he got a second wind and left the house once more, making yet another trip to the storage facility. During the Christmas holidays, he rented the local storage room, and then drove to Hendersonville with a trailer, and hauled everything to Lindle. He hoped to soon have it all moved to the house so he could stop paying for storage. He had plenty of storage in the new garage, and the new RV building. Once he filled, the car he drove home, and when the garage door went up he saw Shane's Hummer in the parking space next to his. He grinned as he backed in and shut the door.

Shane came out the kitchen door with the dogs. "Hey, how are you?"

"I'm pooped. This is my second big load from the storage shed." TJ came up and kissed Shane, and started to turn and open the rear door for SUV, when Shane suddenly bear hugged him and grinned, "I missed you today." He kissed TJ again.

TJ laughed, "I missed you, too. I have big news for you."

"You mean besides Dick coming tomorrow?"

TJ handed him a box of files. "Carry these to the office and hold your stomach tight. No, I talked to Barbara, and I invited them to come see the new house this weekend and stay with us. She is so excited, and she misses her baby."

Shane laughed, "I miss both of them. That is good news. I guess we won't get much rest this week."

"Sure we will. I'll have the office finished by tomorrow night, and maybe the rest of the stuff out of the storage shed by Thursday. The house is pretty good except that if we are going to leave our road clothes on the coach, we need to buy more stuff for the house. When can you go shopping?"

"I usually order most of my good clothes online, but I can go after my workouts tomorrow if you like. What's for supper?"

TJ frowned. "I'm sorry, I forgot. I was going to pick something up on the way home. What would you like, and I'll run out and get it?"

"I was thinking Chinese. We'll get your car unloaded and go together. Come on, let's hustle, as I'm starved."

# TWENTY-THREE

It had been a busy week and every day presented a new opportunity for a learning experience, as TJ and Shane learned more about all the features of their new home. Their bare feet felt the mildly heated tiles, as it was summertime, but they knew how to turn up the temperature for the tile heat for winter. They controlled the heat and air system via programmable thermostats with sensors all over the house. There were four heat and air systems for the building: one for the RV building, one for wet area, one for the great room and bedrooms, and a final one for the office and kitchen. The later with the most potential for extra heat due to the lights for remote studio, computers, digital equipment, and printer, as well as cooking in the kitchen and laundry. While more expensive to install the multiple systems, by working in harmony with each other, they significantly reduced electrical requirements. The gas furnaces were located in two small rooms in the RV building at opposite ends, and provided heat for winter.

They made their first remote interview after Dick Vitale arrived. He loved the house and the motorcoach, as well as the projection television system. He was a kind and gracious as always, and acted more like an extra uncle or grandfather. He gave them a hug when he arrived and was all smiles the entire time. He was also consummate reporter, asking just the right question to lead Shane in the direction he wanted him to go. They did a fifteen-minute interview for his upcoming recruiting show, and then a series of sixty seconds interviews for insertion in the SportsCenter® daily broadcasts, promoting Dick's television special on recruiting. They ended with promo tags of five, fifteen, and thirty seconds promoting the show. Shane and TJ learned a lot by working with Dick. The new system performed flawlessly.

TJ finished emptying the self-storage garage and felt thankful it was the last trip. He put many things in the garage cabinets he planned to list for sale in **I Wanna®** or **EBay®**. He spent the rest of the week organizing the office and catching up on finances with Sam. They were in excellent shape, thanks to the book sales, paying back the money borrowed, including buying the land, and building the house. Al and Shane told TJ to pocket the money from his book and invest it, and they would take care of the house, but TJ refused, saying it would not be fair for him to have the money sitting in the bank when there were bills to be paid. In fact, the book sales for basketball alone paid for everything with an extra million in the bank for renting the jet for the upcoming season. And he was also getting money for the sale of his gay fiction, although a smaller amount, it certainly helped. For the first time in his entire adult life, TJ was totally debt free. He figured he would be making motorcoach payments for the rest of his life, but not anymore. Al and Barbara were proud of TJ's determination to pay the bills, and not in any way take advantage of their son. Shane wanted to argue the point, but TJ threatened no sex if he didn't allow TJ to do this. Shane, while laughing, backed down by saying, "Boy, you really know how hit below the belt!" They both laughed heartily at the double innuendo.

Al and Barbara's visit was a great celebration. They loved the house and motorcoach, and all the things TJ designed for the house. Al and Shane shot many hoops in their indoor gym, while Barbara and TJ went shopping for clothes for TJ and Shane. She had bought most of her son's clothes until he went to college, and knew what to get. Shane showed them what he ordered online for slacks, shirts, shorts, sport coats, and he even ordered two suits after TJ measured every muscle on his body including his penis. They had a big laugh at that. Shane knew where to go on the web for clothes big and tall men. TJ and Barbara bought all his underwear, socks, tee shirts, and belts. She also insisted on buying him a light jacket for rain, and a winter jacket because they were on sale in the June heat. She also helped TJ pick out a completely new wardrobe for tours, ballgames, special functions, and of course, casual wear. She grinned when trying to talk TJ into buying pajamas. She knew that the boys probably slept in the nude, so she settled on buying them both a housewarming present by securing luxurious thick bathrobes. She had them monogrammed simply S&T for Shane and TJ. The foursome enjoyed great meals together, too, including the first with the new grill system. The parents flew out Sunday afternoon, and TJ and Shane already missed them.

With the start of a new week, they finally settled into a summer routine. Shane began the day with morning classes, followed by midday physical strength workouts combining weights and machines. He loved his new training coach. He knew just how hard to push Shane, and did so with wit and humor. Shane had a long meeting with the nutritionist for the athletic department. He did this every year, but he wanted to make sure he was eating the right things in the right portions to maximize his strength and endurance. He also had a long talk with the coach. He received a detail report on exactly what he wanted Shane to work on. Shane made notes from his meetings as if preparing for an exam.

In the afternoons, he would go on long jogs, but as the summer heat rose, he got up early, and often jogged before classes. He also participated in numerous pickup games with former college and NBA players who attended Taylor. This was a basketball tradition at the school and he loved it. The old players, as he called them, were determined to show the little college players how the big boys played. They often tricked him, but all in fun, and of course, they challenged him, which was what he wanted and needed. He had been back only a few weeks, and was already in top form and growing stronger. His schedule would remain the same for the rest of the summer except he would finish his classes in late July for the two sessions, leaving just three classes in the fall and two in the spring to graduate.

TJ also settled into a routine. Before meeting Shane, he often drove the motorcoach in the mornings and wrote in the afternoons. Now that he had a home and office to work out of, and no traveling to plan for, he spent his mornings writing new materials for **The Blackfeet Boys**, and researching for **The War Beyond – Part III** as both stories occur in a similar time with the later mostly in the northern Colorado Rockies, and the former in the northwest in the plains near the Glacier Mountains. He took great delight in spinning his yarns and tales as he called his stories.

He thought of the idea for a story about two Blackfeet Indian boys who grow to become boyfriends in a traditional society that wasn't usually kind to homosexual Indians. If a boy was effeminate and smart, he hung out with the shaman or someone who dealt in good and evil spirits, dreams, and sometimes experienced trances. The Indians often relied on a shaman to tell them what to do, when to hunt, and when to seek winter shelter. However, if two gay boys were caught experiencing sex, the tribe detested and ostracized them, which often meant death without the resources to feed and clothe themselves. Sometimes, they killed the boys to stop their 'disease' from spreading, and to make an example to others. These two boys were not happy with their tribal leadership as they multiple attacks killing innocent white women and children riding among the wagon trains.

They made quick plans, waited patiently for rain to cover their tracks, and in the middle of the night, they packed up their few belongings, took their horses, and left the tribe and quickly went as far away as they could. They found a place to live where they could live and love. TJ quickly edited the storylines for both books, but often added to the storyline while doing more research. He also developed a way for the characters in part three of the sequel to meet the characters in his new Indian storyline. He thought it might be fun and interesting to acknowledge they were not the only gay frontier warriors in the great northwest.

TJ spent the afternoon editing earlier chapters, breaking his tradition of finishing an entire book's rough draft before polishing it. He also began writing the sequel to the basketball book with the first chapter bringing the reader up to date on the things that happen after the team received the championship trophy. He explained Shane's numerous trips around the country, accepting dozens of awards for his achievements this past season. Shane accepted each one, while graciously thanking his teammates and coaches, but soon had boxes of trophies and plaques. TJ retrieved some of the awards and placed them in the office and great room. The rest were in storage in the garage. He thought about having a glass display case made for them.

TJ wrote about the book's release and the phenomenal sales, the team's award banquet, the pressure to turn pro, and Shane's decision to return for his senior year. Shane surprised all by not waiting for a feel of where he would go in the NBA draft in June. He made the decision, then told TJ, Al and

Barbara, the coach, and then called a press conference, and announced his decision to the world just fourteen days after winning the championship.

He did not tell them about the new house or Shane's personal life. He did not want fans attempting to find their home. He also wrote more about Shane's family with great detail about the influence of both Al and Barbara, and how he felt they gave Shane guidance, character, courage, and allowed him to make his own choices, as a way of learning how to make future big decisions. He gave the reader more insight into Shane's thoughts and feelings about sports, and the world in general. He delighted in explaining his sincere discipline when it came to studying for his classes, and his goal of graduating in the spring.

Often, right after lunch, he took his traditional doggie nap. It only lasted about fifteen to twenty minutes, but it recharged his energy for a great afternoon session. He spent some time each day on the business part of their lives. He read the expense reports sent from Sam's office, and downloaded the credit card transactions, and though Sam actually paid the bills, he liked to make sure the charges were accurate. He used Quicken software to help track everything involving money.

He handled about twenty emails a day, as well as requests for speaking engagements at various book events. He declined all of them, but added each to the book databases he created for basketball and fiction. He hoped to repay the requests by putting their stores on next year's tour. He suspected he would have an abbreviated gay fiction tour after Thanksgiving, and the release of **The Blackfeet Boys**. He wondered if there was a way he could make digital appearances instead of speaking engagements using their remote studio. He also began studying podcasts on the Internet, thinking the relative new technology might be a solution. He would give the ideas more thought, and discuss the possibilities with Jake. There were also requests for Shane to attend seminars and basketball camps. Thankfully, Walter's office handled most of these, although TJ and Walter sent emails back and forth. TJ did not pretend to be Shane's manager, and he told Walter he was like an uncle to Shane. That wasn't true, but he did do many things to help Shane as if he was.

TJ's favorite part of their new home was the time they had together, especially on the weekends, but also every night. Shane had homework to do during the week, but usually did it quickly, some of it after lunch while digesting, and the same after supper. TJ did most of the cooking while Shane usually made the salads and cut fresh fruit. With the new larger refrigerator, they could store a lot more prepared food. TJ cooked lean meals with the help from Shane's nutritionist. He, too, was getting in shape, both by his food intake, and using the wet area. He lifted some weights, and spent time on the treadmill and exercise bike. The sauna and steam room helped him lose some water weight, but his workout and diet helped him the most. He'd already dropped fifteen pounds.

They no longer had to take the dogs on numerous daily walks to pee, but often TJ would hike around the property with them, and on weekends, TJ and Shane took the dogs on a road trip to their favorite park. Beeper lost five pounds while J-Henry remained slim and trim. They laughed when Shane tried to teach the dogs how to walk on the treadmill. At night, they enjoyed the sauna, steam and Jacuzzi together, and then watched a movie on the high definition system.

Sleep had been fun, too, as they had no windows in their room, allowing them to sleep deep, and in silence, as their room was near the middle of the building from all outside walls, and the exterior roof. They didn't hear rain, or even the garbage truck. If they had lots of late-night sex, they could easily sleep in the following morning. That was common on the weekend. Occasionally, a dog would slip out for a sip of water or a quick pee, and they never heard him leave or return.

The big shower room, with the multiple heads and endless supply of instant hot water, gave the boys more opportunity for sexual play and caressing their partner. They knew every square inch of their bodies, and TJ knew when Shane had a new purple bruise mark from his battles in the pickup games. TJ attended a summer game or two every now and then, so he could describe the action to his readers.

The second weekend they were home, they cleaned the motorcoach inside and out, enjoying the advantage of a rolling ladder, as well as hot and cold water on both sides of the coach. They did the tires and chrome wheels and touched up every spot on the coach until it was better than the day TJ bought it. They set about reorganizing the RV building until the tool bench was ready as well as the supplies. TJ moved the supply of his books to the back of the RV building in a corner where the big shelves went all the way to the ceiling like a big warehouse home improvement store. They also washed and waxed their cars, and TJ was thrilled at how quick the water ran correctly to the center drain. He sent Henry a big fruit basket, a case of wine, and a dinner for two at Lindale's finest restaurant as thank you present, plus tickets to Taylor's first home ACC game in January. He made sure Henry knew they appreciated his hard work.

The dogs didn't escape their new wash area either. TJ and Shane gave each a bath in the laundry with the new rail to keep their head up and their body still, while they were gently scrubbed, washed, and dried.

TJ's final chore for the new house was to figure out how to take care of the yard. He started by pricing a tractor with a tow behind mower at a price of fifteen thousand dollars and up. He wasn't thrilled at that cost. They would also need more bushes in the front area and the guest parking area, and maybe a bit of privacy in front of the porch. TJ and Shane discussed it and decided to hire a landscaping service that would provide the mowing and maintaining of the yard. Shane felt like they didn't have time to do the work with their schedules in the summer and especially after basketball season started.

280

TJ interviewed numerous expensive landscape companies, and although they had the money, he felt the fees were extravagant and exorbitant. He drove around the nice neighborhoods in Lindle one afternoon until one day he spotted a truck and trailer parked on the street in front of a beautifully landscaped home. The trailer carried a lawn tractor, racks of weed eater trimmers, and yard tools. He spotted two black men working in the flowerbeds. He got out of his car and walked across the lawn to talk to them. The first thing he noticed was they must have been weightlifters, as they were short and stout, with huge arm and neck muscles. They heads were shaved and they both had award winning smiles. He soon learned their hands were very big and strong as well.

As he approached, they both stood up, and he smiled after realizing they were twins. "Please excuse me for interrupting your work. How long have you been maintaining this yard?"

Jerry spoke up first, "About two years. They had just moved in and the yard was brown dust that turned to mud when we started."

"It is beautiful. I'd like to talk with you about doing my property. My name is TJ Johnson. I'm pleased to meet you." TJ walked right up to the flowerbed and shook the dirty hands of the men who were in the middle of planting.

Terry asked, "Where do you live?"

"Not far from here," he replied and then gave them the address. "Do you mind telling me how much you charge for this yard?" They told him and he tried not to smile. "How often do you come by?" They replied once a week. He knew he had found his men.

They agreed to come by after they finished this yard. TJ drove home feeling good about finding two hardworking men, but perhaps a better deal than the big landscaping companies. Jerry and Terry arrived at the gate and TJ buzzed them in. He walked out to meet them by shaking their hands once more. He explained the grass needed cutting weekly, the entrances needed additional bushes, as well as the parking area, and the front area needed a plan to make it look a little more like a home. He explained he did not want big trees that would create more leaves or sap, nor did he want plants that couldn't take care of themselves as they traveled a lot and feared a runaway sprinkler system. Although, with the men handling the yard, he felt they could use the automatic system. He also said he didn't want anything encroaching or congesting the driveway, while scratching or limiting the turning area for the big motorcoach. He showed them the coach as they walked through the kitchen to the front door and outside again so they could see it was indeed a home.

Both men made their notes, did some drawings on the hood of their truck, met privately for a few minutes and came back with two prices. The first price included getting the yard in shape, and the second for the weekly maintenance. TJ was thrilled with both proposals. He also agreed to pay for all the plants and supplies they would need to make the yard beautiful. Finally, they agreed to start right away, and he told them he was flexible as to what day they came for maintenance. He authorized two thousand dollars for plants and gave them a check for it on the spot. They were impressed how quickly he trusted them.

TJ showed them the shed and a pile of water hoses he had brought from his previous house and pointed out that there were numerous farm spigots around the property including the gates, the corners of the building and the front and rear yard. Jerry went to his truck and pulled out a catalog for a wholesaler of lawn equipment. He suggested they buy a couple of industrial hose carts to be wheeled to where water was temporarily needed like planting time, and for a few weeks thereafter until the roots grew deep enough to take are of themselves. TJ liked the idea and authorized the purchase of two carts, plus industrial strength water hoses, sprinklers, showerhead wands, and nozzles. They would buy all the stuff and return in the morning to get started. TJ gave them one of his new business cards with his new address and home number. They gave him their billing address so Sam could send their checks directly to them. He told them his nephew was living with him and going to Taylor University, but he never gave them his name or told him he played basketball. Before they left TJ gave them a unique code to enter the gate at their own will. TJ still marveled at their new security system that logged in the entry and exit of anyone with a pass code, as well as guests.

They arrived early the next morning and worked all day for several days until completing the initial work. The grass was cut and reseeded with special grass that would grow close together like a carpet, and similar to the centipede grass used in the warm coastal areas. They explained it would take a month to grow, but would soon choke out both their old grass and especially the weeds, but they also said they would fertilize the grass to improve growth, kill weeds, and to kill fire ants to protect the dogs. They would also spray for fleas and ticks from time to time. TJ welcomed these ideas and learned they had a spray pump device on the front of the tractor that he hadn't noticed before.

After the yard was completed, TJ and Shane walked the yard with the dogs to inspect their work, and they were thrilled at how beautiful it had become. Shane took pictures and emailed them to his mom. They had solved another big problem without spending huge amounts of money.

Shane's mom encouraged TJ to hire a housekeeper to come once or twice a week to maintain their beautiful home. She knew TJ said he could do it, but they felt it was more important that he continue his work and take advantage of his free time for their relationship growth. TJ went back to Leslie for some referrals. They found a beautiful Spanish housekeeper who came twice a week to maintain the inside of the house and wet area. TJ felt he was truly spoiled to have both a yard crew and housekeeper, as he had always done both chores all his life.

They took a few weekends off to make some trips to the mountains, as it was too hot to go to the beach, and the forecast for the rest of the summer was maybe hotter. There were classes and workouts for Shane, writing and editing for TJ. By the end of July, TJ had dropped a total of twenty pounds since the end of basketball season in the spring, and drastically improved his endurance and strength. He still hated to jog, but on the weekends, he would go on an early morning run with Shane.

They spent a week in Washington after Shane's summer classes ended to see some of the historical sites and museums Shane had never seen. It was hot, but they enjoyed their time on the road again. As soon as classes for the fall started in mid August, TJ flew to New York City to meet with Jake in the morning and his publishers in the afternoon. They knew the publisher wanted to know more about the sequel and TJ's outline. TJ laughed at that, but put many of his new ideas for the book in his computer to show them the depth he would be adding to this year's final story. Jake thought it was important to remind the publishers that this sequel would be the last as Shane was graduating. He would remind the group it was a once in a lifetime opportunity for continuing the behind the scenes story. They were confident that everyone who bought the first book would buy the second, especially if Taylor won a second championship trophy.

The sales of the first book far exceeded expectations, giving TJ the full amount of the first contract and the royalties. The clause for performance kicked in, and now the publisher had to fork up some big bucks to keep the rights for the sequel, or allow the new book to go up for bid. Jake thought they would retain their rights, but wanted to hear from TJ before committing to such a large sum. Jake relished the negotiation. He and TJ agreed to the same promotion schedule with the three-week tour in the spring. TJ would also agree to attend a book convention next month, and a second one in January. TJ and Jake would meet with the gay publisher after the first meeting.

Jake and TJ stopped for lunch, discussed the book business, and TJ listened to Jake's ideas for marketing his gay books. They met the publishers of the basketball book at one-thirty. He met Janet as he approached the conference room. He gave her a big hug as she told him she would again become his project manager. TJ was very happy to work with her again. All the bosses were most cordial, as TJ set up his laptop and linked with the conference room overhead project he requested. He quickly flipped through several camera shots he shot of Shane in the summer pickup games, working out, and shooting. He then brought up his version of an outline, emphasizing new information, and more behind the scenes including recruiting, team surgeries, and strength training. He would also explain how the tutoring system worked, and the class schedules when they were on the road. He included the beginning of the book by showing a rough draft about the events that occurred after the trophy, including a chart of the sixty-six awards, and pictures of the top presentations.

As TJ finished, the president of the company and his associates applauded and thanked him for coming. They wasted no time in offering him four million for the sequel, and they presented him with a check for two million up front. Lots of pictures were taken with TJ holding the check with a huge smile on his face. TJ heard from both Jerome his attorney and Sam his accountant on the legal verbiage for the contract before the meeting, so they were ready for his signature. He gleefully signed, the staff poured champagne, and the president of the company made a toast.

TJ and Jake left their offices with big grins on their faces and took the car service over to the smaller publisher for TJ's gay fiction. He again set up his laptop and showed several pictures of the mountain scenes he researched along with pictures of the Sioux and Blackfeet Indian warriors, and animals like buffalos, bears, and mountain lions. He presented a synopsis of **The Blackfeet Boys**, and closed by adding a twist in the story by presenting the parallel story of **The War Beyond – Part III**. They liked the tie in from one story into the next.

The managing head of development curiously asked if he had another contemporary story in the works, and TJ replied he had created storylines for two more books. "The first story, **Forever Alone, Again**, is about a gay man who sought real love instead of one night stands, but constantly failed at finding a long time companion. The later story would be a fictional story about America's first nationally ranked collegiate gay basketball players, their secret relationship, and the unplanned coming out in the midst of pushing for a national championship.

The gay publishers were very aware of TJ's success with his basketball book, and were pleased to hear he was writing a sequel, as they felt his notoriety there would help his gay books would continue to sell well. They hoped to bounce off the publicity created by the bigger straight publishing company. They felt a gay basketball story could be a megahit for them, too. They began to argue that perhaps he should postpone **The War Beyond** sequel and write the basketball story first. TJ replied he had thought of that, but felt two books about basketball at the same time could be confusing to the readers. He also felt that chaining the stories with the two big basketball stories about Shane, followed the next year by the gay basketball story, could produce far more sales as if it were a sequel. The publishers liked the idea and agreed. He teased them by saying he had no real title for the book yet, but the working title was Ball Three.

TJ's gay books combined sold six hundred thousand copies in six months, becoming a phenomenal success in gay publishing. They offered two hundred and fifty thousand dollars up front for **The Blackfeet Boys**, and the usual royalties. TJ and Jake anticipated there acceptance, the contract had been pre-approved including a clause that gave the gay publisher first look at

TJ's future gay books. This time he signed the contracts without the flair of champagne and toasts. Nonetheless, TJ and Jake were smiling on the way to the ESPN® studio. They had just collected two and quarter million dollars for two future book sales, and more would be coming from his past books as well. TJ knew that all his books by both publishers had been converted to all eBook formats, including Kindle®, and now generated a combine three hundred thousand dollars in the first year. A producer met TJ in the lobby for the interview Jake set up announcing the sequel to his phenomenal sales of his first book about Taylor's championship season. Chad Smith conducted the interview, and TJ knew what he needed to accomplish by answering questions about the last book, talking about the new book, and giving the ESPN® audience some hints as to how Shane was doing this past summer.

Jake gave his performance a top rating as they discussed the day. TJ dropped Jake off at his office, and then the limo took him to Sam's office where he gave him the checks. Sam smiled at the sight of the new money, and quickly made copies of the checks, and the signed contract for his files. He discussed taxes with TJ and suggested he start planning on helping some charities to avoid giving Uncle Sam all his money. He also suggested they find something else to invest in, and he had a portfolio of suggested investments for medium and high risk for him to approve. TJ took Sam's advice on all of it, but the charity idea he liked, and wanted to peruse the possibilities, and begin investigating.

Jerome's office became the final stop of the day. He presented him the contracts for his staff to make copies, brought him up to date on his work and Shane's regimen, and after saying goodbye the limo took him to the executive airport. Steve and Susie flew him home where he landed about seven o'clock. He found Shane asleep in the recliner when he arrived home. During the flight home, TJ devoured dinner, so he and Shane decided to strip and head to the wet area for a long soak in the Jacuzzi. TJ told him all about the day's journey, and the huge amount of money they just made. Shane corrected by saying TJ made, and TJ said no, none of this would have happen had it not been for Shane. Though their accounts were in TJ's name to protect any possible investigation into Shane's amateur status, mentally, he put the money in 'their' accounts.

Shane's schedule returned to normal with classes in the early morning, followed by strength training, lunch, shooting practice, and long jogs until basketball practice started in October. His summer workouts made Shane stronger and more determined than ever to win a second championship for his team, his coach, and his university. He continued to study right after lunch for ninety minutes, and before and after dinner as required. He set a goal to make all A's for his senior year, and he knew could do it if he worked hard enough.

TJ flew out again at the end of the month for the book convention in Las Vegas. Steve flew him out just past six that morning, and he landed near eight o'clock. He would not be staying overnight, so he took the limo directly to the MGM Grand Hotel Convention Center. Upon entering the show area, his mouth dropped at the huge exhibits displaying thousands of books releasing soon, especially those for the Christmas gift-giving season. Janet had met his flight with the limo, and walked him to her company's booth, where he met all the New York staff attending the show. Booksellers were stopping at the booth to pick up promos of the books they were releasing this fall. At the front of the exhibit he noted one of Shane's big cutouts displaying their book. On the corner of the big photograph he spotted a sticker promoting the new sequel to the basketball story to be released in April. TJ signed copies for their visitors until lunch. At two, he made a presentation about the upcoming sequel with his laptop for an audience of a thousand booksellers, and received a warm round of applause.

Afterwards, TJ found his way to the booth for his gay publisher. They were thrilled he paid them a visit, where he signed copies of his gay books for their guests as well. At three, he took the limo back to the airport, and flew home eating dinner in flight. He drove home exhausted. Shane helped him out of his clothes, but while playing fireman, he carried TJ to the sauna he warmed up after receiving an in-flight call updating his arrival time. They sipped on their water bottles and talked about their day. Shane asked lots of questions about the book convention, and TJ asked him questions about his classes and his workouts. They both worked hard at building their relationship, by staying completely interested in their partner's work.

Shane fixed TJ a big bowl of fruit and ice cream while they watched a movie in the great room. Later, they made their way to the bedroom. The sex had been short but good, and after finding their favorite spooning position, they slept well and happy.

# TWENTY-FOUR

Though excited about the beginning of basketball team practice, as usual, Shane dreaded the traditional, foreboding, silly skits on the Friday night basketball season kick-off in the arena filled with students and fans. He had to dance, which he felt he stunk at, even after TJ practiced with him, and he did an impression of an assistant coach hoping the poor man would forgive him. He was thankful when they played the light scrimmage game at the end, giving the fans a thrill with one of his big three hundred sixty degree spins followed by a big dunk. TJ sat in the stands and watched with great excitement for the new season, while lots of laugher at the team's skits.

The following week the entire team attended a Saturday night Taylor University football game, and at halftime Taylor led by two touchdowns. The coaches followed the basketball team onto the football field for the presentation of their National Championship rings, and Shane held the team trophy high over his head. They received a long, standing ovation. The coach spoke briefly, and then called on Shane to say a few words on behalf of the team. Shane thanked the fans for all the support. He told him he was proud of his team's accomplishment, but also expressed they were not done yet. He said they would do all they could and more to win the championship again. This sent the audience to their feet again. TJ used his press pass to watch from the sidelines.

The following week, while Shane was busy with new season practices, TJ met with Walter Mills in his public relations office. He gave TJ a hard copy of this season's media guide, and a CD-ROM edition so he could load it on his laptop. He also gave him a new press pass for this season and a press-parking sticker. Walter told TJ his book had been well received in the sports world, the university's alumni and fans, and congratulated him on drawing such mass attention to the university and the athletic department in particular.

He asked TJ about the numbers for book sales and nearly fell out of his chair when TJ told him they were approaching four million in sales. He had no idea it was that huge. He asked TJ if he would write a behind the scenes update for the team's website, and an article for the team's monthly magazine. TJ was overwhelmed with the opportunity and promised to do so. Finally, Walter told him the coach asked for permission for TJ to fly with the team this year. Coach Timmons, delighted with the book, thought TJ's fans would be interested in what they do during the long flights. TJ thanked him for all his help, and asked Walter if he would once again proof his chapters for this season, Walter said yes, and TJ said he would get back to him about flying with the team.

That night, he and Shane discussed the pros and cons of flying with the team. Shane began, "Well, the plus is simple—you'd get to see my pretty face, all the way there and back."

"I doubt that, as it would be too obvious. You'll have to sit up front, and I would have to sit in the back."

"That would be true on the way out, but I think I could sit with you on the way back by you pretending to interview me. Everyone knows about the book, so that would be easily accepted. The downside as you might fly out earlier than last year, and have to wait to fly home afterwards, so you'd waste a lot of time."

"Would it be harder to write on the team plane?"

"Well, it is noisy when we take off, but we have flown so much that most of us are either doing homework or sleeping. After a big win we are pumped and excited on the way home, but usually sleep takes over quickly, and it is soon quiet. The coach doesn't let us get rowdy. However, the seats are like a commercial flight, and I don't mean first class, so serious writing on the laptop would be hard."

"It would save us a bunch of money."

Shane laughed, "I think we can afford to fly the Learjet again with what you're making on your books, and what I hope to make next year on a NBA contract, so money is not really the issue."

"Maybe we should do both," said TJ.

Shane, "How do you do that?"

"Well, maybe I take a few flights with the team from time to time to tell our readers what it is like, but fly on the Learjet on the rest of the flights, so I can work by doing my research and writing in the air. I am worried that if I can't write on the way home, I might forget something, and I'd be busy into the wee hours upon arrival. I would rather write most of the way home, and be free to make out with you when you arrive."

"I can't argue with that strategy," replied Shane with a sly smile. "How about this, you fly with the team when you want to. You don't even have to ask what I think. Just do it. I trust your instincts. If that's okay, let's head to the wet area. My legs are sore."

"Your butt is going to be sore in the morning!"

Shane laughed, "I'm looking forward to it."


It was near the end of October and TJ was scheduled to deliver **The Blackfeet Boys** to the gay publisher by November first. His friend in Charlotte completed the big editing job, TJ made the marked corrections, and to finish it, he re-edited the book from back to front, forcing him to concentrate on each page individually. He sent the completed book to New York on Halloween via an Acrobat PDF® file, and sighed greatly when he received their email confirmation. He told Shane that finishing his books must be what childbirth felt like. He often felt overwhelmed at the ardent and fervent task before him, but jubilant and delirious when finished. He and Shane didn't celebrate the holiday, but did celebrate the completion of the new western story. TJ always enjoyed writing, but meeting deadlines became

288

a new skill that he was forced to acquire and master. Along with writing the two sequels for basketball and **The War Beyond**, an article for the magazine, and a monthly insert for the website, he felt strained, exhausted mentally and physically, but thanks to Shane, an overwhelming level of confidence, trust, and love. Yesterday's chores were soon forgotten as he began tackling the next assignment on his project list. He also settled on calling the new basketball book, **Twice Is Nice**. It felt perfect by being short and to the point, as well as it had a nice ring to it like a hook for a hit song.

He was, however, looking forward to writing his next two gay books and would work on them when he had a chance during basketball season. **The War Beyond – Part III** would be released with the May tour in the spring. His next gay fiction undertaking would be the gay fiction story **Forever Alone, Again**. He began working on storylines for this story and added to it from time to time. He also began a storyline for the gay basketball story, scheduled for released in eighteen months or so.

Meanwhile he wrote three chapters of the new **Twice Is Nice** basketball sequel, and tomorrow night they were playing the first game of the regular season. The pre-season games had gone well with the team winning by large margins.

TJ decided to ride the bus with the team to Charlotte for the opening game of the NIT Tournament. They were playing Sacred Heart in the first game at seven, and Dick Vitale and the ESPN® crews were broadcasting the game. He already made hotel and flight reservations for all the away games for the season, but planned to drive down to Charlotte, but finally decided to try the bus. He read a book most of the way, as there was no room for him to actually work on his writing. He could have watched a DVD movie and would remember to bring a few next time. Shane sat up front with his dorm roommate. Two hours later, they arrived at the hotel to check-in. At four-thirty, the team continued on to the arena to practice at five, and ate dinner at seven-thirty in a hotel banquet room. A mandatory study hall for ninety minutes followed, and then Shane was free until curfew.

He and TJ talked about practice, the beginning of the season and what Shane thought about tomorrow's game. After that, they cuddled on the bed to watch a movie, that lead to making out, and their first road trip sex of the season. Shane hated to go down two floors to his room afterwards, as he wanted to stay with TJ.

TJ slept late while Shane got up early for breakfast, went through a team meeting and watched video scouting reports. The team went back to the arena for a shooting practice, and then to the Bobcat practice gym for a private one-hour practice. They returned to the hotel and ate their team meal at two, followed by homework, and then ninety minutes of rest before time to leave for the game.

Shane and Taylor University team were comfortable in the Bobcat Arena, and so they were relaxed, as they could be, before their first seasonal game. Sacred Heart's team came to play and beat the National Champions. Every team they met this season hoped to defeat the best and for now, that was Taylor University. The man guarding Shane, beaten by him two years ago, hoped to make the NBA this year. He fouled Shane every chance he could get away with it, and Shane became frustrated the referees weren't calling the infractions. Jerry threw a hard bounce pass down the lane and into Shane's hands. Shane out stepped his man, creating a brief opening in the defense. He snatched the ball and leaped up as he turned. The Sacred Heart player swung hard with his fist to deflect the ball but missed, and caught Shane in the face just below his left eye and knocked him down. The goal missed, and once more the whistles remained silent.

Coach Timmons became exacerbated having seen enough of the lack of accountability and the beating of his star player, and very uncharacteristically stepped out on the court and began berating the nearest referee. They finally blew the whistle, called him for a technical, and he still kept giving them grief. This forced the assistant coaches to contain him and drag him to sidelines before the referees might kick him out of the game. Unfortunately, Sacred Heart made both shots, but Taylor still lead by six with eight minutes to go.

Coach Timmons knelt down in the huddle before his team went back out on the court. "Now maybe they'll call some fouls, but we're not waiting on them. I want you to step up the pressure on every possession. I want a mean full court press, a tenacious tough defense, and I want some solid stops. Jerry, that ball better go from their court to ours in less than two seconds. I want you to run them up and down this court until their tongues reach the floor. Do you hear me?"

"Yes sir!"

Shane came out of the huddle with a grin as TJ flashed a three for go, go, and go! Shane defended the player bringing the ball in. He had been watching him throughout the game, and Sacred Heart had become over confident. He reared back to throw the ball. Shane leaped to his right in a guessed anticipation, and caught the ball with his right hand, dribbled once, and dunked it hard.

They tried to bring the ball in again, but couldn't get a man open, forcing their coach to call a timeout to keep from losing the ball. They tried again, and still couldn't get a good throw, but made a desperate attempt, and Jerry stole it, flipped to Shane, leading to dunk number two with a defensive man hanging on for the ride, but this time the referee called a foul. Shane made the goal, and now they led by eleven.

For the rest of the ball game Sacred Heart only score fourteen points, while Taylor scored on every possession and won by thirty-two points. Dick Vitale enjoyed a field day of commentating, and spoke to TJ after the game.

They would both be back tomorrow for the second game. Dick mentioned TJ's book at the half, and twice he referred to a tidbit of knowledge gained from the book during his color commentating.

The coach granted the team some free time after the game, so Shane called TJ to meet him in the parking garage. They walked out of the back of the hotel to their favorite creamery and enjoyed banana splits. They ate slowly as they walked back to hotel taking the elevator to TJ's room. They made out for a while until time for curfew.

The next game would be against Iona at seven. As usual, the day of a night game remained at best, boring. After writing several pages about last night's game and Shane's comments, he decided to begin work on his new gay novel, **Forever Alone, Again** due out next fall. He just felt like taking a break from the **The War Beyond**. He sat still at first and very deep in thought as he read through his storyline. He began to describe some of the characters until they came to life to him, at least in his brain. He decided to emphasize the point of the title from the very start by beginning with a heated argument between two lovers and their friends. It got ugly—very ugly, as the lead character accused him of having sex with his best friend.

Once TJ made the decision on how it would start, he could not type fast enough. The characters yelled and screamed, threw plates of food, scattering their dinner guests out of the way. It ended as abruptly as It had begun, twelve fast turning pages later when the now ex-boyfriend stormed out, as did the other guests, and the lead character sat down dejectedly on the deck steps, while his heart descended with despair. He pulled his knees to his chest, realizing he was indeed forever alone again.

TJ ate lunch and began writing chapter two. He packed up his stuff late in the day, and boarded the team bus at four-thirty. He would leave his luggage on the bus, and take only his laptop into the game, as they were heading home immediately thereafter. He went up to the pressroom, fixed a plate of food for dinner and sat down alone at a table to eat. A few minutes later, Dick Vitale came by and said hello. He also fixed a plate and came over to eat dinner with TJ. Walter spotted them, brought his plate and joined them.

They talked about last night's game, as well as about the Iona team. Both of them had seen the second game last night and Iona's win, so TJ listened carefully. After a while, they talked about last year's book. Walter asked him about current sales. TJ told them the book had slowed down in the early fall, but with the start of basketball season, and a few well-placed commercials on ESPN®, and a big ad in USA Today®, sales began climbing again. They both shook their head in amazement and wished TJ well with the new one. Dick knew about TJ's gay fiction, but wisely said nothing. Later, he would tell TJ his wife saw his books in a Barnes and Noble in Florida and bought part one, **The War Apart**. She was reading one night in bed waiting for Dick to come to bed. He found her weeping and loving the book. She bought part two before he left. Dick got a kick out of his straight wife reading a book about two gay men. She said the book was about war and love and that she liked it. This compliment touched TJ greatly.

Iona proved to be a tough team. Taylor led by only two points at the half, and Shane uncharacteristically earned two fouls. He would have to be careful in the second half, and yet remain aggressive so they could win. The coach called for full court press and on their third opportunity Jerry got a hand on a misdirected press, fed it to Shane on a long throw and he dunked it. They held Iona to just eight points in the next twelve minutes of play. After the television timeout, Iona hit a pretty three from a long way behind the line, but Larry answered with his own three from the corner. Back and forth they played, and Iona did catch up and tie the game with sixty seconds to play.

Coach Timmons was mad that his team had let their play down, and he didn't mind telling them in the first twenty seconds of their timeout. He then told them they were going to stop Iona from scoring another point. He needed two overpowering defensive stops, and they needed to score once.

Shane came out of the huddle fired up. Iona had the ball and thus the first chance to score. They struggled to bring the ball in. Shane almost got a finger on the inbound pass, but as he came up court, Jerry defended his man so tightly that the guy forgot about Shane. Those long arms of his came in handy as he dove to pull the ball away from behind, rolled over and flipped the ball to Jerry before the referee could call him for traveling. Jerry sprinted down and laid it up for two points.

Shane got back to his feet and began defending the inbound pass again. They had twenty-eight seconds to play and led by two. They needed another stop. The ball was thrown at the last minute and Shane leaped as hard as he could towards center court, getting just a finger on the ball to deflect it right into Larry's hands. Shane rolled and leaped upwards as Larry tossed him the ball. Shane dunked it very hard and fouled by their big man. They now led by five with eight seconds to play. Iona brought the ball in, forced their way down the court, and with two seconds to play they made a long shot that missed and the buzzer sounded. The game ended and Taylor won.

TJ observed from the back of the bus that the team was very excited about their win for two reasons. They had just won two straight and earned themselves a trip to New York City for game three, and maybe the final championship game of the NIT tournament that would take place the Wednesday night before Thanksgiving and the Friday night afterwards.

After a few miles the team settled down for the ride home and most of them fell asleep. Shane moved to the back to sit with TJ. At first, they talked about the game, as they always did, with TJ using his handheld, digital memo recorder for notes.

Afterwards, they talked about Thanksgiving. They safely assumed they would win, so the team had hotel reservations for the tournament in New

York, and Taylor University would have quite a spread for the team's Thanksgiving meal, and two family members. Al and Barbara were flying in. Shane was concerned about TJ missing his family's Thanksgiving to cover his game.

TJ grinned at him saying if he was a reporter he would miss the game, but as the only guy completely in love with Taylor's star player, there was not a chance he would miss a minute of the game. He suggested they make plans to have a Saturday night dinner with his family before his sister left on Sunday to go home. He called his family and they agreed, so they were ready to go win an NIT pre-season tournament.

TJ flew to New York City early on Tuesday while Shane flew with the team leaving around noon. They had an afternoon practice scheduled in Madison Square Garden to prepare for their opening game against Michigan. TJ met with Jake early that afternoon as well as Sam. Wednesday morning he had an appointment with his gay publishers.

He was excited about this meeting, as weeks before he approved the final galley proofs and the cover for **The Blackfeet Boys**. The staff led him to the conference room where several staff members were waiting. They showed him a copy of the new book and he loved the cover, the print style, and the layout of the book. He winced at his picture on the back of the cover. Then they unveiled a new poster promoting the new book, and it was twice the size of his last publication. The staff's excitement encouraged him, and he left with his copy of the new book and a promise that they would send a shipment to the house. He gave the publishing team all the praise he could for their hard work. The president told them the initial shipment would go to two hundred gay bookstores, and all the major chains ordered copies as well.

He returned to his hotel and waited for Shane to call. The team had the evening off. Shane's parents were flying in tomorrow morning. TJ's oldest nephew, lived in New York, and made it to TJ's hotel after work. He sat on the couch thumbing through the new book. Shane finally called stating he was his way up.

He gave TJ a big hug and a kiss, and then bear hugged Ryan as well. They showed him the book and Shane was jubilant at the beautiful cover. They were all excited as they made their way out the back of the hotel and onto the streets of Manhattan. Ryan chose a fantastic Italian restaurant his boss often went to. It was only a few blocks away, so they decided to walk, even though the temperatures were just at freezing, and the wind nearly blew them off the sidewalk.

Thankfully, they found the restaurant was warm and cozy. They decided to order sampler plates and ate until they could eat no more. They had great fun talking and hearing about Ryan's escapades in the city he loved. He joined a gay tennis league, and felt happy making what he called quality gay friends. He went out to the bars far less often, preferring quiet meals with his new friends.

They stayed at the restaurant two hours enjoying the food and company immensely. Ryan was flying out early the next morning to Hilton Head Island, and so they watched him hustle south to the subway before retreating to the hotel to get warm again. TJ and Shane had just enough time before curfew to strip naked, and make love, enjoying it immensely.

Al and Barbara flew in early when most of the city was flying out of town for the Thanksgiving holiday. They paid a high price for the cab ride, but arrived safely at their hotel at noon. They called TJ and he met them in their hotel lobby for lunch. They decided to enjoy the restaurant in the hotel, as it was so cold on the streets. Shane enjoyed an early shoot around in the arena, and ate lunch with the team.

TJ was glad to see them and brought along his copy of his new book so he could show it off. They were thrilled at the new campaign for the release of the book on Tuesday. Shane called right before his lunch to be sure they arrived safely and told them he was doing well. TJ ate a fresh salad and hot potato soup with a cheese and onion topping. It was delicious and he ate it all.

Barbara said she was going to do some shopping after lunch to finish up her Christmas shopping, and maybe do a little shopping for her. They were looking forward to seeing the Macy's Thanksgiving Day Parade on Thursday. TJ said he would pass, as he had been once before on a cold Thursday morning, and thought he might have been close to freezing to death.

TJ wished them well on their shopping trip, and he caught a cab back to his hotel. Shane got a break and came up to see him. He completed his homework early, so there was nothing more for him to do but wait until game time. He was thankful they were playing in the first game.

They stripped down and TJ massaged Shane's muscles hard and deep, and then they napped in each other's arms for a short while. Shane awoke rejuvenated and ready to play. TJ reminded him to stretch well as the cold would tighten him up.

TJ ate dinner in the pressroom and was delighted to see his friend Dick Vitale, so they sat and talked for a while. TJ went down to watch Shane warm-up, smiled and winked at him. Shane did well and hit thirty shots before missing one. TJ made his away around the court and sat with Shane's parents for a while. Dick came over to say hi and they enjoyed talking to him. They didn't talk about the game as much as they did about the new home in North Carolina. TJ would later learn about the Florida mansion Dick lived in. He was kind and generous to them with his compliments, and they were grateful.

Near the start of the game, TJ retreated to his seat after nodding at Shane in the tunnel. The game started fast with Taylor and Michigan trading points back and forth with tough defenses and little mistakes. Every time Shane got the ball, the Michigan defense double-teamed him. He became frustrated as he wanted to score, and made the mistake of trying to go up with the ball and having it stripped away without a foul. The coach took him out for a rest and spoke to him in a gentle way.

"Son, you have the Michigan boys right where we want them."

Shane was puzzled and didn't understand, "How's that?"

"Well, if they are going to swarm you when you get the ball with two and three men, that must mean at last one or two of our men are without defense. All you have to do is throw it to the open man for a clean and pretty shot. We'll hit threes while they beat you up." The coach laughed and slapped Shane's knee. "Keep it up boy and we'll whip 'em!"

Shane smiled. He should have been thinking that way, but with the new season, he wanted to score. He hadn't thought he was helping his team at all, as his scoring was low. Jerry began feeding him the ball as the coach directed. For a while the defense snapped to him like magnets, and he would toss the ball to Larry or Jerry for three points. When they were up by fifteen Michigan began to back off Shane, and he began hitting nice jump shots from six to ten feet out. At the half, they were up by twenty-two.

TJ ate dessert in the pressroom and picked up the latest press releases. The second half was a tough one as they swapped points, but Michigan could make little gain on Taylor's big lead. They fouled Shane so many times that both of their big men were sitting on the bench, and out of the game for the final three minutes of play. Taylor won by thirty-four points.

On Thanksgiving Day, the team ate lunch in the hotel banquet room where the chef had gone to bat for the teams. Al and Barbara were delighted at the privilege to eat the holiday meal with their son and the team he loved. They ate well, too much in fact, and they loved it. The meal took ninety minutes with lots of laugher at the their table, and more when the coach began speaking at the head table. He had something funny to say about every single player, and to the player's delight, the assistant coaches as well.

Meanwhile, TJ decided he would save eating turkey until they arrived at his mom's house on Saturday. He ate an omelet for breakfast, and enjoying the solitude, he wrote twenty pages on **Forever**, and ordered a BLT sandwich for lunch and a bowl of soup. He assumed the staff would be swamped with the Thanksgiving feast downstairs, so he ordered early. He continued writing until about two. His eyes tired, he decided to take a nap.

About three o'clock Shane appeared and gave TJ a huge hug, and began apologizing for the limitation of just two tickets for his parents for the team's Thanksgiving Dinner. TJ laughed and told him about all the writing he accomplished on the new story, and how Shane saved him from gaining ten pounds. He reminded Shane they would enjoy Thanksgiving Dinner together in Greenville on Saturday night.

Shane's parents arrived a few minutes later, so they all sat down to just talk and enjoy each other's company and companionship. They talked and laughed until dinnertime. TJ anticipated dinner might be tough on

Thanksgiving night, but with help from the hotel's concierge, he secured a reservation at superb Chinese restaurant. They offered a large buffet, and though the crowd was small when they arrived, by the time they finished the place was packed.

The wait staff allowed them to stay as long as they wished, so they ate all they wanted, and then sat and talked some more. They caught a cab back to the team's hotel, where Shane and TJ said goodbye for the night, as his parents continued their cab ride to their hotel.

The boys lay in each other's arms, naked and sweating from their sexual play, and now content to just hold the other. Shane had nothing on except his watch, and he checked it often to see how much time he had left. They acted like a couple, now on their second year, and talked about anything but sports. Shane wanted to know where they could go on their next vacation. TJ suggested trips his favorite stops in Yellowstone, Glacier National Park, and places he had yet to visit in Alaska or Canada. It all sounded exciting to Shane.

The Friday after Thanksgiving Day was known as the biggest shopping day of the year. Barbara and Al were out thrashing about with the masses, working their way from Macys to Saks. Shane shot his way through a morning shooting session in Madison Square Garden, and took notes during a scouting meeting in the hotel banquet room. It wasn't a school day, so they had the afternoon off, but were told not to leave the hotel for fear they might get hurt on the street amongst the millions of excited shoppers.

TJ spent the morning writing first on the basketball book after reading the media notes forwarded by an email to him from Walter. Once done, he spent some time editing **The War Beyond**, and then went back to work writing fiction for his new gay book. TJ ate lunch alone in his room, while Shane ate with the team.

Shane soon joined him to rest and wait for the game. They watched SportsCenter® on ESPN® and highlights of their opponents. Wisconsin would be tough, and they had a big guy that would be assigned to Shane. He left at four and just before the start of the consolation game. The final championship game would be at seven.

TJ ate dinner in the pressroom, spent some time with Walter, and later would sit in the seats with Al and Barbara and hear about their day. They were flying out in the morning. Shane looked ready during warm-up, and later the game began with a flurry. Shane caught the tip off and threw it hard to Jerry, who in turn found Larry on the run, who pulled up and drained a three, as Shane arrived under the goal in case of a rebound. Wisconsin also had shooters and swished their first points as well. Back and forth they ran at a furious pace. Dick commented to his broadcasting partner what fine shape both teams were exhibiting, but he knew that Taylor was exceptional, and if Wisconsin didn't find a way to slow the game down, they would be run into

296

the ground. Dick, as usual, made this comment with as much politeness as he could utter.

With four minutes left in the first half, the Wisconsin coach took advantage of a television timeout and immediately followed with his own timeout. He made his boys sit down, sip Gator Aid®, and did all he could to help his winded players. Coach Timmons noted this strategy, so he swapped out a few players for fresh ones, and began a furious run when the whistle blew. They were ahead by twelve at the half.

The second half began as the first, but Wisconsin tired far sooner and Shane was just hitting his stride. He scored twenty-eight points and Taylor won by twenty-two. TJ made his way to Al and Barbara to hug them goodbye, and wish them a safe trip. He made his way back to the hotel where Shane joined him after finishing his late supper.

They flew home the next morning, and the team practiced an hour after landing. After practice, TJ and Shane drove to the airport where Steve and Susie had the Learjet standing by, and they took off at three and landed in Greenville in an hour. Ryan met them at the airport and drove them to the house. They received hugs from TJ's family, and Shane apologized for keeping their son away during Thanksgiving.

The meal was as good as last year with Shane making two trips through the long buffet. Afterwards they sat in the living room and laughed and talked with his parents, sister and nephew until late. They were staying in a hotel, so Ryan gave them a lift. They came for breakfast the next morning, wished them all well, and left for the airport. Elagene and Ryan left an hour later for Hilton Head Island. It had been a successful two-week tournament, and a big win after Thanksgiving in New York City.

# TWENTY-FIVE

Sunday was the last calm day they had for the week, as they had a home game on Wednesday, followed by two very hard practices. They were playing Ohio State as part of the ACC-Big Ten Challenge. Ohio's big man stood barefooted at seven-feet one-inch, and though Shane made it tough for the basketball giant last year, but this year, the big boy finally became a starter. With his chin pointing the way, he was ready to go to war with Shane this year.

At TJ's request, the publisher of **The Blackfeet Boys** set up an Internet videoconference after TJ explained the stores could go online to a conference website, and they could see TJ and ask questions coast to coast, building enthusiasm everywhere at the same time. They decided to test two of them, one for each coast. The response was huge with forty stores setting up a large monitor with the video feed from the Internet, and used a cordless phone to dial a toll-free number to ask questions. TJ used iChat® on his iMac® and used Shane's spare microphone and earpiece so that he not only looked like he was broadcasting on the Today Show®, but he could hear the questions without feedback. He used the audio mixer to raise and lower the telephone questions to prevent an echo. He felt like he was a disk jockey at a radio station, but the audio quality was clear and strong. Each gay bookstore averaged over fifty people in attendance after mailing out thousands of ten percent off coupons for the book, if they attended the half hour broadcast. The big box retail bookstores were mailed the same publicity material, but no one on the staff anticipated any interest in involvement. TJ didn't wait for results, but using his data file from his basketball book tours, he sent emails directly to the store managers with the attached info. Over a hundred big box stores offered the coupons and joined the videoconference. The gay publisher rushed in extra books to all the attendees, and felt astounded at the pre-conference excitement and press coverage.

TJ was nervous as to what they might ask, but they were all good questions, but many of them wanted to know where he got the idea for the story and would their be a sequel story. TJ laughed, and said after doing research in the Northwest, he began to wonder if a gay warrior could survive, and what he would do for love. Later, he decided on a love shared by two gay warriors, facing the wilderness alone. Others asked about the upcoming spring release of **The War Beyond – Part III**. He said he wrote the sequel immediately after the Blackfeet story, after connecting the characters from both stories, as they have an occasion to cross paths. He explained it was a year later, before he finished editing the first book, and that he was still editing the part III sequel that will release in May. When asked about a part IV, he replied he had written a storyline, and there would be a part four if sales were good for the new release. Eventually, the non-book question came up, "Mister Johnson, do you have a longtime partner?" TJ smiled and replied,

"I am pleased to reply…yes!" He paused, laughed, and added, "Next question?"

TJ received a phone call from the publisher the next morning saying they obtained excellent reviews from the stores, and half of the stores sold out of his new book. He said they learned a lot by doing the podcast. He also said many of their regular stores already ordered a second shipment. To TJ's surprise, he said Barnes and Noble® wanted to do a podcast just for their stores. TJ said great and for them to set it up, and he gave them the nights he could do it. He suggested he upload the podcast to them, as he had recorded it, and they could email a copy to the stores that missed the broadcast, or he could put it on his website so they could download it and replay in the stores, especially on the weekends when people were known to browse longer for books. They went right to work on the ideas.

He drove over to the university for tonight's game, ate dinner in the pressroom, watched Shane warm-up, and read through the final changes from Walter about tonight's game. ESPN® was carrying the game, but Dick was not there. TJ noted a quiet, somber mood as the fans began filling the arena. He assumed it either had to do with the holiday travel or the upcoming exams. However, the same kind of mood happened to the team.

Ohio State came to play, and they jumped out with ten straight points to zero for Taylor. His team's poor play enraged Coach Timmons. He yelled and screamed, and at the second television timeout he took out the entire first team. Fired up, the second team jumped at the opportunity to play and caught up to Ohio after just four minutes of play. Coach Timmons chewed on his first team until he felt confident they were ready to play, so he put his first team back in the game, and boy were they on fire.

Ohio only scored six points during the next eight minutes, but Shane and the offense put in twenty-two points. Taylor was ahead by six. The second half was more of the same. Shane had zero fouls, hit eight foul shots, and eighteen from the floor for twenty-five for the night. The big man for Ohio fouled out while trying to stop Shane with three minutes to play. With the big man gone, Shane had it easy for the rest of the night.

Shane came home after the game, but could only stay an hour, as he had to get back in the dorm before curfew. They soaked in the Jacuzzi briefly before moving to the bedroom. TJ didn't bother to set a timer, as Shane had been especially horny, leaving TJ deliciously sore.

This was a tough time of the year for the team. They played Kentucky on Saturday night at home, but the next game was a full week away, and the game after that another full week. The reason was exams. Shane would be studying for three exams, but the last few classes before the exams were always huge for him. So many last minute materials were given, requiring them to learn the stuff quickly. During his freshman year, he was taught to get all his term papers in before the last week of classes, so he could concentrate solely on exams. He continued the practice throughout his college years, and the strategy really saved him this term.

Leading up to the Kentucky game, the practices were hard, but the coach would be forced to lead easy short practices during exam weeks. By the end of the week, Shane felt mentally tired, but thankful he had Friday night and Saturday morning to chill out. The game was at two and TJ arrived in time for a late lunch. Shane stretched well and began his shoot around. He soon realized he was missing a lot of shots and began to get exasperated. TJ, sitting alone in his season ticket seat, saw Shane look up at him. TJ gave him the five-finger signal to chill, and then a two-finger signal for imagining everyone on the other team naked as they discussed a few days earlier.

As annoyed as he was with his performance, Shane smiled. Then TJ simply winked at him and smiled. Shane winked back. He dribbled in for a twelve-foot jump shot and swished it. TJ smiled. Shane caught the ball from the manager and went right back into the air and swished again. He began to get his momentum and confidence going again.

The starting five did not want a repeat of having to sit on the bench for a poor start, so they came out fast and racked up twenty points in four minutes to six for Kentucky. They didn't let up. Shane got a huge dunk from a long beautiful pass from Jerry. They were on a roll, and let by sixteen at the half. Dick was doing color commentating today and excited to see how aggressive they were playing. He was cheering the team on. So was TJ in the stands.

The second half started rough with Kentucky making some hard fouls to try and shake the Taylor team confidence. They pushed Shane and elbowed him, but Shane just kept putting the ball in and making the fouls shots. They won by twenty-two with Shane scoring thirty.

The next morning TJ woke up to find Shane missing from their bed. Shane had come home after the game, and TJ thought he was staying over. Shane loved studying at the house, where he could concentrate without interruption, and a refrigerator nearby. He also liked that he could get a hug and kiss from TJ every now and then. TJ found him in the office flipping through his book and looking at his notes on his computer.

"Good morning," said TJ. "How long have you been up?"

"About two hours."

"Are you hungry?"

"Oh yeah, are you cooking?"

"Yep, how about some omelets?"

"Perfect. Thank you. I love you."

"I love you, too."

While Shane continued studying, TJ went to the kitchen, fed the dogs, and began putting breakfast together. About fifteen minutes later, Shane came to the table to eat his breakfast omelet, some fresh fruit, a huge glass of juice, and a glass of milk. He had learned to eat grits, and now liked them as long as he had butter and cheese to put on them.

Afterwards, he brushed his teeth and went right back to studying. TJ took the dogs into the big back yard and let them explore a while. He walked the property and was pleased to see the new grass had done as expected. The weeds were way down, and it grew like a carpet.

Later he came in and got some work done on his computer, went over his chapter on last week's game, sent a copy to Walter and Dick, and moved on to writing **Forever Alone, Again**.

At lunch, TJ made a bowl of hot vegetable soup, and cut some raw vegetables. Shane devoured the meal, and went back to work. TJ and the dogs took a nap. At four, Shane found TJ washing his car in the RV building while the dogs played chase around and around the motorcoach. TJ was almost done drying the car. Shane laughed the first time he saw TJ use a leaf blower to dry his car, but after he tried it, he decided it was a good idea. TJ was using a dry towel to clean the glass and mirrors.

"That looks like a good idea," said Shane.

"Bring yours around and we'll wash it, too."

"Okay."

Shane jogged back to the kitchen, snapped up his keys, and drove out the first gate and in the second. TJ pulled his car alongside the RV to make plenty of room for Shane's Hummer. He opened the door to let Shane in and quickly brought it back down to keep the heat in.

"What happen to the dogs? I was watching for them."

"Thank you, but they don't know any better about cars. They would try to run up to you, and you're liable to hit them accidentally. I lost Meagan that way. I put them in the backseat of my car." He walked over and let them out.

Shane knelt down to give them a good hug and rub. "That was good thinking. I would never want to hurt them."

Shane quickly vacuumed out the Hummer with the wet-vac, took an air hose and needle gun to bow away the dust in the stereo and vent areas, and then wiped down the inside windows, and the dash. TJ mixed up the rolling mop bucket with more warm water and soap that contained carnauba wax. This was so they could wash and wax at the same time. Other times he used liquid Spic and Span® and swore that stuff did the best job of cleaning a car and leaving a clean sparkling shine.

Shane took the hose and wet down his car splashing away any sand or mud, and then each boy took a mitt glove and dipped it in the mop bucket and began washing the car from top to bottom. In ten minutes, they had each side done. Shane rinsed it, and then they did the running boards and wheels. TJ took care of putting away the cleaning supplies while Shane rinsed the car with warm water. TJ rolled up the hose on the wheel while Shane fired up the leaf blower, blowing away the droplets of water on the car. They finished by toweling it down. It looked great.

"Wow, that puts a great shine on it," said Shane.

"Then I shouldn't tell you it is going to snow tonight."

Shane laughed, "I am not surprised. At least I can study, as I don't have an exam until Wednesday."

"Put the dogs in your back seat, and drive them around to the car garage. I'll follow you in my car so don't worry about the gates. Please don't let them out until after I close the garage door."

After supper, Shane shot hoops for a while on his new basketball court. He loved having the Bose® stereo system in the home gym and cranked it up. Buddy installed the main house Bose® system in the living room, pushing music to all the rooms, but two separate Bose® systems for the RV building, so you can listen while washing or working, and in the wet area so you could listen while shooting, working out, or chilling in the wet area. The later two systems featured an additional input select switch. Shane could hit a select button and pick up the same music playing in the house, which they often did if they were watching a movie, or another button so Shane could plug in his iPod® and listen to his own music. Later, he called TJ to join him in the wet area using the phone intercom system. Ninety minutes later, they were in the recliners watching a movie. Shane decided to stay at the house during exams and Christmas, so for the next few days he studied hard, worked out some, went to the short practices, and studied some more. He aced his chemistry exam, and began studying for calculus.

On Friday afternoon, the team experienced regular full speed workouts to prepare for playing High Point at home. This game and the next at UNC Asheville were what the players called charity games. They were light games to keep their rhythm going, but they were not playing top ranked teams. These meetings were also done to help their opponents earn some cash for their athletic department. A home game in Lindle would make them eighty thousand dollars. A home game in their twenty-five hundred-seat gyms would make them only a few thousand dollars. It was good for the state's university system, and great for the goodwill, however, an unexpected lost would be most embarrassing for the Taylor team.

The coaches hated exam weeks, though they preached the importance of being a good student, so they spent most of their exam time recruiting, as it would be tough to find time to recruit after Christmas. However, Coach Timmons loved practice after exams, as he could work the team as long and as hard as he wanted, as no one had to study. He and his assistant coaches logged over five thousand miles crisscrossing the country, watching high school games, talking to the coaches, and visiting the homes of potential Taylor players. Of course, only one boy would be chosen for every two hundred they looked at it, and they only looked at the best in the country.

The game was at seven and by seven-thirty Taylor was winning by thirty points. Second half was more of the same, and the rest of the squad played the last five minutes. Final score was a hundred and ten to fifty-six. However, the coach still saw plenty of things they needed to work on, but encouraged them all to make top scores on the rest of their exams and workout as often as they could.

Shane took the rest of Saturday night off after eating the after game meal and driving home. He called TJ on his cell phone in route.

"TJ?"

"Yes dear," teased TJ while playing with the dogs. "Congratulations on scoring an hundred and ten points tonight."

"Thanks. I'll be home in three minutes and you'd better naked, cute, and horny." Shane laughed.

TJ grinned, "How about two out of three?"

"Okay," laughed Shane as he continued, "you pick, but I am all three, and that is a warning!"

TJ laughed, "I love it when you talk dirty to me. Hurry home big boy!"

Shane laughed as he hung-up. TJ heard him slide and squeal to a stop in the garage. Shane came in, petted the dogs and sprinted to the bedroom while pulling his shirt over his head. He found TJ lying naked on the bed with a yellow sticky note over his penis.

Shane grinned and continued stripping his clothes off, "I told you to be naked. What's that on your penis?"

TJ said slyly, "You college boys can read, can't you?"

Shane leaned over and read the note. TJ had written 'suck here' on the note in small print. Shane threw the note away, dove on the bed, and went right down on TJ's penis. They made passionate love for over an hour and then Shane threw TJ over shoulder like a fireman again, and took him to the sauna. They were both sore by morning, but very happy.

The following week Shane had two exams. He had studied hard and thought he would get an A in the first but perhaps a B in the second. He was thrilled when he went online and realized he got an A on both. It was Wednesday before their Saturday game with UNC Asheville. He acted like it was summer time on Thursday and Friday by doing strength workouts early in the morning, followed by shooting practice, and after lunch he did more shooting and ended by running. They had a short team practice on Friday afternoon.

The game was at two on Saturday, and though most of the team was rested and ready to go, two of the starters had Friday afternoon final exams and barely made it to practice on time. They were mentally tired and made numerous mistakes in the early drills, causing the entire team to run some laps. After some ragging from their fellow players, they sprung to life.

It snowed all day on Saturday, but TJ put his SUV in four-wheel drive and made it the arena safely. Most of the college students had gone home for Christmas. It was doubtful they were going to fill up the place. The coach had Walter email every student and alumni supporter, and tell them the first hundred in the door would get an autographed Taylor basketball, and any seat without a human in it by five minutes before game time would be offered free to anyone standing in line at door R. This announcement ended up on the radio and television sport shows, as well as the newspapers. The line the following morning was one mile long. People who had never been able to get tickets to a game jumped at the chance. Five thousand of them were let in, and the game became standing room only.

To the coach's dismay, UNC Asheville Bulldogs came to Lindle ready to play. They had a seven-foot giant that could actually play basketball. He was from some European country he had never heard of, and the floor actually shook when he ran by. He pushed Shane out of the lane several times before getting caught with a foul. They also had a hot guard that went ten for ten from the field in the first half. Taylor led by only two at the half, and the coach not at all happy with their play. He grinned as he relished the opportunity to whip his boys back into shape. The first thing he said at half time was there would be two practices tomorrow, which was Sunday, and two practices every day they weren't playing a game. It was the time of the year when he felt the team could improve the most, and take their play up another level or two.

The second half actually saw UNC take the lead, but Shane answered with a powerful dunk over the big giant. The big boy had run out of steam and began moving slower and slower down the court, while Shane kept his motor in a high gear the entire game. Gradually, they took the lead and kept the lead from then on. The game wasn't pretty, but Taylor one by eight. Shane hit only sixteen points, and he was not happy with his performance.

TJ was glad when Shane got home in the snow safely, but Shane was up early the next morning for the first of two practices on Sunday. They did the same on Monday. Florida Atlantic arrived Monday afternoon and shot in the arena that night. The game was for seven on Tuesday night.

They hadn't played this school in a long time and considered it a warm up school, but they had won their conference last year, and like everyone else, they came to beat the National Champions.

Shane made a dive midway through the half, caught the inbound pass, and somehow turned in midair and flipped the ball to a sprinting Jerry. The shortest guy on the starting five dunked it. Meanwhile, Shane hit the floor on his back, but rolled head forward and slid into his team's bench. The coach bent down and made a futile attempt to try and stop him. Shane looked up at him.

The coach looked down at him after he slid to a stop and threw his hands out to his side with palms down, and said, "Safe!"

The bench laughed as the coach acted like a baseball umpire. Shane laughed, rolled to his feet and sprinted back on the floor. He heard the coach say, "Hit one out of the park this time!"

Shane grinned as he went down the court, blocked a shot, caught the ball, flipped it to Larry and took off running. Larry dribbled a little waiting for Jerry to get open, but got a glimpse of Shane's sprint and threw it hard down the court, and into Shane's arms by going over his shoulder like a tight end going for a touchdown. Shane caught it, took one giant step, and leaped high and slammed the ball hard through the net.

The coach yelled, "Home run by the white boy!"

Everyone on the bench cracked up again, and Shane smiled as he went to defend the inbound pass. Taylor won the game by twenty-three at hundred and five to eighty-two. Florida Atlantic fought hard, but the National Champions outgunned them.

Thursday they flew to Saint Louis to play at seven on the following night. It would be their last game before Christmas. TJ had flown up in the Learjet, and gave Steve and Susie game tickets. They had flown back out to handle another passenger, but returned Friday and took their required naptime and woke in time for the game.

TJ was staying in the team hotel as usual, and spent most of the downtime writing in both of his new books. He was working hard to find new angles for the **Twice** sequel, making it feel like the reader was getting a bonus tour behind the scenes pass. He did a whole chapter on the teachers that travel with the players. Another on medical staff and the procedures the managers are trained for in case of an accident. He learned the local hospitals and orthopedic surgeons were always on call as part of the team's pregame check off list. Every precaution would be taken to insure the safety of a player and the correct response for treatment and repair. He included in these chapters one or two players that were in treatment, or obtained an interview of the player's view of his recent emergency treatment.

He arrived at the formerly named Savvis Center, now called Scottrade Center, in plenty of time for the game. He ate dinner in the pressroom, and then opened his laptop to look at a spreadsheet list of his own. He had been working for two weeks on getting things ready for their second Christmas together and the family trips. TJ and Shane selected gifts for their parents, but TJ did the shopping, as Shane had either been studying for exams or working his butt off in the twice a day practices after the tests. He shipped the gifts to the Bradleys with instructions the FedEx boxes were not to be opened. Since the last game before the short Christmas break was in Saint Louis, all the players were flying home after the game. TJ and Shane would simply make a short thirty-minute Learjet flight to Shane's hometown.

TJ also shopped for his side of the family and shipped their gifts as well with similar instructions. They packed for a longer trip than a usual away game excursion, and it would be cold in Missouri. He made sure he had everything as ready as could be. Before leaving he delivered several thank you gifts to the folks who helped them with their new home and life in general. He started with the realtor who helped find their land, Henry and his construction team, Bobby their architect, Leslie who decorated the house so well, and came back to decorate for Christmas. He also sent gifts to Jerry and Terry their new landscapers, and a gift for the housekeeper. He sent packages to Jake, Sam, and Jerome in New York, as well as Janet his project coordinator. He sent special gifts to Walter and Dick who helped them so much with editing, tips and advice. He sent packages to Brian Kenny at ESPN® and their favorite technical guru Buddy Bell. They prepared gifts for all their Learjet flight crews, too. Finally, he sent a package to Bob and Sue in South Dakota.

The boys had hoped they would be back before the snow fell, but they built a new big garage at home this fall, and it wasn't quite finished, and so they just kept working and decided to stay home for Thanksgiving and Christmas. However, she sent email stating they were leaving at six in the morning the day after to Christmas to head south, and thaw out as they traveled, as it was six degrees today in Rapid City. TJ and Shane not only wished them a happy holiday, but also begged them to please be safe driving south. The dogs made the trip, too. TJ took along their pet carrier crates, but they didn't have to climb inside until the car service arrived at the hotel. TJ went inside and checked in, rushed to his room to drop his stuff, and then using his cell phone, he had the driver meet him in the parking garage. He picked up the crates, and went up the back elevator. He would have to sneak them in and out to potty and pee, but he wasn't about to leave them at home in a kennel for Christmas.

The game crowd was not very enthusiastic, and TJ felt there were more Taylor fans than Saint Louis fans in the center, but their team was ready to play. The score went back and forth, and halfway through first half Shane was fouled hard on a short layup. Somehow the ball fell in, and he made the foul shot as well. TJ looked over at the Taylor bench and none of them could believe he had made the shot, even though he had been knocked hard in the air for the foul.

The coach had worked team hard for days, and he was ready to see some results. Eight times in the first half Shane had gotten the rebound and flung it to Jerry or Larry on a fast break and they had scored. The coach got excited. Shane got a steal a few minutes later and ran like a sprinter from theirs goal to his, beating everyone down court. He made the dunk, and waited for the man that was supposed to be guarding him to make it down court and bring the ball in. Shane took advantage of the late player and took the ball out like he was going to bring it in, but the referee laughed at him and took the ball away. Grinning at his coach, Shane stepped to his usual defensive position. Larry was also on fire with his shooting. He hit every shot in the first half, and they were all beautiful three-point field goals. He was six for six. Taylor led at the half by twelve.

Saint Louis found a second wind and came back to tie the score with fourteen minutes to play, but then Taylor went on a wild run. They were running a full court press, making many fast breaks, and flat wore out Saint Louis. TJ spotted Coach Timmons grinning from ear to ear. The coach sat down and enjoyed watching his team. He turned to the players on the bench and used the opportunity to teach them. He loved it.

Taylor stopped at hundred and six points, forty-one more than their opponent. They all hugged in the locker room, wishing their teammates a Merry Christmas, and the place was empty twenty minutes after the game. The bus took all but Shane to the airport, so they could make their connections.

TJ hailed a cab and waited for Shane who sprinted out of the team entrance. They rode back to the hotel and picked up TJ's luggage, the dogs in their carriers, and rode on to the executive airport. Steve and Susie beat them there, and had the plane warmed-up and ready for takeoff. TJ paid the cab driver, and the boys sprinted through the lounge and onto the runway. Steve spotted them and opened the door.

They took off minutes later, and Susie wisely brought them a hot sandwich and soup to tie them over, cheeseburgers for the dogs per TJ's instructions, followed by a bowl of ice cream and bananas for the boys. They landed not long after. The boys wished them a safe flight home. A second flight crew would return on Christmas morning for the flight to Greenville.

Al and Barbara met their flight and greeted them warmly on a frozen runway that barely reached a chilly twenty degrees with a stiff wind. However, Steve had no trouble taking off, but TJ and Shane were freezing after stepping out of the warm jet. Thankfully, Al left the car running so it was warm and ready, so they loaded their gear along with the dogs, and drove home.

This was their second Christmas together, and they easily fell into comfortable laugher as the Bradley family accepted TJ like their own son. Shane was affectionate with TJ in front of his parents, but no suck faces kisses were shown. They also managed to spoil the dogs at every opportunity. The parents knew the next few years might be very different when Shane turned pro, as some teams actually played on Christmas Day. She couldn't imagine why. Football, yes, but not basketball, she thought. Al reminded her it was all about money.  The broadcasters needed games to fill airtime and sell advertising, so they worked holiday games into their big television broadcast package.

This year TJ met some of Shane's relatives as they traveled to a nearby town to visit and eat lunch. They also ate at the country club, and Shane insisted he visit his high school gym for a workout. The coach had given him a key several years ago because the kid loved to practice at odd times. He still did. Shane called to be sure it was okay, so on Christmas Eve morning, TJ was under the goal catching the ball and firing it back to Shane, as the dogs chased each other around the system. They tired quickly and found a tumbling mat to take a nap on. Thankfully, Al came over and relieved TJ after a while. TJ enjoyed resting a spell and watching Shane and his dad workout together. Barbara remained at home working on getting lunch ready. She called and reminded the boys she would have lunch ready at noon.

They all tried to eat light, as they could smell the big Christmas Eve dinner cooking, but it didn't matter, as there was way too much good food for them to enjoy. They did their gift giving after dinner and all went to bed at ten. The next morning TJ, Shane, and the dogs boarded the Learjet for the hop to Greenville, South Carolina. They gave both parents hugs whether they wanted them or not, and thanked them so much. TJ had sat down with Al the night before and logged into his laptop the games they were hoping to attend including home games. TJ invited them to come in the night before the homes games, when they could, and stay in the new house.

The flight crew prepared breakfast for them, but they ate lightly, knowing a second big Christmas dinner awaited their arrival. The dogs ate a nice hot sausage and loved it. The whole family arrived at the airport in two cars and picked them up at ten o'clock eastern time. They did presents first, as Ryan was anxious to see what he received for Christmas. They had lots of fun, and Ryan received several joke presents, while promising to get even next year.

TJ helped his mother and sister prepare lunch with fourteen serving dishes plus a ham and turkey. Shane could not believe it. He went through the line twice with an empty plate each time. They all got a kick out of teasing the boy with the big appetite, but TJ took up for him by saying he would burn off the entire meal in just one practice. TJ on the other hand would endure weeks of treadmill work to try and drop the pounds away.

They spent two full days with TJ's family before catching the jet home after dinner on the twenty-six. TJ and Shane slept in the next morning, but after lunch he warmed up in the home gym. He went to practice at four with the team. They had a minor break for New Year's Day, but after that, it would be time to hustle all the way to the championship.

# TWENTY-SIX

The team endured double practices everyday right up to the their first game after Christmas on Thursday when they played Rutgers at home. It was still a warm-up game for the upcoming league play, but the teams were getting tougher. Three games to get the bugs out of their play before the first ACC game, and Dick often said no league in the country was as tough as the ACC. Usually every single team in the ACC could beat the top ranked teams on any given night. It was exciting, fast paced, brilliant, exhausting, and amazing to watch and play in. Shane loved it. TJ loved it. Dick Vitale loved it. It was great and terrifying!

TJ kept busy at home, writing new fiction in the mornings, and checking sales figures in the afternoon, plus editing on the next release. The gay publisher put a package of his older but recently released books under the new brand for Christmas gifts, and the results were very positive. Since Thanksgiving they sold fifty thousand old titles, and three hundred thousand of **The Blackfeet Boys**. He still couldn't believe those sales numbers. It amazed him last year's basketball book continued selling twenty-five thousand copies a month, and twice that in December due to an ad campaign that basically stated 'For the guy that has everything else, but loves college basketball.'

He also learned from Jake that the big publishing company planned a release of a paperback edition of last year basketball book for the Valentines Day season, with additional pages promoting the new book, and an excerpt from the first chapter.

TJ worked hard on the new book **The War Beyond – Part III**, weaving in more action and detail for all the characters, while blending historical events, including the building of the railroad, the Chinese workers, more Indian trouble, and a mystic mountain lion. There were new characters to describe, and the expansion of their little mountain ranch. He knew there would be heartbreak in part III, as well as plenty of new bad guys, but there would also be the dry wit and humor the gay mountain men were known for. TJ enjoyed the fun of the story, and that was why he wrote any tale, because he wrote things he wanted to read.

Due to the holidays, TJ and Shane were enjoying living with each other full-time, though they knew when school started back, Shane would have a curfew in the dorm making him sleep there. This made the time they did have together so special, and they took advantage of it. On two heavy snow and ice days, Shane figured out that he could jog around the RV building for a pretty good running workout with the dogs chasing him. He had pockets of small treats he would toss to them to keep up the chase. Beeper tired first, and smartly just waited on Shane to come her way before barking at him for her treat. Of course, no matter what the weather was doing in the outside world, inside his own gym, Shane shot hoops. TJ joined him near the end of his workouts to spend some time on the treadmill, and then Shane would spot him lifting some weights and doing some of the exercise machines. Together, they would finish with their usual sauna, steam, and Jacuzzi time.

One night Shane said he wished they had a pool so he could work hard on his aerobic training without stressing his joints like jogging did. TJ told him a few years ago he almost bought a swim spa. He explained the pool measured twenty by ten feet and four feet deep with a jet thruster at one end, and rest stations at the other end. "You adjust the thruster and swim in the wake as if you were a salmon swimming upstream. You can make it hard or easy, and you can do aerobic exercises in the water as well."

Shane wanted to investigate it right away. After they dried off, they put on their terry robes, and TJ brought his laptop in the living room and found the website so Shane could see the demo. He wanted to try one. TJ fired of an email to the manufacturer to find a public place to try one.

Thursday night came with a break in the weather and the fans poured in for the game, even though the students were not yet back for the next semester. However, they would be arriving this weekend and in time for the ACC league play to start. Rutgers arrived with a good squad, but the coach said they were also very smart team. They would mix up their defense to try and slow Taylor down, and they would double-team Shane as often as possible.

Shane studied his man meticulously in the video reports, staying after the team meeting and the scouting report. He replayed certain possessions over and over until he felt like he knew the man better than his teammates did.

Rutgers caught the tip-off, brought the ball down smartly, passed it back and forth, and with time running down on the possession clock, their point guard began moving across the center. Shane's man suddenly broke from down low towards the mid paint with hands out ready for a pass. Shane knew it was a play they had run before, though not often, but they did run it once a game. He quickly stepped in front of his man just as the guard let go of the ball. It came right into Shane's hands and he took it on the run, blazing right past the faster point guard, down the court in three seconds and leaped for a big dunk. The crowd went wild.

Shane didn't even grin. He went over to the inbound slash mark and waited for his man to make it down the court, and take the ball from the referee to try again. Rutgers recovered about midway through the first half and began to hit some pretty three-point shots. They were within eight at the half. Shane scored ten points from the field and three foul shots.

Coach Timmons made several adjustments, and in the second half, the Taylor team began running everything faster. The Rutgers big men were sweating profusely, and at each stop of the game, they bent over panting.

310

A Writer's Fantasy

Shane grinned and told his team it was time for a blitz. The next ten minutes looked like a college team playing a high school team. Taylor scored twenty-two points to six and went on to break a hundred. Everybody on the bench played, and that always made Shane feel great. He scored twenty-nine points and he felt pride at his accomplishments on offense and defense. Coach Timmons noted the progress his team displayed through the hard practices during the holidays. He hoped it was enough for the ACC games.

Sunday's game with Dayton was at two o'clock. Shane spent the night with TJ, and arrived at ten for the game meal rested and ready to go. TJ relaxed by working on the new novel on Sunday morning while listening to the morning news shows. He loved CBS Sunday Morning show, starting with the intro solo trumpet performance. He arrived an hour before the game, ate a late lunch, picked up the notes for Dayton, and went down to watch Shane warm-up. TJ thought he looked loose, calm, and ready, but then he always seem to.

Dayton started at a fast pace and scored point for point with Taylor for over fourteen minutes, but slowly they were beginning to lose their pace, and Taylor kept pouring it on. Shane picked up one foul, but put in eleven points. The Dayton center and forwards elbowed and pushed him hard, and got away with about half of their rough play, but the big man obtained his second foul with three minutes to the break. Their coach took him out of the game. Shane took advantage as Jerry got several quick passes to him for short turn and shoot two-point plays. Taylor led by nine at the half.

Second half started oddly, as Jerry wasn't on the court. Henry was substituting for him, and brought the ball down. They set up their offense, but they were just off. After a foul, Shane asked what happened to Jerry, and Henry said he had diarrhea. Everybody on the team made a sour face, and no one wanted to go to the locker room to see if he was all right. The doctor was with him, and he wondered if it was food poisoning, but everybody else on the team was fine. He checked the food order brought to him by one of the managers, and eight other people ate the same selection as Jerry. The star point guard had a slight temperature, but twice more he fled to the bathroom in a hurry. The doctor finally gave him a pill to plug him up.

Meanwhile, Shane began moving the ball down court by going part of the way, and either setting up the screen or catching a desperate pass. As time was running out on one possession, he rushed to the top of the key, Larry passed him the ball, and he turned and shot a pretty twelve-foot jumper. It went in with a nice swish. It was a shot he did over fifty times in his home gym last night.

With six minutes to play, Rutgers almost caught up, though Taylor still lead by four. Jerry came into the game, looking pale, but ready to play. He moved the ball quickly down the court, ran a play and they scored. Two plays later he made a steal, and fed it to Shane for a quick layup. On and on he

311

went like a machine. Taylor won by fourteen. It wasn't a pretty game, but they won.

After the game, TJ drove home and found Bob and Sue setting up their motorcoach in the new parking spot they made for them. He was thrilled to see them.

"Hey, how are you? How was the trip?"

Bob was plugging in the electricity while Sue gave him a big hug. "It started off a bit scary with a forecast of a big snow coming in. We left early the morning after Christmas as planned, and drove south and east to try and get to warmer weather. The first few days were cold, but after that it wasn't bad. We're tired though. It was too cold to do much sightseeing, although I did get some pretty sunrise pictures, as well as some of ice on the bare trees. We listened to the game on the radio. How are you?"

"I'm fine. Shane is fine. He's happy about beating Dayton, but he'll be very excited that you arrived safely, and so am I. He should be here soon. Are you hungry?"

"Yes, of course we are."

"Come on in and see the dogs, and I'll fix us a quick meal."

"Okay, give us a few minutes to set up and get the heat running, and we'll be over."

"I'll see you soon."

TJ called Shane on his cell phone. "Hey, don't eat too much. Bob and Sue just arrived, and I'm fixing dinner for them. How long before you get here?"

"I just sat down to eat, so I'll eat light and be there in thirty minutes. Do you need anything?"

"No, I think I'll grill steaks, bake some potatoes, and make a big salad."

"Hmm, that sounds good. I can't wait to see them. See you soon."

"Hello?"

TJ replied, "Come on in."

The dogs rushed to the door and welcomed Bob and Sue with wagging tails. They knelt down and petted them furiously. The dogs jumped to give Sue doggie kisses. "I see they didn't forget me."

TJ laughed, "They never forget the people that feed them. Go on down the hall and wash your hands. Shane should be here in a second. The salads are ready, and the steaks will be soon."

They hung their jackets on the coat rack on the wall behind the door, walked through the office and found the hall bathroom. Shane came in the door and gave TJ a kiss.

"Way to go," TJ said. "That was a great game. Are you tired?"

Shane took his jacket off, hung it up, and knelt down to pet the dogs. "I'm good. It was a good workout. " He turned as he heard his name.

312

"Shane!" Sue hustled to him and gave him a big hug. "How are you? Did you grow another foot or something?"

"I'm fine and I think you're getting shorter. How are you?"

Bob came up and gave him a hug as well, "We're fine and glad to be back down south."

TJ brought a platter of salads to the table. "Okay, let's eat. The salads are on the table." TJ served ice tea, which Bob and Sue got the hang off last year, and then brought the steaks and potatoes to the table. The four of them talked easily with lots of humor. Shane brought them up to date on his life, and then TJ talked about the books, and Sue brought them up to date on their new home in South Dakota and their travels.

TJ grinned, "Well, as usual we could use your help from time to time. Thanks to the water jug and a big bowl of dog food, the dogs have been fine on short weekends. They're enjoying the doggie doors and path to the dog pen, we can leave them for a few days at a time, but we know they get lonely. If you don't mind helping from time to time I'll get you a house key, and we'll teach how to turn on the big screen and so forth."

He also gave Sue the password to the Wi-Fi system and urged her to test it when she got back to the coach. They had written down the gate code, but he loaned them a remote control unit for their truck to make it easier. He told them about Jerry and Terry, and what days they usually came for landscaping, the day for trash pickup, the days for the housekeeper, and gave them the official address for the mail. On Monday, he said a man was delivering their new half size dumpster for trash, and they would place it in the midst of the bushes across the way from the garage so it would be out of sight. In the span of just ninety minutes, it was as if Bob and Sue had been there all along.

Shane endured two more hard practices, classes started on Wednesday, and they had a seven o'clock game with Penn State. Thankfully, it was another home game, and they were ready for Penn. It was the last game before the ACC league played started, and the Taylor team was ready to win. Shane surprised Bob and Sue with tickets to the game. They were thrilled. TJ bought them team jerseys with Shane's number, and matching hats.

Dick entertained TJ during their meal together prior to the game in the pressroom. He was there to commentate for the broadcast. He warned TJ that Penn would be tough. They were strong and worked hard together. He added they were not fast as a rule, but had spurts that often caught their opponents off guard.

The game began well for Taylor with a beautiful three-point shot by Jerry at least three feet behind the line. Penn responded with a quick layup and the shooter beating Shane off a screen. Shane was not pleased at being embarrassed, but it must have been good for him. On Penn's next possession, he stole the ball, and ran it home for a big dunk. The crowd loved it. Bob and Sue leaped to their feet screaming and yelling.

Larry was hot and hit twelve points in the first half. Jerry did well at eight, but had nine awesome assists. Shane put ten in, but Taylor led by only two at the half. However, in the second half, the fans saw a war on the court, as the lead swapped back and forth, and though Taylor played hard, Coach Timmons saw room for much improvement. At the final television timeout and three minutes and fifty seconds to play, he chastised his players about defense. He said they had worked hard, but they were not performing what they learned. He called for big defensive stops, fast and furious runs, and high-pressure full court stops. And he would call for trap plays on every other possession for the rest of the game.

The starters returned to the floor with renewed passion. They were bringing the ball in. Shane flipped it to Jerry on the run, and the boy hit a second gear, laying it up just three seconds later. Shane grinned as he ran to the corner, and began attempting to block the inbound pass. The full court press was on, and every one of Penn's men was covered, and before they could bring the ball in, the five-second whistle blew, and it was no Taylor's ball. Shane prepared to bring the ball in. He faked it to Jerry and flung the ball down the line to Larry who turned and shot another three-point play. A frustrated Penn forward fouled him, and Larry put the extra point in as well.

Taylor gained confidence and Penn only got two passes on the next play before Jerry stole the ball and threw it to Shane on the run. A Penn guard fouled Shane, but it must have felt like a gnat as the lay up went in. Shane also made the foul shot. In the final minutes of the game, Penn only scored two points. Taylor won by fourteen. Dick Vitale noted the change in their defensive play in his on-air commentary, and gave them high praise for their total shut down of the Penn offense.

There next game was not until Sunday night, so Shane did his homework at the house, slept over on the weekend, and the coach worked them hard for two days, but they had a light Saturday morning practice. The weather had unseasonably turned warmer, so Shane and TJ loaded the dogs up, and went to their favorite park for a long doggie walk. They laughed as the dogs went left and right while smelling the scents of other dogs or rabbits, and of course, leaving their own mark on top of what they found.

Afterwards, they put their sports bags in the car and drove to Greensboro. They had a four o'clock appointment with a salesman for a Swim Spa® dealer who carried the Endless Pool® brand. They had a good showroom and appeared somewhat use to seriously interested people wanting to try their product. TJ assured them they were very serious, and the person testing it was none other that last year's Most Valuable Player Shane Bradley. They were more than happy for him to try their pools.

TJ arranged to make a call from their car, and someone would meet them at a back door so that Shane would not have to walk through the mall. They immediately took him to a changing room, and minutes later he came out with his bathing suit on, and a towel over his neck. He also had on his lap goggles he used in the summer at the university pool.

They were shown a video about the Endless Pool® system, demonstrating the features of each of their models. TJ held the brochures as they walked around checking out the different models. TJ asked to see a motor and valve compartment so he could inspect them, since he had over a two decades of experience with Jacuzzi spas. He wanted to see how they would drain and fill it.

Shane looked at the smallest one and decided his body length and his reach would mean he could almost touch the sides, so they moved over to their longest one, which also had two sitting areas in the rear to rest and cool down between workouts.

Shane felt the water, threw his towel to TJ, as well as his bathrobe, and quickly slipped over the side into the water. The sales rep showed him how to adjust the speed of the water, and how to hit the start and stop button. Shane stretched for a bit and hit the button. He leaned over and began swimming. TJ knew Shane was a good swimmer, but as he watched the second tallest player on the team stroke through the water, he hadn't realized how graceful and smooth he could be. He swam at a slow speed for eight minutes, paused to adjust the speed upwards, and went back to stroking. He stopped two more times, and each time he made it go faster. After forty minutes, he slowed the flow so he could cool down. Finally, he sat in the cool down area and grinned.

Before the salesman could ask about the workout Shane said, "We'll take it."

TJ laughed. He had known before they got there that Shane wanted it, but he felt better knowing the test went well. Shane went to the dressing room to change while TJ took care of the paperwork. Thankfully, they had the unit in stock and could deliver it right away. TJ paid for it with his credit card and the salesman was a little taken back that he had a card that could pay for the whole thing but he did.

They went out the back door and began driving home. They decided to pick up steak dinners from Texas Roadhouse on the way home. Shane called in the order so it would be ready when they got there. TJ went in and out of the restaurant carrying several large bags with the steaks, salads, and potatoes.

After dinner, they walked to the wet area to figure out where they wanted to put the Endless Pool®. They measured with a long tape measure several times, and realized they could put it between the Jacuzzi and the steam room so that filling and removing the water would be easier, and so the swimmer could move from the swim spa to the Jacuzzi with ease, and without sloshing water all over the wet area. Shane had been afraid it would have to be too close to his new wood floor for his basketball court.

Satisfied with their plan, they went to the bedroom to get naked and head to the sauna, steam and Jacuzzi before watching a movie and going to bed. With a Sunday night game at home with Florida State, Shane knew they could sleep in. They ate a good brunch breakfast and prepared for a noon taping for an interview with two television stations and ESPN's SportsCenter® television program. TJ set up the computer, flipped on the lights and camera, as well as the audio system. He turned on the big LCD HD monitor and muted the sound. He also muted the house audio. He put his headset on as Shane sat on the stool after sliding his microphone under his Taylor basketball shirt, and putting the earpiece in his ear. He turned his controller on and sat down.

"How do I look?"

TJ looked up at the monitor on the wall and smiled, "Sexy. Test your microphone for me."

Shane counted aloud, and began speaking like he was answering a question. TJ told him that was fine. "Are you ready?"

"Yep, let's get them done."

TJ took his headset off and dialed the first number. He gave the waiting producer the link and password, and then hit the software button on his iMac®. Sixty seconds later, they were connected. He went back to his headset and could hear the producer and director in his ear. Soon the local sports reporter for Florida State could be seen in a split screen on the monitor. After a few sound checks, the interview began.

Two minutes later, they were done and said goodbye. They repeated the process for a local Lindle station, and ended by calling ESPN®. He got Fred Archer on the phone, gave him the password and soon they were talking to a reporter in New York. They did a three-minute spot, and then a thirty and fifteen-second tag of short questions they could insert anywhere they needed it. Finally, they asked Shane to cut several five-second spots for promos where he said things like, "This is Shane Bradley and you're watching ESPN®, the leader in sports broadcasting." Shane did all the spots without flaws.

Afterwards, he gave TJ a kiss and headed out the door for his team meal at two, and a team meeting on final scouting notes. TJ liked home games because he could spend the afternoon writing, then rush out the door at the last minute, and get to the game an hour before tip-off, eat a nice hot meal, visit with friends like Walter or Dick, and sometimes Al and Barbara, or Gary and his friends from Asheville. However, today he brought company with him. At the last minute, Shane secured a pair of tickets for Bob and Sue from his dorm roommate. They were thrilled to visit Taylor's big arena and see Shane play in person once again. They were wearing Shane's jerseys once again.

Shane knew that every single team in the ACC could beat them if Taylor played poorly and the other team played well. They were fired up, maybe too pumped, and on the first possession Shane shot a jump shot from twelve feet out, and it missed and fell out. Shane hustled down the court and went to work on defense, feeling highly disappointed he missed a shot he hit twenty-five out of thirty times in practice.

TJ wished he could have told him to just chill out and settle down, the game will come to him, but with the stands full of twenty-five thousand screaming fans, Shane would never have heard him.

Florida State scored first, but Taylor also scored on their next possession. Eight minutes later every one of Taylor's starters had scored, but Shane. Dick had to comment on the situation but he, too, wished he could tell Shane to be patient.

Coach Timmons studied his big man and finally took him out with four minutes to play in the first half. The coach let him sit a second and then knelt down in front of him. "Does your stomach hurt?"

"No sir," replied Shane.

"Does your legs hurt?"

"No sir," replied Shane.

"Are you sick in anyway?"

"No sir."

"Shane, I have seen you score hundreds of points a week in practice. I have seen you hit baskets that were impossible, and with four men hanging on your back. I've seen you run as hard as you can go for an entire game, and hit thirty points, so can I ask you to do just one simple thing for me."

"Sure Coach."

Coach Timmons fought back a temptation to smile, but with his game face on, he moved in until his face was just inches from Shane's and said, "Would you mind going back in the game and just score two points for me?"

"Sure Coach."

"It doesn't have to be fancy—just two points."

"No problem. Go in now?"

Coach Timmons replied, "Unless you'd rather wait until next week."

"No, Coach, now is good."

Shane leaped up and ran to the scoring table. He got in the game with two minutes to play. Thirty seconds later, he stole the ball from their point guard, no easy feat, and out ran everyone on the court, in a fit of exuberance jumped while spinning and completed a three hundred sixty degree spin like an ice skater, and slammed a hard dunk down. He hit the floor and literally growled as he shook his fist in the air like he was the Hulk or something.

The fans went wild, leaping to their feet, and cheering. Coach Timmons fell back into his seat laughing. He normally wasn't a big fan of showboating, but he knew Shane was making a statement. He scored twice more before the half. On the way to the locker room the coach spoke to him again.

"Jeez, Shane, just a little layup would have been fine."

Shane grinned, "That was my layup. I'll get you more in the second half."

Coach Timmons laughed, "I'm counting on it."

Shane led his team by scoring twenty-four points in the second half for an even thirty, and they beat Florida State by eighteen. Dick had gone crazy with Shane's big dunk, but just praised Shane up and down the court during the second half. It was a beautiful game, and after a slow start, Shane showed what he could really do.

Sue could hardly talk after the game. Bob said she yelled louder than the cheerleaders. They enjoyed the game immensely.

The next game would be the end of a long run of home games and the start of a long list of away games. Already the sportscasters said Taylor had the most difficult road schedule of any team in the nation, and a top schedule overall. Every year, Coach Timmons and his staff scheduled the best possible teams they could play to toughen up their squad with the exception of the goodwill games for a few local universities.

Shane did another midday interview for ESPN® prior to the late night start for the Wednesday game with Virginia. TJ gave him kudos, and together, they talked about him chilling at the beginning of the game, and to recall that you can only climb up the victory ladder one rung at a time.

Shane grinned and said, "The next time I get out of whack, just stand up and yell at me."

TJ laughed and replied, "I'd get killed by twenty thousand adoring fans. No thank you. You just do what I say, or you'll be sleeping with the dogs tonight!"

They both laughed, hugged tightly, kissed, and TJ watched him back out of the garage. To keep his mind off the next ACC game, TJ spent the rest of the afternoon writing. He made it a goal to finish the new gay fiction book, **The War Beyond – Part III** by the start of the first weekend of the National Tournament in March. After he edited twenty pages for the new book, he took a break and took the dogs on a long walk around the property, gave them a treat, and fixed himself a snack, and began working harder on the storyline for a future book he recently thought about. He didn't plan to write any of it until after he finished his current books, but sometimes ideas just flowed out of his brain ahead of schedule, forcing him to type swiftly on the new story.

Upon his arrival at the arena, he could feel the buzz in the air, as the place was filling up faster than usual, indicating both a sell out and the beginning of ACC league play. Nothing in basketball was more exciting than the twice a week duals by the teams in the ACC over the next eight weeks. TJ

A Writer's Fantasy

found the pressroom nearly packed, and for the first time this year, he had to stand in line to eat dinner. However, the food choices were better, too. Walter came through at a frantic pace waving and shaking hands with him, but moving on quickly as he handled numerous last minute requests for game updates, comments, and requests for interviews with the coach and players.

TJ knew there would be a press conference after the game, and the press could talk to some of the players, but not for any length of time, as the game would not be over until eleven and most of them, including Shane, had early morning classes the next day.

He watched Shane stretch and he smiled at him. Shane took his time no matter what was going on around him. When he started shooting practice, TJ knew he was feeling good, as he hit sixteen straight shots before missing one. He worked on foul shooting and missed only one of out of twenty. His jump shots were beautiful between the two to three-point zone. Near the end, he shocked even the coaches when he hit five straight jump shots from the three-point range.

The game started at a frenetic pace as they raced up and down the court, but nobody was scoring. Shane was finally fouled and hit the first two shots of the game from the foul line. That opened the flood gates as each team began scoring, but Virginia tried to slow the game down a little, so they could run a few set plays, but the Taylor defense pushed them, snatched at the ball, and sometimes they were caught for hitting a hand, but three times they managed to steal the ball. One such play allowed Jerry to throw it like a quarterback down the court and into Shane's big hands. He dunked it as hard as anyone had ever seen him do. TJ thought sure the backboard would break as Shane swung underneath to keep from falling hard on his back. It was a beautiful assist and play. Shane quickly pointed at Jerry indicating it was all due to him on that play.

The score at the half was Taylor up by one. Coach Timmons was not happy with some of the things he had seen, especially several mental breakdowns like stepping out of bound, stepping into the lane before the ball left the shooter's hands on a foul shot, and at one point, only four men on the court. The later was embarrassing for the coach and the player. But he didn't fuss in the locker room. He just told them they were going to win the game, and what they needed to do to accomplish the win.

The second half began as fast as the first, but soon TJ noted that Virginia became winded and gradually sloppy, and during the last seven minutes, Taylor ran hard on them. Final score put Taylor up by ten, but it had been a hard fought game all the way.

TJ headed home after the game and waited for a text message from Shane after he had eaten a late night dinner, and then they both fell asleep just ten miles apart.

319

# TWENTY-SEVEN

TJ flew up with the team and checked into the hotel Tuesday afternoon before the Wednesday game with Virginia Tech in Blacksburg. That night, Shane and the team had gone to the Cassell Coliseum to practice. They didn't think Tech was as good as Virginia, but they had been beaten here before, so they took the game serious. They would also miss their fan base, although at every game a thousand or more loyal Taylor fans showed up.

The game was in an older building, but as usual, the court measured the same, except there were noticeable squeaks in the floor during practice. However, they knew they wouldn't hear a thing during the game, as the place would be packed to the rafters, as the Hokies hoped this year's team would beat Taylor. It had been six years since Taylor lost in this building. The Virginia Tech team and student body were tired of losing to them.

While Shane practiced, TJ wrote a few pages in the new basketball book after reading the local papers, reading the media guide on the Hokies, and listening to Shane's thoughts about Virginia Tech. He then caught up on his email, and put a movie on the television. He knew Shane would not have free time after practice, mostly likely encouraged to go right to bed. The team would do a shoot around in the morning, attend classes in a banquet hall, and a team meeting would be held right after the game meal. Shane sent TJ a goodnight text message around eleven, and TJ fell asleep shortly thereafter. So did Shane two floors below him.

Though it was twenty degrees outside, it was pretty hot in the coliseum, but not nearly as hot as playing at Duke. The locker room was like a steam bath, as the exposed pipes from the boiler ran just over their heads. The managers had trouble with some of the tape refusing to stick and stay in place. Shane did well during warm-up, hitting his shot at all of his favorite spots. The game started with the Tech team hitting the first shot, but Taylor immediately went on a run and scored the next twelve. Their coach called a timeout just fifteen seconds before the scheduled television timeout.

Coach Timmons told the Taylor boys to keep the pressure up. Tech brought the ball in and began working a play that Shane studied in the team meeting. At the last possible second, he left his man as the ball was thrown across court. When the coach saw him, he almost yelled at him to get back to his position, but his worrisome face soon turn to a smile. He saw Shane intercept the ball and begin his giant stride half court run, and slammed a big dunk with no one around him.

TJ felt the sighs of disappointment all around him as he sat in the midst of the Hokie fans, so he could be in his usual spot directly across the court from the Taylor bench. He tried not to cheer, but he couldn't help but smile. The rest of the half, the Taylor team scored six for Tech's two points. The second half the Virginia team bounced back for a few minutes and then

Taylor ran all over them. Final score was ninety-six to fifty-four. By the end of the game, there were hardly any Hokie fans left in the building. Four hundred brave Taylor fans stood and cheered all the way to the end of the game. Now alone in the stand, TJ stood and cheered, too. Shane smiled and winked at him.

TJ had left his bags in the team bus as they were flying home that night. Everyone hustled out of the locker room, TJ grabbed his laptop from the pressroom, and thirty-five minutes after the end of the game they arrived at the airport.

TJ felt bad because he could sleep-in the following morning, well a little guilty, because Shane had to get up for class. Shane called him after his second class, and told him he was dog tired, but excited about the team's play last night. TJ told him to start getting pumped up about Clemson, because it would be much harder to beat them. Shane agreed and went to the weight room to work on his muscles before lunch.

Shane felt the practices this week were some of the best so far this season. The coach and his staff planned down to the minute, every single aspect of their teaching and execution of new options on offense and tougher defense. On Tuesday afternoon, they spent some time in a team meeting prior to practice going over the scouting reports, assignments, and finally, what the coach called the Taylor battle plan. As they hit the court for practice, the second team did their best to perform as if they were Clemson. Shane called TJ after practice to tell him he thought they finally ready for pesky, but determined Tigers.

TJ was already in route to the arena and got on the bus just minutes before Shane and rest of the team. They flew in and arrived after dark at their hotel, threw their stuff in the room, and set about working on homework. The following morning they did a shoot around, team meeting, class time, and more homework to help the day pass a little faster. Team meal was at three.

TJ woke up early on Wednesday morning, rented a car, and drove to Greenville to see his parents. They were only forty-five minutes away from his hotel. He ate lunch and had a great time talking about how things were going. He tried to get them to commit coming to see the new house, but his dad and mom took turns with health problems, and with dad's three times a week trips to the dialysis center, it just seem to limit how active they could be for traveling. TJ made a note to check out the treatment centers in Lindle.

TJ ate pretty well in the pressroom, but he was really looking forward to the homemade-style ice cream that was a trademark of the trip to Clemson. All the reporters talked about it. TJ watched Shane warm-up and shoot, and thought he looked good. By game time, there were only a thousand Taylor fans and about sixteen thousand Clemson fans in the arena, all dressed in bright orange colors. He never wore team colors because as usual, his seat was in the middle of the opposition.

Clemson loved to beat any school that came to their campus, but not nearly as much as they liked to beat Taylor. Thankfully, it only happen two out of six games at their house, and over a decade at the Taylor arena.

They snagged the tip, but as Shane sprinted to set up his defense and wait for his player, a Clemson player tripped him, and he fell hard on his stomach, but his training paid off as he lifted his head, turned his chin, and raised his feet so he would slide to a stop on his uniform. It did knock the breath out of him, but he never let his eyes lose the ball. He took a quick breath, got back to his feet, and ran hard down the court.

Clemson set up their offense, but Shane and the man he was guarding just kept pounding and bouncing off of each other until finally a guard shot for a three and made it. Shane brought the ball in and Clemson started with a full court press. Taylor practiced against their style of press with the second team, so Shane waited until either Jerry was free or Larry dropped back to catch the ball. Shane made a hard throw to Larry.

Shane jogged up court as Larry flipped the ball to Jerry. Shane set a quick screen for Jerry who blew by him like a tornado, cut around two defensive men, and laid it up among the trees as the coach call the big men.

Back and forth the teams traded the lead, but Clemson made a number of fouls in an effort to contain the Taylor run, and to throw them off their game. It had worked to a certain level because at the half Taylor was only ahead by four.

Before the coach spoke to the team in the locker room, Shane sat by himself and thought about the way he played and what he could do differently to help the defense, and score on the offense. He expected Clemson to continue double-teaming him, so Taylor would follow the usual response by tossing it to Shane, and then he could fling it out quickly to the open man. However, Shane worked hard improving his outside shot, so every now and then he would he would pull up and shoot, or step away from the goal and then turn and shoot for two points. He wanted to force Clemson to keep two men on him.

Jerry flung the ball to him with a fast bounce pass. A Clemson guard tried to snag it, but missed, leaving only one man on Shane. He snatched it and leaned inward as he went up forcing their big man to try and block the shot. The man took a swing, but Shane deftly moved the ball around and away from him. He took the man's palm in his face and still made the shot. When the whistle blew the foul, the Clemson fans booed the referee. TJ knew they weren't really mad at the obvious foul call, but rather frustrated their team could not seem to be able to get ahead of Taylor and stay there.

Three times in the second half Clemson tied the game and appeared on a roll, but Taylor would create numerous defensive stops while scoring on offense. They won the game ninety-six to eight-nine, but to a Clemson fan, it might as well have been a hundred to one.

TJ sprinted to retrieve his laptop in the pressroom and head to the team bus, as they were flying home right after the game. Shane again had morning classes. TJ thought he could sleep in, but woke up at his usual time and could not go back to sleep. After breakfast, he went right to work writing about last night's game in the new basketball book. Road trips to certain schools had become routine, but no one could ever assume Taylor would win automatically. This year, every ACC team focused on beating the National Champions, and Taylor would have to be on guard for the upset opportunity their opponents were trying to create.

The Saturday night game at home against Georgia Tech was a late one at nine, and ESPN® made it a marquee game for the network. Dick Vitale flew in and came by to eat lunch with TJ and Shane. He was surprised at how well the boys cooked and shared duties in the kitchen. TJ handled the hot stuff and Shane the cold salads and fruit slices. They treated him to a variety plate of good quality barbeque, baked beans, and grilled potato wedges. TJ made his famous banana pudding, and Dick ate until finally he pushed back from the table and said no more.

"It was awesome," he said, "but I cannot eat another bite. "Tell me about this Endless Pool® you put in."

Shane and TJ quickly put away the dishes. Shane said, "Come on, I'll show you."

They led him down the hall, with the dogs not far behind with tails wagging, and into the wet area. Dick had seen the room before, but it still amazed him. "This is one of the most beautiful practice gyms I have ever seen, and has all the workout tools and fitness machines you could need. I like the idea of your own sauna, steam, and Jacuzzi. You're definitely taking good care of your bodies. I don't see how you eat like that and not gain a pound. I know Shane burns it off in practice and game time, but how do you keep it off?"

He was talking to TJ so he replied, "Just like my accountant come tax time...I just write it off!"

They all laughed at his pitiful joke, "I just workout the best I can and if I eat a big lunch, then I try to lighten up in the other meals. Shane and I don't eat a lot of sugar snacks. He keeps the refrigerator stocked with fresh cut fruits and vegetables, and if they are already prepared, why not eat them?"

Shane went to his room to change into a swimsuit. TJ and Dick walked over to the new endless pool. "I know you've seen the commercials or clicked on their video online, but the principal is pretty simple. There is a jet water thruster sort of like on the back of a personal water craft, but not that powerful, and it shoots a stream of water across the pool. Shane swims into the rush of water like he was trying to swim upstream. This forces him to work his arms and legs hard to keep from falling back.

"He adjusts the power of the stream from easy to mild, and on to hard as he warms up, and back down again to cool down."

Shane came jogging up, grabbed his goggles off the table, and slid over the edge into the water. "Are you ready?"

Dick started backing up, "I don't look good wet, and you know I like to look good." They all laughed.

"You'll be fine. I just have to hit this waterproof switch and the jet fires up. Then I go to work swimming. I'll start at an easy level."

Shane hit the button and though the jet was pretty quiet they could easily see the stream of water. Shane started swimming and kept a steady pace for about five minutes before hitting the button for the next speed upward. He picked up his pace.

Dick said, "My goodness that is cool."

TJ smiled. "You can also do water aerobics in the pool. Your wife would love that, as it is easier on your joints. You just simulate running or stretching, and the resistance of the water tones you up in a hurry."

Shane hit the button again and was now swimming at a pretty good clip. Dick watched for a while and just shook his head. "How much did this set you back?"

After Shane cooled down, he climbed out of the pool to dry off. TJ replied, "It didn't cost us anything. We told them to bill you!"

They all laughed. Dick asked again, "Okay smart guy. Twenty thousand?"

"More like fifteen because we had to get the longest one they had for my height and arm reach," answered Shane. "I just love it. I normally go a lot longer, but not before a game. After a game is nice, too, as it really stretches my muscles out. Combining it with my strength workouts has helped me increase my stamina, while making a huge difference in my cardiovascular strength. If you watch me closely tonight, you'll rarely catch me breathing hard. My recovery is a lot faster."

"I'm impressed. Very impressed. I think I want one these babies—if my wife will let me. I might have to bring her over to see it."

"Please do. We'd love to meet her," replied TJ.


For the past couple of seasons, Georgia Tech has been rebuilding the basketball program, and they came to town ready to win. They pushed and ran hard during the first half, staying right with Taylor on their home court. At half time, Taylor only led by five.

Walter caught TJ for a few minutes at the break to tell him he loved the new coverage and stories in the new book. He was looking forward to reading more. TJ thanked him, and told him he would send new chapters soon.

Shane started the second half with a determined spirit. On Taylor's first possession, he leaned and pushed, and scored a close basket, while forcing his man to foul him. The next play they threw it inside to him again, and he faked going up and threw the ball hard to Larry in the corner, who downed a pretty three-point play.

Almost every other possession Shane scored. They won by eighteen and Shane had thirty points. He was thrilled with his performance in this game and so was the coach. In fact, he gave good marks to the entire team for their tenacious defensive play, and of course, he still made a list of ten things they wanted to address in tomorrow's practice.

The team took a bus over to Wake Forest for the Saturday game arriving Friday in the late afternoon, and doing a nighttime shoot around in the arena. The game was an early one-thirty game, making mealtime a breakfast affair. Shane ate steak and eggs, with fruit, made notes in the team meeting, and then rested until time to dress out.

TJ did some Saturday morning writing before riding the team bus to the arena. He ate lunch in the pressroom, and read the media notes as prepared by Wake Forest.

A big guy led this year's Wake Forest squad, and three shooting guards, one of which was very deadly from way behind the three-point line. While the score remained close, it appeared Wake could shoot from the floor and Taylor couldn't. Shane put in twelve points in the first half, but they would have to slow down Wake Forest in the second half, if they were going to win this away game.

Second half remained tight, but coach Timmons kept yelling at his boys to run, and by the last four minutes TJ could see the bounce in the Wake team disappear. Shane noted it, too, and he poured it on. He scored twelve more points to finish the game with twenty-eight, and Taylor won by six.

The team flew out at eleven thirty after morning classes. TJ left earlier that morning on the Learjet, so he could work on the long flight. So far, when he traveled with the team, he had only been able to get a few notes written down because there wasn't enough room for laptop work. Susie prepared breakfast for him on the early morning flight, and though he had been able to concentrate and write well, he was glad to step off the plane in Tucson. It was warm, for sure, at seventy-six degrees in Arizona, and he savored the warmth on his face as he peeled out of the warm jacket he needed driving from home to the airport. As he took the car service to the Sheraton hotel, he just marveled at the green grass in the fairways of the numerous golf courses, and he felt a bit astounded at how large the city of Tucson appeared to be. Before arriving, he suspected it be just a small dusty town at the bottom of the state, and a stone's throw from Mexico. Oh sure, there were thousands of Mexicans everywhere in the city, but Spanish was spoken as easily as English.

He put away his stuff in the room, and without a jacket or even a sweater, he took the elevator down at the back of the hotel, and made his way onto the warm streets. He knew from his GPS software the way to go, and he gladly walked three blocks to a grocery store to buy a newspaper, fruit, and Mountain Dew®.

But just before he got there, he crossed a wide street in the downtown district, and a sign caught his eye. It was an Apple® Computer Store. He looked at his watch, and knew that Shane's plane would not land for another hour, so he took a diversion from his planned route and walked a long block to the store. He loved his MacBook Pro® as much as he had learned to love the iMac®, and thought he might just stop in to discover something knew.

He browsed the store and saw the new Leopard Server® and Promise VTrak Raid® storage system. He laughed because eight months ago he knew what a network server was, but not like the awesome one that Buddy Bell installed in their office for all their computers to run on. Buddy told him it was blazing fast, and from TJ's old Novell® days and early NT network software, he found Buddy's quick instructions easy to follow. He especially enjoyed its desktop interface that was similar to the Leopard operating system on all their Macs®.

He had to explain to Shane what a RAID storage system was and mirror drives. Buddy's installed system assured them every thing that was stored on their individual hard drives was also backed up on the RAID system on more than one drive. This was called mirroring and it left nothing to chance. Even the failure of one of its many hard drives was not a problem. Buddy showed him how he could remove a hard drive on the fly, put it back in, and the system would rewrite itself, and soon become totally synched again. It was turbo fast and remarkably efficient. It was even mother earth friendly using far less electricity than some light bulbs.

TJ smiled at the displays, looked through some of the hardware, and failed to notice a handsome male clerk who walked up behind him.

"May I help you find something?"

TJ turned around to see a guy probably four years older than Shane with perhaps the cleanest face he had ever seen. Without a dab of makeup, he face was smooth, flawless, with soft light pink lips, brown eyebrows, chocolate eyes, and soft thin brown hair that the shake of a towel might send it floating to the other side of his head. He had perfect teeth, most likely the result of three years of orthodontics, and a warm wet tongue, or so TJ assumed. He instantly liked the look of him, but he was happily in love with Shane. He remembered the phrase, even though you're on a diet, doesn't mean you can't look at the menu.

TJ replied jokingly, "I was looking for a creamery."

326

The beautiful face changed slightly to a puzzled stare, "Is that a type of software?"

TJ laughed, "No, it is an upscale ice cream shop where they make your favorite banana split, or sundae on a frozen marble slab, mixing it just as you like it, and one spoon will make your cheeks puff out like you just gained a half pound. It is gloriously delicious."

The man laughed, "You're weird, in a nice kind of a way, and you're making me hungry."

TJ blushed a bit realizing he had gone a bit overboard, and said as he stuck his hand out, "My name is TJ. I'm a customer. I try hard not to be customer, but I'm addicted, to Apple®, and I just can't help myself. I admit I often fondle my little white Apple® mouse, and I just can't stop rolling my hot palms over it, while tickling it with my delicate soft fingers."

The man laughed and replied, "I'm John and I'm pleased to meet you. Most of my customers border on the on the boring side, but not you, you're different, pleasantly so. I meant was there a software package you were looking for."

"Boy, if you change those words around a little, it could be a whole lot more interesting, as in a soft package you wear."

John laughed again, "I see, you're gay. Why didn't you say so?"

TJ replied quickly, "I tend to like to prevent personal bleeding from my face and nose after some redneck beats the socks out of me. I've tried hurting people with my face, but after a few punches, their knuckles seem to win out. But to answer your question, no, I wasn't really looking for anything special, just wondering what was new, and if I might be interested in it."

John's iPhone® suddenly rang, "Excuse me, I'll just check it. Sometimes it is the manager." TJ marveled as he quickly shuffled through screens, sent the call to voicemail, and skidded quickly to his text messages."

"Hey, that is cool. I've heard about them, but never actually played with one."

John looked at him kind of funny and smiled, "You're not talking about sex again are you?"

TJ laughed, "No, you big dummy. Tell me about the phone. You're a salesman for god's sake!"

John laughed. "Come on, let's go sit down."

He led TJ back to a comfy couch where he encouraged TJ to sit down beside him. He showed him how the phone worked, flipped back and forth with his finger from messages, to making calls, to zipping across the Internet. TJ became flabbergasted to say the least, but he loved the way John was selling without actually making you feel like he was selling. He especially enjoyed the way John occasionally touched his leg as he said you have to watch this, and so on. When they laughed, John leaned in to him and he smelled good to. He wasn't sure how he knew, but he felt instantly he had met a new friend, a very good friend. He knew Shane would like him, too.

TJ was not normally prone to instant decisions, and he was certainly able to stand his ground against pushy salesman, but John remained far from a typical salesman. TJ was convinced he and Shane needed a pair of iPhones®. The store wasn't busy at this time of the morning, so John took his time and explained every detail of the fancy piece of equipment.

John asked TJ where he was from and surprisingly, he had never heard of Lindle, North Carolina. When TJ told him his boyfriend went to Taylor University John lit up. "You know I love watching college basketball, although I liked it better when they used to play in those short-shorts and not those long things they wear nowadays, but anyhow, I love to watch Taylor basketball, and especially Shane Bradley. He is absolutely gorgeous."

John went on and on about how beautiful Shane was, making TJ feel so wonderful. Suddenly, he missed Shane so much. John made him feel like he was the luckiest guy in the world. He wished he could have told his new friend that his boyfriend was in fact Shane, but the secret had to remain so, and he just smiled and agreed with him.

TJ suddenly stopped him, "I want to buy two of those iPhones®."

John's face went white, "Two?"

"Yeah, one for me, and one for my boyfriend."

"Oh my gosh, I've never sold two at once before. This is really cool. Come on, let's go to my desk, and I'll get you set up."

Using an iMac® John handled the credit card transaction easily, but when he asked for his boyfriend's name, TJ told him to both phones in his name. John gave him a puzzled glance, but processed the order anyhow. It took them a moment to verify connection to their home service, and TJ spoke to the service operator, verifying he wanted to expand their bandwidth for the new iPhone® 3G services. They would continue to have unlimited long distance calling anytime of the day, and the other regular phone features.

After TJ signed all the forms, John said, "That's it. Your phones will be ready in about a half an hour. They have to be programmed and tested before they leave the store. It's part of our quality assurance program."

"Okay, it's lunch time. Are you free for lunch?"

"No, I'm expensive," teased John. "Okay, I know, bad joke." He looked at his watch. "Well, you know, I think I can. Let me just tell my manager."

John left with the orders in his hand, gave them to the tech team so the phones would be ready, walked across the store and spoke to his manager, and returned, "Okay, where shall we go?"

"I'm from North Carolina. How about a nice quiet place where we can get a sandwich, burger, or chef salad."

"I know the place. Let's go."

They went farther down the block, made a right, then a left, and entered a small café. Inside there was a lounge area with small tables, stools, and laptops were everywhere. He also noted a sign that read, "We're Wi-Fi and gay friendly. Help Yourself." TJ grinned.

The host led them to a booth in the back, and handed each man a menu while explaining the specials. After he left, TJ said, "I take it this is a gay café."

"Very gay, but the food is good, and from time to time I see a friend or two, but not this early. Most of the guys in here are probably students."

They made their order and began talking again. TJ told him the truth, as least as far as he was a gay writer, though John had not read any of his books. TJ sensed he didn't believe him, and that wouldn't be the first time. He steered the conversation towards John. He graduated from Arizona State two years ago with a degree in communications, but had yet to find a job he really wanted to do. On a lark, he answered a help wanted ad for the Apple® job and had been with them ever since. He was now an assistant manager and their best salesman.

He had a serious relationship when he first got out of school, but not since then. He did go out to the clubs from time to time, but decided the club scene was not for him. TJ concurred. John joined a gay tennis league and loved it. They met on Sunday afternoons and played both singles and doubles. There were over a hundred men in the league, but usually about sixty played each week. From his tennis friends, he received various invitations to functions and dinners, and met many very successful gay businessmen, doctors, and professors. He had a good group of close friends and except for finding the right career job for him, he was happy. TJ told him that was exactly what his gay nephew did in New York, as he played in a tennis league, too.

John checked his watch as they left the café. "Come on, we have to hurry. I don't want to be late."

He led TJ in the wrong direction when they stepped out of the café, crossed two streets, and turned left and ran right into a Barnes and Noble® store. TJ laughed, as he knew then that John didn't believe him.

"I want to see your books," he said. TJ translated that comment, as I want to see if you're telling the truth, but kept it to himself. John knew where the gay fiction section was and went right to it.

"Last name is Johnson, as in TJ Johnson," stated TJ, as he helped him down the rows until they found the authors beginning with the last name of J.

Suddenly, John's eyes lit up when he saw about forty of TJ's books, and began pulling one from the shelf. He flipped to the back and saw the picture and held it up. "You're him."

TJ replied, "I have been all my life."

John quickly read the back of the book cover to find more about the story and the author.

329

TJ picked up **The War Apart - Part I** and said, "It all began with this one. He began pulling samples of each book in the order he wrote them, "followed by two modern day stories, then part two, another story, and **The Blackfeet Boys** came out right after Thanksgiving. **The War Beyond – Part III** is coming out in late April or early May. Are you convinced now?"

John blushed, "Yes, I'm sorry. As a young gay man you can probably imagine how many pick up lines I've heard, and you just don't look like an author."

"Oh, what do I look like?"

"Tall, dark, and handsome."

"I'll take that as a compliment."

"Which one should I read first?"

"Start with my first one, and if you like it you can decide to jump to the sequel, or intersperse the modern with the historical fiction books. I hope you like them."

John took TJ's first book and they made their way to the counter. On the way, TJ spotted Shane's big cutout advertising their first basketball book. "John, look at this."

John turned around and saw TJ pointing at the big cutout. TJ leaned over and picked up one of the basketball books, and showed him the author's name. John laughed, "I take it you know Shane very well."

"He's the smartest, most amazing basketball player I have ever met."

John replied, "Okay, I'm impressed. I'll take that one, too."

The clerk was handling John's credit card and suddenly looked at TJ oddly. He flipped over the book and saw TJ's picture and smiled. "Oh my. You're him."

John and TJ laughed. TJ replied, "Here we go again."

The clerk turned around and pointed at a poster on the wall for the release of part therein the spring, and said, "I read the first war book, now I'm reading part two, and can't wait to read the third."

"It'll be out in May. I am glad you like them."

TJ and John smiled again. They rushed from the bookstore up the street, and finally into the Apple® store. TJ picked up his phones and received some extra coaching from John. They didn't trade phone numbers, but they did give each other their email. TJ told him to stay in touch and let him know how his career was going. He never imagined he would be hiring John Bunting to work for him four months from now.

Shane obtained some free time later that night and made his way to TJ's room in secret as usual. TJ surprised him with the gift of the iPhone®, and told him about John. They played with the phones for quite a while and finally Shane had to go due to his curfew. He left the phone with TJ to take home, and later, he would bring it with him to school saying he ordered it.

The game was at one the next day and it was another beautiful Saturday in Tucson. CBS Sports® carried the game and the pressroom was busy as the National Champions were in town. The McKale Center was packed to the high windows, and the desert boys were ready to try and whip Taylor University.

The first eight minutes of the game saw the locals performing well and the boys from the east playing sloppy. They just didn't seem to have their rhythm. When they came out of the huddle after a television timeout, TJ gave Shane his chill sign, followed by the infamous two sign for imagining the other team naked. Shane grinned. TJ hoped it would calm him down.

Jerry flung Shane a hard pass into the paint just as Shane got there after a good screen by Larry. Shane went up quickly and shot a simple six-foot jump shot and scored. Next time down the court they did it again. When the defense came out to double-team him, Jerry faked it to him, and caught Larry open for a three-point swish. Next possession, he threw it to Shane and when the double-team came up he flipped it back to Jerry for a long three-point swish.

In the second half, the Taylor boys began a run with twelve minutes to go, and put sixteen points on the board to two for Tucson. It was a slaughter, and the second team put the score to a hundred and six to sixty-four.

TJ flew home in the Learjet right after the game, and was in bed by eleven. Shane had planned to spend the night in the dorm, but they made good time on their flight home. He arrived at their home just a little after eleven, came down the hall and into their bedroom. He went into the walk-in closet, stripped, stepped into the bathroom for a much needed pee, brushed his teeth, and then came back into the room and slipped into bed with TJ.

TJ immediately cuddled up to him, and they kissed passionately, before falling asleep. It had been a long weekend, but they had Sunday off, and they were looking forward to it. They spent most of the following morning learning how to use their new iPhones®.

Thankfully, they had a home game with Miami on Wednesday, giving them a few days to recover from the trip to Arizona. Since joining the ACC league a few years ago, Miami had become tough opponent, and though they had yet to win in Lindle, they were very determined to do so this year. They had a tall center, and a strong forward who would be guarding Shane in a man-to-man defense. They also had a big freshman forward that would rotate with Shane's man to keep both of them fresh for the entire game. Their coach knew that to win, they had to keep Shane from scoring twenty or more points.

Both men bumped against him the entire first half and each man fouled him twice. Shane made both the shots, but he wasn't wearing them down physically. They held him to ten points the first half, and Taylor was up by just four.

Coach Timmons made some adjustments during half in the locker room, and they went immediately to a full court press, and ran their play much harder and faster. Taylor got a run going with six minutes to go, and put themselves up by fourteen. Miami fought back to cut it to six, but Shane hit a pretty jumper with a minute to go, sealing the game with an eight-point lead.

On Saturday, they took a bus over to Raleigh to play NC State and arrived two hours prior to the game. While Shane and the team changed into their uniforms in the locker room, TJ went to the pressroom, which was pretty good hike in the massive RBC Center Arena. TJ hadn't been back to the place since last year's game, and before that to Greg's graduation from NC State, and before that he had seen James Taylor perform on New Year's Eve in 2000. Greg was Gary's twin brother.

The staff handed out excellent media notes to reporters arriving for the game. He set up his laptop and read through the notes highlighting with his yellow marker the quotes and facts he planned to use. The media director for NC State paid him a visit saying he had recently finished reading his basketball book, and wondered if he would consider doing the same for NC State. TJ felt flattered and said he would think about it, but for now he was swamped working on the sequel.

After the sports director left, TJ thought about writing for another team and immediately dismissed it, as traveling with another team, and visiting often to get those behind the scenes story, was not something that interested him. It would require giving up lots of quality time with Shane, and that was not something he wanted to compromise on, but he felt flattered to have been asked. He made a note to write the sports director next week, and sending his regrets he could not accept the invitation.

Shane came out of the locker room early, wanting to spend a lot of time shooting from his favorite spots on the court. The vast and broad arena made a difference to his field of view, and he wanted time to work on it. He stretched carefully and methodically before beginning to shoot close in, working his way backwards from the goal until he began downing sixteen-foot jump shots with ease. He also worked on his foul shots hitting fourteen out of fifteen. By the time the rest of the team came out for their warm-up drills, Shane was ready to play.

The game began with a very uncharacteristic shot by Shane. The possession clock was winding down on Jerry, but the defense successfully covered each of their men. With four seconds to go, Shane suddenly ran from under the goal using Larry's defensive man as a screen to shield his own man away for just a second. Jerry fed him the ball at the top of the key. Shane never hesitated, but snatched the ball, turned, and jumped. It was a high arching shot and TJ could feel the entire arena suck in a breath, as they waited to see if the ball would go in.

Swish! It never touched the rim, and Shane grinned slightly as he ran to guard the man bringing the ball in for State. Taylor now led by two in a game where every point was going to count.

Twelve minutes later, the score was thirty-eight to thirty-six, and Coach Timmons tried not to worry. They had a long time to play and more they could do. At the final television timeout for the first half, he told the team to get tougher on defense and get him some stops. Shane glanced up at TJ as he came out of the huddle. TJ gave him three fingers for time to go. Shane winked at him, but of course, every girl within fifty yards thought he was flirting with her.

On the inbound play, Shane leaped hard and got a finger on the ball, deflecting the pass. He hit the floor in a roll and came right back on his feet. Meanwhile, Jerry left his man and snatched up the ball, and threw a hard bounce pass as Shane broke into a run for the basket. He caught it and went up with State's big man hanging on to him. Shane somehow managed to keep his concentration, put the ball in for a score, and obtain a foul called on his man, and another foul shot point for Shane. Taylor led by six at the half.

Throughout the second half, Taylor never led by more than the six points. Anything could happen, and one of the worst things to happen was at the four-minute mark when Jerry picked up his fourth team foul. TJ thought Jerry's rhythm and timing seem to be off the entire game. He would later learn that Jerry had a stomach virus, and spent a lot of time in the toilet before the game and at the half.

Coach Timmons put a sub in to give Jerry a moment to rest, but the boy never stopped running when he came off the court. The doctor ran behind him as Jerry ran to the locker room. Shane helped Tim bring the ball up court, and it forced Shane to play at the top of the key to keep the ball moving. State had finally gotten within two points and with two minutes to play, Shane was trying to stay focused.

Tim threw the ball in the corner, but Larry couldn't get a shot off, and was close to losing possession on a five second rule. Shane hollered at him, and Tim took a chance and threw it high in Shane's direction. Shane leaped and caught the ball over a State player's head, came down, and right back up with one second to go, took a shot, and obtained another swish and a foul. He made the shot and Taylor led by five, with forty seconds to go.

Coach Timmons called a timeout, and as the Taylor team ran to their bench, Jerry sprinted out of the locker room. "I'm good coach," he said.

"Excellent. Check in," replied the coach with a grin. He called for a defensive stop and controlled ball handling.

State brought the ball in under a strong full court press, but they managed to get the ball into their court. They were trying to score quickly and planned to foul as soon as the ball was brought in. Shane was tight on his man, when suddenly, he saw Jerry driving their man into the corner near the scoring table. Shane took a chance and ran hard up behind the dribbler, and in a flash, he and Jerry had the guard in a trap. The boy twisted left and right trying to find a man to throw the ball to. The clock was ticking down and the referee's hand swung back and forth as he continued counting down the five seconds the boy had to get the ball back in play or lose it. Desperate, he leaped and tried to throw it.

Shane snatched the ball out of his hands like catching a flying bug. He spun around, and in two steps he was already twenty feet ahead of any State player. He continued his rapid run and left the court for the air at the foul line and dunked it hard through the net. Taylor now led by seven with only twenty seconds to play.

Coach Timmons called for yellow defense that meant stay on your man, don't allow an easy shot, but don't foul under any circumstances. The clock ticked down as their guard weaved and bobbed, and finally shot with ten seconds to go. Swish! Taylor now led by only five, but there was only seven seconds left.

Shane grabbed the ball while yelling blue to his teammates. This set up Jerry for an inbound pass expecting to be fouled immediately, but setting up a back door pass to the far court. Tim and Larry spread wide at half court. Shane could not get the ball to Jerry safely, so he yelled blue green that set the play in motion. Without hesitation, he threw the ball high over the man guarding him and aiming for a spot about the foul line in their court. Tim and Larry ran hard crossing each other's path to make the State players guarding have to cross each other. Larry caught the ball as it came down, flipped it over his head to Tim, who was in the midst of a hard run for the basket. He caught the ball and went up for a dunk. Taylor led by seven.

Shane grinned as he ran down to defend in the inbound pass. State got the ball in and made a quick turn to shoot missing the entire backboard and goal. Taylor had won by seven in a very hard fought game.

# TWENTY-EIGHT

TJ changed his writing pattern since meeting Shane and becoming boyfriends. He used to have three books in various stages of production at all times, but with his dual publishing deals, all of his finished books were on the shelves in bookstores across the country. He continued working on the new basketball book, keeping it current at all times, so just like last year, as soon as the final buzzer blew on their last game, he could update the details and send those final pages to the publisher so the presses could roll. He hoped that would be the national championship winning game.

For many years, he wrote an entire rough draft before editing a single phrase, but with time quickly running out, he spent his mornings writing new material and the afternoons editing the book from the beginning. He liked to go through his fiction books many times, creating multiple final drafts. He would then send it to a friend to make a final edit, but his new contract allowed him to send sections of the book to his gay publishers for one of their editors to work on. This sped things up considerably, but he still had a lot of work to do.

If he had time on the road to think for a while, but not time to write new material or edit his writings, he wrote more storylines for his next book. If creatively he felt too tired to write, he continued his extensive research for future stories. He kept journals for all of his books and constantly updated storylines, so that no matter where he was at the moment, in a hotel, the Learjet, or if lucky at home, he could quickly return to the story exactly where he left it.

He wrote his first book without a storyline because it was all in his head from beginning to end. However, every story since then he has used a storyline. Some were more detailed than others, but generally, he wrote about fifty words of either chapters or sequences. He referred back to these storylines during the writing, but by the time he finished, most everything in the storyline was in the book, though embellished, detailed, flushed out, and developed. To TJ, the chore of writing was never as hard as building a house, or plowing a field, but mentally it drained him, while at the same time, it boosted his spirit, and he always enjoyed the journey of the story.

He ran the title by Shane, Walter, Dick, Jake, and finally Janet's team, and they all gave it thumbs up, so the basketball sequel became officially titled **Twice Is Nice**. He delivered seventy percent of the book to the publisher, but the next chapter was one of the most important. Wednesday night at nine, Taylor was playing the tough Duke squad, on an equally tough home court at nine on worldwide television. The game would be shown on the Armed Forces television network, and picked up in the Middle East, Greenland, Australia, and aboard hundreds of ships around the globe.

Previous Duke and Taylor games had been aired to both the space shuttle and the international space station.

To avoid the hassle of a lot of auto traffic, TJ road with the team on the bus, and thanked Walter once again for his travel pass. Though in the middle of winter and a night game at nine, Cameron Indoor Stadium was always hot, and tonight's visit would be no different. TJ wore a light jacket to shield him from the cold on the way to the game, but he left it on the bus, while carrying only his laptop to the pressroom.

He ate the buffet and was shocked to see so many reporters in attendance. Two years ago, the Duke athletic office began limiting the number of reporters and cameramen, so TJ felt fortunate to have a press pass from Walter. He read through the media press releases, made some notes, and went down to find his seat and watch Shane warm-up. Unlike most games, every seat was taken almost an hour before the game. Shane's parents flew in for the big game having obtained tickets through Walter. He felt the parents of a senior player made a great storyline for the broadcast booth, and thus more publicity for the Taylor team.

Forty minutes later, the game began with both squads running a full court press, an extremely tight defense, and a determination to beat the other as severely as possible. Each team experienced good years and bad years, but not on the night they played each other. The phrase 'all bets are off' applied to the players and even the coaches, but not to the sports world, as it was always a big game to bet on all across the country, or the world.

Dick spoke to him in the pressroom. TJ could see the adrenalin already pumping through Dick's veins, as he talked about the excitement leading up to the big match.

A foul marred the tipoff, as a Duke player pushed a Taylor player to try and snatch the ball. It became an omen for the timbre of the game. In the first half alone, fifteen fouls were called, but not one in the favor of Shane, in spite of the obvious scratches, blue marks, and even traces of blood all over his exposed body. Shane argued the first few obvious fouls, but quit arguing with the referees about the lack of calls, preferring to stay focused on defending and scoring. However, Coach Timmons came close to being called for a technical, as he berated every referee within twenty feet of him. He could not believe they were ignoring every foul received by Shane. Dick commented that it appeared that if you're the Player-Of-The-Year, you deserve to get beat up. Coach Timmons began to suspect the referees had been bought, but he forced the thought from his mind because he, too, needed all his energy to call the right strategy for the perfect game.

At the fourth television timeout, and three minutes and forty seconds to play in the first half, Shane acquired only eight points, and Taylor led by two. Coach Timmons told the team not to worry about the lack of called fouls, but he wanted a stop for the rest of the first half on defense, and quality shots on offense. Duke double-teamed Shane when he had the ball, so they ran their offense on the premise they would continue to do so. They would throw the ball to Shane, and if he had a shot he would take it, and if not, he would fling it out to the open man for a shot. It was a simple plan that they used almost every game, because all the teams double-teamed Shane. Coach Timmons also emphasized the need for more offensive rebounds. Shane knew he could do so, but he would have to elbow and push his way into position.

After the timeout, Taylor brought the ball into play. Jerry was on top of his game as he ran his defender all over the place. Shane ran to the top of the key just in time to set up a screen sending the Duke defender into a wall of hard flesh. It gave Jerry a half step lead on his man, and he brought the ball up to shoot. Shane spun down the center of the land, and spread his feet and elbows wide to try and keep position. He jumped just as the ball came over his head. He was ready to leap for the rebound, but Jerry made a swish shot. Taylor was up by four.

They pushed for a strong defensive stop, but Duke's guard came right down the court as if there was no one there, and shot a beautiful three-point shot from so far back that he was almost sitting on the scoring table. The Duke fans went crazy, and they were within one of tying Taylor. Two minutes remained in the first half. Shane brought the ball into Jerry and moved quickly to mid court to set up a screen. After Jerry passed, Shane broke in a hard run for the paint. Jerry flipped him the ball. Duke thought he was going for a dunk and rushed him, but Shane pulled up and shot a pretty soft touch, two-point shot. Swish! They were back up by three with a minute and twenty seconds to go in the half, and they were playing like it was the end of the game.

Duke once again came down the court and their hot guard shot another bomb from way back, and tied the game with forty seconds to play in the half. Coach Timmons was livid that Jerry was not stopping his man. He yelled at him from the sidelines as Jerry hustled the ball down. The coach called for one shot so Jerry began working the ball back and forth, eating the clock up. At one point, he had to pull the ball up close to the sidelines, and Shane realized a trap was about to happen. He broke out in a quick run and Jerry threw it to him. Shane flipped it right back as Jerry sprung past.

Shane broke wide and then across the center with his man inches from him. Shane ran him into the back of another Duke player. Jerry flipped Shane the ball in a hard bullet pass, taking no chances for a steal. Shane caught it like it was pure gold, cut left and leaped. A Duke man pushed him to the right to prevent the dunk. A whistle finally blew, but Shane shifted from a two-hand dunk to a right hand single toss. The ball swished as Shane fell hard to the floor.

TJ heard the collective disappointed sighs from the Duke fans. Shane slowly got to his feet, but walked to the foul line as if nothing spectacular had just happen. Dick practically shouted in his microphone with flowing adjectives on the big man's soft touch and dexterity. Taylor led by three, ten seconds to play, and Shane on the line.

Everyone thought Shane hitting a foul shot was an automatic, but nothing appeared as it seemed in the Taylor and Duke games. Maybe it was nerves, others would speculate Shane did it on purpose, but no matter what the reason, instead of an automatic swish shot from Shane; the ball hit the backboard a bit hard, and kissed the rim just as Shane broke down the center of the lane. He caught his own rebound and slammed it down hard over two Duke players. In the course of a few seconds they went from a tied game to a five-point lead.

Duke tried to score in the final seconds of the half, but their shot went wide. The coach from Duke yelled objections at the officials as his assistants dragged him off the floor. Coach Timmons did his best to hold back a grin until he entered the locker room.

As good as Shane played, as he sat by his locker, he counted ten ways he could do better. Coach Timmons made some adjustments to their battle plan, put in several plays, and urged his team to play the kind of defense they had worked so hard on.

The second half began as the first with fierce tight basketball, and the score remained within four or less apart until the final sixty seconds when Duke's big man was caught holding on to Shane's jersey as he attempted to score. That made five fouls for their big man, and he was out of the game. Shane took a few seconds to calm down and hit both of his foul shots. They were up by five.

Duke brought the ball in and made a quick run down the court. Taylor defense got tough and Jerry was all over their top shooter, and he could not get a shot off. He flipped it to a forward in the corner. Shane rushed him and leaped hard, and somehow managed to get just the tip of his finger to scrape across the bottom of the ball. It hit the rim hard, but Larry brought down rebound. Duke went to foul him, but before they could reach him, he tossed it to Shane. They rushed to foul him, but he flung the ball to Jerry. They fouled Jerry with twenty seconds to play. Dick called the game over, but warned a little magic, a bad foul, and Duke could catch up.

Shane told Jerry to seal the deal. He had to make the both shots as they were in the one and one penalty phase. Jerry sighed heavily, brought the ball up and sunk the first one. Shane grinned. "One more. You can do it, just one more."

Jerry felt the pressure on his shoulders, but he dreamed of playing in games like this since he was six years old. He sighed again and drained the second. The game ended with Taylor winning by seven on Duke's home court. A win never felt better, but TJ had to contain his excitement as he left the stands, retrieved his laptop, and snatched a fresh copy of the game stats. He made his way to the bus and didn't feel safe until he was sitting inside.

TJ slept in Thursday morning after the big game though Shane wished he could. TJ completed the current chapter of **Twice Is Nice** the following morning and sent a copy to Walter and Dick. The corrections returned later that afternoon, so TJ made a few changes, and sent it to Janet in New York. She sent him a spreadsheet of the planned tour to promote the book in late April. His contract called for no more than three weeks on the road, and they packed every possible exposure into the day. The Learjet would be required to keep him on schedule, and Janet would be taking an assistant with her this time.

TJ copied the information into a spreadsheet he designed last year, but with more columns for verifying flights, hotels, and cars. He then copied the signing appearances, and created columns for audience anticipated, quantity of books shipped in, managers name and telephone numbers, as well as their email address, and in between this information, he made narrow columns to be checked off by entering the date accomplished. He sent this list back to Janet and asked to have someone fill in the information required. She knew he was working on the shipments, but he wanted it in writing as to how many books would be there. If he was going to travel and work so hard, he wanted to make sure they maximized the exposure at every opportunity.

When he received the list back from Janet, he planned to call every manager, letting them how excited he was to be coming to their store. Most of the managers never heard from any authors, so TJ's calls certainly got their attention. At each milestone leading up to the publication of the new book, he sent group emails out to the managers keeping them involved, and hopefully building anticipation. He didn't want a single manager waiting to the day before his arrival to begin working on the local publicity for the store signings.

He also created a second spreadsheet for each town, and asked Janet to find out the names of all the local television stations and newspapers, and the name of their sports directors, phone numbers and email addresses. He suggested she begin sending press releases to this group, announcing the date of the tour stop in their town, and set aside some morning time for interviews. He knew early morning book signings were not popular, thus the perfect time to meet the media. She agreed to help and put one of her associates on the assignment. She became impressed with his tenacity, his marketing skills, and though at the moment it was a little more work for her team, it would be TJ doing the extra work in the field.

Thankfully, the next game was against Wake Forest in Lindle, and Shane and the team were glad to be at home after playing Duke in Durham. It was a Saturday one o'clock game, and seemed too soon after playing Duke, as everyone on the starting team displayed purple marks from all the bruises from the Durham matchup. After the Duke game, Shane taped bags of ice to various spots on his shoulders and back, but winning against Duke made the pain of the ice bearable.

Shane spent a lot of extra time stretching out his muscles prior to the Wake Forest game. They were expected to win, but he knew better than to count out any ACC team. The game began as most did with a quick fight for the first possession. Wake got the tip, but Jerry stole it from their guard, and threw it to Shane as he sprinted down the court and dunked it hard sending the Taylor fans in a frenzy of excitement. This year, Wake was no match for the national champions, as Taylor scored four to each one of Wake's points. They led by twenty at the half.

Shane earned twenty-four points in the second half and a total of thirty-two in the game, but didn't even play the last three minutes. Wake caught them at a bad time, as Taylor's confidence was at a season high. Taylor won by thirty-two points.

Three nights later, they played Virginia Tech at home and they, too, received a similar whipping from the mighty Taylor team. Shane scored twenty-eight points, and the top seven players on the team scored in double digits. Shane knew better than to gloat because harder games were coming, and he and his team knew they best be ready. Coach Timmons was not about to let them get the big head. He pushed them harder than before, and Shane loved the way practices were going, and the progress they were making.

The following Friday morning, TJ took the Learjet to New York. The team flew up to Boston for their Saturday night game. They held a practice in the Conte Forum that afternoon. It was snowing outside, but it was hot and exciting inside, and Shane loved the feel of the arena.

TJ met with Jake for a while, and together, they went over to the Janet's office for a morning meeting about the publication and the tour. Afterwards, TJ gave the first of four interviews for the print media for magazines and national newspapers, and sports shows for ESPN® and Fox Sports®.

Each organization signed a document allowing these advance interviews, but only if they agreed to hold their stories until the week of the championship game, and leading up to the release of the new books on the following Tuesday eight days later. By doing the interviews in advance, they could prepare quality pieces, and information from other sources. Each reporter also obtained permission to interview Shane on one of his rare days off via the new remote studio at home in the weeks leading up to the National Championship. Walter approved the project with great enthusiasm, and he loved the idea of the remote studio. TJ invited him over to watch a few of the interviews, and he was led to believe the house was TJ's. They temporarily hid two photos of the boys arm in arm in their bedroom. He was shown the basic tour of the house, but not the wet area or the basketball court. Shane's

Hummer was parked outside and not in his usual garage spot. Walter had been impressed with TJ's setup for writing and broadcasting.

TJ left New York later that afternoon for Boston. It was a short flight and soon he was in his hotel room. Shane ate with the team, but thankfully, the coach gave the team a free evening. TJ was eating in his room when Shane arrived.

Shane grinned, "It's nice to visit a celebrity. How was New York?"

TJ laughed, as they hugged and kissed, "I hope I'm never a celebrity like you. I am doing what I think I have to do to promote the book, brag on my boyfriend, and make us a lot of cash. I'll be glad when the first tour is over, and I still can't believe I have the second tour five days later."

"It'll all be over soon. I think we should start planning a big vacation at the end of the second tour. Where do you want to go?"

"I have been thinking about going to the Northwest to visit Mount Rushmore, the new Crazy Horse Memorial, and over to Yellowstone. Then we could turn north to Glacier National Park and cross over into Canada, and slowly make our way to Alaska. I'd like to spend a couple of weeks there, as who knows when we can get back there once your NBA career cranks up."

"We'll make time, but Alaska sounds exciting to me. Do you have time to set it up?"

"Yeah, you have a championship to win, exams to prepare for, and a graduation to attend. I just have two little old books to finish, and two long tours."

They both laughed. Shane said, "Poor baby. I feel so bad." He paused for a long second and grinned slyly, "How fast can you get naked? I'd like to make it up to you."

TJ laughed, "Faster than you can shoot a jump shot!"

Clothes began flying in the air as they rapidly stripped and dove on the bed. Their lovemaking was intense, tender, wonderful, and thrilling. They were eighteen months into a relationship that had grown by the hour and the days. They were so close they could almost feel what the other was thinking, except for the usual jokes and barbs they teased each other with.

Shane reluctantly toweled off after their shower together and dressed in time to be in his room before the curfew hour. TJ dried off, kissed Shane long and deep, and crawled into the bed deliciously happy. He pulled the pillow where Shane laid his head to his face to smell it, and pulled it to his chest to hold what he could of his lover's scent.

They both wished the game were in the afternoon in Boston, but it was a late game, starting at nine, to pick up the television audience on both coasts. Dick flew in to work the game for ESPN®, and TJ ate lunch with him on Saturday. It was really more of a brunch for Dick, as he had called another game the previous night in Georgia, and flew up late last night and slept in.

The restaurant, Dick's favorite, featured fresh seafood, steaks, and poultry. He ate blacken grouper and lobster. TJ ate surf and turf featuring lobster tail, shrimp, and a nice steak.

"TJ," began Dick between bites of salad, "your book this time is better than last year. It has more detail, and I can tell you've taken great pains to describe the games in a different verse than you did last year. Boy, do I understand trying to avoid repeating yourself. I'm on the air at least four games a week, and at my age, I'm terrified of repeating myself, other than my catch phrases. You have the advantage of the printed word and time to think before you write."

TJ deadpanned, "You're suppose to think?" Dick laughed. TJ added, "Can you think of anything behind the scenes I have missed reporting?"

"No you covered training in the off season, which most fans have no clue how hard these boys work in the hot sun. You gave great insight into the training room, and how they handle bruises, sprains, strained ligaments, and how they prevent future damage. I also liked your chapter on how recruiting affects the current players. Most folks thinks there is animosity when a new star is thinking about attending their school, which could cut them from the starting assignment, and that could be true at some universities, but not at Taylor. There is an instant camaraderie, a bond, and a link to history at Taylor that applies even to guys thinking about playing there. I thought your story about Shane showing a future big man around campus completely hilarious. They met friendly professors, and overly friendly coeds. The new guy became impressed at how many girls flirted with Shane."

"That happens every where we go. They just love him, but although they may have watched every game he played in, they have no concept of how tall he is. When they ask to take a picture with him, and I take the picture with their camera, I have to move way back to get both in the picture. They often find themselves looking up at him like he was standing on a top of a tree. They all say they didn't realize how tall he was, like basketball was a short man's sport."

Dick laughed and asked, "Are you coming my way for vacation this year?"

TJ smiled, "No, opposite end of the country. We're taking the motorcoach to Crazy Horse Memorial, Yellowstone, Glacier National Park, and on to Alaska. We'll be gone three to four weeks or more. We leave the next morning after he graduates."

"Now that is the life. I must say you guys have it all. I have told my wife all about your house."

"Please bring her to come see us, and we'll give her the fifty cent tour for free."

"I will do that," answered Dick. "She could never pass up a bargain." They both laughed and then switched to a conversation about the game tonight.

Shane caught the tipoff and threw it hard to a sprinting Jerry with Larry on his right wing, and only one Boston College defender between them. They played toss until Larry dunked it. Boston College bounced right back, giving the first half a great run and led by eight. Coach Timmons became livid at the poor play his team had done so far. He knew his coaches discussed the records indicating that typically, unless it is a big game, the Taylor team often played sluggish at the nine o'clock tipoff time. He felt at best those facts were just an excuse he'd better fix.

Shane had a list of things he could improve on, and so they returned to the court ready to run, but Boston gave them more of the same, as they upped the lead to ten. However, Shane got a steal and fast break, and slammed the dunk down hard. This seemed to inspire his team. They did a trap play on defense, and got the ball back. Dick proclaimed to his television audience the Taylor team had awoken, and they were already looking at the beginning of a run. He was right, as Jerry scored twice, Larry swished three pretty three-point shots, and Shane scored eight points, plus all three obtained bonus foul shots.

They were tough on defense, too, and held Boston to just four points. Taylor scored sixteen and now led by the third television timeout. Back in the game, they went after it, and TJ noted the wind was out of the Boston team for the last eight minutes of the game. Taylor stretched the lead and won by seventeen points. Shane had twenty-six points.

They were staying over and flying home early in the morning. The team left the hotel at eight, and TJ left about nine. The Learjet touched down before the Taylor team landed. Shane drove straight to the house. They ate lunch, caught up on email, did two television remotes, and went to the wet area to unwind from the long weekend.

# TWENTY-NINE

There were only two more games in February and only four games left in the seasonal play before the ACC Tournament, followed by the NCAA National Championship tournament. For TJ, the season roared by quickly, but he had been writing three books at once, one for fall and two for spring, and editing on the fly, plus spending a lot of time on marketing.

It was Wednesday, and they were playing NC State at home at nine. Shane attended classes in the morning, but came home to rest and eat lunch with TJ. The team game meal was not until five so Shane was hungry. TJ made fresh vegetable soup, with his mother's recipe calling for cornbread baked in an old black iron frying pan. Shane had been leery at first, but with melted butter he loved the southern bread, and once TJ showed him how to mix it in his soup, he really liked it. He ate three bowls plus fresh chopped raw vegetables and fruit.

Shane said between bites, "I have something I want to tell you."

TJ noticed the seriousness of Shane's voice and set his spoon down, "You're breaking up with me?"

Shane grinned, "No, you couldn't drive me off with a pitch fork."

"Now that's an idea. I hadn't thought of that one."

"Would you listen to me? I called my dad last week and told him I had an idea for NBA draft. He says his preliminary scouting reports show that if I play well in the NCAA tournament, I could get the first draft pick."

"That's good."

Shane frowned, "No, that is bad because I would be going to Cincinnati, and they are currently in last place in their division. But it's not just about basketball. I want to play where I want to live. I like North Carolina, and it is easy for us to go north or south, east or west from here. In a few hours we're at the beach or the mountains, and the climate suits me. I don't have to shovel snow here."

"So what is your idea?"

"I want to play in Charlotte for the Bobcats."

"What draft pick do they have this year?"

"Second."

"So how do you keep Cincinnati from picking you while getting the Bobcats to select you?"

"Now that is the question. Here is what I came up with, and this is not my dad's idea—it is mine. I want to know what you think. I propose that my dad fly down to Charlotte, meet with the owner of the Bobcats, and ask him two things: are the Bobcats interested in me playing for them, and would they have any objection if they found out I was gay?"

"Oh my goodness. Are you sure you want to come out before you join the NBA? Isn't it possible no one would hire you?"

344

"I think they will appreciate my honesty, but if they don't hire me, I'll guess we could live off your book income."

"Not the way you eat!" teased TJ. "So there's obviously more to this than what you've said. What's the rest?"

"Well, I think they'll be interested, but how to get Cincinnati not to pick me is the question."

"Is there something or someone they can trade for the number one draft pick?"

"Now you're thinking," began Shane, "because if there is a player they need, then a trade could be done for the right for the Bobcats to choose me."

"But why would Cincinnati pass on you?"

"I think they might if they knew I was gay."

"How so?"

"Well, a few former NBA players have come out of the closet after they retired, but no one has done it while they were playing, and certainly not while starting out as I would be doing. The pressure to play in the NBA is hard enough, but my being the first gay person to play in the NBA would give them and the fans plenty to get excited about."

"Wait a minute, I think this could sell more tickets for the Bobcats because Charlotte has a huge gay population, and if you become their gay role model, they might buy season tickets, and this could start a whole new trend."

"I don't know about a role model, but someone has to break the barrier, and it might just be me, but I'm also considering using my coming out as a deal breaker. I think you and I could live very well in the Charlotte area."

"You mean we'd move to Charlotte?"

"If I can talk you into it. I think we should find a new place, and build perhaps a bigger home. We'll have plenty of money, but we'll also have to worry about where and how we live, especially when it comes to security. There will be some folks who may not like the fact that I'm gay…"

"And living in the Bible belt. So why are you telling me this today?"

"Dad flew down in the Learjet to Charlotte this morning. He has a two o'clock meeting with the owner of the team, and then will fly here to attend the game tonight and bring us up to date. He'll call when he is in the air. Is it okay if he spends the night?"

"Sure. I can't wait to see him. Did you get him a ticket?"

"Yeah, my roommate had an extra one for tonight."

They took a nap, relaxed in the living room watching a movie, and suddenly the phone rang. It was Shane's dad and he would be landing soon. TJ and Shane drove out to meet his flight. After bear hugs in the cold wind, they drove back to the house, fixed him a cup of hot tea, and they sat in the great room with the gas fire logs burning to talk.

Shane couldn't wait any longer. "How'd it go?"

Al smiled, "Well, Bill Johnson is a fine man. I explained your desire to play for him, and he was very happy to get the news. He said he would be thrilled if they could get you, but he feared Cincinnati would certainly pick you. I told him you wanted to play in Charlotte more than anywhere else in the NBA. You wanted to make a home here and stay here for your entire career. He liked the sound of that. So I told him I had an idea of how he could secure Shane. When he asked how, I prefaced my answer by asking if he had anything against gay people. His face lost the warm smile, and for a second I thought I was in big trouble, but he replied his younger brother was gay, and his brother has the same companion for twenty years. He said his family treated the partner like their own. He said he had at least four gay people working on his staff. Then suddenly he paused, his eyes lit up, and he asked if I was telling him Shane was gay."

"I smiled and asked him if I gave him an honest answer would he promise to keep it to himself and no one else. He said he would. So I told him you were. I told him about your relationship with TJ, and you'll be pleased to know he read your book. I wanted him to know that we loved TJ as much as we did Shane and felt the two of you were the perfect couple.

"Then his eyes lit up again, and he began to catch on. I said yeah that was right. Shane will announce he is gay just prior to the draft, and that most likely Cincinnati will pass on him because the owner of that team was a rich redneck. Bill knew him and said our presumption was correct. I asked if he thought the plan would work.

"He said he would like to think it over and would call me soon. I believe he thinks it will work. We'll just have to wait and see."

"Well, this is an exciting possibility, and scary that I would be playing out of the closet, but I will tell both of you, I no longer want to hide the fact that TJ is my boyfriend, and that we are committed lifelong partners."

TJ sat there silent with his face ashen and colorless.

Shane looked at him, and for the moment their eyes seem to say what words could not say. Finally Shane said, "TJ? Say something."

TJ sighed, and smiled a tiny bit and replied, "Al, I think your son is very courageous, and I hope the Bobcats' uniforms will fit over a bullet proof vest."

Shane laughed, "I doubt they would let me wear one on the court. I'll be fine. I know the opposing teams will yell obscenities at me…"

"And so will some of the Bobcat fans. You'll be the poster boy for everything the religious right hates. They will protest, they'll hold up signs, and they will call you names."

"Maybe," Shane replied, "but none of that will be as bad as smelling your breath in the mornings."

TJ and Shane laughed, while Al tried to figure out what they were doing. Shane said, "Dad, TJ is attempting to make sure I know what I'm up against, so that I'll really think it through."

TJ added, "And what Shane is doing is telling me he is going to do it anyhow, and he is now trying to be funny."

Al laughed, "You boys are crazy. Go win the game tonight and try to keep winning, so you'll be exactly what the Bobcats want, and let's hope Bill Johnson finds it in his heart to go out on a limb for you. I think he will, but I don't know for sure. The NBA is big money, and mistakes in recruiting often cause a team to fail. I fear an injury to a key player they want to keep could change their entire recruiting plans. We'll just have to pray it all falls together. I certainly feel my son would be in good hands with Bill."

They began talking about other things, hoping to get Shane's mind off the challenge ahead of him, and back on the game tonight. TJ took Al to the arena, and into the pressroom for dinner. He enjoyed seeing the reporters preparing for the games. Together, they watched Shane warm-up, and then Al moved across court to his seat behind the team for the game. TJ gave Shane his chill and love signal, and Shane winked back at him.

NC State, still pissed they were beaten at home, came to Lindle to even the score. The lead passed back and forth between the two rivals the entire first half with Jerry making a three-point shot just before the buzzer to take a four-point lead at the half.

In the second half, Taylor got a run going early and put the game out of reach for the Wolf Pack. In four minutes, Taylor scored eighteen points. Eight by Shane, Jerry scored six, and Larry put in a long three-point shot while receiving a bad foul, and he made the extra point. NC State fans left early, as the score continued to climb even with the Taylor second team on the floor. Taylor won by twenty-six.

Shane left for class early the next morning after giving his dad a big hug, and thanked him for helping him with the Bobcats. TJ drove Al to the airport where Steve and Susie were waiting for him. He gave him a hug and wished him a safe flight.

TJ returned home to work on both books. He had only ten days left in the regular season play. Two hours later, he sent the latest chapters to Walter and Dick, and after their return, he made corrections and emailed the new version to Janet. He then went on to editing his new gay book **The War Beyond – Part III**. He would finish the final edit this weekend, and ship it to his gay publisher for their editors to work on. They would send back corrections and suggestions for him to work on, and return it by the end of March for publication and release in early May.

On Friday, Shane arrived from practice before dinnertime. He was going to stay overnight, as they both would fly out in the morning to Maryland for the Sunday game. The phone rang and Shane answered, listened, and then called for TJ. "TJ, dad is on the phone, and he wants to talk to both of us. Can you come to the office?"

TJ was brushing his teeth, quickly rinsed, and hustled down the hall. Shane was sitting as his desk with his phone headset on. TJ picked up his wireless headset, and hit the conference button, followed by the lighted line button. "Hey Al. TJ here. How are you?"

"I'm good. Can you both hear me?"

"Yes," they replied in unison.

"I have good news. I just received a call from Bill Johnson. He decided he wants Shane, and while he agrees with your plan, he has come up with a backup plan. He thinks your coming out will change the sport in a positive way to include everyone. He also thinks ticket sales will go up. He is a realist, and knows perhaps a few season ticket holders may cancel, but he believes the rich gay people in the area will flock to the game, and therefore, he expects ticket sales to climb. He said that after people see how hard you work in the NBA, and hopefully help the Bobcats get in the playoffs, that soon everyone will be trying to get tickets."

Shane said, "That is good news. What was his backup plan?"

Al grinned, "He plans to offer a trade of a forward that Cincinnati needs, plus fifty thousand dollars. That's how serious he is about getting you there."

TJ asked, "So you think it is a done deal?"

Al said, "I do. Your coming out may be enough for them to get the number one pick, but if not, he's sure they'll take the trade and the cash."

Shane laughed, "I can't believe he would trade a player and all that cash for just me."

"You're going to share in that trade. He'll give up the player and you'll give up fifty thousand of your dollars."

Shane laughed, "Where do I get fifty thousand dollars?"

"He'll take it out of your signing bonus."

"How much will the signing bonus be?"

"They are working on it. My research says you'll be offered a hundred million for three years and option for a fourth year. You'll also receive a ten million signing bonus, less the fifty thousand you'll owe Bill if he has to sweeten the trade. So you can see how serious the Bobcats want you, but they also don't want anyone else to sign you, and have to play against you."

Shane gulped, "Dad, did you just say a hundred million dollars?"

"Yep, and ten million dollars signing bonus."

Shane laughed, "Well, that would make all that hard work and sweat worth it."

TJ added, "Particularly for a game that you love to play."

"Yep, we'll have to talk with Sam on how to protect as much of that money with tax strategies. Your investment portfolio will be important, too."

"Dad, this is wonderful news. I can't thank you enough. I guess I had better start planning on moving to Charlotte after graduation."

"You'll also have to go to a week-long testing camp in Phoenix in June prior to the draft. Well, I had better go. I promised to take your mom to dinner. Congratulations."

"Thanks again. I love you. Bye."

After they took off their headsets, TJ had some questions, "So it is definite. You'll be playing for the Bobcats?"

"It sounds like it. We can't tell anyone, as some teams might get mad at the pre-draft strategies, but don't be naïve, they all do what they can to get the best players."

"You'll still come out of the closet?"

"Yep. I think that will keep the other teams from offering Cincinnati more than Bill is. I also want to live my life openly. I want to be able to take you dancing."

TJ laughed, "You learned to dance?"

"Well, not really, but I still want to hold you close and grind on you."

TJ teased him, "Would you get your mind off of sex for a minute? So we have to keep our mouths shut to everyone, right?"

"Yes, I'm afraid if anyone other than my parents and us know, then someone could accidentally spill the beans. We have to start making plans to move to Charlotte."

"What do we do with this place?"

"I have been thinking about that for a while, as I had an idea of how much money I would get in the NBA. If you don't mind, I would like to give this house to my parents and try to entice them to move to Lindle. They don't like large cities, but they love Lindle. That would put them within two hours of our home in Charlotte so they can easily visit."

"That sounds fine with me."

Shane grinned slyly, "I have another favor to ask. I would also like for us to give them your motorcoach." He paused as the blood drained from TJ's face. He loved his motorcoach almost as much as he loved Shane and the dogs. "I propose that we order a new Prevost® motorcoach built to your specifications, and we build a new home in Charlotte to store it. How does that sound?"

TJ laughed, "Oh my gosh, a new motorcoach? A Prevost®? This is so exciting."

"Yes, but you have to keep it a secret. Would you be able to take charge once again, and find us a place to live, buy it, build on it, and order the new motorcoach?"

"I think so," replied TJ, "as I'm nearly done with the gay book and the basketball book is up to date. I'll get right on it though."

"I will leave the choices up to you. You did great on this house. The next one will have to be bigger. I hear the NBA stars often have a chef to cook nutrition packed meals, housekeepers, and we'll need more office space as there are requests for a player for appearances, autographs, charities, and more."

"I recall reading a magazine story about Jeff Gordon's setup. We may have to do something like he did. I'll try to research this. Oh my, this is very exciting."

"It is a relief to me. I'll be glad when the coming out and signing stuff is over. I'm going to try and not talk about it, unless you need me to, until we get through the National Championship game. Is that okay with you?"

TJ grinned, "Absolutely. I'll handle it. You just go out there and win."

"Let's go get some takeout."

Later that night, they sat in the living room watching a movie while TJ began using laptop for researching ideas for the house and new motorcoach. He began making a timeline putting in the key dates ahead from his schedule including: tournaments, book deadlines, tours, exams, graduation, and vacation. Online he found the date Shane had to be in Phoenix as June ninth for NBA Rookie Camp. That gave them almost five weeks of vacation. Using his Trailer Life's RV Route planner, he plotted their trip to the west after graduation, on to Canada, and into Alaska, and a different route home. He planned five hundred mile days when crossing the country, and three hundred mile days when they reached part of the area they wanted to explore. And by the time they got to Alaska, perhaps only fifty-mile days with plenty of multi-stay days for exploring. He ordered numerous travel brochures from Canada and Alaska.

He emailed Al and asked him for Bill Johnson's phone number. He wanted his help in finding the right real estate person to help find a place for a new home. He planned to call them in the morning before they flew out.

He researched all the articles he could on the NBA players and NASCAR driver's homes, their offices, and their organizations. Almost all of the drivers were involved in huge charity work, usually forming their own non-profit group to fund many charities. This interested him so he read all he could. He would also consult with Sam, his accountant, on the tax advantages for this type of organization.

He decided the new house would have to have room for: more guest rooms for family and friends, staff housing and room for more office workers, parking for their vehicles inside, parking for staff and guests outside, a chef and a larger cooking area, and a bigger laundry, pantry, phone system, and more.

In his research of the NASCAR drivers, he caught on there was a website for the owners, the drivers, and their charities. The web pages changed often by using the latest technology with rolling screens, dissolving pictures, and high quality slide shows. Some offered blogs with comments from the drivers, so he knew they would need to find a web and print graphics designer. He also recognized that he acted like both Shane's personal assistant and manager, but he knew from his talks with Al they would need a sports agent to complete the deal with the Bobcats and endorsing sponsors, and they may need some other management to help manage Shane's career, as he had no training in that area.

The last thing he did was to begin sketching on the computer crude drawings of how his original house plans for their current home could grow to handle the home and staff of an NBA star. He began recalling some of large RV port homes he saw at some of the fancy motorcoach resorts in Florida. He began downloading designs for ideas. He felt this would be a brick house with everything inside they had now, but a whole lot more.

Shane ate breakfast quickly and drove to school to fly with the team to Maryland. TJ would fly up later in the day. He made a call to Bill Johnson but an answering service picked up the call. TJ left a message he was calling on behalf of Shane after talking to Al, and had a quick question on finding the right realtor. He continued researching the Internet trying to find a realtor, but there were so many, he didn't know whom to choose. Suddenly, the phone rang.

"Hello?"

"TJ, this is Bill Johnson returning your call. How may I help you?"

"I know this deal is extremely confidential, but Shane and Al want me to find a place for him to build a new home. I looked at the list of realtors and it is extremely long. Can you suggest someone that is used to working with NBA players and their homes?"

"I thought about it before I called. I think you should call Nancy Green. She is full of energy and knows everyone, and has done over a dozen player homes. She'll be a big help." He gave him her number.

"Thank you very much."

"If there is anything else you need, please don't hesitate to call me."

It was about only nine-thirty so he gave her a call. She picked up on the second ring, "Hi Nancy. My name is TJ Johnson, and Bill Johnson referred me to you. How are you? Did I call too early?"

"No, of course not. I have a two and four year old. I am on the way to pick up a couple at the airport to see some houses. What can I do for you?"

"I am working for a new NBA star that is relocating to Charlotte. He wants to build a big home there. I have to find and secure the land and get the ball rolling."

"How much land will you need or want?"

"Five acres as a minimum and prefer ten acres or larger."

"Do you want to be on a lake?"

TJ hadn't thought of that. "Is there a lake there big enough to water ski and ride a personal watercraft on?"

"Goodness yes. I probably will suggest Lake Norman. When can you come down, and I'll do the research and get ready for you?"

"I could be in Charlotte on Monday about ten. Is that good for you?"

"Yes. How soon do you need to purchase?"

"Yesterday," replied TJ with a grin.

"Oh my. Well, I'll be ready. Do you know where Lowes Motor Speedway is?"

"Yes, of course."

"Across the street is Fleetwood RV Resort. I have a friend that works in that office. I'll meet you there."

"Thank you and I'll see soon." TJ gave her his phone number in case there was a change in plans.

TJ then left a message with the architect that had helped with their current house. He told Bobby he wanted to start on the plans as soon as possible. When he called back he made an appointment for Tuesday morning. He looked at his drawings for the new house on his computer and printed them out. Using a pencil he began to rapidly modify them. He soon had a concept floor plan he liked.

He created new databases for all the contacts involved in making the house, and another for those in the basketball world or Shane's business. He knew Al had been researching sports agents, so he wasn't worried about that person for now, but he did need to find a business manager or assistant, graphics designer, and secretary. For the house he would need a housekeeper and chef. He made lists of questions for his accountant and lawyer.

He changed clothes, gave the dogs a good rub, and went out to load his stuff in the car, and speak to Bob and Sue. They were outside walking one of their cats that always made TJ laugh. He told them when he would be back, and they said they would check on the dogs. He drove to the airport and met Steve and Susie. On the flight to Maryland, he began looking at various Prevost® motorcoaches, made copies of floor plans, and put them in a folder on his laptop.

He would have three more feet in length to play with, plus huge bays underneath, so he began drawing his ideas from the plans that he saw and a similar desk with some modifications than he had now. He knew right away he would be able to keep the sofa bed in the new coach as the three new feet would give him room for a two two-drawer file cabinets in front of the desk to hold all their working files, his road supply of books, and computer parts and accessories, and on top of the file cabinets he could mount a digital printer and label maker. He became very excited as he continued to modify his drawings for a new motorcoach, and started a new spreadsheet for equipment requests for the new Prevost®.

After he checked into the hotel he made his run to the grocery store, and returned quickly so he could go online continuing his research. Shane was in the Maryland's new arena practicing for the Sunday afternoon game. Afterwards, he attended a late scouting report meeting and dinner at six.

TJ ate in the room after working hard on editing the new gay book and then returned to his projects. He created various checklists of things that had to be done. He wanted construction to start as soon as possible, so he fired off an email to his builder friends to see if they had room in their schedule, and would they work somewhere in Charlotte. He also fired off an email to a contact at Country Coach®, the manufacturer of his current motorcoach.

Shane came up to TJ's room about seven, and they spent the evening watching a movie and making love. Later, they kissed goodnight as Shane return to his room before curfew. They both slept well with Shane dreaming about the game, and TJ dreaming about a new house and motorcoach.

# THIRTY

Maryland began as they always did—in a hurry to win, and they ran at a fast pace from the start, but Taylor kept up with them and shooting was good for both teams. Shane dove for a loose ball and ended up in the second row of a group of Maryland fans. He hustled back to the court with the coach applauding his efforts He finished the half with eleven points and Taylor up by four.

Coach Gary Williams managed to fire up his players once again. They stormed the second half with a big run, and led by six at the second television timeout. Coach Timmons, not very happy with Taylor's play, took a moment to tell them what they did wrong, and finally what they were going to do right. He called for big defensive stops, and the team broke the huddle with a new zeal and eagerness for winning.

A few minutes later, Taylor got a run going and tied the game up with seven minutes to play. Two of Maryland's big men had four fouls. Shane had only two, so nothing slowed down his efforts defensively, but they in turn had to be gentle with him. Jerry threw a hard bounce pass to him just four feet in front of the rim. Shane faked going up twice before he leaped as hard as he could while leaning into one of their big players. The boy took the bait and swatted at the ball catching Shane on the face causing a foul, but Shane remained vigilante on his mission, and scored the basket and the foul shot. They were up by three with six minutes to go.

Back and forth they traded shots and soon Shane noted their big guys were winded, and the guards had slowed down as well. At the next foul shot opportunity, he told his teammates that Maryland's legs were spent, and they should turn up the speed. They agreed and went to a full court press followed by a trap play. They did the trap twice in four minutes, and got a steal and scored both times. Coach Gary Williams was livid and yelled at his team, but nothing could bring them back, and Taylor won by twelve. Shane scored twenty-four points.

They flew home after eating a rushed meal in the locker room. TJ flew back on the Learjet. Once in flight, he ate dinner and went right to work completing his notes on the game, and bringing the book up to date. He emailed the new chapter to Walter and Dick.

Shane arrived about nine and planned to spend the night. TJ quit working, told Shane about his trip to Charlotte in the morning, and then they made their way to the wet area to relax.

TJ took his car to Charlotte early the next morning armed with a pad, his field tape measure, his hand recorder, laptop, and camera. He had just arrived at Fleetwood when Nancy drove up behind him. She looked like a tennis player, tall and thin, long blond hair pulled back into a bund, beautiful tan, and bright blue eyes. She wore a dark green pantsuit, and a big smile. He transferred to her car and she began asking him questions.

"I believe you said five to ten acres. What size house are you going to build?"

"Well we live in four thousand square feet now, but this one will be much larger. I should explain that we are in an RV port home now with a forty-two foot motorcoach, and two bedrooms, large office, two-car garage, big master bedroom and walk-in closet, and a wet area for Jacuzzi, Endless Pool, Steam Room, Sauna, exercise equipment and a half basketball court with a tall ceiling for shooting practice. We plan to build four guest rooms, and four staff rooms, a large laundry and kitchen, a wing for additional staff offices, and we'll fence it in with electric gates. It also has to be in an area where we can get water, electricity, sewer, gas, and T1 telephone transmission lines. A lake would be a plus. Do you have anything in mind?"

Nancy laughed, "Well, I like a man that knows what he wants. I know what a T1 is, and yes, I do know some properties we should look at. Your NBA star probably is a lot like our NASCAR drivers in that he wants to live large…because he is," she laughed at herself. "Let's go and I'll show you some lots for me to judge what you're looking for."

She drove west from the speedway, crossed interstate Eighty-Five and soon they were near Lake Norman. She made several quick turns, while TJ was paying attention to the names of the roads. He had opened his laptop to the GPS software to mark what they found. The computer memorized her route. They began traveling around the lake for several miles until the houses thinned out, and she showed him five or more acre lots on the water. Most of the lots were on the big water, and having had lots on Lake James, he knew the big lake involved a lot of boat traffic. He wanted to find a large private cove to enjoy, but just minutes by boat to the big lake. The lots ran from a quarter million and up. He marked several of the lots, but never quite got excited about any of them.

"Did you consider buying a house and building on?"

TJ answered, "Well, no, but I guess it is possible. Are there homes for sale in a cove and maybe closer to the interstate, so the motorcoach doesn't have to make all these turns?"

She smiled, "Oh, now I get it. Do you tow a car, too?"

"Yes, so pot holes and tight turns are what we try to stay away from, and the closer to the interstate without the noise the better."

"Let me show you some homes for sale on the acreage you're looking for."

They backtracked almost to where they started, and looking at the GPS screen he knew they were a half mile from the highway and less than a quarter mile to the lake. She made a different turn, and he immediately saw some large beautiful homes.

"We have several Bobcat players on this road and a number of racecar drivers." She slowed down, "That's Jeff Gordon's house. He has a nice dock out back, and it is in a cove as you described."

TJ liked the neighborhood and especially the cove. Four houses down, he saw a for sale sign on a ten acre lot with an older four bedroom home. She stopped the car, "This house could be bought and perhaps remodeled for what you want to do."

"Do you have the floor plan?"

Nancy thumbed through her folder and pulled out the listing, and flipped through it until she found it. TJ studied the plan but just couldn't imagine working with the low ceiling and traditional home. It was about twenty years old.

"How much for the house, land, and dock?"

Nancy flipped back to the front of her documents and said, "Five hundred ninety-five thousand, but it has been on the market for over a year after her husband died. She might take less."

"Let me think on this one while you show me what else is available in this cove."

She made some turns and slowed at a newer house but four acres, and on they went, but nothing they looked at had the proximity to the highway, utilities, and the cove like the one with the house on it. They had been looking for three hours and decided to stop for a burger, and look at more listing. They ate and talked, and finally TJ asked, "Nancy, could that house be moved?"

She pulled the listing back out from her briefcase. It was brick veneer with a wood frame, and it was all in a one line and not a T shape. "I think it could."

"Do you know someone that moves houses?"

"Yes, I do."

"Call them and get them to just come take a look from the street and tell me if it can be moved."

She made the call and then TJ said. "Okay, let's change strategies. Find me a half-acre or more lot that as close to this house as possible, but not on the water so the land will be cheaper."

She grinned as she surmised what he was up to, "I can do that. Let's go."

They went back to the house, turned up and away from the lake, and made a left four blocks later, and there she pulled in front of a lot. They got out of the car. TJ said, "This is perfect. How did you know about this lot so quickly?"

She laughed, "Turn around. I just sold the house across the street last week." They both laughed as her cell phone rang. It was the house mover. She asked several questions, and told him they should also check the mileage to here, and price the move. She hung up. "He says the house is movable. He'll be here in a minute, as he is doing the mileage to here to give you a price."

"I'm going to walk across the lot just to be sure. How much is this lot?"

"Ninety thousand."

TJ grinned as he felt he had found his solution. As he began walking, he ran the numbers through his head. He liked the lot and thought it would be perfect for another family. A truck drove up, so TJ walked back to the street.

"Hi, I'm George Shuford. That was only two and half miles. He set his clipboard on the hood of truck, ran some numbers and told them he could move the house for ten thousand."

"How soon can you move it, set it up and make it look as good as it is now?"

"I can move it right away, say five days to prepare for the half day move, and it'll take about two weeks to put it back together again."

TJ shook his hand. "Do you have a card? My name is TJ Johnson. I'm pretty sure we have a deal, but now I have to buy the house, so we'll call you as soon as we can."

The man left and TJ told Nancy, "See if this would be a good time to see the interior of the house."

Nancy replied, "We can see it now as she has already moved to a condo. There's a lockbox on the door."

They drove back and went in. It was a nice well kept home with a deck on the back. He liked it. He felt it would be an easy resell in the new location. "Can we talk directly with the owner?"

"She is one of my listings, but I think you should make an offer to me, and I'll present it to her." Nancy got out her form for an offer. TJ told her to offer five hundred thousand cash as the offer, and he could close Wednesday. He also said he would give Nancy ten thousand dollars as a deposit. After he signed it, she walked away from him, made the call, and thankfully caught the owner at home. They talked for a while and Nancy came back with a grin.

"She said yes. She said she was tired of fooling with it, and worrying about selling the house. I just need to get her signature. Do you want to drive over?"

"Absolutely."

They were there in ten minutes and went into her condo. "Mrs. James, this is TJ Johnson—the buyer."

TJ took her hand warmly, "I'm so pleased to meet you. You have such a beautiful house, and it has been so well taken care of."

"Thank you," she beamed. "We enjoyed living there for twenty years, but after my husband passed, it just wasn't the same. My kids live out west so now that the house is sold, I am thinking of moving near them."

"That sounds like an excellent plan."

She signed the paperwork and they said goodbye. In the car TJ wrote a check for the deposit, and called the house mover while looking at his business card. "George this is TJ Johnson. We met a while ago about moving the house from the lake. The deal is done. Can you start the moving process Thursday?" He waited and smiled, "I'll leave a deposit check with Nancy if that is okay?" he paused again. "Very good, thank you."

He turned to Nancy, "Can you verify there are T1 transmission lines and excellent power in the area? I saw the gas line and I was assuming water and sewer were running since the house already had it. What am I forgetting?" He paused, "Any problems with getting permits for a rebuild on the lot?"

"I don't think you'll have any trouble."

"I may need a builder, but let me make a call first. Do you want to start driving me back to my car?" He flipped through a screen on his laptop after marking the lot on his GPS program. He found the builder of their current home and dialed the number. "Hello, may I speak with Henry please? Yes, I'll hold." He waited. "Henry? This is TJ Johnson. How are you? That's good. I have a quick question for you. I just bought ten acres on Lake Norman to build a bigger RV port home that is also going to have four guest rooms, four staff bedrooms, a huge laundry and kitchen, and two thousand square foot wing for more offices for assistants, secretaries, and graphic designer. It's on the lake so we'll need a new dock, and the usual exterior RV Parking, Shed, and parking for the staff and guests. So it'll be a floor plan slightly similar to what we built last year but much bigger. I think we'll do a brick veneer to match the other homes in the area. My question is simple, would your company build down here?"

TJ waited while Henry spoke and then smiled, "Excellent. I'm calling the architect next, and will get with you once the plans are complete. You know I'm going to want this house completed right away. Is that possible? Yes, thank you. Bye."

Nancy pulled up to his car. "Mr. Johnson, you are a quick decision maker. I'm impressed. What else can I do to help?"

"I don't know, but you've been an excellent help. I hope you enjoyed making a sale quickly. Thank you for your patience. Let me give you my attorney and accountant info, and maybe you can suggest a cheap but fast closing attorney?"

She grinned, "I wouldn't be a good realtor if I didn't have one ready to go. Anything else?"

TJ laughed and said, "How much do you think we can sell the house for after it is moved?"

"I think you could move it fast at four hundred thousand."

"Okay, where's your listing agreement for me to sign. I want you to sell it as soon as George is done. I'll send my landscapers down to clean the property up and make it look nice."

TJ drove home while making calls to Sam and Jerome. TJ's book sales had put so much money in the bank they no longer needed the bank loan. Jerome assured him it would all be done by Wednesday. He would call the local attorney next.

Then he made the call of his dreams by calling Country Coach® in Oregon directly. He got their sales manager on the phone, gave him his unit number, and then said he wanted to order a custom-built Prevost® unit as soon as possible. TJ would email him pictures of his current desk, his drawings for the new desk, and file cabinet area when he got home. The guy suggested TJ fly out to see them as soon as he could. TJ said he would be there when they opened on Wednesday. He arranged for the guy to pick him up at the airport. TJ hung up and called the Learjet number to arrange the flight to Junction City Oregon and back in one day.

TJ arrived home about five, and after playing with the dogs, and fixing some supper, he went right to work on more sketches of the house, and he added what he had in mind for the dock and boathouse.

TJ met with the architect first thing the next morning. He had two assistants in with him drawing and writing as fast as he was, but thanks to TJ's preliminary sketches they knew what he wanted. The only difference in the external construction was instead of a metal skin it would have brick, but still have a painted metal roof and still no gutters, as he didn't want anything to clean. They suggested Leaf Guard® gutter system so TJ said he would check into it. The new design made it easier for the dogs to get out of the house without the tunnel, and it gave them room for an exterior sun deck and pool, as well as the dock at the lake.

He wanted to incorporate some of his ideas like digital lighting to cut down on pulling so many wires, wireless audio, and anything else they could think of he might want. They spent forty-five minutes on building a large kitchen for a chef including a cubby desk, two large refrigerators, eight-burner stove and grill with stainless steel vent, dual microwaves and ovens, four drawer dishwashers, and an ice machine. He also put in a special water fountain for the dogs that circulated and refill the water bowl automatically.

They would have preliminary sketches for him on Monday. TJ knew he was pushing hard and thanked his team several times.

After lunch he was on the phone to ESPN's Brian Kenny. "Brian, how are you?"

"I'm fine, did something break?"

"No, of course not. I need your help." He explained the new house and motorcoach, and wanted to add a remote studio to the motorcoach. He explained it would best if they could light Shane with DC voltage halogens instead of studio lights. The camera and the rest of the equipment didn't pull much wattage. Brian said he would search for some DC spotlights and begin to draw out the plans for both systems.

"Are we taking out the old system?"

"Yeah, but not yet. We'll need it right up to the day we move in. I'll explain later."

Brian made some suggestions for the motorcoach that TJ added to his laptop notes. He then called Buddy Bell and asked if he could come out to the house right away. Buddy was between projects so he agreed to do so. Later, he showed Buddy the sketches for the house, explained the new office wing, staff and guest area, outdoor pool, and dock. He said he wanted to make the house as energy efficient as possible with digital wiring. He asked Buddy what could be done differently to accomplish for them what they did last time, and what else he might do. Buddy thought for a second and grinned. He gave TJ a number of suggestions on new technology they could enjoy. TJ mentioned they would pull in two T1 transmission lines for maintaining excellent bandwidth for broadcast and simultaneous Internet & telephone service. They would also have about a dozen active phone lines. Buddy was getting excited, as he loved a challenge. He promised to work on his ideas and get back to TJ before the end of the week.

TJ then took him out to the motorcoach, and using his drawings he explained what he was going to change for the desk area, and what Brian would be doing with the remote studio onboard. Buddy immediately suggested they go to the larger satellite Internet dish and bandwidth plus faster speeds. They both looked at the Motosat website and he showed TJ the type of dish he had in mind. TJ again made lots of notes and thanked him as he left. They also planned an outside entry port for hooking the various systems from the coach to the office in the house.

Shane came by after practice and his dinner. TJ asked him if he wanted to know. Shane grinned and said, "Okay, give me ten minutes worth."

TJ sped through the work he had done in the last two days, and Shane basically sat there with his mouth open. When TJ finished, Shane smiled and said, "Excellent, and thank you. Everything is falling into place thanks to you. Let's go to the wet area. I'm a little sore."

They spent a few hours enjoying each others company before Shane had to go back to school. TJ spoke to Sue and she agreed to check on the house and the dogs while he was gone. Bob loved watching Shane's games on the projector system. TJ got all his stuff ready for the flight, set the clock, and went to bed.

On the flight across the country to Oregon, TJ worked on all his notes, so he could be as organized as possible for his meeting at Country Coach®. Once satisfied, he continued editing the final version of the new gay book. He hoped to finish it over the weekend. He also caught up on the basketball book. Somehow, he managed to get a thirty-minute nap before they landed at seven-forty local time. A new Hummer with the Country Coach® logo on the side picked him up.

He walked into the corporate offices on time for his appointment at eight o'clock, and the sales manager of the company and the designers for the Prevost® units were in the conference room waiting for him. TJ asked if they would hook his laptop to the overhead projector he requested the previous day, so he could show them some pictures. They quickly did so.

After a welcome speech by their staff, TJ spoke up, "Folks, I'm a Country Coach® fan and love my Allure 470, but I am here to purchase a new custom Prevost® unit, and incorporate some new ideas and technology. I work for a sports star. He is tall at six feet nine inches, so please keep that in mind as you design. He gets around just fine on my coach, but we certainly don't want to go smaller in any way. The desk area is important as I write and work on the road, and the remote studio link, and I'm opened to all of your suggestions. If I can have just a few minutes of your time, I show you what we have in mind for our coach."

On the big screen, TJ showed them a picture of his desk from numerous angles. Then he showed slides of his sketches on how he wanted to change the desk. He demonstrated where he wanted the dual two-drawer file cabinet, the mounting of a digital printer copier fax machine on top of file cabinet, his power requirements, and where he wanted the outlets to be. He explained he wanted a sleeper sofa on the street side near the sink. He also wanted a tray to come up like on an airplane for a person to sit on the couch and operate their laptop or eat a snack. He wanted a big LCD screen up front, and wanted fans pulling cool air behind it, as his sometimes overheated.

He wanted the entertainment cabinet for the electronic gear to be mounted around a nineteen-inch rack with slides, and a turn spindle to make it easier to make changes to the audio/video devices. He also wanted the DirecWay® Internet Satellite system controller and modems mounted in a cabinet over the driver's left side so it wouldn't be on a slide or mounted in the back like his current coach. He wanted Ethernet ports at the main desk, under the dining table, the tray on the couch, and in the bedroom, plus a Wi-Fi system with a switch on/off antenna for the bays for picnic with laptop opportunities.

TJ began asking questions from his long list. He started with the roof layout. They were able to use their computer to bring a picture of the typical roof for the Prevost® units. TJ immediately realized it came with four air condition / heat pump units, or one more than he currently had. He stopped as an idea came to him. "I don't use a lot of windows on my motor coaches. I mostly use the front big window. Can we eliminate the windows over the headboard of the bed, so it would be quieter and easier to cool, and we don't need one on the other side of the bedroom either. Take out the one in the bathroom, and the ones around the dining area and office area. That will keep that area cooler. Leave the one behind the couch and the kitchen. That should save a little time. I do want quad power outlets in the dining, office and kitchen area and the bedroom dresser for all those charger adapters.

"Now as to the roof, I want you to mount a Datastorm® XF3 motorized dish and D3 controller, and we need to put it near the front just behind the in-motion satellite dome dish." He brought up a slide showing the dimensions. "Is there room before the first AC unit?"

An engineer said yes because they may set it back a little from normal, but the duct work would still cover the entrance area to keep the area cool or warm depending on the weather.

TJ asked, "I also want Motosat's new HD Universal DirecTV® mount, and high quality A/B switches so that once we're parked, we can switch to the second system to pick up all three DirecTV® satellites at once. I'd like a DVR HD receiver in the front and the back. Bose® surround system, and separate control for the rear, and outside. Of course we want a HD LCD like I have now in the rear. Forget a VCR. Put in the top of the line Bose® Lifestyle system. It'll have a built in DVD player, but also put in a Sony® HD DVD Player. Also make the XM Player in the dash easy to feed the main stereo system, so you can listen to XM throughout the coach and outside.

"Okay, here's a biggie, I'd like either a better switch panel or patch panel in the entertainment rack for everything coming in to the box, all the equipments in and out ports, and everything going out so it is easier to swap out equipment, pick a different circuit, or trace down a problem."

The Country Coach® staff recorded TJ's requests with a video camera, and wireless microphone they hooked up to him. Various staff members were making notes as well.

"Any questions or suggestions?"

They asked him about multi-controller remote and TJ laughed, "I guess I want one if it works. I had so much trouble with the last few we've tried, but I also want the software to change, add, or fix it. Let's talk about the blinds. They should be dual cone, heavily insulated to prevent the sun heat from getting in, and making it really dark inside when we want it. They might as well be remote controlled.

"The kitchen should have beautiful countertops, electric stove top, Fisher Paykel® dual drawer dishwasher, and the biggest electric refrigerator you can get in the coach. Please put in maximum drawer and cabinet storage, plus a place for mop and broom, stackable washer / dryer units, a garbage disposal for the sink, central vacuum, and trash compactor.

"The bathroom seems to work being in the center for us, so even if we're in a truck stop we can take a shower, and not stepping on each other trying to shave. I want white sink bowls and Corian® countertops everywhere. I know some of the Prevost® come with a second toilet, but we don't need it. Use the back area for a lot more storage for clothes.

"I want marble high gloss tile on the floor everywhere possible from bedroom to the door. It should all be heated tile. Put in a top of the line Aqua Hot® heating and hot water system, and a big generator.

362

"Now this is a special request from a guy that has owned four RV units so far. Please put a water pump on / off switch in the utility bay. So many times I had to go back inside with wet feet to turn it on or off. Okay, gang, that's my wish list. I know there is more you can do with the utility bay, as well as the entertainment bay, so I'm ready to hear your ideas. Oh yeah, please make sure the big inverters have the new air blowing system working from day one." TJ smiled and sat down.

TJ listened to a lady as she talked about colors and fabrics, and showed him suggested samples. He picked all khaki colors hoping to stay away from dark colors. He also picked out the tile he wanted. He fielded questions from an engineer about his desk and the power requirements, and another technical designer asked a few questions about the driver's console. They brought up slides to show the latest electronic dash, tire monitoring and GPS system. He was thankful they weren't using the Pioneer® stereo GPS system, as he had tons of trouble with his. They also added the Vorad® collusion radar technology to prevent accidentally changing lanes on top of someone or hitting a tree or post. He asked about the generator auto start system, and begged for a place to put remote controls, sunglasses, cell phones, and Lifesavers®. He also wanted some small drawers near the driver to put keys, gum, lotion, aspirin, and other pocket things in. He begged for insulated cup holders and grinned when an engineer said they would put in a new electric heat / cold holder for the driver and passenger.

They left the factory and drove over to the Prevost® custom shop. They had several units in production and used them to talk about the bays. TJ suggested four inch white pipes mounted high on the walls for his poles for cleaning, and racks in the top for lounge chairs to keep them up and out of the way. He saw a spot for his toolbox, his fold up ladder, a telescoping ladder to get on the roof for minor emergencies, and he was glad to have hose wheels for water, sewer, and electrical. He told them he wanted a RV Sanicon® Sewer System, and they again made notes. He made sure the coach came with the SmartTire® Sensor System installed inside all the tires, with remote antenna for his SUV.

He was about to return to the factory when he suddenly remembered the awnings and made sure the slide awning were mounted for a big down angle over the slides to keep the water draining off so they could pull the slides in even when it was raining. They showed him the big awning were mounted on top of the roof along the edge to hide all the gear on top and they were full length on both sides, and all the awnings were electric and remote controlled.

Back at the factory, the various team members brought their notes and quotes to the sales manager. They went into a meeting together and an hour later, they asked TJ to come in. The sales manager gave him the quote of one and half million. Before TJ said yes, he asked for a delivery date. They asked if he had a request. He requested May twenty-fifth so they could pick up the coach on the way back from their Alaska trip. They said yes, and then TJ said yes to the deal. He quickly asked how much deposit and when did they want it. They grinned and said half up front and as soon they could get it.

TJ replied, "I need your bank numbers, and I can have it transferred right now." They said sure, and a secretary went to get the information. Meanwhile, TJ called Sam and explained what he was buying, that it would have an office in it so he could write on the road, work on the tours, marketing, provide a remote studio for Shane's interviews, and allow the managing of Shane's career while on the move. TJ gave him the bank information and the phone number of the contact person in case he had a digital error. He said he would call TJ back in fifteen minutes.

While they were waiting, TJ asked if they used iMac® computers with some of their design work, and they said they did. He asked if they could communicate with him with iChat®, so he could see how things were coming on design and assembly, and discussing any new features or modifications. They said that was possible. He asked for the contact information for their electrical engineer so that he could put Buddy Bell in touch with the design team. Together, the three of them could decide where to hang the camera and small monitor. Shane would sit in a chair across from TJ's desk for his interviews. There would be a disappearing screen that would come down from the ceiling as a backdrop behind Shane in case they want him to appear over a video.

The secretary soon came into the room and said the money was in their account. They all marveled at how fast TJ worked. Meanwhile, they printed paperwork for all the things TJ discussed. He asked for a copy of their recordings and that was provided. TJ signed everything, shook a lot of hands, and left for the airport.

TJ flew to Atlanta and arrived as the sun was setting. He bade Steve and Susie goodnight, and took the car service to the team's hotel. Shane arrived at lunchtime and had an afternoon practice in the arena in preparation for Thursday's night. He had a study hall after dinner and then free time, so he headed up to TJ's room. TJ finished eating a late dinner as Shane arrived in the room. Shane thought TJ looked exhausted.

"Tough trip. It's been a long week, and I've spent a lot of money, but I'm very excited about our future. I hope you are."

Shane asked as he went around the couch, and began rubbing and massaging TJ's shoulders, "When is the new coach going to be ready?"

"We'll pick it up on the way back from Alaska on May twenty-fifth."

"Now that is exciting. I can't wait to see that beautiful state. Are you excited about the house?"

"Yes, but I have so much work to do. I'm going to need to hire some folks to work for us out of our new office when we move."

364

"I'm not surprised. I know all the NBA stars have managers, publicists, chefs, drivers, and some have bodyguards."

"I hadn't though of a publicists, and we may need bodyguards for you after you come out."

Shane sighed, "If we do, I hope it is only for a year or two. Surely they will let up on this young gay fellow after that."

TJ smiled at him, "I do, too. I'm sure you're going to help a lot of folks grow out of their gay prejudice, just as they had to do with racial prejudice. I won't let anyone hurt you."

"Come on, let's cuddle a while."

TJ and Shane moved to the bed where they laid down and held each other, and just talked softly for a while. Shane soon had to go due to his curfew, but he said he would talk to TJ again tomorrow. Not long after Shane left, TJ stripped, brushed his teeth, and climbed into the bed. He was physically and mentally exhausted. He fell asleep just a few minutes after his head hit the pillow.

Georgia Tech signed a new coach two years ago, and each season they made big improvements to their play. Tonight's game was going to be a tough one, as they were determined to make it into the NCAA tournament this year, and beating the National Champions was a sure way to get the selection committee's attention.

TJ arrived at the pressroom ninety minutes before the late night game that was going to be broadcast coast to coast. He picked up the latest media information, typed in some notes in his laptop, and shut it down. He walked over to the line at the buffet, and attempted to eat dinner, but mostly he picked at his food. He was still tired, and though the day had been busy, at least he didn't have to go anywhere. He had taken two naps to try and get some additional rest.

He received confirmation from Jerome that the house and land purchase completed yesterday without a hitch. The mover received his check and started work at eight this morning. The architect called about some ideas they had. Later in the day, Country Coach® and their team leaders met and they called with some suggestions and more questions. He called his landscapers and asked them if they wanted the contract for the house at Lake Norman, and would they help him with the yard where the house was moving. They were happy to do so.

He reviewed his checklists, and though he had checked off over a hundred items, he added another fifty. After lunch, he had made a list of the jobs he needed to fill in one column while creating a second column for possible people to hire. The first job on the list was going to be a multi-hat person. He thought of John Bunting, the young man that sold him the iPhones®. He emailed a request for John to call him.

A few minutes later, the phone rang. "Hey, this is TJ Johnson. Do you remember me?"

"Of course, I do. I have read two of your books since we last talked."

"How are you?"

"I'm doing great."

"I wanted to ask you some questions. Your degree is in communications, right? Does that mean you're trained to handle press releases, administrate press conferences, plan ad campaigns, and things like that?"

"Yes, it does."

"Do you also have website design experience?"

"It wasn't a huge part of my degree program, but I have been designing sites for years to supplement my income, and I keep my web skills up to date. I like to be creative."

"Can you manage people?"

"I have been assistant manager here for two years."

"I guess I mean can you hire, mold, and if necessary fire an employee that won't try harder when instructed correctly to do so?"

"Yes I can."

TJ thought for a second and said, "I have a job for you. You'd wear several hats for a while. You'd be our publicist, office manager, web designer, and my right arm assistant. We're building a new home / office complex, and you'd have an office there. You'd have normal days and many not so normal days. You'd travel from time to time, and you'd have all the regular benefits including health, vacation, holidays, and retirement except that during the basketball season you'd be super busy, but you'll be able to take more time off in the off season. You'd have to move to Charlotte. Are you interested?"

There was a long silence on the other end. John didn't say anything. TJ was taken back and asked, "John? Are you there? Are you okay? Did I say something wrong?"

Finally John spoke, "I'm sorry. I'm so overwhelmed. I'm glad you can't see me, as tears are running down my face. I am so excited, I couldn't breathe for a second. Yes," he finally said, "I'm very interested."

"Excellent. I'll start you at fifty thousand a year plus benefits. My accountant is working on a benefit package, as we haven't had one before, so I'll have that for you soon. We will pay all your business and travel expenses, and we'll feed you a lot. Now a personal thought, if you have a partner since we last talked, they are welcome to move with you. What's your status?"

"Unfortunately, I'm still single."

"Well, I guess that will make the move easier. Charlotte has a big gay population with lots of gay professionals like you. I hope you can find the right man. I'll put up a billboard for you if I have to!" They both laughed.

"When do you want me to start?"

"April twenty-fifth. That is just a few days before my partner's graduation and we're leaving on a big vacation the day after. You'll man the phones while we are gone." TJ stopped and suddenly had an idea. "Wait a minute. When do you want to start?"

"As soon as possible. Don't get me wrong. Apple® has been great to me, and I've learned a lot. I took all their management courses, and I know Macs inside and out, but retail sales is a boring job. I am ready to get into my career."

"How soon can you move to Charlotte?"

"I should give them a notice but things are slow, and they'll probably let me go right away. It would take two days to pack, rent a truck, and tow my car there. I don't have enough stuff for a moving company. I would have to find a place to live. I guess I could be there about ten days."

"That sounds great. You're hired. You'll be moving to Lindle until June first, and then we're all moving to Charlotte. I'll rent an RV or an apartment for you to stay in until then. That'll give you time to find a place to live in Charlotte. I will have staff housing for our chef and housekeeper, and you could live there, but it will be like a dorm with a kitchen down the hall. I'm just saying you could do that for a while until you find the right place. Okay, I'm going to have my accountant and attorney send you some forms to sign. Besides the tax stuff, there are two important forms: your contract, and your confidentiality agreement. Let me explain: our company, or my partner and I'll employ you, and he is a major sport professional. Everything we say or do will be held in the strictest confidence. No one we hire can ever talk or write about us. For signing this agreement, we'll pay you a five thousand dollar signing bonus. Do you understand how important our private lives are to us? Do you agree to sign?"

"Not a problem." replied John, though still curious as to whom this sport's star was.

"If you'll email me your banking information I'll wire the five thousand to your bank after the papers are signed."

"I can do that."

"Email your contact information, and I'll quickly send mine to you. My accountant is called Sam. He's a great guy. If you have any question about your pay, ask him. My attorney is Jerome. If you have a question about the contract, he can answer it. Otherwise, email or call me, and I'll send you directions on getting to Lindle. Welcome aboard."

"TJ, I can't thank you enough. I am so excited. I promise to work as hard as I can for you."

"We're lucky to have you. I'll see you soon."

The first half was a mixed bag of excellent play and disasters for Taylor. They got a run and scored fourteen points before Tech scored another point. Then they went cold and Tech caught up. Shane had two fouls on him with two minutes to play in the first half, and for the most part, no one from the Taylor squad could hit anything in the three-point zone. Cool hand Larry had gone cold. Jerry's shots were off as well. Tech led at the half by four.

Coach Timmons pointed out what they were doing wrong on their offense, and what Taylor wasn't doing on defense. He changed a few plays, and fired up the team. Shane knew he could do better, and he hoped his teammates felt the same way.

Taylor brought the ball in and immediately went down the court, set up their offense, passed the ball into Shane and he scored. They went to a full court press. Shane had been watching his man bring the ball in all night and thought he had him figured out. The Tech boy would take a small step forward with his front foot when he was going to throw it. Shane leaped to the center as he threw it and intercepted the pass, dropped it, scooped it up, and as he went for the dunk, the frustrated and embarrassed player that threw it, fouled him. Shane made the dunk and got the foul shot. That was five points in ten seconds by Shane.

They got a defensive stop, brought the ball down in a hurry, and Larry finally hit a nice three-point shot from the corner. They kept up the pressure and three times Shane was involved in successful trap plays. For the next ten minutes, Georgia Tech couldn't do anything right, and Taylor did nothing wrong. The real sinker to Tech's attitude came after Shane hit a long two-point shot while standing alone without a single defender on him.

Taylor won by fifteen, but the game had been closer until the Taylor boys got on fire. They flew home late that night, so they could attend class the next day whether they were awake or not.

# THIRTY-ONE

TJ woke up suddenly in a cold sweat. In all the excitement of building a big home in Charlotte on the east coast, and a big new motorhome on the west coast, he had forgotten to tell the engineers at Country Coach® about both the home and remote connection ports required. He quickly wrote some notes on a sticky pad he kept by his bed, showered, ate breakfast, and after he finished dressing, he went to his computer to create sketches and write a note to Country Coach®.

He wrote they needed to create a small cable port in the bottom of the utility cabinet for external connections for a triple HD satellite ground connections if they are parked under trees, dual cable connections for Internet satellite connection, telephone connection with all four wires terminated for digital service at home, and Internet connection. The roof needed two new rubber ducky antennas for WIFI reception, and a cell phone amplifier external antenna. Inside the coach on the roof should be a cell dome receiver / antenna with the connecting wire pulled to the same cabinet over the driver for connection to the amp. They would need a twelve-volt power receptacle for this amp. That cabinet should also have a heat sensor fan to pull cool air through that cabinet to cool the amp.

He closed by apologizing for his mistake and asked for a quote for the additions. Later that day he got a quick note back stating these types of additions are not unusual. They would bill him for the equipment, but no charge for the installation.

TJ made a call to Leslie to see if she would be interested in handling the interior décor work for the new house. She agreed to come by after lunch. He called Jerome and went over the legal stuff including the contract he needed for new employees and in particular John Bunting, and the confidentially agreement. He had Acrobat PDF® documents in his email by that afternoon for him to use. He also talked to Sam about the purchase of the motorcoach, and the house and two lots in Concord. Sam gave him kudos for quick thinking on moving the house to a cheaper lot. After it sold, he would have actually gotten a valuable piece of property on the lake for peanuts. He asked Sam for the documentation for hiring new staff members. He got more emails from Sam for Acrobat PDF® documents of tax forms, and data information forms he needed on file. He sent instructions that he needed a copy of the Social Security Card, and a copy of the Driver's License or a certified ID like a passport.

TJ decided to make a spreadsheet checklist with the names of the forms and items he needed for each person hired. He sent all copies of the PDF files to John Bunting for him to fill out and fax back, scan and email, or snail mail by the post office. He copied the boilerplate contract from Jerome, typed in the duties and salary, plus the details for the signing bonus.

He called Bob and Sue to see if they were up and asked if they could visit, as he needed a favor. They came into the office a few minutes later. He asked them to sit down as he had a lot to tell them. He brought them up to date on buying the two lots and a house in Concord, just north of Charlotte, and ordering the new motorcoach. They were as excited as TJ about the new Prevost®, since they both loved beautiful motorcoaches. He told them they were moving June first to Concord, and asked if there was anyway they would consider staying until the first week of June to help look after the current home while they were in Alaska, and to help them move to the new place. He told them he had drawn into the new house plans additional parking spots so they could stay there next year. He told Bob about the lake and the fishing possibilities, too.

They said they would talk it over and get back to him, but he felt sure they would. He then asked a big favor. "I have hired John Bunting to work for us, as a man of many hats, but mostly for office manager and right arm assistant. TJ needed help in finding John either a small, furnished apartment to rent for sixty days, or to rent a big camper to put next to their RV on the other lot. They said they would help on that matter. He gave them a signed blank check, so they could find and secure the deal right away.

An hour later, he received multiple emails from John with all the documents signed, scanned and attached. TJ was pleased to have him aboard. He asked Sam to put the five thousand dollars in John's account. He called Bill Johnson, and thankfully, he was in and took the call.

"Bill, I hate to bother you again and hopefully this is the last time, but I have bought land on Lake Norman to build the house. I have the architect working on the plans, the builder is standing by, and we plan to move in June first. I'm hiring some additional help, but there are two areas I'm at a lost for hiring. Where do I find a chef to keep Shane in the best possible health, and Shane wants to set up a non-profit foundation, so he can use his status as a player to help raise money for worthy charities. I also need to learn about handling his publicity, speaking engagements, and whatever else you think we might need. I'm sorry to ask for so much info, and if there is someone on your staff that can help, please pass me to them."

Bill laughed, "Boy, I'm impressed. You are a fast and efficient person. I think I should hire you. Let's start with the chef problem. Call Celebrity Chefs or Chefs Extraordinaire, both in Charlotte, and be sure and tell them he is a professional sports star, because you're not after a pastry or light faire chef. I think I can solve your foundation and publicity questions in one contact. Do you know Jeff Gordon?"

TJ laughed, "Well, I know of Jeff Gordon, and I have one of his hats as I'm a fan, but no, I haven't had the pleasure of meeting him."

Bill grinned, "When you do you'll like him. He is smart, very intelligent, and has a keen sense of humor. He doesn't get enough credit for all the charity work he does. He has an amazing set up for handling both his business side and his foundation work. He'll be at the race track today, but can you meet with him on Monday?"

TJ's face flushed with a pink shade of excitement, "Sure, I can. Anytime."

Bill was not the kind of guy that put things off that could be done now. He had Jeff's cell phone number in his directory. "TJ, if you'll hold a second, I'll get Jeff on the other line."

TJ waited patiently, but knowing that surely Jeff will not have time to meet with him. He realized he was bouncing his leg in nervous anticipation.

"TJ? Bill here. Sorry to keep you holding. I have an appointment for you with Jeff at eleven on Monday morning."

TJ quickly wrote down the address information, and Bill gave him Jeff's cell number in case he got lost or delayed. They were meeting probably just a few miles from the new house location. "Bill, I can't thank you enough. This is a huge help to us. Thanks again."

"One last thing, after we officially sign Shane, then I'll schedule a meeting between my publicity team here and yourself, so you'll have the same information they do on every media event."

"That's great. Thanks again. Bye."

TJ hung up with goose bumps all down his legs. He had a private meeting with Jeff Gordon. How cool was that, he thought. He began making a list of questions for Jeff, and worked on polishing them, and changing the sequence for the next hour.

He called his Concord realtor Nancy Green next, "Hey Nancy. How are you? That's great. I heard from my attorney on Wednesday that the closings went well. I appreciate all your urgent help in the matter."

"No problem. I was by your property this morning and shocked to see the old house up on wheels already. How in the world did you get him to work on your project so quickly?"

TJ laughed, "I offered him a cash thousand dollar tax free bonus if it was gone by Friday. The builders are moving their grading and backhoe equipment there in the morning. Permits were achieved for site grading this morning. I meet with the architect Monday afternoon. I hope to have the plans to the builder Tuesday morning and permits secured shortly thereafter. We could begin pouring the footings on Tuesday if the weather holds."

"That is amazing."

"Nancy, I need a favor. I have hired a new office manager, landscaping team, an interior decorator, and working on a chef, but I need a discrete but excellent housekeeper. I offer housing if they need it for free, and of course an excellent salary and benefit package. Where in the world do I find such a person?"

"Jeez, the job sounds great. Maybe I should apply. You're not the first to ask. There is a service I usually recommend. It's called The Clean

Connection. It's a service for housekeepers. Everyone is carefully screened, bonded, and they must have excellent references. Here's the number."

TJ quickly typed it into his database. He had begun to realize he could never have enough contacts. "Thanks Nancy, this is a huge help. Can you think of anything that I have forgotten?"

"I'll email you a utility list so you can go ahead and get all the services set up and ready to turn on. You'll need to know your power requirements and how much water pressure you'll need."

TJ made additional notes and replied, "Thank you very much. If you think of anything else please let me know."

TJ made a call to the architect firm and got a rough estimate of his utility requirements. He then made the calls to all the utilities, answered all their questions and set up accounts with the billing address to Sam's office. He liked not having to pay bills, although he still kept all their expenses and deposits in Quicken® for Windows on his iMac®. He ran the software in a window created by VMware Fusion® that allowed him to run Microsoft® Windows software on an iMac® on better. He purchased Quicken for Mac and felt cheated, as it was worst written software he had ever experienced. Thankfully, the windows version ran just fine.

Bob and Sue returned after finding a furnished apartment just a few miles away that was open and could be rented for two months as requested. They paid a deposit and two months rent, and gave TJ the paperwork. Sue took pictures of the apartment, so she used her Bluetooth technology to bring them up on TJ's iMac®. In seconds they were all looking at a street view, and inside each room.

TJ grinned, "This is perfect. Excellent job. Are you hungry? I'm starved. How about Chinese?" TJ made the phone order, and then gave Bob the cash. They left to go get it.

TJ emailed John the pictures of the apartment, the address, and asked if this was okay. He also asked what his status was with a cell phone service. John quickly emailed back that the apartment was perfect, and his service was the same as is. TJ asked if he was at home or work? He was at work. He asked if he could call him there, and John said yes.

"John Bunting, please." TJ only had to wait a minute, as he left the workstation where he had gotten the email, and begun walking towards his desk. "Hey, John. How are you?"

"My goodness you are fast."

"I expect you to do the same when you're onboard. Listen, I want to buy another iPhone® for my new office manager. His name is John Bunting. Can you handle that on the phone for me?"

John laughed, "Yes sir, I can."

"Excellent. I'll give you my credit card information for the purchase. I need for you to create a conference call between you, our cell carrier, and myself so I can arrange to pay for your new service and cancel your old one.

Put me on hold and arrange the conference call, and get your tech guy to set up your phone."

"Yes sir," replied John.

TJ was grinning while he waited. He liked treating employees well, and he liked showing them what he expected. After a few minutes, John came back on the line.

"TJ, I have the purchase approved, and my tech guy is activating the phone. Our carrier is on the phone with us. Ma'am?"

"This is Jenifer Anderson. Whom am I speaking with?"

TJ had already pulled his account number. "Jenifer thank you for assistance. My name is TJ Johnson. My account number is 4318-2372-422. Can you pull up my records please? Very good. John is my new employee. I bought another iPhone® for him. I need for you to cancel his current account with his old phone, and create a new account, and have the bills sent to my accountant. The address is on my records. Do you see it?"

"Yes, I do. So I am authorizing you to activate his new phone, and John here is authorizing you to cancel his old one. Is that right John?"

"Yes sir," grinned John.

"Now Jennifer this important. I'm expanding my office and will have a need for more phones soon. Will your company be able to handle these new purchases for me?"

"Yes, of course."

"Good, one last thing, put him on the unlimited calling plan with the web service for iPhone®." He paused for a second and said, "John? Is your tech guy ready for her to activate it?"

John smiled, "Yes, sir. He has just handed it to me?" John gave the lady the serial numbers and code numbers she needed to activate his phone. Soon she made a call to him and the phone was ready."

"Jennifer, you have been terrific. Thank you for helping us. Bye." TJ waited to hear her drop off. "John? Now you're set up. As a former Apple® salesman you probably know you need to charge up this phone before full use."

John laughed aloud, "Yes, sir, I do."

"How's the packing going?"

"I'll be done tonight. This is my last day at the store. They agreed to only a few days notice. I told them you were a big Apple® user, etc. I will be driving soon."

"Do you get paid commission?"

"Yes."

"Okay, I need to make a few more purchases. You'll need a Mac Pro® for your desk to handle our business and work on our websites. Get it loaded with plenty of ram. Storage doesn't have to be big, maybe five hundred gigs, because you'll be on our network. You'll also need an iMac® for a temporary workstation in my office, and you'll need a new laptop. I use the MacBook Pro® loaded. Will that work for you?"

"Yes, sir. I have an old Mac® laptop."

"Add all the software you need for designing websites, and Office for Mac, as I used Word and Excel extensively. Also, go ahead and order copies of VMware Fusion® to run Windows software as well for all three machines. Charge it to my credit card that I used for the phone. If you need a signature, fax me something to sign. Why don't you have the iMacs® shipped here? Do you want to play with the laptop on your trip across the country?" John said yes. "Oh yeah, you won't be able to get this in your store, but go to Best Buy, and get a copy of TravRoute Co-Pilot® for Laptop GPS software. It is what I use. You'll have to have Fusion running to use it. Put it on your card and I'll reimburse you for it. Oh, I'm sorry I didn't ask. Do you have a credit card for expenses and fuel?"

"Yes, I do."

"Very good. Just keep up with your expenses and I'll reimburse you for everything. Take your time coming across, so you're not totally exhausted when you get here, stay in safe hotels, and eat well. Is your car in good shape?"

"Yes, sir. I bought a used 2004 Toyota® Highlander just four months ago and it runs great. I put new tires on it when I bought it."

"I like the sound of that. Excellent choice. You have my cell number. If you incur any problem please don't hesitate to call me. I suspect you'll be here by the ninth or tenth, but take your time and enjoy yourself. I'm going to email you a map on how to get to your new house, and the cell number for my friends who found the apartment for you. They'll meet you there with the key. Please call them a few hours ahead of your arrival so they're not sitting in a movie when you get here. You'll like them. They are known as Bob and Sue. I will be out of town March eighth through the eleventh, but will be home before dark on the eleventh. Why don't we plan to meet at nine the next morning? Have a safe trip."

TJ had started another spreadsheet for office and electronic equipment for the new house. He now had a dozen spreadsheets to try and keep up with all he was doing. He realized it was an arduous, formidable challenge, but he was having fun. He also knew it was a short-term burdensome opportunity and would end after they moved in June first. He could live with that.

While Shane concentrated on playing Duke in the final seasonal game, TJ kept all that he was doing from his ears. Ahead of Shane were five possible weekends of hard work, work that could change his status, and his ranking, but hopefully not his playing for the Bobcats. Satisfied he had done all they could do, he enjoyed the takeout dinner Bob and Sue returned with. He brought them up to date on everything he had done. They told him they had decided to stay until after they got them moved. He thanked them many times over. They were also going to look after the dogs during his time away for the tournaments, and while TJ traveled for each of his book tours. He was so thankful to have them there, and they were thankful for the free parking spot and to be a part of this new exciting life TJ and Shane were experiencing. Bob also liked watching Shane's games on the big projection system in the great room.

That night, TJ shifted gears. He began his final editing of **The War Beyond – Part III**—a book that he was extremely proud of. It was different than anything he had written, and challenging to come up with all the scenarios, and yet find a way to tie it all together. He managed to tie in the previous sequels, and his book **The Blackfeet Boys**. He worked all day Saturday on it, and since they were playing Duke Sunday afternoon at four, and at home, he worked on it right up until time to run to the arena.

Shane spent a few hours with TJ on Saturday, but mostly he worked on his shots. He was mentally and physically geared up for the game, and he told his teammates a lost at home would nullify their victory at Duke. It would only feel like they were better than Duke Blue Devils, if they also won the home game.

The stands were full with no more seats anywhere. CBS carried the game, but Dick Vitale used his press status to get into the game. It was not one that he wanted to miss. He ate a late lunch with TJ in the pressroom. They talked very little about the game. TJ couldn't tell Dick about the Bobcat deal, so he refrained from saying anything about the land and house construction in Concord, but he did tell him about his trip to Country Coach® to purchase a new motorcoach, and that Brian Kenny was going to install a new remote studio in it.

"Now that is something I want to see. I have been telling my wife that she would love to travel in your motorcoach. She comes to some of the tournaments because it gives her time to shop, but my hectic winter travel schedule is too much for, and sometimes too much for me. Thankfully ESPN® takes excellent care of me, but I can't always sleep well in five different hotel rooms a week."

"Just imagine if you could sleep in your own bed onboard a nice motorcoach every night, and have your own refrigerator stocked with food you like."

"You mean travel like John Madden?"

"Well, as I understand it, he doesn't like to fly, and normally calls a game once or twice a week. You do several games a week and sometimes night after night, so that presents a logistic problem. Let's say you had two drivers, so they could drive non-stop while you slept in the back. That would solve everything on the eastern half of the country. If you're doing a game out west, you'd have to fly."

"I only do about six games a year out west, but I do over fifty games on the east coast, and most are in the south for the ACC, and or in the northeast. Hmm…you've given me plenty to think about. I can't wait to see your new coach. May I visit after the arrival?"

"Dick, you're like a wonderful uncle to Shane and me. You're welcome to visit anytime you like, but yes, of course, we want you to come see it when it arrives. We're bringing it home on the way back from our Alaska trip."

"What are doing with the old coach?"

"It's only two years old. Can you keep a secret? We're giving it to Shane's parents. They've always thought about an RV, and they just love ours."

"Now that is some gift. They're going to love it. Okay, we'd better get ready to watch one hell of a game. Old Duke is going to be after revenge. Can Shane and Taylor beat them?"

"I hope so. Thanks for eating with me."

"My pleasure as always."

The game began with a foul. Shane had been pushed hard as the tip was coming his way. Coach K began ranting at the referees, who charged their best forward with the foul, and gave the ball to Taylor. Shane threw it in to Jerry. He drove his man back and forth across the court, and eventually into a screen set up by Shane. Jerry took advantage and drove to the lane. Larry's man left him to stop Jerry, so he made a blind pass to Larry in the corner. Larry hit a beautiful swish shot for three points. Coach Timmons grinned at the beautiful execution, though he could still hear Duke's coach yelling to a referee about the foul.

Taylor went immediately into a full court press and would run it the entire game. On every possession, both teams operated at peak performance and adrenalin was at all time high. There were beautiful shots by both squads, but there were also mistakes. Missed passes, stepping out of bounds, traveling, and close in shots that should have gone in. Both coaches, of course, recognized their boys were under a tremendous amount of pressure, but they demanded excellence and expected to achieve it.

Shane hit six points early, but they began to double-team him when he had the ball. Taylor began faking it to him and feeding Larry or Tim. Jerry managed to drive in for a layup twice in the first half, bringing a volley of curse words from their opponents. Shane was fouled hard on a beautiful speedball pass from Jerry, as he went up to dunk it. He made the shot, though shoved very hard to the floor. TJ and the fans gasped at the loud pop as Shane's body hit the solid wooden floor.

376

To everyone amazement, Shane took only a second to get a good breath before standing up. He pumped his fist in triumph, and walked to the foul line to down another point. Taylor led at the half by just four points.

TJ felt too nervous to eat so he only got another bottle of water. The second half began just where it stopped, except Duke got a short run going, tied up the score, and went ahead by two. After the first television timeout, Taylor bounced back. Shane made a nice layup and a beautiful fifteen-foot jump shot just before the timeout. Taylor was back up by four.

Over the next twelve minutes, the lead changed eight times, but with four minutes to play, Taylor led by two. The fans never sat down during those final minutes. Coach Timmons looked at his huddled squad on the sidelines and smiled at them. "Boys, we're going to win this game. I feel it in my bones. I want to challenge you to an all out effort for a defensive stop. If we can keep Duke from scoring, the game is ours. If we also score some points, then we will win indeed. Don't waste possessions. Get the ball to Shane and if they double-team him, then Shane kick it out to the open man, but wait until you've eat up as much time as possible before actually shooting. We only want clean looks before shooting. We can do this. We can win. We're going to win!"

Shane came out of the huddle displaying a fierce game face, as if he was going to war. TJ had never seen this face before, although Shane was known to wear his version of a 'game face' during all games. TJ could feel the electricity between the players and the fans. It was an awesome exhilarating experience, and he felt lucky to be standing just twelve feet from the court watching it.

Shane was all over the throw in of the ball and he almost stole it. Jerry nearly stole it before they got it across the half court line. Taylor was toe to toe on each of their assignments. Duke could not get a decent shot off, and with two seconds left on the possession clock, they shot a long three but missed. Shane went up for the rebound and snagged the ball just a brief millisecond after it descended below the edge of the rim. He kept the ball high, as Duke tried to steal the ball from him even before his feet touched the ground, and one of them went too far and fouled him.

The whistle blew. It gave their big man four fouls. They were already in the bonus foul category, so Shane had two chances to score. All ten men slowly walked to the far end of the court, and Shane made his way to the foul line as he did every day—with great confidence. Just yesterday, he hit forty-eight out of fifty, but none of those shots counted. It was just he and the manager watching, but it gave him confidence nonetheless.

A few Duke fans hollered as the ball was given to Shane, but the rest of the fans remained calm while waiting and hoping. Shane hit the first shot with a perfect swish. A curse word was heard from the Duke bench. Shane shot the second one as pretty as the first. Swish! Taylor now led by four with three minutes forty seconds to play.

"Now we need a defensive stop!" yelled Coach Timmons from the sidelines.

Shane again jumped and waved his arms as Duke attempted an inbound pass. Shane had been watching every inbound play, and had yet to find a pattern. Perhaps a hunch, better yet a guess, he made a split second decision, and leaped slightly to his right, but with his hand outstretched as far as he could. He caught the ball with just the tip of one finger, but it was enough to deflect it right into a shocked Larry's hands. Shane ran towards the goal, and Larry threw him the ball to the right side of the goal. Duke's inbound player ran after Shane as fast he could. Shane caught the pass and went up with the Duke player in flight. Shane dunked it as the Duke player's forward momentum could not be stopped, and he slammed into Shane knocking him to the floor.

Shane leaped up quickly, but not to fight, as fans might have suspected, but rather tremendously excited he had just scored two more points and gained a foul opportunity. Unfortunately for Duke, it was the fifth foul for their big man, and he was out of the game. Shane hit the foul shot—his twelfth straight for the game. They led by seven.

It would be written in the history books that the mighty Taylor defense completely shut down the impressive Duke offense by not allowing a single point for those last threw minutes. Taylor won by ten in a game that usually measures a victory in single digits. In college basketball, the second meeting of Taylor and Duke each year brought the largest television audience in basketball's regular season games. The battle this year belonged to Taylor by winning both seasonal meetings with Duke.

TJ and Shane enjoyed a Sunday night victory wet party in their house, as they calmed down from the victory over Duke, and celebrated all that happen to them this year. Later in the week, Taylor would begin their quest for a second straight ACC Tournament championship. They already won two season titles in a row. Shane asked TJ to talk a little about his week and accomplishments on the house and motorcoach projects. Shane could see how excited he was. Later, they took turns being the top and slept in their spooning position breathing as one.

# THIRTY-TWO

Shane left for school just seconds before TJ left for Charlotte. TJ waved at Bob as he drove out of his garage. He had his notebooks, camera, and laptop all ready for his meeting with Jeff Gordon. He had read about Jeff's top five finish yesterday, and he just could not wait to meet him, but he drove the speed limit not wishing to take a chance on a ticket.

He arrived in Concord ahead of schedule so he drove by the land at the lake. The house was gone and the entire property had been graded, more dirt hauled in, packed, and the men were working on trenching for utilities. This time there would be one gate on the right side of the house as the main entrance, and the exit for the RV. Farther down the street pass the house and out of view of the house was a second electric gate. This would be entrance for the motorcoach allowing a long steady ride to the back of the house since the new RV port would not be parallel to the house but rather perpendicular. This would also provide a secret private entrance to the house should the press or fans become a problem, especially after Shane came out of the closet. The house would actually be in the shape of a giant H. The RV would exit almost straight to the street while an indention to the center of the property for the three cars and golf cart garage for the house.

The left side of the H would be a huge wet area in the rear, and a basketball half court to the front, a complete reverse from their home in Lindle. This made it possible to enjoy the wet area inside the house, and easily step out to the exterior pool that would be in the center of the property to the rear of the house. There would be a multi level decking for grilling and dining on the deck.

To the right of the RV port, would be two lots for guest RV units and car parking off to right side of the driveway for guests. The new staff office would be beneath the main office and below ground, and leaving a great view out the windows of the main office, and to the rear of the car garage.

TJ could close his eyes and envision it, but with tractors, trucks, and dirt everywhere, it would require his best imagination. He drove over to the new lot, and was pleased to see that the old house made it safely, and they were setting it on the new foundation that was hastily done last week. Checking his watch, he allowed his GPS software to take him to his meeting with Jeff Gordon.

To the rear of a nicely landscaped industrial park, he noted there were no signs indicating anything about Jeff. He found a building labeled simply J, and smiled, as there were only five buildings so the last should have been the E building. So there was a clue after all, he thought. He found twenty cars in the adjacent parking lot. He pulled in and checked his watch. He was five minutes early. He got out of the car to stretch, and just as he lifted his laptop briefcase out of the car, a red corvette pulled into the spot next to him. The top was down and he knew instantly it was Jeff.

Jeff got out of car and smiled, "You must be TJ. I'm pleased to meet you." He came around his car to shake TJ's hand.

"The pleasure is mine. I can't believe you agreed to see me. I just asked Bill a few questions, and he instantly suggested I see you."

"As I understand it, you're working with a basketball superstar that is moving to our area, and you want to learn about management, publicity, and especially about the Jeff Gordon Foundation."

"That's it."

" Do I know this basketball player?"

"I hope so."

"Are you going to tell me who it is, or am I suppose to guess?"

TJ realized it wouldn't be fair to ask for Jeff's help and not trust him at the same time. "Well, we have a problem. He is a major college basketball player that wants to play for the Bobcats, and he is somehow confident that he will get his wish, and thus we are building a new house with a small office and an RV port, but we don't have the training for all the stuff you mention."

"RV port home?"

"Yes, we have a forty-two foot motorcoach, and just ordered a new custom built Prevost®. We like parking it at the property, so we can easily load up and go, to get away from it all. Can I level with you?" Jeff nodded affirmatively. "The basketball player has to remain anonymous to maintain both his NCAA status, and to keep other pro teams from preventing his hope of playing for the Bobcats."

"I see, they would either want him, or try to prevent a good team from getting him."

"That's right. But Bill said I could tell you, if you promised not to reveal it until after the NBA draft."

Jeff laughed, "You have my word. I'm a big a Bobcat fan, but a bigger college basketball fan. I suspect he is from one of the schools in North Carolina. I hope it is Shane Bradley, as he would pack out the stands in the Bobcat arena."

TJ didn't say a word, but his face said it all. Jeff laughed, "TJ, let me give you some advice—never play poker with anyone, especially me. I see by your face my first guess was correct."

TJ said nothing but smiled slightly.

Jeff laughed, "Okay, you didn't tell me, and I won't tell a soul, but now I understand why you knew Bill, and he sent you to me. Congratulations and I hope I get to meet him someday. So let's get started. You're going to need a business side of your work and a charity side. I put both in the same building. I own this industrial center. In the beginning, I had to work hard at the business side of the sport. Most race fans don't know that Dale Earnhardt Senior and I were friends, and business partners. After a few years, more offers came to me than I could handle, and thankfully it remains that way. This allowed me to work on the Jeff Gordon Foundation. We have raised and donated over half billion dollars in the past five years. Come on, I'll show you around.

"I'm going to introduce several people to you, and advise them that you can call on them anytime you wish more help for your questions."

They stepped into his building and into a nice lobby with a receptionist behind a beautiful oak counter. "Libby, this is TJ Johnson. He has clearance from now on to meet with my staff."

He took him through a set of big wooden doors. "My office is at the end of the hall. To the left are several large office areas. At the back is the mail center, and on the right at the back is the project center where I usually sign thousands of items for the fans. Down this hall to the right are all the people who help me with my career."

They went in the first office, met a secretary, and went it to see a man just hanging up his phone. "TJ, this is Bill Smith. He is my publicist, and handles anything to do with press releases, interviews, and requests for media for me, etc. and is in the field with me at the race track and other big events." Jeff introduced TJ and Bill gave him one of his cards and offered to help any way he could.

Down the hall they went to the next office. "This is our scheduling center, which is a nightmare. Sponsors want me on their calendars, my car owner Rick Hendricks and his staff want on theirs, and so does my wife. On the wall were large LCD monitors with the months of the year in sequence starting with the current month. These ladies take the requests from my publicist and my manager, along with sponsor and owner requests, and somehow make it all work. This is Melinda. Call if you have question. They use software to make it happen. It downloads to my PDA so I can keep up."

In the next office, TJ met an older man with no hair, a big smile, and a huge grip. He shook TJ's hand vigorously as they were introduced, "This is Larry Cortez. He is my business manager. He and I are always working on investments and managing money. He overseas my accountant." TJ received another business card before he left.

In the next office he met Tim Alderman. Jeff explained, "Tim handles all my engagements, contract negotiations, and all the office department managers as well. He keeps my career on track, and I consider him my right hand man, which is why he overseas the office as well. He is also on the board of the Jeff Gordon Foundation." TJ shook hands and received another card.

They went in the last door and Jeff said, "And this is my office. I don't really spend a lot of time here, but I need a place to meet folks, and meet with my staff. You have my permission and approval to call on all these folks for advice. Once he starts playing for the Bobcats, your home office won't be large enough and besides, it is good to have most of your business life somewhere away from your home. Have you found a home yet?"

TJ blushed, "Yes, they started construction last Friday. It's just down the street from you on Marian Way. Number one twenty."

Jeff thought for a second, "You bought the Simpson place? But you said you're building?"

"Yes, I bought her house and moved it to a lot on Hilliard Avenue. They are setting it up now. I will sell it once the landscaping is done."

"Now that was clever. So you're building a new house on the land."

"Yes, once I sell her house on the new lot, I will have obtained the ten acres at the lake for about a hundred thousand."

Jeff laughed, "I think you need to go into real estate investments."

"Thank you, but I do have a quick question. The dock is old. I need someone to design and build a good dock. Any suggestions who to call on?"

Jeff picked up the phone and called his secretary. "Judy, what is Larry Mahar's number?" TJ wrote it down as Jeff related it. "He builds the best docks on the lake. He built mine. I'll show it to you when we're done. Let's finish the tour."

They walked to the back of the building and into the project center. There were twenty tables lined up with thousands of miniature Jeff Gordon cars. Deep shelves lined the entire room, filled with Jeff Gordon hats, shirts, jackets, and fifty other items sold online, and in the tractor-trailer souvenir rigs at the tracks.

"I have a warehouse where we buy in bulk, and ship it to the trucks in the field and here as needed." He showed TJ the computers and printers that produced orders and shipping labels, so the items could be instantly shipped. They went to their left into a larger mailing area with big postal machines. They crossed a hall and entered a steel door.

"Now we're in the Jeff Gordon Foundation section. The back is similar in that there is a big mail room, as we have learned that a signed product brings in big donations on our website." They entered a large office with six people working on Mac Pro® computers and screens. "These boys handle our websites both for business and the foundation. It was easier to put it all in one place. This is Mark Johnson, and he is head of the department." Mark shook hands and Jeff got his card for TJ.

There was another project room for the items on sale for the charity, and a mailing center. There was a big conference room for his board of directors to meet in, and offices for about a dozen folks. "These folks handle all the requests from our foundation. They do a ton of research to make sure the dollars we spend are going to help a child or victim in some way, and not to line the pockets of a scam artist. It takes a lot of work. Daily we receive hundreds of requests." They walked up the hall and into a nice office. This is Sally Robertson. She handles the Foundation's investments and works in harmony with Larry Cortez. My goal is to raise money and invest it, so that even after I retire, we're still able to provide funds for our charities from now on. The last office is Jimmy Young. He is the director of my foundation."

TJ shook hands, picked up another business card, and then they made their way out the front of the building. "Any questions? I bet you have a thousand."

"Well, I won't trouble you with my questions, but I will use the contacts you just provided me. I know they will be invaluable. I do have one question. Can you give me a ball park figure on what it cost to set up your offices, staff, and systems, and the annual dollars to keep it running?"

"My business side pays for all the salaries including the non-profit side, as that is a business deduction for us, and it allows the funds raised to go to the charities. We also cover the mailing, telephone, and computer expenses for the same reason. I own the buildings as an investment, but if I were renting them they would run about four thousand a month. My staff is about seventy-five thousand a month, and our utilities are about five thousand a month, plus insurance and stuff. I included a big postage and shipping budget in that last figure."

"Excellent. That is a huge help."

"Let's take my car to the house, as I have to come back here in a little while for a meeting so I can bring you back." After TJ sat in the Corvette, he asked, "Jeff, the race track set up allows you a big opportunity for marketing. I bet you sell a ton at each race."

"You're right. I have an agreement with Hendricks so they get a cut, but they maintain the trucks and hire the driver crews. I pay for the staff running the booth."

"Can you envision how we could do something like that for the NBA?"

"No, I can't, but I can think about it, and I know who to call. You can produce products that they sell in the Bobcat arena and statewide stores, but I imagine you will have to sell more online. That's too bad you can't set up rigs in parking lots. You might look into it."

"Is there anything you suggest we should fight for in our contract when the time comes?"

"Now that is a good question. I would say you should fight for your free time. I fought for the right to fly my own jet to events instead of the team plane. This allows me to leave later, get back faster, and I can take family and friends with me for more time together. I was given good advice early on, and fought for how many personal appearances I do for each sponsor. If they have something come up where they need me a few more times, then they smartly donate heavily to my foundation. I also got my sponsors involved in my foundation, and the key sponsors are on my foundation board. It keeps them associated, and they have been a huge help with tie-ins. That's when I promote their products, and they have a small things about the foundation on their product with the website. Yeah, fight for your time."

They drove to Jeff's house. After he went through the gate he drove down a side road right to the lake. They walked out to the dock. "I had this built a few years ago. The wood is not really wood at all. I think it is hardy plank or something like that. Larry Mahar will know. It is a recycled product, so it is good for our environment. It won't rust, crack, split, peel, and never needs painting or staining. It will always be this color." They walked along the shore dock, down a ramp to this boathouse. Jeff had a few Seadoos, a nice boat, and above was the sun deck with a screened in porch and swings, sink, grill, and music. It was very nice."

"Oh my. This is awesome. I had a boathouse on Lake James for several years, but this is way better. Thank you."

They walked back to the car, but Jeff turned left and drove down to the new house site and stopped, "Well, I just can't get over the deal you put together to get that property. It has an awesome view of the cove, and you got it so cheap. I'm very impressed. Let's go see where the house went. I can't believe they could move it."

TJ showed him where to turn to get to Hilliard Avenue. George now had the house in place, and they were removing boards and jacking it down. Jeff laughed, "That is amazing. You should get your price for it here."

"I hope so. I'm going to landscape it really nice. My crews will be here tomorrow to start. It's already on the market."

They drove back to the office. TJ got out and shook Jeff's hand again, "I am so grateful for the tour, your advice today, and the privilege for calling your staff for answers. We owe you."

"I already have box seats for the Bobcat games, but do you think Shane would help us with some of our charity work?"

"He would be most pleased to do so."

"Excellent. Have a safe trip home, and I'll look forward to seeing you again."

TJ drove straight to Lindle and to the architect's office eating a burger on the run. His head was still spinning with ideas after the tour and time with Gordon. He had a lot more plans and decisions to make, and for now, he would have to make them on his own, as Shane continued preparing for the ACC tournament.

TJ sat in the conference room for the architect as they dazzled him with their plans and sketches. He made some minor changes, explaining some of the technical things they were doing, but overall, it was a beautiful house, RV port, office, and boathouse. They quickly made revisions and their computers soon spit out several sets of office plans. TJ thanked them repeatedly before leaving.

He drove to the builder's office and set down with the owners. Henry just arrived from Concord and went over the plans with TJ. They started with a site plan. He pointed out the gates, the utilities, and the road to the boathouse, and conduit needed to bring water, electrical, telephone, and Ethernet down there. He pointed out the security areas alone the fence line, and then he showed them where the dog pen would be, and how the parking lot would work with the extra spaces for two RV units as well as parking for employees and guests. He explained the RV building was similar to the last one they had done, and the main floor. The second floor in the wing to the left of center would be for houseguests with bathrooms in each of the four suites. To the right would be the staff area. There would be big door separating the guest wing from the staff area as well as the entry staircase. The rooms would have a queen size bed, desk, sitting couch, and television on the wall, computer connection, and a phone. There would be a big laundry on that floor, a room with a kitchen and dining area, a den for watching television or reading, and storage room for supplies, and cleaning carts.

Downstairs the master bedroom would have a bigger walk-in closet, but the bedroom and bath were about the same. There would be a private entrance to the wet area. The second floor guests could walk to the wet area via an end of the hall stairs, but the door had an electrical door lock controlled from the master bedroom. The personal office was a little bigger with a new desk set up at the end of TJ's section for John to work off, but he would also have a desk in the main office. They now had a dining room on the front side next to the main office separated by a stairwell, but a large kitchen and breakfast room with a great view of the lake out the back of the house. The great room was bigger with a center fireplace and windows with a view of the lake. They would have electric blinds to darken the room for the projector system.

The foyer was larger on the front of the house to welcome guests, along with a fancy walkway and car circle around the fountain, so their guests could park, and easily walk in the front door, and continue around the fountain to exit the same gate they came in.

In a very unusual strategy, TJ was willing to pay the builder for all the work they had already done, if their bid was higher than he thought it should be, and he would hire someone else to finish it. However, if they gave him a great bid, then he would give them half the money up front. The next day they called with what TJ thought was an on target price. TJ signed the faxed deal and asked Sam to wire the money. There was a penalty clause if the house wasn't ready to move in by June first. The construction team had no intention of losing out on any money.

TJ spent Tuesday going over **The War Beyond** book very carefully until finally he sent it to the gay publisher. Next week, they would send him an electronic galley. He signed off on the cover last week. Meanwhile, he had just received the last edited chapters of **Twice Is Nice** from Walter and Dick. He made the corrections and sent them to Janet.

He had begun to feel like he was the top of a mountain, and slowly rolling downhill like a big snowball. He fielded calls from everyone involved in the housing project. He obtained all the permits without a hitch, because both his architect and builder were well respected in the industry. He did several remote interviews for the basketball book. Shane also recorded a number of interviews as the first round of the ACC tournament approached. They flew to Atlanta for the tournament on Wednesday. Taylor's first game was not until seven on Thursday night, but they would practice in the arena on Wednesday, and an early practice at a local high school gym on Thursday morning.

TJ set up a command center in his hotel room two floors up from Shane's. He had a beautiful view of Atlanta, but he ate most of his meals in the room. He worked on the basketball book, as well as some of the promotional material for it. He studied his upcoming tour for both books looking for anything he might have forgotten.

He tried to keep everything in digital format, when it came to the two building projects, but he did bring a rolled up tube of the house plans. Henry called about a proposal for the front office, and suggested running the doggie door out the left side of the wet area where they could fence in the pen and angle the slab downhill to help wash it off. The roof water would hit it from the right side of the pen, and should splash hard enough to wash it off. TJ liked the idea and trusted Henry's judgment.

Today he was studying Mahar's revised plans for the dock and boathouse. He had no suggestions other than explaining the electronics he wanted, and his desire for the sink and barbecue, so they cook and wash on the deck. He also put in a rinse shower to wash sweat or the lake water off. They would install a small instant hot water tankless system to provide hot water for the sink, and especially the outdoor shower. Larry began construction and would have it ready by May first, as he was going on a mission trip later that month. TJ and Shane would make a donation to his church's project.

TJ received email pictures of his new Prevost® shell. It looked awful. It was like a gutted fish with all the sides removed so they could install flooring and build upwards. Meanwhile, the bays were being modified for their gear. Wiring trunks had been laid before the installation of the flooring. TJ had seen a team of workers making the wiring trunks on a convention tour at the plant he attended two years before. It was a lot like the wiring done for an airplane. The water and sewer tanks were installed, and the generator. The utility bay was being built to TJ's specifications. They told him the big work would seem to go fast, but everything would get slower as they began tying it in, and working on all the finishing touches. It would take two weeks to test the coach from top to bottom mechanically, electronically, and physically. He wished he could be there to see it. He looked at his calendar, and wondered if he should take the Learjet to Oregon, but decided it was too soon.

Shane received free time after a study hall that night and came up to see him. He was excited and nervous about the start of the tournament. Playing other ACC teams during the season was extremely difficult, but playing three straight games, day after day, would really grind them down. He felt his team had the most experience, and they were a tight unit.

Shane's parents arrived early Thursday morning. TJ ate lunch with them, and afterwards they followed him back to the room to see the details on the house and motorcoach. They were overwhelmed with how much he was handling for the he and Shane. He had told them at dinner about what he learned from Jeff Gordon. Al told him about his final three choices for a sports agent. He said they could meet with them right after the end of the National Championship. TJ suggested they also ask Coach Timmons, Walter, and the athletic lawyer for their picks. Al agreed, and said he would email his files on the sports agents, but not to let Shane see them, so he can honestly say he has not seen or researched any agents, should it come up. TJ remained careful not to say what they were going to do with the Lindle house or his old motorcoach. Al and Barbara assumed they would sell the house, and trade in the RV.

The first game put them against Clemson, and boy did they hate that slot, but at least they were not playing them at Clemson. However, Atlanta is only a two-hour drive from Clemson, so he saw plenty of orange Tiger shirts in the arena. Thankfully, the Taylor fans more than doubled the Clemson fans.

TJ arrived two hours before the game, ate dinner in the pressroom, read the media information that was far more extensive than any had seen this year, and watched Shane warm-up. He then updated his notes in the laptop, locked it up, and made his way to the arena with his usual water bottle.

The Taylor team arrived fired up and ready to win this tournament and move on to the NCAA. Their goal was to play so well, they would once again garner the top seed. Shane missed a short one from six feet out, and TJ knew it was just a case of being hyper and excited. It was two minutes before he had a chance to make up for it, and dunked a big one, picking up a foul. Clemson was being too aggressive, and not used to the speed, so they made mistakes, and had six fouls in seven minutes. Soon their foul numbers put Taylor into the bonus shooting, and Shane made eight foul shots, and went to score six more from the floor in the first half. Taylor led by twelve at the half.

Clemson knew it was win or go home, so they stepped up the pressure in spite of the foul trouble, and went farther in the hole. Two players fouled out with eight minutes to go. Taylor went on to win by twenty, leaving the sea of orange wet with tears.

Shane ate a late dinner with the team, made it up to see TJ for just thirty minutes, called his parents, and went to bed. They had a shoot around and practice at the high school gym the next morning, and would play NC

State Saturday night. TJ ate lunch the next day with Gary and gang, and they experienced lot of laughs as TJ told some war stories about Gary during his early college years. They stayed at the restaurant for two hours, tipped well, and had the best time. TJ was so relaxed after visiting with his old friends. They have such good memories. He begged them to come visit them this summer when he got back from the tours and vacation. He didn't tell them about the new house in Concord.

Shane was shocked they were playing NC State in the Saturday game, as he just didn't think they were as good as Maryland or Florida State, But State beat Maryland in the first round and came fired up to win again.

Shane took the game in stride, staying cool. He stole a pass on the second possession and ran fast down the court for a dunk. Three minutes later, Taylor managed a good run and led by fourteen points. State fought back for the next five minutes getting within six, but that was as close as they would get. Taylor went on another run of sixteen points, and in the second half started yet another run for fourteen points. Shane put in twenty-six and Taylor won by twenty-six points.

In the other game, Miami beat Duke, and would play Taylor in Sunday's final for the ACC title.

Shane arrived in TJ's room after his late night meal, but could only stay a while as they had an earlier curfew since the championship game was a one tomorrow with game meal at eight o'clock. Most of them would eat and go back to sleep. A team meeting was scheduled for ten.

TJ slept in as long as he could, packed and took his stuff down to the team bus at eleven. He was going to fly back with the team immediately after the game. He ate lunch or brunch in his case as he had skipped breakfast, but felt fresh and ready for the game. He typed in some notes he made on the media material, locked his laptop in the locker, and made his way down to his seat to watch Shane warm-up. He spotted Al and Barbara and went over to talk to them. On the way back, he saw Shane in the tunnel, gave him the five and one signal, and Shane pulled his earlobe in response. TJ made it around the court and up to his seat where he found Gary and gang waiting for him. They all were nervous about the game, feeling Miami would be tough after beating Duke.

But everyone was wrong, as it appeared Miami used all their energy in beating Duke, and came in sloppy, with their energy spent in the first half. Shane scored a big eighteen points, as the big man guarding him was exhausted. The second half began with the Miami team showing some pride, but eight minutes into the half Taylor University began a powerful run that put Miami away for good. All of the bench players played in the ninety-four to sixty-eight win.

The team celebrated, but not too much, as their goal remained the National Championship, and now felt with their season title, and league championship, they deserved the number one seed.

On the flight home, the coach announced the NCAA selection committee picked Taylor as the number one seed, and would play in the Friday night game in Raleigh. The team clapped and cheered at the news of this additional accomplishment.

Shane came over for a long while after they landed. They ate dinner together, while he complained they hardly had any time together. TJ reminded him that the ACC tournament marathon of three straight games was over, and they would have more time during the NCAA tournaments, as they only had two games and a day off in between. They watched a movie for a while, did the wet area, made love, and Shane went back to school.

# THIRTY-THREE

After landing on Sunday, TJ called John Bunting on his new cell phone. John arrived at the apartment and remained a happy camper. He unpacked most of his stuff, bought groceries, and set up his house. TJ made notes over the weekend of all the things he wanted to tell John during his training and teaching, and then they would start working on projects. John agreed to meet him at eight o'clock at the house for breakfast.

Recovering from the tension of the weekend ACC tournament, TJ struggled out of bed early, showered and dressed casual business to make a good first impression. He decided to make omelets with ham and cheese, and a plate of fresh fruit. He buzzed John in the gate and walked out to meet him. He showed him where to park his car, so that he wouldn't block the garage, or Bob and Sue. He pointed to the trash dumpster for boxes and the location of the mailbox in the right gatepost structure.

He told him about the dogs, as they came through the garage and into the house. Thankfully, John was a dog lover, so he knelt down and gave the dogs a good rub, and laughed when Beeper yawned. He wasn't a coffee drinker, but liked to sip hot tea in the mornings. TJ asked him what brand and put it on the grocery list he started in the kitchen.

They ate and chatted about his trip across the country and about his apartment. After they cleared the table, TJ took his usual diet Mountain Dew® cup to the office while John decided on a water bottle. He decided to give him the fifty-cent tour, so they went through the house, the wet area, and into the RV building, and even onto the coach. He showed him where the books and supplies were stored. They made their way back through the kitchen to the office. He brought his laptop with him in his briefcase.

TJ had purchased another desk chair for John and set up a work area to the left of his sitting area, and just before the remote studio set up at the end of long horseshoe area for Tom's part of the office. He showed him the network switch area, along with the Apple® Xsan server and RAID hard drives, the digital printer, fax machine, and scanner, and explained the remote studio setup. The new iMac® and Mac Pro® were sitting on the floor. TJ said when he got through orientation John could set up the Mac Pro® next to him, and iMac® on the countertop. John had been successful in setting up VMware Fusion® for his laptop and used the GPS software correctly. TJ was impressed. He wanted him to set up the Macs the same way, and then to work on their sync program so that all their computers would have the same business data available.

He then talked about using the phone. He explained the first four lines were for business, and the last two for personal. He showed him the fax machine and the number for it. He showed him how to buzz someone in the gate, and maintaining their security. If he didn't know who it was, or what it was, ask questions. TJ rattled off a list of names cleared for entry. John wisely typed them in a spreadsheet for printing out later for the housekeeper or other staff.

He talked about ethics, comments, and being careful not to repeat what he and Shane said in private. He reminded him that no one could know about the new house in Concord, and certainly to avoid any discussion of Shane until the NBA draft was over. It was the first time John heard who his other boss was. He was impressed and excited. TJ explained the next few weeks would be absolute chaos with three tournaments, a new house and office, and a new motorcoach, all under construction, plus five weeks of tour, vacation, and the big move in. They decided on a file system, and created a new employee file and applicant section by job. TJ already received several resumes for the housekeeper and chef jobs. He wanted to do interviews in Concord in two weeks. John would be in charge of all employees, their duties, and assignments. He gave him signed copies of the contract and confidentiality paperwork. He also gave him a new credit card for company purchases, and a fuel credit card, as TJ would need for John to use his car for some errands.

TJ decided they would need a company name but coming up with a good name proved difficult. They decided they would ask Shane for his thoughts. TJ wanted John to design some business cards using his company TJI logo, and for now they would use that name to answer the phone, as well as hand out to contacts and business associates as needed. "We can't sound like we're managing Shane at all, as he is not allowed to have an agent or manager until after the tournament is over. So we'll answer TJI," he said. He was told that if someone asked for Shane, he should immediately ask who is calling, and if they weren't on another list TJ dictated to John, then he was to say I'm sorry, there's no one where by that name. People on the list were like Al and Barbara, Dick, and Gary.

He began to talk about the need to expand his gay book website changing it from personal sales to supporting the bookstores around the country. He did want John to design a few items they could sell on his website for charities relating to gay people. He suggested they start with bookmarks using the cover of the book, and on the back listing his other books. TJ hoped to one day begin signing other gay writers; publish their works under his publishing company, and perhaps in harmony or association with his gay publisher in New York. He then wanted to work on a series of postcards promoting his book that could be sold and given away at book signings. He hoped to eventually work on a series of gay greeting cards using witty sayings and phrases.

TJ explained that all the bills were audited and paid by Sam. John should send all receipts to Sam after first getting TJ's approval by phone, email or in person. He would also be authorized for certain expenses maintaining the house, food, and supplies, as well as the office supplies, and repairs less than five hundred dollars. John would be in charge of the computers and network equipment, using Buddy as his contact to go to when he needed something done beyond his training and talents. TJ laughed and said, for TJ, it meant most everything to do with the new server and raid system.

Finally TJ said, "As a manger, right hand man, and all the other hats you wear, there will be a whole lot more we both have to do to get the job done, and take care of our customers and staff, so please expect more. We'll hire more help, and we'll always have the latest greatest whatever to make our jobs more efficient." TJ paused and took a breath, "Okay, you will be required to travel so how is your wardrobe? You'll need a sports jacket or two, good dress shirts, and ties, and cool comfortable walking shoes. You're starting in the warm season, so we won't worry about winter clothes yet. When we finish today, we'll take you shopping and get some new duds for you. Do you have any questions?"

John laughed, "I am very impressed, excited, and can't wait to get started. I do have one important question. Where's the bathroom? I have to pee bad."

TJ laughed and sent him down the hall. When he got back, "You never have to ask to do that again. If you're hungry you eat, and if thirsty you drink. Let's look at the schedule on my iMac® and then I'll leave you alone so you can get your Mac Pro® working, and your MacBook® in sync with my data and calendar. I fly out Wednesday after lunch to Atlanta. Shane is flying out just after his classes. As you can see I have the hotel name, address, and phone on the list. You can generally catch me on the cell, but just in case we have a bad phone signal, or if you have to overnight something to me, you have the shipping info. We have a shipping account with FedEx under business contacts. You'll find some shipping supplies in that right hand lower cabinet, but order more online.

"I'll be delegating a lot of my busy work to you, so I can take on some new stuff, and when we hire a secretary and other workers, you'll delegate to them."

"When will we do that?"

"We're moving June first to our new house and office in Concord. Then we'll have room for an office wing for more desks for your new folks, and a nice new office just for you and some of the electronic gear. We'll start promoting and getting resumes mid April. I'll also be looking for a new manager for our office complex to run our business management, our foundation, and promotions for both. I'll hire top professionals to manage those divisions, but you'll be involved. Jeff Gordon is helping me with that side of the business because I know very little about it."

John laughed, "The Jeff Gordon. You talked to Jeff."

TJ grinned, "He goes by Jeff, but you can call him 'The' Jeff Gordon if you want, and yes, he took me for a ride in his Corvette. Our new house in

392

Concord is just down the street from him. He helped me find my dock builder, too. I'll introduce you."

John nearly fainted. TJ laughed again. "Okay, go to work on synching the Macs before you have a heart attack. I have calls to make.

TJ spun his chair around, put on his wireless headset, "Whoops, I just forgot something. Call Libertel. They are in the database. Tell Marsha we need another headset like mine for you. Have her ship it overnight. I started a list of electronic gear we need for the new house. Find it and add six more headsets for the new office wing."

They only stopped for lunch, which TJ made, and continued hustling afterwards. John got the all three Macs running on the network and synched. He answered the phone without prompting when TJ was on the other line, and sounded very professional. He pulled up TJ's website and made notes and suggestions, and found the files for TJ's book covers and began working on promotion materials for the new release of **The War Beyond – Part III**.

TJ spent most of the day working on the construction projects. He talked with Henry twice about a change Henry wanted to do the house. TJ had a little trouble understanding his idea, so Henry went to his laptop, sketched it out, and emailed it to him. TJ finally understood and gave his okay for the change. He also suggested they build an island in the kitchen with an additional sinks for prepping their food, and building an under counter wine refrigerated cooler. TJ laughed and told him they have never had a drop of wine in the current house, so he asked for two units one for wine, and a second one to stock two liter diet Mountain Dew® bottles. Henry grinned and said no problem.

TJ then called Al Bradley and told him what he had learned from Jeff Gordon. He said all this in front of John, as he wanted him to be aware so he could help, too. TJ hoped Al would agree, as he wanted to emulate Gordon's setup. He knew Shane would. The boys talked many times about using both his fame, and TJ's books to help as many people as they could. They knew there were many projects they could assist, but felt that many gay groups were often over looked. TJ and Shane decided the money from TJ's gay book promotions would go to all gay projects, but with Shane's promotions, it would split between gay and straight groups, hoping to secure as much support as possible.

Al and Barbara were going to meet them in Atlanta for the first round and assuming they won, the second game would be Sunday at two. TJ suggested they change their return ticket to fly out of Lindle, and fly home with him on the Learjet from Atlanta. Monday morning they would get up early and drive to Concord to see Gordon's operation, and the new house project. Al agreed.

TJ emailed Shane he was bringing his folks home Sunday with him. Shane was in the gym lifting weights.

TJ called Larry Cortez, Gordon's business manager, and held his breath, hoping he would he would take TJ's call.

"Hello?"

"Larry, this is TJ Johnson, I met you last Monday while taking the tour of your building with Jeff."

"Oh yes, TJ. I've been expecting your call."

TJ's face puzzled. "You have?"

"Yes, after you left, Jeff came in and he talked excitedly about you. Jeff said for me to expect your call because he was sure you were a guy that likes to get things done correctly, and that you were ready to move forward. So yes, I was expecting this call. So how can I help?"

"Jeff was right. We're moving to Lake Norman on June first, and I have no room here for a staff. Our new house will have room for about six employees, but obviously we hope to capitalize on my friend's fame and increase his investments and business tie-ins, but also create a foundation. Jeff gave me some ballpark figures office space. Jeff is a superstar, so I don't think we'll need quite as big an operation to start, but I hope to find a place where we can continue to expand, with hopes of becoming as big as yours. Where can I find a building that I might pay for small space for now, say half of your business side, and grow as mentioned. I also need your experience as to what I should budget to furnish the office, and set up the necessary equipment from networks to shipping."

Larry grinned, "Are you sitting down?"

"Yes, of course."

"To answer your first question about where you could find suitable office space—you already have."

"I beg your pardon," replied TJ confused.

Larry laughed aloud, "Jeff told me to lease the empty offices next to us to you for three months for free, and after that at twenty percent off market value."

"Oh my gosh. You're kidding. I am overwhelmed. That is so generous."

"Oh don't worry. He'll need your celebrity for a few charity events, but he'll also return the favor when your foundation gets going. It takes quite a bit of work to get a foundation up and running after you obtain your non-profit tax approval. You will want a board to give you clout, and because you want their help and commitment. So the next time you're down, I'll show your new office space to you. It already has suspended ceilings, lighting, and bathrooms, but you'll need to construct offices for your key staff. I suggest you put your managers in a real office, and the rest of your personnel in cubicles. They're easier to move around and expand. You'll need at least one conference room for meetings, and the mailing and shipping center.

"Draw up a floor plan similar to ours if you like, and I bet you end up using at least half of the space we do. We'll try to hold more office space for later, as he predicts you'll grow quickly. As to your budget, you could do it modestly for fifty thousand, and pretty snappy for seventy-five."

"Okay, that will work for us. How long would it take a remodeling crew to do the job?"

"You could push four weeks but eight would be better."

"I have a few associates I'd like to bring through on a faster tour than I had on Monday morning. Would that be possible?"

"Yes, of course."

"Go ahead and draw up the lease, and I'll pick it up Monday."

"I already have."

TJ laughed, "You guys are smart. Larry, I am the first to admit I don't have the experience to do all your staff is capable of doing."

Larry butted in, "Neither did Jeff, but he was smart to hire people that do. Listen, if there was ever a person that was able to delegate authority it is Jeff. He might have learned it from Rick Hendricks, but he is very good at hiring, and motivating his employees."

TJ asked, "Do you have a twin brother?"

Larry laughed, "Heavens no. My parents could barely handle me. Oh, wait a minute, I get it—you need a business manager with my skills."

"That's right. I actually need several people like your key people. I don't know where to start. I don't want to just throw money around. I want to find people that are going to work hard, stick it out, and grow with us. I'm not looking for yes men. I want them to speak their mind and share their ideas."

"I thought you might ask that. This is very smart of you. I'm putting together a folder of people that will do a great job and might be available. How soon do you need it?"

"Can I pick it up Monday as well?"

"Yes, we'll have it and some other things for you, too."

"How about the construction team? Who should I hire? My architect could draw it out for me, but my builder is too busy building the house."

"We used Spearson Construction. He is on our foundation board. I'll call and ask if he'll do it, and he'll be very fair. Once you have your plans, he'll give you a great quote."

"Excellent. Larry, thank you and thank Jeff for his generosity. You guys have been so kind to us. Thank you. I'll see you next week."

TJ turned to John and nearly shouted. "Oh my gosh. Everything is going to fall in place, if I don't go crazy in the process. Okay, John, get the trip to Charlotte on Monday on the schedule, and enter the data for Spearson Construction in the system. You're going to Charlotte with us. Shane won't be able to go, as that would let them know who were doing this for. Only Jeff knows it is Shane."

"Sure no problem. I have some things for you to look at it." He began showing some of his designs for the bookmarks and postcards. TJ made a few minor tweaks, but he loved them. He then showed him his rough suggestion for changing the website to promote the books. TJ liked those ideas, and gave him the info he needed to make and upload the changes. John was going to need more time to create some slide shows and something he called a book viewer. With most web sites you could read a chapter of a new book, but he proposed a trick he called stop and read. A new potential customer could look inside a book, and rapidly scroll pages like he was fanning a book, and stop three times and read the page he stopped on. TJ liked the idea, so John would work on it, along with a slide show and dissolves of his books titles. He asked TJ what he was working on so he could create a better Coming Soon section.

TJ told him to make PDF files of the bookmarks and postcards, so he could send them to his gay publisher. He wanted to make them a deal that if they would print the items for free, he would put both their website for orders and his website for personal promotion and the foundation on the promo products. He would then give them out at signings and online.

Five came soon enough. They were almost done when Shane came in the office. "Hey guys. How's it going?"

TJ grinned, and went over and hugged and kissed him. "Shane, this is John Bunting. My new right arm."

"I'm pleased to meet you John. Right arm? I hope you smell better than his right arm!"

They all laughed. Shane and John talked while TJ went to change clothes to go shopping. TJ came down the hall, "Shane have you eaten?"

"Yes, just did. We got out of practice a little early, so I ate and I'm heading to study at the library, but thought I would swing by and meet John. We're very happy to have you. I hope you can keep up with TJ."

"I hope so, too," began John, "but I am so thrilled to be here."

"We're going shopping to get him some traveling and work clothes. Why don't you come with us? We'll have some fun."

Shane laughed, "Thanks, but no, I don't think so. I'd better study. Practice was hard, and I'm tired, so I'll hit the books and crash."

"Are you sure? Okay, I'll walk you out. I'll be right back John." TJ walked him out to the garage. "So what do you think?"

"He seems all right. How'd he do today?"

"Great, and wait until you see the website suggestions he has, and the new promotion pieces he designed today. He's smart, and he can think on his own. He'll be a big help to me, so I can help the man I love most in the world."

"And who would that be?"

"Santa Claus, you idiot! Give me a kiss."

Shane didn't hesitate. He missed TJ, but he knew they just had to get through the tournament, and things would get easier, at least for him. TJ would need a second wind for the tour. They kissed passionately before Shane finally said, "I miss you so much. We have this big house to share together, and I'm stuck in the dorm. I want to curl up and sleep with you."

"We can sleep together in our dreams, but soon we'll be together all we want. I have so much to tell you, but after you win the championship, or I'm not going to tell you anything."

Shane sighed and smiled, "Go ahead and heap so more pressure on my shoulders."

TJ grinned, "Poor baby. Hang in there, and I'll let you be the top next time."

They both laughed. Shane kissed him again, and climbed in his Hummer® to head back to school. TJ waved goodbye, and watched him drive through the gate. He went back in and fed the dogs, so he and John could leave.

He was still amazed he was flying back to Atlanta on the Learjet on Wednesday afternoon for the first leg of the NCAA championship. Shane arrived at noon, ate a meal with team, attended the team meeting, then performed a fake public practice in the arena for media publicity purposes, and privately practiced at a high school gym. The arena was home to the Atlanta Hawks NBA team.

TJ spent the forty-eight hours with John by working hard in the office, and then driving him around the area, so he would know where the key things were. He suggested he open an account at Wachovia, as they had a branch near Lake Norman, so his banking would be easy. This morning he showed him the house plans, the new office wing, and the staff quarters. While he welcomed him to stay in the staff quarters, he thought as a single guy, he would probably want his own place for overnight company. John agreed, so TJ made a call to Nancy Green and told her about John, and explained John would be in the market for a condo or nice apartment not far from the new house. She promised to work on it and get back to him.

He left John a big to-do-list, and hopefully, plenty of time to work on the website. He would also handle the calls, mail, and anything else that came up. TJ set up his laptop, made his grocery run, and came back to the room. He had just fixed him something to drink when he heard his laptop beeping. He sat down realizing he had an iChat® request. He laughed when he recognized John's face. He accepted and instantly, he was looking and talking to John via a crystal clear image. That's a Mac® feature he had rarely used, and still it impressed him.

"Hey, boss. How was the trip?"

"Excellent. Clear skies. How's it going?"

"Very good. The publisher approved our latest revisions, so I guess it is a go for the bookmarks and postcards. They're interested in your greeting cards, so I guess we should do some mockups for them."

"Okay, I'll try and write something. Do you draw? We may need an artist."

"I know someone that does gay drawings and paintings."

"Can they design on a Mac®? We need to keep it digital if possible, so we can use in multi mediums."

"Yes, he does graphic work at a print shop during the day, and his art at night."

"Okay, let me work on the wording. Did you get the mail?"

"Yes, you got a box from the Over-the-Top Publishing. Shall I open it?"

"Yeah, go ahead." TJ heard the rustling and then a sigh.

He held it up so TJ could see, "It's a big plaque recognizing four million sales of your basketball book. Way to go! You know I was one of those four million."

"Thank you. I started to say hang it up, but we'd just have to pack it soon, so just leave it in the box, and mark it with a Sharpie® as to what it is and fragile. Also put office on the box so we'll know what room it should go to."

He read TJ some of the other mail. John said, "I'm sending you some files of the things I have done today. I also send you a secret link so you can see the new web pages I've completed, and waiting for your perusal before going online. That's about it."

"Very good. Don't forget to pick up your new clothes up from the dry cleaners. Put the bill on the credit card, or as I call it, Mr. Plastic. I'll talk to you soon."

TJ finished the rest of his email, and then yawned heavily as if letting the final steam out of a kettle. He sighed as he realized he had not been alone in a few days, nor was he running from one project to the next. He laid down for a nap, thought of nothing, and was out in seconds.

Shane showed off a bit in the public practice in the arena, followed by a real practice at the high school gym so they could works on plays and end of the game stuff, and followed by a study hall after lunch. He thought the team looked great and was ready to play, but they had entered the boredom zone of any tournament, which is the period where the players wait, wait, and wait some more, until finally the time to play arrives. In Shane's case, the tip off would be Friday at two o'clock and the first game of the day.

TJ worked all day on a new tournament chapter of **Twice Is Nice**, and spent time on the storyline **Forever Along, Again** that was scheduled to release after Thanksgiving. He had written several chapters of the book a few months ago when he had some free time, but for now, he had no creative free time. After a while, he decided to change directions and work on some greetings cards. He had thought it would be easy work, but now he had to say something clever and important in just ten or twenty words or less, instead of a whole paragraph.

He wrote lines like: "I like to wake up first in the morning, just to stare at your beautiful eye lashes, and the curve of your nose, before you have a chance to spoil the view with your sparkling smile."

TJ laughed at his pitiful work, trashed it and tried again: "The touch of your skin sets my heart on fire...every day...every time, and leaves me already longing for tomorrow."

He thought he might be able to fix that one. Next: "I thought nothing could make you more beautiful, until I saw the snowflakes in your hair. Now I'm checking the forecast, hoping for more snow tomorrow."

Ugh, he thought. Trash that one.

He wrote about fifty and kept about two. He wasn't always good with a serious phrase, preferring a bit of humor. So he tried funny: "I liked you better last night, but don't worry, I liked myself better at twenty-one."

"Every person must know his limitations. You should have told me I was too large for ..."

He caught himself grinning at that one but not acceptable. "After noting you left the top off the toothpaste, it gave me an idea for the next time you want oral sex."

Double ugh, thought TJ, this is difficult.

He sat there thinking hard when suddenly an idea came to him. He loaded **Part III** in his laptop, and scrolled through several chapters until he found a line from his story. He copied it to his card document. He kept looking, finding both serious and funny lines to embellish. He knew the phrases had a long way to go, but definitely using his books for the catalyst might be a great tie in, but he knew the project remained a work in progress.

Shane pounded on the door, and TJ greeted him with a big smile. Shane lifted him off his feet, while closing the door with an elbow, and bear hugging him all the way to the couch. They kissed passionately for a long while. When they finally came up for air, TJ said, "We're going to be late for dinner. Your folks and Gary's gang will be waiting."

Shane laughed, "Call them and tell them my dick's too hard for travel."

Without a moment of hesitation, TJ flipped open his cell phone, and hit the speed dial button for Shane. Shane tried to grab the phone, but TJ tried to roll away from him while Shane tried to get to TJ's phone to end the call. Suddenly, Shane's phone began ringing. He froze and almost reached for it, when TJ burst out laughing.

"You rascal. You dialed me, didn't you?"

TJ laughed again, and rolled away, so Shane fell on him and tried to tickle him, but it never worked on him, though Shane was extremely ticklish. They wrestled for a minute or two, and then began kissing again. After another few minutes, they reluctantly climbed off the bed, straighten their hair, and went down the back halls to the elevator. TJ had called a cab and it pulled up just in time for them.

They were eating at a big Italian place. Gary's gang arrived first, and already downed a few beers. Shane and TJ hugged his parents, and the hostess led them to the banquet room, where they set up several tables together. They talked and laughed, made their orders, and laughed some more, before feasting on their dinners. Shane was especially hungry after practice, studying, and waiting. He was ready for the game tomorrow. Gary secured great seats for both games and just prayed Taylor kept winning.

They didn't talk about the games next week, a bit afraid they would jinx the team's luck this weekend, so they shifted to how things were going in Asheville, and Gary again promised to come see the boys in Lindle soon. TJ told them about the big tours coming up, and said he was cleverly leaving town because Shane would be studying for his exams. "I hope I pass", Shane said with a grin, leaving his mother with her mouth open.

"You better pass young man, or I'll jerk a knot in your head, even if I have to rent a step ladder."

Everyone laughed at her, especially Shane. "I'll pass. I can't wait to get it over with, but I'm looking forward to graduating. Most folks believe jocks are stupid, that we all take basket weaving, and have no brains whatsoever."

TJ jumped in, "Oh Shane, they don't think you're stupid...they know you are!"

Shane elbowed him and they all laughed again. The biting banter continued throughout the meal, and TJ was thankful family and friends had come to join them. He knew Shane hid it well, but he was more nervous this year than last year. Last time, many folks thought they couldn't win it all, but now they expected them to win. The relief and comfort of their family and friends helped more than they knew.

TJ asked the cab driver to let them out a block short of the hotel, so he led Shane down the street to a creamery. "This will help you play better tomorrow."

Shane laughed, "I want something to make me horny tonight."

TJ suddenly stopped walking on the street, and let Shane go a step or two alone before he realized TJ stopped walking. He turned and looked at him. TJ began unbuttoning his shirt, his belt, and acted like he was going to strip.

Shane laughed, "What the hell are you doing?"

TJ said with a sly grin, "You said you wanted something to make you horny, so I'm doing the best I can!"

Shane grabbed his arm and pulled him along. "Ice cream first. Sex second."

400

"I think you have the order wrong, but if you insist, I'll take a banana split, and I want a big banana, if you know what I mean!"

They laughed as they went in the store. A few fans recognized Shane, he signed some napkins, and they made a hasty retreated to TJ's room with their ice cream. They made love until time for curfew. After their final kiss, Shane ran down the hall, and TJ fell back on the bed deliriously happy, but sadly alone.

# THIRTY-FOUR

TJ talked to John twice on Friday morning, always thinking of things they need to accomplish. John produced a few more pages on the website, ran a few messages by him, went through the mail, and TJ told him to be sure and watch the game. He told him to go get Bob and Sue, make some lunch, and Bob would show him how to watch the game on the wall with the big High Definition Projector with DLP. John was excited and said he would.

Meanwhile, TJ clicked through the new web pages and gave John kudos on the new web pages, and marveled at how inventive he was. TJ said goodbye, packed up the laptop, and caught a cab to the arena. He made his way to the press entrance, but it was a long hike to the pressroom. Fortunately, they had a beautiful buffet set up, and over two hundred seats for the media. He found a desk, read through the press releases and updates, and locked his laptop in a new locker and went for lunch.

He was almost finished when Dick came up behind him and put his hands on his shoulders and grinned, "Hey, how's the book coming? I hope you plan on adding another winning chapter after this weekend."

"Hey, Dick. How are you? Yes, I'm hoping so, too but we tend to only think about one game at a time, half afraid something bad will happen."

"Nothing will happen. Taylor is on a roll, and Shane has never been better. I'm predicting a big repeat. I'll see you later."

"Ok."

TJ went to watch Shane warm-up. Shane seemed fine, but TJ was already nervous. He couldn't wait until the game started. Playing Michigan in an opening game was not considered a shoe-in, although Taylor had the better record this season, Michigan played some big games, and won a lot this season. TJ fidgeted right up until the ball was tossed into the air. Taylor just missed snatching the ball and getting a quick score. Michigan came down on their offense and set up. Shane hung tight on his man. Back and forth they went with the ball, and Shane and his Michigan man seemed joined to the hip, as they, too, crossed back and forth over the paint waiting for a shot, and preparing to pounce upward for a rebound. The shot came. Shane pushed hard as he leaped upwards, and dug his nails into the ball he clinched it so hard. He quickly tossed it out to his favorite guard.

Jerry brought the ball down the court. Shane set up a midcourt screen, and Larry got free. Jerry threw the ball to him, but his defensive man returned too quickly for a shot. Shane broke through traffic for the lane, tying up the man guarding him. Shane was open for a split second. Larry spotted him. The pass came like a fast bullet and Shane scored a layup. TJ let out a huge sigh. The ice had been broken, and the game took off.

Michigan was strong, but fell into early foul trouble due to what Dick would call big game mental mistakes. Shane made three dunks right before the half because their big man was sitting on the bench with two fouls. They led by twelve at the half. Coach Timmons had a lot to say at halftime in the locker room on how they could shut down Michigan's offense, and he asked everyone to commit to better defensive play. Shane knew he could be better on both ends of the court and challenged himself to do so.

After the break, Michigan had possession first, missed their shot, and Shane snatched the rebound. As he was coming down to the floor, he turned his head and saw Larry sprinting down court. He threw the ball extremely fast before the defense could go after him. Larry caught the ball on the run and dunked it. This began a ten-minute run bringing Taylor's lead to twenty-two points.

Michigan tried several comebacks, but continued having foul trouble with careless mistakes. This was very uncharacteristic for this veteran team, but it was also young team. They would be far better next year. Taylor won by twenty-four points, and everyone on the team played in the first round of the NCAA tournament. This put Taylor in the final thirty-two in the nation.

Relieved, TJ picked up his laptop and caught a ride on the team bus back to the hotel. He and Shane had dinner scheduled with Al and Barbara at six. Shane ate a late lunch after the game, but not too much as they were going to an awesome steakhouse for dinner. TJ spent the rest of the afternoon writing about the game. Shane came up early to his room and added his thoughts and insight into the preplanning for the game, the locker room, and the changes he personally made to his game for the big second half.

TJ and Shane decided tonight would be the night they would tell the folks about their gift. Ironically, they both became very nervous, and Shane feared they wouldn't accept it. The cab dropped the boys off at the Smith Company Steakhouse, where they were whisked to a private area for celebs. TJ tipped the maître d' well as Al and Barbara arrived. They made their orders and after the waiter left, Shane said he had announcement.

"Mom? Dad? TJ and I want to give you something for all the thousands of things you have done for TJ and me. I could never repay you for everything you have done, but this gift is a small attempt to show you how much we both love you. My life is going to change in a few months, my free time will be shorter during the long NBA season, and I want my family and friends to be around when I can get away.

"As you know TJ and I are building a new house and office in Concord, and we have ordered a new motorcoach. After we move, we want to give you our first house and our former motorcoach, and encourage you to move from Missouri to Lindle. Then you'd only be two hours away and can see all my home games, as well as come down and enjoy the lake, and maybe help from time to time. Dad, you know you can now run your business from anywhere, but you could use the Learjet if you need to fly back to Missouri, or you could sell the business and retire. I'll leave that up to you, but please accept this gift with our thanks and our love." Shane paused and said with a grin, "Whew, that was hard."

TJ and Shane looked at Al and Barbara and they were absolutely speechless. They had not seen this coming. Not in their wildest dreams did they ever consider moving to North Carolina. They talked about wanting a motorcoach some day, but they were thinking a small one perhaps.

Al finally gathered his wits about him and smiled, "This is a far too generous gift. We appreciate it so much. It is an opportunity your mother and I need to discuss. We'll get back to you, but please know you didn't have to do anything, but we appreciate it, and the things we have done for you, we did them because we love you. And we love TJ, too. Thank you."

Their salads came and they talked about the house. TJ told them they planned to leave the furniture behind, but Barbara could go through the house and tell them what to keep or move out. It didn't matter to them. He said his interior decorator would be glad to come over, and help her redecorate without the strong male décor they have now. They all got a laugh out of that.

They enjoyed the rest of the meal and discussed their plans to fly back to Lindle with TJ after Sunday's game at one. Afterwards, TJ and Shane made their way up the back elevator to TJ's room. They began taking their clothes off, which was something that happened almost every time they were together on the basketball road, because there were so few times together.

Shane said, "Do you think they were happy about the gift?"

TJ grinned, "I think you stunned them. I once surprised my parents with an eight-day trip to Hawaii, and to present the gift, I had a beautiful fresh flower lei made to present them with the airplane tickets. They didn't say a word for almost a minute. I thought mom was going to have a heart attack. It was the most wonderful thing I have ever done for them. I think your parents are very excited, and I bet they are talking about it right now."

Shane laughed, "I hope so. I would love to have them closer to us. They will be just far enough to prevent popping in on us when we're naked in the Jacuzzi, or making love on the floor in the great room, but not so far they can't be at our home in just ninety minutes to Lake Norman."

Shane fell back on the bed and TJ eased on top of him. They kissed for a long while before TJ began planting kisses gently down Shane chest increasing his erection. They truly loved each other, and cherished their time to be alone together.

Shane practiced on Saturday, but not too hard at the high school gym. They were going to play Connecticut, and they knew it was going to be a tough game, so they began by working on specific plays for inbounding the ball to avoid any chance of a steal, and also working on possession clock countdowns, as well as end of the game and overtime drills. He felt good about the practice. After lunch, they had a team meeting for the scouting report, and no study hall, so he was in TJ's room by three. This gave them time for discussion as to how things were going and a good nap together.

Shane suggested seafood so the reservation was at Bernie's Seafood Restaurant. It was an upscale place providing privacy to special clients, and TJ convinced them Shane was special as a member of the National Championship team, Most Valuable Player, and most likely the number one draft pick. They were pleased to accommodate them with a table in secluded spot away from view from the front.

They made their orders and Al decided it was his turn to talk. "Well, your mother and I graciously accept your gift, though we wish you would let us buy it from you, we thank you so much. Barbara will look forward to seeing the house tomorrow, and making some notes to figure out how she would want to decorate it. So there you have it. Thank you," he said to Shane. "And thank you," he said looking at TJ with a grin. "We love you both very much."

Shane laughed and said, "This is terrific news. I will soon have you close to me again, and you'll love the house. We love it, and if we could move it to Concord we probably would have been happy, but that's not possible. And I know you're going to love the RV. It is so much fun to take a trip in."

TJ added, "Barbara, you just tell us what to pack and get out of your way, and we'll do it. Nothing will hurt our feelings. It is your home to do with as you wish. If you like, we'll leave the audio and video equipment in the living room, as it feeds the rest of the house, and you'll enjoy seeing his games on the big screen. Remind me and we'll show you a playback of the Duke game. I think we should leave the computer network running to make it easier for you, too. We'll take down the remote studio, as it is an eyesore, and I bet you don't want to be on camera."

"Heavens no," laughed Barbara. "Thank you. We're looking forward to spending the night with you, take a new look at the house, and making the trip to Concord to see what you have going on down there."

Shane said, "Dad, if you want to, Henry will visit and give you a quote on bricking the outside of the house to give it a normal look."

Al replied, "Well, I think we'll try it as is for a while. I like the idea of no maintenance, especially if we're going to be traveling in our motorcoach."

Shane replied, "That's great. On our network, you can do iChat® with us so we can see and talk to you at the same time. TJ knows I don't want to talk much about it until after the championship, but from what I have heard, I have no idea how he is keeping up with all of it. He is building a house, a new motorcoach, a home /office, and a new business and foundation office. All at the same time, and in the middle of that, he's doing not one, but two promotional tours, attending my graduation, and taking me to Alaska. Whew, I get tired just thinking of all that."

TJ said to the Bradleys, "I am so excited for you. You'll love the weather in Lindle. The people are nice. Shane and I can visit you often, and you can come see us a lot, too. You'll love the lake and the view."

TJ Johnson

Dinner arrived so they continued talking while enjoying the awesome food. All four were relieved about the house and the motorcoach, but TJ and Shane were most thankful to have them moving closer to them.

The team meal had been at eight o'clock in the morning. Shane ate his usual steak and eggs with fresh fruit. He drank a lot of juice and a glass of milk. They had a final team meeting with questions to be sure everyone knew the Connecticut player they were to cover on defense. Afterwards, they returned to their room to rest, pack, and be ready to leave at eleven.

TJ followed the same orders as he was going to ride with the team, but he was going to leave his stuff in the bellman's closet during the game. Al and Barbara were going to meet him at the executive airport after the game. TJ read the Sunday newspapers and online sporting news, and made some notes that were added to a file on his laptop. Afterwards, he decided he needed a mental diversion, so he began writing the first words of the new gay story to be released next year. He didn't have a title, so he created a spreadsheet for possible titles. Some were stupid, but he put them on the list hoping they would trigger his brain for something far better. His favorites were at the top and the least-liked at the bottom. He didn't usually have trouble coming up with a title, but so far, nothing was quite right. He would have to think a bit more for something with a ring to it. Before he met Shane, he used think of titles while driving the motorcoach all day. He'd keep a memo recorder handy so he could record thoughts and some of those became the titles of his current books. After a bit more thinking, he typed out a few more possible titles.

TJ's laptop alarm went off, giving him fifteen minutes to get downstairs. "Dang!" he said aloud. "This was just getting interesting." He quickly saved his files, grabbed his stuff, and went down to checkout and store his luggage. He was sitting on the bus when the team came aboard. The ride there was mostly silent, as each player took this game very seriously. They knew if they goofed around they could lose, and that would be the sudden end to a great season. For five of them, it could be there last college game forever. TJ respectively remained quiet on the short ride to the arena. Shane nodded and smiled at him before sitting down up front.

At the arena, the fans and cheerleaders turned out to welcome them. TJ remained on the bus until the team exited and watched as the crowd followed the team to the entrance gate. Using his press pass, he came in through the same tunnel as the team and began the long walk to the pressroom. He sat down and began going through a handful of new flyers. He was hungry by the time he read all the media notes, so he locked his laptop and went to the buffet.

Afterwards, he went down into the stands to sit and watch Shane warm-up. He discovered that by watching him slowly stretch, pull, and stretch some more, that Shane gave himself a feeling of calmness. TJ wished he could stretch away the jitters, too. He tried not to worry about this game, but like Shane, the road to the second championship was far more stressful than last year. He grinned when he thought about going down to the court and stretching alongside Shane. He knew that would make his boyfriend laugh, but it would probably result in TJ's arrest. Shane's goal was to win two titles in a row, a very difficult feat. It was also the lynchpin for the publishing of the sequel, **Twice Is Nice**. Jake assured him it would sell well even if they lost, but no one wanted to consider that a remote possibility. A lost might affect Shane's draft status, but they doubted it. The Bobcats wanted him and he wanted to play in Charlotte. TJ never typed out a planning calendar for what he would do if they did lose, as he might have two weeks of free time in front of the tour. It was just not something he allowed his brain to think about at all.

TJ also watched the Connecticut big men warm-up. There were three of them making a double or even triple-team of Shane possible. Defense was going to be demanding, and offense difficult, of that he was sure. He called John to make sure that Bob had the game on. They were excited, too.

The game began easily with Shane getting the tip and tossing it to Jerry, who in turn threw to Larry on the run and he laid it up. They immediately went to a full court press, determined to make Connecticut work hard for every possession. Their starters were going to be difficult for Taylor, but they had little on the bench of the same caliber. Coach Timmons insisted the Connecticut bench was their Achilles heel, but to kick it into play, they had to wear down the starters. They ran hard on offense by pushing the ball down quickly, and often within three seconds of Connecticut shooting, the Taylor team brought the ball down rapidly while attempting to score. They continued running and hustling throughout the game. As the half progressed, they soon saw one of the big men taking longer to get down court. Later, with four minutes to play in second half, and after the final television timeout in the game, Shane told his teammates he thought Connecticut was finally out of gas.

Taylor came back to the court determined to get a defensive stop and run them hard on offense. In the next two minutes, their opponents did not score, and yet Taylor moved the ball rapidly. They called a timeout, a vain attempt to slow them down, but the Connecticut boys couldn't get their legs back. Taylor won as Shane dunked the last basket. No one would have believe they won by sixteen points if they hadn't seen the fine defensive work the Taylor team performed. They were now in the sweet sixteen, and would play next weekend in Memphis, with a chance to win four more games to the title.

After their flight to Lindle, TJ introduced Shane's parents to Bob and Sue, and suggested they join them for dinner. Shane would be over after his plane landed. Shane was going to pick up barbecue takeout for all. After they went inside the house, TJ called Shane and added two more orders for dinner.

TJ helped take their luggage to the guest room, grabbed a pad, and suggested they take the house tour, and he'll make notes for what they want to do.

They went back to the laundry and all was fine there. TJ told them he would leave the new washer / dryer units there, and they were thrilled, and the same for the rest of the appliances in the kitchen area. She didn't want the pot and pan rack hanging from the ceiling, so he made a note to pack it along with their canisters, plates, and silverware. She liked the kitchen table, and the office was fine, minus the hanging remote studio stuff. The living room she liked all the furniture, but wanted to change out the wildlife pictures, so he made a note to pack them.

She liked the guest room furniture and at first didn't like the master bed, so TJ suggested she lay down on it. It was one of those airbeds where you can adjust the resistance with a remote control. She loved it. Al tried the other side and he liked it to. TJ would remove the linens and leave the rest. She even liked the towels and loved the walk-in closet.

The wet area would stay intact, as they would use the exercise equipment and Shane said he would stay over some during summer pickup games. They went into the RV building and agreed everything could stay in place. They went around the coach with TJ demonstrating the bays and the storage, and they were amazed. Inside, they sat down on the couch and just looked all around the front area, and liked everything TJ had done. The same for the kitchen minus some of the canisters and figurines, and he would remove the towels in the bathroom, and they liked the bedroom, matching bed pillows and TJ grinned slyly when she said he did a good job picking them out. He told her the truth, "The coach came with an interior decorator package." They all laughed.

He began slowly demonstrating some of the features, the operation of the slides, and he promised they would receive a lot of training on how to operate, drive, park, and setup the coach. They were thrilled.

Shane arrived with the food. TJ called Bob and Sue over, and they all had a great time eating, talking and celebrating the sweet sixteen victory. Sue told Barbara that she would be happy to teach Barbara how to drive it. She said it was easier for a woman to teach another woman than for a husband to do it. They all laughed and Barbara agreed to try.

John came over early for breakfast on Monday morning with TJ, Shane, and his parents. Shane soon left for class, and the rest of the group got in TJ's car to make the trip to Concord. On the way down, TJ gave John a camera, and told him he was in charge of picture taking of the office set up, and he explained what he had in mind for Shane and TJ's business office, and how they could make more money, and use that to help others by also setting up a foundation.

Larry left word for one of his associates to give them the tour, and he would see TJ before he left. They strolled by the executive offices, and noted the displays of Jeff Gordon's mementoes, including numerous trophies, followed by the conference room, the project room for signing and shipping the stuff sold, the mailing room for publicity materials, the staff that ran it all, then over to the foundation side and the computer room that caught John's eye, where they handled the website designs and updates, and printed graphics, and edited promos Jeff recorded. They rented a studio for production when they needed it. They saw information on the foundation and pleasantly surprised at how many millions Jeff's team raised. They found the walls covered with plaques presented to the foundation for their support.

In the lobby, TJ met with Al and Barbara, and John listening. "This is what we want to do—use Shane's fame for the greater good with a strong emphasis on helping gay charities, but also everyone we can. I suggested we start with about half of what Jeff's office space is and grow from there. Jeff made this easier by offering office space for free for the summer and a low rate from then on. Shane will help him with some charity work in return. They are also helping with construction, staffing, and tons of advice. Do you see any reason not to proceed?"

Al laughed and said, "Hell no. I know the price of office space, and that's a great offer. I think Barbara and I would be pleased to watch Shane grow into charity work. That is wonderful. TJ, you don't need our blessing. We are thrilled that you are willing to help him and help us. Thank you."

TJ gave them a hug, "No, thank you. You gave me the most wonderful partner in the world, and you taught him how to put the cap on the toothpaste!" They laughed at his sense of humor, however, if Shane had been there, he would have told them TJ was deflecting a compliment that was part of his humble nature. "Can I excuse myself for a moment, I need to pick up a folder from Larry, and I'll be right back." They all went outside while TJ went back to the business office to see Larry.

Larry shook his hand and welcomed him. "Larry, thank you so much," began TJ.

"It's our pleasure. Here's a folder of things for you as we discussed. I've put the lease agreement in the back, and I think everything you need to get started is there. Jeff is excited for you."

"Please tell him thank you. My team will go over the lease tonight. We have decided to rent one wing, and get started right away. I'll probably call you tomorrow with some questions on the info, especially the hiring part."

"Well, if you're able to get either of the men I suggested for a business manager, your life could get a lot easier with handling this part of your projects. I'll make some calls for you if you need me to."

"Thank you so much. I'll let you get back to work. I have some associates with me, and I want to show them the new house construction. Thanks again."

TJ went down the hall and when he got to the lobby, he started grinning. On the sidewalk out front were John, Al, and Barbara and they were talking to Jeff Gordon who had just driven up. TJ came out to greet him.

"Ah, Mr. Gordon, welcome to your office. How are you and thank you so much for all you have done and are doing for us?"

Jeff shook TJ's hand vigorously. "Hey, pal. You're welcome, and how are you?"

"Great. Did you meet everyone?"

"Everyone. So when are you moving in?"

"I think early to mid June, but we'll have to start construction soon. Larry gave me the paperwork, and a list of leads to get the job done, staff hired, equipment, and the list goes on and on."

"It'll seem overwhelming but it's not. Once you get the business manager, he'll begin doing the rest for you with your oversight. At least that's how I suggest you do it. I'm good at passing the buck," laughed Jeff.

"Well, thank you, thank you, and thank you."

"You're welcome, and I'll see you soon. Have you seen your house? They are making fast progress. I'm impressed. It was nice to meet you folks. Have a great day."

Jeff went in his office and everyone got in TJ's car. "So what did you guys think of Jeff Gordon?"

They all started talking at once as if they had been dying to say something. TJ said, "Hold it, three at a time. Uh, never mind. I suspect you were impressed. Let's try this, Al, what did you think of the office set up?"

"I give it a big thumb up."

"John, did you get an idea of what we're trying to do?"

"Yes, it helped a lot. I took pictures of everything—even Jeff."

TJ laughed, "I'm not surprised, but we can't do anything without the most important vote, so Barbara what did you think?"

She grinned, paused to make the men lean in for her answer, "I say yes, too. It's a beautiful place and a fantastic idea. I hope we can make my son's foundation as good as Jeff's."

"All right! Well, let's go see how the house is coming. After all, your big boy needs a good place to live."

They drove over to the street for the new house and TJ pointed out Jeff's house, but soon they could see what looked like an army of workers. The house framing was complete, the boarding for the roof was on and the crew was putting on the decorative metal roof. Inside were two wiring crews for electrical, and a specialty wiring crew for networks, alarms, telephone, coax, stereo, intercom, gates, cameras, and more. Two plumbing crews were roughing in all the bathrooms and half baths, all the bedrooms and their baths, and laundry, plus the kitchen. They were also preparing the wet area. The RV plumbing was already complete.

As they walked in from the street, they could see the utility trenches from the street, the conduit to the two gates, and various ditches for cameras, lights, and even motion sensors.

TJ brought a roll of the plans with him. John had the camera and was already taking pictures of the house. TJ began showing them how the entrance would look. They walked to where the fountain would be in the center of the circle drive, and the walkway to the door. They saw a crew of men building the entrance, and at least ten men putting in windows and wall sheathing with the vinyl wrap preventing air leaks. A big truck was unloading thousands of bricks.

They walked to the right of the house where they could see the office framed in, along with the garage, and the RV port going straight towards the lake. There was a heat and air conditioning crew hanging the duck work in the RV building. The ceiling and walls were finished, lights hung, and all the specialty wiring installed. TJ felt most impressed with all the completed work he saw. They turned and walked through the big car garage and into the kitchen, while noting a bigger pantry, the main floor laundry, and then the kitchen. Barbara's mouth fell open as to how big it was. The rough in was done, and TJ showed her where all the pieces would go. They all walked to the bigger breakfast room with a view of the lake out the back. The kitchen sink area sported a good view, too. They noted the formal dining room and then moved to the office while noting a hallway to the front offices. The set up was the same as their old house but larger, with more cabinetry.

The great room was at least thirty percent larger, and two men were busy installing the gas logs and fireplace. There was a view of the lake on both sides. They moved down the hall for the guest half-bath, and into the master suite. The actual bedroom was about the same, but the walk-in closet was at least fifty percent larger. The bath was larger, too. They went out a door and into the wet area. TJ explained the reversal of their current layout with the basketball court up front and the wet area in the rear. You can step out of the Endless pool onto the outside deck and down to the regular outdoor pool. There were men building the rooms for sauna, steam, weights, and exercise equipment. There were six men building the pool, too.

They took the roughed in steps towards the entryway to the second floor. TJ showed them six guest rooms and their baths, through a framed in doorway into the hall. To the right was the under construction doublewide staircase to the foyer and front door. They went straight across the hall, into another framed doorway, and into the six staff rooms, a main laundry, and big kitchen room and lounge area.

Back down the stairs they went and made their way to a partially completed deck that went down a few steps to the pool area, that would sport a privacy fence as well as a bathhouse with a lounge in front with refrigerator, ice machine, bar, and hopefully food. Music would be wired in, as well as big LCD television screen. They went through the garage around the RV exit and he showed them where two more RV's could park with full pedestals for electric, water, sewer, network, and satellite, the future shed, and the road leading down to the lake crossing over the road leading to the RV port from the second gate. They could see the lake and the beautiful view, and TJ waved to Larry Mahar and his crew of four building the boathouse and docks.

Henry came up behind them. "I heard you were here. What do you think?"

"Gang, this is Henry. He is the official construction juggler. He keeps everybody working, while trying to stay out of the way of the next crew. It looks great. Any problems?"

"Oh about twenty today so far, but they're handled. We're hustling today because the insulation crews are coming tomorrow. They did the roof insulation yesterday so the new metal roof will be done by dark."

"Great job, Henry, and thank you so much. Well, we'll get out of your way. Thanks again. Bye."

They boarded the car once more and he drove them over to the house he moved, so they could build their new home. Jerry and Terry lacked about two hours of work to finish the landscaping, and the house looked as if it belonged there. TJ turned around and began the drive home. They stopped for lunch, and then TJ took them to the airport so Steve and Suzy could fly the Bradleys to their old home. He gave them a big hug and congratulated them on their new home and RV.

John loaded the pictures from his camera to the network, and after phone calls and emails, they began studying the pictures of Jeff's office layout. TJ looked through the folder Larry prepared, pulled out Larry's suggestions for a job position list, the resumes, and found a detailed floor plan with all the measurements. Larry just saved him from guessing the size requirements for the various rooms.

They made a copy of the plans, and began making some changes along with TJ naming the rooms by the job title, while checking his personnel list. Thanks to Larry's file, he quickly made decisions for the floor plan he wanted. The biggest change he made was creating adjoining offices for TJ and Shane, with an adjoining pocket doors, and a private bathroom with entry doors from either office. This design created a suite for them to share. This would give Shane a place for displaying some of awards, and great place to meet for business proposals and reporters, and keeping their home private, except for the remote studio.

They also created a computer design room in the first construction as he planned to work hard on developing multiple websites promoting Shane's business side, TJ's books, and their foundation. He had the role of a web master in his hiring list. He emailed the plans to the builder Larry recommended. He got a phone call from the owner a few minutes later.

"TJ? This Bill Jones and we just received your plans. I have been expecting to hear from you. Larry called me last week and said you were leasing the offices next to Jeff's, and needed a similar setup."

"That's right Bill. You did an excellent job on their offices. We're going to build as we grow. I want to develop half of what you did for Jeff, and we'll add the other half later. I made some modifications to floor plans..." began TJ as he explained his drawings.

Bill made a few suggestions and they easily agreed on a plan. He said he would get back to TJ in an hour with a quote. He asked TJ if he wanted to pick out wall colors, carpet, and office furniture. TJ said he had an interior designer he would use. They traded contact information and TJ felt they were off to a good start. He sighed heavily as he hung up, with another big hurdle off his back.

# THIRTY-FIVE

Shane completed two hard practices, but remained motivated and excited about the games coming up later in the week in Memphis. Meanwhile, TJ and John studied the resumes for the business manager role. TJ called and asked the men to come to Lindle for interviews. He did not plan to reveal the sports celebs name until after they were hired.

Both men were from the racing world with over a decade experience in similar roles with top racing teams. After he finished each interview, he asked if they had any trouble working for a gay person, indicating that he was gay. With the first, TJ noted just a slight change in the tension lines around his eyes; a look TJ had seen all his life. The man then said he didn't see any problem working with a gay person, as long as he never saw any gay, uh, and he paused searching for a word, and finally said, event. TJ wasn't impressed. He thanked him for coming. He felt he was hiring for more than talent, but a person that could support Shane and himself, with similar goals. While he knew that he and Shane would always keep the view of their sex away from everyone, they did not want to feel like they couldn't hug, or touch the other affectionately.

There was an hour break between interviews, and TJ needed that to calm down, as he almost questioned the first man's ethics and sincerity, but decided to let it go, as these men were acquaintances of Larry's. The second man, Robby Robertson, was a fifty-year-old former ad executive and stockbroker, with a degree in accounting, and masters in business administration, and currently business manager for TPI Racing. His current duties include managing two hundred workers and supervising all aspects of two racing teams. He was six feet two inches, complete bald, looked physically fit, bright blue eyes, with a warm friendly smile, and a knuckle busting handshake.

TJ liked his comments and friendly approach, and they began to talk about the job, and though he tried not to, he finally had to say he wanted someone like Larry to create an organization as good as Jeff's, and TJ paused and smiled slyly, or better.

The interview went well, so TJ finally said, "Robby, I'm impressed with your credentials, your attitude, and everything you have said, but I wouldn't be fair to you if I didn't tell you something personal about me. I'm a gay man. I'm not effeminate, and I don't push any kind of agenda, and in spite of what you may have heard or read, I don't try to convert people to be gay, which I don't think is possible. I just want to live as normal a life as possible, and let no one tell me how to live. Do you have any problem working for a gay person, or having any gay employees on our staff?"

Robby immediately smiled, "TJ, thank you for sharing with me, and for trusting me with your personal information. I don't have a problem working with any gay person, and on a personal note I'll tell you way. I have a twin brother and he is gay. He was married to a beautiful woman for six years before he nearly had a nervous breakdown, and came out of the closet. It was a shock to me at first, but as I began to look back on our life together, I should have known. After his divorce, he began to rebuild his life, and now has a longtime companion that I like very much. No one will ever harm my brother while I'm around. I've since learned I have a gay cousin, and gay nephew, and a beautiful lesbian neighbor. Do you have any other questions I can answer for you?"

"Just one, when can you start?"

Robby smiled, "Well, you don't waste time."

"Not when I know the correct answer. I'd love to have you run our team. I was told to offer eight-five thousand and full benefits. My accountant is working on a new benefit package for all our employees."

Robby thought for a second, and replied, "I'll trust you on the benefits, and I accept your offer."

TJ grinned broadly, "Very good. I am most excited and happy to have you with us. Here's what I know so far: I am signing a lease for the offices right next door to Jeff. He has generously held them for us. However, I plan to develop just one section to start with." He passed a copy of the floor plan. "We're emulating Jeff's floor plan with some minor changes. You'll be in the executive offices."

During the interviews, John had been working off the desk in the motorcoach, so TJ called him on the phone so he could join them. TJ said to Robby, "I guess I don't have to tell you it is important to keep salary information to yourself." Robby nodded. TJ handed him a confidentially statement. Robby had signed several in his career, scanned through it and signed. "Robby, thank you. Can you trust me a day or two so my accountant and attorney can prepare a proper contract for you. My word is always my bond."

"And that's good enough for me." Robby politely stood as John came in the office.

"Robby, this my right arm, and yes, that is one of his titles. He is my home / office manager, helps with our web design and graphic print needs, and a lot more. At the new house, which is close to Jeff's and thus, the new offices, he'll handle our office staff there, and you'll be over all the business and foundation staff.

"Now that you have signed the confidentially contract, I thought you might interested in who the sports star is. However, you can't tell another soul until after the NBA draft. His name is Shane Bradley."

Robby eyes lit up, "Now that's exciting."

TJ continued, "It is illegal for him to have a sports agent, and so for now you work for me, but in a couple of months you'll work for both of us. I'm an author, and I publish both straight and gay fiction, except that I wrote a non-fiction book about last year's Taylor University Championship team through Shane's eyes, and I'm writing the sequel now. Our goal will be to maximize Shane's sales abilities, and use his status to raise money for the non-profit foundation. We'll need a board of directors and lots of guidance on how to make it work. We really do want to help as many people as possible. It's not just a tax saving plan. Is all this good for you?"

"Yes," replied Robby quickly, "and John it is great to meet you."

"Robby, do you have an office in your home you can work out of until June?"

"I do and I will, but Larry is a step ahead of you. He'll loan us an office for me to do my interviews, and that'll keep me close during construction, if that is all right with you."

"Perfect. How are your computer skills?"

"Good, my daughter taught me a few years ago. At my last job I had to do email, inner office memos, accounting, databases and such, and some experience with graphics, but I'm not a designer."

"Excellent. John, get him a Mac Book® laptop and iPhone® as soon as possible, and set up the security so he can access our data records and so forth from his home and Jeff's office. Send a note to Sam that we need a credit card for him." John replied he would order them right away. TJ added, "Do you need to give notice?"

"I need to offer one, probably two weeks, but in the racing business you're usually shown the door when you give notice."

"If you need to work a notice that is fine with me. I want to be fair. I do need for you to conduct the interviews for the rest of the office staff. John has made copies of Larry's suggestions. John is interviewing a different group for our home staff. Both of you need to choose your people, but please ask if they have a problem working with a gay person. Shane and I want to feel comfortable around every employee on our team. It'll be tough, but we must keep Shane a secret from everyone until after the championship.

"We're moving in the house on June first, so they need to be hired to start as near that date as possible, but I also need a plan on getting the marketing of Shane on the move right after the National Championship game. We'll hire a sports agent in New York to represent him in the negotiations with the team that drafts him, and other sports related activities. We'll have to work with him on sponsors, but I'm sure you have a lot of experience with that. We're looking for a way to tie in the NASCAR® approach to sponsorship, and hoping to find a way to sell our products at the games, but certainly online and in the stores. John has a brief to bring you up to date on Shane.

"Why don't you go tell your wife the news, start putting together a battle plan, and call me with your questions and suggestions. John will call to set up training on your new Mac Book®, iPhone®, and as he is a wizard with that stuff. We'll also use iChat® for conference calls. We'll be able to see each other while talking over important decisions. Thank you for choosing us."

"What is the name of your company?"

"For now, TJI, which is a company I own."

"Very good. I thank you for the opportunity. I think I'm beginning to understand why the secrecy for Shane. I will keep the secret. I'll call tomorrow after I have appointments and interviews set up."

After he left, TJ asked, "So what did you think of Robby?"

John deadpanned, "You hired me to think?" TJ laughed. John continued, "I liked him a lot better than the first guy. Was the first homophobic?"

"I liked Robby, too, and yes, I felt the same about the first. I'm so glad that Robby was way better, making the decision far easier. I'm a gut instinct kind of person, and if I make the wrong judgment on someone, I will fix it, but I was sure on hiring you, as I am Robby.

"Excellent, well, let me make the order for his gear, and I'll be ready to show you some of the web designs I was working on." He paused and said, "Are we ready to order gear for the whole staff?"

"No, just for Robby. The rest of the team won't start until June. Keep your computer and network gear spreadsheet up to date so when I give you a green light, you'll be able to put in the entire order quickly. Do you think we can get a volume discount?"

"Absolutely. We should put out for bids although Apple® is tough on discounts, but if I could use Shane's name, we could get a hell of deal."

"That may be possible but not until after the championships. I think you, Buddy, and I need to meet. Call him and see if he can come in tomorrow. He has a set of house plans, as he is in charge of the specialty wiring at the home / office, but get a floor plan for the business office ready for him, a list of jobs we're filling, and call the rep for the mailing and shipping equipment and get him here for a discussion. Larry put their information in the folder, too."

"Got it. When are you flying to Memphis?"

"Shane flies out after classes Wednesday morning. I think I'll go Thursday morning."

While John went to work, TJ called Larry and told him he hired Robby. Larry said that was an excellent choice and again promised to help all he could. TJ also thanked him for the loan of an office for Robby.

Shane came home Tuesday night with the grim news that Jerry had come up limping in practice. The doctor and the trainer immediately went to work on him, but it was too soon to know if he could play in the Thursday night game. TJ sighed heavily, knowing this could mean the loss of the title, but they tried to remain optimistic. Then went over their schedules for the next few days, and then Shane told him about practice, and his thoughts on the upcoming game in Memphis.

Afterwards, they went to the wet area to spend some time together before Shane left for school with more homework to do. They hugged goodbye a bit longer than usual since they were flying a day apart.

Buddy Bell and John hit it off quickly as they talked about networks, computers, and other electronics. TJ came into the office and they went to work talking about what TJ needed the equipment to do in the new offices, and John and TJ kept spreadsheets busy with notes and lists of the parts required. Buddy was going to order the network gear, while John would order the computers, servers, printers, scanners, and digital phone system.

TJ pulled Larry's file and brought out the mailing and shipping equipment to show it to Buddy. Attached was the name of a company that sold a system to Larry. "Buddy, do you have any experience with this stuff?"

"No, I don't, but I have a friend that runs a similar system for a small distributing company. I could call him and pick his brain on it. I think the networking of the equipment I could handle, but I don't know anything about the forms, postage, and affixing stuff."

TJ's face puzzled, "What's affixing?"

"Well, the shipping system usually works like this. A printer spits out a multipart order ticket. Someone takes the ticket, pulls the items ordered while initialing what they put in the box. One copy goes in the box, and another in basket for their records. The box then goes through a machine that is labeler, and it puts on or affixes the address label, and adds the package to the shipping ticket, and into a cart for the trucks to pick up. As for the mailing, it is similar. The promo letters are printed on high-speed printers, folded, and inserted into an envelope machine, where it is sealed and label affixed. If it is a bigger piece it could go through a second assembly line. It all ends up in a mailing cart for the postal trucks. The more automated, the cheaper it is for you, as machines are just payments, but employees are like elephants, they just keep on eating."

TJ and John laughed, but they understood. "I'd like to meet your friend. John will call you after we get the equipment. Let's aim for Monday. I need you involved in the network, telephone, and security wiring for the offices, and near the end of May the installation of all the equipment. Can you handle that, and of course the new house for me?"

"Sure. I'll take my notes and come up with a bid tomorrow."

"Thank you. I'll see Monday."

TJ got a call from Country Coach® so he said goodbye to Buddy. They had some minor changes they wanted to make, and hoped TJ would be okay with their modifications. He received emails with pictures and drawings of office cabinetry and their suggestions. They were perfect illustrations and

418

TJ easily agreed. He asked if they were still on scheduled and they said yes, and that made him feel much better.

John showed him the website changes for TJ's site, and TJ just about fell out of his chair. John made his book covers almost leap off the screen, and something moved on just about every page. There were new promos for bookmarks and postcards, and room for the greeting cards when they were ready.

John said, "This last section will be uploaded when we're ready because it promotes and ties in the foundation website." He clicked on a few more test pages, "Now this website is for your non-gay books."

"I'll only have two."

John grinned, "I don't think so. Forgive me, but I think you're going to find an opportunity for another book next year. Perhaps a story of what it is like to be a rookie in the NBA, as well as the first out of the closet gay professional basketball player."

TJ looked up at him and said nothing. For a moment John thought he had offended TJ, but TJ slowly smiled, "Maybe you're on to something. Show me what you have."

John used pictures of the Taylor championship team and a lot of Shane, added some live footage and then each book splashed out and over the footage. He also created links for orderings, and adding new bookmarks with Shane's picture on them. For apparel, he created a Shane mannequin or model with his arms outstretched. The various types of clothing appeared in small squares around the edge of the screen. A customer could click on any square and instantly the item changed on the model. It also placed drop boxes to the right of the mannequin to order the item, pick the size and color, and add it to their shopping cart. When they clicked, add to a cart, Shane would grab the order like a basketball, turn and shoot. A shopping cart basketball goal caught the order and disappeared. TJ thought it was very clever and lots of fun.

"John, this looks great but I am not allowed to sell my books anymore. They have to come through the publisher."

"Did you ask?"

"What?"

"Well, I was thinking, since we have the ability to use Shane, we could sell more books, and aren't they interested in making more money? You see, you could offer something that all the stores can't?"

"What's that?"

"You and Shane can autograph a copy for them, and you can throw in bookmarks, post cards, or an autographed picture of Shane. Sorry, I don't think they'd want a picture of you!" John and TJ started laughing hard.

"I think I owe you a steak dinner. Come on, I'm starved."

John managed to jump start TJ's thoughts. With all he was doing, he really had no time to be creative. John helped him with that and more. So far, he was very confident in his new people.

TJ hustle through a flurry of activity all day Wednesday, talked with Shane twice in Memphis, and by the time he caught his Thursday flight he was exhausted, and for the first time slept for the entire ninety minute flight. He yawned as he walked off the jet and said goodbye to Steve and Susie. He checked into the hotel, unpacked, and made his rounds for groceries and newspapers.

Shane finished a shoot around in the arena followed by an excellent practice in a high school. Jerry was there, but did not participate. They worked on the usual drills, and two new plays Coach Timmons put in their arsenal. They also worked on defense assignments with the second team pretending to be the opponent as usual. Over and over they went through their workouts until Coach Timmons was satisfied.

They ate a team meal after they returned to the hotel, followed by a study hall. Shane arrived at TJ's room about nine and woke him up. He had been working on the basketball book, became sleepy, sat on the couch with the television on, and fell asleep. He came to the door with a big yawn. Shane smiled at him, gave him a big hug, and kissed him gently.

Shane said, "I take it you had a bad day."

"No, actually it was good day. It was a good week, but oh my, I have been busy, but what really wore me down…" he paused and smiled, "were too many decisions. I'm happy though. We have a new office, new business manager, and I'm exceptionally proud of John. Do you feel like looking at something?"

"What's it about?"

"Our future. Let me show you this, and then I'll shut up for the rest of the weekend unless you're curious about the construction of the house and motorcoach. Is that okay?"

Shane grinned, "Yes, dear, it is, but thank you for handling so much for me."

"For the both of us." TJ got his laptop and brought it over to the couch so they could sit side by side, and he began demonstrating the new website for Shane's business, TJ's gay books, and then his basketball book. Shane got excited at the flying moving videos that were like small television monitors with each one moving across the screen while playing a different Shane highlight. He saw numerous dunks, beautiful swish shots, and on another, a rapid run down the court after a steal. He saw the championship win, and then book one came out of the center folding into book two and on to the order page. He then showed him the clothing order screen with Shane as the model. Shane could not stop laughing. He loved it and said he had never seen anything like it. When finished, TJ closed his laptop. "So what do you think of that?"

"John did all that?"

"Yes, I've made a few suggestions, but yes, it was his design. He's good and he cares. The goal will be to expand the sales of Shane's business which will be sponsors, basketball camps, and more, while also pushing sales for the basketball books, bookmarks, and post cards, as well a large clothing line, and continuing to sell my gay books. Of course, we'll use all this to increase donations to the foundation. John is researching hiring a full time Webmaster to expand and maintain our websites, and publicity machine."

"I'm impressed. That was a lot of hard work. Please tell John it looks fantastic. So you think we can raise a lot of money from the tie in of all our business?"

"Absolutely. You're going to make a lot of money playing basketball, but you're going to make even more through your sponsor endorsements. You've seen the racecar drivers promote their sponsors at every chance their get. Well, I doubt you can wear patches on your uniform like they do, but we can promote products in many other ways. Then we'll ask the sponsors to also support our foundation."

"I see, with their help, we'll increase the funds in the foundation far faster."

"Right, and there's a whole lot more we can do, but we'll save that until after the championship." TJ paused and grinned slyly, "Did I tell you how handsome you look today?"

Shane laughed, "No, but go right ahead. I'm listening."

"You look awesome!"

Shane laughed harder. "And what is it that you want as the result of all this flattery?"

TJ replied with a straight face, "About six inches."

Shane cackled, "Six? I'd say nine."

"Well, I'd like to see that for myself."

Their lovemaking was intense. TJ's energy renewed. Shane a bit spent from a big effort, but after their kiss goodnight, he walked back to his room like the happiest man on the face of the earth.

TJ arrived at the pressroom ninety minutes before the seven o'clock game with Syracuse. He read the latest media information, made numerous notes, and sat down to type it in the laptop. Once he completed his notes, he made his way to the buffet to eat dinner, while beginning to feel nervous about tonight's game. For the first time this season, Jerry would not start, though dressed out and maybe ready. Tim, with the most experience, had played point guard in high school before a final growth spurt made him a forward instead. The plan was not to act like he was point guard, but rather a forward with the entire team helping to move the ball up the court in a cross court passing pattern. They did a similar drill in practice, passing the ball while moving quickly up and down the court. With success, they could actually move the ball faster than Jerry could, but shifting to this plan could jump start their fast offense, so it became their main objective during practice. It would get a test under fire, where multiple mistakes might become their last game of the season.

TJ walked to his seat and began watching Shane warm-up. He felt a little relief as he noted Shane's solid, confident game face. The stress subsided a little as he gave Shane the five finger signal encouraging him to chill, and to again climb the ladder for success, one careful rung at time and forty minutes of play. Shane winked at him and pulled his earlobe. He knew what he had to do, and with Jerry seating on the bench, as a senior leader, the coach expected him to make floor decisions.

Syracuse possessed a big center, and two tall forwards, so the broadcasters kept talking about how Taylor would have to depend on the team's outside shooting to win the game. Syracuse won the tip after the fancy spotlights and smoke player introductions, and a celebrity sang the National Anthem. They moved the ball quickly. Shane was all over his man and they couldn't get it to him. With four seconds on the possession clock, their point guard made a long three. Swish!

Shane inbounded the ball to Tim who immediately moved it up court with a pass to Larry. Meanwhile, Shane ran right in front of Tim, shaking his man off of his back for a split second. Larry threw a hard pass to Shane who drove towards the basket. Their giant center moved over to stop him. Shane suddenly pulled up short and hit a two-point basket. Taylor immediately ran a full court press. Syracuse had a little trouble bringing the ball in, but their point guard moved a bit faster than Tim and got loose quickly, but the defense held, and they had to shoot from the outside, but again downed a three.

TJ's stomach soured as Syracuse now led six to two. The staggered ball handling continued to work, but Coach Timmons knew it would not work for the entire game. At the first television timeout, with the score eighteen to fourteen, the coach signaled to bring Jerry in. He wanted to discover early on if he could count on Jerry's ankle and his confidence. Jerry wore a stiff support brace on the ankle, that changed just slightly his ability to change direction on a dime, but given an opportunity on the open court, he was still fast.

The starters grinned as their confidence came up immediately. Jerry came back to the huddle after checking in. Their offense changed. Shane still hung back for a half court screen, and Tim prepared for an emergency pass should Jerry get himself in a jam in a corner, but Jerry acted like he had never been hurt. He immediately ran his defensive man right into Shane. The man fell and tried to say Shane fouled him, but Shane had never moved. He was as still and hard as a cement statute, putting a nasty knot on the guard's forehead. Jerry flew on down the court. The big men expected him to pass or shoot, but he didn't. He faked a left, darted back across the lane, and though amongst the giant defensive trees of their big men, he laid it up, making them look slow and stupid. He grinned.

A Writer's Fantasy

This time the defense held and Syracuse missed a long shot. Shane snatched the rebound and threw it quickly to Jerry near the scoring table. He caught it, sprinted down before anyone could catch him, and dunked it in spite of his braced ankle. The score was now tied, and Syracuse immediately called timeout, fearing a run by the Taylor team.

Jerry came to the huddle grinning. Coach Timmons asked, "Jerry, how's the ankle. How does it feel?"

"I can't feel a thing."

Alarmed, Coach Timmons frowned. "Is the brace too tight?"

"No, I'm sorry. That didn't come out right. I don't feel any pain. I'm good coach. Let's go win a ballgame. Their center is tall but slow. I think I can throw it to Shane for the double-team, and if he'll throw it right back I can breeze down the lane."

Syracuse missed another shot. Jerry again ran their guard hard and fast down the court making the boy gasp for air. Jerry faked slowing down before suddenly bursting to the center. Shane ran from the rear to the foul line taking two men with him. Jerry threw him a hard bounce pass. Shane caught it low and bent forward to protect the ball. He dropped his knees like he was going to jump, spin, and shoot, but just as he started upward, the double-team players ran up to him, he tossed it to Jerry like a quarterback handing off to a sliding fullback. Shane continued the ruse by jumping with his back to their double-team, and they wrongly assumed he still had the ball. Jerry cut right beside Shane, and around them, and laid it up. Taylor led by two. Jerry pointed a finger at Shane indicating it was his assist.

Taylor seemed to sprint down the court on every possession and Coach Timmons began calling for defensive stops. By the half, they had turned the game around and led by twelve.

Shane sat in the corner near his locker waiting on the coach to enter for their battle plans for the second half. Jerry sat with his foot elevated just to be sure it remained healthy, but he kept telling everyone he was fine. Shane had a short list of seven things he needed to do in the second. He needed to get open on offense, and he would have to start hitting his twelve-foot jumper. He needed to defeat their double-team by sometimes passing and sometimes shooting. He needed to draw more fouls. He needed to make a least three steals before the game ended, and finally, he needed to fire up the rest of the starters.

Taylor got the ball first in the second half, and set up their offense. Shane was ready to go to work. He moved to the foul line. Jerry tossed him the ball. They double-teamed as expected. Shane threw the ball to Larry who was open, and he hit a swish for three points. Shane studied the tapes, and he had been studying his man bringing the ball in looking for patterns and telegraphs of which way he planned to throw it. This time he glanced back to see where the point guard was waiting, and predicted he was going to break from the scoring table towards the top of the circle, and receive a hard bounce pass on the run. Shane gambled and just as he saw the guard made his move, he looked back at the inbound ball and leaped to the right almost twelve feet sideways, and deflected that hard pass catching it with both hands. He skidded across the floor while flipping to his back and tossing Jerry the ball before a possible call for traveling. Jerry saw the center coming up fast, but he was faster as he sprinted to the right and laid it up. The center had been furious at the defensive play, and stupidly fouled Jerry. Jerry made the basket. Shane grinned because the big guy now had three fouls.

A few plays later, Shane again got the ball, almost waited for the usual two players to run up to block him. He faked to Larry, spun and shot a quick, high arching jump shot over the trees and scored while being bumped by both players. The center took another foul for four, and his coach wisely took him out of the game.

The game moved faster at Coach Timmons's prompting, and with excellent defensive stops, Taylor led by seventeen with three minutes to play. Shane made twenty-five points. Jerry made twelve points, and Larry hit twenty-two points, most of which were beautiful threes as he had been hot all night.

Syracuse attempted a comeback, but Taylor shut them down once again with excellent defensive play and won by eighteen. They just won three of the six games needed to become the National Champions. TJ was elated. Across the court he saw Al and Barbara stand and applaud. Three sections to his right he saw Gary and his group standing and cheering. Shane looked up at TJ and smiled. It was a great game and they were victorious once again.

Earlier in the day, TJ spotted a creamery on the way to the arena. He knew Shane would be in the banquet room eating the after game meal. He left his laptop in the room and made his way to the street, walked two blocks and found the creamery. He waited in a line of a dozen until his turn. He ordered two giant to-go banana splits, put them in a bag, and left the store quickly. He was in hall of the hotel when his cell phone rang.

"TJ? Where are you? I'm in the hall beating on your door."

"I'm on the way. I'm just getting off the elevator. Just keep your britches on! I'll be there shortly." TJ laughed.

"Hurry up. I'm horny."

TJ laughed again. "You're always horny. You act like you just won a big game."

"We did. Now get your ass up here."

"Ooo, I love it when you talk dirty. Got to run," laughed TJ. He clicked his cell phone off before Shane could reply.

Minutes later, they ate furiously their wonderful tubs of the ice cream, then begin stripping each other's clothes off, and with the heart of a champion and a big boner, Shane mounted TJ and grinned from ear to ear.

424

They ate dinner Saturday night with Gary and his gang, along with Al and Barbara. They had a grand time at an Italian Restaurant with TJ enjoying his grilled chicken on top of fettuccini Alfredo. Shane devoured a platter of seafood pasta. The group laughed and celebrated the tough win over Syracuse and their big men. TJ refrained from talking about the new house, so he often asked questions about how things were going in Asheville, and if everyone was ready for the Sunday one o'clock game.

Later in the evening, they gently made love for a while, but Shane had an early curfew and a team meal at eight o'clock in the morning. They once again slept two floors apart, but deliriously in love.

# THIRTY-SIX

TJ packed early Sunday morning after updating his book and sending it first to Walter and Dick, and on to the editors in New York for their perusal. Changes were made and sent back for his final decision. He left his luggage in the bellman's closet as usual, with a nice tip, and caught a cab to the arena. He followed protocol updating his notes, eating the buffet, and then interviewing Walter about the game. He told him Wisconsin was just like Syracuse except they had two excellent guards with great shooting skills. TJ began to worry as he sat in the stands and watched Shane stretch.

The game began about fifty minutes later. TJ wished his seat was with Gary and his gang, but he sat alone in a sea of Wisconsin fans and fidgeted while waiting for the tipoff. Shane anticipated the ball and jumped slightly early in front of his man, and snatched the ball as it was tipped in his direction. He pulled the ball down protecting it, and then catching a glimpse of Tim running in from the sidelines towards their goal, he threw the ball hard in front of him. Tim ran to the ball just in time, snatched it, and laid it up. Taylor scored first. TJ sighed with relief.

Taylor worked hard on defense, but every now and then one of their shooters would catch a screen and score. TJ looked up at the score and sighed, knowing Taylor was leading by eight points. Shane scored two inside shots, and managed to get a steal on a cross-court pass, and lead everyone down the floor for a spectacular dunk. His confidence soared and on the next possession he shot a long sixteen-foot shot. Swish! Taylor went on to lead the half by fourteen.

However, Taylor went cold in the second half while Wisconsin returned to the form that got their team to this final eight game. For ten agonizing minutes, their opponents didn't miss a shot, and Taylor couldn't buy a bucket with a credit card. On the last television timeout, and with just three minutes twenty-five seconds to play, the score was now tied.

Coach Timmons took the long timeout to actually grin at his players. "Boy, I love games like this. I used to shoot hoops when I was eight and dream of the day when I could play in a big game and make the winning score. I did it. You did it. We all did it, but boys, now is the time to make that dream come true. We need, no, we have to have defensive stops on every possession until the end of the game. We have to make our baskets count while eating up the clock. Run the red apple play followed by steeple. You are going to win this game. You are champions and I can't wait to see you play like the champions you are. Let's do it!"

The team left the huddle fired up. TJ gave Shane three fingers for go, go, go and though Wisconsin had the ball first, Shane knew that somehow he was going to get the ball back. Wisconsin was eating up the clock and working a play for their best guard to shoot. At the very last second, Shane broke from his man, darted up the lane, dove forward and got a hand on a pass to their shooting guard. He flipped it up to Jerry. Larry broke into a streak as he sprinted down the other side of the court when he saw Shane leap. Jerry maneuvered around his man, caught sight of Larry, and threw it hard to him. Larry laid it up and was needlessly fouled. Larry made the foul shot. They now led by three as Shane got back to his feet, rubbed the forearm burns, and hustled down the court to block the inbound attempt.

In the next three minutes, Syracuse hit one basket. Taylor got three. Jerry fed Shane the ball at the foul shot line with twenty seconds to play. The double-team came up, but he leaped before they closed in, spun, and then leaned into them with a beautiful one handed high arching shot. They fouled him, but they all watched as he appeared to descend in slow motion, and the ball went through the goal perfectly. Coach Timmons had no idea how Shane could remain so calm with two big men coming at him, bumping him, and making the shot was such skill and finesse. He also made the foul shot.

Taylor won by nine. It wasn't a pretty game, but they made it to the final four. They were excited and thrilled to make it through the second weekend test, and only one weekend to go, and two games to victory.

Bob and Sue met him on the driveway after watching the game on the big screen with the dogs. He gave his friends hugs as they celebrated the victories this past weekend, while trying to remain optimistic for the final two. After playing with the dogs, he took them on a long walk around the big back yard. They returned to the house as Shane drove up. The dogs ran to him so he knelt down and gave each hugs and kisses, and lots of tickling. He waved at Bob and Sue.

The boys enjoyed the wet area and then sat in the recliners just to rest a while. They watched some of the replay on the big screen, but mostly just talked about their upcoming week. Shane said the team would fly out Thursday for Chicago for the Final Four Tournament weekend. TJ thought he would do the same, but wasn't sure yet. He wanted to bring the last chapter up to date and get it off for editing. He also wanted to confirm all aspects of the tour and make reminder calls for live interviews the next week to promote the book. He would fly out on Sunday morning two weeks from today to begin the three-week **Twice Is Nice** basketball book tour.

Shane went to the dorm just before eleven to sleep before classes and big practices for the next three days. TJ felt tired, and a little lonely, but fell asleep with the dogs at his side.

Buddy and his friend arrived at ten and they went over the drawings for the new office, and he showed him the materials he received in overnight mail on the equipment. In a bold move, John asked the sales rep to arrive about thirty minutes later. TJ was grateful. Terry Goodlett was a short rotund man, with big bushy black eyebrows, curly hair, dark tan, and TJ assumed he had Greek ancestry. He was also a take-charge kind of guy. After greetings and a look at the floor plan, he asked John to play a DVD he retrieved from his briefcase on the big LCD screen on the wall.

TJ was impressed with the short videos for the selected equipment Terry thought would be right for his company. Now TJ could see it in action as rapidly the machines printed packing tickets, shipping labels, and finally affixing the label as the boxes rolled down a conveyor belt. Next was the equipment using for mailings. Another high-speed machine that could print both sides in just a quarter of a second, affix a color signature, fold and stuff it, while another machine printed the envelope including postage, and sealed the envelope with the letter inside. The last machine worked in harmony with letter printer, but prepared letter size sheets in full color, collated with pre-printed brochures, stuffed it in a nine and twelve envelopes, sealed it, and affix a shipping label with postage. The last machine was for office mail. It could handle multiple sheets of paper, printing in color, both sides, folding, adding postage to an envelope, stuffing and sealing. He rattled off amazing statistics as to how fast each piece of equipment was, their warranty maintenance program, supplies, and their long history. The last part of the DVD was a long list off companies using their products. He gave TJ hard copies listing over two thousand customers, and brochures for the equipment he suggested.

He asked for questions, but only Buddy could think of a few pertaining to network integration. The man then asked what software they were using or planning to use as their database manager. TJ used Uptrends to keep up with all of his contacts, but he knew it would not handle the volume they were anticipating. He gave John a second DVD and they watched a demonstration of the software he recommended called Fast Data. TJ had seen it on Larry's list. They learned it could handle all the contact information for venders, personal and business contacts, and finally multiple contacts up to a billion names. The accounting and shipping modules also ran all of his equipment.

Well satisfied, the man opened a folder and handed him a beautifully prepared presentation and quote. The entire package and installation was just over two hundred thousand. However, he suggested they lease the equipment on a two or three-year basis, so they could keep updating their equipment and the software programs came with free updates. TJ thanked him for his presentation, and told him he would get back to him in twenty-four hours, but he wanted to send the information to his accountant in New York.

Buddy had his marching orders with a long equipment list to order, so he and his friend left as well. John made Acrobat PDF® files of the equipment and presentation, and emailed it to Sam. TJ followed up with a call, making sure he received all the information. They discussed the plans for the equipment, and whether to buy or lease. Sam had several customers that used the same brand, so he made a few calls to see if they were satisfied and received favorable reviews. He called TJ back and they decided to order, using the lease program. TJ called Terry and gave him the news. John called Buddy at the same time, so TJ sighed with another project off his list. He knew the publicist Robby hired would help with all their promo materials. He called Robby and brought him up to date. He was at Jeff's office. John had finished preparing his computer. They told John they would see him after lunch. TJ and John worked on the rest of their mail and email, and fielded a number of calls and requests for Shane.

Shane came in the door at ten thirty, ate some fruit, and joined them in the office. John congratulated him. TJ asked, "How are you feeling today?"

Shane came over and gave him a kiss, "I'm a little sore, some from the game, and some from the ride back on the plane. That happens when we fly right after an away game. How many remotes do I have?"

TJ looked at him slyly, "Oh, just six."

"Six?" Shane frowned.

"You're very popular today. We had about a dozen calls already. It seems last year's National Champions and Most Valuable Player is on the threshold of doing it again."

Shane laughed, "Don't jinx us. It's one game at a time. Should we get started?"

"Yes." Shane went to his stool, threaded his microphone under his shirt, put in the earpiece. John turned on the camera and lights and began testing. TJ set up the computer, and called ESPN®. Five minutes later, TJ and John sat silently as a reporter in New York quizzed Shane about Sunday's game and their upcoming game with Illinois on Saturday. Once finished, TJ made another call, Shane took a sip from his water bottle, and soon they were into the next interview. When they finished an hour later, Shane completed interviews for four major news organizations, a local station in Lindle, and another in Illinois.

Afterwards, TJ made sandwiches, and the three of them ate lunch together before Shane left for the gym. TJ and John packed up their laptops, notepads, and camera, played with the dogs, and left for Concord in a hurry.

On the road, TJ decided to discuss something with John. "John, let me quickly say Shane and I are most pleased with all facets of your work."

John interrupted, "There's a 'but' coming I suspect."

TJ smiled, "Yes, there is. I especially like your web design work, but as we get closer to moving and going full time with the office and the web sites, I think we should hire a full time Webmaster. Jeff has three and apparently keeps them all busy forty hours a week."

John replied, "I studied their sites, and I think I know why they use three. Jeff's sites are updated daily and maybe hourly, especially on the weekends. After race practice there is an update. After qualifying, more updates, and a wrap-up after the race. When they have a charity event, there are immediate pictures on the websites. They do a great job keeping their supporters and fans informed about all things relating to Jeff."

"Exactly my point. I want to give you a choice. Would you prefer the Webmaster job, or the multi hat job of being my right arm, running the home office, and helping Shane and I personally with…stuff!" He laughed when he couldn't come up with a better description.

John thought for a second, "I'm not an expert at web design. I create with what I know how to do. I think we should hire a real Webmaster, someone I could also learn from, but I would prefer the multi-hat job. I like variety, and I thrive on organized chaos."

TJ laughed, "I like that description. Okay, I agree with your decision. We'll tell Robby to hire one. Do you want to sit in on the interviews for that role?"

"Yeah, that would be cool."

"Okay. I didn't really picture you sitting in an office doing designs all day. We'll keep you involved in all things web related, but I'm excited about your future. Thanks!"


While TJ talked with Robby on his progress, John set up Robby's new laptop and tested the tie in to their office via an Internet connection. Once he was ready, he began training Robby on how to log in securely, and how to use the database for his contacts and interviews. He was impressed that an almost fifty years old man had computer skills. Meanwhile, TJ went to see Larry and bring him up to date on their office plans and the house. He also went next door to see if they had started on the office, and indeed they had begun with several walls of metal two-by-four studs. He also noted the line marks drawn on the floor for the entire floor plan. Later, TJ walked from room to room to get a feel for the place. The men were in the back unloading more construction supplies, so he left them alone and returned to Robby's office to finish their meeting after the computer training.

John and TJ rode over to the house and found themselves amazed at how much progress had been accomplished in another week. John took more photos while TJ talked to Henry. Afterwards, they walked to the dock and walked down the ramp to the newly constructed short dock, and over to the open boat storage, while noting the boatlift, and the PWC slide-up lifts. The men were working on the top deck with storage, plumbing, and wiring. John took more pictures.

They arrived home late in the afternoon, so TJ told John he could go home. Shane called and said he was on the way, and that he already ate dinner with the team after practice. TJ pulled some leftovers from the refrigerator, heated the food, and began eating. He had just finished when Shane arrived. TJ was tired from his day and Shane looked equally tired from practice.

"I've missed you," began TJ. "How are you?"

A Writer's Fantasy

"I'm fine. It was a good practice, but a long day. I have a paper to work on so I can't stay long, but I wanted to see you before my brain turns to Jell-O. Come on, let's go lay down."

Shane led TJ down the hall. TJ brushed his teeth, and then fell on the bed beside Shane. They cuddled up, made small talk, kissed for a while, and just held each other. Their lives were more complicated than last year, but they were happy, very happy, and together counted the days down to their vacation like children marking the days until summer.

After Shane returned to school, TJ did the wet area by himself with a movie playing on the LCD monitors. It was about the only way he was comfortable doing the sauna, steam, and Jacuzzi alone.

The next morning, TJ let John answer the phone while he concentrated on creating a dozen greeting cards. He had been working off and on with the project, throwing away many ideas, but finally finding better ones. He did connect some lines from his books until he and John finally settled on the twelve. John asked his friend to work on ideas for the graphics, and they were on the third set of proofs. TJ knew the first batch must be excellent work for the idea and strategy to catch on with the publishers.

Later, he received a call from Jake, while conferencing the gay publisher. Together, they sold the publisher on printing the bookmarks for free, so TJ could use them at the stores during book signings, and give them away on the website. They also like the idea of post cards, and TJ told him he was sending samples of a new line of greeting cards. He also explained he would like to sell his books on his website, but for the same rate as the other web booksellers. He would also promote a few other gay books that he had read and reviewed. He closed by telling them he was starting a foundation to support predominately gay charities. There would be ties to his books, and he hoped the publisher would help financially when they could, while promoting their other publications. They were also interested.

After the call ended, TJ started telling John what they had said when Jake called back after dropping off the conference call. "Boy," laughed Jake, "you're a born salesman. I am impressed with your marketing skills. Excellent work. Keep me informed as to the progress. Good luck in the tournament. I'll be watching, and I'll see you when you get to New York."

"Thanks. I'll see you Sunday week."

TJ turned back to John and added, "I think deep down I have always hoped to publish other up and coming gay writers. Perhaps I can work a deal with my publisher to print other gay books under my own label. I will have to think about that."

Shane's flight to Chicago left after class on Thursday morning. TJ left earlier that morning so he was on the ground before Shane took off. TJ checked into his room as he always did, making his rounds, buying

431

newspapers and food, and finally settled in his room, ordered room service for lunch, and connected to the Internet to check his email. He was looking forward to spending the afternoon working on **Forever Alone, Again**. He just finished a new chapter when his cell rang. He looked at the iPhone® expecting a call from Shane when they landed, but glancing at the display he saw John's photo.

TJ smiled, "Hey, how are you?"

The immediate change in John's normal tone of voice sent a chill down his spine. "TJ? Turn on CNN® now! The plane carrying the team has an in-flight emergency. Have you got it on?"

TJ was fumbling with the remote. He hadn't turned the television on while writing, choosing to listen to smooth jazz via iTunes Internet service. He rapidly clicked upward through the TV channels until he reached the CNN® Headline news channel. "What happened?"

"Apparently when they took off, one of the main wheels didn't go all the way up. The reporter said they tried to get it back down, but it wouldn't budge. Now it is stuck about half way, and they can't land on the wheels on just one side of the plane."

TJ suddenly pushed himself back deep in the chair, as the plane carrying Shane and the team came into view via another jet chasing them. He could plainly see the wheel partially up and the wheel door open. They both listened to an experienced pilot explain the plane would experience a lot of turbulent shaking of the plane due to the open door, and the wind drag on the obstructed wheels. There was no solution for fixing the wheels, and they would have to crash land. TJ did not like the sound of that. His mind raced for thoughts.

"John? Call me on iChat®. I'm going to hang up, and call Shane's parents. Did they say where they were going to attempt to land?"

John quickly said, "They're coming to Chicago. They are coming to you!"

TJ gulped. "Thanks John. Thank you for calling me. Get going on iChat®. Bye."

TJ loved his iPhone®, and right now it allowed him to speed through and dial Al on his cell phone. It began ringing. "Come on. Pick up!" It rang again. TJ fidgeted. He heard a chime on his laptop and reached over and accepted John's iChat® invitation. In seconds he was looking at him. "Come on. Answer!"

Suddenly Al came on the phone. "Hello?"

"Al, TJ here. Are you driving?"

"Yes, how did you know?"

"Can you pull off and stop? I need to talk to you."

Al became alarmed, "Sure hold just a second. I am doing seventy-five on the freeway. I'm taking this exit." TJ waited impatiently. Finally Al came back on the phone. "Okay, I'm off the road. How are you? What's up?"

432

"Al," began TJ hating what he was about to tell the parent of the man he loved most in the world. "Al, I'm sorry, but Shane's plane has a problem in the air. One side of the plane's wheel structure hung while coming up, and they couldn't get it all the way up, and now they can't get it back down. They are forced to crash-land."

"Oh my god! How in the hell did that happen?"

"I don't know. I'm watching news clips on CNN®. They are coming to Chicago to land, and apparently deliberately spilling fuel, so there is less on board. The runway is being prepared. The airport is on full alert."

Al gulped air, but finally asked, "Where are you?"

TJ's phone suddenly beeped in his ear. "Hold on, Al. I'm getting another call. I'll be right back. Don't hang up." TJ clicked over. "Hello?"

"TJ? TJ? Can you hear me?"

TJ's heart nearly leaped through his chest, "Shane? It's you. Are you okay?"

"No, I am scared shitless. You know I hate to fly in bad weather, but I never imagined on a clear day like today that we would have a plane problem. I knew the plane had a lot of vibration after takeoff, but I never conceived this. The coaches and Walter met up front, and finally they decided to tell us. I'm on the flight phone. We're going to crash, huh…" Shane paused not yet ready to accept what they were going to have to do, "crash-land in Chicago. Are you there?"

"Yes, I am. I've been here a few hours."

"I wish I had flown with you."

"I wish you had, too."

"If I live through this, I want you to work into the contract that I fly with you on the jet."

TJ smiled, "You'll live, and I'll get the contract fixed. I have your dad on the other line. What should I tell him?"

"Tell him I love him and I'm sure everything will be fine. I just hope we make it. I'm pretty tall to stick my head between my knees."

"You do whatever they say. I need for you to be alive when that plane comes to a stop. I love you."

"Me, too. I've got to go. Others need to use the phone. I'll see you soon."

"You'd better, or I'll kick your ass."

Shane had never heard TJ speak like that. Shane repeated, "I'll be there."

TJ flipped over to Al, "Sir, that was Shane. He is reasonably calm though scared. They have no choice but to attempt to crash-land. He said to tell you he loved you and mom very much, and not to worry. He was going to stick his head down to his ankles and hang on."

Al asked, "How long before they land?"

TJ didn't know. He turned to his laptop. "John, do you know what time they are going to do this?"

"Fifteen minutes."

TJ relayed the message. Al spoke, "TJ, don't call Barbara. I'm five minutes from home. She is there fixing some lunch for us. I'll tell her shortly. Can I reach you on your cell?"

"Yes, I'll be right here. Go to CNN® or one of the news channels. Be careful driving, one problem at a time, stay alert, and I'll be right here. Say a prayer and I'll do the same. Bye."

He looked at the laptop so he could see John. "Any news?"

"No. I put the LCD on PIP or dual picture. I have ESPN SportsCenter® on the other channel. They running live footage when it is available, and from time to time they put either the team's picture or Shane on the screen. Bob and Sue just came running in. We're praying, too."

"Thank you." TJ used the remote to figure out the guide on the television, and found ESPN® and hit the button. The hotel didn't have PIP so he put a finger on the 'return' button to go back and forth between the news and the sports channel coverage. They had begun a countdown clock. All the channels were now running the story. He sat there feeling completely helpless. He closed his eyes and prayed. His foot and leg began nervously ticking up and down.

Suddenly, he jumped up and ran to the hotel window. He was on the tenth floor. He yanked all the curtains open and began scanning the horizon recalling he was only ten minutes from the airport. Finally he saw the airport in the distance and wondered which way they would come in from.

He ran back to his laptop and loaded the GPS software. He put in the hotel's location and zoomed back until he could see the runways of the O'Hare Airport. He worked the details until he determined the direction. He ran back to the window and stared intently until he could finally see the airport. He wished he had a pair of binoculars.

He looked back at the television and shuttered. Two minutes to go. He turned the television towards the window. He watched the jet coming down. He looked across the horizon but saw nothing. He looked back at the television. Sixty seconds. He turned back to the window. He waited. He waited some more. Thirty seconds. He saw it. They were coming in from the southeast. They were just a hundred yards into the air. He never let his eyes leave the plane. Down they came…slowly…gently.

TJ began sucking in air as the plane touched the runway, and at first it began to slide across the pavement. Sparks were flying all around the plane. The broken wheel was jammed into the cargo bay storage below Shane's seat causing a terrifying jolt. Suddenly, the plane began a slow clockwise spin and began rocking wing to wing. They had already used up a third of the runway and didn't appear to be slowing down. TJ thought they might run out asphalt.

434

He glanced back at the television. Suddenly, an engine hit the ground and broke off. It bounced on the runway and burst into flames. TJ gasped.

The plane finally reached the section of the runway where the fire department spread fire retardant foam. Nets had been stretched across the runway like those on an aircraft carrier. The plane easily tore through them. They already chewed up two thirds of the long pavement as they continued sliding.

Inside the plane, Shane and the players were screaming, expecting the plane to blow up. TJ put his hands on the windows. He feared an explosion. He glanced back at the television, hoping his eyes hadn't fooled him. The plane had slowed way down and finally came to a stop. He could no longer see the fuselage. He stared at the televisions. Smoke covered the plane. The fire trucks rushed to the scene and began spraying more retardant on the remaining engines. TJ held his breath. He said another prayer.

Suddenly, a door popped open, followed by a bright colored sliding chute that was rapidly filling with air. TJ waited while hoping, praying, and almost willing Shane off that plane. A person abruptly appeared at the door. They hesitated for a second, and then jumped and slid down to the ground. The camera zoomed in and for a brief second TJ saw the face of the man he loved most in the world. He cried out in relief. He fell to his knees, overcome with joy. Shane turned and helped catch his teammates as they began jumping one after the other until finally the coaches came off the plane. Then they ran away from the plane. Next he could see the flight crew drop down the chute. The crews and passengers were scratched, bruised, battered, and numb with fear, but they had all survived.

# THIRTY-SEVEN

The coaches met briefly in the front of the bus as the team made their way to their hotel. They at first thought they should give the boys the afternoon off, but after more discussion decided it might be best to get their minds off the accident, keep them busy, and quickly return the team to normal. They did agree to allow the boys thirty minutes to make phone calls to their families and friends.

Shane called TJ and then his parents from the airport, assuring them he was absolutely fine. Somebody's textbook became loose in the crash and bounced off his head, but he didn't even have a headache. He spent most of the calls assuring his loved ones he was fine.

TJ walked down to the lobby, so he could join the cheerleaders and fans in welcoming the team to the hotel. He gave each of the players a high five, including Shane while desperately trying not to show any emotion. They each gave the other the one finger across the nose and a smile. To know you are loved, is perhaps the best message of all, thought the boys. TJ also wanted to see that Shane was indeed okay. He immediately called Shane's parents and John, and gave them the news. He called Gary to tell him as well.

TJ was spent when he got back to the room, and didn't feel like writing. He lay down and miraculously took a nap. It had been a long day that thankfully ended well. He ate dinner in the room.

Shane had a team meeting after their practice, the team meal, and then a session of study hall. He finally got free and came to see TJ about nine thirty. They held each a long while, talked about what it was like on the plane, and then moved on to how practice went. They made out for a while, but mostly just held the other, feeling grateful they could be together once more.

The next few days were a blur as the team went through public practices in the arena and private practices at a gym. They also had to study for school, and study the scouting reports. With only two games left, they were looking forward to the challenge of winning a second title.

TJ decided to write about the accident into the book so the reader could see what true professionals the coaches were, and especially these young college players. To see them now, you'd never suspect they almost died in a plane crash. Jerry's ankle had steadily improved, and he felt he was at least at ninety-five percent. Larry was draining three-point shots from everywhere. Tim dropped sixteen threes in a row. Shane's confidence was at an all time high as he hit shots from everywhere he wanted. They drilled flawlessly. The coach told them they were more prepared for this semi-final game than they were last year. He told them they were the best they could be.

TJ added his comments to the chapter as well. When he was done, he sent it to Dick and Walter. He wanted to make sure he should put the airplane incident in the book, and if so, did he do it well. The next day after minor corrections, he sent it on to Janet.

Saturday was a long day for the team with an hour of shooting in the arena, and a short easy practice in the gym. There were no study halls, so the day moved slowly as they napped, read, or watched television. Some brought DVD's to watch. A Saturday night game made the long day just creep by.

TJ used the day by moving his brain as far away from basketball as possible. He spent most of it writing the new gay book.

Once he tired, he spent an hour reading his research notes on the killing of a buffalo for a future western story. He downloaded charts, and found an Acrobat PDF® document of a scan of a big buffalo with long lists all around it with lines indicating what the Indians did with each part of the buffalo carcass. Unlike the white men who killed them mostly for their hides, the Indians often survived the entire winter season on just one buffalo per family.

Once satisfied with the knowledge gained from his research, he set about describing the characters and the setting for the story in the great northwest. He continued his research, getting excited with the more he learned. Soon, the storyline began popping out of his head. He typed the notes as fast he could, enjoying the new story, and looking forward to writing it.

TJ looked up at the clock and decided it was time to head to the arena. He packed up his laptop, changed clothes, and caught a cab.

The game sold out, but he felt shocked so many Taylor fans were already there two hours before the game. Taylor University was playing in the first game at seven. He decided to walk through the fan area to see the booths and fun things for the kids to do before making his way up to the pressroom. He picked up the most recent press release, marked it up, and typed in the key facts into his laptop. He secured the laptop, and made his way to the buffet line.

Half way through loading up his plate, Dick Vitale walked up to him. "Hey buddy, how are you?"

"I'm fine," replied TJ. "Are you ready for the game?"

"Yeah, I'm doing some features and wished I was doing the broadcast, but CBS is still in bed with NCAA."

TJ groaned, "That's the best part about seeing the tournament live is you don't have to listen to that knucklehead commentator they use."

"Hey, want some company for supper?"

"Sure, get a plate. I've over near the wall. I'll save you a seat."

TJ and Dick talked for a while between bites before Dick finally said, "I have to tell you something. I was in New York at the ESPN® studios when the story broke about Shane's plane. I was so stunned. I dropped to my knees and prayed for the safety of the Taylor team and the crew. I am so glad they all survived. My wife has been all over me ever since. She wants me to find a way to do less flying."

"You need a big motorcoach," teased TJ.

"You're right, I do," replied a grinning Dick. "When are you picking up the new one?"

"About May twenty-fifth in Junction City, Oregon," replied TJ.

"I can't wait to see it. I ran in to Brian Kenny in New York, and he said he had been on the phone several times with the Country Coach® engineers. He ordered the remote equipment for your coach. He said to tell you he found excellent twelve volt spots for your lighting."

"Excellent. Thank you. We'll get home on June first. We'll have a few projects to do, and Shane is going to rookie drills in Phoenix the second week, and of course there is the big NBA draft later in the month. Why don't you fly up, and we'll give you the tour of the new coach? Maybe your wife would like to see it, too?"

"Now that's an idea. I'll see if I can set it up. I would love for her to travel with me, as I miss her when I'm away so much during the basketball season. Of course, I try to make it up to her in the off-season, but after two weeks at home she starts saying, "Dickie, don't you have somewhere to go?" He laughed as he faked her voice.

"I'd love to have the both of you come up for a visit. It'll be summertime and a great time to get out of hot Tampa."

"Okay, well, time to go to work. I'll see you later. Go Taylor. Go Shane!" he cheered as playfully slapped TJ's back.

"Thanks, Dick. Bye."

Shane told TJ that Illinois would be tough. Unfortunately, he was right. They scored four baskets before Taylor finally settled down and started playing defense. Shane missed his first shot but kept his cool. Three possessions later, Jerry made a fast and hard pass down the line and into Shane's hands. He leaned into the man guarding him, showed him the ball, received a swipe to his head, and laid it in the net as gentle as putting an egg in a basket.

Larry hit a three, Jerry got a quick steal and run, and Taylor tied it up. Then it became and back and forth game with the lead changing over and over again. Taylor ran as fast as possible, but the coach asked for more. So far, the big men from the north were not slowing down. The score at the half was thirty-two all. Many broadcasters considered these two teams the best in the country.

TJ sighed heavily and went for dessert in the pressroom. TJ was sitting alone eating a piece of apple caramel pie when Dick came up behind him. "TJ? I want you to meet a friend of mine."

TJ got up and turned around, expecting to find some little old lady basketball fan. Dick continued, "TJ, this is Michael Jordan."

438

TJ's mouth dropped. Michael said, "I'm so pleased to meet you. I read your book on last year's team and I liked it. Are you doing it again this year?"

TJ finally managed to smile, "Yes, and thank you. I'm so pleased to meet you. Shane and I have been working hard on this year's book. Of course, he is doing the sweat part, and I'm writing the results."

"I'll look forward to reading it. Are they going to win tonight?"

TJ laughed, "Yes, but it is going to be close. Illinois has a great team, but Taylor University usually gets better and better in the second half. I can tell you that right now Shane is sitting in his locker making a list of the things he can do to make his game better."

"I am really enjoying his play. I bet he is a number one draft pick."

"We hope so."

Dick broke in, "Well, we'd better go. I just couldn't resist introducing the greatest to you."

"Thank you, Dick. Michael, thank you for setting the bar high enough for all to seek, but mostly for being such a classy competitor. I wish Shane was here, he would get a thrill out of meeting you."

Michael grinned, "Well, after they win, I'll see him in the locker room. It was a pleasure to meet you, too."

Shane didn't waste any time. He brought the ball into Jerry, went down and set a screen, faked a right spin, then twisted the other way on a set play. The ball came to Larry, who tossed it to Shane who laid it up and received a foul on his man—the third one.

After the shot, Shane dove on the inbound pass, caught it, flipped it to Jerry who dunked it, and another foul on Shane's man, and with four fouls his coach took him out of the game. They sent a sophomore in to keep up with Shane.

A few possessions later, Jerry sent a blinding bullet pass to Shane in the paint. He immediately went up with a high arching shot with the sophomore riding on his shoulder. He made the basket and the foul shot.

Larry got hot from the corner and made four three-point plays in eight minutes. At the third television time out, Coach Timmons exalted his players, but told them they had to get tougher on defense if they were going to stay ahead for good. He told them to run harder and move the ball faster on offense. He could finally see a change in their opponent's legs.

Shane got a rebound and flung it quickly to Larry, who threw the ball hard to Jerry for a fast-break score. Taylor was now up by ten. Shane called for a defensive stop as they came down the court. Jerry bent over and slapped the floor like a bull. He would have snorted if he knew how, but he yelled out, "Come on, try to get pass me. You can't do it. Your legs are spent. You're moving slow. I'm going to take the ball away from you."

The Illinois boy was listening and getting mad, but failed to see Shane run from his man and set a trap on the player. At the last possible second, he tried to throw the ball, but Shane swatted it with a big hand, caught the bounce, sprinted the court and dunked it. The Taylor fans leaped to their feet and cheered loudly. The arena came alive. Shane pointed at Jerry, giving him the credit. Jerry slapped the floor again while grinning.

With four minutes to play, Taylor led by fifteen. There was still time for a team to come back. Coach Timmons again called for defensive stops. Shane watched as the man with four fouls returned to the game. He was about to bring the ball in. Shane had been watching him closely throughout the game. He felt like he had a seventy percent chance of guessing which way he was going to inbound the ball. Shane jumped straight up twice making it difficult for him to think about going over his head. This left only two choices, left or right.

The man suddenly stepped back for a strong leg throw. To Shane that meant across the center court, so he dove right and got a hand on the ball, dribbled once, and as he started for the basket, the player who had thrown the ball angrily pushed him hard across the court, and nearly into his own bench. Whistles blew all across the court.

Shane got up quickly with some spirit showing. Jerry and Larry rushed to him while getting in front of Shane to stop him from responding. Coach came on the floor and did the same. The referee called a two-shot intentional foul and a technical on Illinois. The player left the floor while Shane walked to the foul line. He hit both of his shots, so the coach decided to let him go for the technical. He hit that as well.

Taylor went on to win by fourteen. Shane scored twenty-six points, and now they were in the championship game Monday night, and one win away from repeating their title.

TJ caught a cab to the hotel and immediately sat down and wrote the game into the book. He had just finished when Shane knocked on the door. TJ welcomed him with a big hug. They sat down and talked about the game with TJ making a few notes.

Suddenly, Shane said, "You won't believe who I met in the locker room after the game."

TJ laughed, "Michael Jordan."

"Now how in the world did you know that?"

"Dick brought him over and introduced me at halftime. He said such great things about you. He was pulling for Taylor, and he told me if you won he was going to the locker room. Isn't that cool? We both got to meet him."

"Yes, and it is cool that we won. We have just one more game. Wow!"

TJ wrote all day and loved every second of it. He wrote two new chapters for **Forever Alone, Again** and started a chapter on the western story.

440

A Writer's Fantasy

However, he soon realized it was almost suppertime. Shane and TJ rushed out the door to the back elevator and made their way to big seafood place. There they met Al and Barbara, and Gary and gang. TJ and Shane gave each of them a hug. They were all so glad to see Shane after the plane crash.

After reaching their table in the back, they began talking about the week, and did their best not to talk about the airplane incident. Barbara wanted to sit by her son, so they broke protocol with TJ sitting opposite Shane while he sat between his parents. TJ understood, and didn't mind sharing him every now and then.

They ate some appetizers, big salads, and fresh fruit, a bit of sushi; at least everyone did but TJ, as he hated seafood that smelled like fish, and finally their meal. They laughed and make fun of each other, told stories about things that happen in Asheville, and they all had a great time. Gary had a big sales month and insisted on paying the tab. TJ would try and get him to take some cash later, but he wouldn't succeed.

TJ asked him about how the fishing was this spring and he bragged about how many he caught. Tammy said it was too cold for her, but she would go for a while until he caught her limit of fish, and take those home so he could then work on his limit. He bragged they would soon have a freezer full.

They asked about the basketball book, and he teased and said he would already be done with it if Shane would guarantee they were going to win the last game. He didn't tell them he decided to keep the plane crash in the book.

As they left the restaurant, TJ could tell that Barbara was having a hard time letting her son go. She held his hand, put an arm around him, and Shane allowed her to be a worried mom for a while. TJ suggested the four of them get some ice cream. They walked a few blocks to get there, and though it was still a little cold in Chicago, especially if the wind blew, they enjoyed the walk together after their meal.

They sat inside the creamery enjoying their selection with TJ getting two scoops of pistachio ice cream with bananas and nuts. Shane also went for nuts by ordering pecan ice cream. Afterwards, they called for two cabs and said their goodbyes for now.

Shane visited TJ for about an hour before curfew. They made the most of it. Soon life would change for them, one way or the other. While there was nothing TJ could do to change the outcome of the game, Shane felt there was a lot he could do. He would not lose without giving it his all. He would leave everything on the court. He would make TJ and his parents proud, and he would honor his coach and his team. Tomorrow was championship day. He knew they possessed the advantage of experience, but would it be enough.

TJ wrote emails to Dick and Walter asking for their help in choosing a sports agent for Shane. He knew it was slightly premature, but after studying his calendar, he wanted to get things moving fast, so he could participate before the book tour. He then called Al and told him what he was up to, and asked him to give him his top three choices for sports agent. Al did and he liked the approach, saying it sounded like a great way to pick one. TJ knew they would not select the final choice until they were all in New York. He said he would arrange flights for Al and Barbara arriving Thursday night. He arranged flights and hotels and then fired off emails to Sam, Jerome, and Jake in New York, asking if they could make themselves available on Friday for presentations by three sports agents. He also asked for their top three suggestions. Thankfully, they were all available and working. It was a busy Monday for all. Soon he began to get their replies or nominations, so he created a spreadsheet for the data. With just six voting, TJ grinned when he realized that two of the three they each nominated were the same agents, but added together with all the voters, they selected only three men out of some sixty registered sports agents in the country. The vote was pretty much a tie between two men and close third for the other one. TJ smiled at how his unscientific poll turned out. TJ asked Walter for the contact information for the three selected.

Soon, he was on the phone setting up the presentations. He explained he was the author of last year's book with Shane, and the family asked him to setup the meetings. He also told them that he was currently writing the sequel that would end tonight. Nothing would be official until after the game. The agents agreed and meetings were scheduled for nine, eleven and two o'clock on Friday. He notified Sam, Jerome, and Jake of the offices they were to be at and when. He thanked all by email for their help. He then called John and told him to call the Learjet agency and arrange the flight for Thursday afternoon so Shane could attend class. He would miss Friday classes, but Walter would get him excused. He told John he needed him on the first leg of the tour to pack a bag.

TJ went to each agency's website and read everything about their company. He then began researching everything he could Google® on them. He read articles and reports. He even checked out the Better Business Bureau®. He then called Dick Vitale and asked him how he would find out more on these men and their companies. He made several suggestions and then dropped some names for each one, and gave TJ their phone numbers. These were NBA current players. TJ was immensely grateful. Dick loved TJ's tenacity for knowledge. He wished them luck on tonight's game. He felt Taylor could win, but they would have to work hard on every possession. UCLA would not go down easily, he warned.

TJ spent the next two hours working the phones until he caught most of the players. For the most part, he received polite answers indicating their loyalty to their agent. TJ's final question for all was simply, if your agent could do one more thing for you, what would it be? He made notes on their answers. He studied his previous notes, added in the references, and gave each

442

a score. They were pretty tight. He began to believe they could draw straws and come out fine.

Satisfied he had done all he could do, he ordered room service for lunch, read the newspapers, made some game notes, ate lunch and took a nap. He woke up at two with too much time on his hands. He washed his face, fixed himself a glass of Diet Mountain Dew® for the caffeine, and sat down to work on his gay story. He didn't take him long until he was caught up in the tale, and once again, the therapy of writing was working.

Shane came up for a visit after his team meal, team meeting, and study hall, as it was a school day. They talked for a while about how things were going, what his match up would be with UCLA, and life in general. TJ didn't mention the trip on Thursday or his plan. He wanted Shane thinking about tonight's game. They moved to the couch and cuddled for a while, talking about nothing particular, just spending quality time with the person they loved most, and though the minutes were running out, they both felt revived, confident, and devoted.

For the last time this season, Shane boarded the bus for a game in the arena. TJ rode with the team because he feared getting a cab for the big game might be difficult. Win or lose, they would not fly out until the next morning so no bags were packed. They parted ways as the team was escorted to the locker room, and TJ made the trek to the pressroom. He followed his routine, as if afraid a change or alteration might jinx the game, and he certainly didn't want a lost to be his fault.

Dick came by to wish him luck and TJ thanked him again for all the help. He read the press releases before standing in line for supper. Nervous, he made his way to the court to watch Shane warm-up for his last game as a college player. He knew Shane would miss playing for Taylor, and especially for Coach Timmons and his staff. He trusted the coaching staff when he chose to come there, and they never let him down. He didn't intend to let them down in this last game either. Shane looked good and relaxed, thought TJ. He looked up at the clock counting down to the game starting time.

There were many famous people in attendance and it took an extra ten minutes for all the hoopla preceding the game. Shane was ready to play, and he fidgeted while wishing the game would start. TJ used his press pass to get near the tunnel and spotted Shane in the back. He gave him a three finger sign for chill, and the one on the nose for love. Shane pulled his earlobe, but there was no smile. TJ knew he was in his game zone and nothing would distract him.

When they came out of the huddle to take the court, the fans cheered, the referees went to their spots, the announcer was still blathering, but Shane looked to one chair in the arena of thirty-five thousand and stared at TJ's face. TJ clapped with the fans and yelled go Taylor as loud as he could.

UCLA had some big men and an excellent shooting guard. Jerry would have his hands full slowing that boy down. He had set in his mind half the battle of stopping the guard would be to run him to death on offense. He intended to step on every square inch of that court, zigging and zagging until the boy's tongue was hanging out, and he was panting like a dog.

TJ's man, a senior was about the same height, and possessed excellent game stats. Shane had scored more points this season, but his opponent had more rebounds. They both intended to make the other change their habits and patterns. The ball went up and UCLA tipped the ball, but Larry caught it, flung it to Shane, who threw it hard and fast to Jerry for a quick lay up.

UCLA came back with a pretty three from their shooting guard and Jerry was not happy about it. He came down the court, caught a screen from Shane and shot his own three. Back and forth the lead changed as the score began climbing. Shane was bumping and banging with his man on both ends of the court. The referee warned them to settle down. Jerry threw a hard pass down the lane, and Shane smartly leaned into his man earning a foul from him while Shane made both baskets. Eight possessions later, he did the same thing on the other side, and sent the boy to the locker room at the half with two fouls, and Taylor led by six.

The pundits were changing their minds about a UCLA upset, but TJ knew the game was far from being won. Coach Timmons was preparing a final season speech to fire up his team, worthy of writing and perhaps publishing, but only the team would hear it. Shane made his usual list of things to work on and change. He had been studying the inbound pass, and thought he could make a steal when they needed it. He told Jerry he felt he could dunk over his man, and shoot six-foot jumpers as needed. The coach told them he expected Shane to score some points, and that would force them to double-team him. They knew what to do by getting the ball to the open man be it Larry or Tim. They huddled up in the locker room for the last time, gave a big yell, and returned for the second half.

Everyone in the arena was on their feet as Shane brought the ball in to start the second half. He threw it to Jerry, set up a screen, moved down court, went around Larry's man, and briefly got a step ahead of his defender. Jerry threw it like a flat shot to the rim. No one saw Shane coming with a sudden burst of speed. He caught the alley-oop pass and dunked it, intending to express to UCLA that this game was Taylors.

Again the score became close and twice UCLA took the lead, but each time one of the Taylor men scored again. Shane already scored twenty-four points with four minutes to play. His man had four fouls on him. Shane had two. Coach grinned in the huddle and told them they were going to win. He said, you know, I don't think I'm going to tell you what to do because you already know what I'm going to say, so I'll just go over there and sit down and enjoy the game. They looked at him like he was crazy, but Shane said,

"Boys, it is time for defensive stops. We must make good judgment on offense and score each time, but we must stop them from scoring to win. Can we do that?"

They yelled yes in unison. The coach returned, "See, I told you. This game is ours, so just get those defensive stops. Jerry, be aware of the clock and score in those final two minutes. If it is close, go to our end of game plays we discussed yesterday. Eat up the clock and score. Okay, let's go win a championship!"

They came out of the huddle fired up. UCLA had the ball in the far court after a Taylor score. Taylor put on the full court press as they had all game. Shane watched his man but didn't attempt a steal, however, he made it tough for him to bring the ball in. Jerry almost caught and stole the pass, missing by inches. They hustled down the court and began their defensive stand. Shane called for the stop. Back and forth the ball went, but their opponents could not find an easy shot. With the possession clock down to six seconds they hurried a three-point shot, and it absolutely bounced up high and fell dead center in the net, putting UCLA up by three points. Shane paid no attention to the crowd. He grabbed the ball and brought it in fast. They rushed down the court with Jerry's man barely keeping up with him. Jerry let up like he was going to pass to Larry, the defense adjusted, Shane stepped back out of the paint, Jerry threw him the ball, he jumped, spun, was fouled by his opponent, and made the shot. His man had just fouled out, and Shane had one more foul shot. He tied the game. They sent a junior in to guard him.

At the two-minute mark, the score was tied. UCLA had the ball and their guard wanted to shoot. He passed the ball a few times, but Jerry and Shane knew the boy wanted to be the hero. Shane had a bit more freedom with the junior on his tail. As their forward slung their guard the ball with just four seconds remaining on the possession clock, Shane lunged forward and managed to just tap the ball out of the path of their guard. Jerry scooped it up, ran it down and scored. They were now up by two.

Again the guard wanted to shoot, but Jerry was on him like glue to a shoe. Taylor was holding them down. The possession clock was running down, with four seconds the guard suddenly pulled up, and somehow shot over a leaping Jerry and it went in. UCLA was up by one with ninety seconds to play in the final game.

Coach Timmons had been studying their opponent. Their posture changed, they had lost the spring in their step, they were breathing hard when the whistle blew, and he was proud of his team because they still looked strong. He decided not to call timeout, as that would allow UCLA to rest. He called a play from the sidelines. Shane was to get the ball at the top of the key. If he had a shot he was to take it, but if not, he was to kick it out to Larry as usual, and Jerry would back him up about fifteen feet away. The ball moved a few times back and forth. Jerry waited until six seconds and drove hard to the opposite side like he was going to throw it to Tim. Shane ran up the lane and the pass was there. Jerry began sprinting to the far side in case Shane had to kick it back out. Shane turned as he caught the ball. Two of their men rushed to block him, but Shane remained focused as he shot the ball. UCLA fouled him. The buzzer sounded just a split second after it left his hand. Swish! Taylor was up by one. Shane made the foul shot and now they led by two.

Fifty-five seconds to play, the fans were on their feet cheering and pleading, coaches were chewing the white cotton-like stuff in their dry mouths, hands were fidgeting, and Shane began guarding the new junior player bringing the ball in. He watched him carefully and prevented the player from throwing high. Jerry was all over his man on the court behind him, but somehow they got the ball in play with a wide throw to the center by the junior.

They set up their defense as UCLA hurried the ball down. Again they went back to the left and over to the right, the clock ticking, hearts pounding. Four seconds into the possession, and suddenly Jerry slipped. The UCLA guard couldn't believe he had broken free. He rushed just west of the three-point line and shot. Swish! They had taken the lead by one and twenty-eight seconds to play.

Shane brought the ball in without an ounce of nervousness. He had played in many close games since his first game in the fifth grade. He threw the ball to Jerry, set up a screen, looked down the court, and saw that Larry's man had drifted up court. Jerry threw Larry the ball in the corner. Twelve seconds to play. Larry never hesitated as he leaped from behind the three-point line. Shane noted something different about the arch and ran at lighting speed down the left lane to prepare for a rebound. The ball hit the back of the rim and squirted off to the left just as Shane surprised UCLA's inside men with his sudden appearance. He made a big leap into the air. He caught the ball with six seconds to play. He went down and back up to a jump shot with two seconds to play.

The ball did not swish as he intended. Shane was bumped out of bounds. The ball bounced off the front of the rim to the far side, and fell out with no seconds left, but a whistle had blown. Shane had been obviously fouled, though UCLA would protest loudly, but just short of being called for a technical. The court was cleared. The game was effectively over, but Shane had two foul shots, and a chance to win the championship.

The coach tried not to worry. Many times he had seen his star player shooting foul shots for hours in his gym. Before games he shot foul shots. He had the second best record on the team behind Larry, and for a big man that was saying a lot. His players huddled around him, tried to say words of confidence and encouragement, and then backed away.

Shane bounced the ball once as usual, took his shot, and watched it arch as it had in thousands of other shots and he waited. Swish! The score was tied, with one remaining chance to win.

446

Shane bounced the ball once, sighed, took his shot, and watched it go up and instantly he knew it was off. It barely kissed the back of the rim and bounced out. They were going into overtime. There was a collective sign from the teams and fans in the arena. He walked to the huddle feeling bad. He had already scored more than any other player on the court at thirty-one points, but he missed the one that counted the most.

Coach Timmons grinned at his team. "Shane, I guess you weren't quite ready to give up your college career. Boys, we practiced overtime drills all year long. I betting Shane will score some more points for us, but he can't do it by himself. We need defensive stops on every possession, and quality safe points on offense. They're winded boys. We've got them right where we need them. They are exhausted. Number thirty-two has four fouls on him, so if we can, let's make him foul us. Are you ready for some fun?"

Shane caught the tipoff and without hesitation caught Larry on the run, and they scored the first basket. He watched the junior on the inbound pass and just barely missed steal. On the far end, they worked the clock down taking a shot at the last minute. It was a miss and Shane went higher than he had all season and brought the rebound down. He kicked it out to Jerry and hustled down the court.

Jerry called green. Shane waited to the last second, ran to the foul line, the ball came to him, and he turned and shot, putting two points on the board with a nice swish. They were up by four.

UCLA scored a three-point play from the power hungry guard, but Jerry called green blue. Shane again came to the foul line, but now he was carrying baggage, as not one, but two defensive men came with him. Larry broke from the corner to the goal, and Jerry hit him with a bullet pass for a layup, and they were up by three. UCLA scored two on short jumper. They two teams swapped baskets a few times. Soon the clock was at sixty seconds to play for the second time that night. Taylor was now up by just one.

Coach Timmons was tempted again to call a timeout, but kept to his course, knowing his boys were stronger. The ball was kicked out to Larry who made a long shot with just seconds remaining on the possession clock, it bounced out, but Shane grabbed it, and put it in. They were up by three and twenty-eight seconds remaining.

If UCLA could get the ball down the court, chances are their shooting guard would hit a three and tie the game again. Shane was not about to let that happen. He was again all over the junior bringing the ball in. Shane decided to play the odds. The boy suddenly stepped back telegraphing a long throw perhaps across the mid court. Shane dove as the ball left the junior's fingers. Shane snatched the ball, rolled over, dribbled once, and dunked it hard. They were up by five, ten seconds to go.

The junior brought the ball in successfully. The guard rushed down the court with Jerry all over him. He shot and it hit the rim, the ball bounced high eating up the clock, and Shane pulled down the rebound with one-second left. They couldn't foul him fast enough to stop the clock. The buzzer blew, and Shane had the winning game ball in his hands.

Suddenly, he leaped into the air with such a ferocious visceral scream that thousands of camera flashes lit up the arena. He ran to his teammates and they huddled around him. He ran to his coach and hugged him, told him he loved him, and thanked him. He spotted his parents coming down the aisle, and hugged them. And then he ran all the way across the court, up to the fifth row, and grabbed and hugged TJ, Gary, Tammy, Scrappy, and Meagan who rushed to TJ's seat. Shane was so excited. He gave the ball to TJ, and asked him to hold it for him.

He returned to the court as the Taylor fans cheered. He shook hands with his incredible opponents, and he again hugged his teammates. They had done what seemed impossible by winning not one, but two National Championships in a row. Shane was once again voted the Most Valuable Player. He was so overjoyed and excited that he just could not stop smiling.

TJ finally had to sit down cradling the ball. His energy was spent. He had little voice left, but he was smiling. Gary's gang was still jumping up and down, but TJ just sat there smiling. He waved at Barbara and Al and they, too, sat down while all around them was bedlam. It was a glorious moment they would cherish for many years. The Taylor University team had won in overtime. They were the National Champions.

# THIRTY-EIGHT

After the flight home the following morning, Shane spent most of the afternoon doing interviews via their remote setup while TJ and John researched a commercial trainer. They were disappointed in their Google® skills as they kept coming up empty. TJ wanted to find someone to coach Shane into performing well in front of a camera for video and still photography, and work on his public speaking skills. TJ had learned that sports stars are in high demand for speaking engagements. This skill could be invaluable in all facets of their plans from expanding his commercial success with sponsors, to motivating companies and individuals into donating to the foundation's efforts. Last summer, TJ simply asked Shane how many times did he listen to a sports star talk, and finally, which one motivated him to succeed. Shane smiled and finally agreed he would try.

TJ called Robby and asked him who trains the racecar drivers and explained what he was after. He began rattling off a list of people and companies in the Concord area, but he also put TJ on hold and asked Larry for his suggestions.

"TJ? Larry suggested a studio called Top Line Productions. The owner is Billy Coble. He was a top television director until eight years ago when he had a heart attack. He relocated here on a promise to his wife, and opened his studio. He soon realized there was a niche for high profile drivers to learn how to pitch sponsor products like a pro."

"Does he run a school?"

"Oh no," replied Robby, "much more. Each person is trained individually as if he was his only client. He is like a physical trainer for marketing. He'll take your boy; teach him to work the camera, how to look, how to walk and talk, and how to sell on the air, and even off the air. He'll soon be able to give speeches and motivate his sponsors into spending more money with them."

"Perfect. Can I call him or do I need an introduction?"

Robby laughed, "Larry's talking to him on the other line. Jeff worked with him years ago. They're pals. Hold on." TJ could hear Larry in the background. Robby returned, "Larry said hang up. He said Billy is calling you now. Talk to you later."

TJ clicked off the headset as the phone rang. John answered TJI, put Billy on hold, and TJ picked right up, while grinning at mister cool professional John. "Hello, TJ here. May I help you?"

"TJ this is Billy Coble. Congratulations on winning the National Championship. I take it you were the guy in the stands that was holding on to the game ball?"

TJ laughed, "Yes, sir. Got the ball right here. Shane just had a phenomenal season, ending a great collegiate career, but now it is time to get

449

ready for the big leagues. Shane is very interested in charity work. Jeff Gordon has helped us set up a foundation, we're building offices next to his, and he and Larry have been so kind and wonderful to us. Here's what is going down."

TJ explained the trip to New York to pick an agency, and reviewed the rest of their team to him. He finished by saying, "Shane is pretty good at doing basketball interviews and news spots on our in-house remote studio setup, but I need for him to sell big time sponsors so we can grow our business and in turn mushroom our foundation. Robby tells me you're the guy that can give him the skills he needs."

"I'm a big fan. Shane is incredible, and most of the ballplayers I work with are not half as good looking as he is. They'll just have to zoom back on the camera if they want a full body shot, but that's no problem."

"How does your training work?"

"How soon do you need to start?"

"How about tomorrow after lunch? He has classes in the morning."

"I can do that. Here's the break down on the cost for you. You also need to go to my website and show Shane how run the podcasts so he can start working. I'll see you tomorrow. Tell him to dress casual, but bring a few good shirts, and sports jackets, and tell him to shave well."

TJ hung up, and started laughing. John's face became a huge puzzle. "What are you laughing at?"

"Now all I have to do is convince Shane to really do this."

"He didn't know about it?"

"Well, we talked about it last summer on how he could make a ton of money if he could work a crowd like Jeff does. He just didn't know his training is going to start tomorrow. Bring up those podcasts. Let's see what he is doing. We need to motivate Shane."

They watched about six of them including a promo for his agency with clips from the people he has trained. Shane came in the door grinning.

"Hey guys. How's it going?"

TJ got a hug from him and so did John. "How was school after winning a second championship?"

"It is a zoo over there. Media is everywhere. I did a number of spots for various things. They're doing a whole section in Sunday's newspaper. Sports Illustrated is putting me on the cover. I insisted they put a picture of the team there, too. It is wild."

"I guess you don't have practice today. Are you ready to move on to your new career, mister NBA star?"

Shane grinned, "You're not fooling me. What are you up to?"

TJ laughed, "You're right. I have been on the phone all day setting up all kinds of things. Thursday after your class we're flying to New York City. Your folks are going to meet us there. Sam, Jake, and Jerome are ready to go as well. We have three presentations and companies to visit in one day.

450

One of them is going to be your new sports agent. Here's what went down."
TJ explained how he got the three names from Al, Dick, Walter, and these presentations are by the top three winners.

"So we're flying up and I'm taking John with us. I'm thinking of taking him on the basketball tour or at least the first week, we'll see. We have a number of tie-in products, and I need somebody to push them for us. He has your new website up and running. I need for you to learn how to sell the sponsors on the fact that you can sell their products. You have to learn how to do commercials for television, radio, and photo shoots like a professional model and spokesperson. Just like Jeff and the other racecar drivers."

"How am I going to learn to do that?"

"We got you a trainer?"

"A trainer? Who?"

"The same guy that trained Jeff Gordon, and many other stars. We have a meeting tomorrow right after lunch. We'll leave as soon as you get out of class. Come here. I want you to watch this."

John put the podcasts on the big screen and Shane was soon impressed. "You really think I can do this?"

"I know you can. You'll raise tons of money for our business and foundation. You've seen the NASCAR® guys doing it, and some NBA guys have endorsements, but their commercials suck. I never want you to suck on camera. This will get you ready to start showing the sponsors what you can do. Is this okay?"

"Yeah, sure. It sounds fun, but I'm bound to make an ass of myself."

"You'll be fine as long as they don't ask you to dance!"

Shane laughed, "You're in for it now."

TJ grinned as he continued, "Here's what you need for clothes, and they need for you to shave well."


The three boys laughed and cut up all the way to Concord. The huge yearlong stress finally fell off Shane's shoulders, and TJ noted he was back to having a great time. They told war stories on each other to John. They discovered the studio was just a few miles from their new offices. The lobby was nicely done with lots of photos of his clients. They were ushered into Billy's plush office. TJ noted Billy was dressed business casual, but with great taste. Everything he wore was from top designers. He had blond hair, blue eyes, and a great golf tan, and he was far from shy.

"Hey boys, I'm so glad to meet you. Thank you for coming down. Shane," he began as he shook his hand, "you are an amazing player and will have a great career. Congratulations on your second title. That is staggering." He turned to TJ, "I recognize your voice." He shook TJ's hand as well. "Did you watch the podcasts?"

"Yes, and we are very impressed. Shane watched as well. Billy, this is my personal assistant and office manager, John Bunting. He also designs our websites, graphics, and promotional pieces."

Billy turned to John and shook his hand. "John, you're so talented to be so young. Boy, I wish I had known what I know now when I was your age. I'd own a movie studio in Hollywood. It's a pleasure to meet you."

TJ was impressed that Billy took time to chat with John and make him feel welcomed. TJ explained they were leaving for New York on Thursday, but Shane would be back Sunday night and could return Monday afternoon. Billy explained some guys were naturals and others had to work at it. Jeff was a natural and now he is guest hosting talk shows, and making motivation speeches for big cash. He said they could start right now. Billy picked up his phone and dialed a number and three people came in. This is your training crew, and he made the introductions. They took Shane down the hall to a studio. They began teaching him about lights, cameras, smiles, and more.

Billy sat down with TJ and showed him a number of videos of his team working with sports celebrities. They watched a series of before and after video and photo shoots, and the results impressed TJ and John. Billy gave him a tour of the studio including numerous smaller rooms for training with his teams. The center of the building was a real studio that he leased to various production and agency crews visiting in town and needing a place to work. They watched from an observation window as the crew was taping a home improvement store television commercial with John Herring, a hockey player.

They returned to his office and got down to business. "Billy, you've developed a beautiful facility, and we believe you're the guy to help Shane. What is the cost for the project?"

Billy smiled, "I like the sound of that as the transformation really is a project. It's seventy-five thousand to get him ready. Later, he may want to come back and polish up his performance, and we can do that on a per cost basis. It doesn't matter to us how many hours—it is results you're paying for. Do we have a deal?"

TJ had called Larry to get a ballpark figure, and he hit it right on the nose. "Yes, we do."

"TJ, there's one more thing. I saw some of your interviews in New York promoting your book last year. Did the publisher train you?"

"Yes, I have done some radio and television in the past, and was never shy about speaking in front of a crowd, so yeah, they told me what to do."

Billy frowned, "Well, it was okay, but with your face, and especially your voice, you could do better. I'll tell you what I am going to do—I will train you for free for two reasons. First you need me," he laughed, "and two, I always look for someone in a star's entourage to help him after he leaves our training program. I sense that person is going to be you. Am I right?"

"Yes you are."

"Excellent."

"Just give me your card, and I'll have our accountant overnight a check to you tomorrow."

Billy grinned, "Now that is what I call organization. Very good! I guarantee you are going to get far more than your monies worth." He turned to John, "John, how about you and I putting your boss to work?"

John grinned as they went down the hall to another training room. By dark Shane had completed numerous headshots, plus he learned how to dress for the camera, and they rehearsed several commercial scripts. Thankfully, Shane possessed an incredible memory and recalled everything he was taught. Billy told one of his team members to prepare CD Rom disks for John to take back to their office to prepare promo kits for Friday. He gave TJ several sample kits he had done for other stars. He said in a few weeks he would have top kits prepared for both Shane and TJ.

The trainers had some good laughs at a few flubs by Shane and TJ, and they all laughed together. They explained to Shane the importance of shaking hands with the production crews he would be working with, thanking each one for their efforts, and to be a bit self-deprecating about oneself, and to do so with humor, making the crew want to not only work with you, but to do their best work. TJ learned the same things in a different studio while John watched, answered TJ's phone, checked emails, and using his laptop, he began working on the promo materials they would print for Shane and the trip to New York. He was thankful the new full color digital printer was setup and installed on Monday. It printed on high gloss paper, making the pictures sharp and true. With Billy's help, TJ and John picked out a full color promo folder, added a picture of Shane scoring, and order a hundred folders for overnight delivery.

They returned on Wednesday and continued their training. TJ explained he needed a video promo of Shane's best work in a week or so. Billy said they would obtain that goal. Shane would return on Monday, but tomorrow they were all flying to New York.

While John felt absolutely exhilarated about flying to New York in the Learjet, but it had become old hat to TJ and Shane. They delighted in watching him. TJ went right to work once they were in the air until Susie served lunch. They laughed and enjoyed each other's humor, and Susie thought they were her best customers. They landed in good time and with great weather. Spring had arrived in New York City, and they were glad to be rid of the heavy overcoats they often brought when heading north. The car service loaded up their luggage, and drove to their hotel. TJ arranged a suite with TJ and Shane in one bedroom, and across the living room was the entrance to John's room. Laptops were set up, clothes unpacked, and they waited for Al and Barbara to arrive and call.

About six o'clock Shane's phone rang. "Hi, mom. How was the flight?"

"Excellent and safe. We just arrived in our room. Are you boys hungry?"

"Yes, we are. TJ has reservations. Why don't you freshen up, call us, and we'll meet you in the lobby."

"Okay, just give us about ten minutes. I'm starved, too."

Hugs were exchanged, and they used the car service to take the group to an Italian restaurant Dick suggested. It was a classy place, and void of fans. They devoured appetizers, big salads, and finally their main courses. They discussed all their big adventures, and no longer hid discussions about the NBA, but remained quiet about their new home and office in Concord.

Later in the evening, TJ and Shane were finally alone and cherished the moment. They made love on the eighteenth floor, while laughing and giggling, as they teased and tickled each other. They slept cuddled together, hoping to have as many nights together as possible.

They arrived ten minutes ahead of schedule at the office for the first agency. Sam, Jake, and Jerome arrived and met all of Shane's clan as he called it. They were ushered into a large conference room, a few speeches were made, and then they observed a video presentation explaining how the agency worked, and what they believed they could do for Shane. They were experienced in NBA negotiations, as well as in sponsor endorsements. When they finished, TJ asked a series of questions he worked and contemplated on for weeks. They toured their offices and left the building just under a hundred minutes after they arrived.

In the car, TJ updated his ratings on his spreadsheet, and made notes about the first sports agency. He asked everyone their opinion and a score that he recorded as well.

Agency two followed the same pattern with a similar presentation, beautiful facility, and good roster of professional athletes. TJ again asked questions, and they left for lunch. TJ arranged the tour in the reverse order of his top choice. During lunch at a restaurant Sam picked, they discussed what they had learned, and listened to Sam and Jerome's advice as to the experience of the agencies. They currently worked with clients represented by all three agencies. TJ and Shane listen attentively, hoping they could make the right decision.

The afternoon session began at two. The agency owner handled all the key accounts, and he considered Shane a major player. He was funny as well as smart, pointing out the areas he thought they could improve on, and what sponsors he wanted to go after. Their presentation was far better than the others, and it impressed TJ, as he wanted Shane to be with a team on top of the latest technology, taking advantage of every new medium to propel his company and foundation. TJ and Shane and their guests left two hours later after shaking lots of hands.

They arrived at Jerome's office for a joint meeting in his conference room for their discussion and decision. TJ opened his laptop where he could see his notes and his chart. They discussed the first agency including pros and cons. They followed the same pattern with the second. And finally he brought up the last one. TJ grinned as everyone started talking at once, as if they had been waiting to talk all day. Finally, TJ laughed aloud sensing a decision, but had them vote anyhow. He glanced at his chart, the unanimous selection, and the results were the same.

TJ thanked Sam, Jerome, and Jake, as well as Barbara and Al for their assistance. He let them say goodbye, while he dialed the agency and asked for Alan Anderson. The agent was a tall, dark head former college basketball, with fire in his eyes, and a warm radiating smile. He was sharp and efficient in his choice of words and phrases. TJ congratulated him as their selection for Shane. He asked him to fax over the contract to Jerome's office. He replied he didn't have to, as his assistant was waiting in the lawyer's lobby. TJ laughed. John went to get him, and he returned with a portfolio of information for TJ and Shane, and the contract for Jerome who began reading it immediately.

The contract turned out to be pretty standard, and that's exactly what he wanted. The only things TJ included were they wanted Alan to negotiate support of their foundation, and reimbursement for Shane's Learjet for all functions he attended outside of his trips to the ballgames. He would pay for those flights.

TJ finished his conversation by asking Alan if he had any gay clients. He said yes, most of which were in the closet. He asked if thought he could handle an out of the closet gay person. Alan smiled and replied, "It would be my profound honor. I have a gay son pitching for North Carolina. He's a junior."

They agreed to return to the agency in the morning for a follow-up meeting and lunch together. Jerome approved the contract and faxed a copy over to Sam. They left the office exhausted, and decided to return to the hotel to relax a while before dinner.

Al and Barbara flew home the next morning. TJ, Shane, and John met with Alan at his office and enjoyed discussing their plans for Shane. Alone, TJ met with Alan, and explained the deal with the Bobcats. Alan laughed, and said that was a shrewd accomplishment, and he congratulated them. TJ reminded him the importance of keeping the deal a secret until draft day. Alan laughed, and said, "I don't guess you needed me on that deal, but

I'll be right there for last minute developments, and I'll take care of getting those big endorsements."

TJ explained the house, home office, and the new business and foundation office. He told him they really wanted to do some good in this world, and would welcome his input as to the charities and programs they should go after.

He also discussed the importance of Shane and TJ flying together to the away games. He promised they would always be early and ready to play. Alan knew Billy Coble and approved of his training. He was looking forward to the commercials and promos Shane was working on. He planned to go after first-rate companies. TJ asked what he thought the problems would be businesswise as to Shane coming out.

Alan laughed, "There will be a roar like a shockwave, but everyone is going to want the two-time National Champion, two-time Most Valuable Player, and winner of every collegiate basketball award in the nation. Most of the major companies have learned there are millions of hard working gay folks with plenty of expendable cash. We'll do just fine, don't you worry."

TJ had thought ahead and purchased three awesome seats for a comedy show on Broadway. They arrived just before show time, and sat on the aisle third row from the front. Shane took the aisle to make it easier for those sitting behind him to see. The play was outrageously funny, and the threesome laughed until their jaws ached. Afterwards, they found a creamery, and celebrated their new agent and the launch of a new career for all.

Sunday, TJ and Shane stayed in bed until time for him to shower and prepare for his flight home. They ate lunch together in the room, hugged and kissed for a while, and reluctantly Shane left to fly home, as he had a paper to work on, classes in the morning, and training with Billy in the afternoon in Concord.

TJ waited for Shane to call after a safe landing, and then he took John out to see a few visitor sites since John had never been to the Big Apple. They did the Empire State Building, walked around Times Square, and ate dinner at the Hard Rock Café. They took their time walking back to the hotel, while enjoying being out of their rooms. Tomorrow would be a busy day, followed by Tuesday's release of the new basketball book, **TWICE IS NICE**.

TJ didn't sleep well, perhaps because he and Shane were so far apart, but also because of all the things he was still working on. He got up early and made a call to Henry, to check on construction and thanked him for his excellent progress. He talked to Robby, and brought him up to date on the new agency representing Shane. He sent Shane an email he knew he would get after class, and ordered breakfast for both he and John. He called John on the phone, and he was up and heading to the shower. TJ decided to go ahead shave and shower as well. They both returned to the living room as breakfast arrived.

They arrived at the publisher's office at nine. He expected this year to be easier, but they gave him a refresher course on handling the media, and became amazed to see how polished he was this year for his video and interview rehearsals. TJ insisted John stay with him during all the training so he could help spot bad habits down the road when TJ became tired. At eleven, they were taking a break when the owner came into the conference room with a small box. He set it on the counter and smiled, "Your new books just arrived. I thought you would like to see them. By late afternoon, they will be in the stores of every major bookseller in the country. Congratulations!"

TJ walked over and he handed him a pair of the new books. TJ handed one to John, and together, they began looking at the cover, and flipping through the pages. "It is beautiful. Your staff did a superb job. Are you guys ready to make some money?"

They all laughed at his enthusiasm, and energy. He would need it, as this time he had a dozen print media interviews after lunch. John soon adapted to the situation very well. TJ handed him his phone, so he could answer calls, leaving TJ to give full attention to his job. One after the other, sometimes fielding the same questions, and then suddenly a surprise offbeat question surfaced, but TJ kept his usual calm, composure and a friendly smile, and answered well.

TJ talked to Shane after dinner and went to bed early. The Today Show limo was coming for him at six in the morning. He slept well, but his alarm came early. John was still yawning, as they made their way to the lobby and into the limousine. Janet Wilson met them with a satchel of books and press releases. TJ did makeup, and together they waited in a room until time to move to the studio floor.

John stood behind the cameras and watched as TJ expertly answered their questions, and smiled when they brought in Shane via the remote studio from home. Together, they sold the book to the audience. Next up was the ESPN® studio, and then four book signings before dark. They made it back to their hotel exhausted, but up early and on the way to the airport. Steve flew them to Boston for three books signings and a local television interview.

Day and after day, they began making their way across the country, while marking the days off their electronic calendar, and trying hard not to be anxious for the end, as the book sales provided the money they needed to grow their business and the new foundation. Shane flew out Friday morning after class and caught up with them in Chicago. TJ was thrilled to see him show up at the bookstore and begin signing books with him. John got some pictures of the signings with hundreds of people in line. He had been taking pictures of the entire trip, and uploading to TJ's website, and TJ wrote a daily entry for his new blog. He also placed pictures of Shane on his website as well.

That night the three of them ate a quiet dinner. Shane explained how his training was going at Billy's studio, as well as his schoolwork. He had just a few more weeks until exams, and he was ready to get it over with. The next morning they flew to Cincinnati and four book signings, and quick interviews with local sportscasters. TJ and Shane enjoyed their evening together, and it was sad to see him fly home Sunday afternoon while TJ was still signing books.

The following weekend Shane met them in Seattle for another weekend of bookstores and travel. The following week he met them in Dallas, and the following week TJ and John arrived home. TJ gave John a check for five thousand dollars for the extra work he did at home and on the tour for them. John nearly fainted but quickly hugged TJ. Exhausted, John left for his apartment. TJ and Shane ate barbeque together, did the wet area, and made love for a while before the exhausted TJ fell asleep in his arms.

The following Monday morning, TJ and Shane drove down to Concord to see some of Shane's training results, and to continue his own classes. They laughed and made fun of each other, as they enjoyed the summer ride down to the studio. Once there, they went right to work, and TJ loved the pieces they put together with Shane. They were excellent, but he warned Shane his would never look that good. TJ brought Billy up to speed on the book tour, and promised to be back every day that week before flying out again Sunday for the second tour.

One of the things TJ learned from last year's tour was to ask for a copy of every interview he gave including raw footage. It was an implied requirement, but he made it easy for them by asking for it on a DVD. John prepared a special card for these videos and handed them to the producer wherever they went. Now he had a stack of them to prepare pieces for their book website. He also prepared a special video for Billy so he could see how TJ did under pressure.

Afterwards, they drove over to the new offices and walked through them, marveling at the progress the crews accomplished. Robby joined them and said they would be finished ahead of schedule. He was moving up the arrival of the equipment and the furniture. TJ congratulated him after hearing he had almost filled all the positions. Robby gave them a briefing on each person hired. As they were preparing to leave, a corvette came across the parking lot and pulled alongside the Hummer.

"I take it this is 'the' Shane," began Jeff as he climbed out of the car.

TJ turned to see him, "Just call him Shane, or statue, or tree man." They all laughed, "How are you Jeff?"

"I'm great. How's the roadwork? Robby said you've been to twenty-one cities in as many days. That's sounds very hard."

"No worst than driving in circles all day, and trying not to get hit by Tony Stewart," replied TJ. They laughed again.

"Shane, this is THE Jeff Gordon. Jeff, you have now met THE Shane Bradley, while I remain THE humble servant."

Jeff laughed as he shook Shane's hand firmly, "Does he always act like this?

Shane replied, " I think it was something in the water on the road."

"Your new offices are looking good. I'm impressed, but you need to go see your new house. I was over there this morning. It is beautiful. When are you moving in?"

"June first. I have two more weeks on the second book tour, Shane has exams, graduation, and we celebrate with three weeks on the road to Alaska, and the northwestern section of the United States, and pick up our new motorcoach in Eugene, Oregon, and bringing it home in time to move. Whew, I'm already tired just thinking about it, but it'll be fun."

"I would think so. Well, I'll let you go see your house, and I hope you have a safe trip. I'll see you soon. It was a pleasure to meet you Shane."

"The pleasure was all mine."

Shane had been by the house several times on his journeys to the studio, but it had been almost four weeks since TJ had seen it, and the progress excited him. The entire outside work was complete as to bricks, windows, and doors, and crews were pouring sidewalks. They parked on the street, and walked through the open wrought iron electric gate, and noted the large brick decorative pattern in the cement driveways. Men were building the exterior fancy brick shed, the yard fencing was complete, an electrician was wiring up the RV parking lots, and other men were hanging the garage doors. They walked into the kitchen where the tile was finished, but they were working on the flooring in the office. They could see the heated floor orange mesh stuff that would soon be under the tile.

The kitchen cabinets were in place, but the appliances were not in. The office cabinetry had been installed. They turned left down a hall and at the end you could turn left and go out the staff entrance, or turn right, go down a flight of stairs, and into the new much larger home office where John and his staff will setup shop. After a quick walk around, they returned to see the view out of the breakfast room. They worked their way through the great room and noted the completed fireplace and cabinetry, and on down the hall to see the men installing cabinets in the walk-in closet. The master bathroom was mostly done except for the floor tile.

They went back to the center of the house and up a flight of stairs and viewed the staff rooms, did a u-turn down the hall, across the breezeway, and visited the guest rooms, and took the back stairs to the wet areas, and saw the men working on Shane's new basketball court. In the corner was the rolling ball retrieval system Shane ordered. It was like the one in the gym at school, allowing him to shoot and the machine would collect the balls after feeding him another one. They walked through the area and stepped out the door and saw the outside pool for the first time. It was about fifty feet by forty feet, with beautiful decking, privacy fence, and already filled with clear water with a tinge of reflective sky blue. At the far end, a group of men were installing the bar in front of the bathhouse. They shook their heads feeling amazed at all they saw. It was more than they could have hoped for.

In the RV building they found it pretty much complete though men were tuning up the heating and air systems. They walked down the decorative cement road to the lake. The dock and boathouse were completely finished. They walked across it and up the stairs to the sun and shade deck, noted the sink and countertop. Suddenly, TJ popped out his iPhone® and called John at home in Lindle.

"John? The dock is done. Go to AnyWho.com and tell me where the nearest Yamaha Personal Watercraft dealer is, and find me a couple of nearby boat dealers. Put on the buy list for the house that we need a big grill for the lake and deck furniture. Email the info to my iPhone®. Thanks."

TJ turned to Shane, "Come on, we have some fun shopping to do."

"Where we going?"

"You'll see. Trust me."

They said goodbye and many thanks to Henry, and made their way to the Hummer. TJ's phone chimed as he got in the car. John sent the GPS coordinates for the nearest dealer. TJ cut and paste the info into his GPS function and started giving Shane instructions. Ten minutes later, they pulled into the dealership late in the afternoon. They went up and started looking over the various models of personal watercrafts. A salesman came out and invited them inside so he could show them the differences between his models. They listened carefully. TJ had experience with buying the units before, and began to lean towards three-seat units with the bigger engines. Shane loved them. TJ asked how much for one large one. He got an answer. TJ smiled and asked, "What if I buy two?" The guy smiled and indeed gave them a better deal. TJ said, "What if I buy three?" Again the price got even better, and finally TJ said, "I want an amazing substantial discount for four." The man sat down at his desk, rolled the numbers, and came up with a good answer. TJ grinned, "Now what if I pay cash?" The man knocked another ten percent off, and TJ got him to throw in two dual trailers to haul them. He wrote a check for everything. He told the man to service the boats, and they would be back tomorrow at four to pick them up. He asked for referral for buying a boat. One of the names he mentioned was on John's list.

Back in the car, they drove to the boat dealer and began perusing the long line of boats on the lot of the big dealer. TJ asked Shane, "Can you water ski?"

"Yes, I've been a few times. I can slalom, but you need a big engine to pull me up. I can only kneeboard, but I want to learn to use a wakeboard. Can you?"

460

"I can ski and kneeboard, but I'm a better boat driver. I bet I can sling you off a tube, too. I've owned a few boats. Do you have any boat experience?"

"No, dad wasn't into boats. I went to the lakes with friends. I can drive it."

"Well, come on, let's find one big enough to pull you out of the water, and take a bunch of our family and friends around the lake in style."

For the first time in his life, price was not an issue, but he didn't throw it away either. They got in and out of a few boats before a salesman on a golf cart showed up. The rep began spouting off engine sizes and soon understood they wanted a powerful big boat, with a great stereo, excellent warranty, and comfortable for riding, as well as catching a tan on the open water.

They liked a big red Moomba® Mobius XLV twenty-three foot boat with an inboard engine of three hundred twenty-five-horsepower. The salesman said he had one like it at the company's dock. They decided to go for a test drive. Twenty minutes later, they were on Lake Norman for the first time. It was wide beautiful lake, over thirty-two thousand acres, and North Carolina's largest lake. They could easily see it was a beautiful lake, and the boat was spectacular. The salesman showed off the engine, put it through hard turns and the boat hugged the water like a high performance car. He fired up the powerful stereo with the Kicker® speakers and subwoofers and big beefy power amp. They loved it.

They went back to the dealership, negotiated hard, and bought the boat and trailer, paying cash once again. They also bought all the stuff they needed from lifejackets, skis, and ropes. He asked them to deliver it to their dock tomorrow at four-thirty, and the trailer to the house shed.

TJ immediately drove over to a Lowes store and bought a six-pack of heavy-duty, water resistant pad locks, all keyed to one key, and six four-foot lengths of galvanized chain. He told Shane the locks and chains would secure their new toys when they were away.

They drove home laughing about their new boats. Shane asked why he wanted four Yamahas personal watercrafts. TJ grinned, "I had two before, and that was fun, but many times somebody got left on the dock. We now own a big house on a big lake, and we'll have lots of friends, your parents, my parents, and friends and co-workers over. It'll just be fun." That was good enough for Shane.

It turned out to be a wonderful week they spent together. They played on the lake, spent a lot of training time with Billy, visited the house, and approved final changes with Henry, and Shane did his homework at home. Robby reported more improvements on the office project, and Billy delivered a polished professionally produced promo tape of Shane. TJ and

John studied the tape, and began using pieces of it on Shane's website. He sent a copy of the DVD overnight to Alan in New York.

Alan called after he viewed the video giving it a big thumbs up. They also sent recordings of Shane doing voice work for several pretend commercials, and a short motivation speech. Alan prepared a targeted list of thirty companies he would be sending the info to, plus a number of ad agencies with a large list of clients. His team prepared print ads for newspapers and magazines with goals of introducing Shane as a marketing tool for their companies and clients.

But after all the fun things they accomplished during that short week, it was time for TJ to hit the road again. After having sex one more time, he and Shane slept in on Sunday morning, enjoying cuddling together and kissing. Reluctantly, TJ and John left again for New York City late in the afternoon. Early in the last tour, he thought one week of John's help would be enough, but soon realized what a huge help he was on the road. He asked John if he wanted to do the second tour, and John quickly said yes.

On Monday, he met with the publisher of his gay books, and saw copies of his new book **The War Beyond – Part III** and became overwhelmed at the quality of the production. This was the first of his gay books to be a real hardcover book instead of the usual six by nine soft covers. The embossed cover joyfully stunned him. He also saw new larger posters, and received a report on the delivery of his book to every outlet in the country, and they were ready for today's coast-to-coast release.

They had a wonderful meeting with their staff, and TJ knew he had their full support for his novels. They had a dozen interviews set up for the afternoon, and the following morning TJ and John began the first of four book signings. City by city, they made their way across the country. Shane didn't fly out on the weekends, as TJ would have been in the gay stores all day, and they felt it was best Shane not yet be seen with TJ's gay audience. They worked fourteen cities in as many days, and flew home from their last stop in Atlanta on a Sunday night.

Once home, John went home to rest with another bonus check in hand, and Shane arrived with hot food. TJ was outside catching up with Bob and Sue when he arrived. TJ followed him in, sat down and played with the dogs, and finally set his stuff in the office, and returned to eat. Shane was fixing their plates when TJ came up behind him and put a big bear hug on him. "I've missed you so much I absolutely ache. I love you more than ever." Shane turned around and kissed him passionately, and then kissed his nose, his cheeks, his ears and back to his mouth again.

Shane smiled, "I am thankful I can see you with iChat® every day, but it is nothing compared to holding you. Come on, let's eat and then get naked!"

TJ laughed as he made his way to the table. It was good to have some southern food from their favorite restaurant. It was also good to be home.

# THIRTY-NINE

TJ could hardly move on Monday, somewhat worn out from the exhausting tour, but also from their lovemaking, as he and Shane attempted making up for lost time. They were both sore, but somehow Shane got out of bed and made omelets for their breakfast. TJ had given John some time off, but the day was so beautiful that he called John and asked him to find a bathing suit, and to be at his house in thirty minutes—if he wanted to. John was thrilled, as he was already bored. He also talked Bob and Sue into finding their suits as well. TJ and Shane made a big picnic lunch, loaded the ice chest, and put lots of towels and stuff into the Hummer.

The five friends arrived at the new house a couple of hours later, and took their new drive up to the garage and parked. Jerry and Terry were working on the yard. They had planted over a hundred trees and bushes, hosta, and daylilies, and many others all over the place. It was beautiful. A service truck was pulled up to the utility area, and they were adjusting the underground sprinkler system. Their group toured the house, finding much more completed, and Sue said it smelled new. Leslie was working in the great room, arranging the new furniture and distributing many of the items that gave the house a home kind of feel to it.

Buddy was working on six projects at a time for the phone and network systems, as well as the security system. Henry had a group of men and they were inspecting every room. However, TJ didn't want to worry about the house today, so they evacuated back to the Hummer and drove down to the lake. TJ grinned when he saw their boat in the boathouse slip, and the four Yamahas up on their dry docks. He also noted that Jerry and Terry already finished the new flowerbeds on the bank across from their boathouse. He though they were so beautiful.

Bob and Sue loved the view and she immediately started taking pictures. The boys unloaded the car and everyone followed them down to the dock, and up onto the sun deck. TJ grinned because the new gas grill had been installed, along with the refrigerator, and the lake furniture. They unloaded the ice chest to the refrigerator, everyone chose something to drink, and put down their stuff.

"Let's try out the new boat. Is everybody ready?"

Grabbing hats and sunglasses, they boarded the boat. TJ showed Shane and Bob how to unchain the boat from the dock mooring, and where to throw the switch allowing the boatlift to deflate while lowering the boat into the water. TJ climbed aboard and lifted the engine hood to check for water leaks, but the boat had been tested and ready to go. Everyone left their shoes on the dock and climbed in the new boat. Shane helped Beeper into the boat, while J-Henry jumped in on his own. The dogs went to the front of the boat. TJ fired up the engine, and slowly he backed the boat out of the slip. They cruised slowly out of the cove, while Shane hunted various music stations on the stereo. Once out of the cove, he brought the throttle forward, and they picked up their speed. They cruised around the lake looking at the beautiful houses. It was a very relaxing trip. Sue got some good camera shots of the dogs leaning forward on the front of the boat with their ears flying in the wind.

They returned to the dock so TJ could teach them about the Yamahas, how to start, dock, and safety. They all found lifejackets and prepared for launch. Shane closed the dock gate to keep the dogs on the dock or the nearby grass, while TJ checked their water bowl. He told them to stay. TJ helped John and Shane gets theirs fired up and in the water. He put Bob and Sue on another, and pushed the unit into the water, and finally he got on the last one. He led them out of the cove, and soon they were racing in circles, and flat out straight ahead.

After they returned to the dock, they decided to eat and rest on the lounge chairs, while testing the new cushions. Still exhausted from the two tours, TJ and John fell asleep, while Shane talked to Bob and Sue. He had passed all his classes with A's and did the same on his exams. His folks were flying in Thursday for the Saturday graduation. TJ and Shane were leaving for Alaska on Sunday. He quickly told Bob & Sue they had a new parking spot up by the RV building, and he hoped they would use it often.

Shane asked, "Has TJ asked you about helping us at the end of our vacation?"

"He wanted us to help you guys move before we head north," began Sue.

Shane grinned, "He has something more fun in mind. We are stopping in Junction City, Oregon to pick up our new Country Coach Prevost® on May twenty-fifth. We wondered if we flew you out in the Learjet, would you guys drive our old coach home for us?"

Bob and Sue laughed. "You trust us with your old coach?"

"It's not that old, just three years, but yes we do. We trust you with our lives. We will pay all your expenses from food to fuel. I think you would enjoy the Learjet, and although we'll be in a little bit of a hurry coming back, as we'll be moving the next day, you guys could take your time if you wanted to." Shane smartly closed with a sly grin, "Will you think about it?"

Sue looked to Bob and they both laughed, and said together, "We're done thinking. We'll do it!"

TJ spent Tuesday in Concord doing final interviews with Robby on the team he lined up. He also interviewed housekeepers and chefs that he and John scheduled. It was a long day, but carefully they selected their team, and they were all comfortable working for a gay person. Robby would start some of them in the next few weeks, and the rest of the crew the last week of June. He worked with Jerome in New York on contracts, and a company employee manual. He also obtained paperwork and instructions from Sam. His accounting team put together an excellent benefit program, increasing their hiring package, and in a conference call with TJ and Shane, he explained the tax advantages, plus the benefit of obtaining and keeping quality employees for longer terms. The housekeepers and chef would start the last few days of May, and before the boys returned to get the house and kitchen ready for the final move in day.

Al and Barbara arrived safely for graduation Thursday afternoon, and TJ and Shane welcomed them to Lindle with big hugs. After a steak dinner they toured the house once more with Barbara carrying her digital camera and notepad. TJ and Shane smiled as she made notes, and got Al to measure some of the rooms. She was excited as was Al, and this pleased the boys. TJ taught Al how to maintain the sauna, and steam rooms, as well as the Jacuzzi. Shane had become the expert on Endless Pool®, and proudly showed his dad how to operate the unit.

They moved on to the motorcoach. Shane took his mom inside so she could take more pictures and measure once again. TJ began teaching Al about setting up camp. They disconnected and prepared for a trip, and then set it up again. Al was very smart and remembered everything. They talked about the bays, and TJ showed him what he would get out of their way, but he would leave all the things they need to enjoy sitting outside, like lounge chairs, grill, yard matt, umbrella, and more.

He showed him how to check the oil on the generator with the motorized forward slide. He was impressed. They also checked the oil on the Cummins® engine at the rear. TJ had all the maintenance schedules on spreadsheets. They were going to leave the iMac® on the coach for them, as it operated both the DirecWay® Internet Satellite System and the GPS software to plan their trips.

He showed Al how to change the water filter on the refrigerator and walked him through putting the chemicals in the toilet. He showed both Al and Barbara how to move the slides, and spoke about rain and ice situations, demonstrated the endless hot water unit, floor tiles, water pump and more. They were overwhelmed, but he reminded them he learned all he knew by getting in the RV and trying, reading, and learning.

They went back to the house, changed clothes, and enjoyed the wet area first hand. It was the first time TJ and Shane had worn swimsuits in the area, so they laughed at each other. Later they watched a movie while learning the tricks of the audio / video systems with the HD projector and surround sound systems.

The next morning they went to see the new house at Lake Norman and the progress the crews accomplished, and moved on to the lake and the dock. TJ and Shane once again unloaded the ice chest and their towel duffle bag. Soon Al and Barbara were enjoying a long boat ride with their son at the wheel, and later they chased each other on the Yamaha wave runners. TJ took lots of pictures, as Shane and his family enjoyed the day. As TJ cooked lunch on the grill, he promised them there would be thousands of days like this when they moved to Lindle in June.

Saturday morning finally arrived and Shane was getting nervous. He'd rather go against UCLA again than to march down the aisle for his own graduation. He was not an honors graduate, but proudly receiving a special citation for his athletic performance and dedication during his four years and maintaining a top grade performance. His mother was proud of that award, perhaps as much as his Most Valuable Player awards.

They arrived at the arena early, found their seats while Shane disappeared to make the march wearing his cap and gown. TJ had his small camera ready. John had a press badge, thanks to Walter, to take some digital pictures of Shane crossing the stage and receiving his award. The music was excellent, the speeches fine, but finally they announced his award. TJ's eyes filled with tears of joy and pride when the entire student body, faculty, and all the families and guests gave him a long-standing ovation. TJ noted that Barbara squeezed her husband's hand, as they stood there feeling such pride.

They celebrated with a big dinner at home inviting Bob and Sue, and John. They laughed and cut up like a large family, and TJ noted how Shane just beamed with confidence and security with Al, Barbara, and his friends around. Over the six weeks since winning the second title, Shane had returned to a semi normal life with the exception of his training with Billy Coble for learning how to sell products. He was proud of his accomplishments and yet knew he would do better. He had also started working on his strength, speed, and endurance to get ready for the NBA performance camp in Phoenix.

After everyone went to bed, TJ was still out in the motorcoach still packing, adjusting, checking, and making sure everything was loaded and ready to go. Bob and Sue were taking Shane's parents to the airport at ten, but TJ and Shane would leave at eight for the first leg of the vacation trip.

Two drivers made a huge difference in their stamina and rest, and TJ wondered how he sometimes crossed the entire country in five days by himself. They reached Cincinnati on their second day of their journey north to Winnipeg, Canada. They stopped in Osseo, Wisconsin the next night and experienced spring again as a cool front came through. The dogs were thrilled to be on the road again, and enjoyed their daily walks around the new parks. They also liked that one of the boys was free for an ear or tummy rub at all times. Shane became a more confident driver as the miles ticked by. They were leaving the country tomorrow and had their passports ready, and a folder with all the info and shots records on the dogs, but they had no trouble at the Canadian border. They had reservations at a nice RV resort in Winnipeg. They decided to spend two days and rest a bit before moving west. The scenery at Lake Winnipeg was awesome, and the locals loved to hear the boys talk. TJ would ham it up a bit with a thick southern drawl, leaving Shane in stitches.

They drove on to Calgary in time for the rodeo TJ had been reading about for years. They spent two days there watching all the horse shows, rodeo events, and old western day parade. The beautiful landscapes in Alberta were picture perfect, thought TJ. The next night they were at Dawson's Creek, perhaps known more for dog sleds, but not this time of year. The nights were still cool, so they put their long pants back on. After they crossed into British Columbia, they made it to the Northwest Territory. The hills and valleys were breathtaking, and they began to see animal life including moose, deer, and a few black bears. The next day they crossed from the Canadian border into Alaska. They had to exit the motorcoach for the guards to inspect the coach for drugs and bombs, so the dogs and the boys waited alongside. The guards eventually recognized Shane, so he signed a few autographs, and they escorted their motorcoach on through. TJ could not believe after fifteen years of planning to go to Alaska that he was finally there. They stayed in an RV park for their first night in Alaska and began studying their guidebooks and online materials. They set the GPS for Fairbanks, and made reservations for a five-day stay. They also found a kennel, and made reservations for a plane trip to the top of Alaska.

They went through some steep passes on the highway and traveled much slower after spotting lots of loose gravel that could mar the front of the coach or break a windshield. They took their time but Shane insisted TJ do the driving. He was busy taking pictures of the amazing views. They stopped many times on the way to Fairbanks, finding spectacular, awe inspiring views, but just fifty miles from their destination, they got quite a thrill by spotting a big grizzly bear and her cub fishing in a stream. They took numerous pictures and never ventured away from the road.

TJ had to adjust the DirecWay® Internet satellite to get service in Fairbanks. The folks running the parks were so nice. They spent their winters in Tucson, Arizona and their summers in Alaska. They had a great life and TJ and Shane were envious. They slept in the next morning, took the dogs on jaunts around town, and enjoyed a beautiful park. They couldn't imagine the late June season when the sun never set, and the mid winter when the sun never rose. Just a couple hundred miles from the Arctic Circle, they discovered a beautiful national treasure with wildlife everywhere you looked. Fairbanks, the largest city in the interior region of the state, claimed a population just over thirty-one thousand, but you didn't have to fight for a parking place. The boys only noted a few thousand people in town. They managed to go a cinema to see one of the summer blockbusters, and it was first time they had been able to do so since leaving Key West last year on their previous vacation.

Shane had been running at almost every overnight stop, but he especially enjoyed jogging in Fairbanks. The morning air was cool in the low fifties forcing TJ to fire up the Aqua Hot diesel heating system, which kept them warm and cozy. They had lunch across the street from the Carlson Center that served as host for the preseason college basketball tournament. They walked over to see the arena and discovered summer pickup games in progress. Shane returned after digesting his meal, and played for a couple of hours. There were college players, alumni, and soldiers playing from Eielson Air Force Base. He had a grand time, as everyone was very polite, while marveling at having the National Champion in their little town. Shane and TJ sent photos along the way and read emails. TJ did as little business as possible, but there were decisions he needed to make for house, RV, and office construction, but mostly things at home were going well thanks to John at home, and Robby at the new office.

They signed up for a wilderness trip and boarded Jeeps for rides through the bush that they did the following morning, and then Shane played ball in the afternoons. TJ used the time to do some fun writing, while working on his next story. Their third day in Fairbanks, they put the dogs in the kennel, and boarded a flight to the top of the state at the Arctic Circle, and landed in a town called Barrow. Like the rest of the tourists that visited the cold country, they could not imagine anyone living there year around. They met many Eskimos and found them to be very friendly. They were all so short but wanted their picture taken standing next to Shane. TJ told them Shane used to be a tree. The plane ride made Shane nervous on takeoff with the various crosswinds, but the views from the plane going up and back was just amazing.

They took a riverboat ride the next day and found the Fairbanks area to be amazing. They spotted another grizzly bear washing in the cold water. They decided to head south the next day to Anchorage. It would be a long journey due to the switchbacks and deep gorges they went through, but they were in no hurry and stopped many times for photo opportunities. Their first view of a herd of moose thrilled them. They also saw their first eagles and numerous ground animals.

Anchorage was more of a real city and featured the area's largest indoor dome for soccer games and track events year around. The dome is actually a large inflated facility. Shane worked out there every day. They took daily tours, but also enjoyed long walks through the town and the surrounding scenery left them feeling impressed. It felt good to just be away from it all. They moved on to Juneau, Alaska and spent two days there before leaving the state, crossing through the Northwest Territory and into British Columbia. They worked there way around the coast before reaching Vancouver. It was the largest city they had been to in two weeks. They stayed in a beautiful resort, toured the towns, and finally made it to the Pacific Ocean, and rested for a spell.

A Writer's Fantasy
They reached America and stayed north of Seattle where they found everything green and wet, as it seem to rain all the time. They reached Eugene, Oregon on the night of the twenty-fourth. They stayed overnight just a few miles from the factory, and felt sorely tempted to drive over to check out the coach, but decided to spend the time packing. They planned to transfer all their clothes, and personal gear they did not intend to leave on the coach for Shane's parents. TJ got a call about six from Bob and Sue. They had just flown in, and were staying in a nearby hotel. They would take a cab over to the factory in the morning. They enjoyed their flight on the Learjet immensely, and ate very well on board with Susie.

The next morning they were up early and arrived just before eight o'clock local time. They followed instructions to meet the staff at the Prevost® Custom Facility. They parked their current motorcoach in the parking lot. Shane unhitched the car while TJ gathered up his laptop briefcase with the documents he needed to complete the sale. Several weeks ago, he purchased the insurance for the new coach, and ordered the new license tag. They walked the dogs, and then left them on board with the generator running to keep J-Henry and Beeper cool. They took an excited breath, sighed, and walked through the gate.

The sales staff came out to greet them. There were photographers for both still and video media. They set up a viewing platform where they asked them to stand, as they rolled out the new coach. It had the usual bright shiny chrome lower half with the top black and sleek with the big windows on the street side and front cab, but it also had an amazing swirl of bright colors like streamers in a swirl pattern. To them, it looked amazing.

TJ and Shane endured a slightly slow presentation of the owner keys and more photo opportunities, before finally descending from the stage to get up close with their new purchase. Their staff opened all the bays, rolled out the motorized generator slide, and popped the hood on the big rear diesel engine. They looked for any mistakes, found none, and had lots of questions. They loved the electronics in the deck bay including a motorized thirty-two HD LCD television, and the new utility compartment, and noted the connections they needed for home were in the proper place.

They brought out a rolling ladder so they could see the top of the motorcoach. They engaged the satellite for DirecWay®, as well as the new Motosat® HD three satellite motorized dish for television. The in-motion system was under a dome painted the same black as the top of the coach. They counted off the four air conditioning units and grinned. Down from the ladder, the staff began running out the huge motorized awnings. They were beautiful, bright decorative colors matching the décor and color scheme of the coach.

Finally, the boys went inside and marveled at the details, the marble floors, and the amazing cockpit for the driver, as well as the large HD LCD television screen displaying HBO from a satellite. TJ quickly checked out the new desk area. He grinned, as he finally had the file cabinets and storage he needed with beautiful comfort and organizational features. Shane spotted the new remote studio set up and groaned, knowing he would have to use them to work from to time. The matching Ekornes® recliners were next and opposite a beautiful leather couch. TJ found the high tech stylistic galley completely mindboggling. They had plenty of room, and he especially loved the new dishwasher. They loved the elegantly lighted dining table with soft lighting controls on both sides. The huge refrigerator was on the right, a broom closet, across the aisle they discovered a huge food pantry, and followed by the stackable washer / dryer units. They peeked into the marble bathroom, looked for the requested white sink bowls, as TJ hated the dark ones on his old coach, and finally the bedroom, the air bed, HD LCD television and a huge assortment of closet space. They demonstrated the electric blinds throughout the living area of the coach, and as they looked back towards the front, they saw a good view of the glazed marble tiles. They were so shiny and clean. They almost looked like glass. Of course, they were heated tiles as well.

They quickly noted a short lady coming in the door with a baseball cap on. It was Sue, and she was more excited than they were. She and Bob studied the front and made their own way to them. They hugged in the kitchen area and continued checking out the coach.

TJ told the salesman it looked absolutely perfect, and he was ready for a test drive. They downed the satellite dishes, hit the buttons for the awnings, and did a walk around while closing bays and doors. The Country Coach® Publicity Department took more pictures. A driver took the wheel as he fired up the engine. He turned the generator on to keep everyone on board nice and cool. They pulled out of the lot and made their way to the interstate. After a while, TJ asked him to pull over so he could drive. The driver expected the request. They made it through several exits, turned around, went through town, and everyone held their breath while TJ easily maneuvered through traffic. He turned into a Wal-Mart® parking lot where he had lots of room and practiced backing up and parking. He was impressed at how easy it was to drive.

They went back to the plant where TJ went into the office to do the paperwork and complete the deal. He returned an hour later to begin their systems training with various team members. They shook hands with all the people who participated in the building of their coach. His new state license tag was installed on the rear of the coach to make it legal, but a new two-time National Champion Tag was put on the front by Shane with more pictures taken. TJ asked for a copy of all the pictures, and they promised they would after he explained there use on Shane's website. They began going through page after page of checklists for the outside, and all the systems, slides, and connections. Then another trainer began on the inside, and TJ wanted Bob and Sue to listen, so they could help him later on if needed. The inside required more time with the driver and electronics gear, plus the house functions.

With more than a half day spent on checking and learning the use of every button, switch, knob, and system, they were finally ready to make the transfer. With help from the Country Coach® workers and Bob and Sue, they transferred their personal stuff over in less than an hour, and put it anywhere they could. TJ and Shane would sort it out later. They shook hands once more with the designers and crew, waved goodbye, and shut the door.

They pulled out of the lot with their new coach and car in tow. Bob and Sue were right behind them in TJ's old coach. They drove two hundred miles for their first journey, and they felt like it was Christmas morning. Shane tried to learn all the buttons on the passenger side, and he played with the seat controls including the door entry cover. Once satisfied, he turned the satellite on and began checking the channels. The quality of the high definition picture was far superior to their last coach. The dogs kept checking out the new smells from front to back before settling down on the couch for the ride. As Shane listened to ESPN's SportsCenter® for NBA news, he got out the cheat sheet manual with pictures of the all the electronic arrays around the driver, and a noted the numbers on the picture so he flipped to the correct page and found out what it does.

He asked TJ, "Do you have the radar on?"

TJ laughed, "Are we expecting enemy jet fighters to attack us?"

"Funny," sighed Shane, "no, I'm talking about that Norad® thing, you know, that warns you there is a car around the side or near the front or back, and it helps when you're backing into a spot."

"Point to it for me."

Shane looked at the picture and found it on the right side of the control panel. The light was steady amber. Shane said as he pointed, "I think it is off. Hit the button. It should be flashing green."

TJ hit the button and it began flashing. He grinned, "Okay, mister co-pilot. Radar is ready. What else have you found? How do we launch missiles?"

Shane laughed and then sighed, "I think we could be reading manuals for months."

"It won't be that bad. Most of it is the same as I have seen on other coaches. We just have to learn the new stuff, and figure out where the old stuff is on this coach. Why don't you learn how to operate the GPS? I figured out enough of it to get us to the RV Resort for tonight's stay, but find out how to schedule multiple stops, and how to find fuel stops. Remember, we can only go to the big truck stops to fill this baby up. It holds two hundred and twenty-five gallons of diesel!"

"Holy cow! Are we running out already?"

"Heck no," replied TJ before adding slyly, "we have enough to get us about thirty miles!"

Shane laughed, too. "How many miles to a gallon?"

"Well, that is next on your list to figure out. This baby has a digital dash that displays all the fluid and pressure levels electronically for superb accuracy, and on the right here is the read out for engine performance. It has a section for fuel performance, but I don't know how to set it. We'll need to do that when we fill up."

Shane began flipping through the shortcut manual, as the training rep called it, until he found and followed the instructions. He reached over and pushed a reset button. "I thought we'd have to calculate how much fuel we have used to tell how much fuel we have, but not on this baby. When I hit the reset button, it reads the digital read out of the fuel level, and then converts that to gallons. It has already begun calculating."

"Read a bit more, I want to know how to change the engine monitoring screen for steep grade climbs, so I can keep the engine cool. You're close to that part. Keep going."

They played with just about every knob and button in and around the driver area, so they could find a button or switch when they needed to. Shane was deep in concentration while reading when TJ suddenly tested the air horn. They both got a kick of it, especially when J-Henry and Beeper started barking in response, so TJ hit the horn again.

Late in the afternoon, they followed the GPS directions right into a large new resort. TJ was greatly relieved, as he wasn't quite ready to handle tight turns and back-in spots. The long pull thru sites they reserved were ready for both RVs. TJ paid for the reservations for both coaches, and an old fellow led the way in a golf cart. TJ parked the Prevost® and hit the button for auto level. Shane jumped out and ran over to guide Bob and Sue into their spot right next door. TJ exited as well and began hooking up the electrical only as they had plenty of water and empty black and gray tanks. He wanted to make it easy for an early leave in the morning for a long haul of driving east.

Shane helped Bob hook up the old coach while Sue began putting the slides out. TJ finished and went back inside to move their slides out, and hit the button so the Internet satellite could start motorizing up. Sue did the same. He then brought the dogs out so they could stretch their legs. He led them to a tree so they make an urgent pee. The four laughed about the journey so far, and how each was doing with their coach. Once they had their coaches in a home sweet home operation, they loaded up in TJ's car and headed out to a steakhouse for dinner. They all ate their first buffalo steaks after TJ dared them to. They were fantastic, tender, and so tasty, and they almost ate every bite. However, they each saved a few bites for the dogs. Shane bought two hundred dollars of steaks and divided the stack between the freezer compartments on both coaches. He told Sue to cook what she wanted.

TJ announced that they were going to do five hundred and fifty miles tomorrow. Sue said her limit was three hundred miles. TJ knew that, but laughed any way. He gave Bob a credit card and told him to use it for fuel, parks, food, rental car, and anything else they needed, and to have fun. The boys gave them a hug, after announcing they would see them in Lindle. Bob said it would probably take them two days longer to get there, but they would make it. They went to bed early so TJ and Shane could leave at dawn.

# FORTY

Every day on the road, TJ and Shane learned about twenty more new things about their new motorcoach. To say they loved the Prevost® would definitely be an understatement, but more importantly to them, they were relaxed, together, laughing, and grinning mile after mile. They sailed thru three states on the first day, and by taking turns driving, they were only mildly tired. They celebrated with another great dinner and bit more sex. TJ and Shane felt life just could not get any better.

Shane began jogging after they arrived at the next resort, and shot hoops when he could. He would soon fly out to Phoenix, so although he hoped the deal with the Bobcats would happen as planned, he still wanted to look good in front of his peers.

TJ didn't write a single word in his new book on the trip home, as he spent most of his two hours of free time each night studying the manuals, hoping to learn how to operate everything on the coach. He already created new spreadsheets for the service records for RV mileage and generator hours. Shane spent some time studying the NBA rookie manual. It was a big three-ring binder full of policies and rules. He had a second manual for the player union and their policies.

On the evening of the fifth day, they pulled into their home at Lake Norman for the first time. Previously, Henry gave them both a set of keys and remote controls for the gates and garage doors before they left. They drove on by the first entrance and noted no one was there. They hoped that meant the house was completely finished. As they approached the around the bend second gate, Shane hit the remote button and the big black, fancy wrought gate opened and they drove in grinning. TJ slowed down while watch the gate close in the rear TV monitor. They went through beautiful new landscaped areas that Jerry and Terry had worked so hard on, around the gentle curves where they could see a view of the lake, and then slowly they turned left and slightly upwards. Shane hit another button and the big RV garage door opened in the back of the house. TJ pulled in and Shane hit the button to raise the other door at the far end, so the engine fumes could filter thru to the outside. TJ guided the coach inside the yellow marked lanes and up to the tire stop.

After leveling the coach, Shane put the slides out, and TJ shut down the engine. He and Shane went out and held their breath, but all the electrical, water, sewer, telephone, network, and satellite cable connections were in the correct spot. They were hooked up in no time. Shane hitched up the dogs, and led them to the new dog pen, opened the door, and unhooked them and let them play and mark their new potty area.

They unhitched the car and unloaded a few things they needed, but mostly dog stuff and laptops. Then they went in the house, while marveling at how wonderful it was with every board painted or stained, every doorknob shined, the cabinets glistened, and the huge new appliances in the kitchen blew them away. They thought they were in the kitchen for a nice restaurant. The office looked bigger and better, and so did the great room. The master suite was just a bit better than they currently had, but the walk-in closet was absolutely huge.

They returned to the center of the house and went up the grand staircase to see the staff quarters with the new furniture, kitchen, and big laundry. They turned around and crossed over the foyer to the guest rooms. Leslie created and furnished every room in the house with such amazing care. They took the end of hall stairs to the new wet area that started with the exercise rooms, Shane's new basketball court, and towards the lake but still inside was the sauna, steam, Endless Indoor pool, and large Jacuzzi. They went to the right side of the room at the rear and gazed out the windows at their new swimming pool. The water was sparkling, the changing rooms complete, including the food and beverage bar, and the huge stainless steel outdoor grill. They laughed and hugged each other as they walked across the outdoor deck and took in the sight of the lake below, the pool in front of them, and their beautiful house behind them. They felt very blessed, very lucky, and very happy. They gathered up the dogs, drove out while hitting the button to close the RV garage doors behind them, and headed up the road to Lindle.

The next morning, TJ and John had a lot of business to catch up on, and they spent two days doing it. Shane spent his days working out at Taylor University in the morning, and participating in pickup games in the afternoon. He loved not having to go to class this summer or any other summer for the rest of his life. He also helped with some of the packing in the evenings. Bob and Sue rolled in on the last afternoon in May, and the night before the big move. TJ helped line up the coach, and together they hooked it up, and helped Bob and Sue carry their things to their RV. TJ thanked them over and over for their help. They were excited about moving day, and promised to be up early and ready.

Shane and TJ were up late completing the packing of their personal stuff. TJ and John already packed the office. They would return later to take out the things Barbara didn't need when Shane's parents moved in. They went to bed late, got up early, and soon had three vehicles, and a rental truck driven by John loaded and ready for the ninety-minute trip to Lake Norman and their new home.

Upon arrival, Bob, Sue and John disappeared on their own private tour of the new house. By the time they returned, TJ and Shane had unloaded the first SUV. In a few hours, the group hauled everything in the house. TJ came back out to his car to get his laptop when he saw the gate opening. He didn't recognize the car, but soon noted a second car, followed by another. He waited by his car for the guests to pull into the visitor parking spots. Three ladies got out of their cars and walked over to him. It was then he recognized them as their chef and two housekeepers.

"Hey, ladies how are you? I wasn't expecting your arrival until tomorrow."

Betty Kingsley, the new chef spoke up first, "Well, we were talking yesterday while we were preparing meals for you, and decided all the moving in would probably make you a little hungry. We put a feast together for you in the kitchen, and if it is okay, we'll go set up lunch for you?"

TJ grinned, "I am so grateful. Please go right ahead and introduce yourselves. Shane is the tall one."

As they laughed and went in the house, TJ heard the gate opening again. He recognized Henry's truck followed by Robby's SUV, Leslie's car, and Buddy's truck as they pulled through and parked in the lot.

"Hey, how are you? I wasn't expecting you today. I thought we'd go through the house on Monday," began TJ.

Henry grinned, "I'm not working today. I'm on the welcoming committee. TJ, this is my wife Marilyn." TJ quickly smiled and welcomed her.

Buddy walked alongside him, "So am I? I never miss a party."

"A party?"

Robby caught up with them, "Well, we knew you just finished your vacation with a fast race across the country, and we thought you might need a little help moving in. TJ, this is my wife Sally."

TJ grinned, "That's okay by me. I'm pleased to meet you Sally. We didn't have to move too much, as we're leaving a lot of things for Shane's folks. We filled a truck and a few cars. Come on in."

Leslie came up and gave him a hug. He said, "You have done such a spectacular job on the decorations and choices of everything for the house. I am so proud of your work. I'll be bragging about you for years to come. Well, let's go eat."

When they came into the kitchen, TJ found everyone with a food bowl or platter in their hands and heading for the pool. TJ quickly introduced everyone to each other. Shane said, "I think they're throwing a party for us. You should see the food. I'm starved. I was going to get an ice chest, but Henry said not to bother, as there is ice machine at the pool bar. We have a pool bar?"

"Yeah, I know we hardly drink any alcohol, but the bar will help for the cold drinks and food we'll need when we're entertaining."

When they walked to the pool everyone was waiting for them. Henry spoke up, "TJ? Shane? All of us just wanted to welcome you to your new home. The ladies have prepared a great lunch. Come on and fix your plates, and we'll sit down around the pool and eat."

TJ said, "Thank you. Thank all of you so much. Let's eat."

476

A Writer's Fantasy

They had a wonderful time eating and getting to know their new chef and housekeepers, and were so thankful for the trouble everyone went to. After lunch, they returned to getting unpacked and by dinnertime, they had it all done. Bob and Sue were still tired from their cross-country trip and moving, so they said goodbye and went back to Lindle. They were leaving in a couple of days for South Dakota.

The rest of the gang, including John, began leaving after the boys thanked everyone many times. Soon they were alone and tired. They swam in their outdoor pool, and ate leftovers for dinner, and later they decided to try out the new wet area. Afterwards, they went to the great room to cool down and rest. It took a couple of tries, but soon they had a movie on the new HD projector. The picture quality stunned the boys, and it was forty percent larger than their old one, but the new surround system blew them away. After the movie, the exhausted boys went straight to their new bed.

The next morning after showers, they found themselves standing in the big new walk-in closet. They each had their own side with Shane having extra shelves for his ball cap collection, and numerous long lower shelves for all his basketball shoes. Henry made his suit rack higher because he could reach it and his suits hung longer. TJ had a similar set up on the other side but a bit lower. They had a big dual chest of drawers in the middle for socks, underwear and tee shirts. They had a laundry wheelie cart for dirty clothes, and on the wall was another LCD HD television and speakers.

The staff would return on Monday, so they had Sunday to rest and recover. That strategy didn't last long as ten minutes after finishing breakfast, Shane went to his new gym to shoot hoops, while TJ checked email, and then took the dogs with him to the RV building. He opened the big bay doors and let the dogs run and play outside. Of course, every now and then they would return for a drink of water, so TJ set up a water bowl for them near the door. They didn't have time to clean the coach when they arrived, so he vacuumed out the inside, dusted, cleaned the kitchen, and the bathroom, and hauled laundry to the house for cleaning. He also synched his onboard iMac® with the house network. Following Buddy's instructions, John made a backup for the Lindle network, and together, they loaded it on the new Concord home. TJ grinned when he realized all his files were already on the new network.

After closing the door, he decided to wash the new coach and started with the bugs on the front. He pulled out his cleaning stuff from one of the bays realizing he needed to make an order of new RV garage supplies, as he was leaving his former stuff with Al and Barbara. After making some valve adjustments, he soon enjoyed warm water running through the new hose and began tackling the bugs until the front was spotless. He worked his way around the coach working top to bottom and in an hour he had made it all the way around. He had to admit it was a beautiful coach, and he was thankful he decided to put a water softer unit on their water supply, as it prevented water spots. He pulled out more supplies and began tackling the dirty tires, and chrome wheels. That took another hour.

Shane came into the garage, "Hey, that looks great. You should have called me. I would have helped."

TJ looked up at Shane and grinned. "I know, I was just going to get the bugs off the front, and kept going. Isn't she beautiful?"

"Yes, he is," replied Shane slyly.

"This motorcoach is definitely a she," corrected TJ, without looking up.

"I was talking about you, knucklehead." Shane laughed.

TJ looked at him and grinned, "Thank you. Do you want to help me wash our dusty SUV's?"

"Sure."

They pulled the car to the front of the garage and pulled out the hose, rinsed the cars, and started washing their cars. Forty-five minutes later, the cars were done, the cleaning utensils put away, and they decided to eat lunch. Afterwards, they wandered down to the pool, and both took a short nap in the sun.

Shane wanted to ride the wave runners, so they put on their swimsuits, led the dogs down to the dock, fixed another water bowl, and went for a ride. Later, as they cruised back into the cove, the dogs woke up from their nap and began wagging their tails at them.

"Come on, I'll show you something funny." TJ pulled alongside the dock and called Beeper. The little dog came running and without hesitation jumped into his arms. TJ adjusted the dog, so she sat in front of TJ and put her paws on the middle of the handlebars. TJ made a few laps with her and Beeper leaned just like TJ did, as if they were on a motorcycle. He returned to the dock and Shane was laughing.

"When did you teach her to do that?"

"Oh, they used to ride all the time when I lived in Hendersonville. J-Henry will ride, too but he is not as brave. Here, you take Beeper, and I'll get J-Henry."

TJ handed Beeper over to him, and TJ called J-Henry. He reached out and picked him up and got him situated. They were soon cruising easily across the cove, and then turned around and came back, but passed their place and went deeper into the cove just doing a bit of sightseeing. They were looking at boats and docks, and didn't realize the owner of the next dock was on their sun deck.

"Hey, TJ? Shane? How are you?"

They throttled back on the wave runner, looked up, and spotted Jeff Gordon. TJ said, "Oh, hi. How are you? I wasn't expecting to see you today. Don't you have a race today?"

"It was yesterday."

"Oh, I'm sorry. We just got back from the west coast after picking up our new motorcoach, and yesterday we moved in."

"Great. Welcome to Lake Norman. I want to see your house and motorcoach sometime."

"We'd love to have you over."

"I didn't know you had circus dogs. They're cute. How'd you teach them to ride wave runners?"

TJ grinned, "Oh, they're pretty smart. You should see them water ski!"

They all laughed. Jeff knew he was pulling his leg. "Well, have a great day and I'll see you soon."

"Thank you. I'll call you for dinner."

Shane had one more week to get ready for his trip to Phoenix, so he was up early Monday heading to Lindle to work out and join in the pickup games. TJ met John as he drove in to his new parking spot, and together, they ate breakfast and went to work on getting the office organized in the new house. About nine, Betty and Heather arrived, and came into the kitchen.

"Hey, how are you?"

"We're fine," they replied. "I hope our arrival time is okay today. Robby told us to come a little later since you were getting settled in. We worked out a schedule that I hope is okay with you. As the chef I'll work Monday through Friday, leaving plenty of food for you on the weekends. I'll stay in my quarters upstairs during the week, and go to my house on the weekends. I have my home for sale and when it sells, I'll stay full time. Heather will work three ten-hour days staying here, and then Lindsay will take her place and work four ten hours days, and the next week they will switch so they each have a long week followed by a short and so on. Of course, we know from time to time you'll be entertaining, so just let me know, I'll adjust the schedule, so I can work during the weekend and take other days off. I have a file for temporary wait staff for dinner parties."

"That sounds great to me. You met John yesterday. He is my office / house manager, and well, my right arm. He'll eat a lot of meals with us, but he has an apartment he'll stay in. We'll have other office staff, but they'll take a lunch break and eat out."

"Will there be two or three for lunch?"

TJ sighed, "Just two. Shane went to workout in Lindle and will be home for supper. I'll try to let you know what the plans are as I know them. I suspect you already know how to prepare food for an athlete, but we'll talk about that with Shane when he gets here. He had a nutritionist during his college years, so he loves to eat healthy. I'm so glad to have both of you here."

"Well, we'll get to work and get out of your way. When you have a chance please give me some idea of what you like to eat."

"Okay I will." TJ returned to the office to help John. Once they had the files transferred, they put the supplies they brought with them in the cabinets. John kept a rolling list on his iPhone, as to what he needed to purchase. Once completed, they walked down the stairs to the new office area for employees. The room was large enough for four cubicle workstations, a private office for John, and cabinetry and countertop ran along one wall and across the back. There was also a set of male and female bathrooms, a small kitchen with refrigerator and microwave, and a table with six chairs. There were short windows on the front of the office, letting in some natural light.

The first cubicle was designed for their secretary who would also handle the phones and the electric gate. Buddy installed a television monitor on an arm attached to the wall that displayed four camera positions at a time. The main gate panel remained on at all times, while the other three screen windows rotate various camera angles around the property. John had a similar set up in his private office, and TJ had a second monitor in the main office for the same purpose. He could also hit a button on the remotes for the great room, kitchen, and bedroom to see the surveillance cameras. It worked at the dock.

The cubicles were beautiful with awesome chairs. Each desk featured an iMac® computer tied into the house network. Per TJ instructions, Leslie ordered nice oak furniture for John's office with an expensive office chair. It featured dual Mac Pro® computers and monitors, one on the left side area, so he could work on websites, and print graphics, and the other to work on the Shane and TJ's business. All the computers and printers were tied into the house network that would soon tie into the new main office in the Concord office park. The server, raid hard drives, and switches were mounted in the back of John's office behind smoked glass panel doors, so he could monitor all the systems without seeing all the wires and plugs.

John hadn't seen his office completed and was thrilled. He quickly sat down in his chair and marveled at all the new computers and furnishings. TJ told him to make a list of the office supplies needed for his office and the secretaries. The new secretary was due in shortly. They returned to the house and TJ asked Betty about her computer experience. Thankfully, she could do email and handle the Internet. TJ explained a simple chain of command with Betty and the staff reporting to John, who reported to TJ and Shane. They had already signed their privacy contracts, so he gave her a credit card Sam set up for house expenses. John had two cards for office expenses, one he would give to an associate when they needed to go get something they needed in a hurry.

TJ went on to explain that he would put her in charge of picking up all the groceries, and the smaller cleaning items. On the kitchen desk computer, John showed her how to put the bigger things needed on a spreadsheet he set up on the network. The housekeepers and office staff could add to this list at any time. He would make the order and have the supplies delivered to the house. He also trained her on the phone and gate system in case she was alone in the house. TJ went back to his office to make some calls, while John welcomed Heather, one of the new housekeepers, and trained her on the house and computer systems as well, and explained their chain of command and how to order supplies.

He returned to TJ's office to his work area in their office, and brought up his spreadsheets. He uploaded his list of supplies from his iPhone®, and checked with TJ to see what else they might need. He had opened accounts at the various office supply stores. He went online, made the big order, and asked for urgent delivery. A few minutes later, he got a call to make sure the deliveryman knew where they were. A truck rolled in an hour later. John was impressed with the quick delivery.

He went out to meet them so they could park near the employee entrance and wheel the stuff into the extended office area. They stacked everything along the wall. He and the secretary would sort it out it later. TJ buzzed John on the intercom. "Hey, can you come this way. We need to work on the schedule. Shane has two interviews to do, and I'm calling Alan Anderson, Shane's sports agent."

TJ made a call to Shane and felt shocked that he actually caught him. Shane just finished his strength workout and was taking a water break. He said he would be home by six, so TJ scheduled dinner for his arrival, and set up the two interviews for seven. TJ got Alan on the phone and began asking him about final plans for Phoenix, was there anything he needed to do for Shane, and he wanted to check on Alan's progress for endorsements.

Alan expressed good news and was glad to see they were home and could be reached when needed. He respected their privacy during their vacation with just a few key emails. He said the draft pundits placed Shane as number one in the draft, and that helped a lot with creating a buzz for Shane's endorsement deals. He hoped to close several deals this week for Pepsi, Nike, and Toyota. There were several other companies, too, like Office Depot, Burger King, and a game company that he was negotiating with. He said he would present the numbers for the first three in a few days. He wanted to get those contracts signed before Shane flew out. He asked if they could come to New York for a photo op for the contracts. TJ said he would ask Shane, but he thought they could.

TJ hung up and called Sam to see how things were going with all the construction bills, and income from his books. Sam reported he paid for all the projects with just a few more things for the main offices. The staff would move in on Monday in Concord. John created a new master digital calendar, with cool overlays for TJ's and Shane's schedules, and the calendars could appear on any computer on the network, synched automatically with their laptops via Apple's MobileMe® when traveling anywhere they could connect to the Internet. John ordered 3G cellular air cards for the three laptops for those times when they could not connect via Wi-Fi.

TJ called Jake to check on the status of his book sales. Jake was grinning as he talked and TJ could tell. The basketball book **Twice Is Nice** already outsold last year's book in the same time frame, and now sold over three million books. TJ's mouth dropped. Jake also said the gay book released four weeks later, just hit the four hundred thousand mark. His older books had sold two hundred thousand since the release of the new book. The sales already paid off the advance TJ received, and he was now earning new cash.

"Jake, this is all good news, it is great news! Thank you very much for a job well done." He paused for a second while thinking, "I have something I want to run by you. I need your insight and opinion."

"Sure, how can I help?"

"I'm thinking of writing another sequel to the basketball series about Shane's first year as a rookie beginning with his trip to Phoenix, through the summer leading up to basketball camp in the fall, and of course, the rest of the his first year. Do you think the public would be interested?"

"Hell, yes!" exclaimed Jake. "That's a great idea. It has never been done. I'll call the publisher and see if they're interested. I think we should threaten to bid it again. Can you write me a synopsis?"

"Yeah, sure, I'll get it to you soon."

"How's the new gay story coming?"

"It is coming but I'm behind due to the tournament, tours, vacation, and moving, but we're just settled in, and I'm opening the main office next week. I will to have it ready early fall to release after Thanksgiving like last year. I'll talk to you later this week. Thanks again for all your help."

"Bye and have a great week."

As John listened, he made notes and added to-do memos to the project list that all could see on the network. They shifted gears and began working on Shane's biz website as they called it, and the foundation site. They couldn't release items for sale with a tie to the Bobcats just yet, as that was still a secret, however, thanks to a deal TJ had worked out with Walter and Taylor University, they could sell team products, and licensed products with Shane's name on it like jerseys, hats, and balls. TJ and John ordered a huge shipment of products with samples delivered to the house.

John set up a small area on the counter with lights, so he could take digital pictures of each item. He created a list of sizes, and spent most of last week working on the ordering online shopping system for the products, sizes, and autographs. Every item could be autographed for a five-dollar donation to the foundation. TJ also selected a line of non-Taylor items like basketballs, hats, shirts, and jackets. The clothing item displayed Shane's signature digitally stitched on the garments. John worked on the final pictures so he could finish preparing the photographs for the websites. TJ prepared stacks of clothes for Shane, as he was going to Billy Coble's studio to shoot pictures of him modeling all the new products and other items. TJ set that up for early

Wednesday morning so he could go on to Lindle for his workouts and pickup games in the afternoon.

Betty fixed TJ and John a lunch featuring a cup of her potato soup, a half club sandwich, and slices of fruit. TJ was also pleased she knew how to make good southern sweet tea. After lunch the new secretary arrived. TJ interviewed Sarah Austin before their vacation, and he was excited to have her on the team. She worked for years for the quarterback of Carolina Panthers, who recently retired and moved away this spring. She knew how to work with celebrities, possessed excellent computer and office skills, the dying art of shorthand for quick note taking and composing letters, plus an excellent phone voice. She was also beautiful and very funny. She was married with two kids, and very independent. She also possessed a wonderful dry wit. She worked out daily, looked like a female tennis player, with blond short hair, green eyes, and medium tan.

TJ introduced her to John and Betty, and they sat down in his office to talk about procedures and plans. He showed her how to answer the phone, transfer calls, and operate the gate. After TJ's conversation on privacy and policies, John and Sarah went to their office areas to unpack and set up the office. TJ called Robby to check in with him, and obtain his status on opening the main office. He and John were driving down in the morning to see the new facility. Buddy was meeting them there to complete the computer networking with the installer team of the mailing and shipping systems they ordered. He scheduled TJ, John, Robby, and their new shipping manager to be trained on the equipment. TJ secured Buddy on a maintenance contract including all things electronic at the home / office, and the main office.

Afterwards, he called Dick Vitale and was surprised to catch him quickly. Dick was on the golf course but took his call. "Hey, Dick, how are you?"

"Great, just completed nine holes of golf and eating a sandwich before the back nine. Of course, I'm playing horrible as usual."

TJ laughed, "Just checking to make sure you and your wife were still coming next week to Lake Norman."

"Yes sir. We'll be there Tuesday afternoon."

"Why don't you stay over in one of guestrooms? We'll have a great dinner together."

"That sounds perfect. We'll be there. See you soon, pal."

TJ always came away from a conversation with Dick feeling better about him and the world. The man just had magic for instilling enthusiasm, he thought.

He went to the kitchen and poured himself a glass of a punch Betty had made from scratch. "Oh my," he began after taking a sip, "this is delicious."

"It's all fruit, no preservatives, and no sugar. I did that batch with the blender, but that was a pain. I need several utensils to outfit the kitchen including a juicer."

TJ smiled, "I was expecting this request. Shane and I mostly cook in one or two pots, and that's it. Can you get the gear locally, Charlotte, or online?"

"Charlotte has several excellent restaurant supply houses, but yes, I'll order online as well."

"How much do you estimate?"

"About two thousand. The pots and pans I need are the most expensive part of the order, but they hold their value."

"That's fine. Use the new credit card, give John the receipts, and he'll send the details on to Sam. Tuesday night Shane and I will host Mr. And Mrs. Vitale for dinner. Can you make something special for us? Thanks again for the juice. It is awesome."

TJ went in the office and closed the door to the kitchen, so he could concentrate. He began by writing a synopsis and outline for his proposed new basketball book. The digest would detail Shane's thoughts and comments as a rookie in the NBA. He and Shane discussed the idea on their vacation. Shane was all for it, as he thought the books were good for TJ, but he also knew it would help his foundation. The deal Jake would make with the publisher included a dollar donation from each sale for Shane's foundation. It took him an hour to write the rough draft, and another hour to polish it up. He sent it to Jake.

Afterwards, he looked at the to-do project list and saw the list of things John placed there to remind him. He went to work writing copy for the new websites, and descriptions for the various articles Shane was selling. That took another hour. Next, he tackled the final version of a full-page ad for Friday's edition of the USA Today® national newspaper, and Sunday ads in the sports pages of fifty major newspapers. There were also ads in the leading sports magazines coming out on Monday. John uploaded numerous last minute pictures but by five everything was ready to go.

TJ toured the expanded home / office and was pleased to see the supplies put away, and they were both unpacking items for their desks. John showed him the latest pictures online, and they both checked every single page to see if they could find any errors. TJ gave Sarah a credit card for specialty items TJ or John might need from time to time, and to find a florist and open an account, but for now he had her use the card and go online to Shane's new website, and purchase several items. In seconds, John was watching the order take place, credit card approval achieved, and the customer added to the mailing and emailing list. The money for the items went into their online business account and a dollar transferred to the foundation account as planned. It prompted TJ to tell John to add finding a board of directors to his to-do list. He knew Robby was working on a list, too. He planned to ask Al and Barbara to be on the board, but beyond that he had no idea. He thought he might ask Dick next week.

After dinner, Shane did the remotes studio interviews as planned, and TJ began explaining his hectic but productive day. He showed him the latest changes to the ads, and the websites. He took him on a tour of the expanded home / office, and he met Sarah as she was leaving. John left as well as he would be back early in the morning to go Concord. All this was easier because he had moved from Lindle to a new condo not far from the new house, thanks to TJ paying for a moving service called Two Guy and a Truck. John fell in love with one of the movers and even got his phone number. He planned to call him later tonight. The boys retired early after enjoying a swim in their new pool, and time in the wet area.

The training at the new office went well, and TJ was floored how efficient and quick the new mailing and shipping machines and the network processing were. Together, they processed twenty dummy orders as well as Sarah's order last night. Robby had two staffers stocking the shipping room, and the storage area was full of boxes of everything they were offering on the websites. The computers could print either a business or foundation return address as well as handle all their mail outs with ease.

TJ, Robby, John and their new publicist met in the new conference room. Buddy installed excellent audio /video facilities in the room. John logged on an iMac® in open cubicle at the back end of the conference room. He hit a button on the console, and the electric blinds closed, and a motorized screen descended from the ceiling. The lights dimmed slightly and his presentation began on the screen. He walked back to the conference table with his wireless remote in hand. TJ began explaining to his small staff how the company-wide calendar worked. John demonstrated the overlays, so each person could have their own private schedule, while meetings and such would automatically appear on the master calendar. He also demonstrated how to send a group email, and asked them to please be careful to avoid junk mail, although Buddy installed a master anti-spam and junk module tied to a major company that kept their network clean twenty-four hours a day.

TJ quickly touched on Shane's schedule and TJ's for the next two weeks. Shane would fly out first to Phoenix, and TJ would join him later in the week. He then spoke about the upcoming ads as John displayed copies on the screen, and was followed by a viewing of the four websites: Shane fan site, the foundation site, TJ's straight book site, and TJ's gay book site. He demonstrated the tie in of everything they did with the foundation. Every purchase would automatically donate a dollar to the foundation, but there would also be a spot where they could increase the donation. He passed around bookmarks, postcards, and greeting cards that would also be sold on the sites. He also said the bookmarks would be given away at book signings during the tours.

John began explaining how customers visiting Shane's site could order all kinds of products, and for a five-dollar donation, Shane would autograph it for them. He explained that once a week Shane would visit and sign thousands of autograph items so there would be plenty in stock to fill those special orders.

TJ laughed, "Well, in theory that is how it is supposed to work, but first I have to talk Shane into it." They all laughed assuming he was kidding. He wasn't. "Our goal is to use Shane celebrity to raise funds for many charities." He began listening various charities he and Shane already selected included gay and straight organizations. John clicked on the foundation pages where videos and podcasts displayed the charities and their work with many pictures of children and families benefiting from the money the charities raised. He challenged everyone to help him and Shane raise more funds than any other celebrity.

After the meeting, TJ met with the new publicist, Connie Spearwood. She, too, worked a decade with a major race team until they recently merged with a larger group. She also worked in radio and television, and with ad agencies. She was incredibly bright, articulate, and fun to be around. TJ liked her immediately during her final interview, and he was thrilled when she accepted his offer. He felt she would be a great asset to the team, able to help John with his publicity work, and perhaps after she was up and running, she would help with taking care of TJ and Shane's stuff, as TJ called it.

John taught her how to use the network system, and especially iChat®, so that she and TJ could talk directly on plans and ongoing procedures.

She then gave each a procedure manual she prepared for suggested policy on how they were to each handle the press, especially when under fire. "For example," she said, "Let's suppose Shane has an altercation with the paparazzi, and he is accused of punching a guy out."

TJ started laughing, "I doubt that would happen unless the guy took away some of his prized sushi, but go ahead."

"Shane should try and apologize if he can, and quickly move away. If possible, Shane should never be in the public alone. Too much can happen, and we need to assist him when we can. I'll let you worry about security, but there are a few pages he might want to read to protect him from frivolous and expensive lawsuits. The same applies to us, as we represent him, and representing TJ. Please let me know as far in advance as possible, any situation you think might occur. I will fly out quickly if need be, or I can go online, or I can get to a studio.

"I also will begin updating my vast media files, so a press release goes out about the both of you many times a month. I will also begin a campaign for the foundation. I want to know more about the charities. Each time you pick a board member, we'll use that announcement as another push for the foundation. With the amazing mailing equipment you have here, there is nothing we can't do. Any questions?"

TJ grinned, "I'd say you're right on target. I have one thing I need to tell you about so you can be prepared, but what I am about to tell you cannot be revealed to anyone, at least for a little while longer." He explained the plan for Shane to come out of the closet, and the deal with the Bobcats."

TJ watched her face as the color changed. She sighed, took a deep breath, "Okay, no problem."

TJ laughed, "No problem? I think the media will go crazy."

"Yes," she replied, "but what a great opportunity to promote our business. I admit you threw me a curveball, however, my dad taught me how to hit a curveball when I was fourteen years old. I can handle this, and thanks for the heads up. I will keep the secret, and look forward to the challenge."

TJ shook her hand as the meeting broke up. He walked back once again to the shipping department as the product he and John ordered was unpacked and restocked on the shelves. He knew their business and foundation were about to be launched with a big bang.

# FORTY-ONE

They flew out early on Friday morning with TJ, Shane, John, and Connie aboard. They were on the way to New York City to participate in the signing of Shane to three major sponsors. It had been a busy, but extraordinary and complicated week, including Shane's modeling and handling of all the new products, and the shooting of hundreds of high quality pictures. TJ grinned at how well Shane handled the assignments and the directions of the photographer they hired for the project. John loaded all the digital photos on his Mac Book Pro® and into Adobe's Lightroom® software, so on the ride up to New York they could select the photographs they needed for the websites. They also chose photos for packaging of the products. Connie selected photos for the media kits she continued developing. She explained the kits would constantly grow and change for as long as they continued their careers. John told her he would prepare disks for the photos she needed for inclusion in her media kits. Connie thanked him, but said she would also need a place on the website for media only. She would issue passwords to this backdoor so at any time, the reporters around the country could access it for the latest press releases and pictures. TJ and John liked that idea, and he set about making notes to make it happen.

John quickly created three folders labeled: web, marketing, and promotion, and dropped copies of the photos they selected into the correct folder. Connie recently interviewed both boys to create biographies for her publicity campaign, searching for phrases to describe their talents and skills in various ways. For TJ, it was a matter of books and dates published, while Shane's history included an extensive list of teams he played on, games won, awards, and championship titles. She maintained a long checklist of items she worked tirelessly on. TJ joked the only thing he ever won was Shane. TJ gave her digital copies of last year's media book for Taylor University, which had the statistics and records for Shane. Walter also sent along a supplemental update after the second championship-winning season.

TJ approved each piece for distribution and thanked Connie for her talents and dedication. She brought along two sample cases, often used by salesman to bring their wares in for product demonstrations. However, Connie's cases carried Shane's newly printed media kits with fancy blue covers with his picture on the front dunking a basketball in a big game, as well as wonderful headshot, posed with great lighting.

The limousine service promptly picked them up on the tarmac. TJ and John helped Connie with the heavy cases. John also carried the new expensive digital Sony A700 camera he and TJ selected for their work. They ordered the model and brand suggested by the photographer taking the promo pictures in Concord. It featured a powerful zoom lens at 16-105mm, and could be swapped for a macro lens for close-up work. TJ also ordered extended flash batteries, memory chips, digital portable hard drive, product lights, tripod, and camera case. John could shoot five frames per second in continuous mode. TJ, with a sly grin, told him he looked like a pro. Shane playfully called him a geek, as he constantly studied the camera manuals, learning about another feature or trick. John didn't care what they called him, as he was having a blast figuring out the bells and whistles on this powerful camera.

TJ and John created TJI media security passes for all of them to carry. John shot the pictures for the cards that mimicked TJ's Taylor University Pass including the ID pictures that he shot with the new camera, and their TJI logo. He bought plastic laminated kits and soon produced official looking badges. John also designed business cards for TJ, Shane, John, Connie, and the rest of their office staff to use. He used an online printing service that could print and ship overnight, and they were printed on a thin plastic gloss stock about half the thickness of a credit card. TJ and Shane thought they were very impressive and impervious to liquids. He recently created new email addresses for all the staff, and special addresses for TJ and Shane to keep their business email separate from their personal mail. TJ also maintained a different gay fiction email address. Recently, John secured Shane's name as a website to prevent someone else from grabbing it.

They met Alan at his office. Jerome was there and already perused the contracts, made changes and pronounced all three complete and ready. Yesterday, TJ received an Acrobat PDF® copy of all three agreements, and read them carefully yesterday. In all cases, it was a three-year contract, paying Shane huge amounts of money upfront and so much a month for the term. In exchange, he would perform in two ad campaigns a year, the footage to be shot in his off-season, and make twelve personal appearances a year. They would be allowed to use his photo with their products for print for the term. After the term, they would pay residuals for any promotion containing his voice, image, or likeness, if they did not renew the contract. He would also record a series of radio commercials, and other promotional tapes. TJ heeded Jeff Gordon's advice by insisting the still and movie photography be shot in the same day to cut down on day of travel and obligation.

Alan went over the procedure with them, but basically it was a photo-op for the sponsors, and they would be held an hour apart. In various offices, his staff politely kept the key company heads waiting to be ushered down to the building media room on the main floor where the press assembled, including crews from ESPN® and Fox Sports®. They were amazed that several financial networks were set for the press conferences, too. Soon they were ready and took the elevator downstairs.

Shane and his entourage met with each company individually for about fifteen minutes. Shane shook hands with everyone in attendance for the sponsors, and their media and John took photos. They expressed how pleased they were to have him with their company, and he in turned responded with how grateful he was to join their team. TJ and Shane wished they could tell them about his plans to come out as a gay athlete, but the risk was too great for the NBA Bobcat deal. Shane planned to do so right before the draft. Jerome and Alan agreed with the boys, that they would let the companies cancel their contracts if they had a mind to do so after his announcement. Alan also agreed that Sam would hold the funds received today in escrow until the response by the companies after outing was known.

Secretly, Connie was preparing press releases pronouncing the power of the gay dollar, and a market all three companies needed to break into. Millions of dollars were tappable if they stuck with Shane, she thought. She prepared pages of facts and figures to document her case, as if she was going to court. Alan also prepared for 'the gay day' as he called it. He was confident these companies would stick with them, and if they didn't, he vowed another company would. He prepared a speech that included if they let Shane go, their competition would strike a deal with him in a matter of hours. It was a threat he hoped no one would ever hear. Jerome also prepared several legal briefs in case he needed to get involved.

Shane and TJ were also thanking the companies for their willingness to partner with the foundation's efforts. They began with Office Depot®, and TJ noted a particular paragraph stating Shane's office should use only Office Depot® products provided free to him during the term of the contract. If only he had known that a few days ago, as he and John bought a thousand dollars worth of supplies. He told John they would make up for it in the future. Shane was given a golden Office Depot® credit card for all his future purchases.

Next came Toyota® and they also had a special provision stating Shane should drive only Toyota® products whenever possible. Shane planned to give his Hummer® to his dad. They negotiated a fully loaded Land Cruiser® for Shane, a Sequoia® with leather package for TJ, and a hybrid Highlander® for John, and they signed the deal standing in the bed of a beautiful new Tundra® truck. The Tundra® was a gift for their company, and once a year their cars would be replaced with new ones. Shane would autograph the old ones to be sold on an online auction on their foundation web site. The boys were ecstatic and overjoyed with the offer of the cars for now, and the foundation in the future.

Pepsi® held the last signing and press conference, and their marketing team arrived in a large mass for the announcement. Once the press quieted down, the head of Pepsi® marketing took the podium and began explaining how happy he was to have a high caliber player and person like Shane on their team. He then announced that another sports figure would assist in the official signing. From behind the curtain, Jeff Gordon stepped out. He laughed and smiled at TJ and Shane's face. He surprised them for sure. The Concord Executive Airport was a busy place for everyone connected to NASCAR®. The boys had flown out that morning amongst the beautiful jets of the various teams and drivers heading to a track for the weekend. They hadn't noted that Jeff was among those flying out. He shook their hands and gave hugs as the cameras flashed.

The contract called for Shane to use Pepsi® products including Mountain Dew®. Jeff presented a Pepsi® hat to Shane and TJ, and two leather jackets with the Pepsi® logo on the front and Mountain Dew® on the back. Pepsi® announced a new joint ad campaign with Jeff and Shane for their fall push. Shane and TJ were very excited to be working with their neighbor and mentor. TJ quickly put on his hat and jacket, but did his best to slide away from Shane as the cameras began snapping his picture.

At the conclusion of the press conferences, Connie passed out her press kits until her cases were empty. Shane was tired of smiling, but happy they were over two hundred and fifty million dollars a year richer. After congratulating Alan several times on the acquisitions of these three big companies, they said goodbye, and took the car service to the airport and flew home. Exhausted from the journey and the experience, everyone went home after they landed. On the drive to the house, Shane asked TJ, "Do you think they will cancel when I come out of the closet?"

"There's a chance they will. The contract is a little vague in that regard. They can cancel if you commit a felony, get caught with a hooker..." Shane started laughing while TJ grinned and continued, "though I would have to kill you if you did that. The contract just says you must maintain high moral standards. Bottom line, we're prepared to show these companies the moral obligation they have to support gay people as well, and how profitable it will be. If we have to, we'll throw in an extra set of commercials for free, but I am eighty percent confident they will not turn away the number one draft pick, yah-da, yah-da."

Shane thought for a second, "I hope they stay. It is going to be a tough year as the NBA's first gay rookie. Having these big companies behind me will help us reach our goals a whole lot sooner."

"You're right. Connie, Alan, and I have packages of information to be delivered to the companies the morning of your announcement by courier. It'll begin with an apology for not telling them before the signing, but we'll explain it was part of our strategy to make sure you were drafted onto a team that could win a championship. They all want to be the sponsor of a champion. We will make them a lot of money, and they are responsible to their stockholders. We'll tie the companies into our foundation promotions as well. We'll visit their home offices, shake a lot of employee hands, and you'll speak at some banquets, and whatever else it takes to convince these big boys they need to stick with Shane.

"You'll have to remember to mention your sponsor names when you get a chance. It will be harder in the NBA than it is with NASCAR®, but you can do it. Maybe we need to design a line of public clothes displaying their logos on emblems. Afterwards, we'll have three years to convince everyone to renew your contracts. We'll work hard and always maintain a perfect, cheerful attitude, and we'll win. I think we should talk to Sam about buying stock in all of our sponsor companies, a lot of stock. A little leverage might come in handy later on, but it will also show we are investing our reputation and our money in their companies, too. They will stay. Are you hungry?"

"Starved."

"I will alert Betty of our arrival. I am hungry, too." TJ made the call.

Betty made a chicken casserole with macaroni and cheese, green beans, baby carrots and fresh corn on the cob. The boys devoured it. She also made an apple pie that was equally good. Afterwards, they changed clothes, and took the dogs to the lake. They started with a boat ride with the dogs aboard enjoying the relaxing view as the sun was setting far down the lake. They returned near twilight, put the boat on the lift and made their way back up the hill to the house. They stripped down and went to the wet area, and later settled in the living room for a movie.

TJ spent Saturday morning looking at the photos John uploaded from the trip to New York. He selected several he liked, and dropped copies into a private folder. He began working on a project with Connie on key photos during Shane's career thus far. She found a photographer / designer, who took their selected photos, enlarged and touched up the pictures, and framed each one beautifully. They were all two x three feet and designed for big walls. TJ would put some of them at their home, in their personal quarters and in the home / office, TJ and Shane's space in the new business office, and the rest at the main office in the lobby. Henry helped him find an amazing cabinetmaker that designed beautiful display cases for their home and the big new office in Concord. He planned to exhibit many of Shane's trophies after receiving several shipments from Shane's dad. With the permission of Walter, he ordered duplicates of the National Championship trophies for display at the office. They were put alongside Shane's Most Valuable Player awards, and all the other awards he achieved in the high school and college career. He didn't want to create a museum at home or the new office, but as their clients came to visit, they did want to make an awesome first impression.

John arrived and brought along numerous copies of the Friday edition of USA Today® ad with him, plus copies of the magazines running their ads. Sunday the campaign would continue in both the Parade® and Weekend® newspaper magazines. As TJ flipped through the ads, John turned on his computer, and clicked on the software to load Shane's website statistics. The new site already received over fifty thousand hits since he quietly uploaded the new websites forty-eight hours before the ads ran. He pulled up a sales report and screamed out loud. "TJ! Look at this!"

TJ rolled his chair over to John's work area on his long u-shaped desk and studied the screen as John slowly scrolled down. Every item bearing

Shane's name displayed large sales numbers. In the first two days of unadvertised sales, they already sold two hundred and fifty thousand dollars of product. John scrolled down to the bottom, "Look at that! We have fifty seven thousand for the foundation already."

"How many buyers donated more than the dollar from sales?"

John looked for the column he created for that purpose, and said, "Over twenty thousand customers donated five dollars in addition to their order. That's a hundred thousand dollars!"

"Is your tax program working correctly? Remember, they should not be charged on the donations nor the additional funds."

John scrolled through his reports and found the total for tax sales. "Yes, it is working fine. The tax sales are far less. I will scroll through hundreds of individual reports, but it appears to be working fine."

"Get Robby on the phone." TJ paused, "Wait a minute. This is Saturday. Robby is probably fishing. What are you doing here?"

John looked up from the phone, "I wasn't going to miss this day for nothing in the world. I have thousands of hours in this project. I am excited!"

"Indeed you do. Congratulations and way to go. Tomorrow will be even better when the entire country reads the ads in the newspaper magazines." TJ gave him a hug over the rear of John's desk chair. "I'm so proud of you, and boy was I lucky to shop in your Apple® store."

Shane came in from lifting weights at home and when they showed him the figures he started laughing as well. He wanted to believe their business would grow, but he wasn't quite sure until he saw the results from just two days. He called his dad to give him the report.

TJ asked Shane, "What are you doing today?"

I have another hour of weights and machines to do, then an hour of shooting and I'm done. Why?"

"Well, I have a couple of things in mind. First, all of us have worked very hard to get to and through this exciting week. We secured three major sponsor endorsement contracts, sold our first quarter of million dollars in sales, and our foundation funds are now growing. We moved into the new house, picked up our new motorcoach, and now we are a real business. I propose we celebrate."

Shane laughed, "Okay, how?"

"Well, let's grill some thick steaks by the pool tonight, and spend the afternoon on the lake. Betty left us lunch. We could make up plates and picnic down there. John, you're staying for dinner, too."

John laughed, "You don't have to ask this bachelor twice to dinner."

Shane laughed, "Sounds perfect. I'll go finish my workouts."

Before Shane left, they all heard the chime of the gate intercom button, but they weren't expecting anyone. TJ glanced up at the monitor on the wall and saw three cars and truck at the gate. TJ pushed the button, "May I help you?"

"Yes, sir. My name is Ralph Freeman. I'm from Charlotte Toyota. I have four vehicles to deliver to a Mister Bradley. Is this the right place?"

"Yes, it is. I'll buzz you in." TJ started laughing, and they all quickly went out the door as the cars pulled up to the garage. Ralph climbed out of the first car with a clipboard, and got TJ to sign his paperwork. He then began demonstrating their new toys and the features. A fifth car had come in behind them, and soon the delivery drivers were gone.

TJ laughed, "Well, this just makes the day perfect." TJ took the Highlander keys and said, "John in recognition for your all your hard work, Shane and I would like to present you this brand new Hybrid Highlander. I hope you like it."

John nearly jumped out of shoes he was so excited. He ran to TJ and hugged him. Then did the same to Shane, who swung him around, and then let him go, so he could run see his new car. Shane and TJ laughed, as they were so happy for him. They watched him as he opened all the doors, the hood, the trunk, and finally got in and cranked it up. Since it was a hybrid, they thought it would save fuel for errands and such. TJ said, "Well, go drive it a while and meet us at the lake when you're ready. Be careful, use your seatbelt, and don't speed."

"Thank you!" yelled John as he closed the door, and drove out of the gate after getting his remote controls for the gate out of his old car. Later, TJ would help him put his old car in the I Wanna® classified newspaper to sell it. Shane planned to give his Hummer to his parents. TJ was giving his Sequoia to his parents.

Shane decided to choose the black Land Cruiser as it gave him a bit more headroom with his six foot nine inch frame, plus he thought it looked elegant and the perfect car for him. His big body fit inside just fine, and it featured an in-dash GPS system, Bluetooth® speakerphone, digital stereo with XM Radio®, and rear flip down monitors for watching movies on trips. The leather inside was beautiful.

TJ's new Sequoia was a new color they called Desert Rose, or a shade of khaki with just a slight hint of burgundy. He knew it wouldn't show dust and dirt as easy as the black one would. The following week he would take it to a hitch shop to have it wired for the motorcoach. Inside were the same features as Shane's SUV.

They soon realized that all three cars had Bluetooth technology in the electronic system for GPS, stereo, video, and two cool features: first for safety sake, their iPhones® would link with the car system so that all calls could be answered hands-free by speaking towards the front glass where tiny microphones were hidden in the upholstery above, and also the songs in the iPhone® or an iPod® could be played in the stereo.

494

They quickly scanned through the manuals and TJ figured out how to record the remote signals for the gate and garages. They tested their phones and went for a test drive, one vehicle at a time. After testing their SUV cars, they took Tundra pickup truck for a spin. It would come in handy for the boat and Yamaha® Wave-Runners. After they put the new cars in the garage, and the truck in the workshop, they moved the old vehicles over to guest parking. Shane finished his workout while TJ went to the kitchen. He heard the chime and looked up at the gate monitor. There was a large truck. He buzzed them in and walked out.

TJ laughed when he realized it was a new Pepsi® truck. The guy pulled up and asked, "Is this the Bradley residence?"

"Yes it is. May I help you?"

"Just tell me where you want it?"

"Want what?" asked TJ, half afraid Pepsi® had given them a new truck.

"My boss told me to deliver a truck load of our products to you in our best truck. My helper and I can unload it anywhere you like."

TJ laughed, "Well, let's see, put a about a third in the RV garage just inside the door on the left against the wall, another third down by the pool— just follow the path. You'll find a bar. Just put it against the wall behind the bar, and the final third can go against the far wall in the car garage. Do you need any help?"

"No sir. We can handle it. We have two hand trucks."

"Well, guys thank you very much. Please tell your boss we appreciate it. The gate will automatically open and close when you're ready to leave. Thanks again." He shook their hands vigorously.

TJ went back inside hoping Office Depot® wasn't delivering a truckload of supplies today. He made plates for their lunch and when Shane arrived from the gym soaked in sweat, they picked up the plates he fixed, and walked with the dogs down to the pool.

"Where did all the Pepsi® stuff come from?"

TJ laughed, "This is only a third of it. The rest is in the RV building and the car garage. A Pepsi® truck delivered it for free."

Shane grinned, "I guess they were serious about us drinking Pepsi® products, huh. I guess I had better haul the Sport Drinks to the wet area." He fixed cups of ice, and they sat at one of their new tables under an umbrella, and ate while the dogs chased each other around the pool. All of sudden, Beeper cut a curve too close trying to catch J-Henry and slipped and fell in the pool. Shane jumped up afraid she couldn't swim while TJ started laughing. Beeper came up sputtering and spitting water, swam to the walk up steps, and climbed out of the pool, and promptly tried to shake all the water off. TJ could have sworn he saw J-Henry laughing. The dog had stopped at the far end, and was just sitting there grinning and wagging his tail!

After a while, they went swimming in the new pool. John returned in his new car and couldn't stop smiling. He told the boys all about his new car. TJ told him he would help him set up his remote for the built in controls in his car for the gate. John changed clothes in the new bathhouse. They went down to the lake and chased each other on the wave runners, and finally took a long cruise in the boat with the stereo blasting away. Late in the day, they returned to the pool. TJ brought down steaks for Shane to put on the grill while he went back for the baked potatoes, salad, and fixings. Drinking more Pepsi® they ate and celebrated the week.

Shane flew out early Sunday morning for Phoenix. TJ took him to the airport and sadly said goodbye. TJ would catch up with him Wednesday, but he had a lot of work to do in the meantime, and Dick and his wife were coming in tomorrow afternoon. On Monday morning, the requests from the new sponsors arrived by numerous faxes. TJ responded to each contact person by politely asking them to send their requests and other communications by email so they could easily be distributed to department heads, as well as catch up with them since they travel a lot. John sent copies over to Robby. They studied them over carefully. TJ assumed from now on scheduling was going to be complicated. He called Bill Johnson over at the Bobcat's office asking for a practice and game schedule for the new season. A long PDF document was sent over by email. TJ gasped when he realized Shane would have eight preseason games, and eighty-two regular games plus playoffs and championships. Shane already knew this, but it was a shock to TJ, as that was almost three times what he had played in college. That meant he would play in ninety games for sure.

John used their new software allowing the creation of calendar digital film like the layers used in Adobe's Illustrator® for print designs. He went to work overlapping a game calendar with their master calendar. He brought the game schedule up on the twenty-four inch iMac® on TJ's desk. TJ began studying the photo shoots the sponsors wanted as noted in the faxes. He made phone calls to find out how long each one would be and where was the location. He made sure the requests were bunched together to accomplish as much as possible. He pushed hard for using Billy's studio in Concord. He also noted their requests for personal appearances for company functions, so he requested locations and times emailed to him as soon as possible, and after a game, if Shane was interviewed, he was suppose to have a Pepsi® in his hand, and if he managed to take a sip while on camera, he earned bonus money for the foundation at five thousand dollars per game. It was all mind-boggling. He called Connie and obtained her thoughts, wanting to hear about her experience with the race teams. He also talked to Robby seeking his advice as well. He hoped to have Jeff and his wife over for dinner in the next week or so, and pick his brain, too.

Connie told him most drivers knew they had obligations to sponsors to fulfill, but often resented the wasted time when they went to photo shoots. She said she solved the problem by scheduling more than one company on the same day in the same or nearby location. She said the companies would act all legal and a bit high mighty, but none of them wanted to have an angry and upset celebrity that might make a call to their boss, or worst the newspapers.

Robby gave him some good tips as well, so TJ and John plotted everything on calendars and spreadsheets for the Bobcats and sponsors. They assumed most of September would be for pre-season practices. The first preseason game was October tenth. All of the sponsors wanted commercials ready for the new fall television shows, so shooting had to be completed in August. He made phone calls and persuaded the companies to agree to shoot the commercials in Concord at Billy's studio, except Toyota wanted some rugged mountain terrain for their truck commercials. TJ suggested the Blue Ridge Mountains near Asheville. Their teams went to work researching the idea. He soon planned for Shane spending three days, a day for each company in early August, and later in the month he would do a photo shoot for print media, and record voiceovers and audio commercials. All of which would be done at Top Line Productions. Billy would owe TJ and Shane some favors for all the business they sent his way. The sponsors were pleased with the plan as it save production dollars, too. There were conflicts to workout for the rest of the season, but the worst of it was done. John saved the layers and sent copies to Robby, Connie, their new secretary Sarah, and to Alan in New York. TJ told him to wait until Shane arrived home from rookie camp before sending it to his computer. He felt Shane had enough to worry about out there as it was.

After a fruit snack provided by Betty, TJ and John created a spreadsheet of the away games. There were over forty-five road games. TJ sat there shaking his head as the big number overwhelmed him. He sighed greatly as that was a lot of time away from home, but they would travel and sleep together this time, and make the most of it. He confirmed with the Bobcat office the team always arrived the day before a game, while never taking a chance on a bad weather and flight cancellations. TJ was used to that arrangement after two years with Taylor University. TJ copied the cities over to a new spreadsheet to later study for researching for things to do in each one. They could do museums and sightseeing half-day trips, he thought. They dropped the away game information into TJ's GPS program for plotting on his map, and studying for time from home to each location. They also made adjustments for those games going from one away city to another without coming home. He realized most of the games could be reached in a just a couple of hours by the Learjet. They would spend a fortune on jet rentals this year, but they were making a ton of money, and thankfully could afford it. He made a note to ask Jeff Gordon about the value of owning or leasing a Learjet. He would run that by Sam, too.

The practice schedules were completely different in the NBA, with many morning practices, since there were no school classes or homework to worry about, and he made adjustments for it. On Tuesday morning, they negotiated with the production teams from the sponsor companies until they had a tentative plan to work with. John brought him a printout of the last few days of sales showing online sales continued growing. Robby reported processing on schedule with orders shipped the same day, if they arrived before two, and the next morning if they didn't. All transactions were by credit or debit card, and Robby emailed him a report of the paid orders so far. He also began sending weekly reports to Sam in New York. John told TJ that Sam cursed when he realized how much the bank was charging for the credit card transactions. He said he would make calls and renegotiate a much better deal before the end of the day. TJ smiled.

Dick and Elizabeth arrived around three o'clock on Tuesday. They marveled at the development of the property, and gladly took the house tour. Elizabeth loved the kitchen and big pantry, and made friends quickly with Betty. Dick loved the setup for the new office, the remote studio, and the home /office set up for John and his staff. They liked the great room, the lake view, and grinned at the big master bedroom and walk-in closet. They went up the center stairs to the guest area and down the backstairs to the wet area that gave them a good overview of the entire area. They went out to the pool and walked along the deck, and came in the back way to the RV building.

Dick was anxious to see the new motorcoach, so TJ gave them quick tours of some of the bays, the big engine, and then opened the door while flipping on the lights and letting them wander in. She loved the marble tile and the furnishings, while Dick felt fascinated with the driver's console area, the new desk and remote setup. Elizabeth was shocked at how much room she saw inside, and she liked the kitchen setup. TJ showed her the washer / dryer cabinet, big shower and airbed. He also opened the closets so she could see how much space they had. He then turned on the television in the front and back, and the sound system, and overwhelmed them with beautiful HD pictures.

TJ took them down to the dock along with the dogs, and they went on a boat ride around the lake. They loved Lake Norman and the beautiful homes along the shore. By the time they returned, Betty had set up dinner for them by the pool. They ate roasted chicken, fresh cream corn, green beans, and stuffed potatoes. They ate apple pecan crusts with ice cream for dessert.

Later, they chatted about TJ and Shane's life so far, and Elizabeth wanted to know if the word had gotten out about Shane. He assured her no, but soon everyone on the planet would know. He explained the deal with the Bobcats, and reminded Dick to keep his mouth shut. Elizabeth said she could guarantee he would, but she didn't say how. He told them about negotiations

498

with the sponsors, and the vacation in Alaska. He was proud of the new motorcoach, and Dick had already decided he wanted one, too.

A week later, he planned to call TJ and ask him to fly out to Eugene, Oregon to help him order a new coach. TJ was thrilled to help.

Not long after Dick and Elizabeth Vitale flew out the next morning, TJ flew on the Learjet to Phoenix. Shane was already at morning practice when he arrived, so TJ took a cab over to the workout center. He had a pass to get him in, and sat in the stands with other managers, associates, and wives, and watched Shane go through various speed drills. Shane consistently led his squad in all the drills, and enjoyed the competition in spite of the trash talking he heard. Nothing fazed him. He totally focused his brain and attitude on the task at hand. After a light lunch, they played rapid scrimmage games of ten minutes each. Shane scored twelve points on the first one, and sixteen on the second. He knew it would be tougher when he went against the veterans come September, but he was happy with his progress. As usual, he also made mental notes on what he could improve in his play.

He and TJ ate alone in a nice restaurant that night, and Shane gave him a report on how he thought he was doing. He said the physical the medical doctors gave him was the most intense he had ever experienced. He said they poked and prodded him from head to toe. He said they even looked at his teeth like he was slave, or a horse," he laughed. He was also x-rayed, especially his feet, hands, and limbs. He also took various psychological tests, and sat down with a counselor.

TJ told him about the visit from Dick and Elizabeth. He said Dick left with a serious motorcoach fever, making Shane smile. He thought a coach would be perfect for Dick's career. They walked from the restaurant towards the hotel with a detour to a creamery Shane discovered. They selected big cups and made their way back to the hotel. Since other players were on the same floor as Shane's room, TJ obtained a second room two floors up as usual. They ate their ice cream, talked, and soon made love. They were thankful to be sleeping in the same bed together again as there were no curfews.

The week following their trip to Phoenix allowed a feeling of normalcy as they worked on their business and training during the day, while late afternoons were reserved for rest, relaxation and play. Shane spent a day at Top Line Studio, as each sponsor shot still photos of him promoting their company's products, while preparing for their fall production plans for various marketing campaigns with Shane. They also measured him from head to toe for wardrobe fittings. TJ found time to work on Shane's coming out speech, as the time for it was fast approaching.

Shane had already begun spending a few hours signing products at their main office, where the staff assembled the items on every table and counter possible. He signed each quickly and kept moving. They broke a million dollars in sales by the twentieth day of the month. The foundation banked donations of three hundred thousand. They were already self-sufficient in their new business and foundation organizations. TJ asked Dick and Elizabeth to join their foundation board and they accepted quickly. He and Shane had hosted Jeff and his wife for dinner and a tour of the house. Jeff thought the wet area was amazing, and he also liked the idea of a remote studio in the house and on the motorcoach. His wife loved the view out of the great room as well as the heated marbled floors. She said the boys did a great job on picking the furniture and fabrics. The boys laughed and confessed Leslie did a spectacular job for them.

She was also a dog lover and gave the dogs some good rubs. Later, he asked Jeff if he and his wife would serve on the board. He agreed to do so for two years. "I hope you'll use me to build your foundation up, so you'll find smarter people to replace me." TJ was grateful for his wisdom and support. TJ told him about the sales numbers and wondered how he thought they were doing. Jeff laughed and said he was doing great, and he'd better start building the rest of his office space, and ordering more products.

He asked Bill Johnson, the owner of the Bobcats, to be on the board, as well as Billy Coble. They both agreed to help. He also asked Nancy Green, his realtor, as she knew more rich people than any other, he thought. So now he had his board, and wondered what to do with them. He set up a meeting with Robby, and Larry from Jeff's company. They met in TJ's new public office with pictures of Shane on the wall, along with several Don Balke prints. Balke was one of his favorite western North Carolina artists with an art gallery in Nebo North Carolina. They sat in overstuffed leather chairs in the casual area of his office so they could talk about how the boards work and what he should do. Larry and Robby both had experience with foundations and made numerous suggestions. They did have legal requirements for meeting at least once a year, but TJ liked the idea of a working board. Not so much physically, but using their phones, emails, and contacts attracting others to join their cause.

Bill Johnson called a few days later with news that the deal for the first round drafts pick was secured by offering the trade and fifty thousand dollars. Shane felt relief, but now faced a difficult decision. If things happen as planned, and the deal didn't fall through at the last minute, he really didn't have to come out of the closet. TJ waited patiently for Shane to think about this revelation, as the critical pivotal decision of coming out was his alone. TJ made his far less public decision a decade ago. He told Shane many times that each gay person has to decide if and when they will come out.

Shane may have been tempted not to come out, at least for a few moments, but he knew he wanted to be with TJ as much as he could. He didn't like the lying, sneaking, and hiding they had to do wherever they went.

500

They planned to fly everywhere together, to stay in the same hotel, and to eat dinner wherever they wanted. If he remained in the closet, rumors would start, and that could be more damaging than the truth. He knew he had a chance to create history as the first major player to come out while playing in the NBA. Once again, he steely decided to continue with plans for dramatically coming out to the world. TJ felt great pride at his courage.

They scheduled a press conference for the morning before draft day in Charlotte at a large conference room in a big hotel. John checked the sound system a half hour before Shane's scheduled presentation to the press. All the sports channels, and major newspapers were invited to attend. They were promised a major announcement would be made. Connie personally called everyone on her list, convincing the sports directors they would feel extremely foolish if they missed this opportunity. Over a hundred members of the press hooked up their equipment, and waited patiently for the top of the hour.

Connie prepared a hundred and twenty-five press kits, and hired six pretty college girls to quickly pass the folders out at the end of the announcement. John and their new Webmaster prepared new pages that were ready to upload on all their websites. This would be a major impact, all timed for Shane's moment at the podium.

TJ and Shane nervously waited in a side room for the right time. In a corner near the back of the conference room sat Bill Johnson, anxious to see how the press treated the announcement. Shane would make a short speech followed by an opportunity for the press to ask questions. Dick Vitale flew in to host the event. At the appointed hour, he walked to the podium and called for attention. He made a short speech about the accomplishments of Shane Bradley ending with two National Championships, and two consecutive Most Valuable Player Awards, as well as all the other national basketball awards available. He shared with the press that recently Shane formed a foundation to raise funds for charities, and he read the list of those selected to benefit. He also shared that a portion of Shane's product sales went to the foundation. He told them in just a few weeks he raised over four hundred thousand dollars, and had plans to raise millions. He explained Shane would make an announcement, and would take questions afterwards for fifteen minutes. He then formally welcomed Shane.

Shane received excellent applause as he walked to the podium dressed smartly in a new suit. He began by thanking everyone for coming. He said he had been thinking about this announcement for most of his life. TJ noted that ESPN® and Fox Sports® were carrying the speech live. His palms were sweating, but Shane appeared as always, calm and secure. "I want to make this pronouncement," began Shane, "before tomorrow's draft, so that any team owner choosing me will know exactly what they are getting."

He paused, sighed, took a slight breath, "I, Shane Bradley, am a gay man. I have known I was gay since I was a teenager and felt compelled to keep it a secret until I met my partner. We have been together almost two years, and together, we work very hard at crafting an honorable life by using my status as a sports figure, to try and help the world in any way we can.

"I realize some players may resent having me on their squad, but I promise the players and owners, if they choose me, I will give them my all at every practice and every game, just as I have done all my life. I will be the best possible basketball player I can be, and I hope in time, this announcement will not be a big deal to the next gay person that wants to play in the NBA. I wanted to be fair and honest with any team owner considering drafting me tomorrow. I will live as an honorable gay man, and will represent my team with great respect and dignity. I hope they will provide me with the same courtesy." Shane paused and smiled sheepishly, "I don't suppose there any questions?"

The press chuckled. TJ sighed with great relief. The news was finally out. Shane smiled again as the press appeared so stunned they couldn't think of a question, but after a lady raised her hand and asked the first question, the dam of silence broke, and soon hands were going up everywhere. Dick helped field the questions. Shane was finally asked if he was in love, and he beamed with pride and said yes he was. When asked who his partner was, he responded his partner wished to remain in the background for now. TJ and Shane had anticipated this query, discussed it, and felt it might be perceived that TJ, being older, may have led Shane to become gay, and come out of the closet. Of course, they laughed at such a preposterous notion, since TJ had only know Shane two years, while Shane had known he was gay since his early teens. After twenty minutes, Dick wrapped up the questions. Shane again thanked everyone for coming and left the podium.

When he walked into the back room TJ was waiting for him and gave him a big hug. They both felt greatly relieved. Dick joined them giving the boys a big hug. Dick laughed, "I think I was more nervous than you were. Listen, you were great, and you did a good thing for the future of other gay kids. I've got to get back out there and do my job, but thank you for allowing me to be part of your history-making event. I'll talk to you soon." They left the hotel out the back with John driving the black Lank Cruiser.

Connie remained busy handing out press kits and answering numerous questions. Many of the reporters begged for more in depth interviews. She gave them her card and told them to send their requests to her. A half hour later, the room was empty as the reporters rushed to file their stories. Connie and Dick drove to Shane's house where he and Shane were preparing for a few remote interviews starting with ESPN®. They were the first to interview him live. Dick was gracious, asked good questions, and especially asked why he didn't come out during his college years. Shane responded he had such great respect for Coach Timmons, his teammates, and the Taylor University, and since he had no partner at the time, he really didn't have a reason to risk coming out at that time. He said he remained so focused on winning the championship titles that coming out had to take a back seat.

Connie watched and became a real Shane fan as he flawlessly performed well, and she knew Billy did a great job teaching him. After the interviews were over, she gave them a hug and went back to her office to start fielding the phone calls and requests. They thanked Dick several times for his support and help. They drove him to the airport so he could fly out to Tampa and home.

John brought the newspaper in the following morning with headlines about Shane, and the entire front page of the sports page dedicated to the story. As planned, Shane arrived at their main office at nine for the first of several interviews. They watched ESPN's SportsCenter® as the stories began to unfold. There were some harsh comments from some current NBA players, and worst from some retired veterans, but there were also positive comments from recent college players who played against him. Al and Barbara called to see how they were doing. The parents reported they were almost packed for the trip to Lindle, and the moving company would be coming early next week. Shane told his dad about his gift of the Hummer. They were going to meet Shane in New York tomorrow. Coach Timmons called and said he would meet him in New York, and that he had his highest respect for his coming out. He assured him his Taylor fans, players, and coaches were behind him all the way. Bill Johnson also called and said he felt things would indeed happen as planned.

The next afternoon, Jake called stating all three sponsors were staying with them, and in fact, he had calls from other companies interested in sponsoring as well. Shane and TJ had to sit down as they expected the worst, and this response was so much better. They were so grateful and thankful to their sponsors. TJ fired off letters to company to say how thankful they were.

Shane, TJ, John, Connie, and Robby flew to New York the next day. They met Shane's parents at a restaurant for dinner. Shane arrived at the draft hotel convention center at eight o'clock. He did several interviews and since ESPN® was covering the event, he did a live interview. At nine o'clock, it was announced that a pick trade had transpired, and that the Bobcats now had the first round draft pick. The announcer paused, and read from an envelope. "The first pick in this year's draft is Shane Bradley for the Charlotte Bobcats!" A band began playing as Shane stood, hugged his parents, shook the hand of Coach Timmons, and gave TJ a hug. He then walked to the podium where Bill Johnson presented him with a Bobcat ball cap. He put it on and they walked to the podium. Bill said he felt his team was very lucky to have Shane, and he knew the boy's heart, and that it was the heart of a champion. Shane thanked Bill and his fans, his parents, Coach Timmons, his teammates, Taylor University, and his partner.

Shane was briefly interviewed as he came off the stage, and then followed Bill to the team conference room that was actually a temporary glass cube. Inside, Shane found TJ, Alan Anderson, Jerome, and a few men from Bill's staff. They sat down as the door closed, so they would have privacy.

Bill began, "Well, Shane. We pulled it off. I was so afraid someone would find out and let the cat out of the bag. I must admit I felt more confident after your speech yesterday." He laughed, "I assumed no one would want you, but after I got here today, I had several owners ask me about you, and they were acting like any team would be lucky to have you. So there you have it—I feel very lucky to have you, too. Now this is the part where we negotiate a little, so for cameras peeking into the room, try to look worried for a few minutes, and watch my face." He paused and made a frown, then smiled, "There we just made a deal. I traded a player they needed and fifty thousand of your dollars, for you to play for the Bobcats. Yeah," he laughed. TJ and Shane laughed as well.

Shane's attorney pre-approved the contracts, so Shane signed on the spot, though there would be a formal signing and press conference tomorrow in Charlotte. Buried in the contract were more personal appearance events for Shane to attend. Alan managed to cut them in half from what they wanted, but TJ promised they would do more, if he could fit it into Shane's schedule. Also in the contract were clauses giving TJ and Shane the right to fly to away games in their Learjet, and staying on another floor than the team. Bill easily agreed to their requests.

Shane came out of the room with all smiles. He and Connie went to another room for a short press conference. Afterwards, TJ and Shane shook hands with Coach Timmons and thanked him for coming. They gave Dick Vitale a big hug, and then Al, Barbara, Connie, John, Shane and TJ went to a restaurant for a late dessert to celebrate. Shane just made his dream come true by making it to the NBA, and especially the first draft pick. He felt lucky, grateful, and deeply in love with TJ. Al and Barbara were spending the night in New York, while TJ, Shane, Connie, and John flew home.

Later that night, alone in bed, TJ and Shane celebrated the new contract, and Shane's coming out with a reasonable response to his announcement. They were also grateful for the explosion of sales on their website since the announcement, and the rapid growth of their foundation. They had a great home and staff, and felt lucky to have such wonderful friends. Mostly they celebrated the fact they could now be free to be in love twenty-four hours a day, and Shane was looking forward to one day going to a gay dance club and dancing the night away with TJ, just as soon as he learned how to dance.

# EPILOGUE

It was early fall, and it had been raining most of the day in Chapel Hill, North Carolina. TJ finished a book signing at seven in a local bookstore that carried his gay fiction novels. About forty people bought books, and a few stood around afterwards to talk for a little bit. He thanked the manager for his invitation; packed his things, including the new promotional bookmarks he graciously gave away to patrons, and made his way to the front of the store. It was dark, and the streetlights reflected across the wet pavement. He parked a block down, so he began walking down darken the street.

Almost half way to his car, he noticed a beautiful new truck parked against the curb. Oddly, there was a man sitting inside looking at him. It made him nervous, so he picked up his gait just a little. He tried to recall how much cash in his pocket. He thought perhaps it was just forty bucks. Suddenly, he heard the truck door open, the man climbed out of the car, walked around the back of his car, and stepped to the sidewalk behind a big oak tree. Just as TJ passed, the man asked, "Are you TJ Johnson?"

TJ stopped and gave him a puzzled look, "You're not a murderer are you?"

The man laughed, smiled, and said no. TJ thought he had a beautiful smile, so he answered, "Yes, I am. May I help you?"

The man was wearing a ball cap pulled down tightly and slightly covering his eyes. "You're the guy that wrote the basketball fantasy?"

TJ sighed, "Guilty as charged."

The man laughed a little. "My roommate gave me a copy of your book, and I couldn't stop reading it. It was very funny."

TJ was shocked the man read his book, "Thank you. I'm glad you liked it. Would you like for me sign your copy?" TJ noticed he was carrying it.

"Yes if you don't mind," he replied as he handed TJ the book.

TJ set down his briefcase, took out a Sharpie pen from his pocket, and opened the book to sign it. "Tell me your name and I'll sign it to you."

"Sure," the handsome man replied, "I would like that. My name is Tyler Hansborough."

TJ dropped the pen. Tyler bent down to pick it up. He asked, "Are you okay?"

TJ stuttered, "Uh, you startled me. You're not going to kill me or you?"

"No, of course not," he replied. "I really liked the book. Would you like to go get something to eat? I'm starved."

TJ looked up into the stranger's face. He was indeed "The" Tyler Hansborough—TJ's all time favorite college basketball player. He smiled and said, "Sure, where would you like to go?"

TJ Johnson

"How about the Red, White, and Blue restaurant? I love their food, especially the barbeque."

"Me, too. That's fine, replied TJ.

Tyler suggested, "Come on, we'll take my truck, and I'll bring you back here later to get your car."

TJ slowly climbed in the vehicle feeling a bit surreal. On the drive over, Tyler said, "I liked all the fun things you guys did in the book. Have you been to Alaska?"

"No, it something I want to do as soon as I can. I've only been as far as Seattle so far."

Tyler added, "The gay couple in story really loved each other. I hope I get so lucky someday—you know, to find someone that loves me almost as much as I love them."

TJ sighed and replied, "I hope I do, too."

With these words the fantasy has finally come to an end. The truth is no one has proclaimed to be gay while playing in college basketball, but perhaps one day someone will be brave enough to break new ground. As for Tyler, it has been a pleasure to watch him play with such passion and drive, and with stoic determination to be the best player he can possibly be. As a Tar Heel fan, Tyler has also been a source of great pride, as we watched his amazing attitude towards his coaches and teammates, and the respect he gives family and friends alike. He is exactly what every parent should wish his or her son or daughter would grow up to be. I hope he'll forgive me for making him the secret star of the story. Thank you Tyler for being so much fun to watch and yell for, and best wishes for a great NBA career.

Taylor University substituted for my favorite team the University of North Carolina Tar Heels. I chose the name Taylor after one of Chapel Hill's favorite sons, James Taylor. Lindle is a fictitious town modeled slightly after the hometown of the Tar Heels. I also wished to pay homage to one of my favorite drivers Jeff Gordon. He's a class act on and off the track, and he's the best at what he does. I am also a fan of Dick Vitale, and his genuine support for the college basketball player and his family is so admirable. While other broadcasters criticize these young men as if they were already pros, Dick makes you feel proud you're watching these young stars become exceptional men. My suggestion for better TV: put a college fan in the booth like Dick!

I wish to thank my readers for allowing me this unusual twist in my stories. For me, it's too bad the fantasy has to end!

TJ Johnson
January 30, 2009

506

# Acknowledgements

I finished this story this past spring during basketball season, and spent the rest of the year chopping and editing away. There's nothing better than a good ACC basketball game. It's even better when the Tarheels win!

# Author TJ Johnson

TJ spent most of his early years hating to read, and thinking even less of his senior English class. Fortunately, a special teacher insisted he write a fictional short story, a two-page tale about something he found interesting. Instantly, TJ became hooked on the fun of writing fiction. Thankfully, he now reads constantly, going from one book to the next, with several in queue waiting their turn. His favorite part of writing is the crafting of a rough draft. A period in the process when the words fly from the storage center deep in his brain like a movie stuck on fast-forward. The agonizing part begins with the painstaking restructuring, as TJ edits one sentence at a time until he is either happy, or exhausted into believing he is happy with his conclusion.

His most recent release is **The Raceboys** about a national champion forced to come out as a gay driver. Also available is **The Will** and **Stranded.**

Coming Soon: TJ is currently polishing **Gay Grifters:** Eric learns his new friends not only steal your wallet and gold, but also your heart and soul! With little honor among thieves, these young gay men take pleasure in robbing their tricks, while aiming for bigger scores. Will the biggest thief in America give up a life of crime for a lifetime of love? Only the tale will tell.

Currently TJ is editing Followed by **The Blackfeet Boys** set in the northwest in a time when two young warriors must abandon their home with the most feared and blood thirsty tribe in North America, and search for a safe and isolated world together.

Fans of the War Series (**The War Apart - Part 1**, **The War Ahead - Part 2**) will be pleased to know that the research is finished, and the writing has begun on **The War Beyond - Part 3**.

Future works include **Forever Alone…Again** a funny sentimental tale about a man's countless attempts to find real love, only to watch his new perfect relationship self-destruct before he can move their love from third base to a home.

Requests for additional information and Inquiries can be obtain from **Hard Title Publishing**, at Info@ItsFiction.com

# WWW.ItsFiction.Com

# Contact TJ Johnson at:

## Info@ItsFiction.com

1. I try to answer all my email myself; however please read "Bio & Info" before writing as your question – saving time for all! Many readers ask the same questions repeatedly.

2. Please do not add my email address to any group for jokes, thoughts, prayers, or riddles, etc. I always delete these without reading.

3. I do not open any emails with attachments as these may contain viruses or other nonsense!

4. Please do NOT write suggesting plot lines as I delete these quickly, too. I like to write my own stories. If your plot is good, write it yourself! Do not send your manuscript to me – I am a writer, not a publisher, and I do not have the time.

5. All characters and names are part of my imagination and indicate no one particular. If I like a person's name, I may use the first or the last name but never both at the same time. It is true some of the events in my books are historical in nature but many are not. Choosing which to believe is your job, but this is why fiction is fun.

6. If you do not receive a reply, perhaps "Bio & Info" contain the answer already, or your email address is not functioning correctly.

7. If you have read all the above, I cannot wait to hear from you!

8. If you think a sequel should be added to your favorite story, please send me an email to the above address!

www.ingramcontent.com/pod-product-compliance
Lightning Source LLC
Chambersburg PA
CBHW071628260626
47170CB00001B/13